PENGUIN CLASSICS

FOUR MORALITY PLAYS

JOHN SKELTON (c. 1460–1529) was educated at Oxford and Cambridge and received the title 'laureate' from both universities. From c. 1496 to 1507 he was tutor to Prince Henry (Henry VIII). He took holy orders in 1498 and was rector of Diss in Norfolk from c. 1503 until c. 1511. Skelton's works include the morality play, *Magnyfycence* (1515), and satires on the English clergy, among which are *Collyn Clout* (1522), *Why Come Ye Nat to Courte?* (1522) and *Speke Parott* (1521), which all contain attacks against Cardinal Wolsey, from whose anger he then had to seek sanctuary at Westminster. He is also known for creating his own particular verse form, now called 'Skeltonic Verse'.

JOHN BALE (1495–1563) was educated at a Carmelite convent in Norwich and at Jesus College, Cambridge. He took holy orders but was then converted to Protestantism, abandoned his vows and married. He was imprisoned for his anti-Catholic activities but, helped by Thomas Cromwell, he was released in 1537 and wrote a number of plays, *King Johan* among them, supporting the Reformation. After Cromwell's fall in 1540, Bale took his wife and children to Germany and returned to England about 1547, after the death of Henry VIII. He was appointed Bishop of Ossory in Ireland in 1552 but, with the accession of Mary Tudor, had to go into exile again, returning after Elizabeth's accession in 1558, when he was appointed a Canon at Canterbury in 1560.

SIR DAVID LINDSAY (c. 1490–1555) probably studied at St Andrews University and entered royal service around 1508. From 1512 to 1522 he was usher to Prince James (James V) and in 1529 was appointed Lyon King-of-Arms, chief herald. He was also poet laureate of the Scottish court and wrote several poems attacking the Church and the vices of the court. Amongst these are his first poem, *The Dreme* (1528). His main work, *Ane Satire of the Thrie Estaitis* (1540), which is in the form of a morality play, was very popular and was performed at least three times.

PETER HAPPÉ read English at Cambridge, and afterwards took a Ph.D. at London University with a thesis on Tudor drama. He has lectured on early drama at a number of universities. His publications include an edition of *The Winter's Tale*, and the collections *Tudor Interludes* and *English Mystery Plays* for Penguins. He has completed the first old spelling edition of John Bale's plays, and is working on John Heywood. He is Principal of Barton Peveril College.

FOUR MORALITY PLAYS

*Edited with an
introduction and notes by*
PETER HAPPÉ

PENGUIN BOOKS

Penguin Books Ltd, Harmondsworth, Middlesex, England
Viking Penguin Inc., 40 West 23rd Street, New York, New York 10010, U.S.A.
Penguin Books Australia Ltd, Ringwood, Victoria, Australia
Penguin Books Canada Ltd, 2801 John Street, Markham, Ontario, Canada L3R 1B4
Penguin Books (N.Z.) Ltd, 182–190 Wairau Road, Auckland 10, New Zealand

—

Published in Penguin Books 1979
Reprinted in Penguin Classics 1987

—

—

Made and printed in Great Britain by
Richard Clay Ltd, Bungay, Suffolk
Set in Monotype Fournier

This lyfe, I see, is but a cheyre feyre;
Allthyngis passene and so most I, algate.
To-day I sat full ryall in a cheyere,
Tyll sotell Deth knokyd at my gate,
And onavysed he sayd to me 'Chek-mate!'
Lo, how sotell he maketh a devors —
And wormys to fede he hath here leyd my cors.

This febyll world, so fals and so unstable,
Promoteth his lovers for a lytell while;
But at the last he yeveth hem a bable,
Whene his peynted trowth is torned in-to gile.
Experyence cawsith me the trowth to compile,
Thynkyng this: to late, alas, that I began,
For foly and hope disseyveth many a man.

— Anon, fifteenth century

(From 'Farewell this world', Trinity College, Cambridge MS, 1157
Balliol College MS, 354.)

cheyre feyre Cherry Fairs were held in orchards for the sale of fruit.

CONTENTS

INTRODUCTION

I

DRAMATISTS do not always keep to the categories devised for them by their critics, and this truism holds for the writers of medieval moral plays. 'Morality plays' and 'interludes' have so much in common that to distinguish between the two is bound to be controversial. The term 'morality play' is not genuinely medieval, and yet it is today one of the commonest names for these plays. The term 'interlude' did exist in medieval times, but its scope was so wide that we cannot be sure that it would not be applied to any play with a moral theme, and indeed to some without. It is a matter of convenience, therefore, to call the four plays in this volume morality plays simply because they are examples of long moral plays. The volume is thus complementary to *Tudor Interludes* (Penguin, 1972) in which examples of shorter plays, some with moral themes, were chosen.

Our four morality plays, *The Castle of Perseverance*, *Magnyfycence*, *King Johan*, and *Ane Satire of the Thrie Estaitis*, were written between 1400 and 1562, and so they are more or less contemporary with the plays in the companion volume. It was during these years that the professional drama emerged, a development which had a profound effect upon the nature of the plays and the ways in which they were constructed. *The Castle of Perseverance* is the earliest, and to some extent it stands apart from the others. It is such a complete achievement as a play that it has often been treated as though there were many others like it, but this is not really the case. We cannot tell how many others have been lost, of course, but as things stand there is no play which demonstrably imitates it, and none which uses its particular blend of theme and dramatic presentation. However it is an early example of a play embodying a complex of moral ideas and showing them in dramatic terms. By studying it we can guess at the inheritance of later dramatists, and we can see that its survival is of great importance in the history of

9

moral plays since it shows without doubt that the origin of these plays lay in the didactic impulse found in the sermon and in devotional literature.

Before examining some details of this tradition, however, we ought to take up the matter of the professional theatre. There is no doubt that by the end of the fifteenth century there were professional actors in England. Some of them were working at Court producing such plays as Henry Medwall's *Fulgens and Lucres*, and some appear to have aimed at more rural audiences, as with *Mankind*. As we shall see later it is an open question whether *The Castle of Perseverance* was performed by a travelling company. There is no doubt that *Magnyfycence* was meant for professional actors, and we have evidence that John Bale was paid for performances of *King Johan* even though he was a priest rather than a full-time player. Though the state of the theatre was different in Scotland, it seems reasonable to suppose that some of the actors in *Ane Satire of the Thrie Estaitis* were professional, even though the author himself again had other primary interests. It is likely that Skelton, Bale, and Lindsay, all of whom were substantial and experienced literary figures, found it expedient to use paid actors and to construct their plays so as to make it possible to give scope for the exercise of professional skills. It is against this development of the needs and skills of the professional actor and his company that we must examine the interest in moral ideas which has such a profound effect upon the conventions of the moralities. The effect is discernible in subject matter, construction, and mood.

Didactic Theatre

In considering the relationship between the moral ideas and the dramatic form in which they were embodied in morality plays, it is useful to contrast the mystery cycles which were roughly contemporary with them. The cycles set out to represent the story of the redemption of man from Adam to Doomsday. They were an elaboration of well-established themes. Owing something to the earlier liturgical drama in which scriptural incidents were enacted, and embodying many narrative details from devotional works designed to interpret Scripture, the mystery plays show a consistent and virtually static theology. In spite of the increasing flexibility of character and incident which some of the later additions reveal, the plays had to remain as they were originally conceived. Indeed the last attempts to keep them alive during the first twenty years of Elizabeth I's reign suggest that their appeal was conservative and traditional. They were suppressed because they were associated with Catholic sentiment and with the support of the old religion. The authors of these cycles are now unknown to us, but we may suppose that they were clerics working for the guilds who backed the plays. Although we can occasionally detect individual styles, the overall effect is extraordinarily homogeneous, and the individual author subjects his work to a kind of group consciousness of the ultimate objective, which involves worship and revelation.

The morality – even when the author is unknown – is normally the work of an individual who inherits and contributes to a series of conventions, and whose inspiration causes him to take an independent line. Personal opinion and taste, the direction of criticism towards individuals, and towards political and social matters play a much larger part. The driving force is homiletic, and the subject matter is often to be found in sermons and in books designed to give a wide basis for belief and instruction. From time to time there is evidence of literary influences which lie outside purely theological work. Some of the imagery of the morality play can be traced to specific sources which must have been a matter of personal choice – as in the important images of the castle, the journey or pilgrimage, and the dance of death. Without the unifying discipline of the life of Christ which shaped the mystery cycles, the writers of the morality plays had many opportunities for development. In the sixteenth century the morality plays and interludes became vehicles for theological controversy, whether Protestant or Catholic. At all times there was scope for the invention of plots. Instead of being an act of worship, the moralities moved from theological instruction to polemic, criticism, and satire. The sixteenth century was a period of great social change and the role of the morality was to reflect or even to initiate new social and political ideas. In the end the mystery cycles disappeared because they could not change, while the morality fades imperceptibly at first, but at the last completely into new styles of drama, so that it is possible to detect in the work of Marlowe, Shakespeare, Jonson and many others evidence of dramatic ideas and conventions which were adapted to a new world, in which new philosophies as well as new theatrical techniques took their place.

It appears that the main impulse behind the evolution of the morality plays was an extension of preaching, and it may well be that one of the historical events of importance was the ever-increasing emphasis upon the sermon given by the medieval Church.[1] The extension of the work of the preaching friars, particularly the Dominicans and Franciscans, may well have contributed to this, and coincided with an increasing interest in drama. The material available for the sermon writers is far too complex to analyse here, but it is important to say that some of it went back through the Church's educational collections to the pre-Christian culture of the ancient world (Ovid and Vergil); some of it reflected the new Christian doctrine as it impinged upon the dying Empire (Prudentius); and some of it was evolved in the thousand years between the fall of Rome and the appearance of the medieval sermons and the morality plays which derived from them (St Thomas Aquinas, Hugo of St Victor).

The homiletic impulse was concerned with the salvation of the soul. In order to do this the preacher showed how the soul could fall into temptation and despair, and how these could be overcome by repentance and by the operation of divine grace. To make this apparent to those who listened to the sermons or watched the plays, it was necessary for the art of preaching to lay emphasis upon learning, vivid illustration, subtle argument, and straightforward terror. One of the most notable means was the use of allegory, a term which for the modern reader needs careful consideration.

Allegory is really a representation of an idea by means of a parallel which is similar to the principal features of the idea. It shows itself most clearly by a story which represents an experience, or an illustrative situation which has parallels in real life. The most

1. G. R. Owst, *Literature and Pulpit in Medieval England*, second edition, Oxford, 1961. A. Williams, 'The English Moral Play before 1500', *Annuale Mediaevale* 4, 1963, pp. 5–22.

famous example discovered by scholars looking for the origins of medieval allegory is that of Prudentius in his *Psychomachia* where a description of a battle shows how virtues triumph over vices. The allegory is the battle. This invention of Prudentius – if it is indeed his own idea originally – happens to be of interest in connection with *The Castle of Perseverance* where a battle is also employed to show how virtues triumph over vices, but there are many other allegories such as the dance of death, or the journey of the soul, which represent the means of salvation.

In order to present such allegories it is convenient to use abstract characters which are not really allegories themselves, but become part of the allegory as the parallel unfolds. Abstract characters are therefore a common feature of allegory, and it is interesting to note that a few examples of these have been discovered before the appearance of the earliest English morality play in the middle of the fourteenth century.[2] Here we may look briefly at three cases in which the use of the abstract characters, and an allegorical device of action indicates that on the Continent there had already been some work which showed that the concern for salvation could be revealed in dramatic form. In the *Ludus de Antichristo*,[3] a twelfth-century Latin play from Germany, the story is not so much an allegory as a legend concerning the activities of the Antichrist; however the action involves elaborate debate, and the crafty machinations of Hypocrisy and Heresy who seek to persuade the faithful that the Antichrist is the true Christ. The action is mostly a war of words, but in the end a clap of thunder over the head of Antichrist puts him and his followers to flight. At about the same time Hildegard of Bingen composed her *Ordo Virtutum*, also in Latin.[4] Here all the characters are abstractions, and the allegory is more complete since the action shows how Anima, the soul, has to fight with Satan, and how she must be helped by Humility and other virtues. Satan is enchained –

> Gaudete, o socii, quia antiquus serpens ligatus est
> (Rejoice, o friends, that the ancient serpent is bound)

2. *The Pride of Life* in *T.I.*, pp. 39–62.
3. *Ludus de Antichristo*, ed. R. Enselsing, Stuttgart, 1968.
4. Ed. P. Dronke, *Poetic Individuality in the Middle Ages*, Oxford, 1970, pp. 180–92.

– and so the climax of the play shows by an allegorical device the underlying doctrine that the soul must struggle to pursue the way of virtue. The third example is the anonymous French text of the *Moralité des Sept Péchés Mortels et Des Sept Vertus* (Walloon text of 1380–1420).[5] This gives a much more specific hint of the material of the sermon in the use of the seven deadly sins. The seven vices are condemned to death, but the Hermit prays to the Virgin to intercede for them. The action embodies disputes between the vices and the corresponding virtues.

From these examples it is clear that the dramatization of allegories about salvation had begun long before the English writers began to present their doctrines in dramatic terms. But allegory is only part of the didactic impulse which dominates the moralities, and it plays such a large part because it supports the argument of salvation which is really the main subject matter. It might therefore be wiser to accept that didacticism – the communication of an ethical truth – is the main purpose, and that allegory follows as the most effective mode of communicating.[6] The English morality play placed great emphasis upon a dramatization of the issues of salvation, particularly the process by which the hero is trapped into sin, usually by the misguided exercise of free will which subjects him to the cunning of the vices who seek to destroy him. The destruction is prevented by a change of heart and a repentance which is motivated by divine grace. The dramatic interest often centres upon the evil characters and it is quite clear that the theatrical conventions which were evolved to reveal how evil and cunning they were became a major concern of writers and actors alike. Indeed it is here that the growing professionalism of the English theatre found its chief area of expansion and experimentation. In fact the conventions of the evil characters remained astonishingly consistent throughout the two centuries we are considering, and this is not surprising since conventions are a great convenience to professional actors, giving them an easily assumed means of communicating with their audience. Other examples of the importance

5. Ed. G. Cohen, *Nativités et Moralités Liégeoises du Moyen-Age*, Brussels, 1953.

6. See J. S. Kantrowitz, 'Dramatic Allegory, or exploring the Moral Play', *Comparative Drama* 7, 1973, pp. 68–82.

of a complex of conventions are to be found operating in a similar way in Edwardian melodrama, the modern pantomime, and Wild West films.

The morality vices quickly establish their natures with the audience. Often their physical appearance is a clue, and the style of speech, boasting or crafty, is usually an early indication of where vice is to be found. It is essential that a vice is properly identified and so the evil characters tell the audience exactly what they stand for. To entrap the hero they work upon his weaknesses, often exploiting lust and greed, or indeed any combination of the deadly sins. In soliloquies they often make a declaration to the audience of what they are about to do, and they adopt aliases and disguises which are explained to the audience so that an indication is given of how a sin may be entertained by the hero in ignorance.

But for the hero the action must be concerned not only with his entanglement. He must emerge from it and show true penitence. It is this aspect which takes us back to the sermon, for it illustrates the truth that man may help himself, and that other forces are ready to support him when he does. The psychological effect of this regeneration is profound. If the fall is made so credible by the allegory of the evil characters, the emergence of hope receives support from many aspects of the Church's teaching, particularly confession and forgiveness, which were 'institutionalized in the sacrament of penance'.[7] It is in the choice of particular vices, and of the way in which the penitence of the hero is to be induced and supported that the authors of moralities reveal their particular didactic concern. In the cases of *The Castle of Perseverance*, the Digby *Mary Magdalene*,[8] and the lost *Paternoster Play* of York, the authors placed emphasis upon the seven deadly sins, but in most of the other extant moralities the choice of sin and of virtue is narrower, and dictated by more specific moral or even political preoccupations. In fact in the sixteenth century the villainy is often perpetrated by one leading evil supported by a group of related villains, and the chief became an important conventional role to which the title of 'the Vice' was given.

Inside the broad moral outline sustained by allegorical structures

7. R. Potter, *The English Morality Play*, 1975, p. 16.
8. Ed. F. J. Furnivall, *EETS*, e.s. 70, 1896.

there are a number of other characteristics of morality plays which are exhibited in the plays collected here. The first of these is the emotional effect of the plays. To begin with the hero often shows pride and ignorance. His first state is to rejoice in his strength and the exercise of his free will. It is this which makes him vulnerable, and his fall into sin leads to despair. There is an inevitability in this process which must have been the common experience of the audience. The message is that sin cannot be avoided, and as Man is overwhelmed by the forces which design his destruction he becomes a broken and pathetic figure. But the regeneration which the second part of the play presents is an optimistic process, and the misery of disaster is replaced by relief and rejoicing. The writers of the plays laboured to convey the misery because it was an example to the unwary.

The emotional impact of despair is intensified by a number of devices. The hero is usually alone, deserted by his former false friends, and the despair is often given a particular visual impact, by a change of costume, or some physical affliction. The terror of his situation may be intensified by the appearance of horrific figures who torment him mentally and physically. It is here that Death may intervene as in *The Castle of Perseverance* and *King Johan*, or some other figure like Adversyte in *Magnyfycence*. Indeed the popular medieval allegory of the dance of death which shows how people of all stations in society are subject to death gives an agonizing intensity to Man's suffering.

It is possible that these emotional aspects were made more accessible to the audience by the ritual elements which were shared with folk-drama.[9] The evidence for the existence of medieval folk-drama is not easy to come by, but it is notable that the folk-play in England and other countries repeatedly presented the death of the hero and his revival. The purpose of such rituals was of course to be reassuring and to give confidence in the chances of survival by enacting both death and re-birth. The hero, by his moral folly, becomes a kind of scapegoat, a role which is emphasized by his isolation. Another aspect of this is the combat in which the hero is subdued by his adversaries. The ritual of destruction also liberates forces of ridicule and mockery which are an essential of both folk-

9. Potter, op. cit., p. 10.

play and morality. Within the ritual destruction there is scope for cruelty and abuse, and evil characters often exhibit a licence which implies a magical power to make life intolerable. Again and again we find that vices are comic, quarrelsome, and outrageous. They affront dignity and respectability, and by their disreputable behaviour threaten order and virtue. As in a number of other moral plays, both *Magnyfycence* and *Ane Satire of the Thrie Estaitis* have named Fools who work as part of the evil group of characters. In the former Fansy and Foly act as court fools, but there is little doubt that they incorporate much of the irreverence and destructiveness of the more popular fools who appeared in the various folk-rituals of medieval times.

An extension of this folk fooling is the general function of comedy in the moralities. Two particular traits are the obscenity and the satire. The obscenity is characteristic of the stage devils in the mystery cycles, while the satire has a much wider literary inheritance. In the moralities we find satire is directed at the follies of virtue, at kingship, sexuality, greed and ambition, hypocrisy and the Church. Skelton was a life-long practitioner of satire in many literary forms, and he had a particular interest in the work of his immediate predecessors who wrote in the genre of *The Ship of Fools*.[10] For Bale, satire was a means of theological and political controversy, used ruthlessly to expose the faults he perceived in his opponents. Similarly Lindsay attacked through satire the evils of the Church, especially its oppression of the poor.

It is clear from the elements discussed in this section that the moral allegory provided a framework for a variety of emotional effects. As the morality developed it offered more and more scope for them. The plays embodied much that was human, and it is important to observe that this was done by means of the moral structure, and not in spite of it. Intended as a means of teaching the Church's dogma relating to salvation, the plays dealt with human situations and human dilemmas. Though the central character is usually some generalized figure of Mankind, the stress of circumstances brought about by the plots makes him suffer as

10. Sebastian Brant, *Das Narrenschiff*, 1494; translated by Alexander Barclay as *The Shyp of Folys*, 1509.

a man even though he is not an individual of the kind found in later forms of drama. In this way the moralities occasionally foreshadow the tragedies of later ages. But one should not see their merits as merely a foretaste of greatness to come. The playwrights were writing for their own times, and in doing so they reflected the issues that mattered most to them. They organized their plays in such a way as to make them effective within their own communities whether they were writing for popular or court audiences. Within these objectives we find the dramatists showing skill and care, making good use of the potential response of their audiences and evolving responses by means of the craft of playwriting. In the end the texts of these plays – as with all successful drama – imply a performance and an audience. For us it is still possible to see something of both of these reflected in the texts.

Staging

Some attention has already been given to the growing professionalism which accompanied the development of the moralities. It is now time to turn to the question of staging. In the following paragraphs, we shall consider first some general aspects, and then some individual features of the four plays.

Three of the earliest moral plays, *The Pride of Life*, *The Castle of Perseverance*, and *Mankind*, were intended for outdoor performance. We note the prayer for good weather,[11] and in the first two the action demands raised booth stages probably with a curtain for use when actors temporarily withdraw from the scene. But the chief feature of these in staging is the 'locus' or 'platea', the acting area. This is not usually defined as a particular locality. It is simply the area in which the actors are to perform and from which the audience must be excluded. There is no attempt to give it a name, and the advantage of this is that a change of locality may be assumed as the action demands without the need for visual or scenery changes. Occasionally, as in *The Castle of Perseverance*, the booths were identified with a particular character, and thus the important device of a procession from one booth or scaffold across the 'place' to another could be used. Processions, besides

11. *The Pride of Life*, l. 10; *Ane Satire of the Thrie Estaitis*, Banns, l. 12.

having an obvious visual and dramatic purpose, as in the advance of the warring vices towards the Castle of Perseverance, also allowed for the passage of time, the change of mood, and the division of the action, all necessary parts of the dramatic illusion.

It is probable that this outdoor 'place' preceded its counterpart indoors, though we must be careful about such a generalization, for Henry Medwall's *Nature* (c. 1495) is apparently an indoor play only twenty or so years later than *Mankind*. Once the actors, now perhaps professionals, found themselves working indoors, a number of changes took place. The usual venue for indoor performances was the great hall of castles, houses, and colleges.[12] Instead of an audience grouped around the acting area and arranged according to whatever was available in the way of vantage points, the great halls had a conventional centre for their audiences in the position of the chief of the feast. To some extent the playing of the action must have been directed towards him, seated on the dais at one end, perhaps during or after a meal. However the acting area remained unlocalized and the words and actions of the players had to give to the audience just enough information for its identification without prejudicing transformations which afterwards became necessary.

There were certain regular features of the great hall. At the end opposite the dais would be the screens hiding the kitchens, the two doors providing convenient means of entering the hall. Above the screens in many houses was the minstrel gallery, and music could be easily added. Instead of the public spectacle, with the emphasis upon all ranks of society – an audience characteristic of that for the mystery cycles – the indoor performance was more intimate, and could be tuned more finely towards the particular circumstances of the chief of the feast. Though with later interludes it became the intention to publish the text for a wider audience, many of the extant morality and interlude texts are closely related to a particular audience at a specific time. A close study of the staging details in dialogue and stage direction often yields information about performances. This is particularly so in *Ane Satire of the Thrie Estaitis* where the three versions of the play

12. T. W. Craik, *The Tudor Interlude*, Leicester, 1958; R. Southern, *The Staging of Plays before Shakespeare*, 1973, pp. 48–55.

show the marks of two large-scale outdoor performances and a more intimate indoor one.

The effects of the unlocalized acting place upon the moralities are profound. The writers had to make their effects by spectacle rather than by realism. A great deal of explaining had to be packed into the earlier parts of the plays. The action could be fluid and varied, and it was possible to have only one actor on the stage, or, if the players were sufficient in number, over twenty as in *The Castle of Perseverance.*

The development of professionalism has a significant influence on the structure of the plays, and this is discernible in *Magnyfycence* and *King Johan.* It became financially desirable to keep the number of actors down to a minimum and this led to the practice of doubling parts. Usually the companies tried to work to five or six actors. This meant that there was a limited number of characters who could appear simultaneously. Some characters have to be suppressed from the action so that the actor may be free to appear in another role. The principal effect of this is that the vast confrontation of vices and virtues in the battle scene of *The Castle of Perseverance* could not be imitated by playwrights working for smaller companies. It was thus necessary to arrange the action so that all the virtues could alternate with the vices, and this is what happened in *Magnyfycence* and *King Johan.* For these two plays I give some detail as to how the doubling scheme might have operated.[13] One consequence of this structure is that the vice groups have only themselves to work upon, and this leads to the elaboration of comic business – trickery and brawls – which is a characteristic of later moral plays.

The choice of costume is another aspect which is discernible in these plays. In the first instance the character must be established quickly, and so easily recognizable costumes in terms of colour and symbolism were used: white for Mercy, or clerical robes for doctrinal virtues. Kings could be quickly identified, and so could devils, loose women and the poor. But two kinds of costume change were necessitated by the action. One was the adoption of disguise by the villains in order to deceive the hero (but not usually to deceive the audience), and the other was to underline the change of

13. See Appendix 1 below, pp. 677–83.

fortune, as with Magnyfycence's poor clothing after he is struck by Adversyte. Sometimes the costumes have satirical intention, and this is seen in *Magnyfycence* where the court vices ('the four Cs'), difficult to distinguish on the page, were no doubt easily separable in visual terms. Again the costumes might have importance in identifying fools and separating them from other kinds of characters who were more specific vices or virtues. The matter of costume must also be borne in mind in connection with the procession.

Political Theatre

Since three of the plays included in this volume come from a particular historical circumstance, it is necessary to consider the objective and techniques of the political dramatist. In the first place the morality play was centred upon the Church's role as the medium of salvation. *The Castle of Perseverance* is concerned with all men whatever their rank, and this holds true for most of the other extant early moral plays. They were written by men apparently speaking from within the Church and concerned with the next world and its effect upon this. In doing so they created a powerful vehicle for ideas, one in which one set of values (the good) could be set against another (the bad). One may even suppose that their origin was connected with a particular concern felt by the Church's leaders that it was necessary to make plain and to emphasize the doctrine of penance. It is really upon the fall of the innocent into sin and despair, and his return to grace that the later historical examples of the morality genre are based, and they incorporate many details which were first evolved in the framework of the picture of salvation for all.

We cannot really determine the point at which the morality first became concerned with historical matters. There are hints in Medwall's *Nature* that the Court was taking over pride of place. Skelton may not have been the innovator, but his *Magnyfycence* is very different from anything that has survived from before it. Skelton was concerned early in his life as the instructor of Prince Henry in the virtues of authority. He was a learned man and a skilful poet, and his play sets out to reveal the kingly virtues. He shifted the main direction of the plot away from the salvation of the soul and towards the survival of the king. Yet he preserved within the play the virtues of Good Hope, and the reason and order which were characteristic of the morality. There are no devils or angels, but by a strange irony one of the supporting virtues at the end of the play is Perseverance. As a poet he was keen to indicate his literary sources, especially Horace, and to give scope to the influence of Fortune. As we shall see below there are hints that he had Henry's personality in mind, and for a long time it has been held that he was attacking Wolsey, though there is no clear evidence for this. The real point is that in addressing himself to the virtues necessary for kingship, and in restoring Magnyfycence to his throne, Skelton was seeking to preserve and uphold the monarchy. He obviously expected that his play might have some effect upon the political life of the nation.

This expectation was shared by Bale in his time. Bale was much more of a systematic reformer, and he was one of the earliest clerical supporters of the Reformation. He wrote many plays – perhaps he is the most prolific of our early playwrights - and most of his dramatic works are designed to uphold and further the new religion. He was outspoken, courageous and aggressive, and not at all frightened to enter the political lists in spite of the personal risks he took in doing so. His great innovation was to introduce actual historical characters into the morality. Like most works of historical fiction, what he produced was perhaps not good history, but it was creative as an art form since by the use of a historical parallel, however inaccurate, he illuminated the political issues of his own time. King John interested him because he could see parallels between John's struggle for independence from papal corruption and Henry's support for a Church independent from Rome. Using a wide range of chronicle material, but with the strict application of what he found to support his own protestant polemic, Bale sought to justify and promote the changes which were coming about in his time. It may be that one of his chief sources of inspiration was to adapt from the mystery cycles, in which he is known to have been interested, the notion that in human history there are many parallels, *figurae*, which like Adam and Christ foreshadow and echo one another. It is this ability to break new ground which distinguishes his contribution to the morality.

Sir David Lindsay was a courtier and a gentleman. He served the Scottish crown for many years, often at diplomatic levels. He even visited the English court and created a good impression upon King Henry. Although there is little sign of morality plays in Scotland, his *Ane Satire of the Thrie Estaitis* has many close links with the English type. Like Skelton and Bale, however, his method was to adapt the morality play to his own political ends. Diplomats and courtiers are not normally revolutionaries: they adapt to a system, and perhaps seek to improve it by persuasion. Lindsay has in mind an ideal society in which the three estates, the Spirituality, the Temporality, and the Merchants, would support the monarchy. In the first part of his play the King is shown to be at fault, falling into sensual temptation, and failing to reform the abuses of the clergy whose main object was self-advancement. One can see here two traditional ideas. One is the unity of society with its constituents working together in a balance, an idea which is perhaps a descendant from Plato's *Republic*. The other is the criticism of Church abuses, and here we find him working over similar material to Chaucer and Langland. It is interesting that the figure of the Pardoner is so important in his analysis. In the second part of the play the King's personal fate is much less important, and Lindsay switches attention to the state itself, outlining what is really a programme of reform. Again the techniques of the morality are present: temptation by crafty and successful vices, an elaborate structure of clowning and intrigue by the court vices who are skilled in the art of flattery and lies, and the intervention of the virtues who quickly expose the villains and give the opportunity for a more healthy society. Lindsay also finds room for passages of folly which are not strictly related to the main action but echo the comedy and irreverence we have noted in the folk-elements of the morality plays.

Lindsay's play is the longest of the four: it has a very large scope in the life of the nation, but it never reaches the cosmic scope of *The Castle of Perseverance*. The time had gone by, and circumstances demanded a different approach. It is especially interesting that we have information about three versions of the play, and we can see to some extent how sensitive Lindsay was to political changes. It is obvious too that his play was very popular and successful, and we know something of the people who supported him and invited him to revive the play twice. The revivals were more elaborate and were performed in different circumstances. The performance at Edinburgh in 1554 was in the open air and before a vast audience that presumably contained people from all ranks of society.

The work of these three political dramatists is similar in that it relies heavily upon the conventions of the morality play. Each was a man of great literary experience, learned and skilful, and, being so, not likely to imitate the morality which was more than a hundred years old by 1500 in a slavish way. Instead these three writers transform it to their own ends. But it is clear that what they inherited – their view of the morality play – was substantial and powerful: a flexible dramatic instrument which offered to its practitioners great scope for the achievement of dramatic effects.

II THE CASTLE OF PERSEVERANCE

Text

The manuscript of *The Castle of Perseverance* was written in about 1440, and is now in the Folger Shakespeare Library, Washington, D.C. The eighteenth-century collector, the Rev. Cox Macro of Bury St Edmunds, acquired it, and he also possessed fifteenth-century manuscripts of two other medieval moral plays: *Mankind* and *Wisdom*. In consequence the three plays have become known as the *Macro Plays*. All three have associations with East Anglia, and together they make a significant contribution to our knowledge of moral plays. *The Castle of Perseverance*, the earliest of the three, is thought to have been composed in the years 1400–25, and the reference to 'crakows' at l. 1064 supports this (see note p. 623).

Nothing is known about the author, though we may suppose from the nature of the work that he was a cleric. It is likely that he was responsible for the whole play, but some mention must be made of certain inconsistencies. The style of the Banns, which announce a forthcoming performance, is somewhat different from the rest of the play, but this may be no more than a difference of time and mood, rather than of authorship. One outstanding problem is that the ending of the play described in the Banns is different from the play itself. In the Banns, Our Lady is suggested as the intercessor for the soul of Man, and there is no mention of the debate between Mercy, Peace, Justice, and Truth which occupies the last 550 lines of the play. If these two factors do indicate a change of authorship it may mean that the play was not originally intended for touring and that the Banns were written for a performance or performances subsequent to the author's original conception. As we shall see, there are other difficulties relating to the generally accepted view that the play was intended for a travelling company.

The manuscript has lacunae at lines 1606 and 3053. In each case one leaf is missing, and it is possible that the two leaves were originally one complete sheet which has been lost.

There is a list of characters following the last line of the play. This has been transcribed and translated, and it is printed at the beginning of the text in this edition. The list was arranged by the author or scribe to show the relationship between the World, the Devil, and the Flesh and their followers, the seven deadly sins.

Performance

The drawing on fol. 191^v of the manuscript gives us much information about the way in which the play was performed. Its principal features are the castle, the ditch, and the scaffolds. The castle itself is in the form of a single tower, probably open at the base to reveal a bed for Man: the Soul is to lie under this until his part begins. There is also a cupboard for Avarice at the foot of the bed. The ditch contains water and surrounds the castle: but there is an alternative if a ditch cannot be provided, some form of barrier or barricade, also surrounding the castle. There are five scaffolds apparently outside the ditch, assigned as follows: East for God (the direction of Jerusalem), South for Flesh, West for World, North for Belyal, and North-East for Covetousness.

The interpretation of this drawing is the subject of Richard

Southern's *The Medieval Theatre in the Round*,[14] a book which is distinguished by its remarkable exercise of dramatic imagination and one which cannot be lightly discounted. Briefly, Southern proposed that the ditch be the circumference of the theatre itself, and that the earth from the ditch be thrown inside the circle to make a circular mound. Upon this mound the scaffolds were placed. The audience were allowed to enter the area bounded by the ditch and mound upon payment of an entry charge. They were then marshalled into their places by 'Stytelerys' who arranged them on the bank and on the ground area in such a way as to preserve good visibility and clear passage for the actors moving from the scaffolds to the castle in the centre.

The great merit of Southern's reconstruction is that having evolved this plan, Southern is able to interpret much of the action in a very convincing way and with much detail: the play seems to come to life in this conjectured environment.

As supporting evidence he refers to the Cornish theatre, the *plan-an-guare*, examples of which still survive at St Just-in-Penwith and at Perranporth. These were circular mounds, some of them reputedly having had stone seats in the past. Cornish antiquaries tell of a tradition of productions of the Cornish Passion Play before 1600, the audiences numbering thousands.[15] The extant text of the Cornish plays gives a circular acting space which must be related to the surviving examples of the *plan-an-guare*. Visiting one of them today leaves one in no doubt as to their effectiveness as a setting: indeed *The Castle of Perseverance* was performed at Perranporth in 1969.

However we cannot finally concede that Southern's reconstruction is more than a conjecture since it is open to a number of objections. The Banns imply that the play is to be performed by a large touring company. (This in itself presents difficulties of another kind, because it is not at all clear that there could be a touring company of at least twenty-two players.) If the play were on tour the construction of the ditch and mound would give rise to many practical problems, not the least of which is the sheer size of the

14. Second edition, 1975.

15. See N. Denny, 'Arena Staging and Dramatic Quality in the Cornish Passion Play', in his *Medieval Drama*, 1973.

earth-moving operation at each site. The Cornish rounds are very old, indeed some of them are pre-historic forts or encampments. In an area such as Cornwall it might be possible to rely upon existing works, but the play seems to have originated in eastern England, where there do not seem to be any suitable local sites which could be so adapted.

The drawing itself shows the scaffolds outside the ditch. The main drawback of Southern's concept is that the ditch can play no part in the allegorical and dramatic effects of the action. He makes it simply a barrier against unwanted spectators, but the allegory seems to demand that the castle be strongly defended, and indeed the ditch becomes part of the action during the siege when Sloth tries to remove the water with his spade and so gain entry (ll. 2347–9, 2369–72). It does seem very strange that the diagram should have been drawn with a specific indication that water surround the castle and then its dramatic potential be ignored.

The ditch itself need not be very wide or deep. The action of *Ane Satire of the Thrie Estaitis* makes much of the comic business of crossing a ditch,[16] and there is no good reason to suppose that similar comic effects could not be devised for the discomfiture of the vices during the siege. It could easily be bridged in a number of places if the action symbolically demanded that the characters cross it dry shod. If water were not available – and the fact that it is mentioned in the text implies that it was there on at least one occasion – the barrier given on the plan could be used for the allegorical security of the castle, and a change in the text would have to be made to alter Sloth's foolishness.

It seems fair to conclude therefore that Southern's reconstruction is not entirely self-justifying. If we adopt it we may be overlooking some important effects intended by the dramatist: and it seems wiser to keep as close as possible to the dramatist's intention.

Moral Structure

The three principal features of the plan, the castle, the ditch, and the scaffolds, together with the bed and the cupboard have impor-

16. ll.1377; 1393; 2298; 2439. In *The Pride of Life* there appears to be a ditch over which Mirth leaps: see *T.I.*, p. 53, l. 269.

tant parts to play in the revelation of the moral allegory which lies at the heart of the play. In themselves they are very simple devices, and their origins are not obscure. The image of the castle as a place of spiritual security is widespread in medieval theology.[17] Perhaps the closest parallel is that in Robert Grosseteste's *Le Chasteau d'Amour*. Grosseteste was Bishop of Lincoln (d. 1253) and he was much concerned in the work of educating the clergy. His poem describes an assault upon a castle by the Devil, with Pride, Wrath, and Sloth, the World, with Envy and Covetousness, and the Flesh with 'Fou Delit' and Gluttony.[18] The scaffolds, raised booth stages, with a curtain to be closed when the actor is to withdraw, are commonplace.[19] The skill lies in the juxtaposition of these ideas and the allegorical and dramatic use which is made of them. This is perhaps best described by first reviewing the development of the plot and the accompanying arrangements for staging devices.

In this edition the text is divided into four sections which correspond roughly with the allegorical structure. Clearly it is possible to propose other arrangements (Eccles has 23 scenes), but the one adopted here follows the broad rhythm of the dramatic movement and emphasizes that the play has a very simple structure in general outline in spite of its great length. Looked at in this way the play can be seen as an archetype of much that was to come in the English morality play, based as it was upon the simple pattern of Temptation and Fall, Repentance, and Mercy. Within it there are also contained other episodes which recur elsewhere, notably the coming of Death (as in *Everyman*), the debate of the daughters of God (as in *Respublica*), and the confrontation between vices and virtues (throughout the morality as a genre, though never in the same momentous physical battle as is seen here).

17. G. R. Owst, op. cit., pp. 77–87. Cf. references to Gregory the Great, Honorius of Autun, and Bernard of Clairvaux in R. Cornelius, *The Figurative Castle*, Bryn Mawr, 1930, pp. 58–9.

18. An accessible version is in *The Minor Poems of the Vernon MS*, part 1, ed. C. Horstman, *EETS*, e.s. 98, 1892, ll. 823–58. See also Cornelius, op. cit., pp. 63–4.

19. Such an arrangement is implied in *The Pride of Life*, in *T.I.*, ll. 303–6, and notes 32 and 33.

1. The First Temptation, ll. 157–1723.

World, Belyal, and Flesh each in turn boast from their scaffolds and refer to the deadly sins associated with them (Avarice; Pride, Wrath, and Envy; Gluttony, Lechery, and Sloth). Man, as a child, is provided at birth with the Good and Bad Angels. The World sends Pleasure and Folly to Man, and they tempt him to enter World's scaffold. Backbiter, who is not associated with the three chief enemies of Man, then persuades him to move to the scaffold of Avarice – to do which he has to cross the acting area. Once he is on the scaffold, Avarice invites the other six deadly sins to join him. They make their way from their masters' scaffolds to that of Avarice. When they arrive Man invites each one to come up. Thus the whole action is now concentrated on Avarice's scaffold, except for the two Angels who watch, presumably from near the centre. Good Angel asks for help from Confession and Penitence. The latter strikes Man with a lance, and makes him descend from the scaffold. Man is absolved by Confession who suggests that he enter the Castle of Perseverance. Here he is met by the seven virtues who usher him in and promise to defend him. Probably the castle was large enough to accommodate all the virtues and Man.

2. The Second Temptation, ll. 1724–2800.

Bad Angel calls upon Backbiter for help. Backbiter, true to his name, causes trouble for the seven deadly sins, for his complaints to Belyal, Flesh, and World lead them to beat their followers. Avarice, the last to be beaten, offers hope to his master, World. World moves from his scaffold to attack the castle, Belyal and Flesh (who is on horseback, l. 1949) with the other six sins following. This sets up the central tableau or visual image of the play. Mankind is in the castle, aided by the seven virtues. Outside, probably beyond the ditch, are the three enemies with the seven deadly sins, as well as Pleasure and Folly. Good and Bad Angels observe the scene. There are thus twenty-two actors committed at this point (and God and the Soul are no doubt in their places waiting for their parts in the action to develop).

The siege is not easy to give in detail, but there are indications of the weapons carried by the sins, and some of their individual actions. The fighting is to last a long time, and there is no doubt that the fight involved physical contact, since the sins complain – in a comic style which becomes traditional – of various grievous injuries. In the end the virtues inflict a defeat on the vices by throwing roses. Only Avarice has any further resource. He presumes upon his old acquaintance with Man, and works upon the weakness of Man's increasing age. Mankind descends from the castle in spite of the protest from the virtues. Avarice gives him money (from his cupboard?) and Man puts himself in his power.

3. Death, ll. 2801–3152.

'Coveytyse copboard' is at the foot of the bed which is under the castle. It appears that the action is now concentrated in this area, and the note on the plan warning that people must not sit there draws attention to it. Death strikes Man to the heart. Man, in possession of worldly riches, calls on World to help him. But World sends his servant, Garcio, to drive him out. The servant, in sinister fashion, says he is an heir called I-wot-nevere-Whoo, a total stranger interested only in riches, and he deprives Man of his goods. Man dies, presumably on the bed. The Soul appears, and Bad Angel, rejoicing, carries him off to Hell on his back. Here he would probably go to Belyal's scaffold which could well be decorated in the form of Hell-mouth as in the mystery plays.

4. Mercy, ll. 3153–3700.

The four daughters of God now discuss the case and decide to go to God's scaffold in order to rehearse the arguments for and against the Soul. God gives judgement in the Soul's favour and the daughters ascend to Bad Angel who is in Belyal's scaffold. They remove the Soul and take him up into God's scaffold where he is finally saved.

There is no doubt that the stage-plan in the manuscript gives plenty of opportunity for the visual representation of the moral doctrine. The terrible ranting of the three enemies on their scaffolds, the peculiarly strong appeal of Avarice who turns the action three times, and the final act of judgement in part 4 are all visually effective. Acts of ascending and descending the scaffolds point up moral changes, as do the movements across the 'place'. In the middle of the acting area the castle remains a dominating image, a persistent reminder of the security of good perseverance. Around it the moral battle is waged, and under it Man is born and dies.

Allegory and Theatre

As we have seen, *The Macro Plays* have survived because of the interest of an eighteenth-century book collector. Because of the shortage of data, we cannot tell how many other plays of a similar nature were written. Perhaps because it originated in eastern England where there was a vigorous dramatic tradition, *The Castle of Perseverance* had some chance of becoming widely known and influential. It certainly does contain much material which is common to other morality plays of the fifteenth century. The reason for this lies in the religious background from which the play derives.

There is little doubt that the play is the work of a cleric who set before himself the objective of communicating religious truth, particularly in the matter of sin and repentance. The source material is in all probability devotional manuals such as John Myrc's *Duties of a Parish Priest*. The aim of these works was to make more accessible the central doctrines of the Church, particularly the important matter of penitence. They relied upon a number of symbols or allegories which are widely distributed through the penitential literature, and are echoed in liturgy and sermon, in art forms like the decoration of churches and cathedrals, and in manuscript illustration.[20] Such widely used items are the Seven Deadly Sins, and their corresponding Virtues, the configuration of the World, the Flesh, and the Devil as three enemies of Man, the Coming of Death, the role of confession and penitence, the power of the sin of Avarice, and the Debate of the daughters of God, Mercy, Peace, Truth, and Justice, over the fate of Man's soul. Of purely literary analogues two are especially interesting for their use of some of these images. These are De Guilleville's poem *Le*

20. See E. Mâle, *L'Art Religieux de la Fin du Moyen Age en France*, Paris, 1908; M. D. Anderson, *Drama and Imagery in English Medieval Churches*, Cambridge, 1963, especially pp. 80–84; and J. Evans, *Life in Medieval France*, 1957 (illustrated edition).

Pèlerinage de la Vie Humaine (c. 1330), and the Middle English poem *Of the Seven Ages* which contains some close parallels, especially the two Angels, the role of Avarice, and the cry for mercy.[21] It is important, however, not merely to establish that commonplaces of doctrine are present in the play, but to observe how they are used. The play, after all, is a dramatic sequence, and in presenting these items, various degrees of emphasis are employed, and the figures are used so as to offer a comprehensive dramatic effect.

As I have already said, the central dramatic tableau is the assault of the vices upon the castle, when the resources of actors, space and action are concentrated upon the dramatic climax. It is clear that one of the main objectives is spectacle – a sense of a large and lengthy conflict taking place before the audience, with verbal as well as physical aspects. The vices are not so much tempters as ethical forces aiming at Man's destruction. Indeed one may say that although there is physical conflict and many blows are exchanged, the point is to show in a ritual way the cosmic conflict of good and evil, so as to gain a sense of the huge scale of the forces working for Man's destruction or salvation. Ritual implies not so much realistic conflict as an ordered demonstration of the issues involved. The audience is meant to accept the terms of the conflict, to appreciate that this is a true and vivid picture of how things actually are in the spiritual conflict.[22] To this end the dramatist emphasizes the individual confrontation of Vice and Virtue, and uses many symbolic touches to embody the detail of this demonstration. Thus Pride is the leader of the vices in the assault because traditionally Pride was the sin of Lucifer: and Pride is opposed by Humility who is the leader of the virtues. The same holds for the use of roses as the weapons of the virtues (though clearly the fight is not simply a matter of throwing roses) and for the interrelation between some of the vices (Sloth as the inspirer of Gluttony and Lechery). In this respect the use of allegory in the play reflects the

21. E. T. Schell, 'On the Imitation of Life's Pilgrimage in *The Castle of Perseverance*', *J.E.G.P.* 67, 1968, pp. 235–48; and A. Nelson, '*Of the Seven Ages*: an unknown analogue of *Castle of Perseverance*', *Comparative Drama* 8, 1974, pp. 125–38.

22. R. Potter, op. cit., p. 10.

late-medieval fascination for elaborate decoration. The concern to decorate rather than to clarify is intimately related to the ritual function. This perhaps accounts for the realistic and commonplace details which are frequently incorporated.[23]

It is of course possible to point to analogues of this conflict of Vices and Virtues. The Vices are traceable to the fourth-century writer Evagrius Ponticus, and the *Psychomachia* of Prudentius has often been looked upon as an important step in the development of the iconography since it describes an actual battle.[24] But through sermon, church decoration, and penitential exercise this notion may be too familiar for a particular source to be in question. Langland, for instance, uses the Vices in *Piers Plowman*, Passus V (B text). The lost *Paternoster Play* at York, mentioned in 1389, was probably a series of pageants about the Vices, and there are indications of a similar play at Beverley.[25] The general familiarity emphasizes the importance of the ritual element.

The three enemies of Man, the World, the Flesh, and the Devil, play their part in the assault by beating the Vices and urging them to battle. At the beginning of the play their boasts are used to demonstrate the horrific forces which threaten Man. Though to the modern reader these figures may seem less than horrific on the page, there seems little doubt that in the setting they would produce an enormous impact. They embody a feeling of terror, underlined by occasional touches of ridicule, and their threat is well maintained throughout the play. This happens particularly in World's callous rejection of Man at the point of death, and the savage enjoyment of Garcio as he despoils Man of his property. Backbiter is a servant of World and he becomes Man's page for a time. His skill is flattery and lies, a reminder of the fear of evil language. His service to Man is destructive, and his devilish qualities are illustrated by his sowing discord among the Sins and the

23. M. R. Kelley, 'Fifteenth-Century Flamboyant Style and *The Castle of Perseverance*', *Comparative Drama* 6, 1972, pp. 14–17: other aspects of elaboration are found in the grouping of stanzas, pp. 21–3.

24. Prudentius, *Opera*, ed. H. J. Thomson, Cambridge, Mass., 1949 (Loeb edition). The most comprehensive study of the Sins is M. W. Bloomfield, *The Seven Deadly Sins*, Michigan, 1952.

25. A dramatic representation of a debate between sins and virtues appears in the *Moralité des Sept Péchés Mortels et Des Sept Vertus*.

Enemies, and his consequent rejoicing. He is one of the characters who by their verbal skill and heartless wickedness foreshadow the Vice of the later morality and interlude. World is also served by Folly and Lust-Liking (Voluptas), evils appropriate to the subversion of the young.

A special role is assigned to Avarice, who also serves the Devil. Though he is one of the Sins, he operates from his own scaffold, and is given the special role of persuader. When the siege has failed it is Avarice who persuades Man to leave the castle and indulge in the vice which is traditionally the weakness of age. Man acknowledges the force of his argument—

Thou seyst a good skyl. (l. 2550)

Perhaps the most terrifying moment in the play is the coming of Death. This figure, no doubt costumed like a skeleton, appears widely in medieval art, which generally emphasizes the impermanence of Man, and the inevitability of Death for all levels of society. The Dance of Death was evolved in homiletic literature to point this, and showed Death dancing with individual Popes, Emperors, Cardinals, and other representative figures. It exists as a Latin poem in the fourteenth century in France, and may have appeared as a mime at other places on the Continent, perhaps related to sermons. It was also shown in pictorial terms.[26] As an analogue to the coming of Death in *The Castle of Perseverance* the Dance illustrates widespread terror and apprehension. Death appears as a character in *Everyman* and *The Death of Herod* (Play 20 of *Ludus Coventriae*) and by implication or reference in several others. Often his arrival is sudden and dramatic. In *The Castle of Perseverance* the development of the action draws attention to Death before he arrives. Even Man himself foresees Death, without being wise enough to take a true account. From a didactic point of view Death draws attention to the need for repentance, but his arrival shows that Man has reached the point of no return. There is dramatic tension here, because it is too late for Man to save himself. At the point of death he is isolated and terrified. The reso-

26. See Mâle, op. cit., pp. 390–91; Anderson, op. cit., pp. 75–9; and Potter, op. cit., pp. 20–21.

lution of this crisis in the last sequence of the play is a major feature of the play's overall structure.

The dramatist is concerned to show the large number of forces which influence Man, for both good and evil. The evil side, World, Flesh, and the Devil, the Seven Sins, Backbiter, Lust-Liking, Folly, Garcio, and Death, is co-ordinated by the Bad Angel who usually appears in company with the Good Angel. The Bad Angel, indeed, provides the driving force for most of the play. The Banns give a clear indication of this since they mention his 'Fals entysynge', and show how he is to prompt the actions of Avarice. In the play itself, the Bad Angel speaks of having 'tysyd' (enticed) Man in the role of tempter (l. 540). He persuades Man that repentance can be put off until old age, even though he knows how important confession is (l. 1285). Besides the role of tempter, he also spurs Backbiter to new evil (l. 1733), and rejoices when Man leaves the Castle for Avarice (l. 2671ff.). It is the Bad Angel who takes Man to Hell after death, a function inherited by many later stage Vices, but his promoting the evil in the play is only part of the didactic pattern. He reveals that he does know the truth, and he specifically mentions the importance of penitence (ll. 1282–90). His frequent appearances in company with the Good Angel make his role almost a choric one: to present and underline the moral position, and not merely to be the advocate of evil. It is quite possible that the two Angels are present during most of the action, perhaps located near the middle of the acting area, and observing all that goes on. In this way they provide didactic impulse and dramatic continuity.

The good characters, especially the Virtues, are often used as close parallels to the bad. They do occasionally take the initiative, a notable instance being Confession and Penance (Conscience is mentioned in the Banns, but he does not appear in the play). Confession comes to the aid of Good Angel when the latter laments Man's first submission to Avarice. Penance strikes him to the heart with his lance, thus inducing 'sorwe of hert' which is the essence of true repentance. This intervention changes the course of events for a time, and Man leaves Avarice. But the good characters are circumscribed by Man's weaknesses, and in the end they cannot prevent the exercise of free will by Man: this is a cardinal feature of the didactic purpose of the play, and it offers dramatic flexibility sufficient to maintain the momentum of the plot.[27] If Man wishes to follow evil, he must be allowed to do so –

> For if he wyl to foly flyt
> We may hym not wyth-syt.
> He is of age and can hys wyt. (ll. 2611–3)

In the end the plot and the allegory turn upon the exercise of mercy. Fortunately for Man – and here we touch upon the essential optimism of the play – he cries for mercy at the moment of death. This is tantamount to the contrition which is essential to salvation, and it gives to Mercy and Peace the opportunity of pleading for Man in the last sequence of the play. I have already mentioned that there is something of a change in the last sequence. One of its characteristics is an attempt to consider much of the scriptural teaching which underlines the divine mercy. Perhaps the author was looking at the mystery cycles at this point, for it is notable that he refers to a number of stories which are enacted in the mystery cycles, particularly Lucifer, the Creation, the Crucifixion, the release of the damned (the Harrowing of Hell) and Judgement Day. Thus, though it may lack vigorous action, it succeeds poetically in adducing much material which is relevant to the issue of salvation.

It is not surprising then that the play as a whole is distinguished by religious orthodoxy, and the need to promote the issues of penitence and divine mercy in a period when there was widespread ecclesiastical concern for the spiritual education of religious and lay. An understanding of the play by the modern reader must depend to some extent upon a recognition of this. But we also wish to see the work as a play; as an example of literary and dramatic art it speaks with a powerful voice. The author has the ability to arrange his material in an aesthetically effective way. This is seen not only in the plot and in the organization of the symbolic material which we have been discussing, it also permeates his treatment of the central character. The nature of the play determines that Man should not be presented as an individual, but as a representative of all men. This generality means that he is without individual traits of character. He exhibits only feelings common to all men. As a

27. For an analysis of the function of free will in the morality plays, see M. Fifield, *The Rhetoric of Free Will*, Leeds, 1974.

youth he is foolish and gullible, as an old man he is fearful and ingenuous. But besides moral characteristics of this type he shows intense human emotions. His desires for security, friendship, peace of mind make us sympathize with him. He is subject to suffering and death, and at the end of his life when Death strikes him, he is a pathetic figure. The author is not slow to exploit these emotional aspects, and it is here that the play transcends the moral didacticism of penitential literature, and becomes a genuine work of art.

This is achieved by a dramatic and poetic process. In dramatic terms, as we have seen, the play has some powerful moments. The central siege is particularly effective, but there are other moments when Man and the forces around him are seen in dramatic terms. To some extent this is a visual process. Man hearing but not comprehending the arguments of Avarice and the Angels is an example of this. So too are the movements from one scaffold to another, a processional effect which should not be underestimated, particularly in an age when procession was an important public activity. The skilful use of stage properties like the lance, the bed, the cupboard, trumpets and banners, together with the ascending and descending the scaffolds are all evidence that the author wished to involve the audience in a process which is inescapably dramatic. Notably irony plays its part in this. Man having accepted Avarice for the second time says with more truth than he knows —

> If I myth al-wey dwellyn in prosperyte,
> Lord God, thane wel were me.
> I wolde, the medys, forsake the
> And nevere to comyn in hevene. (ll. 2797–2800)

Thematically the author's control of the allegorical configurations is very closely linked with the theatrical details. The audience can see the three enemies on their scaffolds, and they observe Man in apparent security at the top of the castle. Visual aspects of this kind show that the dramatist was able to control the response of the audience. Moreover he does not merely control the theatrics, he allows tableau, procession, and action to convey Man's aspirations and fears, and to indicate a more general philosophical-religious perception of the human environment. If the forces struggling for Man are numerous and in various ways crafty, generous, callous, sympathetic, the whole effect is finally optimistic. In the end the play avoids tragedy, but it shows despair and folly, and by exploiting the emotional effects of these, it achieves an emotional climax in the release of tension at the moment of mercy. Drama, by means of physical enactment, gives an image of life. By showing changes of intention, and by presenting the consequences of these, it images dynamically an observation of human experience. Conflict is not merely physical, it is also a matter of ideas and attitudes. The audience's response to the enactment submits them to the author's response to life. It does not matter in the case of *The Castle of Perseverance* that this response is really determined by a philosophical-religious interpretation which may not excite universal acceptance today. If this were not so, it would be impossible to appreciate all religious art.

In applying aesthetic considerations to medieval drama it is worth noting that there was no explicit theory of drama for playwrights to turn to. Although the corpus of medieval drama is considerable, and although modern scholarship has revealed many similarities within individual genres, we have no record of how the theory of drama was evolved and transmitted. It may be a task for modern criticism to supply it. Certainly we can observe in *The Castle of Perseverance* a discipline and an order which indicate a deep appreciation of dramatic structure and dramatic effects. The overall control of allegory, the use of structure and contrast, and particularly the sense of the theatrical environment show that the author possesses a remarkable talent for dramatic art. As a reader, one needs to bear constantly in mind the circumstances of the production in the open air, with a large audience. Their attention is directed by surprise, anticipation, silence, movement, and action to the emotions of Man and to the framework of belief and wisdom which surrounds him.

In language too the writer shows his skill. He sums up Man's fear with great pathos —

> I bolne and bleyke in blody ble
> And as a floure fadyth my face.
> To helle I schal bothe fare and fle
> But God me graunte of hys grace.
> I deye certeynly.   (ll. 3023–7)

He writes powerful boasts for the pompous enemies, relying upon strong alliterative effects. The Sins and other evils speak with crafty skill –

> Thou thou syt al day and prey,
> No man schal com to the nor sende;
> But if thou have a peny to pey,
> Men schul to the thanne lystyn and lende
> And kelyn al thi care.   (ll. 2541–5)

Indeed the writer sometimes exhibits a kind of indulgence in the enjoyment of language. But the poetry is not simply language: it is also ideas, invention, and the special potency of expression which comes from the imaginative combination of circumstance and feeling.

III MAGNYFYCENCE BY JOHN SKELTON

Text, Date, and Performance

There is only one surviving early edition of *Magnyfycence* of which one complete copy is in the Cambridge University Library. It is undated, perhaps 1533, and the printer is unknown, though eighteenth-century editors attributed it to John Rastell, and this has not been seriously challenged. The most important subsequent editions are those by Dyce (1843) and Ramsay (1908).

There is some internal evidence for dating, chiefly the probable reference to Louis XII who died in 1515. The play was probably written after his death and before the peace with France in 1518. This was a time of some financial embarrassment as Henry VIII delved deeper into the enormous wealth inherited from his father on his accession in 1509, and there may have been occasion to warn Henry of the need for wisdom in financial matters. However Winser offers an earlier date for the original composition, perhaps in the 1490s when Skelton was Prince Henry's tutor.[28] We can do no better than suppose that the play was written with Henry in mind, since it directs his attention to the kingly virtue of magnificence.

28. L. Winser, 'Skelton's *Magnyfycence*', *Renaissance Quarterly* 23, 1970, pp. 14–25.

It may be that the passage dealing with the king's rage is a specific personal element. It is not now thought that Wolsey is the chief object of Skelton's satire on court vices: these were after all general vices to which all princes are subject, and Wolsey's influence was not at its strongest in the earliest years of Henry's reign.

The indications are that the play is very much a court drama. Not only is the subject matter largely concerned with an allegory on the kingly virtues and their opposite vices, there is also emphasis upon court fools and public affairs which suggests that the play was intended for an élite audience. There is a carefully controlled doubling scheme for five actors. Bevington has suggested that the layout of the list of characters following the text itself gives a clear indication that Skelton saw the play as a series of four sequences each with a doubling plan. The need to write for a small group of actors has meant that the good characters and the bad do not meet.[29]

The stage directions which are full and interesting throw a little more light upon the process of composition. There are fifty-one on the Cambridge copy; of these twenty-three are in Latin, and the rest in English. Whilst it is difficult to be certain why such an arrangement was adopted, it is notable that most of the Latin ones occur before l. 748 or after l. 1966 (there are only two in Latin between these two points). The English directions are thus concentrated in the middle of the play where the doubling scheme shows most signs of stress. The possibility therefore arises that the original version was somewhat different from what we have received, and that some rewriting was necessary in the central episodes of the play where the intrigue and fooling are most carefully developed.

The play shows a remarkable variety of verse forms, a reflection of Skelton's poetic craftsmanship. He uses rime royal for most of the more telling episodes, and various shorter lines and patterns according to mood. Indeed the play is particularly effective in terms of expression as Skelton was a very conscious stylist. The mood varies from lively comedy to severe foreboding. Skelton particularly tries to introduce racy language for the fools. There are

29. See Appendix 1 below, pp. 677–83, and D. M. Bevington, *From 'Mankind' to Marlowe*, Cambridge, Mass., 1962, pp. 132–7.

many proverbs in the play. These offer moral ideas as well as pithiness of expression. Indeed the fool tradition is rich in such expressions, and Skelton is not slow to make use of it.

Moral and Political Allegory

The characters in *Magnyfycence* all represent abstractions. Though there may be implied similarities between the hero and Henry VIII, Skelton's main purpose is to offer a moral doctrine which has general application, and to do this he chooses characters who stand for moral ideas. His concern is mainly with the matter of kingship, and it may be recalled that he had earlier written a *Speculum Principis* for his royal pupil.[30] It is not possible to be sure whether Skelton was the first to turn the morality play in the direction of instruction for kings, but it is clear that other dramatists later in the sixteenth century made much of this new preoccupation.

The strongest influences upon Skelton were the morality plays themselves, the theological exposition of kingly virtues,[31] some poetical conventions relating to Fortune and human impermanence, and the vigorous tradition of satire particularly directed at court vices like flattery. With great subtlety and remarkable ingenuity Skelton set out to combine these well-established modes of thought and expression into a coherent but complex moral scheme for the benefit of kings, and so of all men.

Magnyfycence represents the kingly virtue of magnanimity, the outstanding greatness of soul, and the authority and judgement essential to kingship. But, following the morality tradition, the hero has to be seen to make moral progress through his exposure to the forces which threaten to envelop him. Here, however, there are no angels and devils, and the moral conflict is markedly different from that in other morality plays even though at certain points it shows a precise application of some of the methods and conventions.

The opening speech of Felycyte sets up a number of important themes. He first draws attention to the primary influence of reason

30. W. O. Harris, *Skelton's 'Magnyfycence' and the Cardinal Virtue Tradition*, Chapel Hill, 1965, p. 129 ff.

31. Harris, loc. cit., pp. 71–126.

in human affairs, and then indicates that the proper use of wealth
is a test of wisdom (l. 4), especially as wealth is not permanent,
and the challenge of prosperity may be followed by that of adversity. Only if Sad Cyrcumspeccyon supports prudence can Wealth
be properly used. The main threat is that the influence of reason
may be subject to 'Wyll' and thus prosperity is impermanent.

Felycyte is joined by Lyberte who quickly reveals his impatience
with any form of restraint (l. 73). Measure, apparently aware of the
argument, interrupts their debate, and taking his stand upon support
from Horace he asserts that Measure must control both Felycyte
and Lyberte (l. 114ff.). This Horatian equanimity in the face of
prosperity and adversity shows that Measure must affect 'every
condycyon' (l. 115). Even though Lyberte asks for his 'fre wyll'
it is concluded that Sad Dyrreccyon is necessary.

After this is established, Magnyfycence appears and asserts that
Measure must control the other two, even though Lyberte is
obviously restless at the constraint imposed upon him (ll. 207–8,
232). Magnyfycence is certain that this offers the best chance of
prosperity. Fansy arrives and pretends that he is Largesse, and that
he is indispensable to true nobleness (l. 264–8). He brings a letter
which he says comes from Sad Cyrcumspeccyon and which supports his claim. Magnyfycence accepts the letter and in doing so
opens the way for the first of the court vices, Counterfet Countenaunce. The latter explains in his declaration (ll. 403–493) how his
evil may be exercised and he makes it clear that he knows that
Fansy's trick has worked.

Though the names of the court vices are sometimes frustratingly
similar, there seems little doubt that Skelton made them so in order
to emphasize how closely they work together. Counterfet Coun-
tenaunce is joined by Crafty Conveyaunce and Clokyd Colusyon,
and Fansy cements the alliance. Three more aliases are set up –
Crafty Conveyaunce becomes Sure Surveyaunce (ll. 525–6)
Counterfet Countenaunce becomes Good Demeynaunce (l. 674)
Clokyd Colusyon becomes Sober Sadnesse (l. 681).
While the others leave to join the service of Magnyfycence, Clokyd
Colusyon makes his declaration (ll. 689–744), and in doing so
reveals his connection with Favell, the court vice of flattery (l. 727).
He is joined by his old acquaintance Courtly Abusyon who in turn

makes his declaration (ll. 829–911), and another alias is established
on the advice of Fansy –
Courtly Abusyon becomes Lusty Pleasure (l. 965).

It appears that the vices, offstage, have managed to set Lyberte
free from the control of Measure (ll. 933–950), and they leave
Fansy to make his declaration which is prefaced by his description
of his pet owl which he presents as though it were a hawk. He
shows that he is brain-sick, and this suggests that he is a representation of unrestrained will. This comic exposition is elaborated
further when Foly arrives, and appears even more silly than Fansy.
They exchange purses, and eventually they also exchange pets,
Fansy's owl for Foly's dog, 'Grim' (l. 1136). It appears that the
two fools were at school together. Here we have a notable shift
from the devils of the earlier morality plays, for these two are
examples of the court fool tradition rather than tempters of the
kind found in *The Castle of Perseverance* and *Mankind*. They
demonstrate their skilful fooling at the expense of Crafty Conveyaunce and another alias is established –
Foly becomes Consayte (l. 1310).
Crafty Conveyaunce makes his declaration (ll. 1327–74), and so
completes the organization and revelation of the villains. Skelton
has assembled a complex group here, the two chief influences being
the satire of court vices which perhaps goes back to *Piers Plowman*,
and the fool tradition. The scene is now set for the destruction of
Magnyfycence, but we should note that the play is more than half
run before Skelton is ready to bring it about. This demonstration
of the comic and moral aspects of the villains was one of the chief
purposes of the play.

The action now shows that Magnyfycence has released Lyberte,
in spite of Felycyte's protest: reason is losing control (l. 1387).
Felycyte is placed under the control of Lusty Pleasure (Courtly
Abusyon). Magnyfycence, left alone, makes his boast in which he
shows pride in comparing himself with an impressive list of rulers
and leaders from the past. In the process he defies Fortune (ll. 1459–
61), and so anticipates, or provokes, the form of the disaster which
is to come.

Courtly Abusyon now demonstrates his power over Magnyfycence by acting as a tempter, for he advises him to give way to

Lechery (ll. 1545–86) and Anger (ll. 1601–28). He emphasizes the importance of Wyll and Lust-and-lykyng. Clokyd Colusyon plays his part in this moral sequence by pretending to intercede for Measure, when he is really prompting Magnyfycence to dismiss him in anger (ll. 1723–4). The authority of Sober Sadnesse (Clokyd Colusyon), Lusty Pleasure (Courtly Abusyon) and Surveyaunce (Crafty Conveyaunce) over Lyberte and Largesse (Fansy) is confirmed (ll. 1783–9). This assertion of Appetyte (l. 1793) is followed by another challenge by Magnyfycence to Destiny. The final stupidity is then enacted as Magnyfycence listens indulgently to the rubbish offered to him by Foly (ll. 1803–40). He is ripe for disaster, and Fansy, mournful and apprehensive, reveals the true identities of the villains and tells him that Adversyte has arrived.

Adversyte is a complex figure, and is especially interesting because of the traits combined in the character. He is sent from God, and is a moral force. He acts as a correction for those who are falsely secure. In this way he is a kind of divine justice – like the scourge of God in Marlowe's plays. Because he brings down all powerful men he is similar to Death as shown in the Dance of Death, and the dramatization here recalls the coming of Death in *The Castle of Perseverance*. As we have seen, the latter does have moral overtones, and here Adversyte acts as a punisher of those who fall to folly, and in the case of Magnyfycence himself one who lacks true judgement. Yet there are those whom he strikes who do not deserve to suffer, and for these he is a test of patience. He himself speaks of his affinity with Fortune.

The effect upon Magnyfycence is devastating. Not only is he physically beaten, but he is also despoiled of all his wealth. Poverte comes to mark his degradation, but Magnyfycence fails to respond to promptings to repent. This failure is significant because it leads to further suffering. He now witnesses the rejoicing of Lyberte and three of the court vices. Lyberte reminds him of his errors, particularly his misuse of will, and his dependence upon Fansy and Foly. Magnyfycence has to beg from the villains, and receives nothing. This leads to Wanhope, the despair of the mercy of God (l. 2281). In this sequence following the coming of Adversyte, Magnyfycence thus fails again for he lacks the greatness of soul to survive adversity, and so the second aspect of Horace's ideal is beyond his reach. To mark this, Skelton uses the sinister figures of Dyspare and Myschefe who come to prompt his suicide. It is notable that this is a powerful theatrical moment. In bringing it about Skelton has avoided the clumsiness of much stage-devilry, and at the same time has chosen to mark the moral crisis by a return to strict theological doctrine – that despair and the absence of grace are the companions of suicide. Thus the political morality merges into a wider ethical context which has implications for personal salvation.

Magnyfycence is saved by the intervention of Good Hope who brings the grace of God (l. 2349), and explains that Adversyte tries men's patience, and tests their wisdom (ll. 2368–72). Magnyfycence is reassured and confesses his wilfulness: he is now hopeful of his salvation, Good Hope having brought about a cure. Redresse perceives that Magnyfycence is in a state of grace, and gives him a new garment signifying his restoration. Sad Cyrcumspeccyon, who is wise enough to deal with all fortunes, at last appears, and the letter which Fansy had used to secure Magnyfycence's trust is proved a forgery. It is made clear by Redresse that nobleness should be liberal but not prodigal, and so the theme of the right use of riches is brought home to Magnyfycence. At the same time he is warned to fear God and not to trust Fortune (ll. 2494–7). The changeableness of life is emphasized by Cyrcumspeccyon and Perseverance, and Magnyfycence has learned that wealth can pass away and that the only remedy is wisdom.

Skelton's moral view thus depends upon elements of personal morality and fate which are common in the tradition of the morality plays, but his concern with the particular function of the king's proper use of wealth associates him with the newly emerging political ideas. Although the play shows us that Magnyfycence is tested in the manner of the morality plays, and needs to be restored through repentance, he returns at the end to his palace and to the exercise of his royal authority. The vices he has encountered reflect the threat of his own wilfulness, and also satirize the evils of flattery and corruption which are intimately associated with court life. This mixture of traditional morality structure, depending as it does upon the hero's free choice of the wrong advisers, and of a wider group of ideas relating to the morality of kingship is given a very particular flavour in the play. The ideas themselves may not be original, but the effect is.

Since the evils which confront Magnyfycence are specifically those of the court, there is a general shift in the way in which they are presented. Instead of representations of the deadly sins, or the configuration of the World, the Flesh, and the Devil, we find Magnyfycence is attacked by vices which are themselves the subject of satire.[32] It is here, it seems, that one of Skelton's chief gifts is exercised, for he presents an uncompromising picture of corruption and self-interest. The villains, using some morality devices in disguise and alias, are seen not as devils but as crooks. Perhaps Skelton himself had suffered from these abuses, for it is notable in his other poetry that he reacts very sharply when his own position or reputation are threatened. It may also be that his inspiration for these satirical portraits was not from his predecessors in the drama but from those poets who like him saw themselves as the moral critics of their age, particularly Chaucer and Langland.

The theme of contempt for the world which also arises in *Magnyfycence* is another which has theological and poetic originators. He had used this theme in his earlier treatise, the *Speculum Principis*, which he had offered to Prince Henry. It is one of the medieval reactions to the horror of man's estate. Like the warning against tyranny which is also present in Magnyfycence himself – an echo from Herod in the mystery cycles – it reveals an ascetic reaction against the deception of life.

The variety of elements – which are to some extent self-conflicting – reveal the extraordinary sense of unease in Skelton's play. He was not a comfortable writer. His sense of man's absurdity was too great for him to accept completely a moral order which explained and tidied up the universe. It is therefore all the more surprising that the conventions of the morality play should offer him scope to reveal himself so effectively.

32. For an account of Skelton as a satirical poet, and particularly the sati ical coherence of *Magnyfycence* see A. R. Heiserman, *Skelton and Satire*, Chicago, 1961, especially pp. 124–5.

IV KING JOHAN BY JOHN BALE

Text

The manuscript of *King Johan* which is now in the Huntington Library, San Marino, California (MS. HM3), is a fascinating document with many puzzles and ambiguities to engage the specialist. Our account here must necessarily be brief. It came to light in Ipswich some time after 1831, and was first printed by John Payne Collier in 1838 for the Camden Society. It is written in two hands and really comprises two versions of the play. To begin with Scribe A transcribed his copy, the A-text, from a lost exemplar, and he made up a version of some twenty-two leaves, probably forty-four pages. He then carried out some minor corrections. Later, the second scribe, who has been identified from the handwriting as Bale himself, took the manuscript of this A-text and set about a revision which became the B-text. At first he corrected spellings and other minor blemishes on the pages of the A-text adding a few lines here and there, and sometimes writing longer passages up the margin. On two occasions he wished to insert even longer passages and he wrote them out on smaller sheets, marking them with symbols to show where they were to be inserted. These were MS. p. 23, ll. 991–1011, and MS. p. 26, ll. 1086–1120.

On p. 38 of the manuscript, however, he apparently decided that he must revise more radically than hitherto. The changes he made to five pages corresponding to ll. 1666–1803 are so complicated that I have set them out separately in Appendix 2 (pp. 684–5 below). Much of the new material elaborated the part of Sedicyon, who turns out to be a much bolder character as a result.

It is not surprising that with the text on these five pages in such a complicated state Bale decided that he must write out the rest of the play more clearly as an uninterrupted text, and he began a new copy from MS. p. 41 onwards. Because this final section of the manuscript, MS. pp. 41–63, contains only very minor corrections, it is possible that it is a transcription from the newly evolved B-text.

The original ending of the A-text is now lost, but the cancelled lines on the unnumbered sheets *1–*4 show that in the process of making the B-text Bale incorporated most of his earlier work, expanding as he went along. The A-text probably extended to some 2000 lines, whilst the B-text, which is the basis of this edition, runs to 2691 lines.

The division into Books or Acts as indicated by Bale's notes at l. 1121 and l. 2691 presents a number of problems. The A-text was not divided. The division was made by Bale when he inserted the Interpreter's speech at l. 1086 as he prepared the B-text. However Bale's references in his bibliographical works of 1536, 1548, 1557, and 1559 all mention two books about King John. It was his custom to quote the first line of each work in such lists, and none of those he gives is the same as line 1 of the A-text. This raises the possibility that there is a lost text divided into Books or Acts, or that the A-text is the second part of two originally composed by Bale. There would seem to be a considerable amount of biographical material about King John which is not used in the extant text, notably his military adventures in Ireland and France, the death of Prince Arthur, and Magna Carta.

A list of editions of the play appears in the Note on Books (p. 69). Collier's edition was the chief source for Manly and Farmer, both of whom attempted some modernization. Bang's facsimile has been invaluable in the production of the text here. With Pafford's text, it shares the distinction of including all the known material, including the cancelled sheets. Pafford's text is a very close reprint of the spelling of the original. Creeth and Armstrong both attempt a degree of modernization. Adams' edition is undoubtedly the best available, and a considerable debt must here be acknowledged. It follows the original very closely indeed, prints the continuation of the A-text including the cancelled portion, and derives great strength from a very close scrutiny of the manuscript.

Date

As there was a gap of about twenty years between the two versions of *King Johan* it may be as well to consider the dates of composition against a general view of Bale's varied and eventful life.[33]

33. For a more detailed account see W. T. Davies, 'A Bibliography of John Bale', *Oxford Bibliographical Society Proceedings and Papers* V, 1940, pp. 201–79.

He was born on 21 November 1495 at Cove, near Southwold in Suffolk. After a period in the Carmelite House in Norwich, he was at Jesus College, Cambridge, in about 1513. There he studied philosophy and probably met Thomas Cranmer. He became interested in bibliographical and antiquarian studies, and he also wrote a history of the Carmelites. When the Reformation began to affect the life of the Church in England, Bale was ready to break with the old ways: he abandoned his vows in order to get married, probably in 1536. He rebelled against the Roman Church and took a living at Thorndon in Suffolk. His activities eventually drew hostile attention from the hierarchy, and he was imprisoned and lost his living. However, the interest of Thomas Cromwell was powerful on his behalf, and he was released from prison in 1537.

This seems to have been a critical event in his life for he now became an apologist of the Reformation. Under the patronage of Cromwell he wrote a number of plays in support of the new religion, and took a leading part in the troupe which performed them. It is at this point that we reach the first version of *King Johan*. There is both internal and external evidence to help determine the date of composition. The most important internal evidence is perhaps the reference to

> . . . a joynt of Darvell Gathyron. (l. 1229)

This huge wooden image of a saint was brought from North Wales in April 1538 and burnt at Smithfield on 22 May. There is no reason to suppose that the line concerned is an interpolation, and it therefore fixes the earliest date for the A-text. The reference to the rising in the North of 1536 is another useful pointer (ll. 2514–15). As to external evidence, Adams mentions a letter to Cromwell by Robert Ward dated 9 October 1538.[34] This names 'Mr Bale', and also refers to 'usurped power' and 'sedition'. At the beginning of the next year a letter from Cranmer to Cromwell specifically refers to 'an Interlude concernyng King John' performed on Thursday the second day of January 1539. Cromwell's account books also record two payments to 'Balle and his ffelowes', one on 8 September 1538, and one for 31 January 1539. Neither actually mentions *King Johan*, but it certainly looks as though there were two per-

34. B. B. Adams, (ed.), *John Bale's 'King Johan'*, San Marino, 1969, p. 20.

formances of the play: one at Canterbury early in September, and one on 2 January.

The A-text was probably prepared in close association with these performances. It is not written in Bale's handwriting, but, as we see from the doubling instructions, it seems to bear evidence of some concern for the practicalities of managing the cast. It is of course possible that the play was composed somewhat earlier and that it was updated by the reference to Darvel Gathyron. Other hints of composition earlier in the 1530s come in Imperial Majesty's treatment of Sedition which has been compared with Henry VIII's treatment of Robert Aske who was executed at York in July 1537, and in the reference to the capture of Munster by the Anabaptists in 1532-5. But both these are in the later part of the B-text, and there is no way of telling whether they appeared in the A-text. If they did, they would fit with Bale's support of Henry's pro-Reformation policy in the late 1530s.

With the fall of Cromwell in 1540 Bale felt himself at risk once more as he seems to have had enemies in ecclesiastical circles. He left for the Continent in that year taking his wife and children with him. His exile lasted some eight years, until after the death of Henry when the political climate moved again in favour of the Reformation. He returned to England, and after a period of waiting he obtained preferment, being appointed Bishop of Ossory in Ireland in 1552. On his arrival in Ireland he found himself again in a very hostile environment. The accession of Mary Tudor proved another threat. Bale defiantly produced some of his plays at the Market Cross in Kilkenny. His activities provoked a violent reaction, and he had to go into exile again. After some dramatic adventures which included capture by pirates he eventually reached safety on the Continent. During the next few years he continued his polemical work, perhaps helping Foxe with the *Book of Martyrs*. After Elizabeth's accession in 1558 he returned to England, and was appointed a Canon at Canterbury on 1 January 1560. He was now nearly 65 years of age, and perhaps because of his age he did not resume his see in Ireland. He died in November 1563 and was buried in Canterbury Cathedral.

The B-text belongs to the last few years of his life. The sheets which contain the expanded ending have the date 1558 on the watermark. These pages, and most of the interpolations in Bale's hand in the earlier part of the manuscript seem to have been written out at the same time. The reference to proclamation against the Anabaptists (ll. 2678–81) suggests that the final work of copying and editing took place after September 1560. But this is not to say that the actual composition of the material was not somewhat earlier. The references to 'our late King Henry' and to Leland's slumber (he died in 1552) suggest that Bale may have worked on the text before his final years at Canterbury. The reference to the need to suppress the Anabaptists (ll. 2626–31) implies that he was working on the text before 1560. Perhaps the solution advanced by Adams is the most convincing:[35] most of the B-text modifications were prepared before 1560, and the last lines, a sort of Epilogue, starting at l. 2650, were added in that year as Bale finally put the text in order, possibly in readiness for a performance before Elizabeth. She visited Ipswich in 1561, and this may account for the fact that Collier recovered the manuscript there in the nineteenth century.

Sources

Bale's chief inspiration was William Tyndale's *Obedience of a Christen Man*, 1528, which was a Reformation protest against the tyranny of the Papacy. In extolling the virtues of King John's fight with the Pope, Tyndale gave Bale the theme he wanted in the 1530s, one which no doubt recommended itself to King Henry and perhaps to Cromwell. Especially notable is Tyndale's concept that all the earlier chronicles about John were Catholic and therefore biased.[36]

Tyndale's treatment is however somewhat brief, and Bale looked elsewhere for amplification. As his later bibliographical works show, he was a student of antiquarian and historical authors, and the references at l. 2195 ff. show a wide interest in writings about King John. It is not always easy to see which author Bale

35. op. cit., pp. 23–4.
36. R. Pineas, *Tudor and Early Stuart Anti-Catholic Drama*, New York, 1972, p. 18. For other aspects of Tyndale's influence see the same author's 'William Tyndale: Controversialist', *Studies in Philology* 60, 1963, pp. 117–32.

followed primarily, though a list of some of the works concerned will be found in the note on these lines.

Perhaps the most widely known account of King John is to be found in the English version of *The Brut* which has survived in over 150 manuscripts, and in thirteen printed editions between 1400 and 1528, including those by Caxton and Wynkyn de Worde.[37] The account which runs from chapter cxlvi to chapter clv is particularly detailed in the episode of the poisoning by the monk at Swineshead Abbey (chapter clv).

Structure

In considering *King Johan* from a critical point of view we find much that is similar to *Magnyfycence*. There is very strong evidence that Bale knew the morality play tradition in great detail and, as we shall see, he used many aspects of it. But like Skelton he was concerned with a political objective, and in order to achieve it he had to change the working of the morality pattern in many ways. He was a learned man, but whereas Skelton's learning was primarily that of a poet and philosopher, we may characterize Bale in terms of the propaganda of the Protestant religion. He was also an antiquary, with much interest in rescuing and preserving details of the past. These two aspects lie behind his treatment of the morality tradition, for what he did was to relate allegory to a series of historical events from the life of King John which happened to fit his political and religious objectives. The constraints upon this process were perhaps aesthetic advantages, for he adapts his historical material to give emphasis to the allegory, and he has to make changes in the allegory of temptation and fall so as to keep as near as possible to the historical events. This process was essentially a literary problem, and it is probably the most creative aspect of the play. It may not have been strictly original, but to undertake it asked great intellectual and imaginative powers.

A brief outline of the plot will illustrate how the history and allegory are interwoven. Widow England is much oppressed by the Church and complains to Johan. The chief villain is Sedicyon —

37. *The Brut, or The Chronicles of England*, ed. F. W. D. Brie, *EETS*, o.s. 131 and 136, 1906–8.

he is also an example of 'the Vice' – who explains how extensively the Church operates in support of the Pope (l. 212 ff.). He makes it clear that auricular confession is one of the ways by which the Pope maintains his grip on England (ll. 272–3). The King should be supported by his three estates, Nobylyte, Clergye, and Cyvyle Order, but their allegiance is somewhat doubtful, as is revealed by minor devices like Clergy's verbal slip (l. 512). When they swear allegiance at l. 526 the audience is in no doubt that things are not what they seem.

Sedicyon is aided by Dissymulacyon who reveals how he operates through the religious orders and supports his two followers Privat Welth and Usurpid Power. This alliance is made clear by a typical allegorical device in which Sedicyon is carried by the other three (l. 802 SD). This emphasizes that the Church is deceiving the state in the interests of Rome, an act of sedition which undermines the King's authority and saps his wealth. Sedicyon's speech at l. 813 ff. sums up this position, and so we reach at an early point in the play a clear declaration of the moral and political issues. So far there has been little which can be called historical, but at this point it is revealed that Stephen Langton, the prospective Archbishop of Canterbury, is really Sedicyon, and thus the play takes a great step imaginatively, for we perceive that the abstract characters have an existence outside historical circumstances, and yet they become historical characters from time to time. This must have been made apparent to the audience by means of changes of costume, some parts of Sedicyon's original or basic costume always being detectable under his archiepiscopal disguise. Usurpid Power becomes the Pope, and Privat Welth a Cardinal (l. 1025 SD), and with the threat that Johan will lose his crown when they have undermined allegiance to him we reach the end of the First Part. The Interpretour's speech, which is a later interpolation by Bale, offers a parallel between Johan and Moses, in that they both defend God's people.

In the Second Part, Sedicyon proceeds with his Protean changes: he is not only Stephen Langton, but he also adopts a disguise as Good Perfeccyon (l. 1136). He listens to Nobylyte's confession, and working from the power this gives him, he persuades him under secrecy to be disloyal to Johan. In his role as Langton he

then leads Clergye and Cyvyle Order to declare against the King
(l. 1191 ff.). Privat Welth in the form of a Cardinal curses the King
for resisting him, and releases the people from their allegiance to the
King. Johan asserts the power of Scripture against Papal authority,
and by the same means seeks to challenge the now rebellious
Clergye (l. 1435). Things are now going hard with Johan, and the
Commynalte comes in showing great distress. There is a characteristic allegorical detail in the latter's explanation that he is now
both blind – and might therefore follow the Pope by mistake – and
poor – and therefore unable to support Johan: but such allegory
points inexorably to the political dilemma rather than to a purely
moral one.

There are now further historical elements, for after Johan's
first break with Rome there comes the international league against
him, which, in spite of his defiance, he is powerless to resist because
of the disloyalty of the three estates at home. Sedicyon is trium-
phant, and makes a speech beginning –

Is not thys a sport . . .

which shows the Vice's enjoyment of the successful accomplish-
ment of his schemes: this is followed by an outburst of laughing
which is also a characteristic of the Vice (ll. 1697–1701). The King
is forced to submit to his enemies, and he gives the crown to the
Papal representative, another historical incident (l. 1728 S D). The
Cardynall ruthlessly extorts money from him, and the superiority
of Langton is dramatized by his giving absolution on the Pope's
behalf (l. 1797, and note).

Treason now enters the action, to illustrate that the Church
protects those who are disloyal to the King. Johan preserves a
sober submission to God's will, and prays for help, but the villains
now plot his death. Dissymulacyon reappears, and shows that he
is now Simon of Swynsett, the historical poisoner of the King: thus
allegory and history again come close together. Simon must be
pardoned in advance, which is duly managed by Langton (Sedicyon). Simon persuades the King to drink, but has to take the first
half of the potion himself. He is then grotesquely 'saved' by
Sedicyon (l. 2123 ff.), but Johan's death cannot be prevented. In
itself this is not a major departure from the morality pattern, for

the hero does die in some of them, death being the final test before salvation. But Bale must now restore the ethical balance, and this is done by the introduction of a new series of virtuous characters, notably Verytas who corrects Nobylyte and Cyvyle Order, and Imperyall Majestye who corrects Clergye. Justice is done to the villains: Dissymulacyon is to be hanged at Smithfield (l. 2451) even though he has already 'died' as Simon of Swynsett; and Sedicyon is also condemned though he pours out his crimes in a defiant and careless outburst which really indicates that the particular evil he represents is still full of power (ll. 2508–92). At his last moment he foresees that he will become a saint, a nice Protestant point. The play ends as Imperyall Majestye reunites the three estates, but nothing can be done for Johan save to assert that he defied the antichrist and died nobly.

Bale shows clearly that he can shift quickly and easily between 'history' and allegory. His main purpose is to reveal how the Papacy undermined and destroyed Johan, but since he wanted to draw a parallel between Johan and Henry VIII he could not show that Johan was tempted. His solution is to stick to 'history' where he can, and make as much as possible of the craftiness of the Papacy which is good Henrican material. In fact Johan and Henry are *figurae* of one another in the manner of the mystery cycles. Both are seen as heroic Protestant monarchs relying upon Scripture as their means of following God's will. Johan is the victim of a conspiracy which works like a conspiracy of morality vices in every way except that they do not tempt him. Instead of a fall from innocence, therefore, we have a sense of a closing trap from which Johan, in spite of his virtues, is unable to escape. This, the innocent hero overwhelmed, has been seen by some as an important prototype for tragedy.

The sources of Bale's Protestant attack lie outside the morality play. In this area he was a vigorous propagandist, and it is clear that he saw his dramatic productions in England and in Ireland as contributions to his mission. Trained by the Church himself, he saw many abuses by its members, and he loads his play with details showing the abuses and follies of the religious houses. He attacks vigorously the materialism of the Church, ridicules the liturgy, and especially resents the auricular confession by which the Church controlled the nation's affairs (or so he thought). He sought to express the allegiance which kings owed to God directly, for only in this way could Henry be the ruler of the English Church. He took over the medieval concept of the three estates – which appears more elaborately in Lindsay's play, written at almost the same time as *King Johan* – and as an innovation showed that it is the estates which are tempted and seduced by the vicious agents of the Pope.

Bale was a formidable character. His play is a very clever and effective piece of propaganda. He is not so gifted as Skelton in his powers of expression, but he is his equal in his powers as a playwright. For all his extreme views, and the intolerance that these imply, he puts his play together in a craftsmanlike way, and shows that he could adapt the morality tradition skilfully. It is interesting too that the text of *King Johan* represents his views over a period of about twenty-five years. As he grew older he apparently modified his play more and more successfully, and he never lost the enthusiasm which involved him deeply in the political arena in the prime of his life.

V ANE SATIRE OF THE THRIE ESTAITIS
BY SIR DAVID LINDSAY

Text and Performances

These two aspects of the play are so closely interwoven that it is best to consider them together. The conclusions reached by D. Hamer are still virtually unchallenged, and the following account relies heavily upon his work.[38]

There were certainly three productions of the play during Lindsay's lifetime, and it is highly probable that he was present on each occasion and took an active part in the arrangements, even if he did not appear as an actor.[39] As he was born in 1486, his age at the first known production was 53, and by the time of the later productions he was 65 and 67.

38. D. Hamer, *The Works of Sir David Lindsay of the Mount*, vol. 4, pp. 125–62.

39. As a young man he acted before James IV in 1511; see Hamer, op. cit., p. 246, note 26.

The Performance of 1540 at Linlithgow:
The evidence for this is Sir William Eure's letter written to Thomas Cromwell.[40] Eure was present at Linlithgow Palace at the court of James V at Epiphany –

Ane enterluyde played in the feaste of the Epiphanne of Our Lorde laste paste before the King and Queene at Lighive and the hoole counsaile sprituall and temporall.

The text has not survived, but Eure's letter gives some details of the plot which suggest that it was shorter and simpler than the extant versions. Sensuality, who plays an important part in the later versions, is not mentioned. The circumstances would not perhaps have been very appropriate to the moral of kingly chastity which she was to point up, as the Queen, Mary of Guise, was pregnant, and her coronation was to follow in February.

The Feast of the Epiphany being 6 January, one must accept Hamer's conjecture that the performance took place indoors. The most obvious place at Linlithgow Palace is the Great Hall or Lyon Chalmer on the first floor of the east side. The room is now a ruin, open to the sky, but it is of noble proportions. There is a triple fireplace at the south end with a great window immediately adjacent in the east wall. This would no doubt be the site for the dais and the high table for the royal party. There is a court kitchen at the north end separated by a wall, and probably by screens. A minstrel gallery was formerly placed above the screens. Thus in several respects the Chalmer follows the pattern of baronial halls and the halls of Oxford and Cambridge colleges which had such a profound influence upon the development of the indoor theatre.[41] There are stone seats or benches fixed to the west and east walls of the Chalmer. The west wall provided the main lighting, there being six clerestory windows with a balcony running in front for the length of the wall some twelve feet above the floor. This feature seems to offer possibilities either for seating the audience or for use as an upper stage or an area for commentators, musicians, and the like.

For the production there was a stage ('skaffald'), a dais and a throne for the King in the play, and one must suppose that these

40. 26 January 1540, Hamer, op. cit., vol. 2, pp. 1–6.
41. See Craik, op. cit., p. 9.

were either on the east wall, or, more likely, against the screens to the north. One notices that although the Chalmer is quite large (approximately 120 feet by 30 feet) the production would be for a limited audience – presumably the 'counsaile' would leave little room for others to be present. Eure's account suggests that there were only thirteen players.

Thus we have coherent evidence of an intimate production, on a small scale, expensive, if we consider the Accounts,[42] and suited to a royal entertainment on twelfth night. For the two later productions the style was much changed.

The Performance of 1552 at Cupar in Fife:

The evidence for this and the Edinburgh performance depends upon a consideration of the two extant texts of the play.

1. The Bannatyne MS. George Bannatyne, the compiler of this version in 1568, admits that he has edited and rearranged the play, no doubt because his objective was to compile an anthology of Scottish poetry. He prefaces his edition with a copy of the Banns which make it clear that there was a performance at Cupar (ll. 6, 28), but he does not reconcile this with his other introductory note about the performance at Edinburgh. The Banns do, however, give evidence for date –

> ... the Sevint day of June (l. 11)
> On Witsone tysday (l. 271),

and Hamer indicated that this must have been in 1552.[43]

2. Robert Charteris, Edinburgh, 1602. This printed edition omits the Banns which refer to Cupar, and it modifies some of the references to the town, although some indications of the neighbourhood are still discernible. The arrangements of incidents is much more coherent and the text must therefore be closer to an acting version. This is the text followed in the present edition, as it presumably represents Lindsay's acting version first for Cupar, and then, modified, for the Edinburgh performance.

The text performed at Cupar was more elaborate than the version witnessed by Eure. The Banns indicate that the play was to

42. Hamer, op. cit., vol. 4, p. 126.
43. op. cit., p. 138.

last from seven a.m. until eleven a.m. They also state that the place of performance was 'upone the Castell Hill'. Modern buildings, and the changes of four centuries, make the playing place difficult to locate. But the hill, with a primary school on the top, is still called Castle Hill, though there is no evidence above ground of the medieval castle. Hamer suggests that the playfield was to the north of the castle, on monastic land. Across the Lady Burn to the north, there is still an open space called the Castle Field, and it is possible that this was the place of performance. Although this is some distance from the hill itself (which the Banns designate), G. Wickham's drawing of a possible lay-out is distinctly credible. He places the audience on Cupar Hill by the castle looking across the Burn to the playfield upon which he locates the King's Pavilion, the scaffold and throne, a table and a pulpit. The Burn may thus be the water which is used several times in the action.[44]

It is to be noted that this performance was in the open air, there being concern about fine weather (l. 12). It was a public affair and the Banns are the traditional method of inviting all men and women to attend. The style of this production must have been closer to that of *The Castle of Perseverance* than was the original version. It also contained the piquancy of local allusion, Lindsay's house being three miles from Cupar.

The Performance of 1554 at the Greenside, Edinburgh:
Like the 1540 production, the performance in Edinburgh appeared under royal auspices. Lindsay was now a distinguished senior courtier,[45] having been Lyon King of Arms since 1542. Mary of Guise, the Queen Mother, who was the Queen mentioned in Eure's letter as being present at the Linlithgow performance, assumed the Regency in 1554, and sought to promote dramatic activity in Edinburgh. She required that a playfield be set up at the Greenside. Bannatyne's introductory notes record that the play was 'maid in the Grenesyd besyd Edinburgh'. The actual location appears to be on the low land to the north and west of Calton Hill. The latter is particularly rocky and precipitous and could hardly accommodate

44. G. Wickham, 'The Staging of Saints' Plays in England', in *The Medieval Drama*, ed. S. Sticca, Albany, 1972, p. 114.
45. Hamer, op. cit., pp. 288–90.

a large audience, and it seems clear that room was found on the lower land on the north side now covered by some houses. Hamer refers to expenses incurred in laying out the playfield, and some of the cost may have been due to the necessity of dealing with the marshy nature of the ground.[46] The performance took place on Sunday, 12 August 1554, and it is clear from the Accounts that the Queen was present, and that a special 'hous' was prepared for her. The costs were apparently met by the City and the Guilds. The brief description in Henrie Charteris's Preface to his edition of Lindsay's works (1568) gives an idea of the scope of the performance –

... the play, playit besyde Edinburgh in the presence of the Queen Regent and ane greit part of the Nobilitie with an exceding great nowmer of pepill, lestand fra ix houris afoir none till vi houris at evin.[47]

The play had thus developed from a seasonal court entertainment for King James V to a great public spectacle, and it had been much lengthened in the process. Indeed the stage direction at l. 1911 indicates a break in the performance for refreshment.

The text as we have it contains an aggregation of details about performances, most of them referring to Cupar. It seems clear that the action moves in bursts. There are some 53 named parts, though probably not all the players were visible at any one time. However the number on stage rises to at least thirteen at one point, and therefore extensive doubling seems unlikely. There are a number of highly developed individual roles which would obviously benefit if performed by experienced professionals: roles such as Flatterie, Dissait, Falset, and the two Fools (if they are different).

This kind of structure enables the good and bad characters to meet, which indeed they do on a number of occasions. Moreover the disposition of the stage suggests that there are 'seats' to which the characters retire from time to time. These are available for the King, Chastitie, Veritie, Sensualitie, and the three estates themselves involving seven or more actors. The Second Part of the

46. loc. cit., pp. 140, 151. See also J. Grant, *Old and New Edinburgh*, 1882, vol. 2, p. 102.

47. Hamer, op. cit., p. 139.

play is a Parliament, and this argues a large spectacle with many seats and performers. While the Parliament is in session, certain large public events are enacted, specifically a trial in which pleas are made at the bar, a proclamation of laws, and two sermons. Thus one may envisage that the action takes place in the presence of a large number of seated performers, though dramatic ingenuity could obviously cover for some shortages: when a Bishop retires to his seat, the actor could leave part of the costume or insignia on the seat while he moves off to become another character.

—Moral and Political Themes

The management of the allegory is much less co-ordinated in Lindsay's play than it is in the other three. It may be that the text has suffered somewhat from the modifications which were made for its three performances. There is difficulty also in seeing where Lindsay learned his craft as a writer of a morality play since there is apparently little in Scotland to compare with the state of the English stage in 1540. As a diplomat and courtier he was a travelled man and it may be that he saw morality plays when he visited England and France.[48] What emerged is astonishingly like the English traditions in many respects, showing in fact that Lindsay allied himself to the English convention, and yet this play also comes very close to Scottish political life. There are hints that some of the comic material may have been influenced by French comedy, but the feeling and flavour seem very Scottish indeed, especially as Lindsay writes for all ranks of society, and in a style which is both proverbial and colloquial when dealing with common men.

In a time of great political change, and of some uncertainty for the monarchy, Lindsay was concerned with a programme of modest reform. He was broadly in sympathy with the Reformation, as his attitude to the New Testament in 'Englisch' reveals. He attacks the Church with vigour for its wealth and worldliness, a theme we have

48. Lindsay was in France during the years 1531–7: see V. Harwood, '*Ane Satyre of the Thrie Estaitis* Again', *Studies in Scottish Literature*, 7, 1970, pp. 139–46. For possible French sources for the Fool and Bessy, Fynlaw and Foly's Sermon see A. J. Mill, 'The Influence of the Continental Drama on Lyndsay's *Satyre of the Thrie Estaitis*', *M.L.R.*, 25, 1930, pp. 425–42.

observed in other morality plays, as well as in other satirical writings: the familiar figure of the Pardoner appears again. His political attitudes are related to these concerns, and he seeks to give a picture of the need for change by carefully describing the moral decline which threatens the King. Indeed, in some respects the allegory is very simple, for it shows how the King is subject to sensual pleasures, and that Sensualitie comes so to dominate him and the nation that virtues are constrained and the court vices of flattery – another well tried convention – take over the wealth of the nation for their own advantage. Thus we have another example of the interrelating of political problems with moral principles, and the way through the difficulties lies in the reconciliation of virtue with political objectives.

This description may sound rather like Bale, but there are many differences which in the end make Lindsay's play an individual achievement. Though they share an interest in the Reformation and are both attacking the Church, Lindsay is much less of a propagandist than Bale. He does not make political points with the same committed vigour, and though the language of his comedy is racy, and sometimes obscene, he is not as vituperative as Bale. His political objectives are specific reforms rather than a radical reconstruction, but there is no doubt about his general concern for the good of the kingdom. In pursuance of this he looks for stability through the proper functioning of the three estates, the Spirituality, the Temporality, and the Merchants.

In considering the moral structure of the play we ought first to observe that there are a number of low comedy episodes which involve poor men and fools. These characters are vulgar and form a strong contrast with the elevated political theme of the main part of the play. The Cupar Banns contain such an episode in which the Fuill gets the Auld Man's Wife Bessy in spite of the extreme measures her husband is prepared to adopt in order to preserve her chastity. This really is a kind of folk comedy, perhaps the young superseding the old, and the Fuill is outspoken and bawdy. Its connection with the main theme is remote – lechery perhaps – but it is a piece of entertaining licence, and in this way forms an introduction.

The main action of the First Part of the play shows Rex Humanitas, who is served by Solace, Wantonnes and Placebo, succumbing to the charms of Sensualitie. This crucial act leaves the way open for the chief villains, the court vices Flatterie (l. 601), Falset (l. 634), and Dissait (l. 657). They rapidly take aliases as Devotioun, Sapience, and Discretioun in a mock christening, which is another folk element (l. 785 ff.). When the King accepts their services Gude Counsall is driven away, and the other virtues, Veritie and Chastitie, are also unsuccessful and are put in the stocks. Things begin to go right, however, when King Correctioun arrives to release them.

It is notable that Rex Humanitas is not used very much after the Sensualitie episode. He becomes a rather vague figure who is not fully involved in the action, but remains seated on his throne. The action does not show him experiencing the fate of a typical morality hero. This apart, much of the method of the moral allegory is conventional. Correctioun ends the First Part by revealing the deceptions practised by the three vices.

An 'Interlude' separates the two parts, showing first the Pauper's grievance over the greed of the clergy, and then the Pardoner's crude divorce for the Sowtar and his Wife. Again the tone is colloquial, not to say coarse.

In the Second Part, there is more emphasis upon the three estates, especially as there is a Parliament which is to set things right. This aspect of the action can hardly be regarded as an allegory: the programme of reform which is set out is quite clearly meant to be real and not a parallel. However many subordinate episodes do have an allegorical function, particularly the entry of the three estates at l. 2324 when they are to walk backwards led by the vices. This episode leads to the punishment of the vices who are stocked at l. 2495.

John the Commonweil is a representative figure who comes to the Parliament to present many grievances against the Temporalitie and the Spiritualitie. Although Flatterie, now disguised as a Friar, and therefore still acting in an allegorical way tries to put him off, John justifies his religion and his grievances.

The Spiritualitie continue to be unwilling to give up their lechery and greed, and eventually after the three learned clerks of the Reformation have put their case in sermon form, Correctioun agrees that Flatterie should be despoiled of his friar's habit (l. 3648) thus initiating the final action. Flatterie turns upon Dissait and Falset, and they are hanged. The learned clerks take over the function of the prelates, and John the Commonweil is put in the Parliament. Flatterie, admitting both deception and disguise, escapes. The final sequence is dominated by Folie who is another fool figure. He has matrimonial troubles which he crudely makes much of before giving his sermon on the theme

> Stultorum numerus infinitum
> (The number of fools is infinite.)

Thus the action of the play is episodic. Certain broad themes emerge, but Lindsay's method is to reveal them by a series of allegorical devices, together with the pungent fool passages which really express the moral and political problems without the device of allegory, even though most of the characters are abstractions. Lindsay's use of lechery and greed as symptoms of moral fault is a conventional one however, and the villains are sufficiently like the vices of the English morality plays to use many of their tricks, even to the escape of the chief vice at the end. The play is not without its successful points in allegorical mode, especially when Lindsay makes the truth apparent by means of unexpected contrast, as in Chastitie's rejection by the clerics, and her acceptance by the poor men, whose wives instantly reject her again when they hear about her, for they too hate chastity.

But Lindsay also wanted to speak the plain truth without the benefit of allegory, and by using his abstract characters he satirizes and castigates much that was wrong in contemporary Scotland. Thus though he does criticize the three estates, he also makes them sit in Parliament and bring about a reformed society – one in which there are unmistakable signs of the true Reformation. But he diplomatically keeps the King out of the Second Part almost entirely.

It seems clear that Lindsay's play as we have it is now a kind of compendium representing three performances, and perhaps three texts, one for each performance. In the first, at Linlithgow, the signs are that the play was shorter and more intimate, a court interlude. At Cupar, Lindsay perhaps achieved the highest success from an artistic point of view. Local allusion and local sentiment played a part, and the performance was a great public spectacle, a town play, not dissimilar in some respects to the performances of mystery plays in English towns and cities. The scope of the performance must have made the town of Cupar stand still for a few hours. For this Lindsay could command a wide variety and quality of acting skill, and these, whilst they may have imposed limitations upon some of the scenes, gave him scope for much elaborate and varied entertainment.

The performance at Edinburgh was a royal command, and for this Lindsay had to supply a play able to reflect the central concerns of Reformation Scotland. Probably it was a success, but the text still echoes the triumph in Fife.

VI

In preparing the texts for this volume, I have followed the pattern adopted in *Tudor Interludes* and *English Mystery Plays*. For *The Castle of Perseverance* I have relied upon the facsimiles of Farmer and Bevington, and upon Eccles' edition for the Early English Text Society. For *Magnyfycence* I have worked from the Cambridge University Library copy, and Ramsay's edition. For *King Johan* I have used Bang's facsimile, and the editions by Pafford and B. B. Adams. In the case of *Ane Satire of the Thrie Estaitis* I have relied upon Hamer's edition of the three versions, checked against the printed copy of Charteris's edition in the Bodleian, and the Bannatyne Manuscript in the Scottish National Library in Edinburgh. I wish to make due acknowledgement for the help I have received from all these sources.

In general I have treated texts conservatively and have avoided excessive modernization, and the normalization of spelling, though in the case of the latter some rationalization of speech headings has been necessary, especially for *King Johan*. Brackets are used to indicate departures from the original versions. Modern punctuation and capital letters have been supplied, obsolete letters transliterated, and the modern conventions for 'u' and 'v' and for 'i' and 'j' adopted. All the original stage directions have been included, and some additional ones supplied in brackets.

Difficult words are explained at the foot of the page on their first appearance, and sometimes I have repeated the explanations. A list of these explanations arranged alphabetically is at the end of the volume. Fuller explanations and other comments are gathered together in the Notes which are arranged by line-numbers.

A NOTE ON BOOKS

THE following list includes books found to be most useful in the preparation of this collection. There is however no single bibliography which adequately covers the growing amount of work on the moral plays. The place of publication is London, unless otherwise specified.

1. REFERENCE

W. A. Craigie, *A Dictionary of the Older Scottish Tongue*, Oxford, 1931.

A. Harbage, *Annals of English Drama, 975–1700*, revised by S. Schoenbaum, 1962 (supplements 1966 and 1970).

C. J. Stratman, *A Bibliography of Medieval Drama*, Berkeley, second edition 1972.

M. P. Tilley, *A Dictionary of the Proverbs in England in the Sixteenth and Seventeenth Centuries*, Ann Arbor, 1950.

S. Wells (ed.), *English Drama: Select Bibliographical Guides*, Oxford, 1975.

F. P. Wilson, *The English Drama, 1485–1585*, Oxford, 1969, with a bibliography by G. K. Hunter.

2. FOUR MORALITY PLAYS

A. *The Castle of Perseverance*

i. Texts

MS. V.a. 354, Folger Shakespeare Library, Washington D.C.

Tudor Facsimile Text, ed. J. S. Farmer, 1908.

The Macro Plays, ed. F. J. Furnivall and A. W. Pollard, *EETS* e.s. 91, 1904.

ed. Mark Eccles, *EETS* 262, 1969.

ed. D. M. Bevington (Folger Facsimile), Washington D.C., 1972.

Medieval Drama, ed. D. M. Bevington, Boston, 1975.

ii. Criticism

J. Bennett, '*The Castle of Perseverance*: Redactions, Place, and Date', *Mediaeval Studies* 24, 1962, pp. 141–52.

R. D. Cornelius, *The Figurative Castle*, Bryn Mawr, 1930.

M. R. Kelley, 'Fifteenth-Century Flamboyant Style and *The Castle of Perseverance*', *Comparative Drama* 6, 1972, pp. 14–27.

A. H. Nelson, '*Of the Seven Ages*: an unknown analogue of *The Castle of Perseverance*', *Comparative Drama* 8, 1974, pp. 125–38.

E. T. Schell, 'On the Imitation of Life's Pilgrimage in *The Castle of Perseverance*', *J.E.G.P.* 67, 1968, pp. 235–48.

W. K. Smart, '*The Castle of Perseverance*: Place, Date, and a Source', *Manly Anniversary Studies*, Chicago, 1923, pp. 42–53.

J. Willis, 'Stage Directions in *The Castle of Perseverance*', *M.L.R.* 51, 1956, pp. 404–5.

B. *Magnyfycence*

i. Texts

?J. Rastell, ?1533. Syn. 4.53.12, Cambridge University Library.

ed. A. Dyce, *The Poetical Works of John Skelton*, 1843 (2 vols.).

ed. R. L. Ramsay, *EETS* e.s. 98, 1908.

ed. P. Henderson, *The Complete Poems of John Skelton*, 1959.

ii. Criticism

N. C. Carpenter, 'Skelton and Music: Roty Bully Boys', *R.E.S.* N.S.6, 1955, pp. 279–84.

W. O. Harris, 'Wolsey and Skelton's *Magnyfycence*: a Revaluation', *S.P.* 57, 1960, pp. 99–122.
Skelton's 'Magnyfycence' and the Cardinal Virtue Tradition, Chapel Hill, 1965.

A. R. Heiserman, *Skelton and Satire*, Chicago, 1961.

R. S. Kinsman, 'Skelton's *Magnyfycence*: The Strategy of the 'Olde Sayde Sawe', *S.P.* 63, 1966, pp. 99–125.

M. Pollet, *John Skelton: Poet of Tudor England*, trans. J. Warrington, 1971.

M. West, 'Skelton and the Renaissance Theme of Folly', *P.Q.* 50, 1971, pp. 23–5.

L. Winser, 'Skelton's *Magnyfycence*', *Renaissance Quarterly* 23, 1970, pp. 14–25.

C. *King Johan*

i. Texts

MS. HM3, Huntington Library, San Marino, California.

ed. J. M. Manly, *Specimens of the Pre-Shakespearean Drama*, 1897.

ed. W. Bang, *Kynge Johan nach der Handschrift in der Chatsworth Collection*, in *Materialien* 25, Louvain, 1931.

ed. J. H. Pafford and W. W. Greg, Malone Society Reprint, 1931.

ed. W. A. Armstrong, *English History Plays*, 1965.

ed. B. B. Adams, *John Bale's 'King Johan'*, San Marino, 1969.

ii. Criticism

B. B. Adams, 'Doubling in Bale's *King Johan*', *S.P.* 62, 1965, pp. 111–20.

T. B. Blatt, *The Plays of John Bale: A Study of Ideas, Technique and Style*, Copenhagen, 1968.

W. T. Davies, 'A Bibliography of John Bale', *Oxford Bibliographical Society Proceedings and Papers* 5, 1940, pp. 201–79.

L. P. Fairfield, *John Bale*, West Lafayette, Indiana, 1976.

W. W. Greg, 'Bale's *King Johan*', *M.L.N.* 36, 1921, p. 505.

J. W. Harris, *John Bale*, Urbana, 1940.

M. Mattson, *Five Plays About King John*, Uppsala, 1977.

H. McCusker, *John Bale*, Bryn Mawr, 1942.

E. S. Miller, 'The Roman Rite in Bale's *King Johan*', *PMLA* 64, 1949, pp. 802–22.

J. H. Pafford, 'Two Notes on Bale's *King Johan*', *M.L.R.* 66, 1961, pp. 553–5.

K. Sperk, *Mittelalterliche Tradition und reformatische Polemik in den Spielen John Bales*, Heidelberg, 1973.

D. *Ane Satire of the Thrie Estaitis*

i. Texts

The Bannatyne MS. 1568. National Library of Scotland (contains the Cupar Banns).

Quarto printed by Robert Charteris, Edinburgh, 1603. The Bodleian copy, Gough Scotland 221, is used here. Other copies of this edition are in the Bodleian, the National Library of Scotland, Lincoln Cathedral Library, and the Huntington Library.

ed. D. Hamer, *The Works of Sir David Lindsay of the Mount*, Edinburgh, 1931–5, vols 2 and 4.

ed. J. Kinsley, 1954.

ii. Criticism

A. C. Dessen, 'The Estates Morality Play', *S.P.* 62, 1965, pp. 121–6.

V. Harward, '*Ane Satyre of the Thrie Estaitis* Again', *Studies in Scottish Literature* 7, 1970, pp. 139–46.

J. S. Kantrowitz, 'Encore: Lindsay's *Thrie Estaitis*, Date and New Evidence', *S.S.L.* 10, 1972, pp. 18–32.
Dramatic Allegory: Lindsay's 'Ane Satyre of the Thrie Estaitis', Lincoln, Nebraska, 1975.

A. H. Maclaine, '*Christis Kirk on the Grene* and Sir David Lindsay's *Satyre of the Thrie Estaitis*', *J.E.G.P.* 56, 1957, pp. 596–601.

J. Macqueen, '*Ane Satire of the Thrie Estaitis*', *S.S.L.* 3, 1966, pp. 129–43.

A. J. Mill, *Medieval Plays in Scotland*, 1927.
'The Influence of the Continental Drama on Lyndsay's *Satyre of the Thrie Estaitis*', *M.L.R.* 25, 1930, pp. 425–42.
'Representations of Lyndsay's *Satyre of the Thrie Estaitis*', *PMLA* 47, 1932, pp. 636–51.
'The Original Version of Lyndsay's *Ane Satyre of the Thrie Estaitis*', *S.S.L.* 6, 1969, pp. 67–75.

E. S. Miller, 'The Christening in the *Thrie Estaitis*', *M.L.N.* 60, 1945, pp. 42–4.

R. Mohl, *The Three Estates in Mediaeval and Renaissance Literature*, New York, 1933.

W. Murison, *Sir David Lyndsay, Poet and Satirist*, 1938.

3. OTHER TEXTS

W. L. Braekman, 'The Seven Virtues as Opposed to the Seven Vices – A Fourteenth-Century Didactic Poem', *Neuphilologische Mitteilungen* 74, 1973, pp. 247–68.

G. Cohen (ed.), *Moralité des Sept Péchés Mortels et des Sept Vertus*, in *Nativités et Moralités Liégeoises du Moyen-Age*, (Chantilly MS. 617), Brussels, 1953.

R. Engelsing (ed.), *Ludus de Antichristo*, Stuttgart, 1968.

R. Grosseteste, *The Castle of Love*, ed. R. F. Weymouth, 1862–4.

Hildegard of Bingen, *Ordo Virtutum*, in P. Dronke, *Poetic Individuality in the Middle Ages*, Oxford, 1970.

Prudentius, *Opera*, trans., and ed., by H. J. Thomson, (Loeb), Cambridge, Mass., 1949.

W. Tyndale, *The Obedience of a Christen Man*, Antwerp, 1528, reprinted Scolar Press, 1970.

4. CRITICAL WORKS

P. D. Arnott, 'The Origins of Medieval Theatre in the Round', *Theatre Notebook* 15, 1961, 84–7.

D. Bevington, *From 'Mankind' to Marlowe*, Cambridge, Mass., 1962. *Tudor Drama and Tudor Politics*, Cambridge, Mass., 1968.

R. H. Blackburn, *Biblical Drama under the Tudors*, The Hague, 1971.

M. W. Bloomfield, *The Seven Deadly Sins*, East Lansing, Mich., 1952.

W. Borlase, *Observations on the Antiquities Historical and Monumental of Cornwall*, 1745.

E. K. Chambers, *The Mediaeval Stage*, 2 vols., Oxford, 1903.

L. A. Cormican, 'Morality Tradition and the Interludes', in *The Age of Chaucer*, ed. B. Ford, (Penguin Books), 1954.

T. W. Craik, *The Tudor Interlude*, Leicester, 1958.

L. W. Cushman, *The Devil and the Vice in the English Dramatic Literature before Shakespeare*, Halle, 1900.

N. Denny (ed.), *Medieval Drama*, (Stratford-upon-Avon Studies 16), 1973.

M. Fifield, *The Rhetoric of Free Will*, Leeds, 1974. *The Castle in the Circle*, Muncie, Indiana, 1967.

G. Frank, *The Mediaeval French Drama*, Oxford, 1954.

O. B. Hardison Jr, *Christian Rite and Christian Drama in the Middle Ages*, Baltimore, 1965.

S. J. Kahrl, *Traditions of Medieval Drama*, 1974.

J. S. Kantrowitz, 'Dramatic Allegory or Exploring the Moral Play', *Comparative Drama* 7, 1973, pp. 68–82.

R. Longsworth, *The Cornish Ordinalia: Religion and Dramaturgy*, Cambridge, Mass., 1967.

W. R. Mackenzie, *The English Moralities from the Point of View of Allegory*, Boston, Mass., 1914.

E. Mâle, *L'Art Religieux de la Fin du Moyen Age en France*, Paris, 1908.

R. Morton Nance, 'The Plen-An-Gwary or Cornish Playing Place', *Journal of the Royal Institution of Cornwall* 24, 1935, pp. 190–211.

G. R. Owst, *Literature and Pulpit in Medieval England*, second edition, Oxford, 1961.

R. Pineas, *Tudor and Early Stuart Anti-Catholic Drama*, New York, 1972.

R. Potter, *The English Morality Play*, 1975.

C. Ricks (ed.), *English Drama to 1710*, 1971.

M. Roston, *Biblical Drama in England from the Middle Ages to the Present Day*, 1968.

A. P. Rossiter, *English Drama from early times to the Elizabethans*, 1950.

J. J. Scarisbrick, *Henry VIII*, 1968.

N. C. Schmitt, 'Was There a Medieval Theatre in the Round?', in Taylor and Nelson, op. cit., pp. 292–315.

R. Southern, *The Staging of Plays before Shakespeare*, 1973.
   The Medieval Theatre in the Round, second edition, 1975.

B. Spivack, *Shakespeare and the Allegory of Evil*, New York, 1958.

S. Sticca (ed.), *The Medieval Drama*, Albany, 1972.

J. H. Taylor and A. H. Nelson (eds.), *Medieval English Drama*, Chicago, 1972.

S. Wenzel, 'The Seven Deadly Sins: Some Problems of Research', *Speculum* 43, 1968, pp. 1–22.

B. J. Whiting, *Proverbs in the Earlier English Drama*, Cambridge, Mass., 1928.

G. Wickham, *The Medieval Theatre*, 1974.

A. Williams, 'The English Moral Play before 1500', *Annuale Medievale* 4, 1963, pp. 5–22.

K. Young, 'The Records of the York Play of the Pater Noster', *Speculum* 7, 1932, pp. 541–6.

ABBREVIATIONS

Bann.MS.	Bannatyne Manuscript
Cam.	Cambridge copy of *Magnyfycence*
D.N.B.	*Dictionary of National Biography*
EETS	Publications of the Early English Text Society
E.M.P.	*English Mystery Plays*, ed. Peter Happé, Penguin Books, 1975
J.E.G.P.	*Journal of English and Germanic Philology*
M.L.N.	*Modern Language Notes*
M.L.R.	*Modern Language Review*
N. and Q.	*Notes and Queries*
N.E.B.	*The New English Bible*, 1970
N.E.D.	*The New English Dictonary*
PMLA	Publications of the Modern Language Association of America
R.E.S.	*Review of English Studies*
S D	Stage Direction
S.P.	*Studies in Philology*
S.S.L.	*Studies in Scottish Literature*
T.I.	*Tudor Interludes*, ed. Peter Happé, Penguin Books, 1972
Tilley	M. P. Tilley, *A Dictionary of the Proverbs in England in the Sixteenth and Seventeenth Centuries*, Ann Arbor, 1950

ACKNOWLEDGEMENTS

THE diagram on Fol. 191ᵛ of *The Castle of Perseverance* is reproduced by permission of the Folger Shakespeare Library, Washington, D.C. The title-pages of *Magnyfycence* and *Ane Satire of the Thrie Estaitis* are reproduced by permission of The Syndics of the Cambridge University Library and the Bodleian.

THE CASTLE OF PERSEVERANCE

Written 1400–25

Manuscript V.a.354. Folger Shakespeare Library,
Washington, D.C.

H[a]ec sunt nomina ludentium:

In primis ij Vexillatores.
Mundus et cum eo Voluptas, Stulticia, et Garcio.
Belyal et cum eo Superbia, Ira, et Invidia.
Caro et cum eo Gula, Luxuria, et Accidia.
Humanum Genus et cum eo Bonus Angelus et Malus Angelus.
Avaricia, Detraccio.
Confessio, Penitencia.
Humilitas, Paciencia, Caritas, Abstinencia,
Castitas, Solicitudo et Largitas.
Mors.
Anima.
Misericordia, Veritas, Justicia, et Pax.
Pater sedens in trono.

Summa xxxvj ludentium.

These are the names of the players:*

At first, two Standard-bearers.
World, and with him Lust-liking, Folly, and the Boy.
Belial, and with him Pride, Anger, and Envy.
Flesh, and with him Gluttony, Lechery, and Sloth.
Mankind, and with him the Good Angel and the Bad Angel.
Avarice, Backbiter.
Shrift, Penitence.
Humility, Patience, Charity, Abstinence,
Chastity, Busyness, Generosity.
Death.
The Soul.
Mercy, Truth, Justice, and Peace.
The Father seated on his throne.

A total of 36 players.

* This list appears on the last page of the manuscript. There are actually
only 35 parts in the list and in the play itself. The inconsistency may be explained by l. 44 of the Banns where another character, Conscience, is mentioned.

The wording on the stage diagram, reproduced opposite, is as follows:

Sowth
Caro
skafold

[*Around the circle*] This is the watyr a-bowte the place, if any dyche
may be mad ther it schal be pleyed, or ellys that it be strongely barryd
al a-bowt, and lete nowth ovyr many stytelerys* be wyth-inne the
plase.

[*Above the tower*] This is the castel of perseveraunse that stondyth in
the myddys of the place: but lete no men sytte ther, for lettynge of syt,
for ther schal be the best of all.

Est   [*On either side of the tower*] Coveytyse copbord   West
Deus   be the beddys feet schal be at the ende of   Mundus
skafold   the castel.   skaffold

[*Below the tower*] Mankyndeis bed schal be undyr the castel and ther
schal the Sowle† lye undyr the bed tyl he schal ryse and pleye.

Northe est
Coveytyse   Northe
skaffold   Belyal
                             skaffold

And he that schal pley Belyal loke
that he have gunne-powdyr brennynge
in pypys in hys handys and in hys erys
and in hys ars whanne he gothe to batayl.

The iiij Dowterys schul be clad in mentelys – Mercy in wyth,
    Rythwysnesse in red altogedyr,
Trewthe in sad grene, and Pes al in blake – and thei schul pleye in
    the place
al to-gedyr tyl they brynge up the Sowle.

    * The *stytelerys* are thought to be marshals who controlled the audience,
especially during the processions.
    † The *sowle* (soul) was probably played by a boy, and hence he could more
easily remain in the cupboard for a long time.

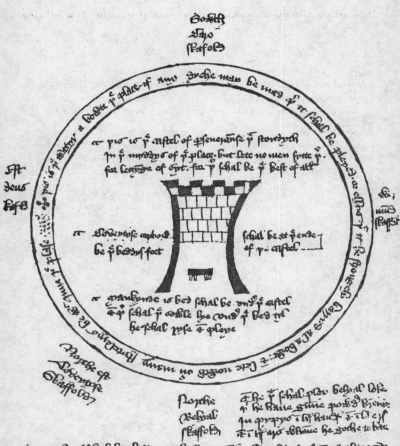

The stage diagram on Folio 191ᵛ of the manuscript

PRIMUS VEXILLATOR: Glorious God, in all degres, lord
        most of myth,
That hevene and erthe made of nowth, bothe se and
    lond,
The aungelys in hevene hym to serve bryth
And mankynde in mydylerd he made wyth hys hond,
And our lofly Lady, that lanterne is of lyth,
Save oure lege lord the kynge, the leder of this londe,
And all the ryall of this reume and rede hem the ryth,
And all the goode comowns of this towne that be-forn
    us stonde
In this place.
We mustyr you wyth menschepe   10
And freyne you of frely frenchepe.
Cryst safe you all fro schenchepe
That knowyn wyl our case.

SECUNDUS VEXILLATOR: The case of oure comynge you
        to declare,
Every man in hym-self for sothe he it may fynde,
Whou Mankynde into this werld born is ful bare
And bare schall beryed be at hys last ende.
God hym gevyth to aungel[ys] ful yep and ful yare,
The Goode Aungel and the Badde to hym for to lende.
The Goode techyth hym goodnesse, the Badde synne
    and sare: 20

1 *myth* power   2 *nowth* nothing   3 *bryth* brightly   4 *mydylerd* earth
5 *lyth* light   7 *ryall* nobility   *reume* realm   *rede* advise   *ryth* right
10   *mustyr* muster   *menschepe* honour   11 *freyne* request
frely noble   *frenchepe* friendship   12 *schenchepe* harm   16 *Whou* how
18 *yep* vigorous   *yare* ready   20 *sare* sorrow

Whanne the ton hath the victory, the tothyr goth
   be-hende,
Be skyll.
The Goode Aungel conveytyth evermore Mans
   salvacion,
And the Badde bysytyth hym evere to hys
   dampnacion,
And God hathe govy[n] Man fre arbritracion
Whethyr he wyl hymse[lf] save or hys soule [spyll].

PRIMUS VEXILLATOR: Spylt is Man spetously whanne
            he to synne asent.
The Bad Aungel thanne bryngyth hym iij enmys so
   stout:
The Werlde, the Fende, the foul Flesche so joly and
   jent.
Thei ledyn hym ful lustyly wyth synnys al abowt.   30
Pyth wyth Pride and Coveytyse, to the World is he
   went,
To mey[n]ten hys manhod all men to hym lout.
Aftyr Ire and Envye the Fend hath to hym lent
Bakbytynge and endytynge, wyth all men for to route,
Ful evyn.
But the fowle Flesch, homlyest of all,
Slawth, Lust and Leccherye gun to hym call,
Glotony and othyr synnys bothe grete and small.
Thus Mans soule is soylyd wyth synnys moo thanne
   sevyn.

SECUNDUS VEXILLATOR: Whanne Mans sowle is soylyd
            wyth synne and wyth sore,   40

21 *ton* ... *tothyr* the one ... the other   22 *skyll* reason, craft
24 *bysytyth* assails   25 *govyn* given   26, 27 *spyll, spylt* destroy(ed)
27 *spetously* shamefully   29 *jent* beautiful   31 *Pyth* placed, furnished
32 *lout* (v) bow   34 *endytynge* (false) accusation   *route* associate
36 *homlyest* most familiar   40 *sore* sorrow

Thanne the Goode Aungyl makyth mykyl mornynge
That the lofly lyknesse of God schulde be lore
Thorwe the Badde Aungell[ys] fals entysynge.
He sendyth to hym Concyens, pryckyd ful pore,
And clere Confescyon wyth Penauns-doynge.
Thei mevyn Man to mendement that he mysdyd
    before.
Thus thei callyn hym to clennesse and to good
    levynge,
Wyth-outyn dystaunce.
Mekenesse, Pacyense, and Charyte,
Sobyrnesse, Besynesse, and Chastyte,   50
And Largyte, vertuys of good degre,
Man callyth to the Castel of Good Perseveraunce.

PRIMUS VEXILLATOR: The Castel of Perseverauns
        wanne Mankynde hath tan,
Wel armyd wyth vertus and ovyrcome all vycys,
There the Good Aungyl makyth ful mery thanne
That Mankynde hath ovyrcome hys gostly e[n]miis.
The Badde Aungyl mornyth that he hath myssyd Man.
He callyth the Werld, the Fende, and the foule Flesch
    i-wys,
And all the sevene synnys, to do that they canne
To brynge Mankynd a-geyn to bale out of blys,   60
Wyth wronge.
Pride a-saylyth Meknesse wyth all hys myth,
Ire a-geyns Paciensse ful fast ganne he fyth,
Envye a-geyn Charyte strywyth ful ryth,
But Coveytyse a-geyns Largyte fytyth ovyr longe.

SECUNDUS VEXILLATOR: Coveytyse Mankynd evere
        coveytyth for to qwell.

41 *mykyl* great   42 *lore* lost   44 *pryckyd* dressed   46 *mevyn* move
mendement amendment   48 *dystaunce* disagreement
53 *wanne* when   *tan* arrived at   56 *gostly* spiritual   60 *bale* torment
63 *fyth* fight   64 *strywyth* strives   66 *qwell* destroy

He gaderyth to hym Glotony a-geyns Sobyrnesse,
Leccherye wyth Chastyte fytyth ful fell,
And Slawthe in Goddys servyse a-geyns Besynesse.
Thus vycys a-geyns vertues fytyn ful snelle.   70
Every buskyth to brynge Man to dystresse.
But Penaunce and Confescion wyth Mankynd wyl
    melle,
The vycys arn ful lyckely the vertues to opresse,
Saun dowte.
Thus in the Castel of Good Perseverance
Mankynd is maskeryd with mekyl varyaunce.
The Goode Aungyl and the Badde be evere at dystaunce;
The Goode holdyth hym inne, the Badde wold brynge
    hym owte.

PRIMUS VEXILLATOR: Owt of Good Perseveraunce
            whanne Mankynde wyl not come,
Yyt the Badde Aungyl wyth Coveytyse hym gan
    asayle,   80
Fyndende hym in poverte and penaunce so be-nome,
And bryngyth hym in beleve in defaute for to fayle.
Thanne he profyrth hym good and gold so gret a
    sowme,
That if he wyl com a-geyn and wyth the Werld dayle,
The badde Aungyl to the Werld tollyth hym downe
The Castel of Perseveraunce to fle fro the vayle
And blysse.
Thanne the Werld be-gynnyth hym to restore.
Have he nevere so mykyl, yyt he wold have more;
Thus the Badde Aungyl leryth hym hys lore.   90
The more a man agyth the harder he is.

68 *fell* fiercely   70 *snelle* vigorously   71 *Every* everyone
buskyth hurries   72 *melle* be concerned with
74 *Saun* without   76 *maskeryd* bewildered   *varyaunce* dispute
81 *be-nome* benumbed   83 *sowme* sum   84 *dayle* deal
85 *tollyth* entices   86 *vayle* benefit   90 *leryth* teaches
lore learning

SECUNDUS VEXILLATOR: Hard a man is in age and
        covetouse be kynde.
Whanne all othyr synnys Man hath forsake,
Evere the more that he hath the more is in hys mynde
To gadyr and to gete good wyth woo and wyth wrake.
Thus the Goode Aungyl caste is be-hynde
And the Badde Aungyl Man to hym takyth,
That wryngyth hym wrenchys to hys last ende,
Tyl Deth comyth foul dolfully and loggyth hym in a
    lake
Ful lowe.   100
Thanne is Man on molde maskeryd in mynde.
He sendyth afftyr hys sekkatours ful fekyl to fynde,
And hys eyr aftyrward comyth evere be-hynde,
I-Wot-Not-Who is hys name, for he hym nowt knowe.

PRIMUS VEXILLATOR: Man knowe not who schal be hys
        eyr and governe hys good.
He caryth more for hys catel thanne for hys cursyd
    synne.
To putte hys good in governaunce he mengyth hys
    mod;
He wolde that it were scyfftyd a-mongys hys ny kynne.
But ther schal com a lythyr ladde wyth a torne hod,
I-Wot-Nevere-Who schal be hys name, hys clothis be
    ful thynne,   110
Schal eryth the erytage that nevere was of hys blod,
Whanne al hys lyfe is lytyd upon a lytyl pynne
At the laste.
On lyve whanne [he] may no lenger lende,
Mercy he callyth at hys laste ende:
'Mercy, God! Be now myn frende!'
Wyth that Mans spyryt is paste.

92 *Hard* mean   *kynde* nature   95 *wrake* pain   98 *wrenchys* deceits
99 *foul* full   *dolfully* cruelly   *lake* pit   101 *molde* earth
102 *sekkatours* executors   *fekyl* untrustworthy   103 *eyr* heir
106 *catel* property   107 *mengyth* troubles   *mod* mind
109 *lythyr* lazy   *hod* hood   111 *eryth* inherit

SECUNDUS VEXILLATOR: Whanne Manys spyryt is past,
     the Badde Aungyl ful fell
Cleymyth that for covetyse Mans sowle schuld ben hys,
And for to bere it ful boystowsly wyth hym in-to hell.   120
The Good Aungyl seyth nay, the spyryt schal to blys
For at hys laste ende of mercy he gan spell
And therefore of mercy schal he nowth mysse,
And oure lofly Ladi if sche wyl for hym mell,
Be mercy and be menys in purgatory he is
In ful byttyr place.
Thus mowthys confession
And hys hertys contricion
Schal save Man fro dampnacion,
Be Goddys mercy and grace.   130

PRIMUS VEXILLATOR: Grace if God wyl graunte us of
     hys mykyl myth,
These parcell[ys] in propyrtes we purpose us to playe
This day sevenenyt before you in syth,
At   on the grene in ryal aray.
Ye haste you thanne thedyrward, syrys, hendly in hyth,
All goode neyborys ful specyaly we you pray,
And loke that ye be there betyme, luffely and lyth,
For we schul be onward be underne of the day,
Dere frendys.
We thanke you of all good dalyaunce   140
And of all youre specyal sportaunce,
And preye you of good contynuaunce
To oure lyvys endys.

SECUNDUS VEXILLATOR: Os oure lyvys we love you,
     thus takande oure leve.

119 *Cleymyth* claims   120 *boystowsly* fiercely   122 *spell* speak
124 *mell* intercede   132 *parcellys* parts   *propyrtes* stage properties
135 *hendly* graciously   *in hyth* extremely   137 *luffely* willing
lyth agreeable   138 *underne* mid-morning   141 *sportaunce* indulgence
144 *Os* as

Ye manly men of   ther Crist save you all!
He maynten youre myrthys and kepe you fro greve,
That born was of Mary myld in an ox stall.
Now mery be all   and wel mote ye cheve,
All oure feythful frendys, ther fayre mote ye fall.
Ya, and welcum be ye whanne ye com prys for to
    preve,
And worthi to be worchepyd in boure and in hall
And in every place.
Fare-wel, fayre frendys,
That lofly wyl lystyn and lendys.
Cryste kepe you fro fendys!
Trumpe up and lete us pace!

150

148 *cheve* thrive   150 *prys* value, worth   154 *lofly* willingly
lendys attend   156 *pace* pass on

THE CASTLE OF PERSEVERANCE

[PART ONE: THE FIRST TEMPTATION]

MUNDUS [*from his scaffold*]:
Worthy wytys in al this werd wyde,
Be wylde wode wonys and every weye-went,
Precyous prinse, prekyd in pride,
Thorwe this propyr pleyn place in pes be ye bent!   160
Buske you, bolde bachelerys, undyr my baner to
    a-byde
Where bryth basnetys be bateryd and backys ar schent.
Ye, syrys semly, all same syttyth on syde,
For bothe be see and be londe my sondys I have sent,
Al the world myn nam[e] is ment.
Al a-bowtyn my bane is blowe,
In every cost I am knowe,
I do men rawyn on ryche rowe
Tyl thei be dyth to dethys dent.

Assarye, Acaye, and Almayne,   170
Cavadoyse, Capadoyse, and Cananee,
Babyloyne, Brabon, Burgoyne, and Bretayne,
Grece, Galys, and to the Gryckysch See;
I meve also Masadoyne in my mykyl mayne,
Frauns, Flaundrys, and Freslonde, and also Normande,
Pyncecras, Parys, and longe Pygmayne,
And every toun in Trage, evyn to the Dreye Tre,
Rodys and ryche Rome.

157 *werd* world   158 *wode* wood   *wonys* places   *weye-went* by-way
159 *prekyd* dressed   162 *basnetys* helmets   164 *sondys* messengers
165 *ment* spoken   166 *bane* summons   168 *rawyn* rave
rowe row, line

All these londys at myn a-vyse
Arn castyn to my werdly wyse.   180
My tresorer, Syr Coveytyse,
Hath sesyd hem holy to me.

Therfor my game and my gle growe ful glad,
Ther is [no] wythe in this werld that my wytte wyl me
    warne.
Every ryche regne rapyth hym ful rad
In lustys and in lykyngys my lawys to lerne.
Wyth fayre folke in the felde freschly I am fadde.
I dawnse doun as a doo be dalys ful derne.
What boy bedyth batayl or debatyth wyth blad
Hym were betyr to ben hangyn hye in hell herne,   190
Or brent on lyth levene.
Who-so spekyth a-geyn the Werd
In a presun he schal be sperd.
Myn hest is holdyn and herd
Into hyge hevene.

BELYAL [*from his scaffold*]:
Now I sytte, Satanas, in my sad synne,
As deuyl dowty, in draf as a drake.
I champe and I cha[f]e, I chocke on my chynne,
I am boystows and bold, as Belyal the blake.
What folk that I grope thei gapyn and grenne,   200
I-wys fro Carlylle into Kent my carpynge thei take,
Bothe the bak and the buttoke brestyth al on brenne,
Wyth werkys of wreche I werke hem mykyl wrake.

182 *sesyd* endowed   183 *gle* pleasure   184 *wythe* person
185 *rapyth* hurries   *rad* readily   187 *fadde* fed   188 *doo* doe
189 *bedyth* threatens   190 *herne* nook   191 *brent* burnt   *lyth* bright
levene lightning   193 *sperd* shut up   194 *hes:* command
195 *hyge* high   197 *draf* filth   *drake* dragon   198 *chocke* thrust out
199 *boystows* fierce   200 *grope* grasp   *gapyn* gape
grenne gnash the teeth, grimace   201 *carpynge* words, commands
202 *brestyth* burst   *on brenne* in flames   203 *wreche* vengeance

In woo is al my wenne.
In care I am cloyed,
And fowle I am anoyed
But Mankynde be stroyed,
Be dykys and be denne.

Pryde is my prince in perlys i-pyth;
Wretthe, this wrecche, wyth me schal wawe;   210
Envye into werre wyth me schal walkyn wyth;
Wyth these faytourys I am fedde, in feyth I am fawe.
As a dyngne devyl in my dene I am dyth.
Pryde, Wretthe, and Envye, I sey in my sawe,
Kyngys, kayserys, and kempys and many a kene
    knyth,
These lovely lordys han lernyd hem my lawe.
To my dene thei wyl drawe.
Al-holy Mankynne
To helle but I wynne,
In bale is my bynne   220
And schent undyr schawe.

On Mankynde is my trost, in contre i-knowe,
Wyth my tyre and wyth my tayl tytly to tene.
Thorwe Flaundris and Freslonde faste I gan flowe,
Fele folke on a flokke to flappyn and to flene.
Where I graspe on the grounde, grym ther schal growe.
Gadyr you togedyr, ye boyis, on this grene!
In this brode bugyl a blast wanne I blowe,
Al this werld schal be wood i-wys as I wene
And to my byddynge bende.   230

204 *wenne* pleasure   205 *cloyed* obstructed   207 *But* unless
208 *dykys* ditches   *denne* valley   209 *i-pyth* adorned   210 *wawe* go
212 *faytourys* deceivers   *fawe* glad   213 *dyth* placed
215 *kayserys* emperors   *kempys* champions   220 *bynne* stall
221 *schent* destroyed   *schawe* ground   223 *tyre* ?equipment
tene (v) harm   225 *Fele* many   *flappyn* beat   *flene* flay
229 *wood* mad

91

Wythly on syde
On benche wyl I byde
To tene, this tyde,
Al-holy Mankende.

CARO [*from his scaffold*]:
    I byde as a brod brustun-gutte a-bovyn on these
        tourys.
    Every-body is the betyr that to myn byddynge is bent.
    I am Mankyndys fayre Flesch, florchyd in flowrys.
    My lyfe is wyth lustys and lykynge i-lent.
    Wyth tapytys of tafata I tymbyr my towrys.
    In myrthe and in melodye my mende is i-ment.   240
    Thou I be clay and clad, clappyd undir clowrys,
    Yyt wolde I that my wyll in the werld went,
    Ful trew I you be-hyth.
    I love wel myn ese,
    In lustys me to plese;
    Thou synne my sowle sese
    I yeve not a myth.

    In Glotony gracyous now am I growe;
    Therfore he syttyth semly here be my syde.
    In Lechery and Lykynge lent am I lowe,   250
    And Slawth, my swete sone, is bent to a-byde.
    These iij are nobyl, trewly I trowe,
    Mankynde to tenyn and trecchyn a tyde.
    Wyth many berdys in bowre my blastys are blowe
    Be weys and be wodys, thorwe this werld wyde,
    The sothe for to seyne.
    But if mans Flesch fare wel

231 *Wythly* quickly   237 *florchyd* decorated   239 *tapytys* tapestries
tymbyr build   240 *i-ment* set   241, 246 *Thou* though   241 *clad* (n) clod
clappyd thrust *clowrys* the ground   243 *be-hyth* tell   247 *yeve* give, care
myth mite   253 *tenyn* harm   *trecchyn* deceive   254 *berdys* nobles

Bot[h]e at mete and at mel,
Dyth I am in gret del,
And browt in-to peyne.   260

And aftyr good fare in feyth thou I fell,
Thou I drywe to dust, in drosse for to drepe,
Thow my sely sowle were haryed to hell,
Wo-so wyl do these werkys, i-wys, he schal wepe
Evyr wyth-owtyn ende.
Be-hold the Werld, the Devyl, and me!
Wyth all oure mythis we kyngys thre,
Nyth and day besy we be
For to distroy Mankende
If that we [may].   270
Ther-for on hylle
Syttyth all stylle,
And seth wyth good wylle
Oure ryche a-ray.

HUMANUM GENUS [*in the middle of the acting area*]:
          Aftyr oure forme-faderys kende
This nyth I was of my modyr born.
Fro my modyr I walke, I wende,
Ful feynt and febyl I fare you beforn.
I am nakyd of lym and lende,
As Mankynde is schapyn and schorn.   280
I not wedyr to gon ne to lende
To helpe my-self mydday nyn morn.
For schame I stonde and schende.
I was born this nyth in blody ble,

258 *mel* meal   259 *del* anguish   262 *drywe* hasten   *drepe* droop
263 *sely* wretched   *haryed* dragged   268 *Nyth* night   273 *seth* watch
278 *fare* go, walk   279 *lende* loin   280 *schorn* made
281 *not* do not know   *lende* stay   282 *nyn* nor
283 *schende* am ashamed   284 *ble* complexion

And nakyd I am, as ye may se.
A, Lord God in trinite,
Whow Mankende is unthende!

Where-to I was to this werld browth
I ne wot, but to woo and wepynge
I am born and have ryth nowth   290
To helpe my-self in no doynge.
I stonde and stodye al ful of thowth.
Bare and pore is my clothynge,
A sely crysme myn hed hath cawth
That I tok at myn crystenynge.
Certys I have no more.
Of erthe I cam, I wot ryth wele,
And as erthe I stande this sele.
Of Mankende it is gret dele.
Lord God, I crye thyne ore.   300

ij aungels bene a-synyd to me:
The ton techyth me to goode –
On my ryth syde ye may hym se,
He cam fro Criste that deyed on rode;
A-nothyr is ordeynyd her to be
That in my foo be fen and flode –
He is a-bout in every degre
[To] drawe me to tho dewylys wode
That in helle ben thycke.
Swyche to hath every man on lyve   310
To rewlyn hym and hys wyttys fyvė.
Whanne man doth ewyl, the ton wolde schryve,
The tothyr drawyth to wycke.

287 *Whow* how   *unthende* unhealthy   294 *crysme* baptismal cloth
cawth wrapped   298 *sele* time   299 *dele* (n) grief   300 *ore* grace
305 *her* here   306 *flode* stream   308 *tho* those   *wode* mad
310 *to* two   312 *schryve* forgive   313 *wycke* wickedness

But syn these aungelys be to me falle,
Lord Jhesu, to you I bydde a bone
That I may folwe, be strete and stalle,
The aungyl that cam fro hévene trone.
Now Lord Jhesu in hevene halle,
Here whane I make my mone.
Coryows Criste to you I calle: 320
As a grysly gost I grucche and grone,
I wene, ryth ful of thowth.
A, Lord Jhesu, wedyr may I goo?
A crysyme I have and no moo.
Alas, men may be wondyr woo
Whanne thei be fyrst forth browth.

BONUS ANGELUS: Ya, forsothe, and that is wel sene.
Of woful wo man may synge,
For iche creature helpyth hym-self be-dene
Save only man at hys comynge.   330
Nevyr-the-lesse turne the fro tene
And serve Jhesu, hevene kynge,
And thou schalt, be grevys grene,
Fare wel in all thynge.
That Lord thi lyfe hath lante,
Have hym alwey in this mynde,
That deyed on rode for Mankýnde,
And serve hym to thi lyfes ende,
And sertys thou schalt not wante.

MALUS ANGELUS: Pes, aungel, thi wordys are not wyse;   340
Thou counselyst hym not a-ryth.
He schal hym drawyn to the Werdys servyse
To dwelle wyth caysere, kynge, and knyth,

315 *bone* boon   320 *Coryows* sensitive, considerate
321 *grysly* frightful *grucche* moan
329 *be-dene* at once 335 *lante* lent, given

That in londe be hym non lyche.
Cum on wyth me, stylle as ston,
Thou and I to the Werd schul goon,
And thanne thou schalt sen a-non
Whow sone thou schalt be ryche.

BONUS ANGELUS: A, pes, aungel, thou spekyst folye.
Why schuld he coveyt werldys goode,   350
Syn Criste in erthe and hys meynye
All in povert here thei stode?
Werldys wele, be strete and stye,
Faylyth and fadyth as fysch in flode,
But heve-ryche is good and trye:
Ther Criste syttyth bryth as blode
Wyth-outyn any dystresse.
To the World wolde he not flyt
But forsok it every whytt.
Example I fynde in holy wryt,   360
He wyl bere me wytnesse.
Divicias et paupertates ne dederis mihi, Domine.

MALUS ANGELUS: Ya, ya, man, leve hym nowth,
But cum wyth me, be stye and strete.
Have thou a gobet of the werld cawth,
Thou schalt fynde it good and swete.
A fayre lady the schal be tawth
That in bowre thi bale schal bete.
Wyth ryche rentys thou schalt be frawth,
Wyth sylke sendel to syttyn in sete.   370
I rede late bedys be.
If thou wylt have wel thyn hele
And faryn wel at mete and mele,

351 *meynye* company   353 *wele* prosperity   *stye* path
355 *heve-ryche* the kingdom of heaven   *trye* tested   363 *leve* believe
365 *gobet* morsel   367 *tawth* instructed   368 *bete* (v) cure
369 *frawth* endowed   370 *sendel* fine quality silk   372 *hele* health

Wyth Goddys servyse may thou not dele
But cum and folwe me.

HUMANUM GENUS: Whom to folwe wetyn I ne may;
I stonde and stodye and gynne to rave.
I wolde be ryche in gret a-ray,
And fayn I wolde my sowle save;
As wynde in watyr I wave.   380
Thou woldyst to the Werld I me toke,
And he wolde that I it for-soke.
Now so God me helpe and the holy boke,
I not wyche I may have.

MALUS ANGELUS: Cum on, man, where-of hast thou
          care?
Go we to the World, I rede the, blyve,
For ther thou schalt mow ryth wel fare;
In case if thou thynke for to thryve,
No lord schal be the lyche.
Take the Werld to thine entent   390
And late thi love be ther-on lent.
Wyth gold and sylvyr and ryche rent
A-none thou schalt be ryche.

HUMANUM GENUS: Now syn thou hast be-hetyn me so,
I wyl go wyth the and a-say.
I ne lette for frende ner fo,
But wyth the Werld I wyl go play,
Certys a lytyl throwe.
In this World is al my trust
To lyvyn in lykyng and in lust.   400
Have he and I onys cust,
We schal not part, I trowe.

376 *wetyn* know   384 *not* do not know   386 *blyve* quickly
387 *mow* be able   394 *be-hetyn* promised   395 *a-say* try
398 *throwe* time   401 *cust* kissed, embraced

BONUS ANGELUS: A, nay, man, for Cristys blod,
    Cum a-gayn, be strete and style.
    The Werld is wyckyd and ful wod
    And thou schalt levyn but a whyle.
    What coveytyst thou to wynne?
    Man, thynke on thyn endynge day
    Whanne thou schalt be closyd undyr clay,
    And if thou thenke of that a-ray,   410
    Certys thou schalt not synne.
    Homo memento finis et in eternum non peccabis.

MALUS ANGELUS: Ya, on thi sowle, thou schalt thynke
        al be-tyme.
    Cum forth, man, and take non hede,
    Cum on and thou schalt holdyn hym inne.
    Thi flesch thou schalt foster and fede
    Wyth lofly lyvys fode.
    Wyth the Werld thou mayst be bold
    Tyl thou be sexty wyntyr hold.
    Wanne thi nose waxit cold,   420
    Thanne mayst thou drawe to goode.

HUMANUM GENUS: I vow to God, and so I may
    Make mery a ful gret throwe.
    I may levyn many a day,
    I am but yonge, as I trowe,
    For to do that I schulde.
    Myth I ryde be sompe and syke
    And be ryche and lord-lyke
    Certys thanne schulde I be fryke
    And a mery man on molde.   430

MALUS ANGELUS: Yys, be my feyth thou schalt be a
        lord,

413 *al be-tyme* in due course   423 *throwe* time   427 *sompe* swamp
syke stream   429 *fryke* daring

And ellys hange me be the hals!
But thou muste be at myn a-cord.
Othyr-whyle thou muste be fals
A-monge kythe and kynne.
Now go we forth swythe a-non,
To the Werld us must gon,
And bere the manly evere a-mong
Whanne thou comyst out or inne.

HUMANUM GENUS: Yys, and ellys have thou my necke   440
But I be manly, be downe and dyche.
And thou I be fals, I ne recke
Wyth so that I be lord-lyche.
I folwe the as I can.
Thou schalt be my bote of bale,
For were I ryche of holt and hale
Thanne wolde I geve nevere tale
Of God ne of good man.

BONUS ANGELUS: I weyle and wrynge and make mone.
This man wyth woo schal be pylt.   450
I sye sore and grysly grone
For hys folye schal make hym spylt.
I not wedyr to gone,
Mankynde hath forsakyn me.
Alas, man, for love of the!
Ya, for this gamyn and this gle
Thou schalt grocchyn and grone.

Pipe up mu[syk].

432 *hals* neck   436 *swythe* at once   442 *recke* (v) care   445 *bote* cure
446 *holt* wood   *hale* hall   447 *tale* concern   449 *weyle* wail
450 *pylt* thrust out   453 *not* do not know   *wedyr* whither
456 *gamyn* sport   457 *grocchyn* moan

MUNDUS [*from his scaffold*]: Now I sytte in my semly
     sale!
  I trotte and tremle in my trew trone;
  As a hawke I hoppe in my hende hale;   460
  Kyng, knyth and kayser to me makyn mone.
  Of God ne of good man gyf I nevere tale.
  As a lykynge lord I leyke here a-lone.
  Wo-so brawle any boste, be downe or be dale,
  Tho gadlyngys schal be gastyd and gryslych grone
  I-wys.
  Lust, Foly, and Veynglory,
  All these arn in myn memory:
  Thus be-gynnyth the nobyl story
  Of this werldys blys.   470

  Lust-Lykyng, and Foly,
  Comly knytys of renoun,
  Be-lyve thorwe this londe do crye
  Al a-bowtyn in tour and toun.
  If any man be fer or nye
  That to my servyse wyl buske hym boun,
  If he wyl be trost and trye
  He schal be kyng and were the croun
  Wyth rycches[t] robys in res.
  Wo-so to the Werld wyl drawe   480
  Of God ne of good man gevyt he not a hawe,
  Syche a man be londys lawe,
  Schal syttyn on my dees.

VOLUPTAS: Lo me here redy, lord, to faryn and to fle,
  To sekyn the a servaunt dynge and dere.

458 *sale* hall   459 *trotte* march   *tremle* quiver, shake (with power?)
463 *lykynge* joyful   *leyke* rejoice   465 *gadlyngys* wretches
gastyd terrified   475 *fer* far   476 *buske* (v) prepare   *boun* quickly
479 *res* haste   481 *gevyt* care   *hawe* hawthorn berry   483 *dees* dais
485 *dynge* noble

Who-so wyl wyth foly rewlyd be
He is worthy to be a servaunt here
That drawyth to synnys sevene.
Who-so wyl be fals and covetouse
Wyth this werld he schal have lond and house.   490
This werldys wy[s]dom gevyth no[t] a louse
Of God nyn of hye hevene.

Tunc descend[ent] in placeam pariter.

Pes, pepyl, of pes we you pray!
Syth and sethe wel to my sawe!
Who-so wyl be ryche and in gret aray
To-ward the Werld he schal drawe.
Who-so wyl be fals al that he may,
Of God hym-self he hath non awe,
And lyvyn in lustys nyth and day
The Werld of hym wyl be ryth fawe,   500
Do dwelle in his howse.
Who-so wyl wyth the Werld have hys dwellynge
And ben a lord of hys clothynge,
He muste nedys ovyr al thynge
Evere-more be covetowse.
Non est in mundo dives qui dicit 'habundo'.

STULTICIA: Ya, covetouse he muste be,
And me, Foly, muste have in mende,
For who-so wyl alwey foly fle
In this werld schal ben unthende.   510
Thorwe werldys wysdom of gret degre
Schal nevere man in werld moun wende
But he have help of me
That am Foly fer and hende;

494 *Syth* sit   *sethe* attend   510 *unthende* unthriving
512 *moun wende* be able to go   514 *fer* fair   *hende* handsome

He muste hangyn on my hoke..
Werldly wyt was never nout
But wyth foly it were frawt.
Thus the wysman hath tawt
A-botyn in his boke.
Sapiencia penes Domini.   520

VOLUPTAS: Now all the men that in this werld wold
          thryve,
For to rydyn on hors ful hye,
Cum speke wyth Lust-and-Lykynge belyve
And hys felaw, yonge Foly.
Late se who-so wyl us knowe.
Who-so wyl drawe to Lykynge-and-Luste
And as a fole in Foly ruste,
On us to he may truste,
And levyn lovely, I trowe.

MALUS ANGELUS: How, Lust-Lykyng and Folye,   530
Take to me good entent!
I have browth, be downys drye,
To the Werld a gret present.
I have gylyd hym ful qweyntly,
For syn he was born I have hym blent.
He schal be serwaunt good and try,
A-monge you his wyl is lent,
To the Werld he wyl hym take.
For syn he cowde wyt, I undirstonde,
I have hym tysyd in every londe.   540
Hys Good Aungel, be strete and stronde,
I have don hym forsake.

516 *nout* nothing   517 *frawt* endowed   527 *ruste* (v) rust, decay
529 *levyn* (v) live   534 *gylyd* tricked   *qweyntly* cunningly
535 *blent* blinded (fig.)   540 *tysyd* enticed

Therfor, Lust, my trewe fere,
Thou art redy al-wey, i-wys,
Of worldly lawys thou hym lere
That he were browth in werldly blys:
Loke he be ryche, the sothe to tell.
Help hym, fast he gunne to thrywe,
And whanne he wenyth best to lywe
Thanne schal he deye and not be schrywe   550
And goo wyth us to hell.

VOLUPTAS: Be Satan, thou art a nobyl knawe
To techyn men fyrst fro goode.
Lust-and-Lykynge he schal have,
Lechery schal ben hys fode,
Metys and drynkys he schal have trye.
Wyth a lykynge lady of lofte
He schal syttyn in sendel softe
To cachen hym to helle crofte
That day that he schal deye.   560

STULTICIA: Wyth ryche rentys I schal hym blynde,
Wyth the Werld tyl he be pytte,
And thanne schal I, longe or hys ende,
Make that caytyfe to be knytte
On the Werld whanne he is set s[ore].
Cum on, man, thou schalt not rewe
For thou wylt be to us trewe.
Thou schalt be clad in clothys newe
And be ryche evere-more.

HUMANUM GENUS: Mary, felaw, gramercy!   570
I wolde be ryche and of gret renoun:
I geve no tale trewly

543 *fere* companion   545 *lere* teach   549 *lywe* live   559 *crofte* enclosure
562 *pytte* placed   566 *rewe* regret

103

So that I be lord of toure and toun,
Be buskys and bankys bro[un].
Syn that thou wylt make me
Bothe ryche of gold and fee,
Goo forthe, for I wyl folow the
Be dale and every towne.

Trumpe up.
Tunc ibunt Voluptas et Stulticia, Malus Angelus et
Humanum Genus ad Mundum, et dicet Voluptas

[VOLUPTAS:] How, lord, loke owt, for we have browth
  A serwant of nobyl fame.   580
  Of worldly good is al hys thouth,
  Of lust and folye he hath no schame.
  He wolde be gret of name.
  He wolde be at gret honour
  For to rewle town and toure.
  He wolde have to hys paramoure
  Sum lovely dynge dame.

MUNDUS: Welcum, syr, semly in syth!
  Thou art welcum to worthy wede.
  For thou wylt be my serwaunt day and nyth,   590
  Wyth my servyse I schal the foster and fede.
  Thi bak schal be betyn wyth besawntys bryth,
  Thou schalt have byggyngys be bankys brede,
  To thi cors schal knele kayser and knyth
  Where that thou walke, be sty or be strete,
  And ladys lovely on lere.
  But Goodys servyse thou must forsake
  And holy to the Werld the take,
  And thanne a man I schal the make,
  That non schal be thi pere.   600

581 *thouth* thought   593 *byggyngys* dwellings   *brede* broad   596 *lere* face

HUMANUM GENUS: Yys, Werld, and ther-to here myn
    honde
  To forsake God and hys servyse.
  To medys thou geve me howse and londe
  That I regne rychely at myn enprise.
  So that I fare wel be strete and stronde
  Whyl I dwelle here in werldly wyse,
  I recke nevere of hevene wonde
  Nor of Jhesu, that jentyl justyse.
  Of my sowle I have non rewthe.
  What schulde I recknen of domysday   610
  So that I be ryche and of gret a-ray?
  I schal make mery whyl I may,
  And ther-to here my trewthe.

MUNDUS: Now sertys, syr, thou seyst wel.
  I holde the trewe fro top to the too
  But thou were ryche it were gret del
  And all men that wyl fare soo.
  Cum up, my serwaunt trew as stel.

Tunc ascendet Humanum Genus ad Mundum.

  Thou schalt be ryche, where-so thou goo.
  Men schul servyn the at mel   620
  Wyth mynstralsye, and bemys blo,
  Wyth metys and drynkys trye.
  Lust-and-Lykynge schal be thin ese;
  Lovely ladys the schal plese.
  Who-so do the any disesse,
  He schal ben hangyn hye.

603 *medys* reward   604 *enprise* power   607 *wonde* rod
618 *stel* steel   621 *bemys* trumpets   *blo* (v) blow

Lykynge, be-lyve
Late clothe hym swythe
In robys ryve
Wyth ryche a-ray.   630
Folye, thou fonde,
Be strete and stronde,
Serve hym at honde
Bothe nyth and day.

VOLUPTAS: Trostyly,
Lord, redy,
Je vous pry,
Syr, I say.
In lyckynge and lust
He schal rust   640
Tyl dethys dust
Do hym to day.

STULTICIA: And I, Folye,
Schal hyen hym hye
Tyl sum enmye
Hym ovyr-goo.
In worldys syt
That in Foly syt
I thynke yyt
Hys sowle to sloo.   650

Trumpe up.

DETRACCIO: All thyngys I crye a-gayn the pes
To knyt and knave, this is my kende.
Ya, dyngne dukys on her des

629 *ryve* generous, ?fine   631 *fonde* ?fool   642 *day* (v) die
644 *hyen* raise   649 *yyt* yet   650 *sloo* slay

In byttyr balys I hem bynde;
Cryinge and care, chydynge and ches
And sad sorwe to hem I sende;
Ya, lowde lesyngys lacchyd in les,
Of talys un-trewe is al my mende.
Mannys bane a-bowtyn I bere.
I wyl that ye wetyn, all tho that ben here,   660
For I am knowyn fer and nere,
I am the Werldys messengere,
My name is Bacbytere.

Wyth every wyth I walke and wende
And every man now lovyth me wele.
Wyth lowde lesyngys undyr lende
To dethys dynt I dresse and dele.
To speke fayre be-forn and fowle be-hynde
A-mongys men at mete and mele
Trewly, lordys, this is my kynde.   670
Thus I renne up-on a whele,
I am feller thanne a fox.
Fleterynge and flaterynge is my lessun,
Wyth lesyngys I tene bothe tour and town,
Wyth letterys of defamacyoun
I bere here in my box.

I am lyth of lopys thorwe every londe,
Myn holy happys may not ben hyd.
To may not to-gedyr stonde
But I, Bakbyter, be the thyrde.   680
I schape yone boyis to schame and schonde,
All that wyl bowyn whanne I hem bydde.
To lawe of londe in feyth I fonde.

655 *ches* quarrelling   658 *mende* thought   660 *wetyn* know
673 *Fleterynge* flitting about   677 *lopys* leaps   678 *happys* fortune
679 *To* two   681 *schonde* (n) disgrace   683 *fonde* tempt

Whanne talys untrewe arn be-tydde
Bakbytere is wyde spronge.
Thorwe the werld, be downe and dalys,
All a-bowtyn I brewe balys.
Every man tellyth talys
Aftyr my fals tunge.

Therfore I am mad massenger   690
To lepyn ovyr londys leye
Thorwe all the world, fer and ner,
Unsayd sawys for to seye.
In this holte I hunte here
For to spye a prevy pley;
For whanne Mankynde is clothyd clere,
Thanne schal I techyn hym the wey
To the dedly synnys sevene.
Here I schal a-bydyn wyth my pese
The wronge to do hym forto chese,   700
For I thynke that he schal lese
The lyth of hey hevene.

VOLUPTAS: Worthy World, in welthys wonde,
Here is Mankynde ful fayr in folde.
In bryth besauntys he is bownde
And bon to bowe to you so bolde.
He levyth in lustys every stounde;
Holy to you he hathe hym yolde.
For to makyn hym gay on grounde,
Worthy World, thou art be-holde.   710
This werld is wel at ese.
For to God I make a vow
Mankynde had lever now
Greve God wyth synys row
Thanne the World to dysplese.

684 *be-tydde* happening 691 *leye* fallow 699 *pese* peace, quit
703 *wonde* rod, control 704 *folde* earth 708 *yolde* submitted
714 *row* ?rough

STULTICIA: Dysplese the he wyl for no man.
   On me, Foly, is al hys thowth.
   Trewly Mankynde nowth nen can
   Thynke on God that hathe hym bowth.
   Worthy World, wyth as swan,   720
   In thi love lely is he lawth.
   Sythyn he cowde and fyrste be-gan
   The forsakyn wolde he nowth,
   But geve hym to Folye.
   And sythyn he hathe to the be trewe,
   I rede the forsakyn hym for no newe.
   Lete us plesyn hym tyl that he rewe
   In hell to hangyn hye.

MUNDUS: Now, Foly, fayre the be-fall!
   And Luste, blyssyd be thou ay!   730
   Ye han browth Mankynde to myn hall
   Sertys in a nobyl a-ray.
   Wyth Werldys welthys wyth-inne these wall
   I schal hym feffe if that I may.
   Welcum, Mankynde, to the I call,
   Clenner clothyd thanne any clay,
   Be downe, dale and dyche.
   Mankynde, I rede that thou reste
   Wyth me, the Werld, as it is beste.
   Loke thou holde myn hende heste   740
   And evere thou schalt be ryche.

HUMANUM GENUS: Whou schul[d] I but I thi hestys
      helde?
   Thou werkyst wyth me holy my wyll.
   Thou feffyst me wyth fen and felde
   And hye hall, be holtys and hyll.
   In werldly wele my wytte I welde,

718 *nen* nor   721 *lely* truly   *lawth* caught   722 *Sythyn* since
734, 744 *feffe, feffyst* endow(est)

In joye I jette wyth juelys jentyll,
On blysful banke my boure is bylde,
In veynglorye I stonde styll.
I am kene as a knyt.   750
Who-so a-geyn the Werld wyl speke
Mankynde schal on hym be wreke;
In stronge presun I schal hym steke,
Be it wronge or ryth.

MUNDUS: A, Mankynde, wel the be-tyde
That thi love on me is sette!
In my bowrys thou schalt a-byde
And yyt fare mekyl the bette.
I feffe the in all my wonys wyde
In dale of dros tyl thou be deth.   760
I make the lord of mekyl pryde,
Syr, at thyn owyn mowthis mette:
I fynde in the no tresun.
In all this worlde, be se and sonde,
Parkys, placys, lawnde and londe,
Here I gyfe the wyth myn honde,
Syr, an opyn sesun.

Go to my tresorer, Syr Covetouse:
Loke thou tell hym as I seye.
Bydde hym make the maystyr in hys house   770
Wyth penys and powndys for to pleye.
Loke thou geve not a lous
Of the day that thou schalt deye.
Messenger, do now thyne use:
Bakbytere, teche hym the weye.
Thou art swetter thanne mede.
Mankynde, take wyth the Bakbytynge.

747 *juelys* ornaments   750 *kene* brave   753 *steke* shut up
758 *bette* better   765 *lawnde* glade   767 *sesun* possession
771 *penys* pennies

Lefe hym for no maner thynge.
Flepergebet wyth hys flaterynge
Standyth Mankynde in stede.   780

DETRACCIO: Bakbytynge and Detracion
Schal goo wyth the fro toun to toun.
Have done, Mankynde, and cum doun.
I am thyne owyn page.
I schal bere the wyttnesse wyth my myth
Whanne my lord the Werlde it behyth.
Lo, where Syr Coveytyse sytt
And bydith us in his stage.

HUMANUM GENUS: Syr Worlde, I wende,
In Coveytyse to chasyn my kende.   790

MUNDUS: Have hym in mende,
And i-wys thanne schalt thou be ryth thende.

BONUS ANGELUS: Alas, Jhesu, jentyl justyce,
Whedyr may mans Good Aungyl wende?
Now schal careful Coveytyse
Mankende trewly al schende.
Hys sely goste may sore a-gryse;
Bakbytynge bryngyth hym in byttyr bonde.
Worldly wyttys, ye are not wyse;
Your lovely lyfe a-mys ye spende   800
And that schal ye sore smert.
Parkys, ponndys, and many pens
Thei semyn to you swetter thanne sens,
But Goddys servyse nyn hys commaundementys
Stondyth you not at hert.

786 *behyth* (v) promises   792 *thende* prosperous   797 *a-gryse* tremble
803 *sens* (n) incense   804 *nyn* nor

MALUS ANGELUS: Ya, whanne the fox prechyth, kepe wel
    yore gees!
He spekyth as it were a holy pope.
Goo, felaw, and pyke of tho lys
That crepe ther up-on thi cope!
Thi part is pleyed al at the dys   810
That thou schalt have here, as I hope.
Tyl Mankynde fallyth to podys prys,
Coveytyse schal hym grype and grope
Tyl sum schame hym schende.
Tyl man be dyth in dethys dow
He seyth nevere he hath i-now.
Ther-fore, goode boy, cum blow
At my nether ende!

DETRACCIO: Syr Coveytyse, God the save,
Thi pens and thi poundys all!   820
I, Bakbyter, thyn owyn knave,
Have browt Mankynde unto thine hall.
The Worlde bad thou schuldyst hym have
And feffyn hym, what-so be-fall.
In grene gres tyl he be grave
Putte hym in thi precyous pal,
Coveytyse, it were ell rewthe.
Whyl he walkyth in worldly wolde
I, Bakbyter, am wyth hym holde.
Lust and Folye, tho barouns bolde,   830
To hem he hath plyth hys trewthe.

AVARICIA: Ow, Mankynde, blyssyd mote thou be!
I have lovyd the derworthly many a day,
And so I wot wel that thou dost me.
Cum up and se my ryche a-ray.
It were a gret poynte of pyte

810 *dys* dice   813 *grype* clutch   *grope* grasp   815 *dow* dough (earth)
825 *gres* grass   827 *ell* else   833 *derworthly* dearly

But Coveytyse were to thi pay.
Sit up ryth here in this se.
I schal the lere of werldlys lay·
That fadyth as a flode.   840
Wyth good i-now I schal the store,
And yyt oure game is but lore
But thou coveyth mekyl more
Thanne evere schal do the goode.

Thou muste gyfe the to symonye,
Extorsion, and false asyse.
Helpe no man but thou have why.
Pay not thi serwauntys here serwyse.
Thi neyborys loke thou dystroye.
Tythe not on non wyse.   850
Here no begger thou he crye;
And thanne schalt thou ful sone ryse.
And whanne thou usyste marchaundyse
Loke that thou be sotel of sleytys,
And also swere al be deseytys,
Bye and sell be fals weytys,
For that is kynde coveytyse.

Be not a-gaste of the grete curse.
This lofly lyfe may longe leste.
Be the peny in thi purs,   860
Lete hem cursyn and don here beste.
What devyl of hell art thou the wers
Thow thou brekyste Goddys heste?
Do after me, I am thi nors.
Al-wey gadyr and have non reste.
In wynnynge be al thi werke.
To pore men take none entent,

838 *se* seat   843 *coveyth* cravest   846 *asyse* measure
850 *Tythe* pay tithes   852 *sone* soon   855 *deseytys* deception
856 *weytys* weights   857 *kynde* natural   864 *nors* nurse   867 *entent* care

For that thou haste longe tyme hent
In lytyl tyme it may be spent;
Thus seyth Caton the grete clerke.   870
Labitur exiguo quod partum tempore longo.

HUMANUM GENUS: A, Avaryce, wel thou spede!
  Of werldly wytte thou canst i-wys.
  Thou woldyst not I hadde nede
  And schuldyst be wrothe if I ferd a-mys.
  I schal nevere begger bede
  Mete nyn drynke, be hevene blys;
  Rather or I schulde hym clothe or fede
  He schulde sterve and stynke i-wys.
  Coveytyse, as thou wylt, I wyl do.   880
  Where-so that I fare, be fenne or flod,
  I make a vow, be Goddys blod
  Of Mankynde getyth no man no good
  But if he synge *si dedero.*

AVARICIA: Mankynd, that was wel songe.
  Sertys thou canst sum skyll.
  Blyssyd be thi trewe tonge!
  In this bowre thou schalt byde and byll.
  Moo synnys I wolde thou undyrfonge:
  Wyth coveytyse the feffe I wyll;   890
  And thanne sum pryde I wolde spronge,
  Hyge in thi hert to holdyn and hyll
  And a-bydyn in thi body.
  Here I feffe the in myn hevene
  Wyth gold and sylvyr, lyth as levene.
  The dedly synnys, all sevene,
  I schal do comyn in hy.

876 *bede* offer 879 *sterve* die 888 *byll* dwell
889 *undyrfonge* undertake 892 *Hyge* deep *hyl!* shelter
895 *lyth* bright *levene* lightning

Pryde, Wrathe, and Envye,
Com forthe, the Develys chyldryn thre!
Lecchery, Slawth, and Glotonye,   900
To mans flesch ye are fendys fre.
Dryvyth downne ovyr dalys drye,
Beth now blythe as any be,
Ovyr hyll and holtys ye you hyge
To com to Mankynde and to me
Fro youre dowty dennys.
As dukys dowty ye you dresse.
Whanne ye sex be comne, I gesse,
Thanne be we sevene and no lesse
Of the dedly synnys.   910

SUPERBIA: Wondyr hyge howtys on hyll herd I houte:
Koveytyse kryeth, hys karpyng I kenne.
Summe lord or summe lordeyn lely schal loute
To be pyth wyth perlys of my proude penne.
Bon I am to braggyn and buskyn a-bowt,
Rapely and redyly on rowte for to renne.
Be doun, dalys, nor dennys no duke I dowt,
Also fast for to fogge, be flodys and be fenne.
I rore whanne I ryse.
Syr Belyal, bryth of ble,   920
To you I recomaunde me.
Have good day, my fadyr fre,
For I goo to Coveytyse.

IRA: Whanne Coveytyse cried and carpyd of care,
Thanne must I, wod wreche, walkyn and wend
Hyge ovyr holtys, as hound aftyr hare.
If I lette and were the last, he schuld me sore schend.
I buske my bold baston, be bankys ful bare.
Sum boy schal be betyn and browth undyr bonde.

904 *hyge* (v) go   908 *comne* come   914 *penne* plume   916 *Rapely* hastily
918 *fogge* go, jog   927 *lette* stop   928 *baston* staff

Wrath schal hym wrekyn and weyin hys ware.   930
For-lorn schal al be for lusti laykys in londe,
As a lythyr page
Syr Belyal, blak and blo,
Have good day, now I goo
For to fell thi foo
Wyth wyckyd wage.

INVIDIA: Whanne Wrath gynnyth walke in ony wyde
          wonys,
     Envye flet as a fox and folwyth on faste.
     Whanne thou steryst[e] or staryst[e] or stumble up-on
          stonys,
     I lepe as a lyon; me is loth to be the laste.   940
     Ya, I breyde byttyr balys in body and in bonys,
     I frete myn herte and in kare I me kast.
     Goo we to Coveytyse, all thre at onys,
     Wyth oure grysly gere a grome for to gast.
     This day schal he deye.
     Belsabubbe, now have good day,
     For we wyl wendyn in good a-ray,
     Al thre in fere, as I the say,
     Pride, Wrath, and Envye.

BELIAL: Farewel now, chy[l]dryn, fayre to fynde.   950
     Do now wel youre olde owse.
     Whanne ye com to Mankynde
     Make hym wroth and envyous.
     Levyth not lytly undyr lynde;
     To his sowle brewyth a byttyr jous.
     Whanne he is ded I schal hym bynde
     In hell, as catte dothe the mows.

930 *wrekyn* destroy   *weyin* measure   *ware* goods   931 *laykys* games
932 *lythyr* idle   936 *wage* reward   938 *flet* runs
941 *breyde* make, 'brew'   942 *frete* gnaw   951 *owse* role
954 *lynde* lime tree   955 *jous* juice

Now buske you forthe on brede.
I may be blythe as any be,
For Mankynde in every cuntre   960
Is rewlyd be my chyldyr thre,
Envye, Wrathe, and Pryde.

GULA: A grom gan gredyn gayly on grounde:
Of me, gay Glotoun, gan al hys gale.
I stampe and I styrte and stynt upon stounde,
To a staunche deth I stakyr and stale.
What boyes wyth here belys in my bondys ben bownd,
Bothe here bak and here blod I brewe al to bale.
I fese folke to fyth tyle here flesch fond.
Whanne summe han dronkyn a drawth thei drepyn in a
    dale;   970
In me is here mynde.
Mans florchynge flesch,
Fayre, frele, and fresch,
I rape to rewle in a rese
To kloye in my kynde.

LUXURIA: In mans kyth I cast me a castel to kepe.
I, Lechery, wyth lykynge, am lovyd in iche a lond.
Wyth my sokelys of swettnesse I sytte and I slepe.
Many berdys I brynge to my byttyr bonde.
In wo and in wrake wyckyd wytys schal wepe   980
That in my wonys wylde wyl not out wende.
Whanne Mankynde is castyn undyr clourys to crepe,
Thanne tho ledrouns for here lykynge I schal al
    to-schende,
Trewly to tell.

958 *on brede* abroad   959 *be* bee   963 *grom* man   *gredyn* call
964 *gale* speech   965 *styrte* leap   *stynt upon stounde* stop suddenly
966 *staunche* firm   *stakyr* stagger   *stale* ?go steadily   967 *belys* bellies
969 *fese* incite   976 *kyth* loins   978 *sokelys* ?honeysuckle flowers
982 *clourys* sods   983 *ledrouns* rascals

Syr Flesch, now I wende,
Wyth lust in my lende,
To cachyn Mankynde
To the Devyl of hell.

ACCIDIA: Ya, w[ha]t seyst thou of Syr Slawth, wyth my
        soure syth?
Mankynde lovyth me wel, wys as I wene.   990
Men of relygyon I rewle in my ryth;
I lette Goddys servyse, the sothe may be sene.
In bedde I brede brothel wyth my berdys bryth;
Lordys, ladys, and lederounnys to my lore leene.
Mekyl of mankynd in my clokys schal be knyth,
Tyl deth dryvyth hem down in dalys be-dene.
We may non lenger a-byde.
Syr Flesch, comly kynge,
In the is al oure bredynge:
Geve us now thi blyssynge,   1000
For Coveytyse hath cryde.

CARO: Glotony and Slawth fare-wel in fere,
Lovely in londe is now your lesse:
And Lecherye, my dowtyr so dere,
Dapyrly ye dresse you so dyngne on desse.
All thre my blyssynge ye schal have here.
Goth now forth and gyve ye no fors.
It is no nede you for to lere
To cachyn Mankynd to a careful clos
Fro the bryth blysse off hevene.   1010
The Werld, the Flesch, and the Devyl are knowe
Grete lordys, as we wel owe,

986 *lende* loins   989 *soure* sour   *syth* appearance   992 *lette* hinder
993 *brothel* wretch, lecher   994 *leene* (v) lean, incline   995 *knyth* tied
1003 *lesse* joy   1005 *Dapyrly* elegantly   1009 *clos* imprisonment
1012 *owe* ought (to be)

And thorwe Mankynd we settyn and sowe
The dedly synnys sevene.

Tunc ibunt Superbia, Ira, Invidia, Gula, Luxuria, et
Accidia ad Avariciam et dicet Superbia

SUPERBIA: What is thi wyll, Syr Coveytyse?
Why hast thou afftyr us sent?
Whanne thou creydyst we ganne agryse
And come to the now parasent.
Oure love is on the lent.
I, Pryde, Wrath, and Envye,   1020
Gloton, Slawth, and Lecherye,
We arn cum all sex for thi crye
To be at thi commaundement.

AVARICIA: Welcum be ye, bretheryn all,
And my sy[s]tyr, swete Lecherye.
Wytte ye why I gan to call?
For ye must me helpe and that in hy.
Mankynde is now com to myn hall
Wyth me to dwell, be downys dry.
Therefore ye must, what-so be-fall,   1030
Feffyn hym wyth youre foly
And ell ye don hym wronge.
For whanne Mankynd is kendly koveytous
He is proud, wrathful, and envyous;
Glotons, slaw and lecherous
Thei arn othyr-whyle a-monge.

Thus every synne tyllyth in othyr
And makyth Mankynde to ben a foole.

1017 *agryse* tremble   1018 *parasent* willingly   1027 *hy* haste
1037 *tyllyth* (v) draws, entices

We sevene fallyn on a fodyr
Mankynd to chase to pyny[n]gys stole.   1040
Therefore Pryde, good brothyr,
And brethyryn all, take ye your tol.
Late iche of us take at othyr
And set Mankynd on a stomlynge stol
Whyl he is here on lyve.
Lete us lullyn hym in oure lust
Tyl he be drevyn to dampnynge dust.
Colde care schal ben hys crust
To deth whanne he schal dryve.

SUPERBIA: In gle and game I growe glad.   1050
Mankynd, take good hed
And do as Coveytyse the bad:
Take me in thyn hert, precyous Pride.
Loke thou be not ovyr-lad,
Late no bacheler the mysbede,
Do the to be dowtyd and drad,
Bete boyes tyl they blede,
Kast hem in careful kettys.
Frende, fadyr and modyr dere,
Bowe hem not in non manere,   1060
And hold no maner man thi pere,
And use these new jettys.

Loke thou blowe mekyl bost
Wyth longe crakows on thi schos.
Jagge thi clothis in every cost,
And ell men schul lete the but a goos.
It is thus, man, wel thou wost,

1040 *pynyngys stole* the place or stool of punishment
1042 *tol* equipment   1044 *stomlynge stol* place for tripping up
1051 *hed* heed   1054 *ovyr-lad* overcome   1055 *mysbede* illtreat
1056 *dowtyd* feared   1062 *jettys* fashions   1065 *Jagge* slash
cost manner

Therfore do as no man dos
And every man sette at a thost
And of thi-self make gret ros.   1070
Now se thi-self on every syde.
Every man thou schalt schende and schelfe
And holde no man betyr thanne thi-selfe.
Tyl dethys dynt thi body delfe
Put holy thyn hert in Pride.

HUMANUM GENUS: Pryde, be Jhesu, thou seyst wel.
Who-so suffyr is ovyrled al day.
Whyl I reste on my rennynge whel
I schal not suffre, if that I may.
Myche myrthe at mete and mel   1080
I love ryth wel, and ryche a-ray.
Trewly I thynke, in every sel,
On grounde to by graythyd gay
And of my-selfe to take good gard.
Mykyl myrthe thou wylt me make,
Lordlyche to leve, be londe and lake.
Myn hert holy to the I take
In-to thyne owyn a-ward.

SUPERBIA: I thi bowre to a-byde
I com to dwelle be thi syde   1090
HUMANUM GENUS: Mankynde and Pride
Schal dwell to-gedyr every tyde.

IRA: Be also wroth as thou were wode:
Make the be dred, be dalys derne.
Who-so the wrethe, be fen or flode,

1069 *thost* dung   1070 *ros* (n) boast   1072 *schende* abuse
schelfe ?push aside   1074 *delfe* pierce   1082 *sel* moment
1083 *graythyd* dressed   1088 *a-ward* protection   1089 *I* in
1094 *dalys* valleys   *derne* secluded   1095 *wrethe* (v) angers

Loke thou be a-vengyd yerne.
Be redy to spylle mans blod.
Loke thou hem fere, be feldys ferne.
Al-way, man, be ful of mod.
My lothly lawys loke thou lerne,   1100
I rede, for any thynge.
A-non take venjaunce, man, I rede,
And thanne schal no man the ovyr-lede,
But of the they schul have drede
And bowe to thi byddynge.

HUMANUM GENUS: Wrethe, for thi councel hende,
Have thou Goddys blyssynge and myn.
What caytyf of al my kende
Wyl not bowe, he schal a-byn.
Wyth myn venjaunce I schal hym schende   1110
And wrekyn me, be Goddys yne.
Rathyr or I schulde bowe or bende
I schuld be stekyd as a swyne
Wyth a lothly launce.
Be it erly or late,
Who-so make wyth me debate
I schal hym hyttyn on the pate
And takyn a-non venjaunce.

IRA: Wyth my rewly rothyr
I com to the, Mankynde, my brothyr.   1120
HUMANUM GENUS: Wrethe, thi fayr fothyr
Makyth iche man to be vengyd on othyr.

INVIDIA: Envye wyth Wrathe muste dryve
To haunte Mankynde al-so.

1098 *fere* frighten   *feldys* fields   *ferne* distant   1100 *lothly* horrible
1109 *a-byn* pay   1111 *yne* eyes   1119 *rothyr* rudder
1121 *fothyr* company

Whanne any of thy neyborys wyl thryve
Loke thou have Envye ther-to.
On the hey name I charge the be-lyve
Bakbyte hym, whow-so thou do.
Kyll hym a-non wyth-owtyn knyve
And speke hym sum schame were thou go,   1130
Be dale or downys drye.
Speke thi neybour mekyl schame,
Pot on hem sum fals fame,
Loke thou un-do hys nobyl name
Wyth me, that am Envye.

HUMANUM GENUS: Envye, thou art bothe good and
          hende
And schalt be of my counsel chefe.
Thi counsel is knowyn thorwe mankynde,
For ilke man callyth othyr hore and thefe.
Envye, thou arte rote and rynde,   1140
Thorwe this werld of mykyl myschefe.
In byttyr balys I schal hem bynde
That to the puttyth any reprefe.
Cum up to me above.
For more envye thanne is now reynynge
Was nevere syth Cryst was kynge.
Cum up, Envye, my dere derlynge.
Thou hast Mankyndys love.

INVIDIA: I clymbe fro this crofte
Wyth Mankynde to syttyn on lofte.   1150
HUMANUM GENUS: Cum, syt here softe,
For in abbeys thou dwellyst ful ofte.

GULA: In gay Glotony a game thou be-gynne,
Ordeyn the mete and drynkys goode.

1138 *thorwe* throughout   1139 *ilke* each   1149 *crofte* enclosure

Loke that no tresour [thou] part a-twynne
But the feffe and fede wyth alkynnys fode.
Wyth fastynge schal man nevere hevene wynne;
These grete fasterys I holde hem wode.
Thou thou ete and drynke, it is no synne.
Fast no day, I rede, be the rode,   1160
Thou chyde these fastyng cherlys.
Loke thou have spycys of goode odoure
To feffe and fede thy fleschly floure,
And thanne mayst thou bultyn in thi boure
And serdyn gay gerlys.

HUMANUM GENUS: A, Glotony, wel I the grete.
    Soth and sad it is, thy sawe.
    I am no day wel, be sty nor strete,
    Tyl I have wel fyllyd my mawe.
    Fastynge is fellyd undyr fete,   1170
    Thou I nevere faste I [ne] rekke an hawe;
    He servyth of nowth, be the rode, I lete,
    But to do a mans guttys to gnawe.
    To faste I wyl not fonde.
    I schal not spare, so have I reste,
    To have a mossel of the beste.
    The lenger schal my lyfe mow leste
    Wyth gret lykynge in londe.

GULA: Be bankys on brede,
    Othyrwhyle to spew the spede!   1180
HUMANUM GENUS: Whyl I lyf lede
    Wyth fayre fode my flesche schal I fede.

    1155 *a-twynne* in two   1156 *alkynnys fode* all kinds of food
    1164 *bultyn* fornicate   1165 *serdyn* serve   1170 *fellyd* struck down
    1171 *hawe* berry   1172 *lete* think   1174 *fonde* try
    1176 *mossel* morsel, dish   1177 *mow* be able
    1180 *Othyrwhyle* sometimes

LUXURIA: Ya, whanne thi flesche is fayre fed,
Thanne schal I, lovely Lecherye,
Be bobbyd wyth the in bed.
Here-of serve mete and drynkys trye.
In love thi lyf schal be led;
Be a lechour tyl th[o]u dye.
Thi nedys schal be the bettyr sped
If [thou] gyf the to fleschly folye 1190
Tyl deth the down drepe.
Lechery syn the werld began
Hath a-vauncyd many a man.
Therfore, Mankynd, my leve lemman,
I my cunte thou schalt crepe.

HUMANUM GENUS: A, Lechery, wel the be.
Mans sed in the is sowe.
Fewe men wyl forsake the
In any cuntre that I knowe.
Spouse-breche is a frend ryth fre, 1200
Men use that mo thanne i-nowe.
Lechery, cum syt be me.
Thi banys be ful wyd i-knowe;
Lykynge is in thi lende.
On nor othyr, I se no wythte
That wyl for-sake [the] day ner nyth.
Therefore cum up, my berd bryth,
And reste the wyth Mankynde.

LUXURIA: I may soth synge
'Mankynde is kawt in my slynge'. 1210
HUMANUM GENUS: For ony erthyly thynge,
To bedde thou muste me brynge.

1185 *bobbyd* bounced   1186 *trye* (adj) choice   1195 *I* into
1200 *Spouse-breche* adultery   1203 *banys* banns
1205 *wythte* person

ACCIDIA: Ya, whanne ye be in bedde bothe,
   Wappyd wel in worthy wede,
   Thanne I, Slawthe, wyl be wrothe
   But ij brothelys I may brede.
   Whanne the messe-belle goth
   Lye styll, man, and take non hede.
   Lappe thyne hed thanne in a cloth
   And take a swet, I the rede,   1220
   Chyrche-goynge thou forsake.
   Losengerys in londe I lyfte
   And dyth men to mekyl unthryfte.
   Penaunce enjoynyd men in schryfte
   Is un-done, and that I make.

HUMANUM GENUS: Owe, Slawthe, thou seyst me skylle.
   Men use the mekyl, God it wot.
   Men lofe wel now to lye stylle
   In bedde to take a morowe swot.
   To chyrche-ward is not here wylle;   1230
   Here beddys thei thynkyn goode and hot.
   Herry, Jofferey, Jone, and Gylle
   Arn leyd and logyd in a lot
   Wyth thyne unthende charmys.
   Al mankynde, be the holy rode,
   Are now slawe in werkys goode.
   Com nere therfore, myn fayre foode,
   And lulle me in thyne armys.

ACCIDIA: I make men, I trowe,
   In Goddys servyse to be ryth slowe.   1240
HUMANUM GENUS: Co[m] up this throwe.
   Swyche men thou schalt fynden i-nowe.

   1214 *wede* clothing   1220 *swet* sweat   1222 *Losengerys* flatterers
   1226 *Owe* Oh   *skylle* argument   1229 *morowe* morning   *swot* sweat
   1234 *unthende* unhealthy   1236 *slawe* lazy   1241 *throwe* time

Mankynde I am callyd be kynde,
Wyth curssydnesse in costys knet.
In sowre swettenesse my syth I sende,
Wyth sevene synnys sadde be-set.
Mekyl myrthe I move in mynde,
 Wyth melody at my mowthis met.
My prowd pouer schal I not pende
Tyl I be putte in peynys pyt,   1250
To helle hent fro hens.
In dale of dole tyl we are downe
We schul be clad in a gay gowne.
I se no man but they use somme
Of these vij dedly synnys.

For comounly it is seldom seyne
Who-so now be lecherows
Of othyr men he schal have dysdeyne
And ben prowde or covetous.
In synne iche man is founde.   1260
Ther is pore nor ryche be londe ne lake,
That alle these vij wyl forsake,
But wyth on or othyr he schal be take
And in here byttyr bondys bownde.

BONUS ANGELUS: So mekyl the werse, wele-a-woo,
That evere Good Aungyl was ordeynyd the.
Thou art rewlyd aftyr the fende that is thi foo
And no thynge certys aftyr me.
Weleaway, wedyr may I goo?
Man doth me bleykyn blody ble.   1270
Hys swete sowle he wyl now slo.
He schal wepe al hys game and gle
At on dayes tyme.
Ye se wel all sothly in syth

1244 *costys* habits   *knet* tied   1249 *pende* limit   1251 *hent* taken
1252 *dole* grief   1270 *bleykyn* make pale   *ble* complexion, pallor

I am a-bowte bothe day and nyth
To brynge hys sowle in-to blis bryth,
And hym-self wyl it brynge to pyne.

MALUS ANGELUS: No, Good Aungyl, thou art not in
      sesun,
Fewe men in the feyth they fynde.
For thou hast schewyd a ballyd resun,   1280
Goode syre, cum blowe myn hol be-hynde.
Trewly man hathe non chesun
On thi God to grede and grynde,
For that schuld cunne Cristis lessoun
In penaunce hys body he muste bynde
And forsake the worldys mende.
Men arn loth on the to crye
Or don penaunce for here folye.
Therfore have I now maystrye
Welny ovyr al mankynde.   1290

BONUS ANGELUS: Alas, Mankynde
Is bobbyd and blent as the blynde.
In feyth, I fynde
To Crist he can nowt be kynde.
Alas, Mankynne
Is soylyd and saggyd in synne.
He wyl not blynne
Tyl body and sowle parte a-twynne.
Alas, he is blendyd,
A-mys mans lyf is i-spendyd,   1300
Wyth fendys fendyd.
Mercy, God, that man were a-mendyd.

1280 *ballyd* bald, barren   1282 *chesun* reason   1283 *grede* call
grynde gnash the teeth   1284 *cunne* know   1286 *mende* thought
1290 *Welny* almost   1292 *bobbyd* mocked   *blent* blinded
1301 *fendyd* defended

CONFESSIO: What, mans Aungel, good and trewe,
Why syest thou and sobbyst sore?
Sertys sore it schal me rewe
If I se the make mornynge more.
May any bote thi bale brewe
Or any thynge thi stat a-store?
For all felechepys olde and newe
Why makyst thou grochynge undyr gore   1310
Wyth pynynge poyntys pale?
Why was al this gretynge gunne
Wyth sore syinge undyr sunne?
Tell me and I schal, if I cunne
Brewe the bote of bale.

BONUS ANGELUS: Of byttyr balys thou mayste me
     bete,
Swete Schryfte, if that thou wylt.
For Mankynde it is that I grete:
He is in poynt to be spylt.
He is set in sevene synnys sete   1320
And wyl certys tyl he be kylt.
Wyth me he thynkyth nevere-more to mete,
He hath me forsake, and I have no gylt.
No man wyl hym amende.
Therfore, Schryfte, so God me spede,
But if thou helpe at this nede
Mankynde gety[t]h nevere othyr mede
But peyne wyth-owtyn ende.

CONFESCIO: What, Aungel, be of counfort stronge,
For thi lordys love that deyed on tre.   1330
On me, Schryfte, it schal not be longe
And that thou schalt the sothe se.
If he wyl be a-knowe hys wronge

1307 *bote* remedy   *brewe* (v) ease   1308 *a-store* restore
1318 *grete* weep   1320 *sete* seat   1321 *kylt* killed
1333 *a-knowe* acknowledge

And no-thynge hele, but telle it me,
And don penaunce sone a-monge,
I schal hym stere to gamyn and gle
In joye that evere schal last.
Who-so sch[r]yve hym of hys synnys alle
I be-hete hym hevene halle.
Therfor go we hens, what so be-falle,   1340
To Mankynde fast.

Tunc ibunt ad Humanum Genus et dicet Confessio

[CONFESSIO:] What, Mankynde, whou goth this?
What dost thou wyth these develys sevene?
Alas, alas, man, al a-mys!
Blysse in the name of God in hevene,
I rede, so have I rest.
These lotly lordeynys a-wey thou lyfte
And cum doun and speke wyth Schryfte
And drawe the yerne to sum thryfte.
Trewly it is the best.   1350

HUMANUM GENUS: A, Schryfte, thou art wel be note
Here to Slawthe that syttyth here-inne
He seyth thou mytyst a com to mannys cote
On Palme Sunday al be-tyme.
Thou art com al to sone.
Therfore, Schryfte, be thi fay,
Goo forthe tyl on Good Fryday.
Tente to the thanne wel I may;
I have now ellys to done.

CONFESCIO: Ow, that harlot is now bold: 1360
In bale he byndyth Mankynd belyve.

1334 *hele* hide   1347 *lotly* horrible   *lyfte* banish   1353 *a* have
cote house

Sey Slawthe I preyd hym that he wold
Fynd a charter of thi lyve.
Man, thou mayst ben undyr mold
Longe or that tyme, kyllyd wyth a knyve,
Wyth podys and froskys many-fold.
Therfore schape the now to schryve
If thou wylt com to blys.
Thou synnyste. Or sorwe the ensense,
Be-hold thynne hert, thi preve spense,   1370
And thynne owyn consyense,
Or sertys thou dost a-mys.

HUMANUM GENUS: Ya, Petyr, so do mo.
We have etyn garlek everychone.
Thou I schulde to helle go,
I wot wel I schal not gon a-lone,
Trewly I tell the.
I dyd nevere so ewyl trewly
That othyr han don as ewyl as I.
Therfore, syre, lete be thy cry   1380
And go hens fro me.

PENITENCIA: Wyth poynt of penaunce I schal hym prene
Mans pride for to felle.
Wyth this launce I schal hym lene
I-wys a drope of mercy welle.
Sorwe of hert is that I mene;
Trewly ther may no tunge telle
What waschyth sowlys more clene
Fro the foul fend of helle
Thanne swete sorwe of hert.   1390
God, that sytty[t]h in hevene on hye,
Askyth no more or that thou dye

1364 *mold* ground   1366 *podys* toads   *froskys* frogs   1369 *Or* before
ensense drives mad   1370 *preve* secret   *spense* store
1382 *prene* pierce

But sorwe of hert wyth wepynge eye
For all thi synnys smert.

Thei that syh in synnynge,
In sadde sorwe for here synne,
Whanne thei schal make here endynge,
Al here joye is to be-gynne.
Thanne medelyth no mornynge
But joye is joynyd wyth jentyl gynne.   1400
Therfore, Mankynde, in this tokenynge,
Wyth spete of spere to the I spynne,
Goddys lawys to the I lerne.
Wyth my spud of sorwe swote
I reche to thyne hert rote.
Al thi bale schal torne the to bote.
Mankynde, go schryve the yerne.

HUMANUM GENUS: A sete of sorwe in me is set:
Sertys for synne I [syhe] sore.
Mone of mercy in me is met: 1410
For werldys myrthe I morne more.
In wepynge wo my wele is wet.
Mercy, thou muste myn stat a-store.
Fro oure lordys lyth thou hast me let,
Sory synne, thou grysly gore,
Owte on the, dedly synne!
Synne, thou haste Mankynde schent.
In dedly synne my lyfe is spent.
Mercy, God Omnipotent,
In youre grace I be-gynne.   1420

1395 *syh* sight   1399 *medelyth* mingles   1400 *gynne* contrivance
1402 *spete* point   *spynne* move   1404 *spud* knife   1407 *yerne* quickly
1410 *Mone* grief   1414 *lyth* brightness   1415 *grysly* frightful
gore wretch

For thou Mankynde have don a-mys,
And he wyl falle in repentaunce,
Crist schal hym bryngyn to bowre of blys
If sorwe of hert lache hym wyth launce.
Lordyngys, ye se wel alle thys,
Mankynde hathe ben in gret bobaunce.
I now for-sake [my] synne i-wys
And take me holy to Penaun[c]e.
On Crist I crye and calle.
A, mercy, Schryfte! I wyl no more.   1430
For dedly synne myn herte is sore.
Stuffe Mankynde wyth thyne store
And have hym to thyne halle.

CONFESCIO: Schryffte may no man forsake:
  Whanne Mankynde cryeth I am redy.
  Whanne sorwe of hert the hathe take
  Schryfte profytyth veryly.
  Who-so for synne wyl sorwe make
  Crist hym heryth whanne he wyl criye.
  Now, man, lete sorwe thyn synne slake   1440
  And torne not a-geyn to thi folye,
  For that makyth dystaunce.
  And if it happe the turne a-geyn to synne,
  For Goddys love lye not longe ther-inne.
  He that dothe alwey ewyl and wyl not blynne,
  That askyth gret venjaunce.

HUMANUM GENUS: Nay, sertys that schal I not do,
  Schryfte, thou schalte the sothe se,
  For thow Mankynde be wonte ther-to
  I wyl now al a-mende me.   1450

Tunc descend[e]t ad Confessionem

1421 *thou* although   1424 *lache* strike   1426 *bobaunce* pomp
1432 *Stuffe* provide   1442 *dystaunce* discord   1445 *blynne* stop

I com to the, Schryfte, al-holy, lo!
I forsake you, synnys, and fro you fle.
Ye schapyn to man a sory scho;
Whanne he is be-gylyd in this degre
Ye bleykyn al hys ble.
Synne, thou art a sory store:
Thou makyst Mankynd to synke sore,
Therfore of you wyl I no more.
I aske schryfte for charyte.

CONFESCIO: If thou wylt be a-knowe here   1460
  Only al thi trespas,
  I schal the schelde fro helle fere
  And putte the fro peyne unto precyouse place.
  If thou wylt not make thynne sowle clere
  But kepe hem in thyne hert cas,
  A-nothyr day they schul be rawe and rere
  And synke thi sowle to Satanas
  In gastful glowynge glede.
  Therfore, man, in mody monys,
  If thou wylt wende to worthi wonys,   1470
  Schryve the now, al at onys,
  Holy of this mysdede.

HUMANUM GENUS: A, yys, Schryfte, trewly I trewe.
  I schal not spare for odde nor even,
  That I schal rekne al on a rowe
  To lache me up to lyvys levene.
  To my Lord God I am a-knowe
  That sytty[t]h a-boven in hey hevene
  That I have synnyd many a throwe
  In the dedly synnys sevene   1480
  Bothe in home and halle.
  Pride, Wrathe, and Envye,

1466 *rawe* raw *rere* rare 1468 *gastful* dreadful *glede* fire
1469 *mody* grieving 1476 *lache* lift *lyvys* life's *levene* light

Coveytyse, and Lecherye,
Slawth, and also Glotonye,
I have hem usyd alle.

The x comaundementys brokyn I have
And my fyve wyttys spent hem a-mys.
I was thanne wood and gan to rave.
Mercy, God, for-geve me thys!
Whanne any pore man gan to me crave   1490
I gafe hym nowt, and that forthynkyth me i-wys.
Now, Seynt Saveour, ye me save
And brynge me to your boure of blys!
I can not alle say.
But to the erthe I knele a-down,
Bothe wyth bede and orison
And aske myn absolucion,
Syr Schryfte, I yow pray.

CONFESCIO: Now Jhesu Cryste, God holy,
And all the seyntys of hevene hende,   1500
Petyr and Powle, apostoly,
To whom God gafe powers to lese and bynde,
He for-geve the thi foly
That thou hast synnyd wyth hert and mynde.
And I up my powere the a-soly
That thou hast ben to God unkynde,
Quantum peccasti.
In Pride, Ire, and Envye,
Slawthe, Glotony, and Lecherye
And Coveytyse continuandelye,   1510
Vitam male continuasti.

I the a-soyle wyth goode entent
Of alle the synnys that thou hast wrowth

1491 forthynkyth causes regret   1496 bede prayer beads
1502 lese (v) loose, release   1505 up upon   a-soly forgive

135

In brekynge of Goddys commaundement
In worde, werke, wyl, and thowth.
I restore to the sacrament
Of penauns weche thou nevere rowt:
Thi v wyttys mys-dyspent
In synne the weche thou schuldyst nowt,
Quicquid gesisti,   1520
Wyth eyne sen, herys herynge,
Nose smellyd, mowthe spekynge,
And al thi bodys bad werkynge,
Vicium quodcumque fecisti.

I the a-soyle wyth mylde mod
Of al that thou hast ben ful madde
In forsakynge of thyn Aungyl Good,
And thi fowle Flesche that thou hast fadde,
The Werld, the Devyl that is so woode,
And folwyd thyne aungyl that is so badde.   1530
To Jhesu Crist that deyed on rode
I restore the a-geyn ful sadde.
Noli peccare.
And all the goode dedys that thou haste don
And all thi tribulacyon
Stonde the in remyssion.
Posius noli viciare.

HUMANUM GENUS: Now Syr Schryfte, where may I dwelle
To kepe me fro synne and woo?
A comly counseyl ye me spelle   1540
To fende me now fro my foo.
If these vij synnys here telle
That I am thus fro hem goo,
The Werld, the Flesche, and the Devyl of hell

1515 *thowth* thought   1517 *weche* which   *rowt* took notice of
1518 *mys-dyspent* spent in an evil way   1521 *sen* seeing   *herys* ears
herynge hearing   1525 *mod* mood

Schul sekyn my soule for to sloo
In-to balys bowre.
Therfore I pray you putte me
In-to sum place of surete
That thei may not harmyn me
Wyth no synnys sowre.   1550

CONFESCIO: To swyche a place I schal the kenne
Ther thou mayst dwelle wyth-outyn dystaunsce
And al-wey kepe the fro synne,
In-to the Castel of Perseveraunce.
If thou wylt to hevene wynne
And kepe the fro werldyly dystaunce,
Goo [to] yone castel and kepe the ther-inne,
For [it] is strenger thanne any in Fraunce.
To yone castel I the seende.
That castel is a precyous place,   1560
Ful of vertu and of grace;
Who-so levyth there hys lyvys space
No synne schal hym schende.

HUMANUM GENUS: A, Schryfte, blessyd mote thou be!
This castel is here but at honde.
Thedyr rapely wyl I tee,
Sekyr ovyr this sad sonde.
Good perseveraunce God sende me
Whyle I leve here in this londe.
Fro fowle fylthe now I fle,   1570
Forthe to faryn now I fonde
To yone precyous port.
Lord, what man is in mery lyve
Whanne he is of hys synnes schrevel
Al my dol a-doun is dreve.
Criste is myn counfort.

1546 *balys bowre* place of torment   1551 *kenne* (v) direct   1566 *tee* go
1567 *sonde* country   1574 *schreve* shriven

MALUS ANGELUS: Ey, what devyl, man, wedyr schat?
  Woldyst drawe now to holynesse?
  Goo, felaw, thi goode gate,
  Thou art forty wyntyr olde as I gesse.   1580
  Goo a-geyn, the develys mat,
  And pleye the a whyle wyth Sare and Sysse.
  Sche wolde not ellys, yone olde trat,
  But putte the to penaunce and to stresse,
  Yone foule feterel fyle.
  Late men that arn on the pyttys brynke
  For-beryn bothe mete and drynke
  And do penaunce as hem good thynke,
  And cum and pley the a-whyle.

BONUS ANGELUS: Ya, Mankynde, wende forthe thi way   1590
  And do no-thynge aftyr hys red.
  He wolde the lede ovyr londys lay
  In dale of dros tyl thou were ded.
  Of cursydnesse he kepyth the key
  To bakyn the a byttyr bred.
  In dale of dol tyl thou schudyst dey
  He wolde drawe the to cursyd-hed,
  In synne to have myschaunce.
  Therfor spede now thy pace
  Pertly to yone precyouse place   1600
  That is al growyn ful of grace,
  The Castel of Perse[ve]raunce.

HUMANUM GENUS: Goode Aungyl, I wyl do as thou wylt,
  In londe whyl my lyfe may leste,
  For I fynde wel in holy wryt
  Thou counseylyste evere for the beste.

    .   .   .   .   .   .

    1577 *schat* are you bound   1581 *mat* mate   1582 *Sare* Sara
    Sysse Cicely   1583 *trat* hag   1585 *feterel* deceiver   *fyle* wretched
    1587 *For-beryn* give up   1592 *lay* fallow   1600 *Pertly* quickly

CARITAS: To Charyte, man, have an eye
   In al thynge, man, I rede.
   Al thi doynge as dros is drye
   But in Charyte thou dyth thi dede.   1610
   I dystroye alwey Envye,
   So dyd thi God whanne he gan blede.
   For synne he was hangyn hye
   And yyt synnyd he nevere in dede,
   That mylde mercy welle.
   Poule in hys pystyl puttyth the prefe,
   'But charyte be wyth the chefe'.
   Therfore, Mankynde, be now lefe
   In Charyte for to dwelle.

ABSTINENCIA: In Abstinens lede thi lyf,   1620
   Take but skylful refeccyon:
   For Gloton kyllyth wyth-outyn knyf
   And dystroyeth thi complexion.
   Who-so ete or drynke ovyr-blyve
   It gaderyth to corrupcion.
   This synne browt us alle in stry[v]e
   Whanne Adam fel in synne down
   Fro precyous paradys.
   Mankynd, lere now of oure lore;
   Who-so ete or drynke more   1630
   Thanne skylfully hys state a-store,
   I holde hym no-thynge wys.

CASTITAS: Mankynd, take kepe of Chastyte
   And move the to maydyn marye.
   Fleschly foly loke thou fle,
   At the reverense of Oure Ladye.
   Quia qui in carne vivunt Domino placere non possunt.
   That curteys qwene, what dyd sche?

   1616 *pystyl* epistle   1617 *chefe* foremost   1624 *ovyr-blyve* too eagerly
   1629 *lere* (v) learn

Kepte hyre clene and stedfastly,
And in here was trussyd the Trin[i]te.   1640
Thorwe gostly grace sche was worthy,
And al for sche was chaste.
Who-so kepyt hym chast and wyl not synne,
Whanne he is beryed in bankys brymmne
Al hys joye is to be-gynne.
Therfore to me take taste.

SOLICITUDO: In besynesse, man, loke thou be,
    Wyth worthi werkys goode and thykke.
    To Slawthe if thou cast the
    It schal the drawe to thowtys wyckke.   1650
    Osiositas parit omne malum.
    It puttyth a man to poverte
    And pullyth hym to peynys prycke.
    Do sum-what al-wey for love of me,
    Thou thou schuldyst but thwyte a stycke.
    Wyth bedys sum-tyme the blys.
    Sum-tyme rede and sum-tyme wryte
    And sum-tyme pleye at thi delyte.
    The Devyl the waytyth wyth dyspyte
    Whanne thou art in i-dylnesse.   1660

LARGITAS: In Largyte, man, ley thi love.
    Spende thi good, as God it sent.
    In worchep of hym that syt a-bove
    Loke thi goodys be dyspent.
    In dale of dros whanne thou schalt drove
    Lytyl love is on the lent;
    The sekatourys schul seyn it is here be-hove
    To make us mery for he is went,
    That al this good gan owle.

1640 *trussyd* packed   1644 *brymmne* brim   1646 *taste* liking
1653 *peynys* of torment   1655 *Thou thou* Though thou
thwyte (v) whittle   1661 *ley* (v) lay   1664 *dyspent* spent
1669 *owle* gather

Ley thi tresour and thi trust   1670
In place where no ruggynge rust
May it dystroy to dros ne dust
But al to helpe of sowle.

HUMANUM GENUS: Ladys in londe, lovely and lyt,
    Lykynge lelys, ye be my leche.
    I wyl bowe to your byddynge bryth:
    Trewe tokenynge ye me teche.
    Dame Meknes, in your myth
    I wyl me wryen fro wyckyd wreche.
    Al my purpose I have pyt,   1680
    Paciens, to don as ye me preche:
    Fro Wrathe ye schal me kepe.
    Charyte, ye wyl to me entende:
    Fro fowle Envye ye me defende.
    Manns mende ye may a-mende,
    Whethyr he wake or slepe.

    Abstynens, to you I tryst:
    Fro Glotony ye schal me drawe.
    In chastyte to levyn me lyst,
    That is Oure Ladys lawe.   1690
    Besynes, we schul be cyste:
    Slawthe, I forsake thi sleper sawe.
    Largyte, to you I tryst,
    Coveytyse to don of dawe.
    This is a curteys cumpany.
    What schuld I more monys make?
    The sevene synnys I forsake
    And to these vij vertuis I me take.
    Maydyn Meknes, now Mercy!

1671 *ruggynge* gnawing   1675 *lelys* lillies   1679 *wryen* twist
1680 *pyt* settled   1691 *cyste* kissed   1692 *sleper* deceitful
1694 *don of dawe* kill

HUMILITAS: Mercy may mende al thi mone.   1700
  Cum in here at thynne owyn wylle.
  We schul the fende fro thi fon
  If thou kepe the in this castel stylle.
  Cum sancto sanctus eris et cetera.

  Tunc intrabit.

Stonde here-inne as stylle as ston,
Thanne schal no dedly synne the spylle.
Whethyr that synnys cu[mm]e or gon,
Thou schalt wyth us thi bourys bylle,
Wyth vertuse we schal the vaunce.
This castel is of so qweynt a gynne   1710
That who-so evere holde hym ther-inne
He schal nevere fallyn in dedly synne:
It is the Castel of Perseveranse.
Qui perseveraverit usque in finem, hic salvus erit.

  Tunc cantabunt 'Eterne rex altissime', et [dicet] Humilitas

[HUMILITAS:] Now blyssyd be Oure Lady, of hevene
    Emperes!
  Now is Mankynde fro foly falle
  And is in the Castel of Goodness.
  He hauntyth now hevene halle
  That schal bryngyn hym to hevene.
  Crist that dyed wyth dyen dos   1720
  Kepe Mankynd in this castel clos
  And put alwey in hys purpos
  To fle the synnys sevene!

    1706 *spylle* destroy   1708 *bourys* dwelling   *bylle* (v) establish
    1709 *vaunce* advance   1718 *hauntyth* inhabits

[PART TWO: THE SECOND TEMPTATION]

MALUS ANGELUS: Nay, be Belyals bryth bonys,
Ther schal he no whyle dwelle:
He schal be wonne fro these wonys
Wyth the Werld, the Flesch, and the Devyl of hell.
Thei schul my wyl a-wreke.
The synnys sevene, tho kyngys thre,
To Mankynd have enmyte.   1730
Scharpely thei schul helpyn me
This castel for to breke.

Howe, Flypyrgebet, Bakbytere!
Yerne oure message loke thou make.
Blythe about loke thou bere.
Sey Mankynde hys synnys hath forsake.
Wyth yene wenchys he wyl hym were,
Al to holynesse he hath hym take.
In myn hert it doth me dere,
The bost that tho moderys crake;   1740
My galle gynnyth to grynde.
Flepyrgebet, ronne up-on a rasche:
Byd the Werld, the Fend, and the Flesche
That they com to fytyn fresche
To wynne ageyn Mankynde.

DETRACCIO: I go, I go on grounde glad,
Swyftyr thanne schyp wyth rodyr.
I make men masyd and mad,

1726 *wonne* won   1728 *a-wreke* perform   1737 *were* defend (himself)
1739 *dere* (v) hurt   1740 *moderys* young women, wenches
crake utter (boasts)   1742 *rasche* (n) haste   1747 *rodyr* rudder
1748 *masyd* confused

And every man to kyllyn odyr
Wyth a sory chere.   1750
I am glad, be Seynt Jamys of Galys,
Of schrewdnes to tellyn talys
Bothyn in Ingelond and in Walys,
And feyth I have many a fere.

    Tunc ibit ad Belial.

Heyl, set in thyn selle!
Heyl, dynge Devyl in thi delle!
Heyl, lowe in helle!
I cum to the talys to telle.

BELYAL: Bakbyter, boy,
Alwey be holtys and hothe,   1760
Sey now, I sey,
What tydyngs? Telle me the sothe.

DETRACCIO: Teneful talys I may the sey,
To the no good, as I gesse:
Mankynd is gon now a-wey
Into the Castel of Goodnesse.
Ther he wyl bothe lyvyn and deye
In dale of dros tyl deth hym dresse;
Hathe the forsakyn, forsothe I sey,
And all thi werkys more and lesse;   1770
To yone castel he gan to crepe.
Yone modyr Meknes, sothe to sayn,
And all yene maydnys on yone playn
For to fytyn thei be ful fayn
Mankynd for to kepe.

    Tunc vocabit Superbiam, Invidiam, et Iram.

1752 *schrewdnes* wickedness   1755 *set* sat   *selle* seat   1756 *dynge* worthy
delle pit (of hell)   1763 *Teneful painful*   1771–3 *yone, yene* that, those

SUPERBIA: Syr kynge, what wytte?
We be redy throtys to kytte.

BELYAL: Sey, gadelyngys, have ye harde grace
And evyl deth mote ye deye —
Why lete ye Mankynd fro you pase   1780
Into yene castel fro us a-weye?
Wyth tene I schal you tey.
Harlotys, at onys
Fro this wonys!
Be Belyals bonys
Ye schul a-beye.

Et verberabit eos super terram.

DETRACCIO: Ya, for God, this was wel goo,
Thus to werke wyth bakbytynge.
I werke bothe wrake and woo
And make iche man othyr to dynge.   1790
I schal goo a-bowte and makyn moo
Rappys for to route and rynge.
Ye bakbyterys, loke that ye do so.
Make debate a-bowtyn to sprynge
Be-twene systyr and brothyr.
If any bakbyter here be lafte,
He may lere of me hys crafte.
Of Goddys grace he schal be rafte
And every man to kyllyn othyr.

Ad Carnem.

1776 *wytte* do you want?   1777 *kytte* cut   1782 *tey* bind
1786 *a-beye* pay   1789 *wrake* ruin   1790 *dynge* beat
1792 *Rappys* strokes   *route* roar, resound   1798 *rafte* deprived

Heyl, kynge, I calle!   1800
Heyl, prinse, proude prekyd in palle!
Heyl, hende in halle!
Heyl, syr kynge, fayre the be-falle!

CARO: Boy Bakbytynge,
  Ful redy in robys to rynge,
  Ful glad tydynge,
  Be Belyalys bonys, I trow thow brynge.

DETRACCIO: Ya, for God, owt I crye
  On thi too sonys and this dowtyr yynge:
  Glotoun, Slawthe, and Lechery   1810
  Hath put me in gret mornynge.
  They let Mankynd gon up hye
  In-to yene castel at hys lykynge,
  Ther-in for to leve and dye,
  Wyth tho ladys to make endynge,
  Tho flourys fayre and fresche.
  He is in the Castel of Perseverauns
  And put hys body to penauns.
  Of hard happe is now thi chauns,
  Syre kynge, Mankyndys Flesche.   1820

        *Tunc Caro clamabit ad Gul[am], Accidiam, et
        Luxuriam.*

LUXURIA: Sey now thi wylle.
  Syr Flesch, why cryest thou so schylle?

CARO: A, Lechery, thou skallyd mare!
  And thou, Gloton, God geve the wo!

  1801 *prekyd* dressed   *palle* robe   1805 *rynge* roar   1809 *yynge* young
  1822 *schylle* shrilly   1823 *skallyd* scurvy

146

And vyle Slawth, evyl mote thou fare!
Why lete ye Mankynd fro you go
In yone castel so hye?
Evele grace com on thi snowte!
Now I am dressyd in gret dowte.
Why [ne] had ye lokyd betyr a-bowte?   1830
Be Belyalys bonys ye schul a-bye.

Tunc verberabit eos in placeam.

DETRACCIO: Now, be God, this is good game!
I, Bakbyter, now bere me wel.
If I had lost my name
I vow to God it were gret del.
I schape these schrewys to mekyl schame:
Iche rappyth on othyr wyth rowtynge rele.
I, Bakbyter, wyth fals fame
Do brekyn and brestyn hodys of stele.
Thorwe this cuntre I am knowe.   1840
Now wyl I gynne forth to goo
And make Coveytyse have a knoke or too,
And thanne I wys I have doo
My dever, as I trowe.

Ad Mundum.

Heyl, styf in stounde!
Heyl, gayly gyrt up-on grounde!
Heyl, fayre flowr I founde!
Heyl, Syr Werld, worthi in wedys wonde!

1837 *rowtynge* violent   *rele* uproar   1839 *brestyn* burst   *hodys* hoods
1844 *dever* duty   1845 *styf in stounde* strong in attack
1848 *wonde* wrapped

147

MUNDUS: Bakbyter in rowte
   Thou tellyst talys of dowte,   1850
   So styf and so stowte.
   What tydyngys bryngyst thou a-bowte?

DETRACCIO: No-thynge goode, that schalt thou wete.
   Mankynd, Syr Werld, hath the for-sake.
   Wyth Schryfte and Penauns he is smete
   And to yene castel he hath hym take
   A-monge yene ladys whyt as la[ke].
   Lo, Syr Werld, ye moun a-gryse
   That ye be servyd on this wyse.
   Go pley you wyth Syr Coveytyse   1860
   Tyl hys crowne crake.

      Tunc buccinabit cornu ad Avariciam.

AVARICIA: Syr bolnynge bowde,
   Tell me why blowe ye so lowde!

MUNDUS: Lowde losel, the Devel the brenne!
   I prey God yeve the a fowl hap!
   Sey why letyst thou Mankynd
   In-to yene castel for to skape?
   I trowe thou gynnyst to rave.
   Now, for Mankynd is went,
   Al oure game is schent.   1870
   Therfore a sore dryvynge dent,
   Harlot, thou schalt have.

     Tunc verbera[b]it eum.

1849 *rowte* crowd   1853 *wete* know, find   1855 *smete* struck
1857 *lake* fine linen   1858 *a-gryse* tremble   1862 *bolnynge* swelling
bowde drunkard   1864 *brenne* burn   1871 *dent* blow

AVARICIA: Mercy, mercy! I wyl no more.
Thou hast me rappyd wyth rewly rowtys.
I snowre, I sobbe, I sye sore.
Myn hed is clateryd al to clowtys.
In al youre state I schal you store
If ye abate youre dyntys dowtys.
Mankynd, that ye have for-lore,
I schal do com owt fro yone skowtys   1880
To youre hende hall.
If ye wyl no more betyn me,
I schal do Mankynd com out fre.
He schal for-sake as thou schalt se,
The fayre vertus all.

MUNDUS: Have do thanne, the Devyl the tere!
Thou schalt ben hangyn in hell herne.
By-lyve my baner up thou bere
And be-sege we the castel yerne
Mankynd for to stele.   1890
Whanne Mankynd growyth good,
I, the Werld, am wyld and wod.
Tho bycchys schul bleryn in here blood
Wyth flappys felle and fele.

Yerne lete flapyr up my fane
And schape we schame and schonde.
I schal brynge wyth me tho bycchys bane:
Ther schal no vertus dwellyn in my londe.
Mekenes is that modyr that I mene,
To hyre I brewe a byttyr bonde.   1900
Sche schal dey up-on this grene

1874 *rewly* grievous *rowtys* (n) blows 1876 *clateryd* rattled
clowtys rags, pieces 1877 *store* restore 1879 *for-lore* lost
1880 *skowtys* whores 1883 *do* cause 1886 *tere* tear 1887 *herne* nook
1893 *bycchys* bitches *bleryn* weep 1894 *flappys* blows *felle* fierce
fele many 1897 *bane* (n) ruin

If that sche com al in myn honde,
Yene rappokys wyth here rumpys.
I am the Werld: it is my wyll
The Castel of Vertu for to spyll.
Howtyth hye upon yene hyll,
Ye traytours, in youre trumpys.

*Tunc Mundus, Cupiditas et Stulticia ibunt ad
castellum cum Vexillo, et dicet Demon*

BELYAL: I here trumpys trebelen al of tene.
The worthi Werld walkyth to werre
For to clyvyn yone castel clene,   1910
Tho maydnys meyndys for to merre.
Sprede my penon up-on a prene
And stryke we forthe now undyr sterre.
Schapyth now youre scheldys schene
Yene skallyd skoutys for to skerre
Up-on yone grene grese.
Buske you now, boyes, be-lyve.
For evere I stonde in mekyl stryve;
Whyl Mankynd is in clene lyve
I am nevere wel at ese.   1920

Make you redy, all thre,
Bolde batayl for to bede.
To yone feld lete us fle
And bere my baner forthe on brede.
To yone castel wyl I te:
Tho mamerynge modrys schul have here mede.
But thei yeld up to me,

1903 *rappokys* wretches   1906 *Howtyth* proclaim
1908 *trebelen* sound shrilly   1910 *clyvyn* ruin   1912 *prene* spike
1915 *skoutys* whores   *skerre* scare   1916 *grese* grass
1925 *te* go   1926 *mamerynge* muttering

Wyth byttyr balys thei schul blede,
Of here reste I schal heme reve.
In woful watyrs I schal hem wasche.   1930
Have don, felaus, and take youre trasche,
And wende we thedyr on a rasche
That castel for to cleve.

SUPERBIA: Now, now, now, go now!
On hye hyllys lete us howte;
For in pride is al my prow
Thi bolde baner to bere a-bowte.
To Golyas I make a vow
For to schetyn yone iche skowte.
On hyr ars raggyd and row,   1940
I schal bothe clatyr and clowte
And geve Meknesse myschanse.
Belyal bryth, it is thyn hest
That I, Pride, goo the nest
And bere thi baner beforn my brest
Wyth a comly contenaunce.

CARO: I here an hydowse whwtynge on hyt
Be-lyve byd my baner forth for to blase.
Whanne I syt in my sadyl it is a selkowth syt:
I gape as a gogmagog whanne I gynne to gase.   1950
This worthy wylde werld I wagge wyth a wyt.
Yone rappokys I ruble and al to-rase.
Bothe wyth schot and wyth slynge I caste wyth a sleyt
Wyth care to yone castel to crachen and to crase
In flode.
I am mans Flesch: where I go
I am mans most fo.

1931 *trasche* course   1939 *schetyn* hit   *skowte* whore   1940 *row* raw
1944 *nest* next, nearest   1947 *whwtynge* shouting   *hyt* high
1949 *selkowth* wonderful   1950 *gase* stare   1952 *ruble* crush
to-rase cut to pieces   1953 *sleyt* skill   1954 *crachen* crack   *crase* shatter

I-wys I am evere wo
Whane he drawyth to goode.

Therfor, ye bolde boyes, buske you a-bowte.   1960
Scharply on scheldys your schaftys ye schevere.
And Lechery ledron, schete thou a skoute.
Help we Mankynd fro yone castel to kevere.
Helpe we moun hym wynne.
Schete we all at a schote
Wyth gere that we cunne best note
To chache Mankynd fro yene cote
In-to dedly synne.

GULA: Lo, Syr Flesch, whov I fare to the felde,
Wyth a faget on myn hond for to settyn on afyre.   1970
Wyth a wrethe of the wode wel I can me welde.
Wyth a longe launce tho loselys I schal lere.
Go we wyth oure gere.
Tho bycchys schul bleykyn and blodyr:
I schal makyn swyche a powdyr
Bothe wyth smoke and wyth smodyr,
Thei schul schytyn for fere.

Tunc descendent in placeam.

MALUS ANGELUS *dicet ad Belyal*: As armys as an
          heyward, hey now I howte.
Devyl, dyth the as a duke to do tho damysely[s] dote.
Belyal, as a bolde boy thi brodde I bere a-bowte: 1980
Helpe to cache Mankynd fro caytyfys cote.

1961 *schevere* shiver, split   1962 *schete* shoot   1963 *kevere* recover
1969 *whov* in what way   1970 *faget* faggot   1974 *bleykyn* grow pale
blodyr (v) blubber   1975 *powdyr* smoke   1976 *smodyr* fumes
1979 *dyth* prepare   1980 *brodde* spike

Pryd, put out thi penon of raggys and of rowte.
Do this modyr Mekenes meltyn to mote.
Wrethe, prefe Paciens, the skallyd skowte.
Envye to Charyte schape thou a schote
Ful yare.
Wyth Pryde, Wrethe, and Envye,
These develys, be downys drye
As comly kyng[ys] I dyscrye
Mankynd to kachyn to care.   1990

Ad Carnem.

Flesch, frele and fresche, frely fed,
Wyth Gloton, Slawthe, and Lechery mans sowle thou
     slo.
As a duke dowty do the to be dred.
Gere the wyth gerys fro toppe to the too.
Kyth this day thou art a kynge frely fedde.
Gloton, sle thou Abstyne[n]sce wyth wyckyd woo.
Wyth Chastyte, thou lechour, be not ovyr-ledde.
Slawthe, bete thou Besynes on buttokys bloo.
Do now thi crafte in coste to be knowe.
     Ad Mundum.
Worthy, wytty, and wys, wondyn in wede,   2000
Lete Coveytyse karpyn, cryen, and grede.
Here ben bolde bacheleris batyl to bede,
Mankynd to tene, as I trowe.

HUMANUM GENUS: That dynge Duke that deyed on rode
This day my sowle kepe and safe!
Whanne Mankynd drawyth to goode
Be-holde what enmys he schal have.
The Werld, the Devyl, the Flesche arn wode,

1990 *kachyn* bring   1995 *Kyth* make plain   1999 *coste* manner
2000 *wondyn* clothed   2001 *karpyn* cry out   *grede* call

To men ben casten a careful kave.
Byttyr balys thei brewyn on brode, 2010
Mankynd in wo to weltyr and wave,
Lordyngys, sothe to sey.
Therfore iche man be war of this,
For whyl Mankynd clene is
Hys enmys schul temptyn hym to don a-mys
If their mown be any wey.
*Omne gaudium existimate cum variis temptacionĭbus
    insideritis.*

Therfore, lordys, beth now glad
Wyth elmes-dede and orysoun
For to don as Oure Lord bad, 2020
Styfly wyth-stonde youre temptacyoun.
Wyth this foul fende I am ner mad.
To batayle thei buskyn hem bown.
Certys I schuld ben ovyr-lad,
But that I am in this castel town,
Wyth synnys sore and smerte
Who-so wyl levyn oute of dystresse
And ledyn hys lyf in clennesse
In this Castel of Vertu and of Goodnesse
Hym muste have hole hys hert. 2030
Delectare in Domino et dabit tibi peticiones cordis tui.

BONUS ANGELUS: A, Mekeness, Charyte, and Pacyens,
Prymrose, pleyeth parlasent:
Chastyte, Besynes and Abstynens
Myn hope, ladys, in you is lent.
Socoure, paramourys, swetter thanne sens,
Rode as rose on rys i-rent.
This day ye dyth a good defens.
Whyl Mankynd is in good entent
His thoutys arn un-hende. 2040

2019 *elmes-dede* charitable acts   2030 *hole* (adj) whole
2040 *thoutys* thoughts   *un-hende* unfitting, unready

Mankynd is browt in-to this walle
In freelte to fadyn and falle.
Therfore, ladys, I pray you alle,
Helpe this day Mankynde.

HUMILITAS: God, that syttyth in hevene on hy,
Save al mankynd be se and sonde!
Lete hym dwellyn here and ben us by
And we schul puttyn to hym helpynge honde.
Yyt forsothe never I sy
That any fawte in us he fonde   2050
But that we savyd hym fro synne sly,
If he wolde be us styfly stonde
In this castel of ston.
Therfore drede the not, mans aungel dere.
If he wyl dwellyn wyth us here
Fro sevene synnys we schul hym were
And his enmys ichon.

Now, my sevene systerys swete,
This day fallyth on us the lot
Mankynd for to schylde and schete   2060
Fro dedly synne and schamely schot.
Hys enmys strayen in the strete
To spylle man wyth spetows spot.
Therfor oure flourys lete now flete
And kepe we hym, as we have het,
Among us in this halle.
Therfor, vij systerys swote,
Lete oure vertus reyne on rote.
This day we wyl be mans bote
A-geyns these develys alle.   2070

2042 *freelte* frailty   2046 *sonde* sand   2049 *sy* saw   2056 *were* protect
2057 *ichon* every one   2060 *schylde* (v) shield   *schete* protect
2063 *spot* disgrace   2064 *flete* float   2065 *het* promised
2067 *swote* sweet   2068 *reyne* (v) rain down   *rote* root

BELYAL: This day the vaward wyl I holde.
A-vaunt my baner, precyous Pride,
Mankynd to cache to karys colde.
Bold batayl now wyl I byde.
Buske you, boyes, on brede.
Alle men that be wyth me wytholde,
Bothe the yonge and the olde,
Envye, Wrathe, ye boyes bolde,
To rounde rappys ye rape, I rede.

SUPERBIA: As armys, Mekenes! I brynge thi bane,   2080
Al wyth pride peyntyd and pyth.
What seyst thou, faytour? Be myn fayr fane,
Wyth robys rounde rayed ful ryth
Grete gounse I shal the gane.
To marre the, Mekenes, wyth my myth,
No werldly wyttys here ar wane.
Lo, thi castel is al be-set.
Moderys, whov schul ye do?
Mekenes, yelde the to me, I rede.
Myn name in londe is precyous Prede.   2090
Myn bolde baner to the I bede.
Modyr, what seyste ther-to?

HUMILITAS: A-geyns thi baner of pride and bost
A baner of meknes and mercy
I putte a-geyns pride, wel thou wost,
That schal schende thi careful cry.
This meke kynge is knowyn in every cost
That was croysyd on Calvary.
Whanne he cam doun fro hevene ost
And lytyd wyth mekenes in Mary,   2100
This lord thus lytyd lowe.

2081 *pyth* decorated   2082 *faytour* deceiver   *fane* banner
2084 *gounse* ?gowns   2086 *wane* reluctant   2098 *croysyd* crucified
2099 *ost* host

Whanne he cam fro the Trynyte
In-to a maydyn lytyd he,
And al was for to dystroye the,
Pride, this schalt thou knowe:
Deposuit potentes de sede et cetera.

For whanne Lucyfer to helle fyl,
Pride, ther-of thou were chesun,
And thou, Devyl, wyth wyckyd wyl
In paradys trappyd us wyth tresun.   2110
So thou us bond in balys ille,
This may I preve be ryth resun,
Tyl this duke that dyed on hylle
In hevene man myth nevere han sesun;
The gospel thus declaryt.
For who-so lowe hym schal ben hy,
Therfore thou schalt not comen us ny,
And thou be nevere so sly,
I schal felle al thi fare.
Qui se exaltat humiliabitur et cetera.   2120

IRA: Dame Pacyens, what seyst thou to Wrathe and Ire?
Putte Mankynd fro thi castel clere,
Or I schal tappyn at thi tyre
Wyth styffe stourys that I have here.
I schal slynge at the many a vyre
And ben a-vengyd hastely here.
Thus Belsabub, oure gret syre,
Bad me brenne the wyth wyld fere,
Thou bycche blak as kole.
Therfor fast, fowle skowte,   2130
Putte Mankynd to us owte,
Or of me thou schalt have dowte,
Thou modyr thou motyhole!

2108 *chesun* cause   2116 *lowe* (v) humble
2123 *tappyn* strike   *tyre* head-dress   2125 *vyre* bolt (for crossbow)

PACIENCIA: Fro thi dowte Crist me schelde
    This iche day, and al mankynde.
    Thou wrecchyd Wrethe, wood and wylde,
    Pacyens schal the schende.
    Quia ira viri justiciam Dei non operatur.
    For Marys Sone, meke and mylde,
    Rent the up, rote and rynde,   2140
    Whanne he stod meker thanne a chylde
    And lete boyes hym betyn and bynde:
    Therfor wrecche be stylle.
    For tho pelourys that gan hym pose,
    He myth a drevyn hem to dros,
    And yyt to casten hym on the cros
    He sufferyd al here wylle.

    Thowsentys of aungell[ys] he myth han had
    To a wrokyn hym ther ful yerne,
    And yyt to deyen he was glad   2150
    Us pacyens to techyn and lerne.
    Therfor, boy, wyth thi boystous blad,
    Fare a-wey be feldys ferne.
    For I wyl do as Jhesu bad,
    Wrecchys fro my wonys werne
    Wyth a dyngne defens.
    If thou fonde to comyn a-lofte
    I schal the cacche from this crofte
    Wyth these rosys swete and softe,
    Peyntyd wyth pacyens.   2160

INVIDIA: Out, myn herte gynnyth to breke,
    For Charyte that stondyth so stowte.
    Alas, myn herte gynnyth to wreke.
    Yelde up this castel, thou hore clowte.
    It is myn offyce fowle to speke,

2144 *pelourys* despoilers   *pose* shove   2149 *yerne* quickly
2152 *blad* blade   2155 *werne* (v) stop   2158 *crofte* enclosure

Fals sklaundrys to bere a-bowte.
Charyte, the Devyl mote the cheke
But I the rappe wyth rewly rowte,
Thi targe for to tere.
Let Mankynde cum to us doun   2170
Or I schal schetyn to this castel town
A ful fowle defamacyon.
Therfore this bowe I bere.

CARITAS: Thou thou speke wycke and fals fame,
The wers schal I nevere do my dede.
Who-so peyryth falsely a-nothyr mans name
Cristys curs he schal have to mede.
Ve homini illi per quem scandalum ven[it].
Who-so wylnot hys tunge tame,
Take it sothe as mes-crede,   2180
Wo, wo to hym and mekyl schame!
In holy wrytte this I rede.
For evere thou art a schrewe.
Thou thou speke evyl, I ne geve a gres;
I schal do nevere the wers
At the last the sothe vers
Certys hym-self schal schewe.

Oure lovely Lord, wyth-owtyn lak,
Gaf example to charyte,
Whanne he was betyn blo and blak   2190
For trespas that nevere dyd he.
In sory synne had he no tak
And yyt for synne he bled blody ble.
He toke hys cros up-on hys bak,
Synful man, and al for the.
Thus he mad defens.

2167 *cheke* choke   2168 *rewly* grievous   2171 *schetyn* shoot
2176 *peyryth* injures   2180 *mes-crede* the Creed
2184 *gres* blade of grass

Envye, wyth thi slaundrys thycke,
I am putte at my lordys prycke;
I wyl do good a-geyns the wycke,
And kepe in sylens.   2200

BELYAL: What, for Belyalys bonys,
Where a-bowtyn chyde ye?
Have done, ye boyes, al at onys.
Lasche don these moderys, all thre.
Werke wrake to this wonys.
The vaunward is grauntyd me.
Do these moderys to makyn monys.
Youre dowty dedys now lete se.
Dasche hem al to daggys.
Have do, boyes blo and blake.   2210
Wirke these wenchys wo and wrake.
Claryouns, cryeth up at a krake,
And blowe your brode baggys.

                Tunc pugnabunt diu.

SUPERBIA: Out, my proude bak is bent.
Mekenes hath me al for-bete.
Pride wyth Mekenes is for-schent.
I weyle and wepe wyth wondys wete;
I am betyn in the hed.
My prowde pride a-doun is drevyn;
So scharpely Mekenes hath me schrevyn   2220
That I may no lengyr levyn,
My lyf is me be-revyd.

INVIDIA: Al my enmyte is not worth a fart:
I schyte and schake al in my schete.

2209 *daggys* shreds   2212 *krake* noise   2213 *baggys* bagpipes
2222 *be-revyd* taken away   2224 *schete* clothes

Charyte, that sowre swart,
Wyth fayre rosys myn hed gan breke.
I brede the malaundyr.
Wyth worthi wordys and flourys swete
Charyte makyth me so meke
I dare neythyr crye noré crepe,   2230
Not a schote of sklaundyr.

IRA: I, Wrethe, may syngyn wele-a-wo.
Pacyens me gaf a sory dynt.
I am betyn blak and blo
Wyth a rose that on rode was rent.
My speche is almost spent.
Hyr rosys fel on me so scharpe
That myn hed hangyth as an harpe.
I dar neythyr crye nor carpe,
Sche is so pacyent.   2240

MALUS ANGELUS: Go hens, ye do not worthe a tord.
Foule falle you alle foure!
Yerne, yerne, let fall on bord,
Syr Flesch, wyth thyn eyn soure.
For care I cukke and koure.
Syr, Flesch, wyth thyn company,
Yerne, yerne, make a cry.
Helpe we have no velony,
That this day may be oure.

CARO: War, war, late mans Flesche go to!   2250
I com wyth a company.
Have do, my chyldryn, now have do,
Glotoun, Slawth and Lechery.
Iche of you wynnyth a scho.

2225 *swart* dark, black person   2227 *malaundyr* scab (disease of horses)
2245 *cukke* excrete   *koure* cower   2254 *scho* shoe

Lete not Mankynde wy[nne] maystry.
Lete slynge hem in a fowl slo .
And fonde to feffe hym wyth foly.
Ðothe now wel youre dede.
Yerne lete se whov ye schul gynne
Mankynde to temptyn to deadly synne. 2260
If ye muste this castelle wynne
Hell schal be your mede.

GULA: War, Syr Gloton schal makyn a smeke
A-geyns this castel, I vowe.
Abstynens, thou thou bleyke,
I loke on the wyth byttyr browe.
I have a faget in myn necke
To settyn Mankynd on a lowe.
My foul leye schalt thou not let,
I wou to God, as I trowe; 2270
Therfor putte hym out here.
In meselynge glotonye,
Wyth goode metys and drynkys trye,
I norche my systyr Lecherye
Tyl man rennyth on fere.

ABSTINENCIA: Thi metys and drynkys arn unthende
Whanne thei are out of mesure take.
Thei makyn men mad and out of mende
And werkyn hem bothe wo and wrake
That for thi fere thou thou here kyndyl, 2280
Certys I schal thi wele a-slake
Wyth bred that browth us out of hell
And on the croys sufferyd wrake:
I mene the sacrament.
That iche blysful bred,

2256 *slo* sloagh 2257 *feffe* endow 2259 *gynne* (v) contrive
2263 *smeke* smoke 2270 *wou* vow 2272 *meselynge* bespotted
2274 *norche* nourish 2281 *a-slake* lessen

That hounge on hyl tyl he was ded,
Schal tempere so myn maydynhed
That thi purpos schal be spent.

In abstynens this bred was browth,
Certys, Mankynde, and al for the.   2290
Of fourty dayes ete he nowth
And thanne was naylyd to a tre.
Cum jejunasset xl^a diebus et cetera.
Example us was be-tawth,
In sobyrnesse he bad us be.
Therfor Mankynd schal not be cawth,
Glotony, wyth thy degre.
The sothe thou schalt se.
To norysch fayre thou thou be fawe,
Abstynens it schal wythdrawe   2300
Tyl thou be schet undyr schawe
And fayn for to fle.

LUXURIA: Lo, Chastyte, thou fowle skowte!
This ilke day here thou schalt deye.
I make a fer in mans towte
That launcyth up as any leye.
These cursyd colys I bere a-bowte
Mankynde in tene for to teye.
Men and wommen hathe no dowte
Wyth pyssynge pokys for to pleye.   2310
I bynde hem in my bondys.
I have no reste, so I rowe,
Wyth men and wommen, as I trowe,
Tyl I, Lechery, be set on a lowe
In al Mankyndys londys.

2296 *cawth* caught   2305 *towte* rump   2306 *leye* flame
2307 *colys* coals, fires   2308 *teye* bind   2314 *lowe* fire
2315 *londys* loins

CASTITAS: I, Chastyte, have power in this place
    The, Lechery, to bynd and bete.
    Maydyn Marye, well of grace,
    Schal qwenche that fowle hete.
    Mater et Virgo, extingue carnales concupiscentias.   2320
    Oure Lord God mad the no space
    Whanne his blod strayed in the strete.
    Fro this castel he dyd the chase
    Whanne he was crounyd wyth thornys grete
    And grene.
    To drery deth whanne he was dyth
    And boyes dyd hym gret dyspyth,
    In lechery had he no delyth,
    And that was ryth wel sene.

    At Oure Lady I lere my lessun   2330
    To have chaste lyf tyl I be ded.
    Sche is qwene and beryth the croun,
    And al was for hyr maydynhed.
    Therfor go fro this castel toun,
    Lechery, now I the rede,
    For Mankynd getyst thou nowth doun
    To soloyen hym[wyth] synful sede.
    In care thou woldys hym cast.
    And if thou com up to me,
    Trewly thou schalt betyn be   2340
    Wyth the yerde of Chastyte
    Whyl my lyf may last.

ACCIDIA: Ware, war, I delve wyth a spade.
    Men calle me the lord Syr Slowe.
    Gostly grace I spylle and schade:
    Fro the watyr of grace this dyche I fowe.
    Ye schulyn com ryth i-nowe
    Be this dyche drye, be bankys brede.

    2337 *soloyen* sully   2345 *schade* pour   2346 *fowe* clean out

xxx^{ti} thousende that I wel knowe,
In my lyf lovely I lede,   2350
That had levere syttyn at the ale
iij mens songys to syngyn lowde
Thanne to-ward the chyrche for to crowde.
Thou Besynesse, thou bolnyd bowde,
I brewe to the thyne bale.

SOLICITUDO: A, good men, be war now all
Of Slugge and Slawthe, this fowl thefe!
To the sowle he is byttyrer thanne gall;
Rote he is of mekyl myschefe.
Goddys servyse that ledyth us to hevene hall,   2360
This lordeyn for to lettyn us is lefe.
Who-so wyl schryvyn hym of hys synnys all,
He puttyth this brethel to mykyl myschefe,
Mankynde he that myskaryed.
Men moun don no penauns for hym this,
Nere schryve hem whanne they don a-mys,
But evyr he wold in synne i-wys
That Mankynd were taryed.

Therfor he makyth this dyke drye
To puttyn Mankynde to dystresse.   2370
He makyth dedly synne a redy weye
Into the Castel of Goodnesse,
But wyth tene I schal hym teye,
Thorwe the helpe of hevene emperesse.
Wyth my bedys he schal a-beye,
And othyr ocupacyons more and lesse
I schal schape hym to schonde,
For who-so wyle Slawth putte doun
Wyth bedys and wyth orysoun
Or sum oneste ocupacyoun,   2380

2354 *bolnyd* swollen   *bowde* fool   2361 *lettyn* hinder   *lefe* willing
2364 *myskaryed* led astray

As boke to have in honde.
Nunc lege nunc hora nunc disce nuncque labora.

CARO: Ey, for B[e]lyalys bonys, the kynge,
Where a-bowte stonde ye al-day?
Caytyvys lete be your kakelynge
And rappe at rowtys of a-ray.
Glotony, thou fowle gadlynge,
Sle Abstynens, if thou may.
Lechery wyth thi werkynge,
To Chastyte make a wyckyd a-ray   2390
A lytyl throwe.
And whyl we fyth
For owre ryth,
In bemys bryth
Late blastys blowe.

        Tunc pugnabunt diu.

GULA: Out, Glotoun, a-down I dryve.
Abstyne[n]s hathe lost my myth
Syr Flesche, I schal nevere thryve;
I do not worthe the develys dyrt;
I may not levyn longe.   2400
I am al betyn toppe and tayl;
Wyth Abstynens wyl I no more dayl.
I wyl gon cowche qwayl
At hom in.your gonge.

LUXURIA: Out on Chastyte, be the rode!
Sche hathe me dayschyd and so drenchyd.
Yyt have sche the curs of God

2399 *worthe* (v) value   2402 *dayl* (v) deal   2403 *cowche* cower
qwayl (like a) quail   2404 *gonge* privy

For al my fere the qwene hath qwenchyd.
For ferd I fall and feynt.
In harde ropys mote sche ryde.   2410
Here dare I not longe a-byde.
Sumwhere myn hed I wolde hyde
As an irchoun that were schent.

ACCIDIA: Out, I deye! Ley on watyr!
I swone, I swete, I feynt, I drulle!
Yene qwene wyth hyr pytyr-patyr
Hath al to-dayschyd my skallyd skulle.
It is as softe a[s] wulle.
Or I have here more skathe,
I schal lepe a-wey, be lurkynge lathe,   2420
There I may my ballokys bathe
And leykyn at the fulle.

MALUS ANGELUS: Ya, the Devyl spede you, al the packe!
For sorwe I morne on the mowle.
I carpe, I crye, I coure, I kacke,
I frete, I fart, I fesyl fowle.
I loke lyke an howle.
    Ad Mundum.
Now, Syr World, what so it cost,
Helpe now, or this we have lost.
Al oure fare is not worth a thost: 2430
That makyth me to mowle.

MUNDUS: How, Coveytyse, banyour a-vaunt!
Here comyth a batayl nobyl and newe;
For syth thou were a lytyl faunt,

2410 *ropys* ropes   2413   *irchoun* brat   2415 *drulle* ?fall
2417 *skallyd* scabby   2419 *skathe* harm   2420 *lathe* by-path
2422 *leykyn* rest   2424 *mowle* ground   2425 *kacke* excrete
2426 *fesyl* break wind   2430 *thost* turd   2431 *mowle* pull faces
2434 *faunt* child

Coveytyse, thou hast ben trewe.
Have do that damysel, do hyr dawnt.
Byttyr balys thou hyr brewe.
The medys, boy, I the graunt,
The galows Canwyke to hangyn on newe,
That wolde the wel be-falle.   2440
Have don, Syr Coveytyse.
Wyrke on the best wyse.
Do Mankynde com and aryse
Fro yone vertuse all.

AVARICIA: How, Mankynde, I am a-tenyde
    For thou art there so in that holde.
    Cum and speke wyth thi best frende,
    Syr Coveytyse, thou knowyst me of olde.
    What devyl schalt thou ther lenger lende
    Wyth grete penaunce in that castel colde?   2450
    In-to the werld if thou wylt wende,
    A-monge men to bere the bolde,
    I rede, be Seynt Gyle.
    How, Mankynde, I the sey,
    Com to Coveytyse, I the prey.
    We to schul to-gedyr pley,
    If thou wylt a-whyle.

LARGITAS: A, God helpe! I am dysmayed.
    I curse the Coveytyse as I can;
    For certys, treytour, thou hast betrayed   2460
    Nerhand now iche erthely man.
    So myche were men nevere a-frayed
    Wyth Coveytyse, syn the werld be-gan.
    God Almythy is not payed.
    Syn thou, fende, bare the Werldys bane,
    Ful wyde thou gynnyst wende.

2436 *dawnt* become tame   2445 *a-tenyde* grieved   2449 *lende* stay
2461 *Nerhand* almost

Now arn men waxyn ner woode.
They wolde gon to helle for werldys goode.
That Lord that restyd on the rode
Is maker of an ende.   2470
Maledicti sunt avariciosi huius temporis.

Ther is no dysese nor debate
Thorwe this wyde werld so rounde,
Tyde nor tyme erly nor late,
But that Covey[ty]se is the grounde.
Thou norchyst pride, envye and hate,
Thou Coveytyse, thou cursyd hounde.
Criste the schelde fro oure gate
And kepe us fro the saf and sounde
That thou no good here wynne.   2480
Swete Jhesu, jentyl justyce,
Kepe Mankynde fro Coveytyse,
For i-wys he is, in al wyse,
Rote of sorwe and synne.

AVARICIA: What eylyth the, Lady Largyte,
  Damysel dyngne, up-on thi des?
  And I spak ryth not to the,
  Therfore I prey the holde thi pes.
  How, Mankynde, cum speke wyth me,
  Cum ley thi love here in my les.   2490
  Coveytyse is a frend ryth fre,
  Thi sorwe, man, to slake and ses.
  Coveytyse hathe many a gyfte.
  Mankynd, thyne hande hedyr thou reche.
  Coveytyse schal be thi leche.
  The ryth wey I schal the teche
  To thedom and to thryfte.

2490 *les* control   2492 *slake* abate   *ses* cease   2495 *leche* physician
2497 *thedom* prosperity

HUMANUM GENUS: Coveytyse, whedyr schuld I wende?
    What wey woldyst that I sulde holde?
    To what place woldyst thou me sende?   2500
    I gynne to waxyn hory and colde;
    My bake gynnyth to bowe and bende;
    I crulle and crepe and wax al colde.
    Age makyth man ful unthende,
    Body and bonys and al unwolde.
    My bonys are febyl and sore.
    I am arayed in a sloppe,
    As a yonge man I may not hoppe,
    My nose is colde and gynnyth to droppe,
    Myn her waxit al hore.   2510

AVARICIA: Petyr, thou hast the more nede
    To have sum good in thyn age:
    Markys, poundys, londys and lede,
    Howsys and homys, castell and cage.
    Therfor do as I the rede;
    To Coveytyse cast thi parage.
    Cum and I schal thyne erdyn bede;
    The worthi Werld schal geve the wage,
    Certys not a lyth.
    Com on, olde man, it is no reprefe   2520
    That Coveytyse be the lefe.
    If thou deye at any myschefe
    It is thi-selfe to wyth.

HUMANUM GENUS: Nay, nay, these ladys of goodnesse
    Wyl not lete me fare a-mys,
    And thou I be a whyle in dystresse,
    Whanne I deye I schal to blysse.

2503 *crulle* ?crawl   2505 *unwolde* infirm   2507 *sloppe* gown
2513 *lede* vassals   2514 *cage* ?stronghold   2516 *parage* share, lot
2517 *erdyn* petition   *bede* (v) present   2519 *lyth* little
2523 *wyth* (v) blame

It is but foly, as I gesse,
Al this werldys wele I wys.
These lovely ladys, more and lesse,   2530
In wyse wordys thei telle me thys.
Thus seyth the bok of kendys.
I wyl not do these ladys dyspyt
To forsakyn hem for so lyt
To dwellyn here is my delyt;
Here arn my best frendys.

AVARICIA: Ya, up and doun thou take the wey
Thorwe this werld to walkyn and wende,
And thou schalt fynde, soth to sey,
Thi purs schal be thi best fre[n]de.   2540
Thou thou syt al day and prey,
No man schal com to the nor sende;
But if thou have a peny to pey,
Men schul to the thanne lystyn and lende
And kelyn al thi care.
Therfore to me thou hange and helde
And be coveytous whylys thou may the welde.
If thou be pore and nedy in elde
Thou schalt oftyn evyl fare.

HUMANUM GENUS: Coveytyse, thou seyst a good skyl.   2550
So grete God me a-vaunce,
Al thi byddynge don I wyl.
I forsake the Castel of Perseveraunce.
In Coveytyse I wyl me hyle
For to gete sum sustynaunce.
A-forn mele men mete schul tyle;
It is good for al chaunce
Sum good owhere to hyde.
Certys this ye wel knowe:

2529 *wele* prosperity   2534 *lyt* little   2545 *kelyn* ease   2546 *helde* obey
2547 *welde* (v) conduct   2554 *hyle* shelter   2556 *tyle* obtain

It is good, whou-so the wynde blowe,   2560
A man to have sum-what of hys owe,
What happe so evere be-tyde.

BONUS ANGELUS: A, ladyse, I prey you of grace,
Helpyth to kepe here Mankynne.
He wyl for-sake this precyous place
And drawe a-geyn to dedly synne.
Helpe, ladys, lovely in lace:
He goth fro this worthi wonnynge.
Coveytyse a-wey ye chac[e]
And schyttyth Mankynd sum-where here-inne,   2570
In youre worthi wyse.
Ow, wrechyd man, thou schalt be wroth,
That synne schal be the ful loth.
A, swete ladys, helpe, he goth
A-wey wyth Coveytyse.

Tunc descend[e]t ad Avariciam.

HUMILITAS: Good Aungyl, what may I do ther-to?
Hym-selfe may hys sowle spylle.
Mankynd to don what he wyl do,
God hath govyn him a fre wylle.
Thou he drenche and hys sowle slo,   2580
Certys we may not do there-tylle.
Syn he cam this castel to,
We dyd to hym that us be-felle
And now he hath us refusyd.
As longe as he was wyth-inne this castel walle,
We kepte hym fro synne, ye sawe wel alle;
And now he wyl a-geyn to synne falle,
I preye you holde us excusyd.

2561 *owe* own   2567 *lace* dress   2570 *schyttyth* shut
2579 *govyn* given   2580 *drenche* drown   *slo* is destroyed

PACIENCIA: Resun wyl excusyn us alle.
 He helde the ex be the helve.   2590
 Thou he wyl to foly falle,
 It is to wytyn but hym-selve.
 Whyl he held hym in this halle,
 Fro dedly synne we dyd hym schelve.
 He brewyth hym-selfe a byttyr galle:
 In dethys dynt whanne he schal delve,
 This game he schal be grete.
 He is endewyd wyth wyttys fyve
 For to rewlyn hym in hys lyve.
 We vertuse wyl not wyth hym stryve,   2600
 A-vyse hym and hys dede.

CARITAS: Of hys dede have we nowt to done;
 He wyl no lenger wyth us be lad.
 Whanne he askyd out, we herd hys bone,
 And of hys presens we were ryth glad.
 But as thou seste he hath for-sakyn us sone;
 He wyl not don as Crist hym bad.
 Mary, thi Sone a-bovyn the mone
 As make Mankynd trewe and sad,
 In grace for to gon.   2610
 For if he wyl to foly flyt
 We may hym not wyth-syt.
 He is of age and can hys wyt,
 Ye knowe wel every-chon.

ABSTINENCIA: Ichon ye knowyn he is a fole,
 In Coveytyse to dyth hys dede.
 Werldys wele is lyke a iij fotyd stole,
 It faylyt a man at hys most nede.
 Mundus transit et concupiscencia eius.
 Whanne he is dyth in dedys dole,   2620

2592 *wytyn* blame   2594 *schelve* (v) shield
2604 *bone* prayer, request   2612 *wyth-syt* prevent

The ryth regystre I schal hym rede;
He schal be tore wyth teneful tole;
Whanne he schal brenne on glemys glede
He schal lere a new lawe.
Be he nevere so ryche of werldys wone,
Hys seketouris schul makyn here mone:
'Make us mery and lete hym gone –
He was a good felawe.'

CASTITAS: Whanne he is ded here sorwe is lest.
 The ton sekatour seyth to the tothyr: 2630
 'Make we mery and a ryche fest
 And lete hym lyn in dedys fodyr.'
 Et sic relinqu[ent] alienis divicias suas.
 So hys part schal be the lest;
 The systyr servyt thus the brothyr.
 I lete a man no betyr thanne a best,
 For no man can be war be othyr
 Tyl he hathe al ful spunne.
 Thou schalt se that day, man, that a bede
 Schal stonde the more in stede   2640
 Thanne al the good that thou mytyst gete,
 Certys undyr sunne.

SOLICITUDO: Mankynde, of on thynge have I wondyr:
 That thou takyst not in-to thyn mende,
 Whanne body and sowle schul partyn on sundyr
 No werldys good schal wyth the wende.
 Non descendet cum illo gloria eius.
 Whanne thou art ded and in the erthe leyd undyr
 Mys-gotyn good the schal schende;
 It schal be weyen as peys in pundyr   2650

2623 *glemys* of bright light *glede* fire 2626 *seketouris* executors
2636 *lete* consider 2638 *spunne* wrought, done
2639 *bede* prayer beads 2650 *peys* weight (?peas) *pundyr* balance

Thi sely sowle to bryngyn in bende
And make it ful unthende.
And yyt Mankynd, as it is sene,
Wyth Coveytyse goth on this grene.
The treytor doth us al this tene
Aftyr hys lyvys ende.

LARGITAS: Out, I crye, and no-thynge lowe,
On Coveytyse, as I wel may.
Mankynd seyth he hath nevere i-nowe
Tyl hys mowthe be ful of clay.   2660
Avarus numquam replebitur pecunia.
Whane he is closyd in dethis dow
What helpyt ryches or gret a-ray?
It flyet a-wey as any snow
A-non aftyr thye endynge day,
To wylde werldys wyse.
Now, good men alle that here be,
Have my systerys excusyd and me,
Thou Mankynde fro this castel fle.
Wyte it Coveytyse.   2670

MALUS ANGELUS: Ya, go forthe and lete the qwenys
          cakle!
Ther wymmen arn are many wordys.
Lete hem gon hoppyn wyth here hakle!
Ther ges syttyn are many tordys.
Wyth Coveytyse thou renne on rakle
And hange thyne hert up-on hys hordys.
Thou schalt be schakyn in myn schakle.
Unbynde thi baggys on hys bordys,
On hys benchys a-bove.
Parde, thou gost owt of Mankynde   2680

2651 *bende* bondage   2655 *tene* harm
2657 *lowe* quietly   2670 *Wyte* blame   2673 *hakle* feathers
2675 *rakle* haste   2676 *hordys* treasures   2677 *schakle* fetters

But Coveytyse be in thi mende.
If evere thou thynke to be thende,
On hym thou ley thi love.

HUMANUM GENUS: Nedys my love muste on hym lende,
Wyth Coveytyse to waltyr and wave.
I knowe non of al my kynde
That he ne coveytyth for to have.
Peny-man is mekyl in mynde;
My love in hym I leye and lave.
Where that evere I walke or wende   2690
In wele and woo he wyl me have;
He is gret of grace.
Where-so I walke in londe or lede
Peny-man best may spede;
He is a duke to don a dede
Now in every place.

BONUS ANGELUS: Alas, that evere Mankynde was born!
On Coveytyse is al hys lust.
Nyth and day, mydnyth and morn,
In Peny-man is al hys trust.   2700
Coveytyse schal makyn hym lorn
Whanne he is dolven al to dust;
To mekyl schame he schal be schorn,
Wyth foule fendys to roten and rust.
Alas, what schal I do?
Alas, alas, so may I say.
Man goth wyth Coveytyse a-way.
Have men excusyd, for I ne may
Trewly not do ther-to.

MUNDUS: A, a, this game goth as I wolde.   2710
Mankynde wyl nevere the World forsake:

2682 *thende* blessed, prosperous   2685 *waltyr* float   2689 *leye* place
lave leave   2702 *dolven* buried

176

Tyl he be ded and undyr molde
Holy to me he wyl hym take.
To Coveytyse he hath hym yolde;
Wyth my wele he wyl a-wake;
For a thousende pounde I nolde
But Coveytyse were mans make,
Certys on every wyse.
All these gamys he schal be-wayle,
For I, the Werld, am of this entayle,   2720
In hys moste nede I schal hym fayle,
And al for Coveytyse.

AVARICIA: Now, Mankynd, be war of this:
 Thou art a party wele in age.
 I wolde not thou ferdyst a-mys.
 Go we now knowe my castel cage.
 In this bowre I schal the blys;
 Worldly wele schal be thi wage.
 More mucke thanne is thyne, i-wys,
 Take thou in this trost terage   2730
 And loke that thou do wronge.
 Coveytyse, it is no sore,
 He wyl the feffen ful of store,
 And alwey, alwey sey 'more and more',
 And that schal be thi songe.

HUMANUM GENUS: A, Coveytyse, have thou good grace!
 Certys thou beryst a trewe tonge.
 'More and more', in many a place,
 Certys that songe is oftyn songe.
 I wyste nevere man, be bankys bace,   2740
 So seyn in cley tyl he were clonge:
 'I-now, i-now' hadde nevere space,
 That ful songe was nevere songe,

2717 *make* mate 2730 *trost* safe *terage* soil 2740 *bace* low
2741 *seyn* to say *clonge* decayed

Nor I wyl not begynne.
Goode Coveytyse, I the prey
That I myth wyth the pley.
Geve me good inow, or that I dey,
To wonne in Werldys wynne.

AVARICIA: Have here, Mankynd, a thousend marke.
I, Coveytyse, have the this gote.   2750
Thou mayst purchase ther-wyth bothe ponde and parke
And do ther-wyth mekyl note.
Lene no man here-of, for no karke,
Thou he schulde hange be the throte,
Monke nor frere, prest nor clerke,
Ne helpe ther-wyth chyrche nor cote,
Tyl deth thi body delve.
Thou he schuld sterve in a cave,
Lete no pore man ther-of have,
In grene gres tyl thou be grave   2760
Kepe sum-what fore thi-selve.

HUMANUM GENUS: I vow to God, it is gret husbondry.
Of the I take these noblys rownde.
I schal me rapyn, and that in hye,
To hyde this gold undyr the grownde.
Ther schal it ly tyl that I dye,
It may be kepte ther save and sownde.
Thou my neygbore schuld be hangyn hye,
Ther-of getyth he neyther peny nor pownde.
Yyt am I not wel at ese.   2770
Now wolde I have castel wallys,
Stronge stedys and styf in stallys.
Wyth hey holtys and hey hallys,
Coveytyse, thou muste me sese.

2748 *wynne* joy   2753 *karke* distress   2764 *rapyn* hasten
2773 *holtys* woods   2774 *sese* endow

AVARICIA: Al schalt thou have al redy, lo,
　At thyn owyn dysposycyoun.
　Al this good take the to,
　Clyffe and cost, toure and toun.
　Thus hast thou gotyn in synful slo
　Of thyne neygborys be extorcyoun.　　　　　　2780
　'More and more' sey yyt, have do,
　Tyl thou be ded and drepyn dounn;
　Werke on wyth werldys wrenchys.
　'More and more' sey yyt, I rede,
　To more thanne i-now thou hast nede.
　Al this werld, bothe lenthe and brede,
　Thi coveytyse may not qwenche.

HUMANUM GENUS: Qwenche nevere no man may:
　Me thynkyth nevere I have inow.
　Ther ne is werldys wele, nyth nor day,　　　　2790
　But that me thynkyth it is to slow.
　'More and more' yit I say
　And schal evere whyl I may blow;
　On Coveytyse is al my lay
　And schal tyl deth me ovyr throw.
　'More and more', this is my stevene.
　If I myth al-wey dwellyn in prosperyte,
　Lord God, thane wel were me.
　I wolde, the medys, forsake the
　And nevere to comyn in hevene.　　　　　　　2800

　2779 *slo* slough, evil　2782 *drepyn* dropped　2783 *wrenchys* tricks
　2796 *stevene* petition　2799 *the medys* as recompense

[PART THREE: DEATH]

MORS: Ow, now it is tyme hye
To castyn Mankynd to Dethys dynt.
In all hys werkys he is unslye;
Mekyl of hys lyf he hath myspent.
To Mankynd I ney ny;
Wyth rewly rappys he schal be rent.
Whanne I com iche man drede for-thi,
But yyt is ther no geyn-went
Hey hyl, holte, nyn hethe.
Ye schul me drede every-chone; 2810
Whanne I come ye schul grone;
My name in londe is lefte a-lone:
I hatte drery Dethe.

Drery is my deth-drawth;
A-geyns me may no man stonde.
I durke and down brynge to nowth
Lordys and ladys in every londe.
Whom-so I have a lessun tawth,
Onethys sythen schal he mowe stonde.
In my carful clothys he schal be cawth 2820
Ryche, pore, fre and bonde.
Whanne I come thei goo no more.
Where-so I wende in any lede,
Every man of me hat drede.
Lette I wyl for no mede
To smyte sadde and sore.

2803 *unslye* foolish   2806 *rewly* grievous   *rappys* blows
2808 *geyn-went* way back   2813 *hatte* am called
2814 *deth-drawth* death blow   2816 *durke* lie in wait
2819 *Onethys* scarcely

Dyngne dukys arn a-dred
Whanne my b[l]astys arn on hem blowe.
Lordys in londe arn ovyr-led;
Wyth this launce I leye hem lowe.   2830
Kyngys kene and knytys kyd,
I do hem delvyn in a throwe.
In banke I buske hem a bed.
Sad sorwe to hem I sowe;
I tene hem, as I trowe.
As kene koltys thow they kynse,
A-geyns me is no defens.
In the grete pestelens
Thanne was I wel knowe.

But now al-most I am for-gete;   2840
Men of Deth holde no tale.
In coveytyse here good they gete;
The grete fyschys ete the smale.
But whane I dele my derne dette,
Tho prowde men I schal a-vale.
Hem schal helpyn nothyr mel nor mete
Tyl they be drewyn to Dethys dale:
My lawe thei schul lerne.
Ther ne is peny nor pownde
That any of you schal save sownde.   2850
Tyl ye be gravyn undyr grownde
Ther may no man me werne.

To Mankynde now wyl I reche;
He hathe hole hys hert on Coveytyse.
A newe lessun I wyl hym teche
That he schal bothe grwcchyn and gryse.
No lyf in londe schal ben hys leche;

2831 *kyd* famous   2836 *koltys* colts   *kynse* ?wince, shy
2845 *a-vale* bring low   2846 *mel* meal   2852 *werne* prevent
2856 *grwcchyn* moan   *gryse* tremble

I schal hym prove of myn empryse;
Wyth this poynt I schal hym broche
And wappyn hym in a woful wyse.   2860
No-body schal ben hys bote.
I schal the schapyn a schenful schappe.
Now I kylle the wyth myn knappe!
I reche to the, Mankynd, a rappe
To thyne herte rote.

HUMANUM GENUS: A, Deth, Deth, drye is thi dryftel
Ded is my desteny!
Myn hed is clevyn al in a clyfte;
For clappe of care now I crye;
Myn eye-ledys may I not lyfte;   2870
Myn braynys waxyn al emptye;
I may not onys myn hod up schyfte;
Wyth Dethys dynt now I dey!
Syr Werld, I am hent.
Werld, Werld, have me in mende!
Goode Syr Werld, helpe now Mankend!
But thou me helpe, Deth schal me schende:
He hat dyth to me a dynt.

Werld, my wyt waxyt wronge.
I chaunge bothe hyde and hewe.   2880
Myn eye-ledys waxyn al outewronge.
But thou me helpe, sore it schal me rewe.
Now holde that thou haste be-hete me longe;
For all felechepys olde and newe,
Lesse me of my peynys stronge.
Sum bote of bale thou me brewe
That I may of the yelpe.
Werld, for olde a-qweyntawns,
Helpe me fro this sory chawns.

2859 *broche* pierce   2860 *wappyn* strike   2863 *knappe* blow
2881 *outewronge* squeezed   2887 *yelpe* boast

Deth hathe lacchyd me wyth hys launce.   2890
I deye but thou me helpe.

MUNDUS: Owe, Mankynd, hathe Dethe wyth the spoke?
A-geyns hym helpyth no wage.
I wolde thou were in the erthe be loke
And a-nothyr hadde thyne erytage.
Oure bonde of love schal sone be broke;
In colde clay schal be thy cage;
Now schal the Werld on the be wroke
For thou hast don so gret outrage.
Thi good thou schalt for-goo.   2900
Werldlys good thou hast for-gon
And wyth tottys thou schalt be torn.
Thus have I servyd here be-forn
A hundryd thousand moo.

HUMANUM GENUS: Ow, Werld, Werld, evere worthe wo!
And thou, synful Coveytyse,
Whanne that a man schal fro you go
Ye werke wyth hym on a wondyr wyse.
The wytte of this werld is sorwe and wo.
Be ware, good men, of this gyse!   2910
Thus hathe he servyd many on mo.
In sorwe slakyth al hys a-syse.
He beryth a tenynge tungge.
Whyl I leyd wyth hym my lott
Ye seyn whou fayre he me be-hett:
And now he wolde I were a clott
In colde cley for to clynge.

MUNDUS: How, boy, a-ryse! Now thou muste wende
On myn erdyn, be steppe and stalle.

2893 *wage* payment   2902 *tottys* devils   2919 *erdyn* errand

Go brewe Mankynd a byttyr bende   2920
And putte hym oute of hys halle.
Lete hym ther-inne no lenger lende.
For-brostyn I trowe be hys galle
For thou art not of hys kende.
All hys erytage wyl the wele be-falle.
Thus faryth myn fayre feres.
Oftyn tyme I have you told,
Tho men that ye arn to lest be-hold
Comynly schal youre wonnynge wold
And ben youre next eyrys.   2930

GARCIO: Werld worthy, in wedys wounde,
I thanke the for thi grete gyfte.
I go glad up-on this grounde
To putte Mankynde out of hys thryfte.
I trowe he stynkyth this ilke stounde.
In-to a lake I schal hym lyfte.
Hys parkys, placys, and penys rounde
Wyth me schul dryven in this dryfte
In baggys as thei ben bownde.
For I thynke for to dele,   2940
I vow to God, neythyr corn nore mele.
If he have a schete he beryth hym wele
Where-inne he may be woun[de].

Tunc iet ad H[u]manum Genus.

Whou faryst, Mankynde? Art thou ded?
Be Goddys body, so I wene.
He is hevyer thanne any led.
I wolde he were gravyn undyr grene.

2923 *For-brostyn* burst to pieces   *galle* gall bladder
2929 *wold* possess

HUMANUM GENUS: A-byde, I breyd uppe wyth myn hed.
What art thou? What woldyst thou mene?
Wheydyr comyst thou for good or qwed?   2950
Wyth peynes prycke thou doste me tene,
The sothe for to sey.
Telle me now, so God the save,
Fro whom comyst thou, good knave?
What dost thou here? Wha[t] woldyst thou have?
Telle me or I deye.

GARCIO: I am com to have al that thou hast,
Ponndys, parkys, and every place.
Al that thou hast gotyn fyrst and last
The Werld hathe grauntyd it me of hys grace   2960
For I have ben hys page.
He wot wel thou schalt be ded,
Nevere more to ete bred;
Therfore he hath for the red
Who schal have thyne erytage.

HUMANUM GENUS: What devyl! Thou art not of my kyn.
Thou dedyst me nevere no maner good.
I hadde lever sum nyfte or sum cosyn
Or sum man hadde it of my blod.
In sum stede I wold it stod.   2970
Now schal I in a dale be delve
And have no good ther-of my-selve.
Be God and be hys apostelys twelve,
I trowe the Werld be wod.

GARCIO: Ya, ya, thi parte schal be the leste.
Deye on, for I am maystyr here.
I schal be makyn a nobyl feste

2948 *breyd* lift   2950 *qwed* bad
2964 *red* decided   2968 *nyfte* nephew

185

And thanne have I do myn devere.
The Werld bad me this gold a-reste,
Holt and hallys and castell clere.   2980
The Werldys joye and hys jenytl jeste
Is now thyne, now myn, bothe fere and nere.
Go hens, for this is myne.
Syn thou art ded and browth of dawe,
Of thi deth, syr, I am ryth fawe.
Thou thou knowe not the Werldys lawe,
He hath gove me al that was thyne.

HUMANUM GENUS: I preye the now, syn thou this good
        schalt gete,
Telle thi name or that I goo.
GARCIO: Loke that thou it not for-gete: 2990
My name is I-Wot-Nevere-Whoo.

HUMANUM GENUS: I-Wot-Nevere-Who! So wele say!
Now am I sory of my lyf.
I have purchasyd many a day
Londys and rentys wyth mekyl stryf.
I have purchasyd holt and hay,
Parkys and ponndys and bourys blyfe,
Goode gardeynys wyth gryffys gay,
To myne chyldyr and to myn wyfe
In dethe whanne I were dyth.   3000
Of my purchas I may be wo,
For, as thout, it is not so,
But a gedelynge I-Wot-Nevere-Who
Hath al that the Werld me by-hyth.

Now, alas, my lyf is lak!
Bittyr balys I gynne to brewe.

2984 *browth* brought   *of dawe* to death   2996 *hay* enclosed land
2997 *blyfe* joyful   2998 *gryffys* groves   3002 *thout* surmised
3004 *be-hyth* promised

Certis a vers that David spak
I the sawter I fynde it trewe:
Tesauriʒat et ignorat cui congregabit ea.
Tresor, tresor, it hathe no tak;   3010
It is othyr mens, olde and newe.
Ow, ow, my good gothe al to wrak!
Sore may Mankynd rewe.
God kepe me fro dyspayr!
Al my good, wyth-out fayle,
I have gadryd wyth gret travayle,
The Werld hathe ordeynyd of hys entayle
I-Wot-Nevere-Who to by myn eyr.

Now, good men, takythe example at me.
Do for youre-self whyl ye han spase.   3020
For many men thus servyd be
Thorwe the werld in dyverse place.
I bolne and bleyke in blody ble
And as a floure fadyth my face.
To helle I schal bothe fare and fle
But God me graunte of hys grace.
I deye certeynly.
Now my lyfe I have lore.
Myn hert brekyth, I syhe sore.
A word may I speke no more.   3030
I putte me in Goddys mercy.

[*Man dies, and the Soul rises from the bed*]

ANIMA: 'Mercy', this was my last tale
    That evere my body was a-bowth.
    But Mercy helpe me in this vale,
    Of dampnynge drynke sore I me doute.

3010 *tak* endurance   3023 *bolne* swell *bleyke* turn pale
ble condition

Body, thou dedyst brew a byttyr bale
To thi lustys whanne gannyst loute.
Thi sely sowle schal ben akale.
I beye thi dedys wyth rewly rowte,
And al it is for gyle.   3040
Evere thou hast be coveytows
Falsly to getyn londe and hows.
To me thou hast browyn a byttyr jows.
So welaway the whyle.

Now swet Aungel, what is thi red?
The ryth red thou me reche.
Now my body is dressyd to ded
Helpe now me and be my leche.
Dyth thou me fro develys drede.
Thy worthy weye thou me teche.   3050
I hope that God wyl helpyn and be myn hed
For 'mercy' was my laste speche;
Thus made my body hys ende.

. . . .

[MALUS ANGELUS:] Wyttnesse of all that ben a-bowte,
Syr Coveytyse he had hym owte.
Therfor he schal, wyth-outyn dowte,
Wyth me to helle pytt.

BONUS ANGELUS: Ye, alas, and welawo!
A-geyns Coveytyse can I not telle.
Resun wyl I fro the goo,   3060
For, wrechyd sowle, thou muste to helle.
Coveytyse, he was thi fo,

3037 *loute* submit   3038 *akale* cold   3043 *jows* juice   3046 *reche* give
3049 *Dyth* save   3055 *owte* owned

He hathe the schapyn a schameful schelle;
Thus hathe servyd many on mo
Tyl thei be dyth to dethys delle,
To byttyr balys bowre.
Thou muste to peyne, be ryth resun,
Wyth Coveytyse, for he is chesun.
Thou art trappyd ful of tresun
But Mercy be thi socowre.   3070

For ryth wel this founnde he have
A-geyns Rythwysnesse may I not holde.
Thou muste wyth hym to careful cave
For grete skyllys that he hathe tolde
Fro the a-wey I wandyr and wave;
For the I clynge in carys colde.
A-lone now I the lave
Whylyst thou fallyst in fendys folde,
In helle to hyde and hylle.
Rytwysnesse wyl that thou wende   3080
Forthe a-wey wyth the fende.
But Mercy wyl to the sende,
Of the I can no skylle.

ANIMA: Alas, Mercy, thou art to longe!
Of sadde sorwe now may I synge.
Holy Wryt it is ful wronge
But Mercy pase alle thynge.
I am ordeynyd to peynys stronge;
In wo is dressyd myn wonnynge;
In helle on hokys I schal honge,   3090
But mercy fro a welle sprynge.
This devyl wyl have me a-way.
Weleaway! I was ful wod
That I forsoke myn Aungyl Good

3063 *schelle* hollow pit   3076 *clynge* waste
3090 *hokys* hooks

And wyth Coveytyse stod
Tyl that day I schuld dey.

MALUS ANGELUS: Ya, why woldyst thou be coveytous
And drawe the a-gayn to synne?
I schal the brewe a byttyr jous;
In bolnynnge bondys thou schalt brenne.   3100
In hye helle schal be thyne hous,
In pycke and ter to grone and grenne;
Thou schalt lye drenkelyd as a mows;
Ther may no man therfro the werne
For that ilke wyll.
That day the ladys thou for-soke
And to my counsel thou the toke,
Thou were betyr an-hangyn on hoke
Up-on a jebet hyll.

Farter fowle, thou schalt be frayed   3110
Tyl thou be frettyd and al for-bled.
Foule mote thou be dysmayed
That thou schalt thus ben ovyrled.
For Coveytyse thou hast a-sayed
In byttyr balys thou schalt be bred.
Al mankynd may be wel payed
Whou Coveytyse makyth the a-dred.
Wyth rappys I the rynge.
We schul to hell, bothe to,
And bey *in inferno*.   3120
Nulla est redempcio
For no kynnys thynge.

Now dagge we hens a dogge trot.
In my dongion I schal the dere.

3100 *bolnynnge* swelling   3102 *pycke* pitch   *ter* tar
3103 *drenkelyd* drowned   3104 *werne* defend   3110 *frayed* bruised
3120 *bey* suffer, pay   3123 *dogge* jog

On the is many a synful spot;
Therfore this schame I schal the schere
Whanne thou comyst to my neste.
Why woldyst thou, schrewe schalt nevere the,
But in thi lyve don aftyr me?
And thi Good Aungyl tawth the   3130
Al-wey to the beste.

Ya, but thou woldyst hym not leve,
To Coveytyse al-wey thou drow.
Therfore schalt thou evyl preve;
That foule synne thi soule slow.
I schal fonde the to greve
And putte the in pey[nn]ys plow.
Have this, and evyl mote thou scheve,
For thou seydyst nevere 'i-now, i-now'
Thus lacche I the thus lowe.   3140
Thow thou kewe as a kat,
For thi coveytyse have thou that!
I schal the bunche wyth my bat
And rouge the on a rowe.

Lo, synful tydynge,
Boy, on thi bak I brynge.
Spedely thou sprynge
Thi placebo I schal synge.
To develys delle
I schal the bere to helle.   3150
I wyl not dwelle.
Have good day! I goo to helle.

3126 *schere* cut off   3128 *the* (v) thrive   3133 *drow* were drawn
3138 *scheve* thrive   3140 *lacche* strike   3141 *kewe* mew
3143 *bunche* strike   3144 *rouge* handle roughly
3148 *placebo* vespers for the dead   3149 *delle* pit

MISERICORDIA: A mone I herd of mercy meve
    And to me, Mercy, gan crye and call.
    But if it have mercy, sore it schal me greve,
    For ell it schal to hell fall.
    Rythwysnes, my systyr cheve,
    Thys ye herde; so dyde we all.
    For we were mad frendys leve
    Whanne the Jewys proferyd Criste eysyl and gall   3160
    On the Good Fryday.
    God grauntyd that remission,
    Mercy, and absolicion,
    Thorwe vertus of hys passion,
    To no man schuld be seyd nay.

    Therfore, my systyr Rytwysnes,
    Pes, and Trewthe, to you I tell,
    Whanne man crieth mercy, and wyl not ses,
    Mercy schal be hys waschynge-well:
    Wytnesse of Holy Kyrke.   3170
    For the leste drope of blode
    That God bledde on the rode
    It hadde ben satysfaccion goode
    For al Mankyndys werke.

JUSTICIA: Systyr, ye sey me a good skyl,
    That mercy pasyt mannys mysdede.
    But take mercy who-so wyl
    He muste it aske wyth love and drede,
    And every-man that wyl fulfyll
    The dedly synnys and folw mysdede,   3180

    3155 *But if* unless   3160 *eysyl* vinegar   3180 *folw* follow

To graunte hem mercy me thynkyth it no skyl.
And therfore, systyr, you I rede
Lete hym a-bye hys mysdede.
For thou he lye in hell and stynke,
It schal me nevere ovyr-thynke.
As he hath browyn lete hym drynke;
The Devyl schal qwyte hym hys mede.
Unusquisque suum honus portabit.

Trowe ye that whanne a man schal deye,
Thanne thow that he mercy crave,
That a-non he schal have mercye?   3190
Nay, nay, so Crist me save!
Non omne qui dicit 'Domine, Domine' intrabit regnum
    celorum.
For schuld no man do no good
All the dayes of hys lyve,
But hope of mercy be the rode
Schulde make bothe werre and stryve
And torne to gret grewaunse.
Who-so in hope dothe any dedly synne
To hys lyvys ende and wyl not blynne,   3200
Rytfully thanne schal he wynne
Crystis gret vengaunse.

VERITAS: Rytwysnes, my systyr fre,
    Your jugement is good and trewe.
    In good feyth, so thynkyth me,
    Late hym hys owyn dedys rewe.
    I am Veritas and trew wyl be
    In word and werke to olde and newe.
    Was nevere man in fawte of me
    Dampnyd nor savyd but it were dew,   3210

3185 *ovyr-thynke* cause to regret   3198 *grewaunse* distress
3200 *blynne* refrain from

193

I am evere at mans ende.
Whanne body and sowle partyn atwynne,
Thanne wey I hys goodys dedys and hys synne,
And weydyr of hem be more or mynne
He schal it ryth sone fynde.

For I am Trewthe and trewthe wyl bere,
As grete God hym-self us byd.
Ther schal no thynge the sowle dere
But synne that the body dyd.
Syth that he deyed in that coveytous synne,   3220
I, Trewthe, wyl that he goo to pyne.
Of that synne cowde he not blynne,
Therfore he schal hys sowle tyne
To the pytte of hell.
Ellys schuld we, bothe Trewthe and Rytwysnes,
Be pu[t] to ovyr mekyl dystresse,
And every man schuld be the wers
That ther-of myth here tell.

PAX: Pes, my systyr Verite.
I preye you, Rytwysnes, be stylle.   3230
Lete no man be you dampnyd be
Nor deme ye no man to helle.
He is on kyn tyl us thre,
Thow he have now not al hys wylle.
For hys love that deyed on tre,
Late save Mankynd fro al peryle
And schelde hym fro myschaunsse.
If ye tweyne putte hym to dystresse
It schuld make gret hevynesse
Be-twene us tweyne, Mercy and Pes,   3240
And that were gret grevaunce.

3212 *atwynne* asunder   3214 *mynne* less   3218 *dere* harm
3233 *on kyn* of the same kind

Rytwysnes and Trewthe, do be my red,
And Mercy, go we to yone hey place.
We schal enforme the hey Godhed
And pray hym to deme this case.
Ye schal tell hym youre entent
Of Trewthe and of Rytwysnesse,
And we schal pray that hys jugement
May pase be us, Mercy and Pes.
All foure, now go we hens   3250
Wytly to the Trinite,
And ther schal we sone se
What that hys jugement schal be
Wyth-outyn any deffens.

*Tunc ascende[n]t ad Patrem omnes pariter et
    dicet Veritas*

VERITAS: Heyl, God al-myth!
    We cum, thi dowterys in syth,
    Trewth, Mercy, and Ryth,
    And Pes, pesyble in fyth.

MISERICORDIA: We cum to preve
    If Man, that was the ful leve,   3260
    If he schal cheve
    To hell or hevene be thi leve.

JUSTICIA: I, Rytwysnes,
    Thi dowtyr as I ges,
    Late me nevere-the-lesse
    At thi dom putte me in pres.

3251 *Wytly* quickly   3258 *fyth* strife   3261 *cheve* attain

PAX: Pesyble kynge,
　I, Pes, thi dowtyr yynge,
　Here my preyinge
　Whanne I pray the, Lord, of a thynge.　　　　　　　3270

DEUS: Welcum in fere,
　Bryther thanne blossum on brere.
　My dowterys dere,
　Cum forth and stand ye me nere.

VERITAS: Lord, as thou art Kyng of kyngys, crownyd
　　　　　wyth crowne,
　As thou lovyste me, Trewthe, thi dowtyr dere,
　Lete nevere me, Trewthe, to fall a-downe,
　My feythful Fadyr, *saunʒ pere*!
　Quoniam veritatem dilexisti.
　For in all trewthe standyth thi renowne,　　　　　3280
　Thi feyth, thi hope, and thi powere.
　Lete it be sene, Lord, now at thi dome,
　That I may have my trewe prayere
　To do trewthe to Mankynd.
　For if Mankynd be dempte be ryth
　And not be mercy, most of myth,
　Here my trewthe, Lord, I the plyth,
　In presun man schal be pynyd.

　Lord, whov schuld Mankynd be savyd
　Syn he dyed in dedly synne　　　　　　　　　　3290
　And all thi comaundementys he depravyd
　And of fals covetyse he wolde nevere blynne?
　Aurum sitisti, aurum bibisti.
　The more he hadde, the more he cravyd,
　Whyl the lyf lefte hym wyth-inne.

3268 *yynge* young　3285 *dempte* judged　3287 *plyth* pledge
3289 *whov* how

But he be dampnyd I am a-bavyd
That Trewthe schuld com of rytwys kynne,
And I am thi dowtyr Trewthe.
Thou he cried mercy, *moriendo,*
Nimis tarde penitendo,   3300
Talem mortem reprehendo.
Lete hym drynke as he brewyth!

Late repentaunce if man save scholde,
Wheythyr he wrouth wel or wyckydnesse,
Thanne every man wold be bolde
To trespas in trost of forgevenesse.
For synne in hope is dampnyd, I holde;
For-gevyn is nevere hys trespase.
He synnyth in the Holy Gost many-folde.
That synne, Lord, thou wylt not reles   3310
In this werld nor in the tothyr.
Quia veritas manet in eternum,
Tendit homo ad infernum,
Nunquam venit ad supernum,
Thou he were my brothyr.

For man on molde halt welthe and wele,
Lust and lykynge in al hys lyfe,
Techynge, prechynge in every sele,
But he forgetyth the Lord be-lyve.
Hye of hert, happe and hele,   3320
Gold and sylvyr, chyld and wyf,
Denteth drynke at mete and mele,
Unnethe the to thanke he can not kyth
In any maner thynge.
Whanne mans welthe gynnyth a-wake
Ful sone, Lord, thou art forsake.

3296 *a-bavyd* amazed   3318 *sele* time   3320 *happe* good fortune
hele well-being   3322 *Denteth* delicious

As he hathe browne and bake,
Trewthe wyl that he drynke.

For if Man have mercy and grace
Thanne I, thi dowtyr Sothfastnesse,   3330
At thi dom schal have no place
But be putte a-bak be wronge dures.
Lord, let me nevere fle thi fayr face
To make my power any lesse!
I pray the, Lord, as I have space,
Late Mankynd have dew dystresse
In helle fere to be brent.
In peyne loke he be stylle,
Lord, if it be thi wylle,
Or ell I have no skylle   3340
Be thi trew jugement.

MISERICORDIA: *O Pater misericordiarum et Deus tocius*
            consolacionis
qui consolatur nos in omni tribulacione nostra.
O thou Fadyr, of mytys moste,
Mercyful God in Trinite!
I am thi dowtyr, wel thou woste,
And mercy fro hevene thou browtyst fre.
Schew me thi grace in every coste.
In this cas my counforte be.
Lete me, Lord, nevere be loste   3350
At thi jugement, whov-so it be,
Of Mankynd.
Ne had mans synne nevere cum in cas
I, Mercy, schuld nevere in erthe had plas.
Therfore graunte me, Lord, thi grace,
That Mankynd may me fynd.

3327 *browne* prepared   3330 *Sothfastnesse* Truth
3332 *dures* hardship, harm   3346 *woste* knowest

And mercy, Lord, have on this man
Aftyr thi mercy that mekyl is,
Un-to thi grace that he be tan,
Of thi mercy that he not mys.   3360
As thou descendyst fro thi trone
And lyth in a maydyns wombe i-wys,
In-carnat was in blod and bone,
Lat Mankynd cum to thi blys,
As thou art Kynge of hevene.
For werldly veyn-glory
He hathe ben ful sory,
Punchyd in purgatory
For all the synnys sevene.

Si pro peccato vetus Adam non cecidisset,   3370
Mater pro nato numquam gravidata fuisset.
Ne had Adam synnyd here be-fore
And thi hestys in paradys had offent,
Nevere of thi modyr thou schuldyst a be bore,
Fro hevene to erthe to have be sent.
But xxx^{ti} wyntyr here and more,
Bowndyn and betyn and al to-schent,
Scornyd and scourgyd sadde and sore,
And on the rode rewly rent,
Passus sub Pilato Poncio.   3380
As thou henge on the croys
On hye thou madyste a voys,
Mans helthe, the gospel seys,
Whanne thou seydyst 'Scitio'.
Scilicet salutem animarum.

Thane the Jeves that were unquert
Dressyd the drynke, eysyl and galle.
It to taste thou myth nowth styrt

3359 *tan* taken 3368 *Punchyd* punished 3373 *offent* offended
3386 *unquert* wicked 3388 *styrt* escape

But seyd '*Consummatum est*' was alle.
A knyt wyth a spere so smert,   3390
Whanne thou forgafe thi fomen thrall,
He stonge the, Lord, un-to the hert.
Thanne watyr and blod gan oute wall,
Aqua baptismatis et sanguis redempcionis.
The watyr of baptomm,
The blod of redempcioun,
That fro thin herte ran doun
Est causa salvacionis.

Lord, thou that man hathe don more mysse thanne
    good,
If he dey in very contricioun,   3400
Lord, the lest drope of thi blod
For hys synne makyth satysfaccioun.
As thou deydyst, Lord, on the rode,
Graunt me my peticioun!
Lete me, Mercy, be hys fode,
And graunte hym thi salv[a]cion,
Quia dixisti ' Misericordiam servabo'.
'Mercy' schal I synge and say
And '*miserere*' schal I pray
For Mankynd evere and ay: 3410
Misericordias Domini in eternum cantabo.

JUSTICIA: Rythwys Kynge, Lord God Almyth,
I am thi dowtyr Rythwysnesse.
Thou hast lovyd me evere, day and nyth,
As wel as othyr, as I gesse.
Justicias Dominus justicia dilexit.
If thou mans kynde fre peyne a-quite,
Thou dost a-geyns thyne owyn processe.
Lete hym in preson to be pyth
For hys synne and wyckydnesse,   3420

3393 *wall* flow   3418 *processe* ?mandate in law

Of a bone I the pray.
Ful oftyn he hathe the, lord, forsake,
And to the Devyl he hathe hym take.
Lete hym lyn in hell lake,
Dampnyd for evere and ay.
Quia Deum qui se genuit dereliquit.

For whanne Man to the werld was bornn
He was browth to Holy Kyrke,
Feythly followd in the funte-ston
And wesch fro orygynal synne so dyrke.   3430
Satanas he forsok as hys fone,
All hys po[m]pe and al hys werke,
And hyth to serve the a-lone;
To kepe thi commandementys he schuld not irke,
Sicut justi tui.
But whanne he was com to mans a-state
All hys behestys he thanne for-gate.
He is worthi be dampnyd for that,
Quia oblitus est [Domini] creatoris sui.

For he hathe for-getyn the, that hym wrout,   3440
And formydiste hym lyke thyne owyn face,
And wyth thi precyous blod hym bowth,
And in this world thou geve hym space.
All thi benefetys he set at nowth
But toke hym to the Develys trase,
The Fl[e]sch, the World, was most in [h]is thowth
And purpose to plese hem in every plase,
So grymly on grounde.
I pray the, Lord lovely,
Of man have no mercy,   3450
But, dere Lord, lete hym ly,
In hell lete hym be bounde.

3429 *funte-ston* font (of baptism)   3434 *irke* resent
3445 *trase* dance

Man hathe forsake the, Kynge of hevene,
And hys Good Aungels governaunce,
And solwyd hys soule wyth synnys sevene
Be hys Badde Aungels comberaunce.
Vertuis he putte ful evyn a-way
Whanne Coveytyse gan hym a-vaunce.
He wende that the schulde a levyd ay,
Tyl Deth trypte hym on hys daunce,   3460
He loste hys wyttys fyve.
Ovyr-late he callyd confescioun,
Ovyr-lyt was hys contricioun,
He made nevere satisfaccioun:
Dampne hym to helle be-lyve.

For if thou take Mans sowle to the
A-geyns thi Rythwysnesse,
Thou dost wronge, Lorde, to Trewth and me
And puttys us fro oure dewnesse.
Lord, lete us nevere fro the fle,   3470
Ner streyne us nevere in stresse,
But late thi dom be by us thre
Mankynde in hell to presse,
Lord, I the be-seche!
For Rytwysnes dwell[ys] evere sure
To deme Man aftyr hys deserviture,
For to be dampnyd it is hys ure:
On Man I crie wreche.
Letabitur justus cum viderit vindictam.

MISERICORDIA: Mercy, my systyr Rythwysnes: 3480
Thou schape Mankynde no schonde.
Leve systyr, lete be thi dresse.
To save Man lete us fonde.

3455 *solwyd* sullied   3456 *comberaunce* temptation
3463 *Ovyr-lyt* too little   3469 *dewnesse* rights   3477 *ure* habit
3481 *schonde* ruin   3483 *fonde* try

For if Man be dampnyd to hell dyrknes,
Thanne myth I wryngyn myn honde
That evere my state schulde be les,
My fredam to make bonde.
Mankynd is of oure kyn.
For I, Mercy, pase al thynge
That God made at the begynnynge,   3490
And I am hys dowtyr yynge:
Dere systyr, lete be thi dyn.
Et Misericordia eius super omnia opera eius.

Of Mankynde aske thou nevere wreche
Be day ner be nyth.
For God hym-self hath ben hys leche,
Of hys mercyful myth.
To me he gan hym be-teche,
Be-syde al hys ryth.
For hym wyl I prey and preche   3500
To gete hym fre respyth,
And my systyr Pese.
For hys mercy is wyth-out be-gynnynge
And schal be wyth-outyn [endynge],
As David seyth, that worthy kynge;
In Scriptur is no les.
Et misericordia eius a progenie in progenies et cetera.

VERITAS: Mercy is Mankynde non worthy,
David thou thou recorde and rede,
For he wolde nevere the hungry   3510
Neythyr clothe nor fede,
Ner drynke gyf to the thrysty,
Nyn pore men helpe at nede.
For if he dyd non of these, for-thy
In hevene he getyth no mede:

3494 *wreche* vengeance   3501 *respyth* respite

So seyth the Gospel.
For he hathe ben unkynde
To lame and to blynde
In helle he schal be pynde:
So is resun and skyl.   3520

PAX: Pesible Kyng in majeste,
  I, Pes thi dowtyr, aske the a boun
Of Man, whou-so it be.
Lord, graunte me myn askynge soun,
That I may evermore dwelle wyth the
As I have evere yyt doun,
And lat me nevere fro the fle,
Sp[e]cialy at thi dome
Of Man, thi creature.
Thou my systyr Ryth and Trewthe   3530
Of Mankynd have non rewthe,
Mercy and I ful sore us mewythe
To cacche hym to oure cure.

For whanne thou madyst erthe and hevyn,
x orderys of aungelys to ben in blys,
Lucyfer, lyter thanne the levyn
Tyl whanne he synnyd, he fel i-wys.
To restore that place ful evyn
Thou madyst Mankynd wyth thys
To fylle that place that I dyd nevene.   3540
If thy wyl be resun it is,
In pes and rest,
Amonge thyne aungels bryth
To worchep the in syth,
Graunt, Lord God al-myth,
And so I holde it best.

3519 *pynde* tormented   3520 *skyl* right   3524 *soun* quickly
3532 *mewythe* prompts   3540 *nevene* mention

For thou Truthe, that is my systyr dere,
Arguyth that Man schuld dwell in wo
And Rytwysnes wyth hyr powere
Wolde fayn and fast that it were so,　　　　　　　　3550
But Mercy and I, Pes, bothe in fere,
Schal nevere in feyth a-corde ther-to.
Thanne schuld we evere dyscorde here,
And stande at bate for frend or foo,
And evere at dystaunce.
Therfore my counseyl is
Lete us foure systerys kys
And restore Man to blys,
As was Godys ordenaunce.
Misericordia et Veritas obviaverunt sibi, Justicia et Pax　3560
osculatae sunt.

For if ye, Ryth and Truthe, schuld have your wylle,
I, Pes, and Mercy schuld evere have travest.
Thanne us be-twene had bene a gret perylle
That oure joyes in hevene schuld a ben lest.
Therfore, gentyl systerys, consentyth me tyll,
Ellys betwene oure-self schuld nevere be rest.
Where schuld be luf and charite, late ther cum non
　　ille.
Loke oure joyes be perfyth, and that I holde the best,
In hevene-ryche blys.　　　　　　　　　　　　　　3570
For ther is pes wyth-owtyn were,
There is rest wyth-owtyn fere,
Ther is charite wyth-owtyn dere.
Oure Fadyris wyll so is.
Hic pax, hic bonitas, hic laus, hic semper honestas.

Therfore, jentyl systerys, at on word,
Truth, Ryth, and Mercy hende,

3554 *bate* strife　3563 *travest* ?opposition
3570 *hevene-ryche* kingdom of heaven　3573 *dere* injury

Lete us stonde at on a-cord,
At pes wyth-owtyn ende.
Late love and charyte be at oure bord,   3580
Alle veniauns a-wey wende,
To hevene that Man may be restoryd,
Lete us be all hys frende
Be-fore oure Fadyrs face.
We schal devoutly pray
At dredful domysday,
And I schal for us say
That Mankynd schal have grace.
Et tuam, Deus, deposcimus pietatem ut ei tribuere
    digneris lucidas et quie[tas] mansione[s].   3590

Lord, for thi pyte and that pes
Thou sufferyst in thi pasciounn,
Boundyn and betyn wyth-out les,
Fro the fote to the crounn,
Tanquam ovis ductus es
Whanne gutte sanguis ran a-dounn,
Yyt the Jues wolde not ses
But on thyn hed thei thryst a crounn
And on the cros the naylyd.
As petously as thou were pynyd,   3600
Have mercy of Mankynd,
So that he may fynde
Oure preyer may hym a-vayle.

PATER *sedens in trono: Ego cogito cogitaciones pacis non*
            affliccionis.
Fayre falle the, Pes, my dowtyr dere.
On the I thynke and on Mercy.
Syn ye a-cordyd beth all in fere,
My jugement I wyl geve you by
Not aftyr deservynge to do reddere,

3609 *reddere* punishment

To dampne Mankynde to turmentry,   3610
But brynge hym to my blysse ful clere
In hevene to dwelle endelesly,
At your prayere for-thi.
To make my blysse perfyth
I menge wyth my most myth
Alle pes, sum treuthe, and sum ryth,
And most of my mercy
Misericordia Domini plena est terra. Amen.

      Dicet filiabus

My dowters hende,
Lufly and lusti to lende,   3620
Goo to yone fende
And fro hym take Mankynd.

Brynge hym to me
And set hym here be me kne,
In hevene to be,
In blysse wyth gamyn and gle.

VERITAS: We schal fulfylle
Thin hestys, as resun and skylle,
Fro yone gost grylle
Mankynde to brynge the tylle.   3630

      *Tunc ascendent ad Malum Angelum omnes pariter et
        dicet*

3610 *turmentry* torment   3615 *menge* mix   3626 *gamyn* pleasure
3629 *grylle* fierce

PAX: A, thou foule wyth,
   Lete go that soule so tyth!
   In he[ve]ne lyth
   Mankynde sone schal be pyth.

JUSTICIA: Go thou to helle,
   Th[o]u devyl bold as a belle,
   Ther-in to dwelle,
   In bras and brimston to welle.

    Tunc ascendent ad tronum.

MISERICORDIA: Lo here Mankynd,
   Lyter thanne lef is on lynde,   3640
   That hath ben pynyd.
   Thi mercy, Lord, lete hym fynde.

PATER *sedens in Iudicio: Sicut sintill[a] in medio maris.*
   My mercy, Mankynd, geve I the.
   Cum syt at my ryth honde.
   Ful wel have I lovyd the,
   Unkynd thow I the fonde.
   As a spark of fyre in the se
   My mercy is synne-quenchand.
   Thou hast cause to love me   3650
   A-bovyn al thynge in land,
   And kepe my comaundement.
   If thou me love and drede
   Hevene schal be thi mede.
   My face the schal fede:
   This is myn jugement.
   Ego occidam et vivificabo percuciam et sanabo et nemo est
      qui de manu mea possit eruere.

   3631 *wyth* creature   3632 *tyth* quickly   3633 *lyth* light
   3638 *welle* boil   3640 *lynde* linden tree

Kyng, kayser, knyt, and kampyoun,
Pope, patriark, prest, and prelat in pes,   3660
Duke dowtyest in dede, be dale and be doun,
Lytyl and mekyl, the more and the les,
All the statys of the werld is at myn renoun;
To me schal thei geve a-compt at my dygne des.
Whanne Myhel hys horn blowyth at my dred dom,
The count of here conscience schal putten hem in pres
And yeld a reknynge
Of here space whou they han spent,
And of here trew talent;
At my gret jugement   3670
An answere schal me brynge.

Ecce requiram gregem meum de manu pastoris.
And I schal inquire of my flok and of here pasture
Whou they have levyd and led here peple sojet.
The goode on the ry[th] syd schul stond ful sure:
The badde on the lyfte syd ther schal I set.
The vij dedys of mercy who-so hadde ure
To fylle, the hungry for to geve mete,
Or drynke to thrysty, the nakyd, vesture,
The pore or the pylgrym hom for to fette,   3680
Thi neybour that hath nede;
Who-so doth mercy to hys myth
To the seke, or in presun pyth,
He doth to me; I schal hym quyth;
Hevene blys schal be hys mede.

*Et qui bona egerunt ibunt in vitam eternam, qui vero mala
in ignem eternum.*
And thei that wel do in thys werld, here welthe schal
    a-wake;
In hevene thei schal [be] heynyd in bounte and blys;

3664 *des* seat   3673 *pasture* pastors   3674 *sojet* subject
3684 *quyth* reward   3689 *heynyd* exalted

And thei that evyl do, thei schul to helle lake   3690
In byttyr balys to be brent: my jugement it is.
My vertus in hevene thanne schal thei qwake.
Ther is no wyth in this werld that may skape this.
All men example here-at may take
To mayntein the goode and mendyn here mys.
Thus endyth oure gamys.
To save you fro synnynge
Evyr at the begynnynge
Thynke on youre last endynge!
Te Deum laudamus!   3700

3693 *skape* escape

🐌 🐌 🐌

MAGNYFYCENCE

JOHN SKELTON

Written 1515–18

Edition ?John Rastell, ?1533. Syn.4.53.12,
Cambridge University Library

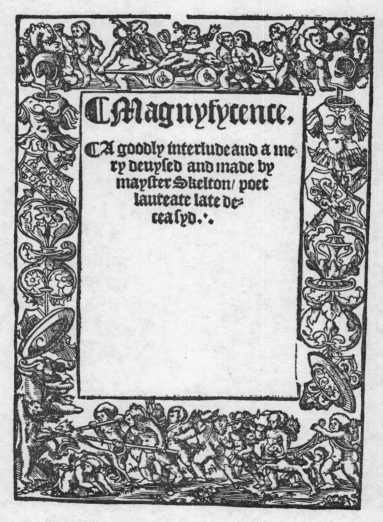

¶Magnyfycence,

¶A goodly interlude and a mery deuysed and made by mayster Skelton/ poet laureate late deceasyd.∴.

The title-page of the Cambridge copy of Magnyfycence

These be the names of the players*:

Felycyte.	Clokyd Colusyon.	Good Hope.
Lyberte.	Courtly Abusyon.	Redresse.
Measure.	Foly.	Cyrcumspeccyon.
	Adversyte.	Perseveraunce.
Magnyfycence.	Poverte.	
	Dyspare.	
Fansy.	Myschefe.	
Counterfet Counte-		
[naunce].		
Crafty Conveyaunce.		

* This list appears after the last line of the play. The layout follows the order of appearance, and is grouped according to the structure (see Introduction pp. 41–6).

MAGNYFYCENCE

[*Enter Felicity.*]

FELYCYTE: Al thyng ys contryvyd by mannys reason,
The world, envyronnyd of hygh and low estate.
Be it erly or late, welth hath a season;
Welth is of wysdome the very trewe probate:
A fole is he with welth that fallyth at debate.
But men nowe-a-dayes so unhappely be uryd
That nothynge than welth may worse be enduryd.

To tell you the cause me semeth it no nede,
The amense therof is far to call agayne.
For when men by welth, they have lytyll drede   10
Of that may come after — experence trewe and playne:
Howe after a drought there fallyth a showre of rayne,
And after a hete oft cometh a stormy colde.
A man may have welth, but not as he wolde

Ay to contynewe and styll to endure.
But yf prudence be proved with sad cyrcumspeccyon,
Welthe myght be wonne and made to the lure,
Yf noblenesse were aquayntyd with sober dyreccyon.
But wyll hath reason so under subjeccyon,
And so dysordereth this worlde over all,   20
That welthe and felicite is passynge small.

1 *contryvyd* controlled   2 *envyronnyd* surrounded   4 *probate* test
5 *at debate* into quarrelling   6 *uryd* disposed   9 *amense* remedy
10 *by* buy   11 *experence* trial, test   20 *dysordereth* corrupts
21 *passynge* exceptionally

217

But where wonnys Welthe, and a man wolde wyt?
For welthfull Felicite truly is my name.

[*Enter Liberty.*]

LYBERTE: Mary, Welthe and I was apoynted to mete,
And eyther I am dysseyved or ye be the same.
FEL: Syr, as ye say. I have harde of your fame;
Your name is Lyberte, as I understande.
LYB: Trewe you say, sir – gyve me your hande.

FEL: And from whens come ye, and it myght be askyd?
LYB: To tell you, syr, I dare not, leest I sholde be
maskyd
In a payre of fetters or a payre of stockys.
FEL: Here you not howe this gentylman mockys?
LYB: Ye, to knackynge ernyst what and it preve?
FEL: Why, to say what he wyll Lyberte hath leve.
LYB: Yet Lyberte hath ben lockyd up and kept in the
mew.
FEL: In-dede, syr, that Lyberte was not worthe a cue.
Howe be it, Lyberte may somtyme be to large,
But yf Reason be regent and ruler of your barge.
LYB: To that ye say I can well condyssende.
Shewe forth, I pray you, here-in what you intende.

FEL: Of that I intende, to make demonstracyon,
It askyth lesure with good advertysment.
Fyrst, I say, we owght to have in consyderacyon
That Lyberte be lynkyd with the chayne of
countenaunce,

22 *wyt* (v) know   25 *dysseyved* deceived   26 *harde* heard
30 *maskyd* enmeshed   33 *knackynge ernyst* downright earnest
35 *mew* pen (for hawks)   36 *cue* ⅛ penny   42 *advertysment* attention
44, 47 *countenaunce* restraint

218

Lyberte to let from all maner offence:
For Lyberte at large is lothe to be stoppyd,
But with countenaunce your corage must be croppyd.

LYB: Then thus to you —
FEL: Nay, suffer me yet ferther to say,
And peradventure I shall content your mynde.
Lyberte, I wote well, forbere no man there may;   50
It is so swete in all maner of kynde.
How be it Lyberte makyth many a man blynde;
By Lyberte is done many a great excesse;
Lyberte at large wyll oft wax reklesse.

Perceyve ye this parcell?
LYB: Ye, syr, passyng wel.
But and you wolde me permyt
To shewe parte of my wyt,
Somwhat I coulde enferre
Your consayte to debarre,   60
Under supportacyon
Of pacyent tolleracyon.
FEL: God forbyd ye sholde be let
Your reasons forth to fet;
Wherfore at Lyberte,
Say what ye wyll to me.

LYB: Brefly to touche of my purpose the effecte:
Lyberte is laudable and pryvylegyd from lawe;
Judycyall rygoure shall not me correcte —
FEL: Softe, my frende; herein your reason is but rawe.   70
LYB: Yet suffer me to say the surpluse of my sawe.
What wote ye where upon I wyll conclude?
I say there is no Welthe where as Lyberte is subdude.

45, 63 *let* prevent(ed)   61 *supportacyon* help   67 *effecte* substance
71 *sawe* wise saying

I trowe ye can not say nay moche to this:
To lyve under lawe it is captyvyte;
Where Drede ledyth the daunce, there is no joy nor
    blysse.
Or howe can you prove that there is Felycyte,
And you have not your owne fre Lyberte
To sporte at your pleasure, to ryn, and to ryde?
Where Lyberte is absent, set welthe asyde.   80

   Hic intrat Measure.

MEASURE: Cryst you assyste in your altrycacyon!
FEL: Why, have you harde of our dysputacyon?
MEAS: I parceyve well howe eche of you doth reason.
LYB: Mayster Measure, you be come in good season.
MEAS: And it is wonder that your wylde insolence
    Can be content with Measure presence.

FEL: Wolde it please you then –
LYB: Us to informe and ken –
MEAS: A, ye be wonders men!
    Your langage is lyke the penne   90
    Of hym that wryteth to fast.
FEL: Syr, yf any worde have past
    Me, other fyrst or last,
    To you I arecte it, and cast

    Therof the reformacyon.
LYB: And I of the same facyon.
    Howe be it, by protestacyon

    Dyspleasure that you none take,
    Some reason we must make.
MEAS: That wyll not I forsake,   100

   79 *ryn* run 81 *altrycacyon* argument 88 *ken* instruct 94 *arecte* refer

So it in measure be.
Come of therfore, let se
Shall I begynne or ye?

FEL: Nay, ye shall begynne, by my wyll.
LYB: It is reason and skyll
We your pleasure fulfyll.

MEAS: Then ye must bothe consent
You to holde content
With myne argument,

And I muste you requyre   110
Me pacyently to here.
FEL: Yes, syr, with ryght good chere.
LYB: With all my herte intere.

MEAS: Oracius to recorde in his volumys olde
With every condycyon Measure must be so[u]ght.
Welthe without Measure wolde bere hymselfe to bolde;
Lyberte without Measure prove a thynge of nought.
I ponder by nomber; by Measure all thynge is wrought,
As at the fyrst orygynall, by godly opynyon;
Whych provyth well that Measure shold have
    domynyon.   120

Where Measure is mayster, Plenty dothe none offence;
Where Measure lackyth, all thynge dysorderyd is;
Where Measure is absent, Ryot kepeth resydence;
Where Measure is ruler, there is nothynge amysse.
Measure is treasure; howe say ye, is it not this?
FEL: Yes, questyonlesse, in myne opynyon:
Measure is worthy to have domynyon.

   102 *of* off   105 *skyll* cause   113 *intere* whole

LYB: Unto that same I am ryght well agrede,
  So that Lyberte be not lefte behynde.
MEAS: Ye, Lyberte with Measure nede never drede.   130
LYB: What, Lyberte to Measure then wolde ye bynde?
MEAS: What ellys? For otherwyse it were agaynst kynde.
  If Lyberte sholde lepe and renne where he lyst
  It were no vertue, it were a thynge unblyst.

  It were a myschefe, yf Lyberte lacked a reyne
  Where with to rule hym with the wrythyng of a rest.
  All trebyllys and tenours be rulyd by a meyne.
  Lyberte without Measure is acountyd for a beste;
  There is no surfet where Measure rulyth the feste;
  There is no excesse where Measure hath his helthe;   140
  Measure contynwyth Prosperyte and Welthe.

FEL: Unto your rule I wyll annex my mynde.
LYB: So wolde I, but I wolde be lothe
  That wonte was to be formyst now to come behynde.
  It were a shame, to God I make an othe,
  Without I myght cut it out of the brode clothe,
  As I was wonte ever, at my fre wyll.
MEAS: But have ye not herde say that wyll is no skyll?

  Take sad dyreccyon, and leve this wantonnesse.
LYB: It i[s] no maystery.
FEL: Tushe, let Measure procede,   150
  And after his mynde herdely your selfe adresse.
  For without Measure, poverte and nede
  Wyll crepe upon us, and us to Myschefe lede:
  For Myschefe wyll mayster us yf Measure us forsake.
LYB: Well, I am content your wayes to take.

  132 *kynde* nature 133 *lepe* leap *renne* run 134 *unblyst* accursed
  136 *wrythyng* twisting · 137 *trebyllys* trebles *meyne* middle voice
  138 *beste* beast 150 *maystery* clever device 151 *herdely* firmly

MEAS: Surely I am joyous that ye be myndyd thus.
   Magnyfycence to mayntayne, your promosyon shalbe.
FEL: So in his harte he may be glad of us.
LYB: There is no prynce but he hath nede of us thre:
   Welthe, with Measure, and plesaunt Lyberte.   160
MEAS: Nowe pleasyth you a lytell whyle to stande;
   Me semeth Magnyfycence is comynge here at hande.

Hic intrat Magnyfycence.

MAGNYFYCENCE: To assure you of my noble porte and
      fame,
   Who lyst to knowe, Magnyfycence I hyght.
   But Measure, my frende, what hyght this mannys
      name?
MEAS: Syr, though ye be a noble prynce of myght,
   Yet in this man you must set your delyght.
   And, syr, this other mannys name is Lyberte.
MAG: Welcome, frendys, ye are bothe unto me.

But nowe let me knowe of your conversacyon.   170
FEL: Pleasyth your grace, Felycyte they me call.
LYB: And I am Lyberte, made of in every nacyon.
MAG: Convenyent persons for any prynce ryall.
   Welthe with Lyberte, with me bothe dwell ye shall,
   To the gydynge of my Measure you bothe
      commyttynge;
   That Measure be mayster us semeth it is syttynge.

MEAS: Where as ye have, syr, to me them assygned,
   Suche order I trust with them for to take,

---

157 *promosyon* advancement   163 *porte* reputation   164 *hyght* am called
173 *Convenyent* suitable   *ryall* royal   176 *syttynge* suitable

So that Welthe with Measure shalbe conbyned,
And Lyberte his large with Measure shall make.   180
FEL: Your ordenaunce, syr, I wyll not forsake.
LYB: And I my selfe hooly to you wyll inclyne.
MAG: Then may I say that ye be servauntys myne.

For by Measure I warne you we thynke to be gydyd;
Wherin it is necessary my pleasure you knowe:
Measure and I wyll never be devydyd,
For no dyscorde that any man can sawe.
For Measure is a meane, nother to hy nor to lawe,
In whose attemperaunce I have suche delyght,
That Measure shall never departe from my syght.   190

FEL: Laudable your consayte is to be acountyd,
    For Welthe without Measure sodenly wyll slyde.
LYB: As your grace full nobly hath recountyd,
    Measure with Noblenesse sholde be alyde.
MAG: Then, Lyberte, se that Measure be your gyde,
    For I wyll use you by his advertysment.
FEL: Then shall you have with you Prosperyte resydent.

MEAS: I trowe good fortune hath annexyd us together,
    To se howe greable we are of one mynde.
    There is no flaterer nor losyll so lyther,   200
    This lynkyd chayne of love that can unbynde.
    Nowe that ye have me chefe ruler assyngned,
    I wyll endevour me to order every thynge
    Your noblenesse and honour consernynge.

179 *conbyned* combined   182 *hooly* wholly   187 *sawe* (v) sow
188 *lawe* low   189 *attemperaunce* moderation   191 *consayte* idea
194 *alyde* allied   196 *advertysment* advice   200 *losyll* lout
lyther wicked

LYB: In joy and myrthe your mynde shalbe inlargyd,
And not embracyd with pusyllanymyte.
But plenarly all thought from you must be
   dyschargyd,
If ye be lyst to lyve after your fre Lyberte.
All delectacyons aquayntyd is with me;
By me all persons worke what they lyste.   210

MEAS: Hem, syr, yet beware of 'Had I wyste!'
Lyberte in some cause becomyth a gentyll mynde,
Bycause course of Measure, yf I be in the way.
Who countyd without me is caste to fer behynde
Of his rekenynge, as evydently we may
Se at our eye the worlde day by day.
For defaute of Measure all thynge dothe excede.
FEL: All that ye say is as trewe as the Crede.

For how be it Lyberte to Welthe is convenyent,
And from Felycyte may not be forborne,   220
Yet Measure hath ben so longe from us absent,
That all men laugh at Lyberte to scorne.
Welth and wyt, I say, be so threde bare worne,
That all is without Measure and fer beyonde the mone.
MAG: Then noblenesse, I se well, is almoste undone,

But yf therof the soner amendys be made;
For dowtlesse I parceyve my Magnyfycence
Without Measure lyghtly may fade,
Of to moche Lyberte under the offence.
Wherfore, Measure, take Lyberte with you hence,   230
And rule hym after the rule of your scole.
LYB: What, syr, wolde ye make me a poppynge fole?

206 *pusyllanymyte* cowardice   207 *plenarly* fully
209 *delectacyons* pleasures   212 *becomyth* befits   214 *countyd* calculates
fer far   224 *mone* moon   226 *But yf* unless   232 *poppynge* blabbing
fole fool

MEAS: Why, were not your selfe agreed to the same,
    And now wolde ye swarve from your owne
    ordynaunce?
LYB: I wolde be rulyd and I myght for shame.
FEL: A, ye make me laughe at your inconstaunce.
MAG: Syr, without any longer delyaunce,
    Take Lyberte to rule, and folowe myne entent.
MEAS: It shalbe done at your commaundement.

> *Itaque Measure exeat locum cum Libertate, et*
> *maneat Magnyfycence cum Felicitate.*

MAG: It is a wanton thynge, this Lyberte.   240
    Perceyve you not howe lothe he was to abyde
    The rule of Measure, notwithstandynge we
    Have deputyd Measure hym to gyde?
    By Measure eche thynge duly is tryde.
    Thynke you not thus, my frende Felycyte?
FEL: God forbede that it other wyse sholde be!

MAG: Ye coulde not ellys, I wote, with me endure
FEL: Endure? No, God wote, it were great payne.
    But yf I were orderyd by just Measure,
    It were not possyble me longe to retayne.   250

> *Hic intrat Fansy.*

FANSY: Tusche, holde your pece, your langage is vayne.
    Please it your grace to take no dysdayne
    To shewe you playnly the trouth as I thynke.
MAG: Here is none forsyth whether you flete or synke.

    237 *delyaunce* delay   253 *trouth* truth   254 *flete* float

FEL: From whens come you, syr, that no man lokyd
       after?

MAG: Or who made you so bolde to interrupe my tale?

FAN: Nowe, *benedicite*, ye wene I were some hafter,
   Or ellys some jangelynge Jacke of the Vale;
   Ye wene that I am dronken bycause I loke pale.

MAG: Me semeth that ye have dronken more than ye have
      bled.   260

FAN: Yet amonge noble men I was brought up and bred.

FEL: Nowe leve this jangelynge and to us expounde
   Why that ye sayd our langage was in vayne.

FAN: Mary, upon trouth my reason I grounde,
   That without Largesse Noblenesse can not rayne;
   And that I sayd ones yet I say agayne,
   I say without Largesse Worshyp hath no place,
   For Largesse is a purchaser of pardon and of grace.

MAG: Nowe, I beseche the, tell me what is thy name?

FAN: Largesse, that all lordes should love, syr, I hyght.   270

FEL: But hyght you Largesse, encrease of noble fame?

FAN: Ye, syr, undoubted.

FEL: Then of very ryght
   With Magnyfycence, this noble prynce of myght,
   Sholde be your dwellynge, in my consyderacyon.

MAG: Yet we wyll therin take good delyberacyon.

FAN: As in that, I wyll not be agaynst your pleasure.

FEL: Syr, hardely remembre what may your name
      avaunce.

MAG: Largesse is laudable, so it in measure be.

FAN: Largesse is he that all prynces doth avaunce:
   I reporte me herein to Kynge Lewes of Fraunce.   280

    255 *lokyd after* expected   257 *wene* think   *hafter* sharper
    258 *jangelynge* chattering   280 *reporte* refer

FEL: Why have ye hym named, and all other refused?
FAN: For, syth he dyed, Largesse was lytell used.

Plucke up your mynde, syr; what ayle you to muse?
Have ye not Welthe here at your wyll?
It is but a maddynge, these wayes that ye use,
What avayleth lordshyp, yourselfe for to kyll
With care and with thought howe Jacke shall have Gyl?
MAG: What! I have aspyed ye are a carles page.
FAN: By God, syr, ye se but fewe wyse men of myne age.

But Covetyse hath blowen you so full of wynde,   290
That *colyca passyo* hath gropyd you by the guttys.
FEL: In fayth, broder Largesse, you have a mery mynde.
FAN: In fayth, I set not by the worlde two Dauncaster cuttys.
MAG: Ye wante but a wylde flyeng bolte to shote at the
        buttes.
Though Largesse ye hyght, your langage is to large;
For whiche ende goth forwarde ye take lytell charge.

FEL: Let se this checke yf ye voyde canne.
FAN: In faythe, els had I gone to longe to scole
But yf I coulde knowe a gose from a swanne.
MAG: Wel, wyse men may ete the fysshe, when ye shal
        draw the pole.   300
FAN: In fayth, I wyll not say that ye shall prove a fole,
But ofte tymes have I sene wyse men do mad dedys.
MAG: Go shake the, dogge, hay, syth ye wyll nedys!

You are nothynge mete with us for to dwell,
That with your lorde and mayster so pertly can prate!
Gete you hens, I say, by my counsell.

285 *maddynge* madness   288 *carles* careless, trivial   291 *gropyd* seized
297 *checke* taunt   *voyde* escape

228

I wyll not use you to play with me checke mate.

FAN: Syr, yf I have offended your noble estate,
I trow I have brought you suche wrytynge of recorde
That I shall have you agayne my good lorde.　　　　310

To you recommendeth Sad Cyrcumspeccyon,
And sendeth you this wrytynge closed under sele.
MAG: This wrytynge is welcome with harty affeccyon!
Why kepte you it thus longe? Howe dothe he? Wele?
FAN: Syr, thanked be God, he hath his hele.
MAG: Welthe, gete you home and commaunde me to
　　　　Mesure;
Byd hym take good hede to you, my synguler tresure.

FEL: Is there ony thynge elles your grace wyll
　　　　commaunde me?
MAG: Nothynge, but fare you well tyll sone,
And that he take good kepe to Lyberte.　　　　320
FEL: Your pleasure, syr, shortely shall be done.
MAG: I shall come to you myselfe, I trowe, this after-
　　　　none.
I pray you, Larges, here to remayne,
Whylest I knowe what this letter dothe contayne.

> [*Exit Felycyte.*]
> *Hic faciat tanquam legeret litteras tacite. Interim*
> *superveniat cantando Counterfet Countenaunce*
> *suspenso gradu, qui viso Magnyfycence sens[i]m*
> *retrocedat; a[t] tempus post pusillum rursum*
> *accedat Counterfet Countenaunce prospectando et*
> *vocitando a longe; et Fansy animat silentium cum*
> *manu.*

315 *hele* health　　316 *commaunde* commend　　318 *commaunde* command

COUNTERFET COUNTENAUNCE: What, Fansy! Fansy!

MAG: Who is that that thus dyd cry?
　Me thought he called Fansy.

FAN: It was a Flemynge hyght Hansy.

MAG: Me thought he called Fansy me behynde.

FAN: Nay, syr, it was nothynge but your mynde.　　　　330
　But nowe, syr, as touchynge this letter –

MAG: I shall loke in it at leasure better;
　And surely ye are to hym beholde,
　And for his sake ryght gladly I wolde
　Do what I coude to do you good.

FAN: I pray God kepe you in that mood!

MAG: This letter was wryten ferre hence.

FAN: By lakyn, syr, it hathe cost me pence
　And grotes many one or I came to your presence.

MAG: Where was it delyvered you? Shewe unto me.　　　340

FAN: By God, syr, beyond the se.

MAG: At what place, nowe, as you gesse?

FAN: By my trouthe, syr, at Pountesse.
　This wrytynge was taken me there,
　But never was I in gretter fere.

MAG: Howe so?

FAN:　　　　　By God, at the see syde
　Had I not opened my purse wyde,
　I trowe, by Our Lady, I had ben slayne,
　Or elles I had lost myne eres twayne.

[MAG:] By your soth?

[FAN:]　　　　　Ye, and there is suche a wache　　　　350
　That no man can scape but they hym cache.
　They bare me in hande that I was a spye;
　And another bade put out myne eye;
　Another wolde myne eye were blerde;
　Another bade shave halfe my berde;
　And boyes to the pylery gan me plucke,
　And wolde have made me Freer Tucke,
　To preche out of the pylery hole

338 *By lakyn* By Our Lady　345 *fere* fear　350 *wache* guard
354 *blerde* blinded

230

Without an antetyme or a stole;
And some bade sere hym with a marke: 360
To gete me fro them I had moche warke.

MAG: Mary, syr, ye were afrayde.

FAN: By my trouthe, had I not payde and prayde,
And made largesse, as I hyght,
I had not ben here with you this nyght.
But surely largesse saved my lyfe;
For Largesse stynteth all maner of stryfe.

MAG: It dothe so sure, nowe and than;
But Largesse is not mete for every man.

FAN: No, but for you grete estates   370
Largesse stynteth grete debates;
And he that I came fro to this place
Sayd I was mete for your grace;
And in dede, syr, I here men talke
By the way, as I ryde and walke,
Say howe you excede in noblenesse,
If you had with you Largesse.

MAG: And say they so, in very dede?

FAN: With ye, syr, so God me spede.

MAG: Yet Mesure is a mery mene.   380

FAN: Ye, syr, a blannched almonde is no bene.
Measure is mete for a marchauntes hall,
But Largesse becometh a state ryall.
What, sholde you pynche at a pecke of otes,
Ye wolde sone pynche at a pecke of grotes.
Thus is the talkynge of one and of oder,
As men dare speke it hugger mugger,
'A lorde a negarde, it is a shame':
But Largesse may amende your name.

MAG: In faythe, Largesse, welcome to me.   390

FAN: I pray you, syr, I may so be,
And of my servyce you shall not mysse.

MAG: Togyder we wyll talke more of this.

359 *antetyme* text, theme   367 *stynteth* stops
370, 383 *estates, state* person(s) of rank   383 *becometh* befits
387 *hugger mugger* secretly   388 *negarde* miser, niggard

Let us departe from hens home to my place.
FAN: I folow even after your noble grace.

Hic discedat Magnificens cum Fansy, et intrat
Counterfet Countenaunce.

COUNTERFET C.: What, I say, herke a worde.
FAN: Do away, I say, the devylles torde!
COUNTERFET C.: Ye, but how longe shall I here awayte?
FAN: By Goddys body, I come streyte;
  I hate this blunderyng that thou doste make.   400
COUNTERFET C.: Nowe to the devyll I the betake,
  For in fayth ye be well met.

  Fansy hath cachyd in a flye net
  This noble man Magnyfycence,
  Of Largesse under the pretence.
  They have made me here to put the stone,
  But nowe wyll I, that they be gone,
  In bastarde ryme, after the dogrell gyse,
  Tell you where-of my name dothe ryse.

  For Counterfet Countenaunce knowen am I;   410
  This worlde is full of my foly.
  I set not by hym a fly
  That can not counterfet a lye,
  Swere, and stare, and byde therby,
  And countenaunce it clenly,
  And defende it manerly.

  A knave wyll counterfet nowe a knyght,
  A lurdayne lyke a lorde to fyght,
  A mynstrell lyke a man of myght,

  401 *betake* send   416 *manerly* in a courtly way   418 *lurdayne* vagabond

A tappster lyke a lady bryght: 420
Thus make I them wyth thryft to fyght;
Thus at the laste I brynge hym ryght
To Tyburne where they hange on hyght.

To counterfet I can by praty wayes:
Of nyghtys to occupy counterfet kayes,
Clenly to counterfet newe arayes,
Counterfet eyrnest by way of playes.
Thus am I occupyed at all assayes.
What so ever I do, all men me prayse,
And mekyll am I made of nowe-adays.   430

Counterfet maters in the lawe of the lande,
Wyth golde and grotes they grese my hande,
In stede of ryght that wronge may stande;
And counterfet fredome that is bounde.
I counterfet suger that is but [sa]nde;
Counterfet capytaynes by me are mande;
Of all lewdnesse I kyndell the brande.

Counterfet kyndnesse, and thynke dyscayte;
Counterfet letters by the way of sleyght;
Subtelly usynge counterfet weyght;   440
Counterfet langage, *fayty bone geyte.*
Counterfetynge is a proper bayte;
A counte to counterfet in a resayte,
To counterfet well is a good consayte.

Counterfet maydenhode may well be borne,
But counterfet coynes is laughynge to scorne:

420 *tappster* barmaid   425 *kayes* keys   426 *arayes* clothing
428 *assayes* matters   430 *mekyll* much   436 *mande* given followers
438 *dyscayte* deceit   439 *sleyght* trick, stratagem   442 *bayte* temptation

It is evyll patchynge of that is torne.
Whan the noppe is rughe it wolde be shorne.
Counterfet haltynge without a thorne;
Yet counterfet chafer is but evyll corne.   450
All thynge is worse whan it is worne.

What, wolde ye wyves counterfet
The courtly gyse of the newe jet?
An olde barne wolde be underset;
It is moche worthe that is ferre fet.
What, wanton, wanton, nowe well ymet!
What, Margery Mylke Ducke, mermoset!
It wolde be masked in my net!

It wolde be nyce, thoughe I say nay.
By crede, it wolde have fresshe aray,   460
'And therfore shall my husbande pay.'
To counterfet she wyll assay
All the newe gyse, fresshe and gaye,
And be as praty as she may,
And jet it joly as a jay.

Counterfet prechynge, and byleve the contrary;
Counterfet conscyence, pevysshe pope holy;
Counterfet sadnesse, with delynge full madly;
Counterfet holynes is called ypocrysy;
Counterfet reason is not worth a flye;   470
Counterfet wysdome and workes of Foly;
Counterfet Countenaunce every man dothe occupy.

Counterfet worshyp outwarde men may se;
Ryches rydeth, at home is Poverte;

448 *noppe* nap   449 *haltynge* limping   450 *chafer* merchandise
453 *jet* fashion   454 *underset* supported   458 *masked* enmeshed
459 *nyce* extravagant

Counterfet pleasure is borne out by me,
Coll wolde go clenly and it wyll not be
And Annot wolde be nyce, and laughes 'tehe, wehe.'
Your Cou[n]terfet Countenaunce is all of nysyte,
A plummed partrydge all redy to flye.

A knokylbonyarde wyll counterfet a clarke;   480
He wolde trotte gentylly, but he is to starke;
At his cloked counterfetynge dogges dothe barke.
A carter a courtyer, it is a worthy warke,
That with his whyp his mares was wonte to yarke;
A custrell to dryve the devyll out of the derke,
A counterfet courtyer with a knaves marke.

To counterfet this freers have lerned me.
This nonnes nowe and then, and it myght be,
Wolde take in the way of co[u]nterfet charyte,
The grace of God under *benedicite*.   490
To counterfet thyr counsell they gyve me a fee.
Chanons can not counterfet but upon thre;
Monkys may not for drede that men sholde them se.

Hic ingrediatur Fansy properanter cum Crafty
Conveyaunce cum famine multo adinvicem
garrulantes; tandem viso Counterfet Countenaunce
dicat Crafty Conveyaunce

CRAFTY C.: What! Counterfet Countenaunce!
COUNTERFET C.: What! Crafty Conveyaunce!
FAN: What the devyll! are ye two of aquayntaunce?
   God gyve you a very myschaunce!

476 *clenly* innocently   478 *nysyte* pretended modesty
480 *knokylbonyarde* clumsy fellow   481 *starke* clumsy, stiff
484 *yarke* beat   485 *custrell* base fellow, groom   *derke* dark

CRAFTY C.: Yes, yes, syr, he and I have met.

COUNTERFET C.: We have bene togyder bothe erly and
    late.

But Fa[n]sy, my frende, where have ye bene so longe?   500

FAN: By God, I have bene about a praty pronge –

Crafty Conveyaunce, I should say, and I.

CRAFTY C.: By God, we have made Magnyfycence to ete
    a flye.

COUNTERFET C.: Howe could ye do that and [I] was
    away?

FAN: By God, man, bothe his pagent and thyne he can
    play.

COUNTERFET C.: Say trouth?

CRAFTY C.:   Yes, yes, by lakyn, I shall the
    warent,

As longe as I lyve, thou haste an heyre parent.

FAN: Yet have we pyckyd out a rome for the.

COUNTERFET C.: Why, shall we dwell togyder all thre?

CRAFTY C.: Why, man, it were to great a wonder   510

That we thre galauntes sholde be longe asonder.

COUNTERFET C.: For cockys harte, gyve me thy hande.

FAN: By the masse, for ye are able to dystroy an hole
    lande.

CRAFTY C.: By God, yet it muste begynne moche of the.

FAN: Who that is ruled by us, it shalbe longe or he thee.

COUNTERFET C.: But I say, kepest thou the olde name
    styll that thou had?

CRAFTY C.: Why wenys t thou, horson, that I were so
    mad?

FAN: Nay, nay – he hath chaunged his, and I have
    chaunged myne.

COUNTERFET C.: Nowe what is his name, and what is
    thyne?

FAN: In faythe, Largesse I hyght,   520

And I am made a knyght.

COUNTERFET C.: A rebellyon agaynst Nature –

So large a man, and so lytell of stature!

    501 *pronge* device   505 *pagent* part   515 *thee* thrive

But, syr, howe counterfetyd ye?

[CRAFTY C.:] Sure Surveyaunce I named me.

[COUNTERFET C.:] Surveyaunce! Where ye survey
    Thryfte hathe lost her cofer kay.

FAN: But is it not well? Howe thynkest thou?

COUNTERFET C.: Yes, syr, I gyve God avowe,
    Myself coude not counterfet it better.   530
    But what became of the letter
    That I counterfeyted you underneth a shrowde?

FAN: By the masse, odly well alowde.

CRAFTY C.: By God, had not I it convayed
    Yet Fansy had ben dysceyved.

COUNTERFET C.: I wote thou arte false ynoughe for one.

FAN: By my trouthe, we had ben gone!
    And yet, in fayth, man, we lacked the,
    For to speke with Lyberte.

COUNTERFET C.: What, is Largesse without Lyberte?   540

CRAFTY C.: By Mesure mastered yet is he.

COUNTERFET C.: What, is your conveyaunce no better?

FAN: In faythe, Mesure is lyke a tetter
    That overgroweth a mannes face,
    So he ruleth over all our place.

CRAFTY C.: Nowe therfore, whylest we are togyder –
    Counterfet Countenaunce, nay, come hyder –
    I say, whylest we are togyder in same –

COUNTERFET C.: Tushe, a strawe! It is a shame
    That we can no better than so!   550

FAN: We wyll remedy it, man, or we go.
    For lyke as mustarde is sharpe of taste,
    Ryght so a sharpe fansy must be founde,
    Wherwith Mesure to confounde.

CRAFTY C.: Can you a remedy for a tysyke,
    That sheweth yourselfe thus spedde in physyke?

COUNTERFET C.: It is a gentyll reason of a rake.

FAN: For all these japes yet that we make –

527 *cofer kay* key of treasure chest   533 *alowde* received
543 *tetter* skin disease   555 *tysyke* phthisis, consumption
556 *spedde* learned, versed

CRAFTY C.: Your fansy maketh myne elbowe to ake.
FAN: Let se, fynde you a better way.   560
COUNTERFET C.: Take no dyspleasure of that we say.
CRAFTY C.: Nay, and you be angry and overwharte
  A man may beshrowe your angry harte.
FAN: Tushe, a strawe! I thought none yll.
COUNTERFET C.: What, shall we jangle thus all the day
      styll?
CRAFTY C.: Nay, let us our heddes togyder cast.
FAN: Ye, and se howe it may be compast
  That Mesure were cast out of the dores.
COUNTERFET C.: Alasse, where is my botes and my
      spores?
CRAFTY C.: In all this hast whether wyll ye ryde?   570
COUNTERFET C.: I trowe it shall not nede to abyde.
  Cockes woundes! Se, syrs, se, se!

*Hic ingrediatur Cloked Colusyon cum elato aspectu,
deorsum et sursum ambulando.*

FAN: Cockes armes, what is he?
CRAFTY C.: By cockes harte, he loketh hye.
  He hawketh, me thynke, for a butterflye.
COUNTERFET C.: Nowe, by cockes harte, well abyden.
  For had you not come, I had ryden.
CLOKED COL: Thy wordes be but wynde, never they have
      no wayght.
  Thou hast made me play the jurde hayte.
COUNTERFET C.: And yf ye knewe howe I have mused,   580
  I am sure ye wolde have me excused.
CLOKED COL.: I say com hyder. What are these twayne?
COUNTERFET C.: By God, syr, this is Fansy Small-
      Brayne;
  And Crafty Convayaunce, knowe you not hym?

562 *overwharte* irritable, wrangling   565 *jangle* chatter
567 *compast* brought about

CLOKED COL: 'Knowe hym, syr?' quod he. Yes by
   Saynt Sym!
 Here is a leysshe of ratches to renne an hare!
 Woo is that purse that ye shall share.
FAN: What call ye him, this?
CRAFTY C.: I trowe that he is –
COUNTERFET C.: Tushe! Holde your pece.   590
 Se you not howe they prece
 For to knowe your name?
CLOKED COL: Knowe they not me? They are to blame.
 Knowe ye not me, syrs?
FAN: No, in dede.
CRAFTY C.: Abyde – lette me se – take better hede!
 Cockes harte! It is Cloked Colusyon!
CLOKED COL: A, syr, I pray God gyve you confusyon!
FAN: Cockes armes, is that your name?
COUNTERFET C.: Ye, by the masse, this is even the same,
 That all this matter must under grope.   600
CRAFTY C.: What is this that he wereth? A cope?
CLOKED COL: Cappe, syr. I say you be to bolde.
FAN: Se howe he is wrapped for the colde.
 Is it not a vestment?
CLOKED COL: A, ye wante a rope.
COUNTERFET C.: Tushe, it is Syr John Double-Cloke!
FAN: Syr, and yf ye wolde not be wrothe –
CLOKED COL: What sayst?
FAN: Here was to lytell clothe.
CLOKED COL: A, Fansy, Fansy, God sende the brayne!
FAN: Ye, for your wyt is cloked for the rayne.
CRAFTY C.: Nay, lette us not clatter thus styll.   610
CLOKED COL: Tell me, syrs, what is your wyll?
COUNTERFET C.: Syr, it is so that these twayne
 With Magnyfycence in housholde do remayne;
 And there they wolde ha[v]e me to dwell.
 But I wyll be ruled after your counsell.
FAN: Mary, so wyll we also.

  586 *leysshe* leash (of three) 591 *prece* (v) press
  600 *under grope* grasp 610 *clatter* argue

CLOKED COL: But tell me where aboute ye go.

COUNTERFET C.: By God, we wolde gete us all thyder,
Spell the remenaunt, and do togyder.

CLOKED COL: Hath Magnyfycence ony tresure? 620

CRAFTY C.: Ye, but he spendeth it all in Mesure.

CLOKED COL: Why, dwelleth Mesure where ye two
dwell?
In faythe, he were better to dwell in hell.

FAN: Yet where we wonne, nowe there wonneth he.

CLOKED COL: And have you not amonge you Lyberte?

COUNTERFET C.: Ye, but he is a captyvyte.

CLOKED COL: What the devyll! Howe may that be?

COUNTERFET C.: I can not tell you; why aske you me?
Aske these two that there dothe dwell.

[CLOKED COL:] Syr, the playnesse you tell me. 630

[CRAFTY C.:] There dwelleth a mayster men calleth
Mesure —

FAN: Ye, and he hath rule of all his tresure.

CRAFTY C.: Nay, eyther let me tell, or elles tell ye.

FAN: I care not I; tell on for me.

COUNTERFET C.: I pray God let you never to thee!

CLOKED COL: What the devyll ayleth you? Can you not
agree?

CRAFTY C.: I wyll passe over the cyrcumstaunce
And shortly shewe you the hole substaunce.
Fansy and I, we twayne,
With Magnyfycence in housholde do remay[n]e; 640
And counterfeted our names we have,
Craftely all thynges upryght to save:
His name Largesse, Surveyaunce myne.
Magnyfycence to us begynneth to enclyne,
Counterfet Countenaunce to have also,
And wolde that we sholde for hym go.

COUNTERFET C.: But shall I have myne olde name styll?

CRAFTY C.: Pease, I have not yet sayd what I wyll.

FAN: Here is a pystell of a postyke!

619 *Spell* expel 624 *wonne, wonneth* dwell(s) 626 *a* in
635 *thee* (v) thrive

CLOKED COL: Tusshe, fonnysshe Fansy, thou arte
       frantyke!   650
  Tell on, syr; howe then?
CRAFTY C.: Mary, syr, he told us, when
  We had hym founde, we sholde hym brynge,
  And that we fayled not for nothynge.
CLOKED COL: All this ye may easely brynge aboute.
FAN: Mary, the better and Mesure were out.
CLOKED COL: Why, can ye not put out that foule freke?
CRAFTY C.: No; in every corner he wyll peke,
  So that we have no Lyberte;
  Nor no man in courte, but he,   660
  For Lyberte he hath in gydyng.
COUNTERFET C.: In fayth, and without Lyberte there is
       no bydyng.
FAN: In fayth, and Lybertyes rome is there but small.
CLOKED COL: Hem! That lyke I nothynge at all.
[CRAFTY C.:] But, Counterfet Countenaunce, go we
       togyder,
  All thre, I say.
COUNTERFET C.: Shall I go? Whyder?
[CRAFTY C.:] To Magnyfycence with us twayne,
  And in his servyce the to retayne.
COUNTERFET C.: But then, syr, what shall I hyght?
CRAFTY C.: Ye and I talkyd therof to nyght.   670
FAN: Ye, my Fansy was out of owle flyght,
  For it is out of my mynde quyght.
CRAFTY C.: And nowe it cometh to my remembraunce:
  Syr, ye shall hyght Good Demeynaunce.
COUNTERFET C.: By the armes of Calys, well conceyved!
CRAFTY C.: When we have hym thyder convayed,
  What and I frame suche a slyght
  That Fansy with his fonde consayte
  Put Magnyfycence in suche a madnesse
  That he shall have you in the stede of Sadnesse,   680
  And Sober Sadnesse shalbe your name?

650 *fonnysshe* foolish   657 *freke* man   658 *peke* peep
677 *slyght* trick

CLOKED COL: By cockys body, here begynneth the game!
  For then shall we so craftely cary
  That Mesure shall not there longe tary.
FAN: For cockys harte, tary whylyst that I come agayne.
CRAFTY C.: We wyll se you shortly, one of us twayne.
COUNTERFET C.: Now let us go, and we shall, then.
CLOKED COL: Nowe let se; quyte you lyke praty men.

> [*Exeunt Fansy, Crafty Conveyaunce, Counterfet*
> *Countenaunce.*]
> *Hic deambulat* [*Cloked Colusyon*].

To passe the tyme and order whyle a man may talke
Of one thynge, and other to occupy the place,   690
Then for the season that I here shall walke
As good to be occupyed as up and downe to trace
And do nothynge. How be it full lytell grace
There cometh and groweth of my comynge,
For Clokyd Colusyon is a perylous thynge.

Double delynge and I be all one;
Craftynge and haftynge contryved is by me.
I can dyssemble, I can bothe laughe and grone;
Playne delynge and I can never agre.
But Dyvysyon, Dyssencyon, Dyrysyon – these thre   700
And I, am counterfet of one mynde and thought,
By the menys of Myschyef to brynge all thynges to
   nought.

And though I be so odyous a geste,
And every man gladly my company wolde refuse,
In faythe, yet am I occupyed with the best;
Full fewe that can themselfe of me excuse.

688 *quyte* acquit   697 *haftynge* tricking

Whan other men laughe than study I and muse,
Devysynge the meanes and wayes that I can,
Howe I may hurte and hynder every man.

Two faces in a hode covertly I bere;   710
Water in the one hande and fyre in the other.
I can fede forth a fole and lede hym by the eyre:
Falshode-in-felowshyp is my sworne brother.
By Cloked Colusyon, I say, and none other,
Comberaunce and trouble in Englande fyrst I began:
From that lorde to that lorde I rode and I ran,

And flatered them with fables fayre before theyr face,
And tolde all the myschyef I coude behynde theyr
    backe,
And made as I had knowen nothynge of the case.
I wolde begyn all myschyef, but I wolde bere no lacke. 720
Thus can I lerne you, syrs, to bere the devyls sacke;
And yet, I trowe, some of you be better sped than I
Frendshyp to fayne and thynke full lytherly.

Paynte to a purpose good countenaunce I can,
And craftely can I grope howe every man is mynded.
My purpose is to spy and to poynte every man;
My tonge is with favell forked and tyned.
By Cloked Colusyon thus many one is begyled.
Eche man to hynder I gape and gaspe.
My speche is all pleasure, but I stynge lyke a waspe.   730

I am never glad but whan I may do yll,
And never am I sory but whan that I se
I can not myne appetyte accomplysshe and fulfyll

712 *eyre* ear   715 *Comberaunce* distress   720 *lacke* blame
723 *fayne* pretend   *lytherly* wickedly   727 *tyned* pronged

In hynderaunce of Welthe and Prosperyte.
I laughe at all Shrewdenes, and lye at Lyberte.
I muster, I medle amonge these grete estates;
I sowe sedycyous sedes of dyscorde and debates.

To flater and to flery is all my pretence
Amonge all suche persones as I well understonde
Be lyght of byleve and hasty of credence.   740
I make them to startyll and sparkyll lyke a bronde.
I move them, I mase them, I make them so fonde,
That they wyll here no man but the fyrst tale;
And so by these meanes I brewe moche bale.

Hic ingrediatur Courtly Abusyon cantando.

COURTLY AB: Huffa, huffa taunderum, taunderum tayne,
      huffa, huffa!
CLOKED COL: This was properly prated, syrs. What sayd
      a?
COURTLY AB: Rutty bully joly rutterkyn, heyda!
CLOKED COL: *De que pays este vous?*

Et faciat tanquem ex[u]at beretum ironice.

COURTLY AB: Decke your hofte and cover a lowce.
CLOKED COL: *Say vous chaunter 'Venter tre dawce?'*   750
COURTLY AB: *Wyda, wyda.*
  Howe sayst thou, man? Am not I a joly rutter?
CLOKED COL: Gyve this gentylman rome, syrs, stonde
      utter!
  By God, syr, what nede all this waste?
  What is this, a betell, or a batowe, or a buskyn lacyd?
COURTLY AB: What! Wenyst thou that I knowe the not,
      Clokyd Colusyon?

737 *debates* quarrels   738 *flery* fawn
741 *to startyll* to be startled, disturbed   746 *a* he   752 *rutter* gallant
753 *utter* aside   755 *betell* ?staff   *batowe* ?boot   *buskyn* half boot

CLOKED COL: And wenyst thou that I knowe not the,
cankard Abusyon?

COURTLY AB: Cankard Jacke Hare, loke thou be not
rusty;

For thou shalt well knowe I am nother durty nor dusty.

CLOKED COL: Dusty! Nay, syr, ye be all of the lusty.   760

Howe be it, of scape thryfte your clokes smelleth musty.

But whether art thou walkynge, in fayth unfaynyd?

COURTLY AB: Mary, with Magnyfycence I wolde be
retaynyd.

CLOKED COL: By the masse, for the cowrte thou art a
mete man;

Thy slyppers they swap it, yet thou fotys it lyke a
swanne.

COURTLY AB: Ye, so I can devyse my gere after the
cowrtly maner.

CLOKED COL: So thou art personable to bere a prynces
baner.

By Goddes fote, and I dare well fyght, for I wyll not
start.

COURTLY AB: Nay, thou art a man good inough but for
thy false hart.

CLOKED COL: Well, and I be a coward, ther is mo than I.   770

COURTLY AB: Ye, in faythe, a bolde man and a hardy.

CLOKED COL: A bolde man in a bole of newe ale in
cornys.

COURTLY AB: Wyll ye se this gentylman is all in his
skornys?

CLOKED COL: But are ye not avysed to dwell where ye
spake?

COURTLY AB: I am of fewe wordys; I love not to barke.

Beryst thou any rome? Or cannyst thou do ought?

Cannyst thou helpe in faver that I myght be brought?

CLOKED COL: I may do somwhat, and more I thynke
shall.

757 *cankard* evil   761 *scape thryfte* spendthrift
772 *in cornys* strong, malty   775 *barke* ?exclaim

*Here cometh in Crafty Conveyaunce poyntyng with his
fynger, and sayth*

[CRAFTY C.:] Hem, Colusyon!
COURTLY AB: Cockys hart! Who is yonde that for the
    dothe call? 780
[CRAFTY COL:] Nay, come at ones, for the armys of the
    dyce!
COURTLY AB: Cockys armys! He hath callyd for the
    twyce.
CLOKED COL: By cockys harte! And call shall agayne;
  To come to me I trowe he shalbe fayne.
COURTLY AB: What, is thy harte pryckyd with such a
    prowde pynne?
CLOKED COL: Tushe, he that hath nede, man, let hym
    rynne.
CRAFTY C.: Nay, come away, man; thou playst the
    Cayser.
[CLOKED COL:] By the masse, thou shalt byde my leyser.
CRAFTY C.: Abyde, syr, quod he? Mary, so I do.
COURTLY AB: He wyll come, man, when he may tende to. 790
CRAFTY C.: What the devyll! Who sent for the?
CLOKED COL: Here he is nowe, man; mayst thou not se?
CRAFTY C.: What the devyll, man, what thou menyst?
  Art thou so angry as thou semyst?
COURTLY AB: What the devyll! Can ye agre no better?
CRAFTY C.: What the devyll! Where had we this joly
    jetter?
CLOKED COL: What sayst thou, man? Why dost thou not
    supplye?
  And desyre me thy good mayster to be?
COURTLY AB: Spekest thou to me?
CLOKED COL: Ye, so I tell the. 800
COURTLY AB: Cockes bones! I ne tell can
  Whiche of you is the better man,
  Or whiche of you can do most.

   796 *jetter* swaggerer   797 *supplye* beg

CRAFTY C.: In fayth, I rule moche of the rost.

CLOKED COL: Rule the roste! Ye, thou woldest,
As skante thou had no nede of me.

CRAFTY C.: Nede? Yes, mary. I say not nay.

COURTLY AB: Cockes ha[r]te! I trowe thou wylte make a
fray.

CRAFTY C.: Nay, in good faythe; it is but the gyse.

CLOKED COL: No; for or we stryke, we wyll be advysed
twyse.   810

COURTLY AB: What the devyll! Use ye not to drawe no
swordes?

CRAFTY C.: No, by my trouthe; but crake grete wordes.

COURTLY AB: Why, is this the gyse nowe adayes?

CLOKED COL: Ye, for surety; ofte peas is taken for
frayes.
But, syr, I wyll have this man with me.

CRAFTY C.: Convey yourselfe fyrst, let se.

CLOKED COL: Well, tarry here tyll I for you sende.

CRAFTY C.: Why, shall he be of your bende?

CLOKED COL: Tary here; wote ye what I say?

COURTLY AB: I waraunt you I wyll not go away.   820

CRAFTY C.: By Saynt Mary, he is a tawle man.

CLOKED COL: Ye, and do ryght good servyce he can.
I knowe in hym no defaute
But that the horson is prowde and hawte.

And so they go out of the place.

COURTLY AB: Nay, purchace ye a pardon for the pose;
For Pryde hath plucked the by the nose
As well as me; I wolde, and I durste —
But nowe I wyll not say the worste.

Courtly Abusyon alone in the place.

809 *gyse* fashion   818 *bende* band   824 *hawte* haughty
825 *pose* cold in the head

COURTLY AB: What nowe? Let se
  Who loketh on me 830
  Well rounde aboute,
  Howe gay and howe stoute
  That I can were
  Courtly my gere.

  My heyre bussheth
  So plesauntly,
  My robe russheth
  So ruttyngly,
  Me seme I flye
  I am so lyght 840
  To daunce delyght.

  Properly drest
  All poynte devyse,
  My persone prest
  Beyonde all syse
  Of the newe gyse,
  To russhe it oute
  In every route.

  Beyonde Measure
  My sleve is wyde, 850
  Al of pleasure
  My hose strayte tyde,
  My buskyn wyde,
  Ryche to beholde,
  Gletterynge in golde.

  Abusyon
  Forsothe I hyght;

837 *russheth* rustles   838 *ruttyngly* ostentatiously   844 *prest* neat
848 *route* assembly

Confusyon
Shall on hym lyght
By day or by nyght   860
That useth me:
He can not thee.

A very fon,
A very asse
Wyll take upon
To compasse
That never was
Abusyd before;
A very pore

That so wyll do,   870
He doth abuse
Hym-selfe to [d]o;
He dothe mysse-use
Eche man take a fe
To crake and prate;
I befoule his pate.

This newe fonne jet
From out of Fraunce
Fyrst I dyd set,
Made purveaunce   880
And suche ordenaunce,
That all men it founde
Through out Englonde.

All this nacyon
I set on fyre;
In my facyon

863 *fon* fool   880 *purveaunce* provision

This theyr desyre
This newe atyre;
This ladyes have
I it them gave.   890

Spare for no coste:
And yet in dede
It is coste loste
Moche more than nede
For to excede
In suche aray.
Howe be it, I say,

A carlys sonne,
Brought up of nought,
Wyth me wyll wonne   900
Whylyst he hath ought.
He wyll have wrought
His gowne so wyde
That he may hyde

His dame and his syre
Within his slyve;
Spende all his hyre
That men hym gyve;
Wherfore I preve
A Tyborne checke   910
Shall breke his necke.

Here cometh in Fansy craynge

[FAN:] Stow, stow!
[COURTLY AB:] All is out of harre

   906 *slyve* sleeve   911 SD *craynge* crying out

And out of trace,
Ay warre and warre
In every place.

But what the devyll art thou
That cryest 'Stow, stow?'
FAN: What! Whom have we here, Jenkyn Joly?
Nowe welcom, by the God holy!   920
COURTLY AB: What! Fansy, my frende! Howe doste thou
        fare?
FAN: By Cryst, as mery as a Marche hare.
COURTLY AB: What the devyll hast thou on thy fyste?
        An owle?
FAN: Nay, it is a farly fowle.
COURTLY AB: Me thynke she frowneth and lokys sowre.
FAN: Torde! Man, it is an hawke of the towre.
She is made for the malarde fat.
COURTLY AB: Methynke she is well becked to catche a rat.
But nowe what tydynges can you tell? Let se.
FAN: Mary, I am come for the.
COURTLY AB: For me?   930
FAN: Ye, for the, so I say.
COURTLY AB: Howe so? Tell me, I the pray.
FAN: Why, harde thou not of the fray
That fell amonge us this same day?
COURTLY AB: No, mary; not yet.
FAN: What the devyll! Never a whyt?
COURTLY AB: No, by the masse; what, sholde I swere?
FAN: In faythe, Lyberte is nowe a lusty spere.
COURTLY AB: Why, under whom was he abydynge?
FAN: Mary, Mesure had hym a whyle in gydynge,   940
Tyll, as the devyll wolde, they fell a chydynge
With Crafty Convayaunce.
COURTLY AB: Ye, dyd they so?
FAN: Ye, by Goddes sacrament; and with other mo.

915 *warre* worse   924 *farly* wonderful   928 *becked* beaked
938 *spere* stripling

COURTLY AB: What! Neded that, in the dyvyls date?

FAN: Yes, yes; he fell with me also at debate.

COURTLY AB: With the also? What! He playeth the state?

FAN: Ye; but I bade hym pyke out of the gate;
  By Goddes body, so dyd I.

COURTLY AB: By the masse, well done and boldely.

FAN: Holde thy pease! Measure shall frome us walke.   950

COURTLY AB: Why, is he crossed than with a chalke?

FAN: Crossed? Ye, checked out of consayte.

COURTLY AB: Howe so?

FAN: By God, by a praty slyght,
  As here after thou shalte knowe more.
  But I must tary here; go thou before.

COURTLY AB: With whom shall I there mete?

FAN: Crafty Conveyaunce standeth in the strete
  Even of purpose for the same.

COURTLY AB: Ye, but what shall I call my name?

FAN: Cockes harte! Tourne the, let me se thyne aray.   960
  Cockes bones! This is all of John de Gay.

COURTLY AB: So I am poynted after my consayte.

FAN: Mary, thou jettes it of hyght.

COURTLY AB: Ye, but of my name let us be wyse.

FAN: Mary, Lusty Pleasure, by myne advyse
  To name thyselfe; come of, it were done.

COURTLY AB: Farewell, my frende.

FAN: Adue tyll sone.

  [*Exit Courtly Abusyon.*]

FAN: Stowe, byrde, stowe, stowe!
  It is best I fede my hawke now.
  There is many evyll faveryd, and thou be foule!   970
  Eche thynge is fayre when it is yonge; all hayle, owle!

Lo, this is
My Fansy, iwys.
Nowe Cryst it blysse!
It is, by Jesse,

  947 *pyke* go   962 *poynted* equipped

A byrde full swete,
For me full mete.
She is furred for the hete
All to the fete;

Her browys bent,   980
Her eyen glent.
Frome Tyne to Trent,
From Stroude to Kent,

A man shall fynde
Many of her kynde,
Howe standeth the wynde,
Before or behynde;

Barbyd lyke a nonne
For burnynge of the sonne;
Her fethers donne.   990
Well faveryd bonne!

Nowe let me se about
In all this rowte
Yf I can fynde owt
So semely a snowte

Amonge this prese —
Even a hole mese —
Pease, man, pease!
I rede we sease.

981 *glent* glittering   989 *For* against   990 *donne* dun coloured
991 *bonne* beauty, bonny   997 *hole* whole   *mese* group

So farly fayre as it lokys!   1000
And her becke so comely crokys!
Her naylys sharpe as tenter hokys!
I have not kept her yet thre wokys,

And howe styll she dothe syt!
Te[w]yt, te[w]yt!
Where is my wyt?
The devyll spede whyt!

That was before I set behynde:
Nowe to curteys, forwith unkynde;
Somtyme to sober, somtyme to sadde,   1010
Somtyme to mery, somtyme to madde;
Somtyme I syt as I were a solempe prowde,
Somtyme I laughe over lowde;
Somtyme I wepe for a gew-gaw,
Somtyme I laughe at waggynge of a straw;
With a pere my love you may wynne,
And ye may lese it for a pynne.
I have a thynge for to say,
And I may tende therto for play.
But, in faythe, I am so occupyed   1020
On this halfe and on every syde
That I wote not where I may rest.
Fyrst to tell you what were best,
Frantyke Fansy Servyce I hyght:
My wyttys be weke, my braynys are lyght,
For it is I that other whyle
Plucke down lede and theke with tyle.
Nowe I wyll this, and nowe I wyll that,
Make a wyndmyll of a mat.
Nowe I wolde — and I wyst what.   1030

1001 *crokys* (v) bends, curves   1003 *wokys* weeks
1009 *to curteys* too courteous, courtly   1012 *solempe* (adj) ceremonious
1014 *gew-gaw* trifle   1016 *pere* pear   1017 *lese* lose   1019 *tende* attend

Where is my cappe? I have lost my hat!
And within an houre after,
Plucke downe an house and set up a rafter.
Hyder and thyder, I wote not whyder;
Do and undo, bothe togyder.
Of a spyndell I wyll make a sparre;
All that I make forthwith I marre.
I blunder, I bluster, I blowe, and I blother,
I make on the one day, and I marre on the other.
Bysy, bysy, and ever bysy,   1040
I daunce up and downe tyll I am dyssy;
I can fynde fantasyes where none is.
I wyll not have it so, I wyll have it this.

*Hic ingrediatur Foly qu[at]iendo crema et faciendo
multum feriendo tabulas et similia.*

FOLY: Maysters, Cryst save everychone!
    What Fansy, arte thou here alone?
FAN: What fonnysshe Foly! I befole thy face.
FOLY: What frantyke Fansy, in a foles case?
    What is this? an owle or a glede?
    By my trouthe, she hathe a grete hede.
FAN: Tusshe, thy lyppes hange in thyne eyen;   1050
    It is a Frenche butterflye.
FOLY: By my trouthe, I trowe well;
    But she is lesse a grete dele
    Than a butterflye of our lande.
FAN: What pylde curre ledest thou in thy hande?
FOLY: A pylde curre!
FAN: Ye, so I tell the, a pylde curre.
FOLY: Yet I solde his skynne to Mackemurre
    In the stede of a budge furre.

1038 *blother* gabble   1046 *befole* ridicule   1047 *case* dress, habit
1048 *glede* kite   1055 *pylde* bald   1058 *budge* lambskin

FAN: What, fleyest thou his skynne every yere?

FOLY: Yes, in faythe, I thanke God I may here.   1060

FAN: What, thou wylte coughe me a dawe for forty pens?

FOLY: Mary, syr, Cokermowthe is a good way hens.

FAN: What, of Cokermowth spake I no worde.

FOLY: By my faythe, syr, the frubyssher hath my sworde.

FAN: A, I trowe ye shall coughe me a fole.

FOLY: In faythe, trouthe ye say, we wente togyder to
    scole.

FAN: Ye, but I can somwhat more of the letter.

FOLY: I wyll not gyve an halfepeny for to chose the
        better.

FAN: But, Broder Foly, I wonder moche of one thynge,
    That thou so hye fro me doth sprynge,   1070
    And I so lytell alway styll.

FOLY: By God, I can tell the, and I wyll:
    Thou art so feble-fantastycall,
    And so braynsyke therwithall,
    And thy wyt wanderynge here and there,
    That thou cannyst not growe out of thy boyes gere.
    And as for me, I take but one folysshe way,
    And therfore I growe more on one day
    Than thou can in yerys seven.

FAN: In faythe, trouth thou sayst nowe, by God of heven!   1080
    For so with fantasyes my wyt dothe flete
    That wysdome and I shall seldome mete.
    Nowe of good felowshyp, let me by thy [d]ogge.

FOLY: Cockys harte, thou lyest; I am no [h]ogge.

FAN: Here is no man that callyd the hogge nor swyne.

FOLY: In faythe, man, my brayne is as good as thyne.

FAN: The devyls torde for thy brayne!

FOLY: By my syers soule, I fele no rayne.

FAN: By the masse, I holde the madde.

FOLY: Mary, I knew the when thou waste a ladde.   1090

FAN: Cockys bonys, herde ye ever syke another?

FOLY: Ye, a fole the tone, and a fole the tother.

    1059 *fleyest* flayest   1064 *frubyssher* furbisher (who renovated swords)
    1081 *flete* abound   1091 *syke* such

FAN: Nay, but wotest thou what I do say?

FOLY: Why, sayst thou that I was here yesterday?

FAN: Cockys armys, this is warke, I trowe.

FOLY: What, callyst thou me a donnyshe crowe?

FAN: Nowe, in good faythe, thou art a fonde gest.

FOLY: Ye, bere me this strawe to a dawys nest.

FAN: What, wenyst thou that I were so folysshe and so
       fonde?

FOLY: In fayth, ellys is there none in all Englonde.   1100

FAN: Yet for my Fansy sake, I say,
  Let me have thy dogge, what soever I pay.

FOLY: Thou shalte have my purse, and I wyll have thyne.

FAN: By my trouth, there is myne.

FOLY: Nowe, by my trouth, man, take, there is myne;
  And I beshrowe hym that hath the worse.

FAN: Torde, I say, what have I do?
  Here is nothynge but the bockyll of a sho,
  And in my purse was twenty marke.

FOLY: Ha, ha, ha! Herke, syrs, harke!   1110
  For all that my name hyght Foly,
  By the masse, yet art thou more fole than I.

FAN: Yet gyve me thy dogge, and I am content;
  And thou shalte have my hauke to a botchment.

FOLY: That ever thou thryve, God it forfende!
  For Goddes cope, thou wyll spende.
  Nowe take thou my dogge and gyve me thy fowle.

FAN: Hay, Chysshe, come hyder!

FOLY: Nay torde, take hym be tyme.

FAN: What callest thou thy dogge?

FOLY: Tusshe, his name is Gryme.

FAN: Come, Gryme! Come, Gryme! It is my praty
       dogges.   1120

FOLY: In faythe, there is not a better dogge for hogges,
  Not from Anwyke unto Aungey.

FAN: Ye, but trowest thou that he be not maungey?

FOLY: No, by my trouthe; it is but the scurfe and the scabbe.

1096 *donnyshe* dunnish   1097 *gest* fellow
1114 *botchment* make-weight   1115 *forfende* forbid

FAN: What? He hathe ben hurte with a stabbe?
FOLY: Nay, in faythe; it was but a strype
    That the horson had for etynge of a trype.
FAN: Where the devyll gate he all these hurtes?
FOLY: By God, for snatchynge of puddynges and wortes.
FAN: What, then he is some good poore mannes curre?   1130
FOLY: Ye, but he wyll in at every mannes dore.
FAN: Nowe thou hast done me a pleasure grete.
FOLY: In faythe, I wolde thou had a marmosete.
FAN: Cockes harte, I love suche japes.
FOLY: Ye, for all thy mynde is on owles and apes;
    But I have thy pultre, and thou hast my catell.
FAN: Ye, but thryfte and we have made a batell.
FOLY: Remembrest thou not the japes and the toyes —
FAN: What, that we used whan we were boyes?
FOLY: Ye, by the rode, even the same.   1140
FAN: Yes, yes, I am yet as full of game
    As ever I was, and as full of tryfyls
    Nil, nichelum, nihil, anglice, nyfyls.
FOLY: What, canest thou all this L[a]tyn yet
    And hath so mased a wandrynge wyt?
FAN: Tushe, man! I kepe some Latyn in store.
FOLY: By cockes harte, I wene thou hast no more?
FAN: No? Yes in faythe; I can versyfy.
FOLY: Then I pray the hartely
    Make a verse of my butterfly;   1150
    It forseth not of the reason, so it kepe ryme.
FAN: But wylte thou make another on Gryme?
FOLY: Nay, in fayth fyrst let me here thyne.
FAN: Mary, as for that, thou shalte sone here myne.
    Est snavi snago with a shrewde face *vilis imago.*
FOLY: *Grimbald[us]* gredy snatche a puddyng tyl the rost
        be redy.
FAN: By the harte of God, well done!
FOLY: Ye, so redely and so sone!

1129 *wortes* vegetables   1133 *marmosete* monkey   1137 *batell* bargain
1144 *canest thou* do you know?   1151 *forseth* (v) matters

Here cometh in Crafty Conveyaunce.

CRAFTY C.: What, Fansy! Let me se who is the tother.
FAN: By God, syr, Foly, myne owne sworne brother.   1160
CRAFTY C.: Cockys bonys, it is a farle freke;
   Can he play well at the hoddypeke?
FAN: Tell by thy trouth what sport can thou make.
FOLY: A, holde thy peas! I have the tothe ake.
CRAFTY C.: The tothe ake! Lo, a torde ye have.
FOLY: Ye, thou haste the four quarters of a knave.
CRAFTY C.: Wotyst thou, I say, to whom thou spekys?
FAN: Nay, by cockys harte, he ne reckys.
   For he wyll speke to Magnyfycence thus.
CRAFTY C.: Cockys armys! a mete man for us.   1170
FOLY: What, wolde ye have mo folys, and are so many?
FAN: Nay, offer hym a counter in stede of a peny.
CRAFTY C.: Why, thynkys thou he can no better skyll?
FOLY: In fayth, I can make you bothe folys, and I wyll.
CRAFTY C.: What haste thou on thy fyst? A [k]esteryll?
FOLY: Nay, iwys, fole; it is a doteryll.
CRAFTY C.: In a cote thou can play well the dyser.
FOLY: Ye, but thou can play the fole without a vyser.
FAN: Howe rode he by you? Howe put he to you?
CRAFTY C.: Mary, as thou sayst, he gave me a blurre.   1180
   But where gatte thou that mangey curre?
FAN: Mary, it was his, and now it is myne.
CRAFTY C.: And was it his, and nowe it is thyne?
   Thou must have thy fansy and thy wyll,
   But yet thou shalt holde me a fole styll.
FOLY: Why, wenyst thou that I cannot make the play the
      fon?
FAN: Yes, by my faythe, good Syr John.
CRAFTY C.: For you bothe it were inough.
FOLY: Why, wenyst thou that I were as moche a fole as
      thou?

1161 *farle* marvellous   *freke* fellow   1162 *hoddypeke* fool, noodle
1168 *reckys* cares   1172 *counter* token coin   1175 *kesteryll* kestrel
1177 *dyser* scoffer, one who mocks others

FAN: Nay, nay; thou shalte fynde hym another maner of
      man.   1190
FOLY: In faythe, I can do mastryes, so I can.
CRAFTY C.: What canest thou do but play Cocke Wat?
FAN: Yes, yet he wyll make the ete a gnat.
FOLY: Yes, yes, by my trouth I holde the a grote
  That I shall laughe the out of thy cote.
CRAFTY C.: Than wyll I say that thou haste no pere.
FAN: Nowe, by the rode, and he wyll go nere.
FOLY: Hem, Fansy! *Regardes, voyes.*

*Here Foly maketh semblaunt to take a lowse from
Crafty Conveyaunce showlder.*

FAN: What hast thou founde there?
FOLY: By God, a lowse.
CRAFTY C.: By cockes harte, I trowe thou lyste.   1200
FOLY: By the masse, a Spaynysshe moght with a gray
        lyste!
FAN: Ha, ha, ha, ha, ha, ha!
CRAFTY C.: Cockes armes! It is not so, I trowe.

Here Crafty Conveyaunce putteth of his gowne.

FOLY: Put on thy gowne agayne, for nowe thou hast lost.
FAN: Lo, John a Bonam, where is thy brayne?
  Nowe put on, fole, thy cote agayne.
FOLY: Gyve me my grote, for thou hast lost.

*Here Foly maketh semblaunt to take money of Crafty
Conveyaunce saynge to hym*

1191 *mastryes* tricks   1200 *lyste* liest
1201 *moght* moth   *lyste* stripe, border

Shyt thy purse, dawe, and do no cost.

FAN: Nowe hast thou not a prowde mocke and a starke?

CRAFTY C.: With yes, by the rode of Wodstocke Parke.　　1210

FAN: Nay, I tell the, he maketh no dowtes
To tourne a fole out of his clowtes.

CRAFTY C.: And for a fole a man wolde hym take.

FOLY: Nay, it is I that foles can make;
For be he cayser, or be he kynge,
To felowshyp with Foly I can hym brynge.

FAN: Nay, wylte thou here nowe of his scoles,
And what maner of people he maketh foles?

CRAFTY C.: Ye, let us here a worde or twayne.

FOLY: Syr, of my maner I shall tell you the playne:　　1220
Fyrst I lay before them my bybyll
And teche them howe they sholde syt ydyll
To pyke theyr fyngers all the day longe;
So in theyr eyre I synge them a songe
And make them so longe to muse
That some of them renneth strayght to the stuse;
To thefte and bryboury I make some fall,
And pyke a locke and clyme a wall;
And where I spy a nysot gay
That wyll syt ydyll all the day　　1230
And can not set herselfe to warke,
I kyndell in her suche a lyther sparke
That rubbed she must be on the gall
Bytwene the tap[pet] and the wall.

CRAFTY C.: What horson, arte thou suche a one?

FAN: Nay, beyonde all other set hym alone.

CRAFTY C.: Hast thou ony more? Let se, procede.

FOLY: Ye, by God, syr, for a nede
I have another maner of sorte,
That I laugh at for my dysporte;　　1240
And those be they that come up of nought –

1208 *Shyt* shut　1209 *starke* (adj) perfect, unqualified
1212 *clowtes* clothes　1223 *pyke* pick　1226 *stuse* stews
1227 *bryboury* pilfering　1229 *nysot* ?lascivious wench
1233 *gall* sensitive spot　1234 *tappet* tapestry

As some be not fer[r]e and yf it were well sought –
Suche dawys, what soever they be,
That be set in auctorite,
Anone he waxyth so hy and prowde,
He frownyth fyersly brymly browde.
The knave wolde make it koy, and he cowde
All that he dothe muste be alowde;
And 'This is not well done, syr; take hede';
And maketh hym besy where is no nede.   1250
He dawnsys so long 'Hey troly loly,'
That every man lawghyth at his foly.
CRAFTY C.: By the good Lorde, truthe he sayth.
FAN: Thynkyst thou not so, by thy fayth?
CRAFTY C.: Thynke I not so, quod he? Ellys have I
          shame,
For I knowe dyverse that useth the same.
FOLY: But nowe, forsothe, man, it maketh no mater;
For they that wyll so bysely smater,
So helpe me God, man, ever at the length
I make hym lese moche of theyr strength.   1260
For with Foly so do I them lede
That wyt he wantyth when he hath moste nede.
FAN: Forsothe, tell on; hast thou any more?
FOLY: Yes, I shall tell you or I go
Of dyverse mo that hauntyth my scolys.
CRAFTY C.: All men beware of suche folys!
FOLY: There be two lyther, rude and ranke:
Symkyn Tytyvell and Pers Pykthanke.
Theys lythers I lerne them for to lere,
What he sayth and she sayth to lay good ere,   1270
And tell to his sufferayne every whyt;
And then he is moche made of for his whyt.
And, be the mater yll more or lesse,
He wyll make it mykyll worse than it is;
But all that he dothe, and yf he reken well,
It is but Foly every dell.

1246 *brymly* fiercely   1247 *koy* disdainful   1258 *smater* chatter
1267 *lyther* evil men   *ranke* corrupt   1269 *lere* learn   1271 *whyt* ?bit

FAN: Are not his wordys cursydly cowchyd?
CRAFTY C.: By God, there be some that be shroudly
     towchyd;
  But, I say, let se and yf thou have any more.
FOLY: I have an hole armory of suche haburdashe in   1280
     store,
  For there be other that Foly dothe use,
  That folowe fonde fantasyes and vertu refuse.
FAN: Nay, that is my parte that thou spekest of nowe.
FOLY: So is all the remenaunt, I make God avowe;
  For thou fourmest suche fantasyes in theyr mynde
  That every man almost groweth out of kynde.
CRAFTY C.: By the masse, I am glad that I came hyder
  To here you two rutters dyspute togyder.
FAN: Nay, but Fansy must be eyther fyrst or last.
FOLY: But whan Foly cometh, all is past.   1290
FAN: I wote not whether it cometh of the or of me:
  But all is Foly that I can se.
CRAFTY C.: Mary, syr, ye may swere it on a boke.
FOLY: Ye, tourne over the lefe, rede there, and loke
  Howe frantyke Fansy fyrst of all
  Maketh man and woman in Foly to fall.
CRAFTY C.: A, syr, a, a! Howe by that?
FAN: A peryllous thynge, to cast a cat
  Upon a naked man and yf she scrat.
FOLY: So how, I say, the hare is squat!   1300
  For, frantyke Fansy, thou makyst men madde;
  And I Foly bryngeth them to *qui fuit* gadde,
  With *qui fuit* brayne seke I have them brought,
  From *qui fuit aliquid* to shyre shakynge nought.
CRAFTY C.: Well argued and surely on bothe sydes!
  But for the, Fansy, Magnyfycence abydes.
FAN: Why, shall I not have Foly with me also?
CRAFTY C.: Yes, perde, man, whether ye ryde or go.
  Yet for his name we must fynde a shyfte.

1277 *cowchyd* expressed   1280 *haburdashe* cheap merchandise
1288 *rutters* gallants   1297 *Howe* Stop   1300 *squat* cowering
1308 *perde* by God

FAN: By the masse, he shall hyght Consayte.   1310
CRAFTY C.: Not a better name under the sonne.
  With Magnyfycence thou shalte wonne.
FOLY: God have mercy, good godfather.
CRAFTY C.: Yet I wolde that ye had gone rather;
  For as sone as you come in Magnyfycence syght,
  All mesure and good rule is gone quyte.
FAN: And shall we have Lyberte to do what we wyll?
CRAFTY C.: Ryot at Lyberte russheth it out styll.
FOLY: Ye, but tell me one thynge.
CRAFTY C.:   What is that?
FOLY: Who is mayster of the masshe fat?   1320
FAN: Ye, for he hathe a full dry soule.
CRAFTY C.: Cockes armes! Thou shalte kepe the
       brewhouse boule.
FOLY: But may I drynke therof whylest that I stare?
CRAFTY C.: When Mesure is gone, what nedest thou
       spare?
  Whan Mesure is gone, we may slee care.
FOLY: Nowe then goo we hens. Away the mare!

           [*Exeunt Fansy and Foly.*]
           Crafty Conveyaunce alone in the place.

CRAFTY C.: It is wonder to se the worlde aboute,
  To se what Foly is used in every place;
  Foly hath a rome, I say, in every route.
  To put where he lyst, Foly hath fre chace.   1330
  Foly and Fansy all where every man dothe face and
    brace;
  Foly fotyth it properly, Fansy ledyth the dawnce,
  And next come I after, Crafty Conveyaunce.

  Who so to me gyveth good advertence
  Shall se many thyngys donne craftely.

   1322 *boule* bowl   1329 *route* crowd   1331 *brace* embrace

By me conveyed is wanton insolence

. . . .

Pryvy poyntmentys conveyed so properly,
For many tymes moche kyndnesse is denyed
For drede, that we dare not ofte, lest we be spyed.

By me is conveyed mykyll praty ware: 1340
Somtyme, I say, behynde the dore for nede.
I have an hoby can make larkys to dare;
I knyt togyther many a broken threde.
It is grete almesse the hunger to fede,
To clothe the nakyd where is lackynge a smocke,
Trymme at her tayle or a man can turne a socke.

'What howe! Be ye mery; was it not well conveyed?'
'As oft as ye lyst, so honeste be savyd
'Alas, dere harte, loke that we be not perseyvyd!'
Without crafte nothynge is well behavyd.   1350
'Though I shewe you curtesy, say not that I crave,
'Yet convey it craftely, and hardely spare not for me,'
So that there knowe no man but I and she.

Thefte also and pety brybery
Without me be full ofte aspyed.
My inwyt delynge there can no man dyscry.
Convey it be crafte, lyft and lay asyde.
Full moche flatery and falsehode I hyde,
And by Crafty Conveyaunce I wyll, and I can,
Save a stronge thefe and hange a trew man.   1360

But some man wolde convey, and can not skyll,
As malypert tavernars that checke with theyr betters;
Theyr Conveyaunce weltyth the worke all by wyll.

1356 *inwyt* secret   1362 *malypert* impudent   *checke* quarrel
1363 *weltyth* ?overturns, confuses

And some wyll take upon them to conterfet letters,
And therwithall convey hymselfe into a payre of fetters.
And some wyll convey by the pretence of sadnesse,
Tyll all theyr Conveyaunce is turnyd into madnesse.

Crafty Conveyaunce is no chyldys game:
By Crafty Conveyaunce many one is brought up of
    nought.
Crafty Conveyaunce can cloke hymselfe frome shame,   1370
For by Crafty Conveyaunce wonderful thynges are
    wrought.
By Convayaunce Crafty I have brought
Unto Magnyfy[cen]ce a full ungracyous sorte,
For all hokes unhappy to me have resorte.

*Here cometh in Magnyfycence with Lyberte and
Felycyte.*

MAG: Trust me, Lyberte, it greveth me ryght sore
    To se you thus ruled and stande in suche awe.
LYB: Syr, as by my wyll, it shall be so no more.
FEL: Yet Lyberte without rule is not worth a strawe.
MAG: Tushe! Holde your peas; ye speke lyke a dawe;
    Ye shall be occypyed, Welthe, at my Wyll.   1380
CRAFTY C.: All that ye say, syr, is reason and skyll.

MAG: Mayster Survayour, where have ye ben so longe?
    Remembre ye not how my Lyberte by Mesure ruled
      was?
CRAFTY C.: In good faythe, syr, me semeth he had the
      more wronge.
LYB: Mary, syr, so dyd he excede and passe,
    They drove me to lernynge lyke a dull asse.

   1374 *hokes* people   1379 *dawe* fool

FEL: It is good yet that Lyberte be ruled by Reason.
MAG: Tushe! Holde your peas – ye speke out of season.

Yourselfe shall be ruled by Lyberte and Largesse.
FEL: I am content so it in Measure be.   1390
LYB: Must Mesure, in the mares name, you furnysshe and
          dresse?
MAG: Nay, nay, not so, my frende Felycyte.
CRAFTY C.: Not and your grace wolde be ruled by me.
LYB: Nay he shall be ruled even as I lyst.
FEL: Yet it is good to beware of 'had I wyst'.

MAG: Syr, by Lyberte and Largesse I wyll that ye shall
          Be governed and gyded; wote ye what I say?
          Mayster Survayour, Largesse to me call.
CRAFTY C.: It shall be done.
MAG: Ye, but byd hym come away
          At ones, and let hym not tary all day.   1400

          Here goth out Crafty Convayaunce.

FEL: Yet it is good wysdome to worke wysely by welth.
LYB: Holde thy tonge, and thou love thy helth.

MAG: What! Wyll ye waste wynde and prate thus in
          vayne?
          Ye have eten sauce, I trowe, at the Taylers Hall.
LYB: Be not to bolde, my frende; I counsell you, bere a
          brayne.
MAG: And what so we say, holde you content withall.
FEL: Syr, yet without Sapyence your substaunce may be
          smal,
          For where is no Mesure, how may worshyp endure?

          Here cometh in Fansy.

FAN: Syr, I am here at your pleasure.

Your grace sent for me, I wene; what is your wyll?   1410
MAG: Come hyther, Largesse; take here Felycyte.
FAN: Why, wene you that I can kepe hym longe styll?
MAG: To rule as ye lyst, lo, here is Lyberte.
LYB: I am here redy.
FAN: What! Shall we
    Have Welth at our gydnge to rule as we lyst?
    Then fare well thryfte, by Hym that crosse kyst!

FEL: I truste your grace wyll be agreabyll
    That I shall suffer none impechment
    By theyr demenaunce, nor loss repryvable.
MAG: Syr, ye shall folowe myne appetyte and intent.   1420
FEL: So it be by Mesure, I am ryght well content.
FAN: What, all by Mesure, good syr, and none excesse?
LYB: Why, Welth hath made many a man braynlesse.

FEL: That was by the menys of to moche Lyberte.
MAG: What, can ye agree thus and appose?
FEL: Syr, as I say, there was no faute in me.
LYB: Ye, of Jacke a Thrommys bybyll can ye make a
        glose.
FAN: Sore sayde, I tell you, and well to the purpose.
    What sholde a man do with you? Loke you under
    [k]ay?
FEL: I say it is Foly to gyve all welth away.   1430

LYB: Whether sholde Welth be rulyd by Lyberte
    Or Lyberte by Welth? Let se, tell me that.
FEL: Syr, as me semeth, ye sholde be rulyd by me.

    1419 *repryvable* reprovable, blameworthy   1425 *appose* argue
    1427 *glose* gloss

MAG: What nede you with hym thus prate and chat?
FAN: Shewe us your mynde then, howe to do and what.
MAG: I say that I wyll ye have hym in gydynge.
LYB: Mayster Felycyte, let be your chydynge;

And so as ye se it wyll be no better,
Take it in worthe suche as ye fynde.
FAN: What the devyll, man, your name shalbe the greter: 1440
For Welth without Largesse is all out of kynde.
LYB: And Welth is nought worthe yf Lyberte be behynde.
MAG: Nowe holde ye content, for there is none other
        shyfte.
FEL: Then waste muste be welcome, and fare well thryfte!

MAG: Take of his substaunce a sure inventory,
And get thou home togyther; for Lyberte shall byde
And wayte upon me.
LYB: And yet for a memory,
Make indentures howe ye and I shal gyde.
FAN: I can do nothynge but he stonde besyde.
LYB: Syr, we can do nothynge the one without the other.   1450
MAG: Well, get you hens than, and sende me some other.

FAN: Whom? Lusty Pleasure, or mery Consayte?
MAG: Nay, fyrst Lusty Pleasure is my desyre to have,
And let the other another [time] awayte;
Howe be it, that fonde felowe is a mery knave.
But loke that ye occupye the auctoryte that I you gave.

Here goeth out Felycyte, Lyberte, and Fansy.
Magnyfycence alone in the place.

[MAG:] For nowe, syrs, I am lyke as a prynce sholde be:
I have Welth at wyll, Largesse and Lyberte.

Fortune to her lawys can not abandune me,
But I shall of Fortune rule the reyne.   1460
I fere nothynge Fortunes perplexyte.
All honour to me must nedys stowpe and lene.
I synge of two partys without a mene.
I have wynde and wether over all to sayle;
No stormy rage agaynst me can prevayle.

Alexander, of Macedony kynge,
That all the Oryent had in subjeccyon,
Though al his conquestys were brought to rekenynge,
Myght seme ryght wel under my proteccyon
To rayne, for all his marcyall affeccyon,   1470
For I am prynce perlesse, provyd of porte
Bathyd with blysse, embracyd with comforte.

Syrus, that somme tyme kyng of Babylo.
That Israell releysyd of theyr captyvyte,
For al his pompe, for all his ryall trone,
He may not be comparyd unto me.
I am the dyamounde dowtlesse of dygnyte.
Surely it is I that all may save and spyll,
No man so hardy to worke agaynst my wyll.

Porcenya, the prowde provoste of Turky lande,   1480
That ratyd the Romaynes and made them yll rest,
Nor Cesar July, that no man myght withstande,
Were never halfe so rychely as I am drest.
No, that I assure you; loke who was the best.
I reyne in my robys, I rule as me lyst,
I dryve down th[e]se dastardys with a dynt of my fyste.

Of Cato the counte, acountyd the cane,
Daryus, the doughty cheftayn of Perse,

1470 *marcyall affeccyon* warlike interest   1471 *porte* reputation
1478 *spyll* destroy   1487 *cane* khan   1488 *doughty* valiant

I set not by the prowdest of them a prane,
Ne by non other that any man can rehersse.   1490
I folowe in Felycyte without reve[r]sse;
I drede no daunger; I dawnce all in delyte:
My name is Magnyfycence, man most of myght.

Hercules the herdy, with his stobburne clobbyd mase,
That made Cerberus to cache, the cur dogge of hell,
And Thesius, th[at] prowde was Pluto to face,
It wolde not become them with me for to mell.
For of all barones bolde I bere the bell;
Of all doughty I am doughtyest duke as I deme;
To me all prynces to lowte man be sene.   1500

Cherlemayne, that mantenyd the nobles of Fraunce,
Arthur of Albyan, for all his brymme berde,
Nor Basyan the bolde, for all his brybaunce,
Nor Alerycus, that rulyd the Gothyaunce by swerd,
Nor no man on molde, can make me aferd.
What man is so maysyd with me that dare mete,
I shall flappe hym as a fole to fall at my fete.

Galba, whom his galantys garde for agaspe,
Nor Nero, that nother set by God nor man,
Nor Vaspasyan, that bare in his nose a waspe,   1510
Nor Hanyball, agayne Rome gates that ranne,
Nor yet [C]ypyo, that noble Cartage wanne;
Nor none so hardy of them with me that durste crake,
But I shall frounce them on the foretop and gar them to
    quake.

*Here cometh in Courtly Abusyon doynge reverence
and courtesy.*

1489 *prane* prawn   1494 *mase* mace   1497 *mell* mix
1503 *brybaunce* plundering   1513 *crake* boast   1514 *gar* cause

271

COURTLY AB: At your commaundement, syr, wyth all
        dew reverence.

MAG: Welcom, Pleasure, to our Magnyfycence.

COURTLY AB: Plesyth it your grace to shewe what I do
        shall?

MAG: Let us here of your Pleasure, to passe the tyme
        withall.

COURTLY AB: Syr, then, with the favour of your benynge
        sufferaunce,

To shewe you my mynde myselfe I wyll avaunce,   1520
If it lyke your grace to take it in degre.

MAG: Yes, syr; so good man in you I se,
And in your delynge so good assuraunce,
That we delyte gretly in your dalyaunce.

COURTLY AB: A, syr, your grace me dothe extole and
        rayse,

And ferre beyond my merytys ye me commende and
        prayse.
Howe be it, I wolde be ryght gladde, I you assure,
Any thynge to do that myght be to your Pleasure.

MAG: As I be saved, with Pleasure I am supprysyd
Of your langage, it is so well devysed;   1530
Pullyshyd and fresshe is your ornacy.

COURTLY AB: A, I wolde to God that I were halfe so
        crafty,

Or in electe utteraunce halfe so eloquent,
As that I myght your noble grace content.

MAG: Truste me, with you I am hyghly pleasyd,
For in my favour I have you feffyd and seasyd.
He is not lyvynge your maners can amend;
Mary, your speche is as pleasant as though it were pend,
To here your comon it is my hygh comforte,
Poynt devyse all pleasure is your porte.   1540

COURTLY AB: Syr, I am the better of your noble reporte.
But of your pacyence under the supporte
If it wolde lyke you to here my pore mynde —

1521 *in degre* kindly   1524 *dalyaunçe* conversation   1536 *feffyd* invested
seasyd put in possession   1538 *pend* written   1539 *comon* speech

MAG: Speke, I beseche the; leve nothynge behynde.
COURTLY AB: So as ye be a prynce of great myght,
  It is semynge your pleasure ye delyte,
  And to aqueynte you with carnall delectacyon;
  And to fall in aquayntaunce with every newe facyon,
  And quyckely your appetytes to sharpe and adresse;
  To fasten your fansy upon a fayre maystresse   1550
  That quyckly is envyved with rudyes of the rose,
  Inpurtured with fetures after your purpose,
  The streynes of her vaynes as asure inde blewe,
  Enbudded with beautye and colour fresshe of hewe,
  As lyly whyte to loke upon her [l]eyre,
  Her eyen relucent as carbuncle so clere,
  Her mouthe enbawmed, dylectable, and mery,
  Her lusty lyppes ruddy as the chery:
  Howe lyke you? Ye lacke, syr, suche a lusty lasse.
MAG: A, that were a baby to brace and to basse!   1560
  I wolde I had, by Hym that hell dyd harowe,
  With me in kepynge suche a Phylyp Sparowe.
  I wolde hauke whylest my hede dyd warke,
  So I myght hobby for suche a lusty larke.
  These wordes, in myne eyre they be so lustely spoken,
  That on suche a female my flesshe wolde be wroken.
  They towche me so thorowly and tykyll my consayte,
  That weryed I wolde be on suche a bayte.
  A cockes armes! Where myght suche one be founde?
COURTLY AB: Wyll ye spende ony money?
MAG: Ye, a
  thousande pounde.   1570
COURTLY AB: Nay, nay; for lesse I waraunt you to be
  sped,
  And brought home and layde in your bed.
MAG: Wolde money, trowest thou, make suche one to the
  call?

1551 *rudyes* redness   1552 *Inpurtured* endowed   1555 *leyre* face
1557 *enbawmed* sweet tasting   1560 *brace* embrace   *basse* kiss
1564 *hobby* hunt   1566 *wroken* fulfilled   1568 *weryed* wearied
bayte temptation

COURTLY AB: Money maketh marchauntes, I tell you,
      over all.

MAG: Why, wyl a maystres be wonne for money and for
      golde?

COURTLY AB: Why, was not for money Troy bothe
      bought and solde?

Full many a stronge cyte and towne hath be wonne
By the meanes of money without ony gonne.
A maystres, I tell you, is but a small thynge:
A goodly rybon, or a golde rynge   1580
May wynne with a sawte the fortresse of the holde.
But one thynge I warne you, prece forth and be bolde.

MAG: Ye, but some be full koy and passynge harde harted.

COURTLY AB: But blessyd be our Lorde, they wyll be
      sone converted.

MAG: Why, wyll they then be intreted, the most and the
      lest?

COURTLY AB: Ye, for *omnis mulier meritrix si celari potest.*

MAG: A, I have spyed ye can moche broken sorowe.

COURTLY AB: I coude holde you with suche talke hens
      tyll to-morowe;

But yf it lyke your grace more at large
Me to permyt my mynde to dyscharge,   1590
I wolde yet shewe you further of my consayte.

MAG: Let se what ye say; shewe it strayte.

COURTLY AB: Wysely let these wordes in your mynde be
      wayed.

By waywarde wylfulnes let eche thynge be convayed.
What so ever ye do, folowe your owne wyll;
Be it reason or none, it shall not gretely skyll.
Be it ryght or wronge, by the advyse of me,
Take your pleasure and use fre lyberte;
And yf you se ony thynge agaynst your mynde,
Then some [o]ccacyon or quarell ye must fynde,   1600
And frowne it and face it, as thoughe ye wolde fyght.
Frete yourselfe for anger and for dyspyte,
Here no man what so ever they say,

    1578 *gonne* gun   1581 *sawte* assault   1602 *Frete* fret, make angry

But do as ye lyst and take your owne way.
MAG: Thy wordes and my mynde odly well accorde.
COURTLY AB: What sholde ye do elles? Are not you a
    lorde?
Let your lust and lykynge stande for a lawe.
Be wrastynge and wrythynge, and away drawe.
And ye se a man that with hym ye be not pleased,
And that your mynde can not well be eased —   1610
As yf a man fortune to touche you on the quyke —
Then feyne yourselfe dyseased, and make yourselfe seke.
To styre up your stomake you must you forge,
Call for a candell, and cast up your gorge,
With 'Cockes armes! Rest shall I none have
'Tyll I be revenged on that horson knave.
'A, howe my stomake wambleth! I am all in a swete.
'Is there no horson that knave that wyll bete?'
MAG: By cockes woundes, a wonder felowe thou arte;
For ofte tymes suche a wamblynge goth over my harte, 1620
Yet I am not harte seke, but that me lyst.
For myrth I have hym coryed, beten, and blyst,
Hym that I loved not, and made hym to loute;
I am forthwith as hole as a troute.
For suche abusyon I use nowe and than.
COURTLY AB: It is none abusyon, syr, in a noble man:
It is a pryncely pleasure and a lordly mynde.
Suche lustes at large may not be lefte behynde.

Here cometh in Cloked Colusyon with Mesure.

CLOKED COL: [*To Measure*]: Stande styll here, and ye shall
    se
That for your sake I wyll fall on my kne.   1630
COURTLY AB: Syr, Sober Sadnesse cometh; wherfore it
    be?

1612 *seke* sick   1613 *forge* pretend   1617 *wambleth* heaves   *swete* sweat
1622 *coryed* drubbed   *blyst* thumped, thrashed   1623 *loute* bow, submit

MAG: Stande up, syr; ye are welcom to me.

CLOKED COL: Please it your grace at the contemplacyon
    Of my pore instance and supplycacyon,
    Tenderly to consyder in your advertence,
    Of our blessyd Lorde, syr, at the reverence,
    Remembre the good servyce that Mesure hath you done,
    And that ye wyll not cast hym away so sone.

MAG: My frende, as touchynge to this your mocyon,
    I may say to you I have but small devocyon.   1640
    Howe be it, at your instaunce I wyll the rather
    Do as moche as for myne owne father.

CLOKED COL: Nay, syr; that affeccyon ought to be
           reserved,
    For of your grace I have it nought deserved.
    But yf it lyke you that I myght rowne in your eyre,
    To shewe you my mynde I wolde have the lesse fere.

MAG: Stande a lytell abacke, syr, and let hym come hyder.

COURTLY AB: With a good wyll, syr; God spede you
           bothe togyder.

CLOKED COL: Syr, so it is: this man is here by,
    That for hym to laboure he hath prayde me hartely.   1650
    Notwithstandynge to you be it sayde,
    To trust in me he is but dyssayved;
    For so helpe me God, for you he is not mete.
    I speke the softlyer because he sholde not wete.

MAG: Come hyder, Pleasure; you shall here myne entent.
    Mesure, ye knowe wel, with hym I can not be content:
    And surely, as I am nowe advysed,
    I wyll have hym rehayted and dyspysed.
    Howe say ye, syrs? Herein what is best?

COURTLY AB: By myne advyse, with you in fayth he shall
           not rest.   1660

CLOKED COL: Yet, syr, reserved your better advysement,
    It were better he spake with you or he wente,
    That he knowe not but that I have supplyed
    All I can his matter for to spede.

    1635 *advertence* notice   1645 *rowne* whisper   1646 *fere* fear
    1654 *wete* know   1658 *rehayted* rebuked   1662 *or* before

MAG: Nowe by your trouthe, gave he you not a brybe?
CLOKED COL: Yes, with his hande I made hym to
       subscrybe
A byll of recorde for an annuall rent.
COURTLY AB: But for all that, he is lyke to have a glent.
CLOKED COL: Ye, by my trouthe, I shall waraunt you for
       me.
And he go to the dev[y]ll, so that I may have my fee,   1670
What care I?
MAG: By the masse, well sayd.
COURTLY AB: What force ye, so that he be payde?
CLOKED COL: But yet, lo, I wolde, or that he wente,
Lest that he thought that his money were evyll spente,
That he wolde loke on hym, thoughe it were not longe.
MAG: Well cannest thou helpe a preest to synge a songe.
CLOKED COL: So it is all the maner nowe a dayes
For to use suche haftynge and crafty wayes.
COURTLY AB: He telleth you trouth, syr, as I you ensure.
MAG: Well, for thy sake the better I may endure   1680
That he come hyder, and to gyve hym a loke
That he shall lyke the worse all this woke.
CLOKED COL: I care not howe sone he be refused,
So that I may craftely be excused.
COURTLY AB: Where is he?
CLOKED COL: Mary, I made hym abyde,
Whylest I came to you, a lytell here besyde.
MAG: Well, call hym, and let us here hym reason,
And we wyll be comonynge in the mene season.
COURTLY AB: This is a wyse man, syr, where so ever ye
       hym had.
MAG: An honest person, I tell you, and a sad.   1690
COURTLY AB: He can full craftely this matter brynge
       aboute.
MAG: Whylest I have hym, I nede nothynge doute.
    Hic introducat Colusion, Mesure, Magnyfycence
    aspectant[e] vultu elatissimo.

1668 *glent* fall   1678 *haftynge* trickery   1688 *comonynge* conversing

CLOKED COL: By the masse, I have done that I can,
　And more than ever I dyd for ony man.
　I trowe ye herde yourselfe what I said.
MEAS: Nay, indeede, but I sawe howe ye prayed,
　And made instance for me be lykelyhod.
CLOKED COL: Nay, I tell you, I am not wonte to fode
　Them that dare put theyr truste in me;
　And thereof ye shall a larger profe se.　　　　　　1700
MEAS: Syr, God rewarde you as ye have deserved!
　Byt thynke you with Magnyfycence I shal be reserved?
CLOKED COL: By my trouth, I can not tell you that.
　But and I were as ye, I wolde not set a gnat
　By Magnyfycence nor yet none of his.
　For go when ye shall, of you shall he mysse.
MEAS: Syr, as ye say.
CLOKED COL:　　　　Nay, come on with me.
　Yet ones agayne I shall fall on my kne
　For your sake, what so ever befall;
　I set not a flye and all go to all.　　　　　　　　1710
MEAS: The Holy Goost be with your grace.
CLOKED COL: Syr, I beseche you let Pety have some place
　In your brest towardes this gentylman.
MAG: I was your good lorde tyll that ye beganne
　So masterfully upon you for to take
　With my servauntys, and suche maystryes gan make,
　That holly my mynde with you is myscontente.
　Wherfore I wyll that ye be resydent
　With me no longer.
CLOKED COL:　　　　Say somwhat nowe, let se,
　For your selfe.
MEAS:　　　　　Syr, yf I myght permytted be,　　　1720
　I wolde to you say a worde or twayne.
MAG: What! Woldest thou, lurden, with me brawle
　　　　agayne?
　Have hym hens, I say, out of my syght!
　That day I se hym I shall be worse all nyght.

1698 *fode* deceive　1716 *maystryes* tricks

278

*Here Mesure goth out of the place [with Courtly
Abusyon].*

COURTLY AB: Hens, thou haynyarde! Out of the dores
      fast!
MAG: Alas! My stomake fareth as it wolde cast.
CLOKED COL: Abyde, syr, abyde: let me holde your hede.
MAG: A bolle or a basyn, I say, for Goddes brede!
  A, my hede! But is the horson gone?
  God gyve hym a myscheffe! Nay, nowe let me alone.   1730
CLOKED COL: A good dryfte, syr; a praty fete!
  By the good Lorde, yet your temples bete.
MAG: Nay, so God helpe, it was no grete vexacyon;
  For I am panged ofte tymes of this same facyon.
CLOKED COL: Cockes armes! Howe Pleasure plucked hym
      forth!
MAG: Ye, walke he must; it was no better worth.
CLOKED COL: Syr, nowe me thynke your harte is well
      eased.
MAG: Nowe Measure is gone, I am the better pleased.
CLOKED COL: So to be ruled by Measure, it is a payne.
MAG: Mary, I wene he wolde not be glad to come agayne.   1740
CLOKED COL: So I wote not what he sholde do here.
  Where mennes belyes is mesured, there is no chere;
  For I here but fewe men that gyve ony prayse
  Unto Measure, I say, nowe a days.
MAG: Measure? Tut! What the devyll of hell!
  Scantly one with Measure that wyll dwell.
CLOKED COL: Not amonge noble men, as the worlde
      gothe.
  It is no wonder, therfore, thoughe ye be wrothe
  With Mesure. Where as all noblenes is, there I have
    past.
  They catche that catche may, kepe and holde fast,   1750
  Out of all measure themselfe to enryche;
  No force what thoughe his neyghbour dye in a dyche.

1725 *haynyarde* ?wretch ?niggard   1728 *bolle* bowl

With pollynge and pluckynge out of all measure,
Thus must ye stuffe and store your treasure.
MAG: Yet somtyme, parde, I must use Largesse.
CLOKED COL: Ye, mary, somtyme: in a messe of
        vergesse,
As in a tryfyll or in a thynge of nought,
As gyvynge a thynge that ye never bought.
It is the gyse nowe, I say, over all,
Largesse in wordes, for rewardes are but small.   1760
To make fayre promyse, what are ye the worse?
Let me have the rule of your purse.
MAG: I have taken it to Largesse and Lyberte.
CLOKED COL: Than is it done as it sholde be
But use your largesse by the advyse of me
And I shall waraunt you welth and lyberte.
MAG: Say on; me thynke your reasons be profounde.
CLOKED COL: Syr, of my counsayle this shall be the
        grounde:
To chose out ii, iii, of suche as you love best,
And let all your fansyes upon them rest.   1770
Spare for no cost to gyve them pounde and peny;
Better to make iii ryche than for to make many.
Gyve them more than ynoughe, and let them not lacke;
And as for all other, let them trusse and packe.
Plucke from an hundred, and gyve it to thre;
Let neyther patent scape them nor fee.
And where soever you wyll fall to a rekenynge,
Those thre wyll be redy even at your bekenynge;
For then shall you have at Lyberte to lowte.
Let them have all, and the other go without;   1780
Thus joy without mesure you shall have.
MAG: Thou sayst truthe, by the harte that God me gave!
For as thou sayst, ryght so shall it be.
And here I make the upon Lyberte
To be supervysour, and on Largesse also;
For as thou wylte so shall the game go.
For in Pleasure and Surveyaunce and also in the

1753 *pollynge* extortion   1774 *trusse* pack up   1779 *lowte* stoop

I have set my hole felycyte;
And suche as you wyll shall lacke no promocyon.
CLOKED COL: Syr, syth that in me ye have suche
    devocyon,   1790
Commyttynge to me and to my felowes twayne
Your Welthe and Felycyte, I trust we shall optayne
To do you servyce after your appetyte.
MAG: In faythe, and your servyce ryght well shall I
    acquyte;
And therfore hye you hens, and take this oversyght.
CLOKED COL: Nowe Jesu preserve you, syr, prynce most
    of myght!

    Here goth Cloked Colusyon awaye, and leveth
    Magnyfycence alone in the place.

MAG: Thus, I say, I am envyronned with Solace;
I drede no dyntes of fatall Desteny.
Well were that lady myght stande in my grace,
Me to enbrace and love moost specyally;   1800
A Lorde, so I wolde halse her hartely!
So I wolde clepe her! So I wolde kys her swete!

    Here cometh in Foly.

FOLY: Mary, Cryst graunt ye catche no colde on your
    fete!
MAG: Who is this?
FOLY: Consayte, syr, your owne man.
MAG: What tydynges with you, syr? I befole thy brayne
    pan.
FOLY: By our lakyn, syr, I have ben a howkyng for the
    wylde swan.

1792 *optayne* succeed   1795 *oversyght* authority   1801 *halse* embrace
1802 *clepe* kiss   1805 *befole* call a fool   1806 *howkyng* hawking

My hawke is rammysshe, and it happed that she ran —
Flewe I sholde say — in to an olde barne
To reche at a rat — I coude not her warne;
She pynched her pynyon, by God, and catched harme.   1810
It was a ronner; nay, fole, I warant her blode warme.
MAG: A, syr, thy jarfawcon and thou be hanged togyder!
FOLY: And, syr, as I was comynge to you hyder,
    I saw a fox sucke on a kowes ydder,
    And with a lyme rodde I toke them bothe togyder.
    I trowe it be a frost, for the way is slydder.
    Se, for God avowe, for colde as I chydder.

MAG: Thy wordes hange togyder as fethers in the wynde.
FOLY: A, syr, tolde I not you howe I dyd fynde
        A knave and a carle, and all of one kynde?   1820
    I sawe a wethercocke wagge with the wynde!
    Grete mervayle I had, and mused in my mynde.
    The houndes ranne before, and the hare behynde.
    I sawe a losell lede a lurden, and they were bothe
      blynde.
    I sawe a sowter go to supper, or ever he had dynde.

MAG: By cockes harte, thou arte a fyne mery knave.
FOLY: I make God avowe ye wyll none other men have.
MAG: What sayst thou?
FOLY: Mary, I pray God your
        mastershyp to save.
    I shall gyve you a gaude of a goslynge that I gave,
    The gander and the gose bothe grasynge on one grave.   1830
    Than Rowlande the reve ran, and I began to rave,
    And with a bristell of a bore his berde dyd I shave.

1807 *rammysshe* wild   1811 *ronner* runner
1812 *jarfawcon* gerfalcon (large falcon)   1814 *ydder* udder
1816 *slydder* slippery   1817 *chydder* shiver   1825 *sowter* shoemaker
1829 *gaude* trick   1830 *grasynge* grazing   1831 *reve* reeve, bailiff

MAG: If ever I herde syke another, God gyve me shame.
FOLY: Sym Sadyglose was my syer, and Dawcocke my
　　　dame.
　I coude, and I lyst, garre you laughe at a game:
　Howe a wodcocke wrastled with a larke that was lame;
　The bytter sayd boldly that they were to blame;
　The feldfare wolde have fydled and it wolde not frame;
　The crane and the curlewe therat gan to grame;
　The snyte snyveled in the snowte and smyled at the
　　　game.　　　　　　　　　　　　　　　　　　　　1840

MAG: Cockes bones, herde ye ever suche another?
FOLY: Se, syr, I beseche you, Largesse my brother.

　　　Here Fansy cometh in

MAG: What tydynges with you, syr, that you loke so sad?
FAN: When ye knowe that I knowe, ye wyll not be glad.
FOLY: What, Brother Braynsyke; how farest thou?
MAG: Ye, let be thy japes, and tell me howe
　The case requyreth.
FAN:　　　　　　　　Alasse, alasse, an hevy metynge!
　I wolde you and yf I myght for wepynge.
FOLY: What, is all your myrthe nowe tourned to sorowe?
　Fare well tyll sone, adue tyll to morowe.　　　　　1850

　　　Here goth Foly away.

MAG: I pray the, Largesse, let be thy sobbynge.
FAN: Alasse, syr, ye are undone with stelyng and
　　　　robbynge!
　Ye sent us a supervysour for to take hede;

　1833 *syke* such　1839 *grame* fret

Take hede of your selfe, for nowe ye have nede.
MAG: What, hath Sadnesse begyled me so?
FAN: Nay, madnesse hath begyled you and many mo:
    For Lyberte is gone, and also Felycyte.
MAG: Gone? Alasse, ye have undone me!
FAN: Nay, he that ye sent us, Clokyd Colusyon,
    And your payntyd Pleasure, Courtly Abusyon,   1860
    And your demenour with Counterfet Countenaunce,
    And your supervysour, Crafty Conveyaunce,
    Or ever we were ware, brought us in adversyte,
    And had robbyd you quyte from all felycyte.
MAG: Why, is this the largesse that I have usyd?
FAN: Nay, it was your fondnesse that ye have usyd.
MAG: And is this the credence that I gave to the letter?
FAN: Why, coulde not your wyt serve you no better?
MAG: Why, who wolde have thought in you suche gyle!
FAN: What? Yes, by the rode, syr; it was I all this whyle   1870
    That you trustyd, and Fansy is my name;
    And Foly, my broder, that made you moche game.

Here cometh in Adversyte.

MAG: Alas, who is yonder that grymly lokys?
FAN: Adewe, for I wyll not come in his clokys.
    [*Exit Fansy.*]
MAG: Lorde, so my flesshe trymblyth nowe for drede!

Here Magnyfycence is beten downe and spoylyd from
all his goodys and rayment.

ADVERSYTE: I am Adversyte, that for thy mysdede
    From God am sent to quyte the thy mede.
    Vyle velyarde, thou must not nowe my dynt withstande:

1873 *lokys* looks   1874 *clokys* clutches   1878 *velyarde* old man

Thou mayst not abyde the dynt of my hande
Ly there, losell, for all thy pompe and pryde;   1880
Thy pleasure now with payne and trouble shalbe tryde.
The Stroke of God, Adversyte, I hyght;
I plucke downe kynge, prynce, lorde, and knyght;
I rushe at them rughly and make them ly full lowe;
And in theyr moste truste I make them overthrowe.
Thys losyll was a lorde and lyvyd at his lust,
And nowe lyke a lurden he lyeth in the duste.
He knewe not hymselfe, his harte was so hye;
Nowe is there no man that wyll set by hym a flye.
He was wonte to boste, brage, and to brace;   1890
Nowe he dare he not for shame loke one in the face.
All worldy welth for hym to lytell was;
Nowe hath he ryght nought, naked as an asse.
Somtyme without Measure he trusted in golde;
And now without Mesure he shall have hunger and
    colde.
Lo, syrs, thus I handell them all
That folowe theyr fansyes in foly to fall:
Man or woman, of what estate they be,
I counsayle them beware of Adversyte.
Of sorowfull servauntes I have many scores: 1900
I vysyte them somtyme with blaynes and with sores;
With botches and carbuckyls in care I them knyt;
With the gowte I make them to grone where they syt;
Some I make lyppers and lazars full horse;
And from that they love best some I devorse;
Some with the marmoll to halte I them make;
And some to cry out of the bone-ake;
And some I vysyte with brennynge of fyre;
Of some I wrynge of the necke lyke a wyre;
And some I make in a rope to totter and walter;   1910
And some for to hange themselfe in an halter;
And some I vysyte [with] batayle, warre, and murther,

1890 *brace* domineer   1901 *blaynes* swellings   1902 *botches* boils
carbuckyls tumours   1904 *lyppers and lazars* lepers   1906 *marmoll* ulcer
1907 *bone-ake* pain in the bones   1910 *walter* stagger

And make eche man to sle other;
To drowne or to sle themselfe with a knyfe:
And all is for theyr ungracyous lyfe.
Yet somtyme I stryke where is none offence,
Bycause I wolde prove men of theyr pacyence.
But nowe a dayes to stryke I have grete cause,
Lydderyns so lytell set by Goddes lawes.
Faders and moders that be neclygent,   1920
And suffre theyr chyldren to have theyr entent,
To gyde them vertuously that wyll not remembre,
Them or theyr chyldren ofte tymes I dysmembre.
Theyr chyldren, bycause that they have no mekenesse,
I vysyte theyr faders and moders with sekenesse;
And yf I se therby they wyll not amende,
Then Myschefe sodaynly I them sende.
For there is nothynge that more dyspleaseth God
Than from theyr chyldren to spare the rod
Of correccyon, but let them have theyr wyll.   1930
Some I make lame, and some I do kyll,
And some I stryke with a franesy;
Of some theyr chyldren I stryke out the eye;
And where the fader by wysdom worshyp hath wonne,
I sende ofte tymes a fole to his sonne.
Wherfore of Adversyte loke ye be ware,
For when I come, comyth sorowe and care.
For I stryke lordys of realmes and landys,
That rule not by mesure that they have in theyr
    handys,
That sadly rule not theyr howsholde men.   1940
I am Goddys Preposytour; I prynt them with a pen;
Because of theyr neglygence and of theyr wanton vagys,
I vysyte them and stryke them with many sore plagys.
To take, syrs, example of that I you tell
And beware of Adversyte by my counsell;
Take hede of this caytyfe that lyeth here on grounde:
Beholde howe Fortune o[n] hym hath frounde.

1919 *Lydderyns* rascals   1932 *franesy* frenzy
1941 *Preposytour* prefect (as in school)   1942 *vagys* strayings

For though we shewe you this in game and play,
Yet it proveth eyrnest, ye may se, every day.
For nowe wyll I from this caytyfe go,   1950
And take Myscheffe and vengeaunce of other mo
That hath deservyd it as well as he.
Howe, where art thou? Come hether, Poverte:
Take this caytyfe to thy lore.

[*Exit Adversyte.*]
Here cometh in Poverte.

POVERTE: A, my bonys ake! My lymmys be sore.
Alasse, I have the cyatyca full evyll in my hyppe!
Alasse, where is youth that was wont for to skyppe?
I am lowsy and unlykynge and full of scurffe;
My colour is tawny, colouryd as a turffe.
I am Poverte, that all men doth hate.   1960
I am baytyd with doggys at every mannys gate;
I am raggyd and rent, as ye may se;
Full fewe but they have envy at me.
Nowe must I this carcasse lyft up;
He dynyd with Delyte, with Poverte he must sup.
Ryse up, syr, and welcom unto me.

Hic accedat ad levandum Magnyfycence, et locabit
eum super locum stratum.

MAG: Alasse where is now my golde and fe?
Alasse, I say, where to am I brought?
Alasse, alasse, alasse! I dye for thought.
POV: Syr, all this wolde have bene thought on before;   1970
He woteth not what Welth is that never was sore.
MAG: Fy, fy, that ever I sholde be brought in this snare!

1954 *lore* teaching 1956 *cyatyca* sciatica
1958 *unlykynge* out of condition 1959 *turffe* turf

I wenyd ones never to have knowen of care.
POV: Lo, suche is this worlde! I fynde it wryt,
    In welth to beware; and that is wyt.
MAG: In welth to beware yf I had had grace,
    Never had I bene brought in this case.
POV: Nowe, syth it wyll no nother be
    All that God sendeth, take it in gre;
    For thoughe you were somtyme a noble estate,   1980
    Nowe must you lerne to begge at every mannes gate.
MAG: Alasse that ever I sholde be so shamed!
    Alasse that ever I Magnyfycence was named!
    Alasse that ever I was so harde happed
    In mysery and wretchydnesse thus to be lapped!
    Alasse that I coude not myselfe no better gyde!
    Alasse in my cradell that I had not dyde!
POV: Ye, syr, ye; leve all this rage,
    And pray to God your sorowes to asswage.
    It is foly to grudge agaynst his vysytacyon.   1990
    With harte contryte make your supplycacyon
    Unto your Maker that made bothe you and me:
    And when it pleaseth God, better may be.
MAG: Allasse, I wote not what I sholde pray.
POV: Rem[e]mbre you better, syr; beware what ye say,
    For drede ye dysplease the hygh Deyte.
    Put your wyll to His wyll, for surely it is He
    That may restore you agayne to felycyte,
    And brynge you agayne out of adversyte.
    Therefore Poverte loke pacyently ye take,   2000
    And remembre He suffered moche more for your sake,
    Howe be it, of all synne He was innocent,
    And ye have deserved this punysshment.
MAG: Alasse, with colde my lymmes shall be marde!
POV: Ye, syr, nowe must ye lerne to lye harde,
    That was wonte to lye on fetherbeddes of downe.
    Nowe must your fete lye hyer than your crowne.
    Where you were wonte to have cawdels for your hede,

1975 *wyt* wise   1979 *in gre* willingly   1985 *lapped* wrapped
2008 *cawdels* warm, nourishing drinks

Nowe must you monche mamockes and lumpes of
    brede.
And where you had chaunges of ryche aray,   2010
Nowe lap you in a coverlet, full fayne what you may.
And where that ye were pomped with what that ye
    wolde,
Nowe must ye suffre bothe hunger and colde.
With curteyns of sylke ye were wonte to be drawe,
Nowe must ye lerne to ly on the strawe.
Your skynne that was wrapped in shertes of Raynes,
Nowe must ye be stormy beten with showres and
    raynes.
Your hede that was wonte to be happed moost drowpy
    and drowsy,
Now shal ye be scabbed, scurvy, and lowsy.
MAG: Fye on this worlde full of trechery!   2020
    That ever Noblenesse sholde lyve thus wretchedly!
POV: Syr, remembre the tourne of Fortunes whele,
    That wantonly can wynke, and wynche with her hele.
    Nowe she wyll laughe; forthwith she wyll frowne;
    Sodenly set up and sodenly pluckyd downe.
    She dawnsyth varyaunce with mutabylyte,
    Nowe all in welth, forwith in poverte.
    In her promyse there is no sykernesse;
    All her delyte is set in doublenesse.
MAG: Alas, of Fortune I may well complayne.   2030
POV: Ye, syr, yesterday wyll not be callyd agayne.
    But yet, syr, nowe in this case
    Take it mekely, and thanke God of his grace;
    For nowe go I wyll begge for you some mete.
    It is foly agaynst God for to plete.
    I wyll walke nowe with my beggers baggys,
    And happe you the whyles with these homly raggys.

      Di[sce]dendo dicat ista verba

2009 *mamockes* scraps   2011 *fayne* glad   2012 *pomped* pampered
2018 *happed* fortuned   2019 *scabbed* mangy *scurvy* covered with scurf
2023 *wynke* blink *wynche* kick 2035 *plete* plead

A, howe my lymmys be lyther and lame!
Better it is to begge than to be hangyd with shame.
Yet many had lever hangyd to be,   2040
Then to begge theyr mete for charyte.
They thynke it no shame to robbe and stele,
Yet were they better to begge, a great dele;
For by robbynge they rynne to *in manus tuas* quecke;
But beggynge is better medecyne for the necke.
Ye, mary, is it, ye, so mote I goo.
A Lorde God, howe the gowte wryngeth me by the
    too!

[*Exit Poverte.*]
Here Magnyfycence dolorously maketh his mone.

MAG: O feble Fortune, O doulfull Destyny!
    O hatefull happe, O carefull cruelte!
    O syghynge sorowe, O thoughtfull mysere!   2050
    O rydlesse rewthe, O paynfull poverte!
    O dolorous herte, O harde adversyte!
    O odyous dystresse, O dedly payne and woo!
    For worldly shame I wax bothe wanne and bloo.

Where is nowe my welth and my noble estate?
Where is nowe my treasure, my landes, and my rent?
Where is nowe all my servauntys that I had here a late?
Where is nowe my golde upon them that I spent?
Where is nowe all my ryche abylement?
Where is nowe my kynne, my frendys, and my noble
    blood?   2060
Where is nowe all my pleasure and my worldly good?

2038 *lyther* withered   2044 *quecke* quickly   2046 *mote* may
2047 *gowte* gout   2051 *rydlesse* ?hopeless, destitute
rewthe pitifulness   2054 *bloo* blue   2059 *abylement* clothing

Alasse my foly, alasse my wanton wyll!
I may no more speke tyll I have wept my fyll!

[*Enter Lyberte.*]

LYB: With ye, mary, syrs, thus shold it be:
I kyst her swete, and she kyssyd me;
I daunsed the darlynge on my kne;
I garde her gaspe, I garde her gle
With daunce on the le, the le!
I bassed that baby with harte so free;
She is the bote of all my bale.   2070
A, so, that syghe was farre fet!
To love that lovesome I wyll not let;
My harte is holly on her set;
I plucked her by the patlet;
At my devyse I with her met;
My fansy fayrly on her I set;
So merely syngeth the nyghtyngale!

In lust and lykynge my name is Lyberte.
I am desyred with hyghest and lowest degre.
I lyve as me lyst, I lepe out at large;   2080
Of erthely thynge I have no care nor charge.
I am presydent of prynces; I prycke them with pryde.
What is he lyvynge that Lyberte wolde lacke?
A thousande pounde with Lyberte may holde no tacke.
At Lyberte a man may be bolde for to brake;
Welthe without Lyberte gothe all to wrake.
But yet, syrs, hardely one thynge lerne of me;
I warne you beware of to moche Lyberte:
For *totum in toto* is not worth an hawe;

2067 *garde* made, caused   *gle* (v) rejoice   2069 *bassed* kissed
2070 *bote* cure   *bale* ill   2702 *let* omit   2074 *patlet* ruff

To hardy, or to moche, to free of the dawe, 2090
To sober, to sad, to subtell, to wyse,
To mery, to mad, to gyglynge, to nyse,
To full of fansyes, to lordly, to prowde,
To homly, to holy, to lewde, and to lowde,
To flatterynge, to smatterynge, to to out of harre,
To claterynge, to chaterynge, to shorte, and to farre,
To jettynge, to jaggynge, and to full of japes,
To mockynge, to mowynge, to lyke a jackenapes.
Thus *totum in toto* groweth up, as ye may se,
By meanes of madnesse and to moche lyberte. 2100
For I am a vertue yf I be well used,
And I am a vyce where I am abused.

MAG: A, woo worthe the, Lyberte! Nowe thou sayst full
      trewe;
That I used the to moche sore may I rewe.
LYB: What! A very vengeaunce! I say, who is that?
What brothell, I say, is yonder bounde in a mat?
MAG: I am Magnyfycence, that somtyme thy mayster was.
LYB: What is the worlde thus come to pass?
Cockes armes, syrs, wyll ye not se
Howe he is undone by the meanes of me? 2110
For yf Measure had ruled Lyberte as he began,
This lurden that here lyeth had ben a noble man.
But he abused so his free Lyberte,
That nowe he hath loste all his felycyte.
Not thorowe Largesse of lyberall expence,
But by the way of Fansy-Insolence.
For Lyberalyte is most convenyent
A prynce to use with all his hole intent,
Largely rewardynge them that have deservyd:
And so shall a noble man nobly be servyd. 2120
But nowe adayes as huksters they hucke and they
      stycke,

2090 *dawe* ?fooling   2092 *nyse* foolish
2095 *smatterynge* talking idly   2097 *jettynge* boastfull
jaggynge slashing   *japes* tricks   2098 *mowynge* grimacing
2106 *brothell* wretch   2121 *huksters* hagglers   *hucke* haggle

And pynche at the payment of a poddynge prycke.
A laudable Largesse, I tell you, for a lorde
To prate for the patchynge of a pot sharde!
Spare for the spence of a noble that his honour myght
    save,
And spende C.s for the pleasure of a knave.
But so longe they rekyn with theyr reasons amysse
That they lose theyr Lyberte and all that there is.

MAG: Alasse that ever I occupyed suche abusyon!

LYB: Ye, for nowe it hath brought the to confusyon;   2130
For where I am occupyed and usyd wylfully
It can not contynew long prosperyously.
As evydently in retchlesse youth ye may se
Howe many come to Myschefe for to moche Lyberte.
And some in the worlde, theyr brayne is so ydyll
That they set theyr chyldren to rynne on the brydyll,
In youth to be wanton, and let them have theyr wyll:
And they never thryve in theyr age, it shall not gretly
    skyll.
Some fall to foly them selfe for to spyll,
And some fall prechynge at the Toure Hyll.   2140
Some hath so moche lyberte of one thynge and other,
That nother they set by father and mother;
Some have so moche lyberte that they fere no synne,
Tyll, as ye se many tymes, they shame all theyr kynne.
I am so lusty to loke you, so freshe and so fre,
That nonnes wyll leve theyr holynes and ryn after me.
Freers, with Foly I make them so fayne
They cast up theyr obedyence to cache me agayne.
At Lyberte to wander and walke over all,
That lustely they lepe somtyme theyr cloyster wall.   2150

Hic aliquis buccat in cornu a retro post populum.

2122 *poddynge prycke* skewer for pudding bag
2125 *spence* expenditure   2133 *retchlesse* heedless
2138 *skyll* (v) matter

Yonder is a horson for me doth rechate.
Adewe, syrs, for I thynke leyst that I come to late.

[*Exit Lyberte.*]

MAG: O good Lorde, how longe shall I indure
This mysery, this carefull wrechydnesse?
Of worldly welthe, alasse, who can be sure?
In Fortunys frendshyppe there is no stedfastnesse;
She hath dyssayvyd me with her doublenesse.
For to be wyse all men may lerne of me,
In welthe to beware of herde Adversyte.

Here cometh in Crafty Conveyaunce [and] Cloked
Colusyon with a lusty laughter.

CRAFTY C.: Ha, ha, ha! For laughter I am lyke to brast.   2160
CLOKED COL: Ha, ha, ha! For sporte I am lyke to spewe
and cast.
CRAFTY C.: What hast thou gotted, in faythe, to thy
share?
CLOKED COL: In faythe, of his cofers the bottoms are
bare.
CRAFTY C.: As for his plate of sylver, and suche trasshe,
I waraunt you I have gyven it a lasshe.
CLOKED COL: What, then he may drynke out of a stone
cruyse.
CRAFTY C.: With ye, syr, by Jesu, that slayne was with
Jewes!
He may rynse a pycher, for his plate is to wed.
CLOKED COL: In faythe, and he may dreme on a
daggeswane for ony fether bed.

2151 *rechate* horn call to recall dogs   2152 *leyst* lest
2154 *carefull* full of care   2159 *herde* hard, severe   2166 *cruyse* pot
2168 *wed* pledged   2169 *daggeswane* coarse coverlet

CRAFTY C.: By my trouthe, we have ryfled hym metely
    well.   2170

CLOKED COL: Ye, but thanke me therof every dele.

CRAFTY C.: Thanke the therof, in the devyls date!

CLOKED COL: Leve they pratynge, or els I shall lay the on
    the pate.

CRAFTY C.: Nay, to wrangle, I warant the, it is but a
    stone caste.

CLOKED COL: By the messe, I shall cleve thy heed to the
                                        waste.

CRAFTY C.: Ye, wylte thou clenly clene me in the clyfte
    with thy nose?

CLOKED COL: I shall thrust in the my dagger —

CRAFTY C.:   Thorowe
    the legge in to the hose.

CLOKED COL: Nay, horson, here is my glove; take it up
    and thou dare.

CRAFTY C.: Torde! Thou arte good to be a man of
    warre.

CLOKED COL: I shall skelpe the on the skalpe; lo, seest
    thou that?   2180

CRAFTY C.: What, wylte thou skelpe me? Thou dare not
    loke on a gnat.

CLOKED COL: By cockes bones, I shall blysse the and
    thou be to bolde.

CRAFTY C.: Nay, then thou wylte dynge the devyll and
    thou be not holde.

CLOKED COL: But wottest thou, horson? I rede the to be
                                         wyse.

CRAFTY C.: Nowe I rede the beware; I have warned the
                                         twyse.

CLOKED COL: Why, wenest thou that I forbere the for
    thyne owne sake?

CRAFTY C.: Peas, or I shall wrynge thy be in a brake.

CLOKED COL: Holde thy hande, dawe, of thy dagger, and
    stynt of thy dyn,

2170 *metely* moderately   2180 *skelpe* (v) strike   2182 *blysse* hit
2184 *rede* advise

Or I shal fawchyn thy flesshe and scrape the on the
    skyn.

CRAFTY C.: Ye, wylte thou, ha[n]gman? I say, thou
                                        cavell?   2190

CLOKED COL: Nay, thou rude ravener! Rayne beten
                                      javell!

CRAFTY C.: What, thou Colyn Cowarde, knowen and
    tryde!

CLOKED COL: Nay, thou false harted dastarde! Thou dare
    not abyde.

CRAFTY C.: And yf there were none to dysplease but
    thou and I,

Thou sholde not scape, horson, but thou sholde dye.

CLOKED COL: Nay, iche shall wrynge the, horson, on the
    wryst.

CRAFTY C.: Mary, I defye thy best and thy worst.

[*Enter Counterfet Countenaunce.*]

[COUNTERFET C.:] What a very vengeaunce nede all
    these wordys?

Go together by the heddys, and gyve me your swordys.

CLOKED COL: So he is the worste brawler that ever was
    borne.   2200

CRAFTY C.: In fayth, so to suffer the, it is but a skorne.

COUNTERFET C.: Now let us be all one, and let us lyve
    in rest;

For we be, syrs, but a fewe of the best.

CLOKED COL: By the masse, man, thou shall fynde me
    resonable.

CRAFTY C.: In faythe, and I wyll be to reason agreable.

COUNTERFET C.: Then truste I to God and the holy rode,

Here shalbe not great sheddynge of blode.

CLOKED COL: By our lakyn, syr, not by my wyll.

2189 *fawchyn* cut   2190 *cavell* low fellow   2191 *ravener* plunderer
javell worthless wretch   2196 *iche* I

CRAFTY C.: By the fayth, that I owe to God, and I wyll
    syt styll.

COUNTERFET C.: Well sayd; but in fayth, what was your
    quarell?   2210

CLOKED COL: Mary, syr, this gentylman called me javell.

CRAFTY C.: Nay, by Saynt Mary, it was ye called me
    knave.

CLOKED COL: Mary, so ungoodly langage you me gave.

COUNTERFET C.: A, shall we have more of this maters
    yet?

Me thynke ye are not gretly acomberyd with wyt.

CRAFTY C.: Goddys fote! I warant you I am a gentylman
    borne.

And thus to be facyd I thynke it great skorne.

COUNTERFET C.: I cannot well tell of your dysposycyons:

And ye be a gentylman, ye have knavys condycyons.

CLOKED COL: By God, I tell you, I wyll not be out facyd.   2220

CRAFTY C.: By the masse, I warant the, I wyll not be
    bracyd.

COUNTERFET C.: Tushe, tushe, it is a great defaute;

The one of you is to proude, the other is to haute.

Tell me brefly where upon ye began.

CLOKED COL: Mary, syr, he sayd that he was the pratyer
    man

Then I was, in opynynge of lockys;

And I tell you, I dysdayne moche of his mockys.

CRAFTY C.: Thou sawe never yet but I dyd my parte,

The locke of a caskyt to make to starte.

COUNTERFET C.: Nay, I know well inough ye are bothe
    well handyd   2230

To grope a gardevyaunce, though it be well bandyd.

CLOKED COL: I am the better yet in a bowget.

CRAFTY C.:   And I the
    better in a male.

2215 *acomberyd* encumbered, loaded   2221 *bracyd* defied
2223 *haute* hawty   2231 *gardevyaunce* chest
2232 *bowget* bag, pouch   *male* large, travelling bag

COUNTERFET C.: Tushe, these maters that ye move are
    but soppys in ale.
Your trymynge and tramynge by me must be tangyd,
For had I not bene, ye bothe had bene hangyd,
When we with Magnyfycence goodys made
    chevysaunce.
MAG: And therfore our Lorde sende you a very
    wengeaunce!
COUNTERFET C.: What begger art thou, that thus doth
    banne and wary?
MAG: Ye be the thevys, I say, away my goodys dyd cary.
CLOKED COL: Cockys bones, thou begger, what is thy
    name?   2240
MAG: Magnyfycence I was, whom ye have brought to
    shame.
COUNTERFET C.: Ye, but trowe you, syrs, that this is he?
CRAFTY C.: Go we nere and let us se.
CLOKED COL: By cockys bonys, it is the same.
MAG: Alasse, alasse, syrs, ye are to blame.
I was your mayster, though ye thynke it skorne,
And nowe on me ye gaure and sporne.
COUNTERFET C.: Ly styll, ly styll nowe, with yll hayle!
CRAFTY C.: Ye, for thy langage can not the avayle.
CLOKED COL: Abyde, syr, abyde, I shall make hym to   2250
    pysse.
MAG: Nowe gyve me somwhat, for God sake, I crave.
CRAFTY C.: In faythe, I gyve the four quarters of a knave.
COUNTERFET C.: In faythe, and I bequethe hym the
    tothe ake.
CLOKED COL: And I bequethe hym the bone ake.
CRAFTY C.: And I bequethe hym the gowte and the gyn.
CLOKED COL: And I bequethe hym sorowe for his syn.
COUNTERFET C.: And I gyve hym Crystys curse,
With never a peny in his purse.

    2236 *chevysaunce* booty   2238 *banne* curse   *wary* swear
    2247 *gaure* stare   *sporne* spurn   2248 *yll hayle* bad fortune
    2255 *gyn* rack

CRAFTY C.: And I gyve hym the cowghe, the murre, and
the pose.

CLOKED COL: Ye, for *requiem eternam*, groweth forth of
his nose.   2260

But nowe let us make mery and good chere.

COUNTERFET C.: And to the taverne let us drawe nere.

CRAFTY C.: And from thens to the halfe strete,

To get us there some freshe mete.

CLOKED COL: Why, is there any store of rawe motton?

COUNTERFET C.: Ye, in faythe, or ellys thou arte to great
a glotton.

CRAFTY C.: But they say it is a queysy mete:

It wyll stryke a man myschevously in a hete.

CLOKED COL: In fay, man, some rybbys of the motton be
so ranke

That they wyll fyre one ungracyously in the flanke.   2270

COUNTERFET C.: Ye, and when ye come out of the
shoppe,

Ye shall be clappyd with a coloppe

That wyll make you to halt and to hoppe.

CRAFTY C.: Som be wrestyd there that they thynke on it
forty dayes,

For there be horys there at all assayes.

CLOKED COL: For the passyon of God, let us go thyther!

Et cum festinacione discedant a loco.

MAG: Alas, myn owne servauntys to shew me such
reproche,

Thus to rebuke me and have me in dyspyght!

So shamfully to me, theyr mayster, to aproche,

That somtyme was a noble prynce of myght!   2280

Alasse, to lyve longer I have no delyght,

2259 *cowghe* cough   *murre* severe cold   *pose* catarrhal cold
2267 *queysy* causing sickness   2273 *halt* limp
2274 *wrestyd* afflicted with pain

For to lyve in mysery, it is herder than dethe.
I am wery of the worlde, for unkyndnesse me sleeth.

Hic intrat Dyspare.

DYSPARE: Dyspare is my name, that Adversyte dothe
       felowe.
  In tyme of dystresse I am redy at hande;
  I make hevy hertys, with eyen full holowe.
  Of farvent Charyte I quenche out the bronde;
  Faythe and Good Hope I make asyde to stonde.
  In Goddys Mercy, I tell them, is but foly to truste;
  All grace and pyte I lay in the duste.   2290

  What, lyest thou there lyngrynge, lewdly and lothsome?
  It is to late nowe thy synnys to repent.
  Thou hast bene so waywarde, so wranglyng, and so
       wrothsome,
  And so fer thou arte behynde of thy rent,
  And so ungracyously thy dayes thou hast spent,
  That thou arte not worthy to loke God in the face.
MAG: Nay, nay, man, I loke never to have parts of his
       grace,
  For I have so ungracyously my lyfe mysusyd;
  Though I aske mercy, I must nedys be refusyd.

DYS: No, no; for thy synnys be so excedynge farre,   2300
  So innumerable, and so full of dyspyte,
  And agayne thy Maker thou hast made suche warre,
  That thou canst not have never Mercy in his syght.
MAG: Alasse my wyckydnesse! That may I wyte!
  But nowe I se well there is no better rede,
  But sygh and sorowe and wysshe my selfe dede.

  2293 *wrothsome* angry   2304 *wyte* blame

DYS: Ye, ryd thy selfe rather than this lyfe for to lede.
The worlde waxyth wery of the; thou lyvest to longe.

Hic intrat Myschefe.

MYSCHEFE: And I, Myschefe, am comyn at nede,
Out of thy lyfe the for to lede.   2310
And loke that it be not longe
Or that thy selfe thou go honge
With this halter good and stronge;
Or ellys with this knyfe cut out a tonge
Of thy throte bole, and ryd the out of payne.
Thou arte not the fyrst hymselfe hath slayne.
Lo, here is thy knyfe and a halter, and or we go
      ferther,
Spare not thy selfe, but boldly the murder.
DYS: Ye, have done at ones without delay
MAG: Shall I myselfe hange with an halter? Nay: 2320
Nay, rather wyll I chose to ryd me of this lyve
In styckynge my selfe with this fayre knyfe.

Here Magnyfycence wolde slee hymselfe with a knyfe.

[MYS:] Alarum, alarum! To longe we abyde!
DYS: Out harowe! Hyll burneth! Where shall I me hyde?

*Hic intrat Good Hope, fugientibus Dyspayre and
Myschefe; repente Good Hope surripiat illi gladi[o],
et dicat*

GOOD HOPE: Alas, dere sone! Sore combred is thy
            mynde,

2315 *throte bole* Adam's apple   2324 *Hyll* hell

Thyselfe that thou wolde sloo agaynst Nature and
    Kynde.

MAG: A, blessyd may ye be, syr! What shall I you call?

G.H.: Good Hope, syr, my name is; remedy pryncypall
    Agaynst all fautes of your goostly foo.
    Who knoweth me, hymselfe may never sloo.   2330

MAG: Alas, syr, so I am lapped in Adversyte
    That Dyspayre well nyghe had myscheved me.
    For had ye not the soner ben my refuge,
    Of dampnacyon I had ben drawen in the luge.

G.H.: Undoubted ye had lost yourselfe eternally:
    There is no man may synne more mortally
    Than of Wanhope thrughe the unhappy wayes,
    By Myschefe to brevyate and shorten his dayes.
    But, my good sonne, lerne from Dyspayre to flee;
    Wynde you from Wanhope and aquaynte you with me.   2340
    A grete mysadventure thy Maker to dysplease,
    Thyselfe myschevynge to thyne endlesse dysease!
    There was never so harde a storme of mysery,
    But thrughe Good Hope there may come remedy.

MAG: Your wordes be more sweter than ony precyous
        narde,
    They molefy so easely my harte that was so harde.
    There is no bawme ne gumme of Arabe
    More delectable than your langage to me.

G.H.: Syr, your fesycyan is the Grace of God,
    That you hath punysshed with his sharpe rod.   2350
    Good Hope, your potecary, assygned am I,
    That Goddes Grace hath vexed you sharply
    And payned you with a purgacyon of odyous Poverte,
    Myxed with bytter alowes of herde Adversyte.
    Nowe must I make you a lectuary softe,
    I to mynyster it, you to recyve it ofte,
    With rubarbe of repentaunce in you for to rest;

2329 *goostly* spiritual   2332 *myscheved* destroyed   2334 *luge* prison
2338 *brevyate* abbreviate   2340 *Wynde* go   2345 *narde* nard
2349 *fesycyan* physician   2354 *alowes* aloes (a purgative)
2355 *lectuary* electuary (sweetened medicine)

With drammes of devocyon your dyet must be drest,
With gommes goostly of glad herte and mynde,
To thanke God of his sonde; and comforte ye shal
    fynde. 2360
Put fro you presumpcyon and admyt humylyte,
And hartely thanke God of your Adversyte;
And love that Lorde that for your love was dede,
Wounded from the fote to the crowne of the hede.
For who loveth God can ayle nothynge but good;
He may helpe you, He may mende your mode.
Prosperyte to Hym is gyven solacyusly to man,
Adversyte to hym therwith nowe and than,
Helthe of body his besynesse to acheve,
Dysease and sekenesse his conscyence to dyscryve, 2370
Afflyccyon and trouble to prove his pacyence,
Contradyccyon to prove his sapyence,
Grace of assystence his Measure to declare,
Somtyme to fall, another tyme to beware;
And nowe ye have had, syr, a wonderous fall,
To lerne you hereafter for to beware withall.
Howe say you, syr, can ye these wordys grope?
MAG: Ye, syr, nowe am I armyd with Good Hope,
  And sore I repent me of my wylfulnesse.
I aske God mercy of my neglygence, 2380
Under Good Hope endurynge ever styll,
Me humbly commyttynge unto Goddys wyll.
G.H.: Then shall you be sone delyvered from dystresse,
For nowe I se comynge to youwarde Redresse.

    Hic intrat Redresse.

REDRESSE: Cryst be amonge you, and the Holy Gostel
G.H.: He be your conducte, the Lorde of myghtys mostel
RED: Syr, is your pacyent any thynge amendyd?

2359 *gommes* remedies   2360 *sonde* sending   2365 *ayle* ?suffer
2367 *solacyusly* as a comfort   2370 *dyscryve* probe

G.H.: Ye, syr, he is sory for that he hath offendyd.
RED: How fele you your selfe, my frend? How is your
  mynde?
MAG: A wrechyd man, syr, to my Maker unkynde.   2390
RED: Ye, but have ye repentyd you with harte contryte?
MAG: Syr, the repentaunce I have no man can wryte.
RED: And have ye banyshed from you all Dyspare?
MAG: Ye, holly to Good Hope I have made my repare.
G.H.: Questyonles he doth me assure
 In Good Hope alway for to indure.
RED: Then stande up, syr, in Goddys name!
 And I truste to ratyfye and amende your fame.
 Good Hope, I pray you with harty affeccyon
 To sende over to me Sad Cyrcymspeccyon.   2400
G.H.: Syr, your requeste shall not be delayed.

   Et exiat.

RED: Now, surely Magnyfycence, I am ryght well apayed
 Of that I se you nowe in the state of grace.
 Nowe shall ye be renewyd with solace:
 Take nowe upon you this abylyment,
 And to that I say gyve good advysement.

   Magnyfycence accipiat indumentum.

MAG: To your requeste I shall be confyrmable.
[RED:] Fyrst, I saye, with mynde fyrme and stable
 Determyne to amende all your wanton excesse;
 And be ruled by me, whiche am called Redresse, 2410
 Redresse my name is, that lytell am I used
 As the world requyreth, but rather I am refused.

  2390 *unkynde* unnatural 2402 *apayed* contented
  2407 *confyrmable* conformable

Redresse sholde be at the rekenynge in every accompte,
And specyally to redresse that were out of joynte.
Full many thynges there be that lacketh Redresse,
The whiche were to longe nowe to expresse.
But Redresse is redlesse and may do no correccyon.
Nowe welcome, forsoth, Sad Cyrcumspeccyon.

Here cometh in Sad Cyrcumspeccyon, sayenge

SAD CYRCUMSPECCYON: Syr, after your message I hyed
    me hyder streyght,
  For to understande your pleasure and also your mynde.   2420
RED: Syr, to accompte you the contynewe of my consayte
  Is from Adversyte Magnyfycence to unbynde.
CYRC: How fortuned you, Magnyfycence, so far to fal
    behynde?
MAG: Syr, the longe absence of you, Sad Cyrcumspeccyon,
  Caused me of Adversyte to fall in subjeccyon.

RED: All that he sayth of trouthe doth procede,
  For where Sad Cyrcumspeccyon is longe out of the
    way,
  Of Adversyte it is to stande in drede.
CYRC: Without fayle, syr, that is no nay:
  Cyrcumspeccyon inhateth all rennynge astray.   2430
  But, syr, by me to rule ye fyrst began.
MAG: My wylfulnesse, syr, excuse I ne can.

CYRC: Then ye repent you of foly in tymes past?
MAG: Sothely to repent me I have grete cause.
  Howe be it, from you I receyved a letter [sent],
  Whiche conteyned in it a specyall clause
  That I sholde use Largesse.

2421 *contynewe* content   2430 *inhateth* hates intensely

CYRC: Nay, syr, there a pause.
RED: Yet let us se this matter thorowly ingrosed.
MAG: Syr, this letter ye sent to me at Pountes was
         enclosed.

CYRC: Who brought you that letter? Wote ye what he
         hyght?   2440
MAG: Largesse, syr, by his credence was his name.
CYRC: This letter ye speke of never dyd I wryte.
RED: To gyve so hasty credence ye were moche to blame.
MAG: Truth it is, syr; for after he wrought me moch
         shame,
   And caused me also to use to moche Lyberte,
   And made also Mesure to be put fro me.

RED: Then Welthe with you myght in no wyse abyde.
CYRC: A ha! Fansy and Foly met with you, I trowe.
RED: It wolde be founde so yf it were well tryde.
MAG: Surely my Welthe with them was overthrow.   2450
CYRC: Remembre you, therfore, howe late ye were low.
RED: Ye, and beware of unhappy Abusyon.
CYRC: And kepe you from counterfaytynge of Clokyd
         Colusyon.

MAG: Syr, in Good Hope I am to amende.
RED: Use not then your countenaunce for to counterfet.
CYRC: And from crafters and hafters I you forfende.

      Hic intrat Perseveraunce.

MAG: Well, syr, after your counsell my mynde I wyll set.
RED: What, Brother Perceveraunce! Surely well met!

    2438 *ingrosed* arranged

CYRC: Ye com hether as well as can be thought.
PERSEVERAUNCE: I herde say that Adversyte with
    Magnyfycence had fought.   2460

MAG: Ye, syr; with Adversyte I have bene vexyd,
  But Good Hope and Redresse hath mendyd my estate,
  And Sad Cyrcumspeccyon to me they have a[nn]exyd.

. . . .

RED: What this man hath sayd, perceyve ye his sentence?
MAG: Ye, syr, from hym my corage shall never flyt

. . . .

CYRC: Accordynge to treuth they be well devysed.
MAG: Syrs, I am agreed to abyde your ordenaunce:
  Faythfull assuraunce with good peradvertaunce.
PERS: Yf you be so myndyd, we be ryght glad.
RED: And ye shall have more worshyp then ever ye had.   2470

MAG: Well I perceyve in you there is moche sadnesse,
  Gravyte of counsell, provydence, and wyt.
  Your comfortable advyse and wyt excedyth all
    gladnesse;
  But frendly I wyll refrayne you ferther, or we flyt,
  Whereto were most metely my corage to knyt;
  Your myndys I beseche you here in to expresse.
  Commensynge this processe at Mayster Redresse.

RED: Syth unto me formest this processe is erectyd,
  Herein I wyll aforse me to shewe you my mynde:
  Fyrst, from your Magnyfycence syn must be abjected,   2480
  In all your warkys more grace shall ye fynde,
  Be gentyll, then, of corage, and lerne to be kynde;

2468 *peradvertaunce* close attention   2474 *refrayne* ask
2479 *aforse* exert

For of Noblenesse the chefe poynt is to be lyberall,
So that your Largesse be not to prodygall.

CYRC: Lyberte to a lorde belongyth of ryght,
But wylfull waywardnesse muste walke out of the way.
Measure of your lustys must have the oversyght,
And not all the nygarde nor the chyncherde to play.
Let never negarshyp your noblenesse affray;
In your rewardys use suche moderacyon   2490
That nothynge be gyven without consyderacyon.

PERS: To the increse of your honour then arme you with
ryght,
And fumously adresse you with magnanymyte;
And ever let the drede of God be in your syght,
And knowe your selfe mortal for all your dygnyte.

·   ·   ·   ·   ·   ·   ·   ·   ·

Set not all your affyaunce in Fortune full of gyle;
Remember this lyfe lastyth but a whyle.

MAG: Redresse, in my remembraunce your lesson shall
rest;
And Sad Cyrcumspeccyon I marke in my mynde:
But, Perseveraunce, me semyth your probleme was best;   2500
I shall it never forget nor leve it behynde,
But hooly to Perseveraunce my selfe I wyll bynde,
Of that I have mysdone to make a redresse,
And with Sad Cyrcumspeccyon correcte my
wantonnesse.

RED: Unto this processe brefly compylyd,
Comprehendyng the worlde casuall and transytory,

2488 *nygarde* niggard   *chyncherde* miser
2493 *fumously* zealously   2506 *casuall* precarious

Who lyst to consyder shall never be begylyd
Yf it be regystryd well in memory.
A playne example of worldly vaynglory,
Howe in this worlde there is no sekernesse,   2510
But fallyble flatery enmyxyd with bytternesse.

Nowe well, nowe wo, nowe hy, nowe lawe degre;
Nowe ryche, nowe pore, nowe hole, nowe in dysease;
Nowe pleasure at large, nowe in captyvyte;
Nowe leve, nowe lothe, now please, nowe dysplease;
Now ebbe, now flowe, nowe increase, now dyscrease:
So in this worlde there is no sykernesse,
But fallyble flatery enmyxyd with bytternesse.

CYRC: A myrrour incleryd is this interlude,
This lyfe inconstant for to beholde and se: 2520
Sodenly avaunsyd, and sodenly subdude,
Sodenly ryches, and sodenly poverte,
Sodenly comfort, and sodenly adversyte,
Sodenly thus Fortune can bothe smyle and frowne,
Sodenly set up, and sodenly cast downe;

Sodenly promotyd, and sodenly put backe;
Sodenly cherysshyd, and sodenly cast asyde;
Sodenly commendyd, and sodenly fynde a lacke;
Sodenly grauntyd, and sodenly denyed;
Sodenly hyd, and sodenly spyed: 2530
Sodenly thus Fortune can bothe smyle and frowne,
Sodenly set up, and sodenly cast downe.

PERS: This treatyse, devysed to make you dysporte,
Shewyth nowe adayes howe the worlde comberyd is,

2510 *sekernesse* security   2512 *lawe* low   2515 *leve* pleasant
2519 *incleryd* clear   2528 *lacke* fault

To the pythe of the mater who lyst to resorte:
To-day it is well, to-morowe it is all amysse;
To-day in delyte, tomorowe bare of blysse;
To-day a lorde, to-morowe ly in the duste:
Thus in this worlde there is no erthly truste.

To-day fayre wether, to-morowe a stormy rage;   2540
To-day hote, to-morowe outragyous colde;
To-day a yoman, to-morowe made of page;
To-day in surety, to-morowe bought and solde;
To-day maysterfest, to-morowe he hath no holde:
To-day a man, to-morowe he lyeth in the duste:
Thus in this worlde there is no erthly truste.

MAG: This mater we have movyd you myrthys to make,
  Precely purposyd under pretence of play,
  Shewyth wysdome to them that wysdome can take:
  Howe sodenly worldly welth dothe dekay;   2550
  How wysdom thorowe wantonesse vanysshyth away;
  How none estate lyvynge of hymselfe can be sure,
  For the welthe of this worlde can not indure.

Of the tereste rechery we fall in the flode,
Beten with stormys of many a frowarde blast,
Ensordyd with the wawys savage and wode.
Without our shyppe be sure it is lykely to brast.
Yet of Magnyfycence oft made is the mast;
Thus none estate lyvynge of hym[selfe] can be sure,
For the welthe of this worlde can not indure.   2560

RED: Nowe semyth us syttynge that ye then resorte
  Home to your paleys with joy and ryalte.

2544 *maysterfest* bound to a master   2548 *Precely* seriously
2554 *tereste* earthly   *rechery* riches   2556 *wawys* waves

CYRC: Where every thyng is ordenyd after your noble
        porte.
PERS: There to indeuer with all felycyte.
MAG: I am content, my frendys, that it so be.
RED: And ye that have harde this dysporte and game,
  Jhesus preserve you frome endlesse wo and shame.

Amen.

2563 *porte* reputation   2564   *indeuer* endure

🐟 🐟 🐟

KING JOHAN

JOHN BALE

Written 1538–60

Manuscript HM3. Huntington Library, San Marino, California

'This seist thou, that it is the bloudy doctrine of the Pope which causeth disobedience, rebelion and insurreccion. For he teacheth to fighte and to defende his tradicions and what so ever he dreameth with fire, water and swerde, and to dis-obeye father, mother, master, lorde, kynge, and emperour.'

W. Tyndale, *The Obedience of a Christen Man*, f. xxiiij

King Johan.
Englande.
Sedicyon, also Stevyn Langton (or the Monke).
Nobylyte.
Clergye.
Cyvyle Order.
Dissymulacyon, also Raymundus, also Simon of Swinsett.
Usurpid Power, also The Pope.
Privat Welth, also Cardynall Pandulphus.
Treason.
Commynalte.
Veritas.
Imperyall Majestye.
The Interpretour.

KING JOHAN

[ACT ONE]

[Enter King John.]

KYNGE JOHAN: To declare the powres and their force to
   enlarge
The Scriptur of God doth flow in most abowndaunce;
And of sophysteres the cauteles to dyscharge,
Bothe Peter and Pawle makyth plenteosse utterauns;
How that all pepell shuld shew there trew alegyauns
To ther lawfull kyng, Christ Jesu dothe consent,
Whych to the hygh powres was evere obedyent.

To shew what I am I thynke yt convenyent:
Johan, Kyng of Ynglond, the cronyclys doth me call.
My granfather was an emperowre excelent,   10
My fathere, a kyng by successyon lyneall,
A kyng my brother, lyke as to hym ded fall;
Rychard Cur-de-lyon, they callyd hym in Fraunce,
Whych had over enymyes most fortynable chaunce.

By the wyll of God, and his hygh ordynaunce
In Yerlond and Walys, in Angoye and Normandye,
In Ynglond also, I have had the governaunce
I have worne the crowne and wrowght vyctoryouslye,
And now do purpose by practyse and by stodye

1 *declare* reveal, prove 3 *sophysteres* false reasoners
cauteles tricks 12 *ded* did 14 *fortynable* fortunate
18 *wrowght* succeeded 19 *practyse* skill, care *stodye* study, care

317

To reforme the lawes and sett men in good order,　　20
That trew justyce may be had in every bordere.

[*Enter*] *Ynglond Vidua.*

[ENGLANDE:] Than I trust yowr Grace wyll waye a poore
　　　　　wedowes cause,
Ungodly usyd, as ye shall know in short clause.
K. JOHAN: Yea, that I wyll swer, yf yt be trew and just.
ENGLANDE: Lyke as yt beryth trewth, so lett yt be dyscust.
K. JOHAN: Than, gentyll wydowe, tell me what the mater ys.
ENGLANDE: Alas, yowr clargy hath done very sore amys
In mysusyng me ageynst all ryght and justice;
And for my more greffe therto they other intyce.
K. JOHAN: Whom do they intyce for to do the injurye?　　30
ENGLANDE: Soch as hath enterd by false hypocrysye,
Moch worse frutes havyng than hathe the thornes
　　　　　unplesaunt,
For they are the trees that God dyd never plant,
And, as Christ dothe saye, blynd leaders of the blynd.
K. JOHAN: Tell me whom thow menyst, to satysfy my
　　　　　mynd.
ENGLANDE: Suche lubbers as hath dysgysed heades in their
　　　　　hoodes,
Whych in ydelnes do lyve by other menns goodes:
Monkes, chanons, and nones, in dyvers coloure and
　　　　　shappe,
Bothe whyght, blacke and pyed – God send ther
　　　　　increase yll happe!
K. JOHAN: Lete me know thy name or I go ferther with
　　　　　the.　　40
ENGLANDE: Ynglond, syr, Ynglond my name is; ye may
　　　　　trust me.

24 *swer* sure　25 *dyscust* considered　29 *greffe* grief　30 *the* thee
32 *Moch* much　36 *lubbers* louts　38 *chanons* canons　*nones* nuns
39 *pyed* pied　40 *or* before

K. JOHAN: I mervell ryght sore how thow commyst
  chaungyd thus.

[*Enter Sedition.*]

SEDICYON: What, you ij alone? I wyll tell tales, by
  Jesus!
And saye that I see yow fall here to bycherye.
K. JOHAN: Avoyd, lewde person, for thy wordes are
  ungodlye.
SEDICYON: I crye yow mercy, sur. I pray yow be not
  angrye.
Be my fayth and trowth, I cam hyther to be merye.
K. JOHAN: Thow canst with thy myrth in no wysse
  dyscontent me,
So that thow powder yt with wysdom and honeste.
SEDICYON: I am no spycer, by the messe! Ye may
  beleve me.   50
K. JOHAN: I speke of no spyce, but of cyvyle honeste.
SEDICYON: Ye spake of powder, by the Holy Trynyte!
K. JOHAN: Not as thow takyst yt, of a grosse capasyte,
But as Seynt Pawle meanyth unto the Collessyans
  playne:
'So seasyne yowr speche, that yt be with-owt
  dysdayne.'
Now, Ynglond, to the: go thow forth with thy tale
And showe the cawse why thow lokyst so wan and pale.
ENGLANDE: I told yow be-fore the faulte was in the clergye
That I, a wedow, apere to yow so barelye.
SEDICYON: Ye are a Wylly Wat, and wander here full
  warelye!   60
K. JOHAN: Why in the clargye, do me to understande.
ENGLANDE: For they take from me my cattell, howse and
  land,

---

44 *bycherye* wickedness 49 *So that* provided that *powder* mix
53 *grosse* coarse *capasyte* understanding 55 *seasyne* season
59 *barelye* poorly dressed 60 *warelye* cunningly

My wodes and pasturs, with other commodyteys.
Lyke as Christ ded saye to the wyckyd Pharyseys,
'Pore wydowys howsys ye grosse up by long prayers,'
In syde cotys wandryng lyke most dysgysed players.

SEDICYON: They are well at ese that hath soch
    soth-sayers.
K. JOHAN: They are thy chylderne; thou owghtest to say
    the[m] good.
ENGLANDE: Nay, bastardes they are, unnaturall, by the
    rood!
Sens ther begynnyng they ware never good to me.   70
The wyld bore of Rome – God let hym never to thee –
Lyke pyggys they folow, in fantysyes, dreames and
 lyes,
And ever are fed with his vyle cerymonyes.
SEDICYON: Nay, sumtyme they eate bothe flawnes and
    pygyn-pyes.
K. JOHAN: By the bore of Rome, I trow thow menyst the
    Pope.
ENGLANDE: I mene non other but hym, God geve hym a
    rope!
K. JOHAN: And why dost thow thus compare hym to a
    swyne?
ENGLANDE: For that he and his to such bestlynes
    inclyne.
They forsake Godes word whych is most puer and cleane,
And unto the lawys of synfull men they leane.   80
Lyke as the vyle swyne the most vyle metes dessyer
And hath gret plesure to walowe them-selvys in myre,
So hath this wyld bore, with his church unyversall,
His sowe with hyr pygys and monstres bestyall,
Dylyght in mennys draffe and covytus lucre all.
Yea, *aper de sylva* the prophet dyd hym call.
SEDICYON: Hold yowr peace, ye whore, or ellys, by
    masse, I trowe,

---

63 *commodyteys* possessions 65 *grosse up* appropriate
71 *bore* boar *thee* thrive 74 *flawnes* flat cakes *pygyn-pyes* pigeon pies
79 *puer* pure 81 *metes* food *dessyer* desire 85 *draffe* (n) refuse

I shall cawse the Pope to curse the as blacke as a
  crowe.

K. JOHAN: What arte thow, felow, that seme so braggyng
    bolde?

SEDICYON: I am Sedycyon, that with the Pope wyll hold   90
So long as I have a hole within my breche.

ENGLANDE: Commaund this felow to avoyd, I yow
    beseche,
For dowghtles he hath don me great injury.

K. JOHAN: A-voyd, lewd felow, or thow shalt rewe yt
    truly.

SEDICYON: I wyll not awaye for that same wedred wytche;
She shall rather kysse whereas it doth not ytche.
Quodcumque ligaveris I trow wyll playe soch a parte
That I shall abyde in Englond, magry yowr harte.
Tushe, the Pope ableth me to subdewe bothe kyng and
  keyser.

K. JOHAN: Off that thow and I wyll common more at
    leyser.   100

ENGLANDE: Trwly of the devyll they are that do
    onythyng
To the subdewyng of ony Christen kyng;
For be he good or bade, he is of Godes apoyntyng:
The good for the good, the badde ys for yll doyng.

K. JOHAN: Of that we shall talke here-after: say forth thy
    mynd now
And show me how thou art thus be-cum a wedowe.

ENGLANDE: Thes vyle popych swyne hath clene exyled
    my hosband.

K. JOHAN: Who ys thy husbond? Tel me, good gentyll
    Yngland.

ENGLANDE: For soth, God hym-selfe, the spowse of every
    sort
That seke hym in fayth to ther sowlys helth and
  comfort.   110

95 *wedred* withered   98 *magry* in spite of
99 *ableth* empowers   *keyser* caesar, emperor
100 *common* (v) speak   *leyser* leisure

SEDICYON: He ys scant honest that so many wyfes wyll
    have.

K. JOHAN: I saye hold yowr peace and stond asyde lyke a
    knave!

    Ys God exylyd owt of this Regyon? Tell me.

ENGLANDE: Yea, that he is, ser, yt is the much more pete.

K. JOHAN: How commyth yt to passe that he is thus
    abusyd?

ENGLANDE: Ye know he abydyth not where his word ys
    refusyd,

    For God is his word, lyke as Seynt John dothe tell
    In the begynnyng of his moste blyssyd gospell.
    The Popys pyggys may not abyd this word to be hard,
    Nor knowyn of pepyll, or had in anye regard.   120
    Ther eyes are so sore they maye not abyd the lyght,
    And that bred so hard ther gald gummes may yt not
      byght.
    I, knowyng yowr grace to have here the governance
    By the gyft of God, do knowlege my allegeance,
    Desyeryng yowr Grace to waye suche injuryes
    As I daylye suffer by thes same subtyll spyes.
    And lett me have ryght as ye are a ryghtfull kyng,
    Apoyntyd of God to have such mater in doyng;
    For God wyllyth yow to helpe the pore wydowes cause,
    As he by Esaye protesteth in this same clause: 130
    Querite iudicium, subvenite oppresso,
    Iudicate pupillo, defendite viduam.
    Seke ryght to poore, to the weake and faterlesse,
    Defende the wydowe whan she is in dystresse.

SEDICYON: I tell ye, the woman ys in great hevynes.

K. JOHAN: I may not in no wyse leve thi ryght undyscuste,
    For God hath sett me by his apoyntment just
    To further thy cause and to mayntayne thi ryght,
    And therefor I wyll supporte the daye and nyght.
    So long as my symple lyffe shall here indewer,   140

---

114 *pete* pity   119 *hard* heard   122 *gald* galled, sore   *byght* bite
124 *knowlege* acknowledge   133 *faterlesse* fatherless
136 *undyscuste* without legal inquiry   140 *indewer* endure

I wyll se the have no wrong, be fast and swer.
I wyll fyrst of all call my nobylyte,
Dwkis, erlyes and lordes, yche on in ther degre;
Next them the clargy, or fathers spirituall,
Archebysshopes, bysshoppes, abbottes, and pryers all;
Than the great juges, and lawers everychon,
So opyny[n]g to them thi cause and petyfull mone,
By the meanys wherof I shall ther myndes understande.
Yf they helpe the not, my-selfe wyll take yt in hande,
And sett such a waye as shall be to thi comforte.   150

ENGLANDE: Than for an answare I wyll shortly ageyne
        resort.
K. JOHAN: Do, Ynglond, hardly, and thow shalt have
        remedy.
ENGLANDE: God reward yowr Grace, I be-seche hym
        hartely,
And send yow longe dayes to governe this realme in
        peace!
K. JOHAN: Gramercy, Yngland, and send the plentyus
        increse.

Go owt Ynglond and drese for Clargy.

SEDICYON: Of bablyng matters, I trow, yt is tyme to cease.
K. JOHAN: Why dost thow call them bablyng maters?
        Tell me.
SEDICYON: For they are not worth the shakyng of a
        per-tre
Whan the peres are gon; they are but dyble-dable.
I marvell ye can abyd suche byble-bable.   160
K. JOHAN: Thow semyst to be a man of symple
        dyscrescyon.

---

143 *Dwkis* dukes   145 *pryers* priors   146 *Than* then
lawers lawyers   *everychon* everyone   147 *opynyng* revealing
mone complaint   152 *hardly* certainly   158 *per-tre* pear-tree
159 *dyble-dable* trifles   160 *byble-bable* idle talk

SEDICYON: Alas, that ye are not a pryst to here
    confessyon.

K. JOHAN: Why for confessyon? Lett me know thi fantasye.

SEDICYON: Becawse that ye are a man so full of mercye,
    Namely to women that wepe with a hevy harte
    Whan they in the churche hath lett but a lytyll farte.

K. JOHAN: I perseyve well now thow speakyst all this in
    mockage
    Becawse I take parte with Englandes ryghtfull
    herytage.
    Say thu what thow wylt, her mater shall not peryshe.

SEDICYON: Yt is joye of hym that women so can
    cheryshe.   170

K. JOHAN: God hathe me ordeynned in this same princely
    estate
    For that I shuld helpe such as be desolate.

SEDICYON: Yt is as great pyte to se a woman wepe
    As yt is to se a sely dodman crepe,
    Or, as ye wold say, a sely goose go barefote.

K. JOHAN: Thow semyste by thy wordes to have no more
    wytt than a coote.
    I mervell thow arte to England so un-naturall:
    Beyng her owne chyld, thou art worse than a best
    brutall.

SEDICYON: I am not her chyld! I defye hyr, by the messe!
    I her sonne, quoth he? I had rather she were hedlesse.   180
    Thowgh I sumtyme be in Englond for my pastaunce,
    Yet was I neyther borne here, in Spayne nor in
    Fraunce,
    But under the Pope in the holy cyte of Rome,
    And there wyll I dwell un-to the daye of dome.

K. JOHAN: But what is thy name? Tell me yett onys
    agayne.

SEDICYON: As I sayd afore, I am Sedycyon playne:
    In every relygyon and munkysh secte I rayne,

163 *fantasye* caprice, silly notion   167 *mockage* mockery
171 *ordeynned* ordained   174 *sely* humble   *dodman* snail   178 *best* beast
181 *pastaunce* pastime, pleasure

Havyng yow prynces in scorne, hate and dysdayne.

K. JOHAN: I pray the, good frynd, tell me what ys thy
      facyon.

SEDICYON: Serche and ye shall fynd in every
      congregacyon   190
That long to the Pope, for they are to me full swer,
And wyll be so long as they last and endwer.

K. JOHAN: Yff thow be a cloysterer, tell of what order thow
      art.

SEDICYON: In every estate of the clargye I playe a part:
Sumtyme I can be a monke in a long syd cowle;
Sumtyme I can be a none and loke lyke an owle;
Sumtyme a channon in a syrples fayer and whyght;
A chapterhowse monke sumtym I apere in syght;
I am ower Syre John sumtyme, with a new shaven
      crowne;
Sumtyme the person, and swepe the stretes with a syd
      gowne;   200
Sumtyme the bysshoppe with a myter and a cope;
A graye fryer sumtyme, with cutt shoes and a rope;
Sumtyme I can playe the whyght monke, sumtyme the
      fryer,
The purgatory prist and every-mans wyffe desyer.
This cumpany hath provyded for me morttmayne,
For that I myght ever among ther sort remayne.
Yea, to go farder, sumtyme I am a cardynall
Yea, sumtyme a Pope, and than am I lord over all,
Bothe in hevyn and erthe and also in purgatory,
And do weare iij crownes whan I am in my glorye.   210

K. JOHAN: But what doeste thow here in England? Tell
      me shortlye.

SEDICYON: I hold upp the Pope, as in other places many,
For his ambassador I am contynwally,
In Sycell, in Naples, in Venys and Ytalye,
In Pole, Spruse and Be[r]ne, in Denmarke and
      Lumbardye,

189 *facyon* sect, allegiance   191 *long* belong   197 *syrples* surplice
201 *myter* mitre   205 *morttmayne* inalienable right

In Aragon, in Spayne, in Fraunce and in Germanye,
In Ynglond, in Scotlond, and in other regyons elles.
For his holy cawse I mayntayne traytors and rebelles,
That no prince can have his peples obedyence,
Except yt doth stand with the Popes prehemynence.   220

K. JOHAN: Gett the hence, thow knave, and moste
       presumptuows wreche,
Or as I am trew kyng, thow shalt an halter streche!
We wyll thow know yt, owr powr ys of God,
And therfor we wyll so execute the rod
That no lewde pryst shall be able to mayneteyne the.
I se now they be at to mych lyberte;
We wyll short ther hornys, yf God send tyme and
      space.

SEDICYON: Than I in Englon[d] am lyke to have no
      place?

K. JOHAN: No, that thow arte not, and therfor a-voyd
      apace!

SEDICYON: By the holy masse, I must lawgh to here
      yowr grace!   230
Ye suppose and thynke that ye cowd me subdewe.
Ye shall never fynd yowr supposycyon trewe,
Thowgh ye wer as strong as Hector and Diomedes,
Or as valyant as ever was Achylles.
Ye are well content that bysshoppes contynew styll?

K. JOHAN: We are so in dede, yf they ther dewte fullfyll.

SEDICYON: Nay than, good inowgh! Yowr awtoryte and
      powrr
Shall passe as they wyll; they have sawce bothe swet and
      sowr.

K. JOHAN: What mennyst thow by that? Shew me thi
      intente this howre.

SEDICYON: They are Godes vycars: they can both save
      and lose.   240

K. JOHAN: Ah, thy meenyng ys that they maye a prynce
      despose.

220 *stand with* accord with   225 *lewde* ignorant   236 *dewte* duty
237 *inowgh* enough   239 *howre* hour   240 *lose* destroy

SEDICYON: By the rood, they may, and that wyll appere
      by yow.

K. JOHAN: Be the helpe of God, we shall se to that well
      i-now.

SEDICYON: Nay, that ye can not, thowgh ye had Argus
      eyes,

In abbeyes they have so meny suttyll spyes.

For ones in the yere they have secret vysytacyons,

And yf ony prynce reforme ther ungodly facyons,

Than ij of the monkes must forthe to Rome by and by

With secrett letters to avenge ther injury.

For a thowsand pownd they shrynke not in soch
      matter,   250

And yet for the tyme the prynce to his face, they
      flater.

I am ever-more ther gyde and ther advocate.

K. JOHAN: Than with the bysshoppes and monkes thou
      art checke mate?

SEDICYON: I dwell among them and am one of ther sorte.

K. JOHAN: For thy sake they shall of me have but small
      comforte;

Loke, wher I fynd the, that place wyll I put downe.

SEDICYON: What yf ye do chance to fynd me in every
      towne

Where as is fownded any sect monastycall?

K. JOHAN: I pray God I synke yf I dystroye them not all!

SEDICYON: Well yf ye so do, yett know I where to
      dwell.   260

K. JOHAN: Thow art not skoymose thy fantasy for to tell.

SEDICYON: Gesse at a venture, ye may chance the marke to
      hytt.

K. JOHAN: Thy falssed to shew, no man than thy selfe more
      fytt.

SEDICYON: Mary, in confessyon under-nethe *benedicite*.

K. JOHAN: Nay tell yt ageyne that I may understond the.

---

243 *i-now* enough   247 *ony* any   *facyons* conspiracies
252 *ther* their   253 *checke mate* equal   261 *skoymose* reluctant
263 *falssed* falsehood, falseness

SEDICYON: I saye I can dwell whan all other placys fayle
    me
  In ere confessyon undernethe *benedicite*,
  And whan I am ther the pryst may not bewray me.

K. JOHAN: Why, wyll ere confesshon soch a secret traytor
    be?

SEDICYON: Whan all other fayle, he is so swre as stele.   270
  Offend Holy Churche and I warant ye shall yt fele;
  For by confessyon the Holy Father knoweth
  Throw-out all Christendom what to his holynes growth.

K. JOHAN: Oh, where ys Nobylyte, that he myght knowe
    thys falshed?

SEDICYON: Nay, he is becum a meyntener of owr godhed.
  I know that he wyll do Holy Chyrch no wronge,
  For I am his gostly father and techear amonge.
  He belevyth nothyng but as Holy Chyrch doth tell.

K. JOHAN: Why, geveth he no credence to Cristes holy
    Gospell?

SEDICYON: No, ser, by the messe, but he callyth them
    herytyckes   280
  That preche the Gospell, and sedycyows scysmatyckes;
  He tache them, vex them, from preson to preson he
    turne them,
  He indygth them, juge them, and in conclusyon he
    burne them.

K. JOHAN: We rewe to here this of owr Nobylyte;
  But in this behalfe what seyst of the spretuallte?

SEDICYON: Of this I am swer: to them to be no stranger,
  And spesyally, whan ther honor ys in dawnger.

K. JOHAN: We trust owr lawers have no such wyckyd
    myndes.

---

267 *ere* ear (i.e. auricular confession)   268 *bewray* reveal
270 *swre* sure   275 *meyntener* defender, supporter
277 *gostly* spiritual   *techear* teacher   *amonge* at the same time
279 *geveth* giveth   281 *sedycyows* seditious
scysmatyckes schismatics, those who divide the Church
282 *tache* arrests   283 *indygth* indicts   284 *here* hear
285 *behalfe* matter   *seyst* sayest   *spretuallte* spirituality

SEDICYON: Yes, they many tymys are my most secrett
    fryndes.
  With faythfull precheres they can play leger-demayne,   290
  And with falce colores procure them to be slayne.

K. JOHAN: I perseyve this worlde is full of iniquite.
  As God wold have yt, here cummyth Nobylyte.

SEDICYON: Doth he so in dede? By owr Lord, than wyll
    I hence!

K. JOHAN: Thow saydest thou woldyst dwell where he
    kepyth resydence.

SEDICYON: Yea, but fyrst of all I must chaunge myn
    apparell
  Unto a bysshoope, to maynetayene with my quarell,
  To a monke or pryst or to sum holy fryer.
  I shuld never elles accomplych my dysyre.

K. JOHAN: Why, art thow goyng? Naye, brother, thow
    shalte not hence.   300

SEDICYON: I wold not be sene as I am for fortye pence.
  Whan I am relygyouse I wyll returne agayne.

K. JOHAN: Thow shalt tary here, or I must put the to
    payne.

SEDICYON: I have a great mynd to be a lecherous man –
  A wengonce take yt! I wold saye a relygyous man.
  I wyll go and cum so fast as evyre I can.

K. JOHAN: Tush, dally not with me! I saye thou shalt
    abyde.

SEDICYON: Wene yow to hold me that I shall not slyppe
    asyde?

K. JOHAN: Make no more prattyng, for I saye thou shalt
    abyde.

SEDICYON: Stoppe not my passage, I must over see at the
    next tyde.   310

K. JOHAN: I wyll ordeyne so, I trowe, thou shalt not
    over.

SEDICYON: Tush, tush, I am sewer of redy passage at
    Dover.

290 *leger-demayne* trickery   308 *Wene* think   309 *prattyng* chattering

Her go owt Sedwsion and drese for Syvyll Order.

K. JOHAN: The devyll go with hym! The unthryftye
      knave is gon.

[*Enter Nobility.*]

NOBYLYTE: Troble not yowr-sylfe with no soch
      dyssolute persone,
For ye knowe full well, very lyttell honeste
Ys gote at ther handes in every commynnalte.
K. JOHAN: This is but dallyaunce; ye do not speke as ye
      thynke.
NOBYLYTE: By my trowthe I do, or elles I wold I shuld
      synke.
K. JOHAN: Than must I marvell at yow of all men
      lyvynge.
NOBYLYTE: Why mervell at me? Tell me yowr very
      menyng.   320
K. JOHAN: For no man levyng is in more famylyerite
With that wycked wrech, yf it be trew that he told me.
NOBYLYTE: What wrech speke ye of? For Jesus love,
      intymate.
K. JOHAN: Of that presumtous wrech that was with me
      here of late,
Whom yow wyllyd not to vexe my-selfe with-all.
NOBYLYTE: I know hym? Not I, by the waye that my
      sowll to shall!
K. JOHAN: Make yt not so strange, for ye know hym wyll
      inow.
NOBYLYTE: Beleve me yff ye wyll! I know hym not, I
      assuer yow.
K. JOHAN: Ware ye never yett aquantyd with Sedissyon?

316 *commynnalte* community   317 *dallyaunce* joking, trifling
321 *levyng* living   323 *intymate* reveal   327 *wyll* well

NOBYLYTE: Syns I was a chyld, both hym and his
     condycyon   330
I ever hated for his iniquite.
K. JOHAN: A clere tokyn that is of trew nobelyte;
But I pray to God we fynde yt not other-wyse.

[*Enter Clergye.*]

Yt was never well syns the clargy wrowght by practyse
And left the Scriptur for mens ymagynacyons,
Dyvydyng them-selvys in so many congrygacyons
Of monkes, chanons and fryers, of dyvers colors and
     facyons.
CLERGYE: I do trust yowr grace wyll be as lovyng now
As yowr predysessours have bene to us before yow.
K. JOHAN: I wyll suer wey my love with yowr behavers: 340
Lyke as ye deserve, so wyll I bere yow favers.
Clargy, marke yt well, I have more to yow to say
Than, as the sayeng is, the prist dyd speke a Sonday.
CLERGYE: Ye wyll do us no wrong, I hope, nor injurye.
K. JOHAN: No, I wyll do yow ryght in seyng yow do
     yowr dewtye.
We know the cawtelles of yowr sotyll companye.
CLERGYE: Yf ye do us wrong we shall seke remedy.
K. JOHAN: Yea, that is the cast of all yowr company.
Whan kynges correcte yow for yowr actes most
     ungodly,
To the Pope, syttyng in the chayer of pestoolens,   350
Ye ronne to remayne in yowr concupysens.
Thus sett ye at nowght all princely prehemynens,
Subdewyng the ordere of dew obedyens.
But with-in a whyle I shall so abate yowr pryde

334 *practyse* treachery   340 *wey* weigh   345 *seyng* seeing
346 *cawtelles* tricks   350 *chayer* chair   pestoolens *pestilence*
351 *ronne* run   *concupysens* desires   352 *prehemynens* superior rank
353 *dew* due

That to yowr popet ye shall noyther runne nor ryde;
But ye shall be glad to seke to me, yowr prynce,
For all such maters as shall be with in this provynce,
Lyke as God wyllyth yow by his Scripture evydente.

NOBYLYTE: To the Church I trust ye wyll be obedyent.

K. JOHAN: No mater to yow whether I be so or no. 360

NOBYLYTE: Yes, mary, is yt, for I am sworne therunto.
I toke a great othe whan I was dubbyd a knyght
Ever to defend the Holy Churches ryght.

CLERGYE: Yea, and in her quarell ye owght onto deth to
fyght.

K. JOHAN: Lyke backes, in the darke y[e] alweys take
yowr flyght,
Flytteryng in fanseys, and ever abhorre the lyght.
I rew yt in hart that yow, Nobelyte,
Shuld thus bynd yowr-selfe to the grett captyvyte
Of blody Babulon, the grownd and mother of whordom,
The Romych Churche I meane, more vyle than ever
was Sodom, 370
And to say the trewth, a mete spowse for the fynd.

CLERGYE: Yowr grace ys fare gonne; God send yow a
better mynd!

K. JOHAN: Hold yowr peace, I say! Ye are a lytyll to
fatte.
In a whyle, I hope, ye shall be lener sumwhatte.

[*Enter Cyvyle Order.*]

We shall loke to yow, and to Civyle Order also.
Ye walke not so secrett but we know wher abowght ye
goo.

CYVYLE ORDER: Why, yowr grace hath no cawse with me
to be dysplesyd.

355 *popet* pope   365 *backes* bats   366 *Flytteryng* fluttering
371 *mete* suitable   *fynd* fiend   373 *to* too   374 *lener* leaner

K. JOHAN: All thynges consyderyd, we have small cause
    to be plesyd.
CYVYLE ORDER: I be-sech yowr grace to graunt me a
    word or too.
K. JOHAN: Speke on yowr pleasur and yowr hole mynd
    also.   380
CYVYLE ORDER: Ye know very well to set all thynges in
    order
I have moche ado, and many thynges passe fro me
For yowr common welth, and that in every border,
For offyces, for londes, for lawe, and for lyberte.
And for traun[s]gressors I appoynt the penalte,
That cytes and townes maye stand in quiotose peace,
That all theft and murder, with other vyce, maye seace.

Yff I have chaunsed for want of cyrcumspeccyon
To passe the lymytes of ryght and equite,
I submyte my-selfe unto yowr Graces correccyon,   390
Desyryng pardon of yowr benyngnyte.
I wot I maye fall throwgh my fragylyte;
Therfor, I praye yow, tell me what the mater ys,
And amendes shall be where as I have done amyse.

K. JOHAN: Aganste amendement no resounable man can be.
NOBYLYTE: That sentence rysyth owt of an hygh charyte.
K. JOHAN: Now that you are her assembled all together,
    Amongeste other thynges ye shall fyrst of all consyder
    That my dysplesure rebounyth on to yow all.
CLERGYE: To yow non of us ys prejudycyall.   400
K. JOHAN: I shall prove yt. Yes, how have ye usyd
    Englond?
NOBYLYTE: But as yt becommyth us, so fare as I
    understond.

380 *hole* whole   386 *quiotose* quiet   387 *seace* cease
392 *fragylyte* frailty   397 *her* here   399 *rebounyth* rebounds
402 *fare* far

K. JOHAN: Yes, the pore woman complayneth her grevosly,
And not with-owt cawse, for she hath great injurye.
I must se to yt, ther ys no remedy,
For it ys a charge gevyn me from God Allmyghtye.
Howe saye ye, Clargye? Apperyth it not so to yow?

CLERGYE: Yf it lykyth yowr Grace, all we knowe that
well ynow.

K. JOHAN: Than yow, Nobelyte, wyll affyrme yt, I am
suer.

NOBYLYTE: Ye, that I wyll, sur, so long as my lyfe
indure.   410

K. JOHAN: And yow, Cyvyll Order, I thynke wyll graunte
the same?

CYVYLE ORDER: Ondowghted, sir; yea, elles ware yt to
me gret shame.

K. JOHAN: Than for Englandes cause I wyll be sumewhat
playne.

Yt is yow, Clargy, that hathe her in dysdayne
With yowr Latyne howrrs, sermonyes, and popetly
playes.
In her more and more Godes holy worde decayes,
And them to maynteyn unresonable ys the spoyle
Of her londes, her goodes, and of her pore chylderes
toyle.
Rekyn fyrst yowr tythis, yowr devocyons and yowr
offrynges,
Mortuaryes, pardons, bequestes and other thynges,   420
Besydes that ye cache for halowed belles and
purgatorye,
For jwelles, for relyckes, confessyon and cowrtes of
baudrye,
For legacyes, trentalls, with Scalacely messys,
Wherby ye have made the people very assys;
And over all this ye have browght in a rabyll

409 *suer* sure   410 *sur* sir   412 *Ondowghted* undoubtedly   *elles* else
ware were   413 *playne* frank   415 *popetly* popish
418 *chylderes* children's   422 *jwelles* jewels   424 *assys* asses
425 *rabyll* rabble

334

Of Latyne mummers and sectes desseyvabyll,
Evyn to dewore her and eat her upp attonnys.

CLERGYE: Yow wold have no Churche, I wene, by thes
sacred bones.

K. JOHAN: Yes, I wold have a Churche, not of dysgysyd
shavelynges,
But of faythfull hartes and charytable doynges;   430
For whan Christes Chyrch was in her hyeste glory,
She knew neyther thes sectes nor ther ipocrysy.

CLERGYE: Yes, I wyll prove yt by David substancyally:
Astitit Regina a dextris tuis in vestitu
Deaurato circumdata varietate.
A quene, sayth Davyd, on thy ryght hond, Lord, I se,
Apparrellyd with golde and compassyd with
dyversyte.

K. JOHAN: What ys yowr meanyng by that same
Scriptur? Tell me.

CLERGYE: This quene ys the Chyrch, which thorow all
Cristen regions
Ys beawtyfull, dectyd with many holy relygyons: 440
Munkes, chanons and fryeres, most excellent dyvynis,
As Grandy Montensers and other Benedictyns,
Primonstratensers, Bernardes and Gylbertynys,
Jacobytes, Mynors, Whyght Carmes and Augustynis,
Sanbonites, Cluniackes, with holy Carthusyans,
Heremytes and auncors, with most myghty Rodyans,
Crucifers, Lucifers, Brigettes, Ambrosyanes,
Stellifers, Ensifers, with Purgatoryanes,
Sophyanes, Indianes, and Camaldulensers,
Jesuytes, Joannytes, with Clarimontensers,   450
Clarynes and Columbynes, Templers, Newe
Ninivytes,
Rufyanes, Tercyanes, Lorytes and Lazarytes,
Hungaryes, Teutonyckes, Hospitelers, Honofrynes,
Basyles and Bonhams, Sclavons and Celestynes,

426 *sectes* sects   *desseyvabyll* deceiving   427 *dewore* devour
attonnys at once   429 *shavelynges* tonsured ecclesiastics
440 *dectyd* decked

Paulynes, Hieronymytes, and Monkes of Josaphathes
    Valleye,
Fulgynes, Flamynes, with Bretherne of the Black
    Alleye,
Donates and Dimysynes, with Canons of S. Mark,
Vestals and Monyals, a worlde to heare them barke,
Abbottes and doctors, with bysshoppes and
    cardynales,
Arche-decons and pristes, as to ther fortune falles.   460
CYVYLE ORDER: Me thynkyth yowr fyrst text stondeth
            nothyng with yowr reson,
For in Davydes tyme were no such sectes of relygyon.
K. JOHAN: Davyd meanyth vertuys by the same diversyte,
As in the sayd psalme yt is evydent to se,
And not munkysh sectes; but yt is ever yowr cast
For yowr advauncement the Scripturs for to wrast.
CLERGYE: Of owr Holy Father in this I take my grownd,
Which hathe awtoryte the Scripturs to expond.
K. JOHAN: Naye he presumyth the Scripturs to confownd.
Nowther thow nor the Pope shall do pore Englond
    wronge,   470
I beyng governor and kyng her peple amonge.
Whyle yow for lucre sett forth your popysh lawys
Yowr-selves to advaunce, ye wold make us pycke strawes.
Nay, ipocrytes, nay. We wyll not be scornyd soo
Of a sort of knavys; we shall loke yow otherwyse too!
NOBYLYTE: Sur, yowr sprytes are movyd, I persayve by
        yowr langage.
K. JOHAN: I wonder that yow for such veyne popych
        baggage
Can suffyr Englond to be impoveryshyd
And mad a begger; ye are very yll advysyd.
NOBYLYTE: I marvell grettly that ye saye thus to me.   480
K. JOHAN: For dowghtles ye do not as becummyth
        Nobelyte;
Ye spare nouther landes nor goodes, but all ye geve

461 *stondeth* agrees   465 *cast* trick   466 *wrast* twist
475 *sort* group, company   479 *mad* made

To thes cormerantes; yt wold any good man greve
To see yowr madnes, as I wold God shuld save me.
NOBYLYTE: Sur, I suppose yt good to bylde a perpetuite
For me and my frendes, to be prayed for evermore.
K. JOHAN: Tush, yt is madnes all to dyspayre in God so
        sore
And to thynke Christes deth to be unsufficient.
NOBYLYTE: Sur, that I have don was of a good intent.
K. JOHAN: The intente ys nowght which hath no sewer
        grounde.   490
CLERGYE: Yff yow continue, ye wyll Holy Chyrch
        confunde.
K. JOHAN: Nay, no Holy Chyrch, nor feythfull
        congregacyon,
But an hepe of adders of Antecristes generacyon.
CYVYLE ORDER: Yt pyttyth me moche that ye are to
        them so harde.
K. JOHAN: Yt petyeth me more that ye them so mych
        regarde.
They dystroye mennys sowlles with damnable
        supersticyon,
And decaye all realmys by meyntenaunce of sedycon.
Ye wold wonder to know what profe I have of this.
NOBYLYTE: Well amenment shalbe wher any thyng is
        amysse,
For, undowtted, God doth open soche thynges to
        prynces   500
As to none other men in the Cristyen provynces,
And therfor we wyll not in this with yowr Grace
        contend.
CYVYLE ORDER: No, but with Godes grace we shall owr
        mysededes amend.
CLERGYE: For all such forfetes as yowr pryncely mageste
For yowr owne person or realme can prove by me,
I submytte my-selfe to yow, bothe body and goodes.

485 *perpetuite* perpetual right   491 *confunde* confound
494/5 *pyttyth petyeth* grieves   499 *amenment* amendment

Knele.

K. JOHAN: We pety yow now, consyderyng yowr
repentante modes,
And owr gracyous pardone we grante yow upon
amendment.

CLERGYE: God preserve yowr Grace and Mageste
excelent!

K. JOHAN: Aryse, Clargy, aryse, and ever be obedyent, 510
And, as God commandeth yow, take us for yowr
governere.

CLERGYE: By the Grace of God, the Pope shall be my
rulare.

K. JOHAN: What saye ye, Clargy? Who ys yowr
governer?

CLERGYE: Ha, ded I stomble? I sayd my prynce ys my
ruler.

K. JOHAN: I pray to owr Lord this obedyence maye
indewre.

CLERGYE: I wyll not breke yt, ye may be fast and suer.

K. JOHAN: Than cum hether all thre: ye shall know more
of my mynde.

CLERGYE: Owr kyng to obeye the Scriptur doth us
bynde.

K. JOHAN: Ye shall fyrst be sworne to God and to the
crowne
To be trew and juste in every cetye and towne, 520
And this to perfor[m]e set hand and kysse the bocke.

CYVYLE ORDER: With the wyffe of Loth we wyll not
backeward locke
Nor turne from owr oth, but ever obeye yowr grace.

K. JOHAN: Than wyll I gyve yow yowr chargys her in
place
And accepte yow all to be of owr hyghe councell.

---

514 *stomble* stumble   515 *indewre* endure

CLERGYE:
NOBYLYTE: } To be faythfull, than, ye us more
CYVYLE ORDER: } streytly compell.

K. JOHAN: For the love of God, loke to the state of
        Englond!
Leate non enemy holde her in myserable bond.
Se yow defend her as yt becommyth nobilite,
Se yow instrutte her acordyng to yowr degre,   530
Fournysh her yow with a cyvyle honeste.
Thus shall she florysh in honor and grett plente.
With godly wysdom yowr maters to conveye
That the commynnalte the powers maye obeye,
And ever be-ware of that false thefe Sedycyon,
Whych poysennyth all realmes and bryng them to
        perdycyon.
NOBYLYTE: Sur, for soche wrecches we wyll be so
        circumspectte
That neyther ther falsed nor gylle shall us infecte.
CLERGYE: I warrant yow, sur, no, and that shall well
        apere.
CYVYLE ORDER: We wyll so provyde yff anye of them
        cum here   540
To dysturbe the realme, they shall be full glad to fle.
K. JOHAN: Well, yowr promyse includeth no small
        dyffyculte.
But I put the case that this false thefe Sedycyon
Shuld cum to yow thre and call hym-selfe Relygyon.
Myght he not under the pretence of holynes
Cawse yow to consent to myche ungodlynes?
NOBYLYTE: He shall never be able to do yt veryly.
K. JOHAN: God graunt ye be not deceyvyd by
        hypocresye.
I say no more, I. In shapes aparell sum walke
And seme relygeyose that deceyvably can calke.   550

526 *streytly* strictly   530 *instrutte* instruct   538 *falsed* falsehood
gylle guile   546 *myche* much   550 *relygeyose* religious   *calke* calculate

Beware of soche hipocrites as the kyngdom of hevyn
from man
Do hyde for a-wantage, for they deceyve now and than.
Well I leve yow here; yche man consyder his dewtye.

NOBYLYTE: With Godes leve, no faute shall be in this
companye.

K. JOHAN: Cum, Cyvyle Order, ye shall go hence with me.

CYVYLE ORDER: At yowr commandmente I wyll gladlye
wayte upon ye.

*Here Kyng Johan and Sivile Order go owt: and
Syvile Order drese hym for Sedewsyon.*

NOBYLYTE: Me thynke the kyng is a man of a
wonderfull wytt.

CLERGYE: Naye, saye that he ys of a vengeable craftye
wytt,
Than shall ye be sure the trewth of the thyng to hytt.
Hard ye not how he of the Holy Church dyd rayle?   560
His extreme thretynynges shall lytyll hym avayle:
I wyll worke soch wayes that he shall of his purpose
fayle.

NOBYLYTE: Yt is meet a prince to saye sumwhat for his
plesure.

CLERGYE: Yea, but yt is to moch to rayle so withowt
mesure.

NOBYLYTE: Well, lett every man speke lyke as he hathe a
cawse.

CLERGYE: Why, do ye say so? Yt is tyme for me than to
pawse.

NOBYLYTE: This will I saye, sur, that he ys so noble a
prince
As this day raygneth in ony Cristyne provynce.

CLERGYE: Mary, yt apereth well by that he wonne in
Fraunce!

NOBYLYTE: Well, he lost not ther so moche by marcyall
chaunce   570

But he gate moche more in Scotland, Ireland and
    Wales.

CLERGYE: Yea, God, sped us well: Crystmes songes are
    mery tales!

NOBYLYTE: Ys dysdayne soche mater as ye know full
    evydent.

Are not bothe Ireland and Wales to hym obedyent?
Yes, he holdyth them bothe in pessable possessyon,
And – by cause I wyll not from yowr tall make
    degressyon –
For his lond in Fraunce he gyveth but lytell forsse,
Havyng to Englond all his love and remorse;
And Angoye he gave to Artur his nevy in chaunge.

CLERGYE: Owr changes are soch that an abbeye turneth
    to a graunge.   580

We are so handled we have scarce eyther horse or male.

NOBYLYTE: He that dothe hate me the worse wyll tell my
    tale.

Yt is yowr [f]assyon soche kynges to dyscommend
As yowr abuses reforme or reprehend.
Yow pristes are the cawse that Chronycles doth defame
So many prynces and men of notable name,
For yow take upon yow to wryght them evermore;
And therfor Kyng Johan ys lyke to rewe yt sore
Whan ye wryte his tyme, for vexcyng of the clargy.

CLERGYE: I mervell ye take his parte so ernestlye.   590

NOBYLYTE: Yt becommyth Nobelyte his prynces fame to
    preserve.

CLERGYE: Yf he contynew, we lyke in a whyle to
    starve:

He demaundeth of us the tenth parte of owr lyvyng.

NOBYLYTE: I thynke yt is then for sum nessessary thyng.

CLERGYE: Mary, to recover that he hath lost in Fraunce,
As Normandy dewkedom and his land beyond
    Orleaunce.

NOBYLYTE: And thynke ye not that a mater nessesary?

575 *pessable* peaceful   576 *tall* tale   581 *male* (n) pack
587 *wryght* (v) correct

CLERGYE: No, sur, by my trowth, he takyng yt of the
    clergy.

NOBYLYTE: Ye cowde be content that he shuld take yt of
    us?

CLERGYE: Yea, so that he wold spare the clargy, by swet
    Jesus!   600

  This takyng of us myght sone growe to a custom,
  And than Holy Churche myght so be browght to
    thraldom,
  Whych hath ben ever from temporall prynces free
  As towchyng trybute or other captyvyte.

NOBYLYTE: He that defendeth yow owght to have parte
    of yowr goodes.

CLERGYE: He hath the prayers of all them that hathe
    hoodes.

NOBYLYTE: Why, ys that inowgh to helpe hym in his
    warre?

CLERGYE: The Churche he may not of lyberte debarre.

NOBYLYTE: Ded not Crist hym-selfe paye trybytt unto
    Cesere?

  Yf he payd trybute, so owght his holy vycar.   610

CLERGYE: To here ye reson so ondyscretlye I wonder.
  Ye must consyder that Cryst that tyme was under,
  But his vycar now ys above the prynces all;
  Therfor be ware ye do not to herysy fall.
  Ye owght to beleve as Holy Churche doth teche yow,
  And not to reason in soche hygh materes now.

NOBYLYTE: I am unlernyd, mȳ wyttes are sone
    confowndyd.

CLERGYE: Than leve soch materes to men more depely
    growndyd.

NOBYLYTE: But how wyll ye do for the othe that ye have
    take?

CLERGYE: The keyes of the Church can all soche materes
    of shake.   620

602 *thraldom* servitude   611 *ondyscretlye* unwisely
620/1 *keyes, kyes* keys   620 *of shake* shake off

NOBYLYTE: What call ye those kyes? I pray yow hartly,
    tell me!
CLERGYE: Owr Holy Fathers powr and his hygh autoryte.
NOBYLYTE: Well, I can no more say; ye are to well
    lernyd for me.
My bysynes ys soche that here now I must leve ye.
CLERGYE: I must hence also so fast as ever maye be,
To sewe unto Rome for the Churches lyberte.

Go owt Nobylyte and Clar[gy].
Here Sedycyon commyth in.

SEDICYON: Have in onys ageyne, in spyght of all myn
    enymyes,
For they can not dryve me from all mennys companyes;
And thowgh yt wer so that all men wold forsake me,
Yet dowght I yt not but sume good women wold take
    me.   630
I loke for felowys that here shuld make sum sporte.
I mervell yt is so longe ere they resorte.
By the messe, I wene the knaves are in the bryers,
Or elles they are fallen in to sum order of fryers.
Naye shall I gesse ryght? They are gon into the stwes.
I holde ye my necke, anon we shall here newes.

[A voice heard] seyng the Leteny.

Lyst, for Godes passyon! I trow her cummeth sum
    hoggherd
Callyng for his pygges – such a noyse I never herd!

Here cum Dyssymulacy[on] syngyng of the Le[t]any.

633 *bryers* briars   635 *stwes* stews   637 *hoggherd* swineherd

DISSYMULACYON: *syng: Sancte Dominice, ora pro nobis.*

SEDICYON: *syng: Sancte* pyld *monache,* I beshrow *vobis.*   640

DISSYMUL: *syng: Sancte Francisse, ora pro nobis.*

SEDICYON: Here ye not? Cockes sowle, what meaneth
      this ypocryte knave?

DISSYMUL: *Pater noster,* I pray God bryng hym sone to
      his grave;

  Qui es in celis, with an vengeable *sanctyficetur,*

Or elles Holy Chyrche shall never thryve, by Saynt
  Peter.

SEDICYON: Tell me, good felowe, makyste thou this
      prayer for me?

DISSYMUL: Ye are as ferce as thowgh ye had broke yore
      nose at the buttre.

I medyll not with the, but here to good sayntes I
  praye,

Agenst soch enmyes as wyll Holy Churche decaye.

Here syng this:

A Johanne Rege iniquo, libera nos, Domine.   650

SEDICYON: Leve, I saye, or by the messe I wyll make yow
      grone.

DISSYMUL: Yff thow be jentyll, I pray the leate me alone,

For with-in a whyle my devocyon wyll be gone.

SEDICYON: And wherfor dost thow praye here so bytterly,

Momblyng thy *Pater noster* and chauntyng the Letany?

DISSYMUL: For that Holy Chyrch myght save hyr
      patrymonye,

And to have of Kyng Johan a tryumph[a]nt vyctorye.

SEDICYON: And why of Kyng Johan? Doth he vexe yow
      so sore?

DISSYMUL: Bothe chyrchys and abbeys he oppressyth
      more and more,

640 *pyld* bald, shaven   647 *buttre* ?tilting
648 *medyll* concern (myself) with   651 *Leve* stop   *grone* groan

And take of the clergye – yt is onresonable to tell.   660

SEDICYON: Owte with the Popys bulles, than, and cursse
          hym downe to hell.

DISSYMUL: Tushe, man, we have done so, but all that
          wyll not helpe.

He regardyth no more the Pope than he dothe a whelpe.

SEDICYON: Well, lett hym a-lone; for that wyll I geve
          hym a scelpe.

But what arte thou callyd of thyn owne munkych
          nacyon?

DISSYMUL: Kepe yt in counsell: Dane Davy
          Dyssymulacyon.

SEDICYON: What, Dyssymulacyon? Cockes sowle myn
          old aquentaunce!

Par me faye, mon amye, je tote ad voutre plesaunce.

DISSYMUL: Gramercyes, good frend, with all my very hert.

I trust we shall talke more frely or we deperte.   670

SEDICYON: Why, vylayn horson! Knowyst not thi cosyn
          Sedycyon?

DISSYMUL: I have ever loved both the and thy condycyon.

SEDICYON: Thow must nedes, I trowe, for we cum of ij
          bretherne:

Yf thou remember, owr fatheres were on manns
          chylderne –

Thow commyst of Falsed and I of Prevy Treason.

DISSYMUL: Than In-fydelyte owr grandfather ys by
          reason.

SEDICYON: Mary, that ys trewe, and his begynner
          Antycrist,

The great Pope of Rome or fyrst veyne popysh prist.

DISSYMUL: Now welcum, cosyn, by the waye that my
          sowle shall to!

SEDICYON: Gramercy, cosyn, by the holy bysshope
          Benno.   680

Thow kepyst thi old wont; thow art styll an abbe mann.

663 *whelpe* puppy   664 *scelpe* blow   666 *Dane* Don, Lord
670 *or* before   *deperte* separate   671 *vylayn* villain   674 *on* one
677 *begynner* originator   678 *veyne* vain   681 *wont* fashion

DISSYMUL: To hold all thynges up I play my part now
  and than.
SEDICYON: Why, what manere of offyce hast thou with
  in the abbey?
DISSYMUL: Of all relygyons I kepe the chyrch dore keye.
SEDICYON: Than of a lykelyhod thow art ther generall
  porter.
DISSYMUL: Nay, of munkes and chanons I am the suttyll
  sorter.
Whyle sum talke with Besse the resydewe kepe sylence.
Thowgh we playe the knavys, we must shew a good
  pretence.
Where so ever sum eate, a serten kepe the froyter;
Where so ever sum slepe, sum must nedes kepe the
  dorter.   690
Dedyst thou never know the maner of owr senyes?
SEDICYON: I was never with them aqueyntyd, by Seynt
  Denyes.
DISSYMUL: Than never knewyst thou the knavery of owr
  menyes.
Yf I shuld tell all, I cowd saye more than that.
SEDICYON: Now, of good felowshyppe, I beseche the show
  me what.
DISSYMUL: The profytable lucre cummyth ever in by me.
SEDICYON: But by what meane? Tell me, I hartely pray
  the.
DISSYMUL: To wynne the peple I appoynt yche man his
  place:
Sum to syng Latyn, and sum to ducke at grace;
Sum to go mummyng, and sum to beare the crosse; 700
Sum to stowpe downeward as ther heades ware stopt
  with mosse;
Sum to rede the epystle and gospell at hygh masse;
Sum syng at the lectorne, with long eares lyke an asse.

685 *ther* there 689 *froyter* refectory 690 *dorter* dormitory
691 *senyes* language of fingers 693 *menyes* tricks 699 *ducke* bob
701 *stopt* ?filled

The pawment of the Chyrche the aunchent faders
   tredes,
Sumtyme with a portas, sumtyme with a payre of bedes;
And this exedyngly drawth peple to devoycyone,
Specyally whan they do se so good relygeon.
Than have we imagys of Seynt Spryte and Seynt
   Savyer:
Moche is the sekynge of them to gett ther faver;
Yong whomen berfote and olde men seke them
   brecheles.   710
The myracles wrowght ther I can in nowyse expresse.
We lacke neyther golde nor sylwer, gyrdles nor rynges,
Candelles nor tapperes, nor other customyd offerynges.
Thowgh I seme a shepe, I can play the suttle foxe:
I can make Latten to bryng this gere to the boxe.
Tushe, Latten ys alone to bryng soche mater to passe;
Ther ys no Englyche that can soche profyghtes
   compasse.
And therfor we wyll no servyce to be songe,
Gospell nor pystell, but all in Latten tonge.
Of owr suttell dryftes many more poyntes are behynde;   720
Yf I tolde yow all, we shuld never have an ende.

SEDICYON: *In nomine Patris*, of all that ever I hard
   Thow art alone yet of soche a dremyng bussard!
DISSYMUL: Nay, dowst thou not se how I in my colours
   jette?
To blynd the peple I have yet a farther fette.
This is for Bernard, and this is for Benet,
This is for Gylbard, and this is for Jhenet;
For Frauncys this is, and this is for Domynyke,
For Awsten and Elen, and this is for Seynt Partryk.
We have many rewlles, but never one we kepe;   730

704 *pawment* pavement   *tredes* treads
705 *portas* portable breviary   *payre of bedes* rosary
710 *whomen* women   *berfote* barefoot   *brecheles* without breeches
713 *tapperes* tapers   715 *gere* matter   720 *dryftes* purposes
723 *dremyng* dreaming   *bussard* buzzard, fool   724 *jette* swagger
725 *fette* device

Whan we syng full lowde owr hartes be fast aslepe.
We resemble sayntes, in gray, whyte, blacke and blewe,
Yet unto prynces not one of owr nomber trewe —
And that shall kyng Johan prove shortly by the rode.

SEDICYON: But in the meane tyme yowr-selves gett
    lytyll good;
Yowr abbeys go downe, I here saye, every where.

DISSYMUL: Yea, frynd Sedysyon, but thow must se to that
    gere.

SEDICYON: Than must I have helpe, by swete Saynt
    Benettes cuppe.

DISSYMUL: Thow shalt have a chyld of myn owne
    bryngyng uppe.

SEDICYON: Of thy bryngyng uppe! Cokes sowle, what
    knave is that?   740

DISSYMUL: Mary, Pryvat Welth; now hayve I tolde the
    what.
I made hym a monke and a perfytt cloysterer,
And in the abbeye he becam fyrst celerer,
Than pryor, than abbote, of a thowsand pownd land,
    no wors.
Now he is a bysshoppe and rydeth with an hondryd
    hors,
And, as I here say, he is lyke to be a cardynall.

SEDICYON: Ys he so in dede? By the masse, than have
    att all!

DISSYMUL: Nay, fyrst, Pryvat Welth shall bryng in
    Usurpyd Powr
With his autoryte, and than the gam ys ower.

SEDICYON: Tush, Usurpyd Powr dothe faver me of all
    men,   750
For in his trobles I ease his hart now and then.
Whan prynces rebell agenste hys autoryte,
I make ther commons agenst them for to be.
Twenty M^d men are but a mornyng breckefast
To be slayne for hym, he takyng his repast.

732 *blewe* blue   743 *celerer* cellarer, steward   749 *ower* over
753 *ther* their   *commons* common people

DISSYMUL: Thow hast, I persayve, a very suttyll cast.

SEDICYON: I am for the Pope as for the shyppe the mast.

DISSYMUL: Than helpe, Sedycyon, I may styll in Englond
be.

Kyng Johan hath thre[t]ned that I shall over see.

SEDICYON: Well yf thow wylte of me have remedy this
owr,   760

Go feche Pryvat Welth and also Usurpyd Powr.

DISSYMUL: I can bryng but one, be Mary, Jesus mother.

SEDICYON: Bryng thow in the one and let hym bryng in
the other.

*Here cum in Usurpyd Powr and Private Welth
syngyng on after another.*

USURPID POWR *syng this: Super flumina Babilonis
suspendimus organa nostra.*

PRIVAT WELTH *syng this: Quomodo cantabimus canticum
bonum in terra aliena?*

SEDICYON: By the mas, me thynke they are syngyng of
placebo.

DISSYMUL: Peace, for with my spectakles *vadam et
videbo.*

Cokes sowll, yt is they; at the last I have smellyd them
owt.

Her go and bryng them.

SEDICYON: Thow mayst be a sowe yf thow hast so good
a snowt.

Sures, marke well this gere for now yt begynnyth to
worke: 770

756 *cast* trick   760 *owr* hour   770 *Sures* certainly

False Dyssymulac[y]on doth bryng in Privat Welth;
And Usurpyd Powr, which is more ferce than a Turcke,
Cummeth in by hym to decayve all spyrytuall helth;
Than I by them bothe, as clere experyence telth.
We iiij by owr craftes Kyng Johan wyll so subdwe
That for iij.C yers all Englond shall yt rewe.

DISSYMUL: Of the clergy, fryndes, report lyke as ye se,
That ther privat welth cummyth ever in by me.
SEDICYON: But by whom commyst thou? By the messe,
    evyn by the devyll,
For the grownd thou arte of the Cristen peplys evyll.   780
DISSYMUL: And what are you, ser? I praye yow say good
    be me.
SEDICYON: By my trowth, I cum by the and thy affynyte.
DISSYMUL: Feche thow in thy felow so fast as ever thow
    can.
PRIVAT WELTH: I trow thow shalt se me now playe the
    praty man.
Of me, Privat Welth, cam fyrst Usurpyd Powr:
Ye may perseyve yt in pagent here this howr.
SEDICYON: Now welcum, felowys, by all thes bonys and
    naylys!
USURPID POWR: Among companyons good felyshyp
    never faylys.
SEDICYON: Nay, Usurpid Powr, thou must go backe
    ageyne,
For I must also put the to a lytyll payne.   790
USURPID POWR: Why, fellaue Sedycyon, what wyll thou
    have me do?
SEDICYON: To bare me on thi backe and bryng me in
    also,
That yt maye be sayde that fyrst Dyssymulacyon
Browght in Privat Welth to every Cristen nac[y]on,
And that Privat Welth browght in Usurpid Powr

772 *ferce* fierce   774 *telth* tells   782 *affynyte* kin
791 *fellaue* fellow, brother

And he Sedycyon, in cytye, towne and tower,
That sum man may know the feche of all owr sorte.

USURPID POWR: Cum on thy wayes, than, that thow
    mayst mak the fort.

DISSYMUL: Nay, Usurped Powr, we shall bare hym all
    thre,
    Thy selfe he and I, yf ye wyll be rewlyd by me,   800
    For ther is non of us but in hym hath a stroke.

PRIVAT WELTH: The horson knave wayeth and yt were a
    croked oke!

Here they shall bare hym in, and Sedycyon saythe

SEDICYON: Yea, thus it shuld be. Mary now [I am] alofte
    I wyll beshyte yow all yf ye sett me not downe softe.
    In my opynyon, by swete Saynt Antony,
    Here is now gatheryd a full honest company.
    Here is nowther Awsten, Ambrose, Hierom nor
        Gregory,
    But here is a sorte of companyons moch more mery.
    They of the Chirch than wer fower holy doctors,
    We of the Chirch now are the iiij general proctors.   810
    Here ys fyrst of all good father Dyssymulacyon,
    The fyrst begynner of this same congregac[y]on;
    Here is Privat Welthe, which hath the Chyrch infecte
    With all abusyons and brought yt to a synfull secte;
    Here ys Usurpid Powr, that all kynges doth subdwe,
    With such autoryte as is neyther good ner trewe;
    And I last of all am evyn sance pere Sedycyon.

USURPID POWR: Under hevyn ys not a mor knave in
        condycyon.
    Wher as thou dost cum, that common welth can not
        thryve.

797 *feche* craftiness, devices   *sorte* company   798 *fort* ?strong, brave
802 *oke* oak-tree   810 *proctors* stewards   817 *sance pere* unequalled
818 *mor* more

By owr Lord, I marvell that thow art yet alyve!   820
PRIVAT WELTH: Wher herbes are pluckte upp the wedes
        many tymes remayne.
DISSYMUL: No man can utter an evydence more playn.
SEDICYON: Yea, ye thynke so, yow? How Godes blyssyng
        breke yowr heade!
I can do but lawgh to her yow, by this breade!
I am so mery that we are mett, be Saynt John,
I fele not the ground that I do go uppon.
For the love of God, lett us have sum mery songe.
USURPID POWR: Begyne thy self, than and we shall lepe
        in amonge.

Here syng.

SEDICYON: I wold ever dwell here to have such mery
        sporte.
PRIVAT WELTH: Thow mayst have yt, man, yf thow wylt
        hether resorte,   830
For the Holy Father ys as good a felowe as we.
DISSYMUL: The Holy Father! Why, I pray the, whych is
        he?
PRIVAT WELTH: Usurpid Powr here, which thowgh he
        apparaunt be
In this apparell, yet hathe he autoryte
Bothe in hevyn and erth, in purgatory and in hell.
USURPID POWR: Marke well his saynges, for a trew tale
        he doth tell.
SEDICYON: What, Usurpid Powr? Cockes sowle, ye are
        owr Pope?
Where is yowr thre crounys, yowr crosse keys and
        yowr cope?
What meanyth this mater? Me thynke ye walke astraye.
USURPID POWR: Thou knowest I must have sum
        dalyaunce and playe,   840

    830 *hether* hither

For I am a man lyke as an other ys.
Sumtyme I must hunt, sumtyme I must Alysen kys.
I am bold of yow, I take ye for no straungers.
We are as spirituall; I dowght in yow no daungers.
DISSYMUL: I owght to conseder yowr Holy Father-hode,
From my fyrst infancy ye have ben to me so good.
For Godes sake, wytsave to geve me yowr blyssyng
here,
A pena et culpa that I may stand this day clere.

Knele.

SEDICYON: From makyng cuckoldes? Mary, that wer no
mery chere.
DISSYMUL: *A pena et culpa*: I trow thow canst not here. 850
SEDICYON: Yea, with a cuckoldes wyff ye have dronke
dobyll bere.
DISSYMUL: I pray the, Sedycyon, my pacyens no more
stere;
A pena et culpa I desyre to be clere,
And than all the devylles of hell I wold not fere.
USURPID POWR: But tell me one thyng: dost thou not
preche the Gospell?
DISSYMUL: No, I promyse yow, I defye yt to the devyll
of hell!
USURPID POWR: Yf I knewe thow dedyst, thou shuldest
have non absolucyon.
DISSYMUL: Yf I do, abjure me or put me to execucyon.
PRIVAT WELTH: I dare say he brekyth no popyshe
constytucyon.
USURPID POWR: Soche men are worthy to have owr
contrybucyon: 860
I assoyle the here, behinde and also beforne.
Now art thou as clere as that daye thow wert borne.

844 *dowght* fear   847 *wytsave* vouchsave   850 *here* hear
852 *stere* (v) stir up, trouble   859 *constytucyon* decree
861 *assoyle* absolve

Ryse Dyssymulacyon, and stond uppe lyke a bold
   knyght.
Dowght not of my powr thowgh my aparell be lyght.
SEDICYON: A man, be the messe, can not know yow
       from a knave;
Ye loke so lyke hym as I wold God shuld me save.
PRIVAT WELTH: Thow arte very lewde owr father so to
   deprave.
Thowgh he for his pleasure soche lyght apparell have,
Yt is now sommer and the heate ys with-owt mesure,
And among us he may go lyght at his owne pleasure.   870
Felow Sedycyon, thowgh thou dost mocke and scoffe,
We have other materes than this to be commyned of,
Frynd Dyssymulacyon, why dost thou not thy massage
And show owt of Englond the causse of thi farre
   passage?
Tush, blemysh not, whoreson, for I shall ever assyst the.
SEDICYON: The knave ys whycht-leveryd, by the Holy
      Trynyte!
USURPID POWR: Why so, Privat Welth? What ys the
      mater? Tell me.
PRIVAT WELTH: Dyssymulacyon ys a massanger for the
   clergy;
I must speke for hym ther ys no remedy.
The clargy of Ynglond, which ys yowr specyall frynde   880
And of a long tyme hath borne yow very good mynde,
Fyllyng yowr coffars with many a thowsande p[o]wnde,
Yf ye sett not to hand, he ys lyke to fall to the
   grownde.
I do promysse yow truly, his harte ys in his hose;
Kyng Johan so usyth hym that he reconnyth all to lose.
USURPID POWR: Tell, Dyssymulacyon, why art thow so
      asshamed
To shewe thy massage? Thow art moch to be blamed.
Late me se those wrytynges. Tush, man, I pray the cum
   nere.

867 *deprave* defame   872 *commyned of* discussed   873 *massage* message
875 *blemysh* discredit   876 *whycht-leveryd* white-livered

DISSYMUL: Yowr horryble holynes putth me in
    wonderfull fere.
USURPID POWR: Tush, lett me se them, I pray the
    hartely.   890

Here Dissimulacyon shall delever the wrytynges to
Usurpyd Powr.

I perseyve yt well, thow wylt lose no ceremony.
SEDICYON: Yet is he no lesse than a false knave, veryly.
I wold thow haddyst kyst his ars, for that is holy.
PRIVAT WELTH: How dost thow prove me that his arse
    ys holy now?
SEDICYON: For yt hath an hole evyn fytt for the nose of
    yow.
PRIVAT WELTH: Yowr parte ys not elles but for to playe
    the knave,
And so ye must styll contynew to yowr grave.
USURPID POWR: I saye, leve yowr gawdes and attend to
    me this howre.
The bysshoppes writeth here to me, Usurped Powr,
Desyryng assystence of myne auctoryte   900
To save and support the Chyrches lyberte.
They report Kyng Johan to them to be very harde
And to have the Church in no pryce nor regarde.
In his parlament he demaundeth of the clargy
For his warres the tent of the Chyrches patrymony.
PRIVAT WELTH: Ye wyll not consent to that, I trow, by
    Saynt Mary!
SEDICYON: No, drawe to yow styll, but lett none from
    yow cary.
USURPID POWR: Ye know yt is cleane agenst owr holy
    decrees
That princes shuld thus contempne owr lybertees.
He taketh uppon hym to reforme the tythes and
    offrynges   910

898 *gawdes* pranks   905 *tent* tenth   909 *contempne* (v) scorn

And intermedleth with other spyrytuall thynges.

PRIVAT WELTH: Ye must sequester hym, or elles that
      wyll mare all.

USURPID POWR: Naye, besydes all this, before juges
      temporall

He conventeth clarkes of cawses crymynall.

PRIVAT WELTH: Yf ye se not to that, the Churche wyll
      have a fall.

SEDICYON: By the masse, than pristes are lyke to have a
      pange;

For treson, murder, and thefte they are lyke to hange.

By cockes sowle, than I am lyke to walke for treason

Yf I be taken. Loke to yt therfor in seasone.

PRIVAT WELTH: Mary, God forbyd that ever yowr holy
      anoynted   920

For tresone or thefte shuld be hanged, racked or
      joynted

Lyke, the rascall sorte of the prophane layete.

USURPID POWR: Naye, I shall otherwyse loke to yt, ye
      may trust me.

Before hymselfe also the bysshoppes he doth convent,

To the derogacyon of ther dygnyte excelent,

And wyll suffer non to the court of Rome to appele.

DISSYMUL: No, he contemnyth yowre autoryte and seale

And sayth in his lond he wyll be lord and kyng,

No prist so hardy to enterpryse any thyng.

For the whych of late with hym ware at veryaunce   930

Fower of his bysshoppes, and in maner at defyaunce:

Wyllyum of London, and Eystace Bysshope of Hely,

Water of Wynchester, and Gylys of Hartford, trewly.

Be yowr autoryte they have hym excominycate.

USURPID POWR: Than have they done well, for he is a
      reprobate.

To that I admytt he ys alwayes contrary.

912 *sequester* excommunicate   *mare* mar
914 *conventeth* summons   921 *joynted* dismembered
922 *sorte* group, company   925 *derogacyon* disparagement
930 *veryaunce* difference   935 *reprobate* one rejected by God

I made this fellow here the Archebysshope of
  Canterbury,
And he wyll agree therto in no condycyon.
PRIVAT WELTH: Than hathe he knowledge that his name
  ys Sedycyon?
DISSYMUL: Dowtles he hath so, and that drownnyth his
  opynyon.   940
USURPID POWR: Why do ye not saye his name ys Stevyn
  Langton?
DISSYMUL: Tush, we have done so but that helpyth not
  the mater;
The Bysshope of Norwych for that cawse doth hym
  flater.
USURPID POWR: Styke thow to yt fast, we have onys
  admytted the.
SEDICYON: I wyll not one iote from my admyssyon fle;
The best of them all shall know that I am he.
Naye, in suche maters lett men beware of me.
USURPID POWR: The monkes of Caunterbe[r]y ded more
  at my request
Than they wold at his concernyng that eleccyon.
They chase Sedycyon, as yt is now manyfest,   950
In spytt of his harte. Than he for ther rebellyon
Exyled them all and toke ther hole possessyon
Into hys owne handes, them sendyng over see,
Ther lyvynges to seke in extreme poverte.

This custum also he hath, as it is tolde me:
Whan prelates depart, yea bysshope, abbott, or curate,
He entreth theyr landes withowt my lyberte,
Takyng the profyghtes tyll the nexte be consecrate,
Instytute, stallyd, indeucte or intronyzate.
And of the pyed monkes he entendeth to take a dyme.   960
And wyll be marryd yf I loke not to yt in tyme.

945 *iote* jot   950 *chase* chose   956 *curate* parish priest
960 *dyme* tithe

DISSYMUL: Yt is takyn, ser. The somme ys
   un-resonnable –
A nynne thowsand marke; to lyve they are not able.
His syggesteon was to subdew the Yrysh men.
PRIVAT WELTH: Yea, that same peple doth ease the
   Church now and then;
For that enterpryse they wold be lokyd uppon.
USURPID POWR: They gett no mony but they shall have
   clene remyssion,
For those Yrysh men are ever good to the Church;
Whan kynges dysobeye yt, than they begynne to worch.
PRIVAT WELTH: And all that they do ys for indulgence
   and pardon.   970
SEDICYON: By the messe, and that is not worth a rottyn
   wardon!
USURPID POWR: What care we for that? To them yt is
   venyson.
PRIVAT WELTH: Than lett them have yt, a Godes dere
   benyson!
USURPID POWR: Now how shall we do for this same
   wycked kyng?
SEDICYON: Suspend hym and curse hym, both with
   yowr word and wrytyng;
Yf that wyll not holpe, than interdyght his land
With extrem cruellnes; and yf that wyll not stand,
Cawse other prynces to revenge the Churchys wronge.
Yt wyll profytte yow to sett them aworke amonge;
For clene remyssyon one kyng wyll subdew another. 980
Yea, the chyld sumtyme wyll sle both father and mother.
USURPID POWR: This cownsell ys good; I wyll now
   folow yt playne.
Tary thow styll here tyll we returne agayne.

*Her go owt Usurpid Powr and Privat Welth and
Sedycyon: Usurpyd Powr shall drese for the Pope,*

962 *somme* sum 969 *worch* work 971 *wardon* warden pear
973 *benyson* blessing 976 *interdyght* interdict

*Privat Welth for a Cardinall, and Sedycyon for a
monke. The Cardynall shall bryng in the crose, and
Stevyn Launton the bocke, bell and candell.*

DISSYMUL: This Usurpid Powr, whych now is gon from
        hence,
For the Holy Church wyll make such ordynance
That all men shall be under his obedyens.
Yea, kynges wyll be glad to geve hym their alegyance,
And than shall we pristes lyve here with-owt dysturbans.
As Godes owne vyker anon ye shall se hym sytt,
His flocke to avaunse by his most polytyke wytt.   990

He shall make prelates, both byshopp and cardynall,
Doctours and prebendes with furde whodes and syde
    gownes.
He wyll also create the orders monastycall,
Monkes, chanons and fryers, with gaye coates and
    shaven crownes,
And buylde them places to corrupt cyties and townes.
The dead sayntes shall shewe both visyons and myracles;
With ymages and rellyckes he shall work sterracles.

He wyll make mattens, houres, masse and evensonge,
To drowne the Scriptures for doubte of heresye;
He wyll sende pardons to save mennys sowles amonge,   1000
Latyne devocyons, with the holye rosarye.
He wyll apoynt fastynges and plucke downe matrimonye;
Holy water and breade shall dryve awaye the devyll;
Blessynges with blacke bedes wyll helpe in every evyll.

989 *vyker* vicar, substitute   990 *polytyke* crafty
992 *prebendes* prebendaries, holders of church stipend   *furde* furred
whodes hoods   997 *sterracles* spectacle shows   999 *doubte* fear

Kynge Johan of Englande, bycause he hath rebelled
Agaynst Holy Churche, usynge it wurse than a stable,
To gyve up hys crowne shall shortly be compelled.
And the Albygeanes, lyke heretykes detestable,
Shall be brent bycause agaynst Our Father they babble;
Through Domynyckes preachynge an xviij thousande
   are slayne   1010
To teache them how they shall Holye Churche disdayne.

All this to performe he wyll cawle a generall cowncell
Of all Cristendom to the church of Laternense.
His intent shall be for to supprese the Gospell,
Yett wyll he glose yt with a very good pretens:
To subdwe the Turkes by a Cristen vyolens.
Under this coloure he shall grownd ther many thynges,
Whych wyll at the last be Cristen mennys undoynges.

The Popys powr shall be abowe the powrs all,
And eare confessyon a matere nessessary.   1020
Ceremonys wyll be the ryghtes ecclesyastycall.
He shall sett up ther both pardowns and purgatory;
The Gospell prechyng wyll be an heresy.
Be this provyssyon and be soch other kyndes
We shall be full suere all waye to have owr myndes.

> [*Usurped Power returns as the Pope, Private
> Wealth as a Cardinal, and Sedition as Stephen
> Langton.*]

THE POPE: Ah, ye are a blabbe! I perseyve ye wyll tell all.
   I lefte ye not here to be so lyberall.
DISSYMUL: *Mea culpa, mea culpa, gravissima mea culpa!*
   Geve me yowr blyssyng *pro Deo et Sancta Maria.*

   1009 *brent* burnt   1012 *cawle* call   1015 *glose* gloss
   1020 *eare* ear, auricular   1024 *Be* by   1026 *blabbe* babbler

Knele and knoke on thi bryst.

THE POPE: Thow hast my blyssyng, aryse now and stond
    asyde.   1030
DISSYMUL: My skyn ys so thyke yt wyll not throw glyde.
THE POPE: Late us goo abowght owr other materes now.
SAY THIS ALL THRE: We wayte her upon the greate
    holynes of yow.
THE POPE: For as moch as Kyng Johan doth Holy
    Church so handle,
Here I do curse hym wyth crosse, boke, bell and
    candle;
Lyke as this same roode turneth now from me his face,
So God I requyre to sequester hym of his grace;
As this boke doth speare by my worke maanuall,
I wyll God to close uppe from hym his benyfyttes all;
As this burnyng flame goth from this candle in syght,   1040
I wyll God to put hym from his eternall lyght;
I take hym from Crist, and after the sownd of this bell,
Both body and sowle I geve hym to the devyll of hell.
I take from hym bapty[s]m with the othere
    sacramentes
And suffrages of the Churche, bothe ember dayes and
    lentes.
Here I take from hym bothe penonce and confessyon,
Masse of the v. wondes with sensyng and processyon.
Here I take from hym holy water and holy brede,
And never wyll them to stande hym in any sted.
This thyng to publyshe I constytute yow thre,   1050
Gevyng yow my powr and my full autoryte.
SAY THIS ALL THRE: With the grace of God we shall
    performe yt, than.
THE POPE: Than gett yow foreward so fast as ever ye can
Uppon a bone vyage; yet late us syng meryly.

1029 SD *bryst* breast   1038 *speare* close   *maanuall* by hand
1046 *penonce* penance   1054 *bone vyage* successful journey

SEDICYON: Than begyne the song and we shall folow
    gladly.

Here they shall syng.

THE POPE: To coloure this thyng, thow shalte be callyd
      Pandulphus;
  Thow, Stevyn Langton; thy name shall be Raymundus.
  Fyrst thow, Pandolphus, shalt opynly hym suspend
  With boke, bell and candle; yf he wyll not so amend,
  Interdycte his lande and the churches all up speare.   1060
PRIVAT WELTH: I have my massage; to do yt I wyll not
    feare.

Here go owt and dresse for Nobylyte.

THE POPE: And thow, Stevyn Langton, cummaund the
      bysshoppes all
  So many to curse as are to hym benefycyall,
  Dwkes, erles, and lordes, wherby they may forsake hym.
SEDICYON: Sur, I wyll do yt, and that, I trow, shall
    shake hym.

    [*Exit.*]

THE POPE: Raymundus, go thow forth to the Crysten
      princes all;
  Byd them in my name that they uppon hym fall,
  Bothe with fyre and sword, that the Churche may hym
    conquarre.
DISSYMUL: Yowr plesur I wyll no lengar tyme defarre.
THE POPE: Saye this to them also: Pope Innocent the
    Thred   1070

1060 *up speare* close up   1068 *conquarre* conquer
1069 *lengar* longer   *defarre* defer

Remyssyon of synnes to so many men hath graunted
As wyll do ther best to slee hym yf they may.
DISSYMUL: Sur, yt shall be don with-owt ony lenger
          delay.

          [*Exit.*]

THE POPE: In the meane season I shall soch gere a-vaunce
          As wyll be to us a perpetuall furderaunce:
          Fyrst eare confessyon, than pardons, than purgatory,
          Sayntes worchyppyng than, than sekyng of ymagery,
          Than Laten servyce with the cerymonyes many,
          Wherby owr bysshoppes and abbottes shall get mony.
          I wyll make a law to burne all herytykes,   1080
          And kynges to depose whan they are sysmatykes.
          I wyll all-so reyse up the fower beggyng orderes
          That they may preche lyes in the Cristen borderes.
          For this and other I wyll call a generall cownsell
          To ratyfye them in lyke strength with the Gospell.

          Here the Pope go owt.

THE INTERPRETOUR: In thys present acte we have to yow
          declared,
          As in a myrrour, the begynnynge of Kynge Johan,
          How he was of God a magistrate appoynted
          To the governaunce of thys same noble regyon,
          To see maynteyned the true faythe and relygyon.   1090
          But Satan the Devyll, whych that tyme was at large,
          Had so great a swaye that he coulde it not discharge.

          Upon a good zele he attempted very farre
          For welthe of thys realme to provyde reformacyon

1075 *furderaunce* aid, advantage 1076–8 *than* ... *Than* then ... then
1079 *mony* money 1082 *reyse* raise 1093 *farre* far

In the Churche therof, but they ded hym debarre
Of that good purpose; for, by excommunycacyon,
The space of vij yeares they interdyct thy nacyon.
These bloudsuppers thus, of crueltie and spyght,
Subdued thys good kynge for executynge ryght.

In the second acte thys wyll apeare more playne,   1100
Wherein Pandulphus shall hym excommunycate
Within thys hys lande, and depose hym from hys
    reigne.
All other princes they shall move hym to hate
And to persecute after most cruell rate.
They wyll hym poyson in their malygnyte
And cause yll report of hym alwayes to be.

Thys noble Kyng Johan, as a faythfull Moyses,
Withstode proude Pharao for hys poore Israel,
Myndynge to brynge it out of the Lande of
    Darkenesse.
But the Egyptyanes ded agaynst hym so rebell   1110
That hys poore people ded styll in the desart dwell,
Tyll that Duke Josue, whych was our late Kynge
    Henrye,
Clerely brought us in to the lande of mylke and honye.

As a stronge David at the voyce of verytie,
Great Golye, the Pope, he strake downe with hys slynge
Restorynge agayne to a Christen lybertie
Hys lande and people, lyke a most vyctoryouse kynge,
To hir first bewtye intendynge the Churche to brynge,
From ceremonyes dead to the lyvynge wurde of the
    Lorde.
Thys the seconde acte wyll plenteously recorde.   1120

Finit Actus Primus.

1105 *malygnyte* malignity   1119 *wurde* word

364

[ACT TWO]

[Sedition] and Nobylyte cum in and say

NOBYLYTE: It petyeth my hart to se the controvercye
    That now-a-dayes reygnethe be-twyn the kyng and the
      clargy.
    All Cantorbery monkes are now the realme exyled,
    The prystes and bysshoppes contyneally revyled,
    The Cystean monkes are in soche perplexyte
    That owt of Englond they reken all to flee.
    I lament the chaunce as I wold God shuld me save.
SEDICYON: Yt is gracyously sayd; Godes blyssyng myght
      ye have!
    Blyssyd is that man that wyll graunte or cond———
    To h———

SEDICYON: From Innocent, the Pope, I am cum from
        Rome evyn now.
  A thowsand tymes, I wene, he commendyth Hym unto
    yow,
  And sent yow clene remyssyon to take the Chyrches
    parte.
NOBYLYTE: I thanke his Holynes. I shall do yt with all
        my harte.
  Yf ye wold take paynes for heryng my confessyon,
  I wold owt of hand resayve this cleane remyssyon.
SEDICYON: Mary, with all my hart, I wyll be full glad to
        do ytt.
NOBYLYTE: Put on yowr stolle, then, and I pray yow in
        Godes name sytt.

Here sett down, and Nobelyte shall say Benedycyte.

To helpe relygyon or Holy Churche defend.

NOBYLYTE: For there mayntenance I have geyvn londes
full fayere,
And have dysheryted many a la[w]full ayere.

SEDICYON: Well, yt is yowr owne good; God shall
reward yow for ytt,
And in hevyn full hyghe for soch good workes shall ye
sytt.

NOBYLYTE: Yowr habyte showythe ye to be a man of
relygeon.

SEDICYON: I am no worse, sur; my name is Good
Perfeccyon.

NOBYLYTE: I am the more glad to be aquented with ye.

SEDICYON: Ye show yowr-selfe here lyke a noble man,
as ye be.
I perseyve ryght well yowr name ys Nobelyte.

NOBYLYTE: Yowr servont and umfrey. Of trewthe, father,
I am he.

1132 *ayere* heir   1135 *habyte* habit

NOBYLYTE: *Benedicite.*

SEDICYON: *Dominus: In nomine domini pape, amen.* Say
forth yowr mynd, in Godes name. 1150

NOBYLYTE: I have synnyd agaynst God; I knowlege
my-selfe to blame:

In the vij dedly synnys I have offendyd sore;

Godes ten commaundymentes I have brokyn ever more;

My v. boddyly wytes I have on-godly kepte;

The workes of charyte in maner I have owt-slepte.

SEDICYON: I trust ye beleve as Holy Chyrch doth teache
ye?

And from the new lernyng ye are wyllyng for to fle?

NOBYLYTE: From the new lernyng? Mary, God of
hevyn save me!

I never lovyd yt of a chyld, so mote I the.

SEDICYON: Ye can saye yowr crede? And yowr Laten
Ave Mary? 1160

1146 *resayve* receive 1148 *stolle* stole (vestment) 1148 SD *sett* sit

NOBYLYTE: Yea, and dyrge also, with sevyn psalmes and
    letteny.

SEDICYON: Do ye not beleve in purgatory and holy bred?

NOBYLYTE: Yes, and that good prayers shall stand my
    soule in stede.

SEDICYON: Well than, good inowgh; I warant my soulle
    for yowr.

NOBYLYTE: Than execute on me the Holy Fatheres powr.

SEDICYON: Naye, whyll I have yow here underneth
    benedicite,

In the Popes be-halfe I must move other thynges to ye.

NOBYLYTE: In the name of God, saye here what ye wyll
    to me.

SEDICYON: Ye know that Kyng Johan ys a very wycked
    man

And to Holy Chyrch a contynuall adversary.   1170

The Pope wyllyth yow to do the best ye canne

To his subduyng, for his cruell tyranny;

And for that purpose this prevylege gracyously

Of clene remyssyon he hath sent yow this tyme,

Clene to relesse yow of all yowr synne and cryme.

NOBYLYTE: Yt is clene agenst the nature of Nobelyte

To subdew his kyng with-owt Godes Autoryte,

For his princely astate and powr ys of God.

I wold gladly do yt, but I fere his ryght-full rode.

SEDICYON: Godes Holy Vycare gave me his whole
    autoryte.   1180

Loo, yt is here, man; beleve yt, I beseche the,

Or elles thow wylte faulle in danger of damnacyon.

NOBYLYTE: Than I submyt me to the Chyrches
    reformacyon.

SEDICYON: I assoyle the here from the kynges obedyence

By the auctoryte of the Popys magnifycence:

Auctoritate Romani Pontyficis ego absolvo te

1171 *canne* can 1178 *astate* estate 1179 *rode* rod, punishment
1182 *faulle* fall

From all possessyons gevyn to the spiritualte,
In nomine Domini Pape, Amen.
Kepe all thynges secrett, I pray yow hartely.

Go owt Nobelyte.

NOBYLYTE: Yes, that I wyll, sur, and cum agayne hether
    shortly.   1190

*Here enter Clargy and Cyvyll Order together; and
Sedysyon shall go up and down a praty whyle.*

CLERGYE: Ys not yowr fatherhod Archebysshope of
    Canterbery?
SEDICYON: I am Stevyn Langton. Why make ye here
    inquyry?

Knele and say both

[CLERGY:]   } Ye are ryght welcum to this same
[CIVIL ORDER:] } regyon, trewly.
SEDICYON: Stond up, I pray yow. I trow thou art the
    Clargy.
CLERGYE: I am the same, sur, and this is Cyvyle Order.
SEDICYON: Yf a man myght axe yow, what make yow in
    this bordere?
CLERGYE: I here tell yester-daye ye were cum in to the
    lond.
    I thowght for to se yow, sum newes to understand.
SEDICYON: In fayth, thow art welcum. Ys Cyvyll Order
    thy frynd?

1196 *axe* ask   *bordere* country

368

CLERGYE: He is a good man and beryth the Chyrch good
　　mynd.　　　　　　　　　　　　　　　　　　　　　1200

CYVYLE ORDER: Ryght sory I am of the great
　　controvarsy

Betwyn hym and the kyng, yf I myght yt remedy.

SEDICYON: Well. Cyvyll Order, for thy good wyll
　　gramercy;

That mater wyll be of an other facyon shortly.

Fyrst, to begynne with we shall interdyte the land.

CYVYLE ORDER: Mary, God forbyde we shuld be in soche
　　band!

But who shall do yt, I pray yow hartyly?

SEDICYON: Pandulphus and I; we have yt in owr legacy.

He went to the kyng for that cawse yester-daye,

And I wyll folow so fast as ever I maye.　　　　　　1210

Lo, here ys the Bull of myn auctoryte.

CLERGYE: I pray God to save the Popes holy majeste.

SEDICYON: Sytt downe on yowr kneys and ye shall have
　　absolucyon

A pena et culpa, with a thowsand dayes of pardon.

Here ys fyrst a bone of the blyssyd Trynyte,

A dram of the tord of swete Seynt Barnabe;

Here ys a feddere of good Seynt Myhelles wyng,

A toth of Seynt Twyde, a pece of Davyds harpe
　　stryng,

The good blood of Haylys and owr blyssyd ladys
　　mylke,

A lowse of Seynt Fraunces in this same crymsen sylke,　1220

A scabbe of Saynt Job, a nayle of Adams too,

A maggott of Moyses, with a fart of Saynt Fandigo;

Here is a fygge leafe and a grape of Noes vyneyearde,

A bede of Saynt Blythe with the bracelet of a
　　berewarde,

The Devyll that was hatcht in maistre Johan Shornes
　　bote,

1205 *interdyte* excommunicate　1208 *legacy* legal authority
1216 *tord* excrement　1217 *feddere* feather　1218 *toth* tooth
1224 *berewarde* bearward, bear-keeper

That the tree of Jesse ded plucke up by the roote;
Here ys the lachett of swett Seynt Thomas shewe,
A rybbe of Seynt Rabart, with the huckyll bone of a
  Jewe;
Here ys a joynt of Darvell Gathyron,
Besydes other bonys and relyckes many one.　　　　1230
In nomine Domini Pape, Amen.
Aryse now lyke men and stande uppon yowr fete,
For here ye have caught an holy and a blyssyd hete.
Ye are now as clene as that day ye were borne
And lyke to have increase of chylderne, catell and
  corne.

CYVYLE ORDER: Chyldryn? He can have non, for he ys
  not of that loade.

SEDICYON: Tushe, thowgh he hath non at home, he maye
  have sume abroade.
Now Clargy, my frynd, this must thow do for the Pope
And for Holy Chyrch: thow must mennys conscyence
  grope,
And as thow felyst them, so cause them for to wurcke.　　1240
Leat them show Kyng Johan no more faver than a
  Turcke;
Every wher sture them to make an insurreccyon.

CLERGYE: All that shall I do, and to provoke them more,
This interdyccyon I wyll lament very sore
In all my prechynges, and saye throwgh his occacyon
All we are under the danger of dampnacyon;
And this wyll move peple to helpe to put hym downe,
Or elles compel hym to geve up septur and crowne.
Yea, and that wyll make those kynges that shall succede
Of the Holy Chyrche to stonde ever more in drede.　　1250
And bysydes all this, the chyrch dores I wyll upseale,
And closse up the belles that they ryng never a pele.
I wyll spere up the chalyce, crysmatory, crosse and all.

1228 *huckyll* hip　1233 *hete* heat　1235 *catell* property
1240 *wurcke* work　1242 *sture* stir　1245 *occacyon* cause, fault
1248 *septur* sceptre　1251 *upseale* seal up　1253 *spere* lock
crysmatory chrismatory (vessel containing unction)

That masse they shall have non, bapty[s]m nor beryall.
And thys I know well wyll make the peple madde.

SEDICYON: Mary, that yt wyll; soche sauce he never had.
And what wylte thow do for Holy Chyrche, Cyvyll
Ordere?

CYVYLE ORDER: For the clargyes sake I wyll in every
border
Provoke the gret men to take the comonnys parte.
With cautyllys of the lawe I wyll so tyckle ther hart   1260
They shall thynke all good that they shall passe upon,
And so shall we cum to ower full intent anon;
For yf the Church thryve than do we lawers thryve,
And yf they decay, ower welth ys not alyve.
Therfor we must helpe yowr state, masters, to uphold,
Or elles owr profyttes wyll cache a wynter colde.
I never knew lawer whych had ony crafty lernyng
That ever escapte yow with-owt a plentyows levyng
Therfore we may not leve Holy Churchys quarell,
But ever helpe yt, for ther fall ys owr parell.   1270

SEDICYON: Godes blyssyng have ye! This ger than wyll
worke, I trust.

CYVYLE ORDER: Or elles sum of us are lyke to lye in the
dust.

SEDICYON: Let us all avoyde! Be the messe the kyng
cummyth her!

CLERGYE: I wold hyde my selfe for a tyme yf I wyst
where.

CYVYLE ORDER: Gow we hence apace, for I have spyed a
corner.

Here go owt all, and Kyng Johan cummyth in.

K. JOHAN: For non other cawse God hathe kynges
constytute

1254 *beryall* burial   1260 *cautyllys* tricks   1268 *levyng* living
1270 *parell* peril   1271 *ger* device   1274 *wyst* knew

And gevyn them the sword but forto correct all vyce.
I have attempted this thyng to execute
Uppon transgressers accordyng unto justyce,
And be cawse I wyll not be parcyall in myn offyce   1280
For theft and murder to persones spirytuall,
I have ageynst me the pristes and the bysshoppes all.

A lyke dysplesure in my fatheres tyme ded fall
Forty yeres ago for ponnyshment of a clarke.
No cunsell myght them to reformacyon call,
In ther openyon they wer so stordy and starke,
But ageynst ther prynce to the Pope they dyd so barke
That here in Ynglond, in every cyte and towne,
Excomminycacyons as thonder boltes cam downe.

For this ther captayn had after a pared crowne   1290
And dyed upon yt, with-owt the kynges consent.
Than interdiccyons wer sent from the Popes renowne
Whych never left hym tyll he was penytent
And fully agreed unto the Popes apoyntment,
In Ynglond to stand with the Chyrches lyberte
And suffer the pristes to Rome for appeles to flee.

They bownd hym also to helpe Ierusalem cyte
With ij hundrid men the space of a yere and more,
And thre yere after to maynteyne battell free
Ageynst the Sarazens, whych vext the Spannyardes sore.   1300
Synce my fatheres tyme I have borne them groge
    therfor,
Consydryng the pryde and the capcyose dysdayne
That they have to kynges, whych owghte over them to
    rayne.

Privat Welth cum in lyke a cardynall.

1280 *parcyall* partial   1286 *stordy* fierce   *starke* rigid
1290 *pared* damaged, split   *crowne* head   1296 *appeles* appeals
1301 *groge* grudge   1302 *capcyose* great

[PRIVATE WEALTH:] God save yow, sur kyng, in yowr
        pryncly mageste.
K. JOHAN: Frynd, ye be welcum. What is yowr plesur
        with me?
PRIVAT WELTH: From the Holy Father, Pope Innocent
        the Thred
As a massanger I am to yow dyrectyd
To reforme the peace betwyn Holy Chyrch and yow.
And in his behalfe I avertyce yow here now
Of the Chyrchys goodes to make full restytucyon,   1310
And to accepte also the Popes holy constytucyon
For Stevyn Langton, Archebysshop of Canturbery,
And so admytt hym to his state and primacy.
The monkes exilyd ye shall restore agayne
To ther placys and londes, and nothyng of theres
        retayne.
Owr Holy Fatheres mynde ys that ye shall agayne
        restore
All that ye have ravyshyd from Holy Chyrche with the
        more.
K. JOHAN: I reken yowr father wyll never be so harde,
But he wyll my cawse as well as theres regarde.
I have done nothyng but that I may do well;   1320
And as for ther taxe, I have for me the Gospell.
PRIVAT WELTH: Tushe, Gospell or no, ye must make a
        recompens.
K. JOHAN: Yowr father is sharpe and very quycke in
        sentence
Yf he wayeth the word of God nomor than so.
But I shall tell yow in this what Y shall do:
I am well content to receyve the monkes agayne
Upon amendement; but as for Stevyn Langton, playne,
He shall not cum here, for I know his dysposycyon.
He is moche inclyned to sturdynesse and sedicyon.
Ther shall no man rewle in the lond wher I am kyng   1330
Withowt my consent, for no mannys plesur lyvyng.

1309 *avertyce* warn   1311 *constytucyon* laws   1325 *Y* I
1329 *sturdynesse* fierceness

Never the less yet upon a newe behaver,
At the Popes request here aftere I may hym faver
And graunt hym to have sum other benyfyce.

PRIVAT WELTH: By thys I perseyve ye bare hym groge
and malyce.

Well, thys wyll I say by cause ye are so blunte:
A prelate to dyscharge Holy Chyrche was never wonnt,
But her custome ys to mynyster ponnyshment
To kynges and princes beyng dyssobedyent.

K. JOHAN: Avant, pevysh prist! What, dost thow
thretten me?   1340
I defye the worst, both of thi Pope and the!
The powr of princys ys gevyn from God above,
And, as sayth Salomon, ther hartes the Lord doth move.
God spekyth in ther lyppes whan they geve jugement.
The lawys that they make are by the lordes
appoyntment.
Christ wylled not his the princes to correcte,
But to ther precepptes rether to be subjecte.
The offyce of yow ys not to bere the sword,
But to geve cownsell acordyng to Godes word.
He never tawght his to weare nowther sword nor
sallett,   1350
But to preche abrode with-owt staffe, scrypp or
walett;
Yet ar ye becum soche myghty lordes this howr
That ye are able to subdewe all princes powr.
I can not perseyve, but ye are becum Belles prystes,
Lyvyng by ydolles; yea, the very Antychrystes.

PRIVAT WELTH: Ye have sayd yowr mynd, now wyll I
say myn also.
Here I cursse yow for the wronges that ye have do
Unto Holy Churche, with crosse, bocke, bell and
candell;
And by sydes all thys, I must yow otherwyse handell.

1332 *behaver* conduct   1337 *dyscharge* release   1347 *rether* rather
1350 *sallett* helmet   1351 *scrypp* bag   1358 *bocke* book
1359 *handell* deal with

374

Of contumacy the Pope hath yow convyt;   1360
From this day forward yowr lond stond interdytt.
The Bysshope of Norwyche and the Bysshope of
    Wynchester
Hath full autoryte to spred it in Ynglond here;
The Bysshope of Salysbery and the Bysshope of
    Rochester
Shall execute yt in Scotlond every where;
The Bysshope of Landaffe, Seynt Assys and Seynt Davy
In Walles and in Erlond shall puplyshe yt openly.
Throwgh owt all Crystyndom the bysshoppes shall
    suspend
All soche as to yow any mayntenance pretend;
And I cursse all them that geve to yow ther harte,   1370
Dewkes, erlles and lordes, so many as take yowr parte;
And I assoyle yowr peple from yowr obedyence,
That they shall owe yow noyther fewte nor reverence.
By the Popys awctoryte I charge them with yow to
    fyght
As with a tyrant agenst Holy Chyrchys ryght;
And by the Popes auctoryte I geve them absolucyon
A pena et culpa, and also clene remyssyon.

Extra locum.

SEDICYON: Alarum! Alarum! Tro ro ro ro ro, tro ro ro
            ro ro, tro ro ro ro ro!
    Thomp, thomp, thomp! Downe, downe, downe! to go,
        to go, to go!
K. JOHAN: What a noyse is thys that without the dore is
            made?   1380
PRIVAT WELTH: Suche enmyes are up as wyll your realme
                invade.
K. JOHAN: Ye cowde do nomor and ye cam from the
            devyll of hell

1369 *mayntenance* support   *pretend* offer   1373 *fewte* loyalty

Than ye go abowt here to worke by yo[w]r wyckyd
  cownsell.
Ys this the charyte of that ye call the Churche?
God graunt Christen men not after yowr wayes
  to worche.
I sett not by yowr curssys the shakyng of a rod,
For I know they are of the devyll and not of God.
Yowr curssys we have, that we never yet demaundyd,
But we can not have that God hath yow commaundyd.
PRIVAT WELTH: What ye mene by that I wold ye shuld
          opynlye tell.   1390
K. JOHAN: Why, know ye it not? The prechyng of the
      Gospell.
Take to ye yowr traysh, yowr ryngyng, syngyng and
  pypyng,
So that we may have the Scryptures openyng.
But that we can not have; yt stondyth not with yowr
  avantage.
PRIVAT WELTH: Ahe! Now I fell yow for this heretycall
        langage:
I thynke noyther yow nor ony of yowres, iwys,
We wyll so provyd, shall ware the crowne after this.

    Go owt and dresse for Nobylyte.

K. JOHAN: Yt becum not the Godes secret workes to deme.
Gett the hence, or elles we shall teche the to blaspheme!
Oh lord, how wycked ys that same generacyon   1400
That never wyll cum to a godly reformacyon.
The prystes report me to be a wyckyd tyrant
Be-cause I correct ther actes and lyfe unplesaunt.
Of thy prince, sayth God, thow shalt report non yll,
But thy selfe applye his plesur to fulfyll.
The byrdes of the ayer shall speke to ther gret shame,

1386 *sett* care   1392 *traysh* trash   1395 *fell* bring down
1398 *the* thee   *deme* judge   1399 *the* thee

As sayth Ecclesyastes, that wyll a prince dyffame.
The powrs are of God, I wot Powle hath soch sentence;
He that resyst them agenst God maketh resystence.
Mary and Joseph at Cyrinus appoyntment,   1410
In the descripcyon to Cesar wer obedyent.
Crist ded paye trybute, for hymselfe, and Peter to,
For a lawe prescrybyng the same unto pristes also;
To prophane princes he obeyed unto dethe.
So ded John Baptyst so longe as he had brethe.
Peter, John and Powle, with the other apostles all,
Ded never withstand the powers imperyall.

[*Enter Civil Order.*]

Prystes are so wycked they wyll obeye no powr,
But seke to subdewe ther prynces day and howr,
As they wold do me; but I shall make them smart,   1420
Yf that nobelyte and law wyll take my parte.

CYVYLE ORDER: Dowghtles we can not tyll ye be
      reconcylyd
Unto Holy Chyrche, for ye are a man defylyd.

K. JOHAN: How am I defylyd? Tel me, good gentyll mate.

CYVYLE ORDER: By the Popes hye powr ye are
      excomynycate.

K. JOHAN: By the word of God, I pray the, what powr
      hath he?

CYVYLE ORDER: I spake not wyth hym, and therfor I
      cannot tell ye.

K. JOHAN: With whom spake ye not? Late me know yowr
      intent.

CYVYLE ORDER: Mary, not with God sens the latter
      wecke of Lent.

[*Enter Clergy.*]

1407 *dyffame* defame   1412 *to* also   1424 *mate* friend   1428 *Late* let
1429 *sens* since

K. JOHAN: Oh mercyfull God, what an unwyse clawse ys
     this,   1430
  Of hym that shuld se that nothyng ware amys.
  That sentence or curse that Scriptur doth not dyrect,
  In my opynyon, shall be of non effecte.
CLERGYE: Ys that yowr beleve? Mary, God save me from
     yow!
K. JOHAN: Prove yt by Scriptur, and than wyll I yt alowe.
  But this know I well: whan Balaam gave the curse
  Uppon Godes peple, they war never a whyt the worse.
CLERGYE: I passe not on the Scriptur: that ys inow for
     me
  Whyche the Holy Father approvyth by his auctoryte.
K. JOHAN: Now alas, alas! What wreched peple ye are   1440
  And how ygnorant yowr owne wordes doth declare.
  Woo ys that peple whych hath so wycked techeres.
CLERGYE: Naye, wo ys that peple that hathe so cruell
     rewlars.
  Owr Holy Father, I trow, cowd do no lesse,
  Consyderyng the factes of yowr owtragyosnes.

     [Enter Nobility.]

NOBYLYTE: Com awaye, for shame, and make no more
     ado.
  Ye are in gret danger for commynnyng with hym so.
  He is acursyd; I mervell ye do not waye yt.
CLERGYE: I here by his wordes that he wyll not obeye yt.
NOBYLYTE: Whether he wyll or no, I wyll not with hym
     talke.   1450
  Tell he be assoyllyd. Com on, my fryndes, wyll ye
     walke?
K. JOHAN: Oh, this is no tokyn of trew nobelyte,
  To flee from yowr kyng in his extremyte.

   1431 *ware* were   1434 *beleve* belief   1437 *whyt* jot   1438 *passe* rely
   1445 *factes* actions   1447 *commynnyng* conversing

NOBYLYTE: I shall dyssyer yow as now to pardone me;
 I had moche rather do agaynst God, veryly,
 Than to Holy Chyrche to do any injurye.
K. JOHAN: What blyndnes is this? On this peple, Lord,
  have mercy!
 Ye speke of defylyng, but ye are corrupted all
 With pestylent doctryne or leven pharesayycall.
 Good [and] faythfull Susan sayd that yt was moche
  bettere   1460
 To fall in daunger of men than do the gretter,
 As to leve Godes lawe, whych ys his word most pure.
CLERGYE: Ye have nothyng, yow to allege to us but
  Scripture?
 Ye shall fare the worse for that, ye may be sure.
K. JOHAN: What shuld I allege elles, thu wycked Pharyse?
 To yowr false lernyng no faythfull man wyll agree.
 Dothe not the Lord say *nunc reges intelligite?*
 The kynges of the erthe that worldly cawses juge,
 Seke to the Scriptur; late that be yowr refuge.
CYVYLE ORDER: Have ye nothyng elles but this? Than
  God be with ye!   1470
K. JOHAN: One questyon more yet ere ye departe from me
 I wyll fyrst demaund of yow, Nobelyte;
 Why leve ye yowr prince and cleave to the Pope so sore?
NOBYLYTE: For I toke an othe to defend the Chyrche
  ever more.
K. JOHAN: Clergy, I am sure than yowr quarell ys not
  small.
CLERGYE: I am proffessyd to the ryghtes ecclesyastycall.
K. JOHAN: And yow, Cyvyle Order, oweth her sum offyce
  of dewtye?
CYVYLE ORDER: I am hyr feed man; who shuld defend her
  but I?
K. JOHAN: Of all thre partyes yt is spokyn resonably:
 Ye may not obeye becawse of the othe ye mad, 1480
 Yowr strong professyon maketh yow of that same trad,

 1454 *dyssyer* desire 1462 *leve* leave 1463 *allege* call upon
 1476 *proffessyd* sworn 1478 *feed* bound by payment 1481 *trad* trade

Yowr fee provokyth yow to do as thes men do.
Grett thynges to cawse men from God to the devyll to
    go!
Yowr othe is growndyd fyrst uppon folyshenes,
And yowr professyon uppon moche pevyshenes;
Yowr fee, last of all, ryseth owt of covetusnes,
And thes are the cawses of yowr rebellyosnes.
CLERGYE: Cum, Cyvyll Order, lett us too departe from
            hence.
K. JOHAN: Than are ye at a poynt for yowr obedyence?
CYVYLE ORDER: We wyll in no wysse be partakeres of
            yowr yll.   1490

*Here go owt Clargy, and dresse for Ynglond, and
Syvyll Order for Commynalte.*

K. JOHAN: As ye have bene ever, so ye wyll contynew
            styll.
    Thowgh they be gone, tarye yow with me a whyle;
    The presence of a prynce to yow shuld never be vyle
NOBYLYTE: Sir, nothyng grevyth me but yowr
            excomynycacyon.
K. JOHAN: That ys but a fantasy in yowr ymagynacyon.
    The Lord refuse not soch as hath his great cursse,
    But call them to grace and faver them never the worsse.
    Saynt Pawle wyllyth yow whan ye are among soch sort
    Not to abhore them, but geve them wordes of comfort.
    Why shuld ye than flee from me, yowr lawfull kyng,   1500
    For plesur of soch as owght to do no suche thyng?
    The Chyrches abusyons, as holy Seynt Powle do saye,
    By the princes powr owght for to be takyn awaye;
    He baryth not the sword withowt a cawse, sayth he.
    In this neyther bysshope nore spirituall man is free;
    Offendyng the lawe, they are under the poweres, all.

1482 *fee* feudal benefice   1485 *pevyshenes* obstinacy
1489 *at a poynt* confirmed, decided

NOBYLYTE: How wyll ye prove me that the fatheres
        sprytuall
    Were under the princes ever contynewally?

K. JOHAN: By the actes of kynges I wyll prove yt by and
        by:
    David and Salomon the pristes ded constitute,   1510
    Commandyng the offyces that they shuld execute.
    Josaphat the kyng the mynysters ded appoynt;
    So ded Kyng Ezechias, whom God hym-selfe ded
        anoynt.
    Dyverse of the princes for the pristes ded make
        decrees,
    Lyke as yt is pleyn in the fyrst of Machabees.
    Owr pristes are rysyn throwgh lyberte of kynges
    By ryches to pryd and other unlawfull doynges,
    And that is the cawse that they so oft dysobeye.

NOBYLYTE: Good lord, what a craft have yow thes
        thynges to convaye!

K. JOHAN: Now, alas, that the false pretence of
        superstycyon   1520
    Shuld cawse yow to be a mayntener of sedycyon.
    Sum thynkyth nobelyte in natur to consyst,
    Or in parentage; ther thowght is but a myst.
    Wher habundance is of vertu, fayth and grace,
    With knowlage of the Lord, nobelyte is ther in place,
    And not wher as is the wylfull contempte of thynges
    Pertaynyng to God in the obedyence of kynges.
    Beware ye synke not with Dathan and Abiron
    For dysobeyng the powr and domynyon.

NOBYLYTE: Nay, byd me be-ware I do not synke with
        yow here;   1530
    Beyng acurssyd, of trewth ye put me in fere.

K. JOHAN: Why are ye gone hence, and wyll ye no
        longar tarrye?

NOBYLYTE: No, wher as yow are in place, by swete Seynt
        Marye!

    1517 *pryd* pride   1519 *convaye* remove

Here Nobelyte go owt and dresse for the Cardynall.
Here enter Ynglond and Commynalte.

K. JOHAN: Blessed Lorde of heaven, what is the
        wretchednesse
Of thys wycked worlde! An evyll of all evyls, doubtlesse.
Perceyve ye not here how the clergye hath rejecte
Their true allegeaunce to maynteyne the popysh secte?
See ye not how lyghte the lawers sett the poure,
Whome God commaundeth them to obeye yche daye
        and howre?
Nobylyte also, whych ought hys prynce to assyste,   1540
Is vanyshed awaye, as it we[re] a wynter myste.
All they are from mee; I am now left alone,
And, God wote, knowe not to whome to make my mone.
Oh, yet wolde I fayne knowe the mynde of my
        Commynnalte,
Whether he wyll go with them or abyde with me.
ENGLANDE: He is here at hond, a symple creatur as may
        be.
K. JOHAN: Cum hether, my frynde, stand nere. Ys
        thi-selfe he?
COMMYNNALTE: Yf it lyke yowr grace, I am yowr pore
        Commynnalte.
K. JOHAN: Thow art poore inowgh. Yf that be good, God
        help the!
Me thynke thow art blynd. Tell me, frynde, canst thou
        not see?   1550
ENGLANDE: He is blynd in dede. Yt is the more rewth
        and pytte.
K. JOHAN: How cummyst thow so blynd? I pray the, good
        fellow, tell me.
COMMYNNALTE: For want of knowlage in Christes lyvely
        veryte.
ENGLANDE: This spirituall blyndnes bryngeth men owt of
        the waye

1538 *poure* power   1541 *myste* mist   1543 *wote* knows   *mone* complaint
1553 *lyvely* living

And cause them oft tymes ther kynges to dyssobaye.

K. JOHAN: How sayst thow, Commynnalte? Wylt not thou
    take my parte?

COMMYNNALTE: To that I cowd be contented with all
    my hart,

But, alas, in me are two great impedymentes.

K. JOHAN: I pray the, shew me what are those,
    impedymentes.

COMMYNNALTE: The fyrst is blyndnes, wherby I myght
    take with the Pope   1560

Soner than with yow, for, alas, I can but grope,

And ye know what full well ther are many nowghty
    gydes.

The nexte is poverte, whych cleve so hard to my sydes

And ponych me so sore that my powr ys lytyll or non.

K. JOHAN: In Godes name, tell me how cummyth thi
    substance gone?

COMMYNNALTE: By pristes, channons and monkes, which
    do but fyll ther bely

With my swett and labour for ther popych purgatory.

ENGLANDE: Yowr grace promysed me that I shuld have
    remedy

In that same mater whan I was last here, trewly.

K. JOHAN: Dowghtles I ded so; but, alas, yt wyll not be.   1570

In hart I lament this great infelycyte.

ENGLANDE: Late me have my spowse and my londes at
    lyberte,

And I promyse yow my sonne here, yowr Commynallte,

I wyll make able to do ye dewtyfull servyce.

K. JOHAN: I wold I ware able to do to the that offyce,

But, alas, I am not, for why my nobelyte,

My lawers and clargy hath cowardly forsake me.

And now last of all, to my most anguysh of mynd,

My Commynnalte here I fynd both poore and blynd.

ENGLANDE: Rest upon this, ser, for my governor ye shall
    be   1580

1560 *take with* side with   1562 *nowghty* wicked   *gydes* guides
1564 *ponych* punish

So long as ye lyve; God hath so apoynted me.
His owtward blyndness ys but a syngnyficacyon
Of blyndnes in sowle for lacke of informacyon
In the word of God, which is the orygynall grownd
Of dyssobedyence, which all realmies doth confund.
Yf yowr grace wold cawse Godes word to be tawght
    syncerly
And subdew those pristes that wyll not preche yt
    trewly,
The peple shuld know to ther prynce ther lawfull dewty;
But yf ye permytt contynuance of ypocresye
In monke[s], chanons and pristes, and mynysters of the
    clargy,   1590
Yowr realme shall never be withowt moch traytery.

K. JOHAN: All that I persceyve and therfor I kepe owt
        fryers,
Lest they shuld bryng the moch farder into the bryers.
They have mad labur to inhabytt this same regyon;
They shall for my tym not enter my domynyon.
We have to many of soch vayne lowghtes allredy.
I beshrew ther hartes, they have made yow ij full nedy!

Here enter Pandwlfus, the cardynall, and sayth

CARDYNALL: What, Commynalte, ys this the covnaunt
        kepyng?
Thow toldyst me thou woldest take hym no more for
    thi kyng.
COMMYNNALTE: *Peccavi, mea culpa!* I submyt me to yowr
        holynes.   1600
CARDYNALL: Gett the hence than shortly, and go abowt
        thi besynes!
Wayet on thy capttaynes, Nobelyte and the Clargy,
With Cyvyll Order and the other company.

1585 *realmies* kingdoms   1591 *traytery* treachery   1596 *lowghtes* louts
1598 *covnaunt* covenant

Blow owt yowr tromppettes and sett forth manfully,
The frenche kyng Phelype by sea doth hether apply
With the powr of Fraunce to subdew this herytyke.

K. JOHAN: I defye both hym and the, lewde scysmatyke!
Why wylt thou for-sake thi prince or thi prince leve the?

COMMYNNALTE: I must nedes obbay whan Holy Chirch
    commandyth me.

Go owt Commynulte.

ENGLANDE: Yf thow leve thy kyng, take me never for
    thy mother.   1610

CARDYNALL: Tush, care not thu for that, I shall provyd
    the another.
Yt ware fytter for yow to be in another place.

ENGLANDE: Yt shall becum me to wayte upon his grace
And do hym servyce where as he ys resydente,
For I was gevyn hym of the Lord Omnypotente.

CARDYNALL: Thow mayst not abyde here, for whye we
    have hym curssyd.

ENGLANDE: I beshrow yowr hartes so have ye me
    onpursed.
Yf he be acurssed than are we a mete cuppell,
For I am interdyct. No salve that sore can suppell.

CARDYNALL: I say, gett the hence, and make me no more
    pratyng.   1620

ENGLANDE: I wyll not a-waye from myn owne lawfull
    kyng.
Appoyntyd of God tyll deth shall us departe.

CARDYNALL: Wyll ye not in dede? Well than, ye are
    lyke to smarte.

ENGLANDE: I smarte all redy throw yowr most suttell
    practyse,

1616 *for whye* because   1617 *onpursed* robbed   1618 *mete* fine, suitable
cuppell couple   1619 *salve* remedy   *suppell* mollify
1622 *departe* separate   1624 *practyse* craftiness

And am clene ondone by yowr false merchandyce –
Yowr pardons, yowr bulles, yowr purgatory
    pyckepurse,
Yowr lent fastes, yowr schryftes – that I pray God geve
    yow his cursse!

CARDYNALL: Thou shalt smart better or we have done
        with the,
For we have this howr great navyes upon the see
In every quarter, with this loller here to fyght   1630
And to conquarre hym for the Holy Chyrchis ryght.
We have [i]n the northe Alexander, the Kynge of
    Scottes,
With an armye of men that for their townnes cast
    lottes;
On the sowthe syde we have the French kyng with his
    powr,
Which wyll sle and burne tyll he cum to Londen towr;
In the west partes we have Kyng Alphonse with the
    Spanyardes,
With sheppes full of gonepowder now cummyng hether
    towardes;
And on the est syde we have Esterlynges, Danes, and
    Norwayes,
With soch powr landynge as can be resystyd nowayes.

K. JOHAN: All that is not true that yow have here
        expressed.   1640

CARDYNALL: By the messe, so true as I have now
        confessed.

K. JOHAN: And what do ye meane by such an hurly
        burlye?

CARDYNALL: For the Churches ryght to subdue ye
    ma[n]fullye.

      [*Enter Sedition.*]

1627 *schryftes* penances   1628 *or* before   1630 *loller* heretic
1635 *sle* slay   1637 *sheppes* ships

SEDICYON: To all that wyll fyght I proclame a Jubyle
 Of cleane remyssyon, thys tyraunt here to slee.
 Destroye hys people, burne up both cytie and towne,
 That the Pope of Rome maye have hys scepture and
  crowne.
 In the Churches cause to dye thys daye be bolde;
 Your sowles shall to heaven ere your fleshe and bones
  be colde.

K. JOHAN: Most mercyfull God as my trust is in The, 1650
 So comforte me now in this extremyte!
 As thow holpyst David in his most hevynes,
 So helpe me this hour of thy grace, mercye and goodnes.

CARDYNALL: This owtward remorse that ye show here
   evydent
 Ys a grett lykelyhod and token of amendment.
 How say ye, Kyng Johan? Can ye fynd now in yowr
  hart
 To obaye Holy Chyrch and geve ower yowr froward
  part?

K. JOHAN: Were yt so possyble to hold thes enmyes
   backe,
 That my swete Ynglond perysh not in this sheppwracke?

CARDYNALL: Possyble, quoth he? Yea, they shuld go bake
   indede, 1660
 And ther gret armyse to some other quarteres leede,
 Or elles they have not so many good blyssynges now,
 But as many cursynges they shall have, I make God a
  vowe.
 I promyse yow, sur, ye shall have specyall faver
 Yf ye wyll submyt yowr sylfe to Holye Chyrch here.

K. JOHAN: I trust than ye wyll graunt some delyberacyon
 To have an answere of thys your protestacyon.

SEDICYON: Tush, gyve upp the crowne and make
   nomore a-do.

K. JOHAN: Your spirytuall charyte wyll be better to me
  than so.

1652 *hevynes* grief 1657 *froward* perverse 1659 *sheppwracke* shipwreck
1660 *bake* back 1667 *protestacyon* assertion

The crowne of a realme is a matter of great wayght;   1670
In gyvynge it upp we maye not be to slayght.

SEDICYON: I saye gyve it up! Lete us have nomore a-do.

CARDYNALL: Yea, and in our warres we wyll no farder go.

K. JOHAN: Ye wyll gyve me leave to talke first with my
    clergye?

SEDICYON: With them ye nede not; they are at a poynt
    alreadye.

K. JOHAN: Than with my lawers to heare what they wyll
    tell.

SEDICYON: Ye shall ever have them as the clergye gyve
    them counsell.

K. JOHAN: Then wyll I commen with my nobylyte.

SEDICYON: We have hym so jugled he wyll not to yow
    agree.

K. JOHAN: Yet shall I be content to do as he counsell me.   1680

CARDYNALL: Than be not to longe from hence, I wyll
    advyse ye.

[*Exeunt King John and England.*]

SEDICYON: Is not thys a sport? By the messe, it is, I
    trowe.

What welthe and pleasure wyll now to our kyngedom
    growe!

Englande is our owne, whych is the most plesaunt
    grounde

In all the rounde worlde! Now maye we realmes
    confounde.

Our Holye Father maye now lyve at hys pleasure

And have habundaunce of wenches, wynes and
    treasure.

He is now able to kepe downe Christe and hys Gospell,

True fayth to exyle and all vertues to expell.

Now shall we ruffle it in velvattes, golde and sylke,   1690

1671 *slayght* crafty   1678 *commen* consult   1690 *ruffle* swagger

With shaven crownes, syde gownes, and rochettes
    whyte as mylke.
By the messe, Pandulphus, now maye we synge
    Cantate,
And crowe *Confitebor*, with a joyfull *Iubilate*!
Holde me, or els for laughynge I must burste.
CARDYNALL: Holde thy peace, whorson, I wene thu art
    accurst.
Kepe a sadde countenaunce. A very vengeaunce take the!
SEDICYON: I can not do it, by the messe, and thou
    shuldest hange me.
If Solon were here I recken that he woulde laugh,
Whych never laught yet; yea, lyke a whelpe he woulde
    waugh.
Ha, ha, ha! Laugh, quoth he! Yea, laugh and laugh
    agayne!   1700
We had never cause to laugh more free, I am playne.
CARDYNALL: I praye the, nomore, for here come the
    kynge agayne.

[*King John and England return.*]

Ye are at a poynt wherto ye intende to stande?
SEDICYON: Yea, hardely sir: gyve up the crowne of
    Englande.
K. JOHAN: I have cast in mynde the great displeasures of
    warre,
The daungers, the losses, the decayes both nere and
    farre,
The burnynge of townes, the throwynge downe of
    buyldynges,
Destructyon of corne and cattell, with other thynges,
Defylynge of maydes and shedynge of Christen blood,
With suche lyke outrages, neyther honest, true nor
    good.   1710

1691 *rochettes* surplices   1699 *waugh* ?bark

389

These thynges consydered, I am compelled thys houre
To resigne up here both crowne and regall poure.

ENGLANDE: For the love of God, yet take some better
advysement.

SEDICYON: Holde your tunge, ye whore, or by the messe
ye shall repent!

Downe on your mary bones and make nomore a-do!

ENGLANDE: If ye love me, sir, for Gods sake do never so.

K. JOHAN: O Englande, Englande, shewe now thyselfe a
mother;
Thy people wyll els be slayne here without nomber
As God shall judge me, I do not thys of cowardnesse
But of compassyon, in thys extreme heavynesse.   1720
Shall my people shedde their bloude in suche
habundaunce?
Nay, I shall rather gyve upp my whole governaunce.

SEDICYON: Come of apace, than, and make an ende of it
shortly.

ENGLANDE: The most pytiefull chaunce that hath bene
hytherto, surely.

K. JOHAN: Here I submyt me to Pope Innocent the Thred,
Dyssyering mercy of hys holy fatherhed.

CARDYNALL: Geve up the crowne, than; yt shalbe the
better for ye.
He wyll unto yow the more favorable be.

Here the Kyng delevyr the crowne to the Cardynall.

K. JOHAN: To hym I resygne here the septer and the
crowne
Of Ynglond and Yrelond, with the powr and renowne,   1730
And put me wholly to his mercyfull ordynance.

CARDYNALL: I may say this day the Chyrch hath a full
gret chaunce.

1715 *mary* marrow

390

Thes v dayes I wyll kepe this crowne in myn owne
    hande,
In the Popes behalfe upseasyng Ynglond and Yerlond.
In the meane season ye shall make an oblygacyon
For yow and yowr ayers, in this synyficacyon:
To resayve yowr crowne of the Pope for ever more
In maner of fefarme; and for a tokyn therfor
Ye shall every yere paye hym a thowsand marke
With the peter pens, and not agenst yt barke.   1740
Ye shall also geve to the Bysshoppe of Cantorbery
A thre thowsand marke for his gret injury.
To the Chyrch besydes, for the great scathe ye have
    done,
Forty thowsand marke ye shall delyver sone.

K. JOHAN: Ser, the taxe that I had of the hole realme of
    Ynglond
Amownted to no more but unto xxxti thowsand.
Why shuld I than paye so moche unto the Clargy?

CARDYNALL: Ye shall geve yt them; ther is no remedy.

K. JOHAN: Shall they paye no tribute yf the realme stond
    in rerage?   1750

CARDYNALL: Sir, they shall paye none; we wyll have no
    soch bondage.

K. JOHAN: The Pope had at once thre hundred thowsand
    marke.

CARDYNALL: What is that to yow? Ah, styll ye wyll be
    starke.
Ye shall paye yt sir; ther is no remedy.

K. JOHAN: Yt shall be performed as ye wyll have yt,
    trewly.

ENGLANDE: So noble a realme to stande tributarye, alas,
To the Devyls vycar! Suche fortune never was.

SEDICYON: Out with thys harlot! Cockes sowle, she hath
    lete a fart!

1734 *upseasyng* taking possession of
1738 *fefarme* subject to rent, homage   1743 *scathe* harm
1750 *rerage* debt   1753 *starke* rigid

ENGLANDE: Lyke a wretche thu lyest; thy report is lyke
    as thu art.

[*Exit Sedition.*]

CARDYNALL: Ye shall suffer the monkes and channons to
    make re-entry
  In to ther abbayes and to dwell ther peacebly.   1760
  Ye shall se also to my great labur and charge.
  For other thynges elles we shall commen more at large.
K. JOHAN: Ser, in every poynt I shall fulfyll yowr plesur.
CARDYNALL: Than plye yt apace and lett us have the
    tresur.
ENGLANDE: Alacke for pyte that ever ye grantyd this.
  For me, pore Ynglond, ye have done sore amys;
  Of a fre woman ye have now mad a bonde mayd.
  Yowr selfe and heyres ye have for ever decayd.
  Alas, I had rether be underneth the Turke
  Than under the wynges of soch a thefe to lurke.   1770
K. JOHAN: Content the, Ynglond, for ther ys no remedy.
ENGLANDE: Yf yow be plesyd than I must consent gladly.
K. JOHAN: If I shoulde not graunt here woulde be a
    wondrefull spoyle;
  Every where the enemyes woulde ruffle and turmoyle.
  The losse of people stycketh most unto my harte.
ENGLANDE: Do as ye thynke best; yche waye is to my
    smarte.
CARDYNALL: Are ye at a poynt with the same
    oblygacyon?
K. JOHAN: Yt is here redye at yowr interrogacyon.

Here Kyng Johan shall delevyr the oblygacyon.

1774 *ruffle* rage   *turmoyle* agitate

CARDYNALL: Wher is the mony for yowr full
      restytucyon?

K. JOHAN: Here, ser, accordyng to yowr last
      constutucyon.   1780

CARDYNALL: Cum hether, my lorde. By the Popys
      autoryte
Assoyll this man here of irregularyte.

Here the bysshop Stevyn Langton cum in.

K. JOHAN: Me thynke this bysshope resembleth moch
      Sedycyon.

CARDYNALL: I cownsell yow yet to be ware of wrong
      suspycyon.
This is Stevyn Langton yowr meteropolytan.

K. JOHAN: Than do the offyce of the good samarytan,
And pore oyle and wyne in my old festerd wownd.
Releace me of synne that yt doth not me confownd.
Confiteor Domino Pape et omnibus cardinalibus eius et
   vobis, quia peccavi nimis exigendo ab ecclesia tributum,   1790
   mea culpa. Ideo precor sanctissimum dominum Papam
   et omnes prelatos eius et vos, orare pro me.

STEVYN LANGTON: *Misereatur tui omnipotens Papa, et*
   dimittat tibi omnes erratus tuos, liberetque te a
   suspencione, excominicacione et interdicto, et restituat te
   in regnum tuum.

K. JOHAN: *Amen*

STEVYN LANGTON: *Dominus Papa noster te absolvat, et ego*
   absolvo te auctortibate eius, et apostolorum Petri et Pauli in   1800
   hac parte mihi comissa, ab omnibus impietatibus tuis, et
   restituo te corone et regno, in nomine Domini Pape, amen.

CARDYNALL: Ye are well content to take this man for
      yowr primate?

K. JOHAN: Yea, and to use hym accordyng to his estate.

I am ryght sory that ever I yow offendyd.

SEDICYON: And I am full gladde that ye are so welle
amended.

Unto Holy Churche ye are now an obedyent chylde,

Where ye were afore with heresye muche defyelde.

ENGLANDE: Sir, yonder is a clarke whych is condempned
for treason.

The shryves woulde fayne knowe what to do with hym
thys season.

[*Enter Treason.*]

K. JOHAN: Come hyther, fellawe. What? My thynke thou
art a pryste.

TREASON: He hath ofter gessed that of the truthe have
myste. 1810

K. JOHAN: A pryste and a traytour? How maye that wele
agree?

TREASON: Yes, yes, wele ynough underneth *Benedicite.*

Myself hath played it, and therfor I knowe it the better

Amonge crafytye cloyners there hath not bene a gretter.

K. JOHAN: Tell some of thy feates; thou mayest the better
escape.

SEDICYON: Hem! Not to bolde yet; for a mowse the catte
wyll gape.

TREASON: Twenty thousande traytour I have made in my
tyme

Undre *Benedicite* betwyn hygh masse and pryme.

I made Nobylyte to be obedyent

To the Churche of Rome, whych most kynges maye
repent. 1820

I have so convayed that neyther priest nor lawer

Wyll obeye Gods wurde, nor yet the Gospell faver.

In the place of Christe I have sett up supersticyons:

1808 *shryves* sherrifs 1814 *cloyners* cheats 1821 *convayed* contrived

394

For preachynges, ceremonyes; for Gods wurde, mennys
    tradicyons;
Come to the temple and there Christe hath no place;
Moyses and the paganes doth utterly hym deface.

ENGLANDE: Marke wele, sir. Tell what we have of
              Moyses.

TREASON: All your ceremonyes, your copes and your
              sensers, doubtlesse,
Your fyers, your waters, your oyles, your aulters, your
    ashes,
Your candlestyckes, your cruettes, your salte with suche
    lyke trashes;   1830
Ye lacke but the bloude of a goate or els a calfe.

ENGLANDE: Lete us heare sumwhat also in the paganes
              behalfe.

TREASON: Of the paganes ye have your gylded ymages all,
In your necessytees upon them for to call
With crowchynges, with kyssynges and settynge up of
    lyghtes,
Bearynge them in processyon and fastynges upon their
    nyghtes;
Some for the tothe-ake, some for the pestylence and
    poxe,
With ymages of wax to brynge moneye to the boxe.

ENGLANDE: What have they of Christe in the Churche, I
              praye the tell.

TREASON: Marry nothynge at all but the Epystle and the
              Gospell,   1840
And that is in Latyne that no man shoulde it knowe.

SEDICYON: Peace, noughty whoreson, peace; thou
              playest the knave, I trowe.

K. JOHAN: Hast thou knowne suche wayes and sought no
              reformacyon?

[TREASON:] It is the lyvynge of our whole congregacyon.
If supersticyons and ceremoneys from us fall,
Farwele, monke and chanon, priest, fryer, byshopp and
    all.

    1824 *tradicyons* teaching

Our conveyaunce is suche that we have both moneye and
　　ware.
SEDICYON: Our occupacyon thou wylt marre! God gyve
　　the care.
ENGLANDE: Very fewe of ye wyll Peters offyce take?
TREASON: Yes, the more part of us our maistre hath
　　forsake.　　　　　　　　　　　　　　　　　　　　1850
ENGLANDE: I meane for preachynge. I praye God thu be
　　curste.
TREASON: No, no, with Judas we love wele to be purste.
　　We selle our maker so sone as we have hym made,
　　And as for preachynge, we meddle not with that trade
　　Least Annas, Cayphas, and the lawers shulde us blame,
　　Callynge us to a reckenynge for preachynge in that
　　　name.
K. JOHAN: But tell me, person, whie wert thu cast in
　　preson?
[TREASON:] For no great matter, but a lyttle petye
　　treason:
　　For conjurynge, calkynge, and coynynge of newe
　　　grotes
　　For clippynge of nobles with suche lyke pratye motes.　　1860
ENGLANDE: Thys is hygh treason, and hath bene evermore.
K. JOHAN: It is suche treason as he shall sure hange fore.
TREASON: I have holy orders; by the messe I defye your
　　wurst!
　　Ye can not towche me but ye must be accurst.
K. JOHAN: We wyll not towche the, the halter shall do yt
　　alone.
　　Curse the rope, therfor, whan thu begynnest to grone.
TREASON: And sett ye nomore by the holy ordre of
　　prestehode?
　　Ye wyll prove your-selfe an heretyke, by the rode.
K. JOHAN: Come hyther, Englande, and here what I saye
　　to the.
ENGLANDE: I am all readye to do as ye commaunde me.　　1870

　　1847 *ware* goods　1852 *purste* counted
　　1859 *calkynge* calculating by astrology　*coynynge* coining

396

K. JOHAN: For so much as he hath falsefyed our coyne,
As he is worthie lete hym with an halter joyne.
Thu shalt hange no priest nor yet none honest man,
But a traytour, a thefe, and one that lyttle good can.

CARDYNALL: What, yet agaynst the Churche? Gett me
boke, belle, and candle;
As I am true priest, I shall ye yett better handle.
Ye neyther regarde hys crowne nor anoynted fyngers,
The offyce of a priest nor the grace that therin lyngers.

SEDICYON: Sir, pacyent yourselfe, and all thynge shall be
well.
Fygh, man! To the Churche that ye shulde be styll a
rebell!   1880

ENGLANDE: I accompt hym no priest that worke such
haynouse treason.

SEDICYON: It is a worlde to heare a folysh woman reason.

CARDYNALL: After thys maner ye used Peter Pomfrete,
A good symple man and as they saye, a profete.

K. JOHAN: Sir, I ded prove hym a very supersticyouse
wretche
And blasphemouse lyar; therfor ded the lawe hym
upstretche.
He prophecyed first I shulde reigne but xiiij years,
Makynge the people to beleve he coulde bynde bears;
And I have reigned a seventene years and more.
And anon after he grudged at me very sore,   1890
And sayde I shulde by exylded out of my realme
Before the Ascencyon, whych was turned to a
fantastycall dreame,
Saynge he woulde hange if hys prophecye were not true.
Thus hys owne decaye hys folyshnesse ded brue.

CARDYNALL: Ye shoulde not hange hym whych is a frynde
to the Churche.

K. JOHAN: Alac, that ye shoulde counte them fryndes of
the Churche
That agaynst all truthe so hypocrytycally lurche;
An yll churche is it that hath suche fryndes indede.

1894 *brue* cause

397

ENGLANDE: Of Maister Morres suche an-other fable we
      reade,
That in Morgans fyelde the sowle of a knyght made
    verses,   1900
Apearynge unto hym and thys one he rehearces:
Destruet hoc regnum rex regum duplici plaga –
Whych is true as God spake with the Ape at Praga.
The sowles departed from thys heavye mortall payne
To the handes of God returneth never agayne.
A marvelouse thynge that ye thus delyght in lyes.
SEDICYON: Thys queane doth not els but mocke our
      blessed storyes.
That Peter angred ye whan he called ye a devyll
    incarnate.
K. JOHAN: He is now full sure nomore so uncomely to
      prate.
Well as for thys man because that he is a priste   1910
I gyve hym to ye; do with hym what ye lyste.
CARDYNALL: In the Popes behalfe I wyll sumwhat take
      upon me:
Here I delyver hym by the Churches lyberte,
In spyght of your hart. Make of it what ye lyste.
K. JOHAN: I am pleased, I saye, because he ys pryste.
CARDYNALL: Whether ye be or no, it shall not greatly
      force.
Lete me see those cheanes. Go thy waye, and have
    remorce.
TREASON: God save your lordeshypps, I trust I shall
      amende
And do nomore so, or els, sir, God defende.

   [*Exit Treason.*]

SEDICYON: I shall make the, I trowe, to kepe thy
      benefyce.   1920

     1916 *force* matter   1917 *cheanes* chains   1919 *defende* forbid

By the Marye Messe, the knave wyll never be wyse!

ENGLANDE: Lyke lorde, lyke chaplayne; neyther barrell
better herynge.

SEDICYON: Styll she must trattle; that tunge is alwayes
sterynge

A wurde or two, sir, I must tell yow in your eare.

CARDYNALL: Of some advauntage I woulde very gladly
heare.

SEDICYON: Releace not Englande of the generall
interdictyon

Tyll the Kynge hath graunted the dowrye and the
pencyon

Of Julyane, the wyfe of Kynge Richarde Cour de Lyon.

Ye knowe very well she beareth the Churche good
mynde.

Tush, we must have all, manne, that she shall leave
behynde.   1930

As the saynge is, he fyndeth that surely bynde.

It were but folye suche louce endes for to lose;

The lande and the monye wyll make well for our
purpose.

Tush, laye yokes upon hym more than he is able to
beare;

Of Holy Churche so he wyll stande ever in feare.

Suche a shrewe as he it is good to kepe undre awe.

ENGLANDE: Woo is that persone whych is undreneth your
lawe!

Ye maye see good people what these same merchauntes
are;

Their secrete knaveryes their open factes declare.

SEDICYON: Holde thy peace, callet; God gyve the sorowe
and care!   1940

CARDYNALL: Ere I releace yow of the interdyctyon heare,

In the whych your realme contynued hath thys seven
yeare,

Ye shall make Julyane, your syster in lawe, thys bande,

1923 *trattle* chatter   1932 *louce* loose   1937 *undreneth* underneath
1940 *callet* whore

399

To gyve hir the thirde part of Englande and of Irelande.

K. JOHAN: All the worlde knoweth, sir, I owe hir no suche
   dewtye.

CARDYNALL: Ye shall gyve it to hir; there is no remedye.

Wyll ye styll withstande our Holy Fathers precepte?

SEDICYON: In peyne of dampnacyon hys commaundement
   must be kepte.

K. JOHAN: Oh, ye undo me, consyderynge my great
   paymentes.

ENGLANDE: Sir, disconfort not, for God hath sent
   debatementes;   1950

Your mercyfull maker hath shewed upon ye hys powere,

From thys heavye yoke delyverynge yow thys howre.

The woman is dead; suche newes are hyther brought.

K. JOHAN: For me, a synnar thys myracle hath God
   wrought.

In most hygh paryls he ever me preserved,

And in thys daunger he hath from me swerved.

In genua procumbens Deum adorat dicens

As David sayth, Lorde, thu dost not leave thy servaunt

That wyll trust in the and in thy blessyd covenaunt.

SEDICYON: A vengeaunce take it! By the messe, it is
   unhappye

She is dead so sone. Now is it past remedye.   1960

So must we lose all now that she is clerely gone.

If that praye had bene ours, oh, it had bene alone!

The chaunce beynge suche, by my trouth, even lete it
   go;

No grote, no *Pater Noster*, no penye, no *placebo*.

The devyll go with it, seynge it wyll be no better.

ENGLANDE: Their myndes are all sett upon the fylthie
   luker.

   1950 *debatementes* strife   1955 *paryls* perils   1962 *praye* prey
   1966 *luker* money

400

CARDYNALL: Than here I releace yow of your
          interdictyons all,
  And strayghtly commaunde yow upon daungers that
    maye fall
  Nomore to meddle with the Churches reformacyon,
  Nor holde men from Rome whan they make appellacyon,   1970
  By God and by all the contentes of thys boke.
K. JOHAN: Agaynst Holy Churche I wyll nomore speake
          nor loke.
SEDICYON: Go, open the churche dores and lete the
          belles be ronge,
  And through-out the realme see that *Te Deum* be songe.
  Pryck upp your candels before Saynt Loe and Saynt
    Legearde,
  Lete Saynt Antonyes hogge be had in some regarde.
  If your ale be sower and your breade moulde, certayne,
  Now wyll they waxe swete, for the Pope hath blest ye
    agayne.
ENGLANDE: Than within a whyle I trust ye wyll preache
          the Gospell?
SEDICYON: That shall I tell the – kepe thu it in secrete
          counsell –   1980
  It shall neyther come in churche nor yet in chauncell.
CARDYNALL: Goo your wayes a pace and see our
          pleasure be done.
K. JOHAN: As ye have commaunded all shall be
          perfourmed sone.

[King John and England go out.]

CARDYNALL: By the messe, I laugh to see thys cleane
          conveyaunce!
  He is now full glad, as our pype goeth, to daunce;
  By cockes sowle, he is now become a good parrysh
    clarke.

1968 *strayghtly* strictly   1970 *appellacyon* appeal   1981 *chauncell* chancel

SEDICYON: Ha, ha, wylye whoreson, dost that so busyly
      marke?
  I hope in a whyle we wyll make hym so to rave
  That he shall become unto us a commen slave,
  And shall do nothynge but as we byd hym do.   1990
  If we byd hym slea I trowe he wyll do so;
  If we bydde hym burne suche as beleve in Christe,
  He shall not saye naye to the byddynge of a priste.
  But yet it is harde to trust what he wyll be,
  He is so crabbed, by the Holye Trinyte.
  To save all thynges up I holde best we make hym more
    sure
  And gyve hym a sawce that he no longar endure.
  Now that I remembre we shall not leave hym thus.
CARDYNALL: Whye, what shall we do to hym els, in the
      name of Jesus?
SEDICYON: Marry, fatche in Lewes, Kynge Phylyppes
      sonne of Fraunce,   2000
  To fall upon hym with hys menne and ordynaunce,
  With wyldefyer, gunpouder, and suche lyke myrye
    tryckes,
  To dryve hym to holde and searche hym in the quyckes.
  I wyll not leave hym tyll I brynge hym to hys yende.
CARDYNALL: Well, farwele Sedicyon, do as shall lye in
      thy myende.

[*Exit Cardinal.*]

SEDICYON: I marvele greatly where Dissymulacyon is.
DISSYMUL: I wyll come anon if thu tarry tyll I pysse.

[*Enter Dissimulation.*]

SEDICYON: I beshrewe your hart! Where have ye bene so
      longe?

    1991 *slea* slay   2003 *quyckes* tenderest part   2004 *yende* end

DISSYMUL: In the gardene, man, the herbes and wedes
  amonge,
And there have I gote the poyson of toade.   2010
I hope in a whyle to wurke some feate abroade.

SEDICYON: I was wonte sumtyme of thy prevye counsell
  to be.
Am I now-adayes become a straunger to the?

DISSYMUL: I wyll tell the all undreneth *Benedicite*
What I mynde to do in case thu wylt assoyle me.

SEDICYON: Thu shalt be assoyled by the most Holy
  Fathers auctoryte.

DISSYMUL: Shall I so in dede? By the masse, than, now
  have at the!
Benedicite.

SEDICYON: *In nomine Pape, Amen.*

DISSYMUL: Syr, thys is my mynde: I wyll gyve Kyng
  Johan thys poyson,   2020
So makynge hym sure that he shall never have foyson.
And thys must thu saye to colour with the thynge,
That a penye lofe he wolde have brought to a
  shyllynge.

SEDICYON: Naye, that is suche a lye as easely wyll be
  felte.

DISSYMUL: Tush, man, amonge fooles it never wyll be
  smelte,
Though it be a foule great lye. Set upon it a good face,
And that wyll cause men beleve it in every place.

SEDICYON: I am sure, than, thu wylt geve it hym in a
  drynke.

DISSYMUL: Marry, that I wyll, and the one half with hym
  swynke
To encourage hym to drynke the botome off.   2030

SEDICYON: If thu drynke the halfe thu shalt fynde it no
  scoff;
Of terryble deathe thu wylt stacker in the plashes.

2021 *foyson* plenty   2029 *swynke* drink deep   2032 *stacker* stagger
plashes puddles

DISSYMUL: Tush, though I dye, man, there wyll ryse
more of my ashes.
I am sure the monkes wyll praye for me so bytterlye
That I shall not come in helle nor in purgatorye.
In the Popes kychyne the scullyons shall not brawle
Nor fyght for my grese. If the priestes woulde for me
yewle
And grunt a good pace *placebo* with Requiem Masse,
Without muche tarryaunce I shulde to paradyse passe,
Where I myght be sure to make good cheare and be
myrye,   2040
For I can not away with that whoreson purgatorye.
SEDICYON: To kepe the from thens thu shalt have fyve
monkes syngynge
In Swynsett Abbeye so longe as the worlde is durynge.
They wyll daylye praye for the sowle of Father Symon,
A Cisteane monke whych poysened Kynge Johan.
DISSYMUL: Whan the worlde is done what helpe shall I
have than?
SEDICYON: Than shyft for thy self so wele as ever thou
can.
DISSYMUL: Cockes sowle, he cometh here! Assoyle me
that I were gone then.
SEDICYON: *Ego absolvo te in nomine Pape, Amen.*

[*Exeunt Sedition and Dissimulation.*
Enter King John and England.]

K. JOHAN: No prynce in the worlde in suche captivyte   2050
As I am thys houre, and all for ryghteousnesse.
Agaynst me I have both the lordes and commynalte,
Byshoppes and lawers, whych in their cruell madnesse
Hath brought in hyther the Frenche kynges eldest sonne
Lewes.

2037 *grese* grease, fat   *yewle* howl   2043 *durynge* lasting

The chaunce unto me is not so dolorrouse,
But my lyfe thys daye is muche more tedyouse.

More of compassyon for shedynge of Christen blood
Than any thynge else, my sceptre I gave up latelye
To the Pope of Rome, whych hath no tytle good
Of jurisdyctyon, but of usurpacyon onlye.　　　　　　　　　2060
And now to the, Lorde, I would resygne up gladlye

Flectit genua.

Both my crowne and lyfe; for thyne owne ryght it is,
If it woulde please the, to take my sowle to thy blys.

ENGLANDE: Sir, discomfort ye not in the honour of
　　　　　Christe Jesu:
　　God wyll never fayle yow, intendynge not els but
　　　vertu.
K. JOHAN: The anguysh of sprete so pangeth me every
　　　　　where
　　That incessauntly I thyrst tyll I be there.
ENGLANDE: Sir, be of good chere, for the Pope hath sent
　　　　　a legate
　　Whose name is Gualo, your foes to excommunycate;
　　Not only Lewes whych hath wonne Rochestre,　　　　　2070
　　Wynsore and London, Readynge and Wynchestre,
　　But so manye els as agaynst ye have rebelled
　　He hath suspended and openly accursed.
K. JOHAN: They are all false knaves; all men of them be
　　　　　ware
　　They never left me tyll they had me in their snare,
　　Now have they Otto the Emproure so wele as me,
　　And the French Kynge Phylypp, undre their captivyte.

2055 *dolorrouse* painful　2066 *sprete* spirit　*pangeth* hurts

All Christen princes they wyll have in their bandes.
The Pope and hys priestes are poyseners of all landes.
All Christen people be ware of trayterouse pristes,　　　　2080
For of truthe they are the pernicyouse Antichristes.

ENGLANDE: Thys same Gualo, sir, in your cause doth
　　　　stoughtly barke.

K. JOHAN: They are all nought, Englande, so many as
　　　　weare that marke.
From thys habytacyon, swete lorde, delyver me,
And preserve thys realme, of thy benygnyte.

DISSYMUL: [sings offstage.] Wassayle, wassayle, out of the
　　　　mylke payle,
Wassayle, wassayle, as whyte as my nayle,
Wassayle, wassayle, in snowe, froste, and hayle,
Wassayle, wassayle, with partriche and rayle.
Wassayle, wassayle, that muche doth avayle,　　　　2090
Wassayle, wassayle, that never wyll fayle.

K. JOHAN: Who is that, Englande? I praye the stepp
　　　　fourth and see.

ENGLANDE: He doth seme a farre some relygyouse man
　　　　to be.

DISSYMUL: [Enters.] Now Jesus preserve your worthye
　　　　and excellent grace,
For doubtlesse there is a very angelyck face.
Now forsoth and God, I woulde thynke my self in
　　　　heaven
If I myght remayne with yow but yeares alevyn;
I woulde covete here none other felicyte.

K. JOHAN: A lovynge persone thu mayest seme for to be.

DISSYMUL: I am as gentle a worme as ever ye see.　　　　2100

K. JOHAN: But what is thy name, good frynde? I praye
　　　　the tell me.

DISSYMUL: Simon of Swynsett my very name is, per dee.
I am taken of men for monastycall devocyon,
And here have I brought yow a marvelouse good
　　　　pocyon,

2089 _partriche_ partridge　　_rayle_ rail　　2097 _alevyn_ eleven
2104 _pocyon_ potion

For I hearde ye saye that ye were very drye.

K. JOHAN: In dede I wolde gladly drynke. I praye the
come nye.

DISSYMUL: The dayes of your lyfe never felt ye suche a
cuppe,

So good and so holsome if ye woulde drynke it upp.

It passeth malmesaye, capryck, tyre or ypocras.

By my faythe, I thynke a better drynke never was.   2110

K. JOHAN: Begynne, gentle monke; I praye the drynke half
to me.

DISSYMUL: If ye dronke all up it were the better for ye.

It woulde slake your thirst and also quycken your
brayne.

A better drynke is not in Portyngale nor Spayne.

Therfor suppe it of and make an ende of it quycklye.

K. JOHAN: Naye, thu shalte drynke half. There is no
remedye.

DISSYMUL: Good lucke to ye than; have at it by and bye.

Halfe wyll I consume if there be no remedye.

K. JOHAN: God saynt the, good monke, with all my very
harte.

DISSYMUL: I have brought ye half; conveye me that for
your parte.   2120

Where art thu, Sedicyon? By the masse, I dye, I dye!

Helpe now at a pynche. Alas, man, cum awaye shortlye.

[*Enter Sedition*]

SEDICYON: Come hyther apace, and gett thee to the
farmerye.

I have provyded for the, by swete Saynt Powle,

Fyve monkes that shall synge contynually for thy
sowle,

That I warande the thu shalt not come in helle.

2119 *saynt* bless   2122 *shortlye* quickly   2123 *farmerye* infirmary

DISSYMUL: To sende me to heaven goo rynge the holye
    belle
And synge for my sowle a masse of *Scala Celi*,
That I maye clyme up aloft with Enoch and Heli.
I do not doubte it but I shall be a saynt;   2130
Provyde a gyldar, myne image for to paynt.
I dye for the Churche with Thomas of Canterberye;
Ye shall fast my vigyll and upon my daye be merye.
No doubt but I shall do myracles in a whyle,
And therfor lete me be shryned in the north yle.
SEDICYON: To the than wyll offer both crypple, halte
    and blynde,
Mad men and mesels, with suche as are woo behynde.

Exeunt [Dissimulation and Sedition.]

K. JOHAN: My bodye me vexeth; I doubt muche of a
    tympanye.
ENGLANDE: Now alas, alas, your grace is betrayed
    cowardlye!
K. JOHAN: Where became the monke that was here with
    me latelye?   2140
ENGLANDE: He is poysened, sir, and lyeth a dyenge
    surelye.
K. JOHAN: It can not be so, for he was here even now.
ENGLANDE: Doubtlesse, sir, it is so true as I have tolde
    yow.
A false Judas kysse he hath gyven yow and is gone.
The halte, sore and lame thys pitiefull case wyll mone.
Never prynce was there that made to poore peoples uses
So many masendewes, hospytals and spyttle howses
As your grace hath done yet sens the worlde began.

2131 *gyldar* gilder   2135 *yle* aisle   2137 *mesels* lepers
2138 *tympanye* swelling   2141 *dyenge* dying   2145 *mone* moan
2147 *masendewes* i.e. *maisondieus* hospitals for the poor
spyttle howses lazar-houses

K. JOHAN: Of priestes and of monkes I am counted a
        wycked man
  For that I never buylte churche nor monasterye,   2150
  But my pleasure was to helpe suche as were nedye.
ENGLANDE: The more grace was yours, for at the daye of
        judgement
  Christe wyll rewarde them whych hath done hys
    commaundement.
  There is no promyse for voluntarye wurkes,
  Nomore than there is for sacrifyce of the Turkes.
K. JOHAN: Doubtlesse I do fele muche grevaunce in my
        bodye.
ENGLANDE: As the Lorde wele knoweth, for that I am
        full sorye.
K. JOHAN: There is no malyce to the malyce of the
        clergye.
  Well, the Lorde God of heaven on me and them have
    mercye.

For doynge justyce they have ever hated me.   2160
They caused my lande to be excommunycate
And me to resygne both crowne and princely dygnyte,
From my obedyence assoylynge every estate,
And now, last of all, they have me intoxycate.
I perceyve ryght wele their malyce hath none ende.
I desyre not els but that they maye sone amende.

I have sore hungred and thirsted ryghteousnesse
For the offyce sake that God hath me appoynted,
But now I perceyve that synne and wyckednesse
In thys wretched worlde, lyke as Christe prophecyed,   2170
Have the overhande; in me is it verefyed.
Praye for me, good people, I besych yow hartely,
That the Lorde above on my poore sowle have mercy.

    2164 *intoxycate* poisoned   2171 *overhande* upper hand

Farwell, noble men, with the clergye spirytuall;
Farwell, men of lawe, with the whole commynnalte;
Your disobedyence I do forgyve yow all
And desyre God to perdon your iniquyte.
Farwell, swete Englande, now last of all to the;
I am ryght sorye I coulde do for the nomore.
Farwele ones agayne, yea, farwell for evermore.   2180

ENGLANDE: With the leave of God I wyll not leave ye
          thus,
    But styll be with ye tyll he do take yow from us,
    And than wyll I kepe your bodye for a memoryall.
K. JOHAN: Than plye it, Englande, and provyde for my
          buryall.
    A wydowes offyce it is to burye the deade.
ENGLANDE: Alas, swete maistre, ye waye so heavy as leade.
    Oh horryble case, that ever so noble a kynge
    Shoulde thus be destroyed and lost for ryghteouse
      doynge
    By a cruell sort of disguysed bloud souppers,
    Unmercyfull murtherers, all dronke in the bloude of
      marters.   2190
    Report what they wyll in their most furyouse madnesse,
    Of thys noble kynge muche was the godlynesse.

          Exeunt.
          [*Enter Verity.*]

VERITAS: I assure ye, fryndes, lete men wryte what they
          wyll,
    Kynge Johan was a man both valeaunt and godlye.
    What though Polydorus reporteth hym very yll
    At the suggestyons of the malicyouse clergye?
    Thynke yow a Romane with the Romanes can not lye?

2190 *marters* martyrs

410

Yes! Therfor, Leylande, out of thy s[l]umbre awake,
And wytnesse a trewthe for thyne owne contrayes sake.

For hys valeauntnesse many excellent writers make   2200
As Sigebertus, Vincentius and also Nauclerus;
Giraldus and Mathu Parys with hys noble vertues take –
Yea, Paulus Phrigio, Johan Maior and Hector Boethius.
Nothynge is allowed in hys lyfe of Polydorus
Whych discommendeth hys ponnyshmentes for trayterye,
Advauncynge very sore hygh treason in the clergye.

Of hys godlynesse thus muche report wyll I:
Gracyouse provysyon for sore, sycke, halte and lame
He made in hys tyme, he made both in towne and cytie,
Grauntynge great lyberties for maytenaunce of the same   2210
By markettes and fayers in places of notable name.
Great monymentes are in Yppeswych, Donwych and
    Berye,
Whych noteth hym to be a man of notable mercye.

Thy cytie of London through hys mere graunt and
    premye
Was first privyleged to have both mayer and shryve,
Where before hys tyme it had but baylyves onlye.
In hys dayes the brydge the cytiezens ded contryve.

[*Enter Nobility, Clergy and Civil Order.*]

Though he now be dead hys noble actes are alyve.
Hys zele is declared as towchynge Christes religyon
In that he exyled the Jewes out of thys regyon.   2220

2205 *discommendeth* censures   2214 *mere* sole   *premye* gift
2215 *shryve* sherrif   2216 *baylyves* bailiffs

NOBYLYTE: Whome speake ye of, sir, I besyche ye
hartelye?

VERITAS: I talke of Kynge Johan, of late your prynce
most worthye.

NOBYLYTE: Sir, he was a man of very wycked sorte.

VERITAS: Ye are muche to blame your prynce so to
reporte.

How can ye presume to be called Nobilyte,
Diffamynge a prynce in your malygnyte?
Ecclesiastes sayth, If thu with an hatefull harte
Misnamest a kynge, thu playest suche a wycked parte
As byrdes of ayer to God wyll represent
To thy great parell and excedynge ponnyshment.   2230
Saynt Hierome sayth also that he is of no renowne
But a vyle traytour that rebelleth agaynst the crowne.

CLERGYE: He speaketh not agaynst the crowne but the
man, per dee.

VERITAS: Oh, where is the sprete whych ought to reigne
in the!

The crowne of it-selfe without the man is nothynge.
Learne of the Scriptures to have better undrestandynge.
The harte of a kynge is in the handes of the Lorde,
And he directeth it, wyse Salomon to recorde.
They are abhomynable that use hym wyckedlye.

CLERGYE: He was never good to us, the sanctifyed
clergye.   2240

VERITAS: Wyll ye knowe the cause before thys
worshypfull cumpanye?

Your conversacyon and lyves are very ungodlye.
Kynge Salomon sayth, who hath a pure mynde,
Therin delyghtynge, shall have a kynge to frynde.
On thys wurde *Cleros*, whych signyfieth a lott
Or a sortynge out into a most godly knott,
Ye do take your name, for that ye are the lordes
Select, of hys wurde to be the specyall recordes,
As of Saynt Mathias we have a syngular mencyon,
That they chose hym out anon after Christes ascencyon.   2250
Thus do ye recken. But I feare ye come of *Clerus*,

412

A very noyfull worme, as Aristotle sheweth us,
By whome are destroyed the honycombes of bees;
For poore wydowes ye robbe as ded the Pharysees.

CYVYLE ORDER: I promyse yow it is uncharytably
    spoken.

VERITAS: Treuthe ingendereth hate; ye shewe therof a
    token.

Ye are suche a man as ought every where to see
A godly order, but ye loose yche commynalte.
Plato thought alwayes that no hyghar love coulde be
Than a man to peyne hymself for hys own countreye.   2260
David for their sake the proude Phelistyan slewe,
Aioth made Eglon hys wyckednesse to rewe,
Esdras from Persye for hys owne contreys sake
Came to Hierusalem, their stronge-holdes up to make;
But yow, lyke wretches, cast over both contreye and
    kynge.
All manhode shameth to see your unnaturall doynge.
Ye wycked rulers, God doth abhorre ye all.
As Mantuan reporteth in hys Egloges Pastorall,
Ye fede not the shepe, but ever ye pylle the flocke
And clyppe them so nygh that scarsely ye leave one
    locke.   2270
Your jugementes are suche that ye call to God in vayne
So longe as ye have your prynces in disdayne.
Chrysostome reporteth that nobylyte of fryndes
Avayleth nothynge, except ye have godly myndes.
What profiteth it yow to be called spirytuall
Whyls yow for lucre from all good vertues fall?
What prayse is it to yow to be called Cyvylyte
If yow from obedyence and godly order flee?
Anneus Seneca hath thys most provable sentence:
The gentyll free hart goeth never from obedyence.   2280

CYVYLE ORDER: Sir, my bretherne and I woulde gladly
    knowe your name.

VERITAS: I am Veritas, that come hyther yow to blame

2252 *noyfull* harmful   2256 *ingendereth* engenders

For castynge awaye of our most lawfull kynge.
Both God and the worlde detesteth your dampnable
    doynge.
How have ye used Kynge Johan here now of late?
I shame to rehearce the corruptyons of your state.
Ye were never wele tyll ye had hym cruelly slayne,
And now beynge dead, ye have hym styll in disdayne.
Ye have raysed up of hym most shamelesse lyes,
Both by your reportes and by your written storyes.   2290
He that slewe Saul through fearcenesse vyolent
Was slayne sone after at Davids just commaundement,
For bycause that Saul was anoynted of the Lorde.
The Seconde of Kynges of thys beareth plenteouse
    recorde.
He was in those dayes estemed wurthie to dye
On a noynted kynge that layed handes violentlye.
Ye are not ashamed to fynde fyve priestes to synge
For that same traytour that slewe your naturall kynge.
A trayterouse knave ye can set upp for a saynte,
And a ryghteouse kynge lyke an hatefull odyouse
    tyraunt paynte.   2300
I coulde shewe the place where yow most spyghtfullye
Put out your torches upon hys physnomye.
In your glasse wyndowes ye whyppe your naturall
    kynges.
As I sayde afore, I abhorre to shewe your doynges.
The Turkes, I dare saye, are a thousande tymes better
    than yow.
NOBYLYTE: For Gods love, nomore! Alas, ye have sayde
    ynough.
CLERGYE: All the worlde doth knowe that we have done
    sore amys.
CYVYLE ORDER: Forgyve it us, so that we never heare
    more of thys.
VERITAS: But are ye sorye for thys ungodly wurke?
NOBYLYTE: I praye to God, els I be dampned lyke a
    Turke.   2310

    2302 *physnomye* portrait

VERITAS: And make true promyse ye wyll never more do
so?

CLERGYE: Sir, never more shall I from true obeyence goo.

VERITAS: What saye yow, brother? I must have also your
sentence.

CYVYLE ORDER: I wyll ever gyve to my prynce due
reverence.

VERITAS: Well, than, I doubt not but the Lorde wyll
condescende

To forgyve yow all, so that ye mynde to amende.

Adewe to ye all, for now I must be gone.

[*Enter Imperial Majesty.*]

IMPERYALL MAJESTYE: Abyde, Veryte. Ye shall not
depart so sone.

Have ye done all thynges as we commaunded yow?

VERITAS: Yea, most gracyouse prynce, I concluded the
whole even now.   2320

IMP MA: And how do they lyke the customs they have used
With our predecessours, whome they have so abused,
Specyally Kynge Johan? Thynke they they have done
well?

VERITAS: They repent that ever they folowed sedicyouse
counsell

And have made promes they wyll amende faultes.

IMP MA: And forsake the Pope with all hys cruell
assaultes?

VERITAS: Whie do ye not bowe to Imperyall Majeste?
Knele and axe pardon for your great enormyte.

NOBYLYTE: Most godly governour, we axe your gracyouse
pardon,

Promysynge nevermore to maynteyne false Sedicyon.   2330

CLERGYE: Neyther Prvyate Welthe, nor yet Usurped
Poure

2313 *sentence* opinion, intention   2328/9 *axe* ask

Shall cause me disobeye my prynce from thys same
    houre.
False Dissymulacyon shall never me begyle;
Where I shall mete hym I wyll ever hym revyle.

IMP MA: I perceyve, Veryte, ye have done wele your part,
Refourmynge these men. Gramercyes with all my hart.
I praye yow take paynes to call our commynalte
To true obedyence, as ye are Gods Veryte.

VERITAS: I wyll do it, sir. Yet shall I have muche a-doo
    With your Popish prelates. They wyll hunte me to and
    fro.   2340

IMP MA: So longe as I lyve they shall do yow no wronge.

VERITAS: Than wyll I go preache Gods wurde your
    commens amonge.
But first I desyre yow their stubberne factes to remytt.

IMP MA: I forgyve yow all, and perdon your frowarde
    wytt.

OMNES UNA: The heavenly Governour rewarde your
    goodnesse for it!

VERITAS: For Gods sake obeye lyke as doth yow befall,
For in hys owne realme a kynge is judge over all
By Gods appoyntment, and none maye hym judge
    agayne
But the Lorde hymself. In thys the Scripture is playne.
He that condempneth a kynge condempneth God
    without dought;   2350
He that harmeth a kynge to harme God goeth abought;
He that a prynce resisteth doth dampne Gods
    ordynaunce
And resisteth God in withdrawynge hys affyaunce.
All subjectes offendynge are undre the kynges
    judgement;
A kynge is reserved to the Lorde Omnypotent.
He is a mynyster immedyate undre God,
Of hys ryghteousnesse to execute the rod.

2342 *commens* common people   2343 *factes* crimes   2344 *perdon* pardon
frowarde perverse   2353 *affyaunce* fidelity, faith

I charge yow, therfor, as God hath charge me,
To gyve to your kynge hys due supremyte
And exyle the Pope thys realme for evermore.   2360
OMNES UNA: We shall gladly doo accordynge to your loore.
VERITAS: Your grace is content I shewe your people the
          same?
IMP MA: Yea, gentle Veryte, shewe them their dewtye, in
          Gods name.

[*Exit Verity.*]

To confyrme the tale that Veryte had now
The Seconde of Kynges is evydent to yow.

The yonge man that brought the crowne and bracelett
Of Saul to David, saynge that he had hym slayne,
David commaunded, as though he had done that forfett,
Strayght waye to be slayne. Gods sprete ded hym
          constrayne
To shewe what it is, a kynges bloude to distayne.   2370
So ded he those two that in the fyelde hym mett
And unto hym brought the heade of Isboset.

Consydre that Christe was undre the obedyence
Of worldly prynces so longe as he was here,
And always used them with a lowly reverence,
Paynge them tribute, all hys true servauntes to stere
To obeye them, love them, and have them in reverent
          feare.
Dampnacyon it is to hym that an ordre breake
Appoynted of God, lyke as the Apostle speake.

2361 *loore* teaching   2368 *forfett* misdeed   2370 *distayne* defile
2376 *stere* stir

No man is exempt from thys, Gods ordynaunce;   2380
Bishopp, monke, chanon, priest, cardynall, nor pope,
All they, by Gods lawe, to kynges owe their
    allegeaunce.
Thys wyll be wele knowne in thys same realme, I hope.
Of Verytees wurdes the syncere meanynge I grope:
He sayth that a kynge is of God immedyatlye;
Than shall never pope rule more in thys monarchie.
CLERGYE: If it be your pleasure, we wyll exyle hym
      cleane,
That he in thys realme shall nevermore be seane:
And your grace shall be the supreme head of the
    Churche;
To brynge thys to passe ye shall see how we wyll
    wurche.   2390
IMP MA: Here is a nyce tale: he sayth, if it be my pleasure
He wyll do thys acte, to the Popes most hygh
    displeasure;
As who sayth I woulde, for pleasure of my persone
And not for Gods truthe, have suche an enterpryse done.
Full wysely convayed! The crowe wyll not chaunge her
    hewe.
It is marvele to me and ever ye be trewe.
I wyll the auctoryte of Gods holy wurde to do it:
And it not to aryse of your vayne slypper wytt.
That Scripture doth not is but a lyght fantasye.
CLERGYE: Both Daniel and Paule calleth hym Gods
      adversarye;   2400
And therfor ye ought, as a devyll, hym to expell.
IMP MA: Knewe ye thys afore, and woulde it never tell?
Ye shoulde repent it, had we not now forgyven ye.
Nobylyte, what saye yow? Wyll ye to thys agree?
NOBYLYTE: I can no lesse, sir, for he is wurse than the
      Turke,

2384 *grope* examine   2390 *wurche* work   2391 *nyce* foolish
2398 *slypper* slippery   2407 *bocher* butcher   *bayte* strife

Whych none other wayes but by tyrannye doth wurke.
Thys bloudy bocher, with hys pernycyouse bayte,
Oppresse Christen princes by frawde, crafte, and
    dissayte,
Tyll he compell them to kysse hys pestylent fete,
Lyke a levyathan syttynge in Moyses sete.   2410
I thynke we can do unto God no sacrifyce
That is more accept nor more agreynge to justyce
Than to slea that beaste and slauterman of the Devyll,
That Babylon boore, whych hath done so muche evyll.

IMP MA: It is a clere sygne of a true nobilyte
To the wurde of God whan your conscyence doth agree;
For, as Christe ded saye to Peter, *caro et sanguis*
Non revelavit tibi, sed Pater meus celestis:
Ye have not thys gyfte of carnall generac[y]on,
Nor of noble bloude, but by Gods owne
    demonstracyon.   2420
Of yow, Cyvyle Order, one sentence woulde I heare.

CYVYLE ORDER: I rewe that ever any harte I ded hym
    beare.
I thynke he hath spronge out of the bottomlesse pytt,
And in mennys conscyence in the stede of God doth
    sytt,
Blowynge fourth a swarme of grassopers and flyes,
Monkes, fryers and priestes, that all truthe putrifyes.
Of the Christen faythe playe now the true defendar.
Exyle thys monster and ravenouse devourar
With hys venym wormes, hys adders, whelpes, and
    snakes,
Hys cuculled vermyne, that unto all myschiefe wakes.   2430

IMP MA: Than in thys purpose ye are all of one mynde?

CLERGYE: We detest the Pope and abhorre hym to the
    fynde.

IMP MA: And are wele content to disobeye hys pryde?

NOBYLYTE: Yea, and hys lowsye lawes and decrees to sett
    asyde.

2408 *dissayte* deceit   2413 *slauterman* executioner
2429 *venym* poisonous   *wormes* snakes   2430 *cuculled* hooded, cowled

IMP MA: Than must ye be sworne to take me for your
    heade.

CYVYLE ORDER: We wyll obeye yow as our governour in
    Gods steade.

IMP MA: Now that ye are sworne unto me, your
    pryncypall,
  I charge ye to regarde the wurde of God over all,
  And in that alone to rule, to speake, and to judge,
  As ye wyll have me, your socour and refuge.   2440

CLERYGE: If ye wyll make sure, ye must exyle Sedicyon,
  False Dyssymulacyon, with all vayne superstycyon,
  And put Private Welthe out of the monasteryes;
  Than Usurped Power maye goo a-birdynge for flyes.

IMP MA: Take yow it in hande; and do your true
    dilygence,
  Iche man for hys part: ye shall wante no assystence.

CLERGYE: I promyse yow here to exyle Usurped Powre,
  And your supremyte to defende yche daye and howre.

NOBYLYTE: I promyse also out of the monasteryes
  To put Private Welthe, and to detect hys mysteryes.   2450

CYVYLE ORDER: False Dissymulacyon I wyll hange up in
    Smythfylde,
  With suche supersticon as your people hath begylde.

IMP MA: Than I trust we are at a very good conclusyon:
  Vertu to have place, and vyce to have confusyon.
  Take Veryte wyth ye for every acte ye doo,
  So shall ye be sure not out of the waye to goo.

    Sedicyon intrat.
    [*Sings.*]

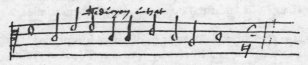

    Pepe,   I   see ye! I   am glad I have spyed ye.

2446 *Iche* each   **2450** *mysteryes* secrets   **2457** *Pepe* peep

NOBYLYTE: There is Sedicyon. Stande yow asyde a whyle.
Ye shall see how we shall catche hym by a wyle.

SEDICYON: No noyse amonge ye? Where is the mery
chere   2460
That was wont to be, with quassynge of double bere?
The worlde is not yet as some men woulde it have.
I have bene abroade, and I thynke I have playde the
knave.

CYVYLE ORDER: Thu canyst do none other, except thu
change thy wunte.

SEDICYON: What myschiefe ayle ye that ye are to be so
blunte?
I have sene the daye ye have favoured me, Perfectyon.

CLERGYE: Thy-selfe is not he; thu art of an-other
complectyon.
Sir, thys is the thiefe that first subdued Kynge John,
Vexynge other prynces that sens have ruled thys regyon;
And now he doth prate he hath so played the knave   2470
That the worlde is not yet as some men woulde it have.
It woulde be knowne, sir, what he hath done of late.

IMP MA: What is thy name, frynde? To us here intymate.

SEDICYON: A sayntwary! A sayntwary! For Gods dere
passyon, a sayntwarye!
Is there none wyll holde me, and I have made so
manye?

IMP MA: Tell me what thy name is; thu playest the knave,
I trowe.

SEDICYON: I am wyndelesse, good man; I muche peyne
to blowe.

IMP MA: I saye tell thy name, or the racke shall the
constrayne.

SEDICYON: Holy Perfectyon my godmother called me
playne.

NOBYLYTE: It is Sedicyon! God gyve hym a very
myschiefe!   2480

2459 *wyle* trick   2461 *quassynge* drinking   2464 *wunte* custom
2465 *ayle* (v) troubles   2467 *complectyon* nature
2474 *sayntwary* sanctuary

CYVYLE ORDER: Undre heaven is not a more detestable
        thiefe.

SEDICYON: By the messe, ye lye. I see wele ye do not
        knowe me.

IMP MA: Ah, brother, art thu come? I am ryght glad we
        have the.

SEDICYON: By bodye, bloude, bones, and sowle, I am not
        he!

CLERGYE: If swearynge myghte helpe he woulde do we[ll]
        ynough.

IMP MA: He scape not our handes so lyghtly, I waraunde
        yow.

CLERGYE: Thys is that thiefe, sir, that all Christendome
        hath troubled,

And the Pope of Rome agaynst all kynges maynteyned.

NOBYLYTE: Now that ye have hym, nomore but hange
        hym uppe.

CYVYLE ORDER: If ye so be content, it shall be done ere
        I suppe.   2490

IMP MA: Loo, the Clergye accuseth the; Nobylyte
        condempneth the;

And the lawe wyll hange the. What sayst now to me?

SEDICYON: I woulde I were now at Rome, at the sygne of
        the cuppe,

For heavynesse is drye! Alas, must I nedes clymbe
    uppe?

Perdon my lyfe and I shall tell ye all,

Both that is past, and that wyll herafter fall.

IMP MA: Aryse. I perdon the, so that thu tell the trewthe.

SEDICYON: I wyll tell to yow suche treason as ensewthe.

Yet a ghostly father ought not to bewraye confessyon.

IMP MA: No confessyon is but ought to discover treason.   2500

SEDICYON: I thynke it maye kepe all thynge save
        heresye.

IMP MA: It maye holde no treason, I tell the verelye,

And therfor tell the whole matter by and bye.

2498 *ensewthe* follows   2499 *bewraye* reveal

Thu saydest now of late that thu haddest played the
    knave,
And that the worlde was not as some men woulde it have.

SEDICYON: I coulde playe Pasquyll but I feare to have
    rebuke.

IMP MA: For utterynge the truthe feare neyther byshopp
    nor duke.

SEDICYON: Ye gave injunctyons that Gods wurde myghte
    be taught.
But who observe them? Full manye a tyme have I
    laught
To see the conveyaunce that prelates and priestes can
    fynde.   2510

IMP MA: And whie do they beare Gods wurde no better
    mynde?

SEDICYON: For if that were knowne than wolde the
    people regarde
No heade but their prynce. With the Churche than were
    it harde.
Than shoulde I lacke helpe to maynteyne their estate,
As I attempted in the Northe but now of late,
And sens that same tyme in other places besyde
Tyll my setters on were of their purpose wyde.
A vengeaunce take it! It was never well with me.
Sens the cummynge hyther of that same Veryte.
Yet do the byshoppes for my sake vexe hym amonge.   2520

IMP MA: Do they so in dede? Well, they shall not do so
    longe.

SEDICYON: In your parlement commaunde yow what ye
    wyll,
The Popes ceremonyes shall drowne the Gospell styll:
Some of the byshoppes at your injunctyons slepe;
Some laugh and go bye; and some can playe boo pepe;
Some of them do nought but searche for heretykes,
Whyls their priestes abroade do playe the scysmatykes.
Tell me, in London how manye their othes discharge
Of the curates there? Yet is it muche wurse at large.

2517 *setters on* promoters

If your true subjectes impugne their trecheryes, 2530
They can fatche them in anon for Sacramentaryes,
Or Anabaptystes. Thus fynde they a subtyle shyfte
To helpe proppe up their kyngedome; suche is their
 wyly dryfte.
Get they false wytnesses, they force not of whens they
 be,
Be they of Newgate, or be they of the Marshall-see.
Paraventure a thousande are in one byshoppes boke,
And agaynst a daye are readye to the hooke.

IMP MA: Are those matters true that thu hast spoken here?
SEDICYON: What can in the worlde more evydent
   wytnesse bere?
First of all consydre the prelates do not preache, 2540
But persecute those that the Holye Scriptures teache.
And marke me thys wele: they never ponysh for popery,
But the Gospell readers they handle very coursely,
For on them they laye by hondred poundes of yron
And wyll suffer none with them ones for to common.
Sytt they never so longe, nothynge by them cometh
 fourthe
To the truthes furtheraunce that any-thynge ys wourthe.
In some byshoppes howse ye shall not fynde a testament;
But yche man readye to devoure the innocent.
We lyngar a tyme, and loke but for a daye 2550
To sett upp the Pope, if the Gospell woulde decaye.

CLERGYE: Of that he hath tolde hys selfe is the very
   grounde.
IMP MA: Art thu of counsell in thys that thu hast spoken?
SEDICYON: Yea, and in more than that if all secretes
   myght be broken,
For the Pope I make so muche as ever I maye do.
IMP MA: I praye the hartely, tell me why thu doest so.
SEDICYON: For I perceyve wele the Pope is a jolye
   fellawe,
A trymme fellawe, a ryche fellawe, yea, and myry
 fellawe.
IMP MA: A jolye fellawe? How dost thu prove the Pope?

SEDICYON: For he hath crosse keyes, with a tryple
        crowne and a cope,   2560
  Trymme as a trencher, havynge hys shoes of golde,
  Ryche in hys ryalte and angelyck to beholde.

IMP MA: How dost thu prove hym to be a fellawe myrye?

SEDICYON: He hath pypes and belles, with *kyrye, kyrye,*
        kyrye.
  Of hym ye maye bye both salt, creame, oyle and waxe;
  And after hygh masse ye maye learne to beare the paxe.

IMP MA: Yea, and nothynge heare of the Pystle and the
        Gospell?

SEDICYON: No, sir, by the Masse; he wyll gyve no suche
        counsell.

IMP MA: Whan thu art a-broade where doest thy lodgynge
        take?

SEDICYON: Amonge suche people as God ded never make;   2570
  Not only cuckoldes, but suche as folowe the Popes
    lawes
  In disgysed coates, with balde crownes lyke
    jacke-dawes.

IMP MA: Than every where thu art the Popes altogyther.

SEDICYON: Ye had proved it ere thys if I had not
        chaunced hyther.
  I sought to have served yow lyke as I ded Kynge John,
  But that Veryte stopte me, the Devyll hym poyson.

NOBYLYTE: He is wurthie to dye and there were men
        nomore.

CYVYLE ORDER: Hange up the vyle knave and kepe hym
        no longar in store.

IMP MA: Drawe hym to Tyburne. Lete hym be hanged
    and quartered.

SEDICYON: Whye, of late dayes ye sayde I shoulde not so
        be martyred.   2580
  Where is the pardon that ye ded promyse me?

IMP MA: For doynge more harme thu shalt sone pardoned
        be.
  Have hym fourth, Cyvyle Ordre, and hange hym tyll he
    be dead,

And on London Brydge loke ye bestowe hys head.

CYVYLE ORDER: I shall see it done, and returne to yow
        agayne.

SEDICYON: I beshrewe your hart for takynge so muche
        payne.
Some man tell the Pope, I besyche ye with all my harte,
How I am ordered for takynge the Churches parte,
That I maye be put in the Holye Letanye
With Thomas Beckett, for I thynke I am as wurthye.   2590
Praye to me with candels for I am a saynt alreadye.
O blessed Saynt Partryck, I see the, I, verylye.

[*Civil Order leads Sedition away.*]

IMP MA: I see by thys wretche there hath bene muche
        faulte in ye.
Shewe your-selves herafter more sober and wyse to be.

Kynge Johan ye subdued for that he ponnyshed treason,
Rape, theft, and murther in the holye spirytualte:
But Thomas Becket ye exalted without reason
Because that he dyed for the Churches wanton lyberte,
That the priestes myght do all kyndes of inyquyte
And be unponnyshed. Marke now the judgement   2600
Of your ydle braynes, and for Gods love repent.

NOBYLYTE: As God shall judge me, I repent me of my
       rudenesse.
CLERGYE: I am ashamed of my most vayne folyshenesse.

NOBYLYTE: I consydre now that God hath for Sedicyon
Sent ponnyshmentes great. Examples we have in Brute,
In Catilyne, in Cassius, and fayer Absolon,

Whome of their purpose God alwayes destytute,
And terryble plages on them ded execute
For their rebellyon. And therfor I wyll be ware,
Least hys great vengeaunce trappe me in suche lyke
    snare.   2610

[*Civil Order returns.*]

CLERGYE: I pondre also that sens the tyme of Adam
  The Lorde evermore the governours preserved.
  Examples we fynde in Noe and in Abraham,
  In Moyses and David, from whome God never swerved.
  I wyll therfor obeye least he be with me displeased.
  Homerus doth saye that God putteth forth hys shyelde,
  The prynce to defende whan he is in the fyelde.
CYVYLE ORDER: Thys also I marke whan the priestes had
        governaunce
  Over the Hebrues, the sectes ded first aryse,
  As Pharisees, Sadducees, and Essees, whych wrought
    muche grevaunce   2620
  Amonge the people by their most devylysh practyse,
  Tyll destructyons the prynces ded devyse,
  To the quyetnesse of their faythfull commens all,
  As your grace hath done with the sectes papistycall.
IMP MA: That poynt hath in tyme fallen to your memoryes.
  The Anabaptystes, a secte newe rysen of late,
  The Scriptures poyseneth with their subtle allegoryes,
  The heades to subdue after a sedicyouse rate.
  The cytie of Mynster was lost through their debate.
  They have here begonne their pestilent sedes to sowe,   2630
  But we trust in God to increace, they shall not growe.
CLERGYE: God forbyd the[y] shoulde, for they myght do
      muche harme.
CYVYLE ORDER: We shall cut them short if they do hyther
    swarme.
IMP MA: The adminystracyon of a princes governaunce

Is the gifte of God and Hys hygh ordynaunce,
Whome with all your power yow thre ought to support
In the lawes of God to all hys peoples comfort:
First yow, the Clergye, in preachynge of Gods worde;
Than yow, Nobilyte, defendynge with the sworde;
Yow, Cyvyle Order, in executynge justyce.   2640
Thus, I trust we shall seclude all maner of vyce.
And after we have establyshed our kyngedome,
In peace of the Lorde and in Hys godly fredome,
We wyll confirme it with wholesom lawes and decrees,
To the full suppressynge of Antichristes vanytees.

      Hic omnes rex osculatur.

Farwele to ye all; first to yow Nobilyte,
Than to yow, Clergye, then to yow, Cyvylyte.
And above all thynges, remembre our injunctyon.
OMNES UNA: By the helpe of God, yche one shall do hys
          functyon.

    [*Exit Imperial Majesty.*]

NOBYLYTE: By thys example ye maye see with your eyes   2650
How Antichristes whelpes have noble princes used.
Agayne ye maye see how they, with prodigyouse lyes
And craftes uncomely, their myschiefes have excused.
Both nature, manhode, and grace they have abused,
Defylynge the lawe, and blyndynge Nobilyte
No Christen regyon from their abusyons free.

CLERGYE: Marke wele the dampnable bestowynge of their
        masses,

   2656 *abusyons* abuses

              428

With their foundacyons for poysenynge of their kynge.
Their confessyon driftes all other traytery passes.
A saynt the[y] can make of the most knave thys daye
    lyvynge,   2660
Helpynge their market. And to promote the thynge
He shall do myracles. But he that blemysh their glorye
Shall be sent to helle without anye remedye.

CYVYLE ORDER: Here was to be seane what ryseth of
    Sedicyon,
And howe he doth take hys mayntenaunce and grounde
Of ydle persones brought upp in supersticyon,
Whose daylye practyse is alwayes to confounde
Such as myndeth vertu and to them wyll not be bounde.
Expedyent it is to knowe their pestylent wayes,
Consyderynge they were so busye now of late dayes.   2670

NOBYLYTE: Englande hath a quene, thankes to the Lorde
    above,
Whych maye be a lyghte to other princes all
For the godly wayes whome she doth dayly move
To hir liege people, through Gods wurde specyall.
She is that Angell, as Saynt Johan doth hym call,
That with the Lordes seale doth marke out Hys true
    servauntes,
Pryntynge in their hartes Hys holy wourdes and
    covenauntes.

CLERGYE: In Danyels sprete she hath subdued the papistes,
With all the ofsprynge of Antichristes generacyon.
And now of late dayes the secte of Anabaptistes   2680
She seketh to suppresse for their pestiferouse facyon.
She vanquysheth also the great abhomynacyon
Of supersticyons, witchcraftes, and hydolatrye,
Restorynge Gods honoure to Hys first force and bewtye.

CYVYLE ORDER: Praye to the Lorde that hir grace maye
      contynewe
  The dayes of Nestor to our sowles consolacyon,
  And that hir ofsprynge maye lyve also to subdewe
  The great Antichriste, with hys whole generacyon,
  In Helias sprete, to the confort of thys nacyon;
  Also to preserve hir most honourable counsell,   2690
  To the prayse of God, and glorye of the Gospell.

Thus endeth the ij. playes of Kynge Johan.

❧ ❧ ❧

ANE SATIRE OF THE THRIE ESTAITIS

SIR DAVID LINDSAY

Written 1539–54

Manuscript by George Bannatyne, 1568, National Library of Scotland, Edinburgh. (Incomplete version)

Edition by Robert Charteris, Edinburgh, 1602, Gough Scotland 221, Bodleian Library, Oxford

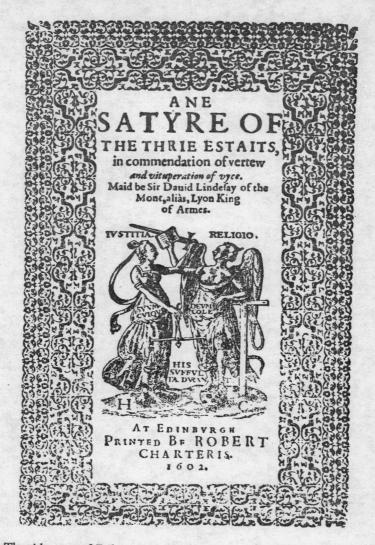

ANE
SATYRE OF
THE THRIE ESTAITS,
in commendation of vertew
and vituperation of vyce.
Maid be Sir Dauid Lindesay of the
Mont, aliàs, Lyon King
of Armes.

IVSTITIA.　　RELIGIO.

SVM
CVIQ

DEVM
COLE

HIS
SVFFVL
TA DVRAN

H　　C

AT EDINBVRGH
PRINTED BE ROBERT
CHARTERIS.
1602.

The title-page of Robert Charteris's edition of 1602 in the Bodleian
(Gough Scotland 221)

CHARACTERS

In the Cupar Banns

Nuntius

Cotter

Cotter's Wife

Fynlaw of the Fute Band

Fule

Auld Man

Bessy

Courtier

Merchand

Clerk

In the Play

Diligence

Rex Humanitas

Wantonnes

Placebo

Solace

Sensualitie

Hamelines

Danger

Fund-Jonet

Gude Counsall

Flatterie

Falset

Dissait

Veritie

Spiritualitie: Bishop

    Abbot (Abbasse)

    Persone

Chastitie

Priores

Temporalitie

Sowtar

Sowtar's Wyfe

Taylour

Taylour's Wyfe

Jennie

Discretioun

Correctioun's Varlet

Divyne Correctioun

Pauper

Pardoner

Wilkin

Merchand (perhaps as in Banns)

Johne the Common-weill

Covetice

Public Oppressioun

First Sergeant

Secund Sergeant

Scrybe

Common Thift

Clerks: Doctour

    First Licentiate

    Batcheler

Foly

SCHIR DAVID LYNDSAYIS PLAY

Proclamatioun maid in Cowpar of Fyffe.

    [Enter Nuntius saying]

Richt famous pepill, ye sall undirstand
How that ane prince richt wyiss and vigilent
Is schortly for to cum in-to this land,
And purpossis to hald ane Parliament.
His Thre Estaitis thairto hes done consent
In Cowpar Town in to thair best array,
With support of the Lord Omnipotent
And thairto hes affixt ane certaine day.

With help of Him that rewlis all abone,
That day salbe within ane litill space.   10
Our purpos is on the Sevint day of June,
Gif weddir serve, and we haif rest and pece,
We sall be sene in till our playing place,
In gude array abowt the hour of sevin.
Off thriftiness that day I pray yow ceiss,
Bot ordane ws gude drink aganis allevin.

Fail nocht to be upone the Castell Hill
Besyd the place quhair we purpoiss to play.
With gude stark wyne your flacconis see ye fill,

2 *wyiss* wise   5 *hes* has   9 *rewlis* rules   *abone* above
12 *weddir* weather *haif* have   *pece* peace   15 *thriftiness* business
ceiss cease   16 *ws* us   *aganis allevin* for eleven (o'clock)
17 *nocht* not   18 *quhair* where   19 *stark* strong   *flacconis* flaggons

437

And hald yourself the myrieast that ye may. 20
Be not displeisit quhat evir we sing or say,
Amang sad mater howbeid we sumtyme relyie.
We sall begin at sevin houris of the day,
So ye keip tryist: forswth we sall nocht felyie.

[*Enter Cotter.*]

COTTER: I salbe thair with Goddis grace,
   Thocht thair war nevir so grit ane prese
     And formest in the fair,
   And drink ane quart in Cowpar Toun
   With my gossep Johnne Willamsoun,
     Thocht all the nolt sowld rair. 30
   I haif ane quick divill to my wyfe,
   That haldis me evir in sturt and stryfe.
     That warlo and scho wist
   That I wald cum to this gud toun,
   Scho wald call me fals ladrone loun,
     And ding me in the dust.
   We men that hes sic wickit wyvis,
   In grit langour we leid our lyvis,
     Ay dreifland in diseiss.
   Ye preistis hes grit prerogatyvis, 40
   That may depairt ay fra your wyvis,
     And cheiss thame that ye pleiss.
   Wald God I had that liberty,
   That I micht pairt, als weill as ye,
     Withowt the Constry Law.
   Nor I be stickit with ane knyfe,

20 *myrieast* merriest   21 *displeisit* displeased   22 *howbeid* even though
relyie (v) joke   24 *tryist* trust, agreement   *forswth* forsooth   *felyie* fail
26 *Thocht* though   *prese* press, crowd   27 *formest* foremost
30 *nolt* cattle   *rair* roar   32 *sturt* vexation   33 *warlo* devil   *scho* she
wist knew   34 *gud* good   35 *ladrone* slovenly   *loun* fellow, lout
36 *ding* strike   38 *langour* distress   39 *dreifland* raving
diseiss discomfort   42 *cheiss* choose   44 *pairt* (v) separate

For to wad ony uder wyfe,
    That day sowld nevir daw.
NUNTIUS: War thy wyfe deid I see thow wald be fane.
COTTER: Ye that I wald, sweit sir, be Sanct Fillane.   50
NUNTIUS: Wald thow nocht mary fra hand ane uder
        wyfe?
COTTER: Na, than the dum divill stik me with ane knyfe.
  Quha evir did mary agane the feind mot fang thame,
  Bot as the preistis dois ay, stryk in amang thame.

NUNTIUS: Than thow mon keip thy chestety as effeiris?
COTTER: I sall leif chest as Abbottis, Monkis, and
        Freiris.
  Maister, quhairto sowld I my self miskary
  Quhair I, as preistis, may swyve and nevir mary.

[*Enter Cotter's Wife.*]

WYFE: Quhair hes thow bene, fals ladrone loun?
  Doyttand and drinkand in the toun.
  Quha gaif the leif to cum fra hame?   60
COTTER: Ye gaif me leif, fair lucky dame.
WYFE: Quhy hes thow taryit heir sa lang?
COTTER: I micht not thrist owtthrow the thrang,
  Till that yone man the play proclamit.
WYFE: Trowis thow that day, fals cairle defamit,
  To gang to Cowpar to see the play?
COTTER: Ye, that I will deme, gif I may.
WYFE: Na, I sall cum thairto sickerly,
  And thow sall byd at hame and keip the ky.   70
COTTER: Fair lucky dame, that war grit schame,

48 *daw* dawn 49 *War* were *fane* glad 51 *fra hand* at once
53 *Quha* who *fang* catch *thame* them 55/6 *chestety, chest* chastity, chaste
56 *leif* (v) live 58 *swyve* copulate 60 *Doyttand* fooling
64 *thrist* push *owtthrow* through 69 *sickerly* surely 70 *ky* cow

Gif I that day sowld byid at hame.
Byid ye at hame, for cum ye heir
Ye will mak all the toun a steir.
Quhen ye ar fow of barmy drink
Besyd yow nane may stand for stink.
Thaifoir byid ye at hame that day,
That I may cum and see the play,

WYFE: Fals cairle, be God that sall thow nocht,
And all thy crackis sall be deir coft.   80
Swyth, cairle, speid the hame speidaly,
Incontinent, and milk the ky,
And muk the byre or I cum hame.

COTTER: All salbe done, fair lucky dame,
I am sa dry, dame, or I gae,
I mon ga drink ane peny or twae.

WYFE: The divill a drew sall cum in thy throte
Speid hand, or I sall paik thy cote;
And to begin, fals cairle, tak thair ane plate.

COTTER: The feind ressaif the handis that gaif me that.   90
I beseik yow, for Goddis saik, lucky dame,
Ding me na mair this day till I cum hame,
Than sall I put me evin in to your will.

WYFE: Or evir I stynt thow sall haif straikis thy fill.

*Heir sal the Wyfe ding the Carle and he sall cry
Goddis mercy.*

[COTTER:] Now wander and wa be to thame all thair
          lyvis,
The quhilk ar maryit with sic unhappy wyvis.

WYFE: I ken foure wyvis, fals ladrone loun,
Baldar nor I, dwelland in Cowpar Toun.

74 *a steir* astir 75 *fow* full *barmy* frothy
80 *crackis* boasts *coft* bought 81 *Swyth* quickly 87 *drew* drop
89 *plate* blow 90 *ressaif* receive 91 *beseik* beg 94 *Or* before
stynt stop *straikis* blows 95 *wander* misfortune *wa* woe
98 *Baldar* bolder

COTTER: Gif thay be war ga thow and thay togidder.
I pray God nor the feind ressaif the fidder.   100

[*She drives him away. Enter Findlaw.*]

FYNLAW OF THE FUTE BAND: Wow, mary, heir is ane
        fellone rowt;
  Speik, schiris, quhat gait may I get owt?
    I rew that I come heir.
My name, schiris, wald ye undirstand,
Thay call me Findlaw of the Fute Band,
    A nobill man of weir.
Thair is na fyifty in this land
Bot I dar ding thame hand for hand,
    Se sic ane brand I beir.
Nocht lang sensyne besyd ane syik,   110
Upoun the sonny syd of ane dyk,
    I slew with my richt hand
Ane thousand, ye and ane thousand to.
My fingaris yit ar bludy, lo,
    And nane durst me ganestand.
Wit ye it dois me mekill ill
That can nocht get fechting my fill,
    Nowdir in peax nor weir?
Will na man for thair ladyis saikis
With me stryk twenty markit straikis   120
    With halbart, swerd or speir?
Quhen Inglismen come in-to this land
Had I bene thair with my bricht brand,
    Withowttin ony help
Bot myne allane, on Pynky Craiggis
I sowld haif revin thame all in raggis,

100 *fidder* load   102 *schiris* sirs   *gait* way   103 *rew* regret
106 *weir* war   109 *brand* sword   110 *sensyne* since then
syik marshy stream   111 *dyk* ditch   115 *ganestand* withstand
117 *fechting* fighting   118 *peax* peace   121 *halbart* halbert
126 *sowld* should   *haif* have   *revin* ruined

And laid on skelp for skelp.
Sen nane will fecht, I think it best
To ly doun heir and tak me rest,
　　Than will I think nane ill.
I pray the grit God of his grace
To send ws weir and nevir peace,
　　That I may fecht my fill.

130

Heir sall he ly doun.
[Enter the Fool.]

THE FULE: My Lord, be him that ware the croun of
　　　　thorne,
A mair cowart was nevir sen God was borne.
He lovis him-self and uthir men he lakkis.
I ken him weill, for all his boistis and crakkis.
Howbeid he now be lyk ane captane cled
At Pyncky Clewch he was the first that fled.
I tak on hand or I steir of this steid
This crakkand cairle to fle with ane scheip heid.

140

Heir sall the Auld Man cum in leidand his Wyfe
in ane dance.

[AULD MAN:] Bessy my hairt, I mon ly doun and sleip,
And in myne arme se quyetly thow creip.
Bessy my hairt, first lat me lok thy cunt,
Syne lat me keip the key as I was wount.
BESSY: My gud husband, lock it evin as ye pleiss;
I pray God send yow grit honor and eiss.

127 *skelp* blow　135 *mair* greater, more　*cowart* coward
136 *lakkis* reproaches　147 *eiss* ease

*Heir sall he lok hir cunt and lay the key under his
heid: he sall sleip and scho sall sit besyd him.*
[*Enter Courtier, Merchant and Clerk.*]

THE COURTEOUR: Lusty lady, I pray yow hairtfully
    Gif me licence to beir yow cumpany.
    Ye sie I am ane cumly courteour,   150
    Quhilk nevir yit did woman dishonour.
MARCHAND: My fair maistres, sweitar than the lammer,
    Gif me licence to luge in to your chalmer.
    I am the richest marchand in this toun:
    Ye sall of silk haif kirtill, hude and goun.
CLERK: I yow beseik, my lusty lady bricht,
    To gif me leif to ly with yow all nicht,
    And of your quoman lat me schut the lokkis,
    And of fyne gold ye sall ressaif ane box.
FWILL: Fair damessell, how pleiss ye me!   160
    I haif na mair geir nor ye sie.
    Swa lang as this may steir or stand
    It sall be ay at your command.
    Na it is the best that evir ye saw.
BESSY: Now welcome to me aboif thame aw
    Was nevir wyf sa straitly rokkit?
    Se ye not how my cunt is lokkit?
FULE: Thinkis he nocht schame, that brybor blunt,
    To put ane lo upoun your cunt?
BESSY: Bot se gif ye can mak remeid,   170
    To steill the key fra undir his heid.
FULE: That sall I do, withowttin dowt.
    Lat se gif I can get it owte,
    Lo, heir the key, do quhat ye will.
BESSY: Na than, lat ws ga play our fill.

151 *Quhilk* who   152 *lammer* amber   153 *luge* lodge   *chalmer* chamber
155 *kirtill* skirt   158 *quoman* pudenda   162 *Swa* so   165 *aboif* above
aw all   166 *straitly* strictly   *rokkit* ?rocked, ?wracked
168 *brybor* briber   170 *gif* if

Heir sall thay go to sum quyet place.
[*Exeunt Courtier and Merchant.*]

FYNLAW OF THE FUTE BAND: Will nane with me in
        France go to the weiris,
  Quhair I am captane of ane hundreth speiris?
  I am sa hardy, sturdy, strang, and stowt,
  That owt of hell the Divill I dar ding owt.

CLERK: Gif thow be gude or evill I can not tell: 180
  Thay ar not sonsy that so dois ruse thame sell.
  At Pyncky Clewch I knew richt woundir weill
  Thow gat na creddence for to beir a creill.
  Sen sic as thow began to brawll and boist,
  The commoun weill of Scotland hes bene loist.
  Thow cryis for weir, bot I think peax war best.
  I pray to God till send ws peice and rest,
  On that conditioun that thow and all thy fallowis
  War be the craiggis heich hangit on the gallowis,
  Quha of this weir hes bene the foundament.   190
  I pray to the grit God Omnipotent
  That all the warld and mae mot on thame wounder,
  Or ding thame deid with awfull fyre of thunder.

FYNLAW: Domine doctor, quhair will ye preiche to
        morne?
  We will haif weir and all the warld had sworne.
  Want we weir heir I will ga pass in France,
  Quhair I will get ane lordly governance.
CLERK: Sa quhat ye will, I think seuer peax is best.
  Quha wald haif weir God send thame littill rest.
  Adew crakkar, I will na langar tary: 200

176 *weiris* wars   181 *sonsy* lucky   *ruse* rouse   *sell* self
183 *creill* basket   184 *Sen* since   *sic* such   189 *craiggis* necks
heich high   190 *foundament* cause   192 *mae* more   *mot* may

I trest to see the in ane firy fary.
I trest to God to see the and thy fallowis
Within few dayis hingand on Cowpar gallowis.

[*Exit Clerk.*]

FYNLAW: Now art thow gane; the dum divill be thy gyd.
 Yone brybour was sa fleit he durst not byid.
 Be woundis and passionis had he spokkin mair ane
  word,
 I sowld haif hackit his heid af with my swerd.

Heir sall the Gudman walk in and cry for Bessy.

[AULD MAN:] My bony Bessy, quhair art thow now?
 My wyfe is fallin on sleip I trow.
 Quhair art thow Bessy, my awin sweit thing,   210
 My bony, my hairt, my dayis darling?
 Is thair na man that saw my Bess?
 I trow scho be gane to the mess.
 Bessy my hairt, heiris thow not me?
 My joy, cry keip, quhairevir thow be.
 Allace for evir now am I fey,
 For of hir cunt I tynt the key.
 Scho may call me ane jufflane Jok:
 Or I swyve I mon brek the lok.

BESSY: Quhat now, gudman, quhat wald ye haif?   220
AULD MAN: No thing, my hairt, bot yow I craif.
 Ye haif bene doand sum bissy wark?
BESSY: My hairt, evin sewand yow ane sark
 Of holland claith baith quhyt and tewch.
 Lat pruve gif it be wyid annewch.

201 *firy* wonderful *fary* confusion 205 *fleit* fleet 207 *af* off
210 *awin* own 213 *mess* mass 216 *fey* troubled 217 *tynt* lost
223 *sark* shift 224 *quhyt* white *tewch* tough 225 *annewch* enough

*Heir sall scho put the sark ovir his heid and the
Fuill sall steill in the key agane.*

AULD MAN: It is richt verry weill, my hairt,
  Oure Lady, lat ws nevir depairt.
  Ye ar the farest of all the flok,
  Quhair is the key Bess of my lok?
BESSY: Ye reve, gudman; be Goddis breid,   230
  I saw yow lay it undir your heid.
AULD MAN: Be my gud faith, Bess, that is trew.
  That I suspectit yow sair I rew.
  I trow thair be no man in Fyffe
  That evir had sa gude ane wyfe.
  My awin sweit hairt, I ha[l]d it best
  That we sitt doun and tak ws rest.
FYNDLAW: Now is nocht this ane grit dispyte,
  That nane with me will fecht nor flyte.
  War Golias in to this steid   240
  I dowt nocht to stryk of his heid.
  This is the swerd that slew gray steill
  Nocht half ane myle beyond Kynneill.
  I was that nobill campioun
  That slew Schir Bews of Sowth Hamtoun.
  Hector of Troy, Gawyne, or Golias
  Had nevir half sa mekle hardiness.

*Heir sall the Fuile cum in with ane scheip heid on ane
staff and Fynlaw sall be fleit.*

[FYNLAW:] Wow, wow, braid benedicitie,
  Quhat sicht is yone, schiris, that I see?
  I[n] *nomine patris et filii.*   250
  I trow yone be the spreit of Gy.

230 *reve* rave   233 *sair* sore   *rew* regret   238 *dispyte* pity
249 *sicht* sight

Na, faith, it is the spreit of Marling,
Or sum scho gaist, or gyr garling.
Allace for evir, how sall I gyd me?
God sen I had ane hoill till hyd me.
Bot dowt my deid yone man hes sworne,
I trow yone be grit Gowmakmorne.
He gaippis, he glowris; howt welloway;
Tak all my geir and lat me gay.
Quhat say ye, schir, wald ye have my swerd?   260
Ye mary sall ye at the first word,
My gluvis of plait and knapskaw, to.
Your pressonar I yeild me; lo
Tak thair my purss, my belt, and knyfe.
For Goddis saik, maister, save my lyfe.
Na, now he cumis evin for to sla me.
For Godis saik, schiris, now keip him fre me.
I see not ellis bot tak and slae.
Wow, mak me rowme and lat me gae.

[*Findlaw runs away.*]

NUNTIUS: As for this day I haif na mair to say yow.   270
On Witsone tysday cum see our play, I prey yow.
That samyne day is the sevint day of June,
Thairfoir get up richt airly and disiune;
And ye ladyis, that hes na skent of leddir,
Or ye cum thair, faill nocht to teme your bleddir.
I dreid or we haif half done with our wark,
That sam of yow sall mak ane richt wait sark.

[*Exit Nuntius.*]

255 *hoill* hole *till* to 259 *gay* go 262 *plait* plate (armour)
knapskaw head-piece 268 *tak* capture *slae* death 272 *samyne* same
273 *disiune* (v) breakfast 274 *skent* shortage *leddir* pudenda
277 *wait* wet *sark* shift

447

ANE SATIRE OF THE THRIE ESTAITIS

[PART ONE]

[*Enter Diligence, the Messenger.*]

DILIGENCE: The Father and founder of faith and
             felicite,
That your fassioun formed to his similitude,
And his Sone our Saviour, scheild in necessitie,
That bocht yow from baillis ranson rude,
Repleadgeand his presonaris with his hart-blude,
The Halie Gaist, governour and grounder of grace,
Of wisdome and weilfair baith fontaine and flude,
Gif yow all that I sie seasit in this place,
    And scheild yow from sinne;
And with his Spreit yow inspyre,   10
Till I have shawin my desyre.
Silence, Soveraine, I requyre,
    For now I begin.

Pausa.

Tak tent to me my freinds, and hald yow coy,
For I am sent to yow, as messingeir,
From ane nobill and rycht redoubtit Roy,
The quhilk hes bene absent this monie yeir,
Humanitie, give ye his name wald speir:
Quha bade me shaw to yow but variance,

2 *fassioun* shape   *similitude* shape   4 *baillis* woes
5 *Repleadgeand* pledging   8 *sie* see   *seasit* seated   14 *tent* heed
coy quiet   18 *give* if   *speir* ask   19 *but* without   *variance* quarrelling

448

That he intendis amang yow to compeir,   20
With ane triumph and awfull ordinance,
With crown and sword and scepter in his hand,
Temperit with mercie quhen penitence appeiris:
Howbeit that hee lang tyme hes bene sleipand,
Quhairthrow misreull hes rung thir monie yeiris,
That innocentis hes bene brocht on thair beiris,
Be fals reporteris of this natioun:
Thocht young oppressouris at the elder leiris,
Be now assurit of reformatioun.

Sie no misdoeris be sa bauld   30
As to remaine into this hauld:
For quhy be him that Judas sauld
   Thay will be heich hangit.
Now faithfull folk for joy may sing:
For quhy it is the just bidding
Of my soveraine lord the king
   That na man be wrangit.
Thocht he ane quhyll, into his flouris
Be governit be vylde trompouris,
And sumtyme lufe his paramouris,   40
   Hauld ye him excusit.
For quhen he meittis with Correctioun,
With Veritie and Discretioun,
Thay will be banisched aff the toun,
   Quhilk hes him abusit.

And heir be oppin proclamatioun,
I wairne in name of his magnificence,
The Thrie Estaitis of this natioun,
That thay compeir with detfull diligence,

20 *compeir* appear   25 *Quhairthrow* through which   *rung* reigned
thir these   26 *beiris* biers   28 *leiris* learn   30 *misdoeris* evil-doers
31 *hauld* place   37 *wrangit* wronged   38 *flouris* flower, prime
39 *vylde* vile   *trompouris* deceivers   40 *lufe* love   49 *detfull* dutiful

And till his grace mak thair obedience.   50
And first I wairne the Spritualitie,
And sie the Burgessis spair not for expence:
Bot speid thame heir with Temporalitie.
Als I beseik yow famous auditouris,
Conveinit in this congregatioun,
To be patient the space of certaine houris,
Till ye have hard our short narratioun.
And als we make yow supplicatioun,
That na man tak our wordis intill disdaine,
Althocht ye hear be declamatioun   60
The common-weill richt pitiouslie complaine.

Rycht so the verteous Ladie Veritie
Will mak ane pitious lamentatioun:
Als for the treuth sho will impresonit be,
And banischit lang tyme out of the toun:
And Chastitie will mak narratioun
How sho can get na ludging in this land,
Till that the heavinlie King Correctioun
Meit with the king and commoun, hand for hand.

Prudent peopill, I pray yow all,   70
Tak na man greif in speciall:
For wee sall speik in general,
    For pastyme and for play.
Thairfoir till all our rymis be rung,
And our mistoinit sangis be sung,
Bet everie man keip weill ane toung,
    And everie woman tway.

    [*Enter Rex Humanitas.*]

50 *till* to   55 *Conveinit* gathered   59 *intill* in   60 *be* by
64 *Als* as   *sho* she   75 *mistoinit* out of tune   *sangis* songs
77 *tway* two

REX HUMANITAS: O Lord of Lords, and King of Kingis
    all,
  Omnipotent of power, Prince but peir,
  Ever ringand in gloir celestial: 80
  Quha, be great micht, and haifing na mateir,
  Maid heavin and eird, fyre, air and watter cleir:
  Send me thy grace with peace perpetuall,
  That I may rewll my realme to thy pleaseir,
  Syne, bring my saull to joy angelicall.

  Sen thow hes givin mee dominatioun
  And rewll of pepill subject to my cure,
  Be I nocht rewlit be counsall and ressoun,
  In dignitie I may nocht lang indure.
  I grant my stait my self may nocht assure,   90
  Nor yit conserve my lyfe in sickernes:
  Have pitie, Lord, on mee thy creature,
  Supportand me in all my busines.

  I thee requeist, quha rent wes on the Rude,
  Me to defend from the deidis of defame:
  That my pepill report of me bot gude,
  And be my saifgaird baith from sin and shame.
  I knaw my dayis induris bot as ane dreame,
  Thairfoir, O Lord, I hairtlie the exhort,
  To gif me grace to use my diadeame   100
  To thy pleasure and to my great comfort.

[*Enter Wantonness and Placebo.*]

WANTONNES: My Soveraine Lord and Prince but peir,
  Quhat garris yow mak sic dreirie cheir?

79 *but peir* without equal   80 *ringand* reigning   81 *Quha* who
82 *eird* earth   85 *Syne* then   87 *cure* care   91 *sickernes* security
103 *garris* causes

Be blyth sa lang as ye ar heir,
    And pas tyme with pleasure:
For als lang leifis the mirrie man
As the sorie, for ocht he can:
His banis full sair, Sir, sall I ban
    That dois yow displeasure.
Sa lang as Placebo and I   110
Remaines into your company,
Your grace sall leif richt mirrely:
    Of this haif ye na dout.
Sa lang as ye have us in cure,
Your grace, sir, sall want na pleasure:
War Solace heir, I yow assure,
    He wald rejoyce this rout.

PLACEBO: Gude brother myne, quhair is Solace,
    The mirrour of all mirrines?
I have great mervell be the Mes,   120
    He taries sa lang.
Byde he away wee ar bot shent:
I ferlie how he fra us went:
I trow he hes impediment
    That lettis him nocht gang.

WANTONNES: I left Solace, that same greit loun,
    Drinkand into the burrows toun:
It will cost him halfe of ane croun,
    Althocht he had na mair.
And als he said hee wald gang see   130
Fair ladie Sensualitite,
The buriall of all bewtie
    And portratour preclair.

106 *leifis* lives   108 *banis* (n) bones   *ban* (v) curse
116 *War* were   117 *rout* company   122 *shent* disgraced
123 *ferlie* (v) wonder   125 *gang* go   132 *buriall* brightest
133 *portratour* portraiture   *preclair* famous

PLACEBO: Be God I see him at the last
   As he war chaist rynnand richt fast;
   He glowris evin as he war agast
      Or fleyit of ane gaist.
   Na, he is wod drunkin I trow.
   Se ye not that he is wod fow?
   I ken weill be his creischie mow   140
      He hes bene at ane feast.

   [*Enter Solace.*]

SOLACE: Now quha saw ever sic ane thrang?
   Me thocht sum said I had gaine wrang.
   Had I help I wald sing ane sang
      With ane rycht mirrie noyse.
   I have sic pleasour at my hart,
   That garris me sing the troubill pairt:
   Wald sum gude fallow fill the quart
      It wald my hairt rejoyce.
   Howbeit my coat be short and nippit,   150
   Thankis be to God I am weill hippit,
   Thocht all my gold may shone be grippit
      Intill ane pennie pursse.
   Thocht I ane servand lang haif bene,
   My purchais is nocht worth ane preine:
   I may sing Peblis on the Greine:
      For ocht that I may tursse.
   Quhat is my name can ye not gesse?
   Sirs, ken ye nocht Sandie Solace?
   Thay callit my mother Bonie Besse,   160
      That dwelt betwene the bowis.

135 *chaist* chased   *rynnand* running   136 *glowris* glowers
137 *fleyit* frightened   *gaist* ghost   138 *wod* mad   *fow* drunk
140 *creischie* greasy   *mow* mouth   147 *troubill* treble   148 *quart* pot
150 *nippit* cut short   151 *hippit* large hipped   152 *shone* soon
155 *preine* pin   157 *tursse* carry

Of twelf yeir auld sho learnit to swyfe,
Thankit be the great God on lyve:
Scho maid me fatheris four or fyve:
    But dout, this is na mowis.
Quhen ane was deid, sho gat ane uther:
Was never man had sic ane mother.
Of fatheris sho maid me ane futher
    Of lawit men and leirit.
Scho is baith wyse, worthie and wicht,   170
For scho spairis nouther kuik nor knycht:
Yea four and twentie on ane nicht,
    And ay thair eine scho bleirit:
And gif I lie, sirs, ye may speir.
Bot saw ye nocht the King cum heir?
I am ane sportour and playfeir
    To that royall young king:
He said he wald within schort space
Cum pas his tyme into this place:
I pray the, Lord, to send him grace,   180
    That he lang tyme may ring.

PLACEBO: Solace, quhy taryit ye sa lang?
SOLACE: The feind a faster I micht gang:
    I micht not thrist out throw the thrang
        Of wyfes fyftein fidder:
    Then for to rin I tuik ane rink,
    Bot I felt never sik ane stink:
    For our Lordis luif gif me ane drink,
        Placebo, my deir brother.

REX HUMANITAS: My servant Solace, quhat gart yow
        tarie?   190

    162 *swyfe* copulate   168 *futher* load   169 *lawit* humble, lay
leirit learned   170 *wicht* brave   171 *kuik* cook   173 *eine* eyes
bleirit blurred   176 *sportour* companion   *playfeir* playfellow
185 *fidder* load   186 *tuik* took   *rink* run

SOLACE: I wait not, sir, be sweit Saint Marie:
  I have bene in ane feirie farie,
    Or ellis intill ane trance:
  Sir, I have sene, I yow assure,
  The fairest earthlie creature
  That ever was formit be nature
    And maist for to advance.
  To luik on hir is great delyte,
  With lippis reid and cheikis quhyte.
  I wald renunce all this warld quyte   200
    For till stand in hir grace:
  Scho is wantoun and scho is wyse,
  And cled scho is on the new gyse.
  It wald gar all your flesche up ryse,
    To luik upon hir face.
  War I ane king it sould be kend
  I sould not spair on hir to spend,
  And this same nicht for hir to send
    For pleasure:
  Quhat rak of your prosperitie   210
  Gif ye want Sensualitie?
  I wald nocht gif ane sillie flie
    For your treasure.

REX: Forsuith, my friends, I think ye are not wyse,
  Till counsall me to break commandement
  Directit be the Prince of Paradyce:
  Considering ye knaw that my intent
  Is for till be to God obedient,
  Quhilk dois forbid men to be lecherous.
  Do I nocht sa perchance I will repent.   220
  Thairfoir I think your counsall odious,
    The quhilk ye gaif mee till.
  Becaus I have bene to this day

203 *cled* clothed   *gyse* fashion   210 *rak* counts, is of value
212 *sillie* simple   222 *quhilk* which

Tanquam tabula rasa:
That is als mekill as to say,
   Redie for gude and ill.

PLACEBO: Beleive ye that we will begyll yow,
  Or from your vertew we will wyle yow,
  Or with evill counsall overseyll yow,
    Both into gude and evill?   230
  To tak your graces part wee grant
  In all your deidis participant,
  Sa that ye be nocht ane young sanct
    And syne ane auld devill.

WANTONNES: Beleive ye, Sir, that Lecherie be sin?
  Na, trow nocht that: this is my ressoun quhy.
  First at the Romane Kirk will ye begin,
  Quhilk is the lemand lamp of lechery:
  Quhair Cardinals and Bischops generally
  To luif ladies thay think ane pleasant sport,   240
  And out of Rome hes baneist Chastity,
  Quha with our Prelats can get na resort.

SOLACE: Sir, quhill ye get ane prudent Queine,
  I think your Majestie serein
  Sould have ane lustie concubein,
    To play yow withall:
  For I knaw be your qualitie,
  Ye want the gift of chastitie.
  Fall to *in nomine Domini:*
    This is my counsall.   250
  I speik, Sir, under protestatioun
  That nane at me haif indignatioun:

225 *mekill* much   228 *wyle* (v) snare   229 *overseyll* cover
233 *sanct* saint   238 *lemand* shining

For all the Prelats of this natioun,
  For the maist part,
Thay think na schame to have ane huir,
And sum hes thrie under thair cuir:
This to be trew Ile yow assuir
  Ye sall heir efterwart.
Sir, knew [ye] al the mater throch
To play ye wald begin: 260
Speir at the Monks of Bamirrinoch,
  Gif lecherie be sin.

PLACEBO: Sir send ye for Sandie Solace,
  Or ells your monyeoun Wantonnes,
And pray my Ladie Priores,
  The suith till declair:
Gif it be sin to tak [ane] Kaity,
Or to leif like ane bummillbaty.
The buik sayis *Omnia probate*
  And nocht for to spair.   270

  [*Enter Sensuality, Homeliness and Danger to one side
  of the stage.*]

SENSUALITIE: Luifers awalk! Behald the fyrie spheir,
Behauld the naturall dochter of Venus:
Behauld, luifers, this lustie ladie cleir,
The fresche fonteine of knichtis amorous,
Repleit with joyis dulce and delicious:
Orquha wald mak to Venus observance
In my mirthfull chalmer melodious?
Thair sall thay find all pastyme and pleasance.

255 *huir* whore   256 *cuir* care   264 *monyeoun* minion
266 *suith* truth   267 *Kaity* mistress   268 *bummillbaty* booby

457

Behauld my heid, behauld my gay attyre,
Behauld my halse, lu[f]sum and lilie quhite: 280
Behauld my visage flammand as the fyre,
Behauld my papis of portratour perfyte.
To luke on mee luiffers hes greit delyte;
Rycht sa hes all the Kinges of Christindome:
To thame I haif done pleasouris infinite,
And speciallie unto the Court of Rome.

And kis of me war worth in ane morning
A milyioun of gold to Knicht or King.
And yit I am of nature sa towart
I lat no luiffer pas with ane sair hart. 290
Of my name wald ye wit the veritie,
Forsuith thay call me Sensualitie.
I hauld it best now or we farther gang,
To Dame Venus let us go sing ane sang.

HAMELINES: Madame, but taryng,
For to serve Venus deir,
We sall fall to and sing.
Sister Danger, cum neir.

DANGER: Sister, I was nocht sweir
To Venus observance. 300
Howbeit I mak Dangeir,
Yit be continuance
Men may have thair pleasance.
Thairfoir let na man fray:
We will tak it, perchance,
Howbeit that wee say nay.

279 *heid* head   280 *halse* neck   *lufsum* lovable   *quhite* white
283 *luiffers* lovers   289 *towart* free   290 *lat* let   *sair* sore
293 *or* before   295 *but* without   299 *sweir* lazy   304 *fray* fear

HAMELINES: Sister, cum on your way,
    And let us nocht think lang:
    In all the haist wee may
    To sing Venus ane sang.   310

DANGER: Sister, sing this sang I may not,
    Without the help of gude Fund-Jonet:
    Fund-Jonet, hoaw cum tak a part.

    [*Enter Fund-Jonet.*]

FUND-JONET: That sall I do with all my hart:
    Sister, howbeit that I am hais,
    I am content to beir a bais.
    Ye twa sould luif me as your lyfe,
    Ye knaw I lernit yow baith to swyfe:
    In my chalmer, ye wait weill quhair,
    Sen syne the feind ane man ye spair.   320

HAMELINES: Fund-Jonet, fy, ye ar to blame:
    To speik foull wordis think ye not schame?
FUND-JONET: Thair is ane hundreth heir sitand by
    That luifis geaping als weill as I,
    Micht thay get it in privitie:
    Bot quha begins the sang let se.

REX: Up Wantonnes, thow sleipis to lang,
    Me thocht I hard ane mirrie sang:
    I the command in haist to gang
    Se quhat yon mirth may meine.   330

309 *haist* haste   315 *hais* hoarse   316 *bais* bass   319 *wait* know
324 *geaping* sexual intercourse

WANTONNES: I trow, Sir, be the Trinitie,
   Yon same is Sensualitie,
   Gif it be scho sune sall I sie
     That Soverance sereine.

*Heir sall Wantones ga spy thame and cum agane to
the King*

REX: Quhat war thay gon, to me declair?
WANTONNES: Dame Sensuall, baith gude and fair.

PLACEBO: Sir, scho is mekill to avance,
   For scho can baith play and dance,
   That perfyt patron of plesance,
     Ane perle of pulchritude: 340
   Soft as the silk is hir quhite lyre,
   Hir hair is like the goldin wyre:
   My hart burnis in ane flame of fyre
     I sweir yow be the Rude.
   I think scho is sa wonder fair
   That in earth scho hes na compair.
   War ye weill leirnit at luifis lair
     And syne had hir anis sene,
   I wait, be cokis passioun,
   Ye wald mak supplicatioun,   350
   And spend on hir ane millioun
     Hir lufe for till obteine.

SOLACE: Quhat say ye sir? Ar ye content
   That scho cum heir incontinent?
   Quhat vails your kingdome and your rent,
     And all your great treasure,

337 *mekill* great   341 *lyre* skin   347 *lair* lore   348 *anis* once
355 *vails* avails

Without ye haif ane mirrie lyfe,
And cast asyde all sturt and stryfe?
And sa lang as ye want ane wyfe,
    Fall to and tak your pleasure. 360

REX: Gif that be trew quhilk ye me tell,
    I will not langer tarie,
Bot will gang preif that play my sell
    Howbeit the warld me warie.
Als fast as ye may carie
Speid with all diligence:
Bring Sensualitie,
    Fra-hand, to my presence.
Forsuth I wait not how it stands,
Bot sen I hard of your tythands, 370
My bodie trimblis feit and hands,
    And quhiles is hait as fyre.
I trow Cupido with his dart
Hes woundit me out-throw the hart;
My spreit will fra my bodie part,
    Get I nocht my desyre.
Pas on away with diligence,
And bring hir heir to my presence:
Spair nocht for travell nor expence,
    I cair not for na cost. 380
Pas on your way schone Wantonnes,
And tak with yow Sandie Solace,
And bring that ladie to this place,
    Or els I am bot lost.
Commend me to that sweitest thing,
And present hir with this same ring,
And say I ly in languisching,
    Except scho mak remeid:
With siching sair I am bot schent,

358 *sturt* vexation   363 *preif* prove   364 *warie* curse   365 *carie* go
368 *Fra-hand* at once   370 *tythands* tidings   372 *hait* hot
381 *schone* soon

Without scho cum incontinent,
My heavie langour to relent,
   And saif me now fra deid.
WANTONNES: Or ye tuik skaith, be God[i]s goun,
  I lever thair war not, up nor doun,
  Ane tume cunt into this toun,
   Nor twentie myle about.
  Doubt ye nocht, Sir, bot wee will get hir,
  Wee sall be feirie for till fetch hir,
  Bot faith wee wald speid all the better,
   Till gar our pursses rout.

400

SOLACE: Sir, let na sorrow in yow sink,
  Bot gif us Ducats for till drink:
  And wee sall never sleip ane wink
   Till it be back or eadge.
  Ye ken weill, Sir, wee have no cunye.
REX: Solace, sure that sall be no sunyie;
  Beir ye that bag upon your lunyie:
   Now sirs win weill your wage:

I pray yow speid yow sone againe.
WANTONNES: Ye, of this sang, sir, wee ar faine,

410

  Wee sall nether spair [for] wind nor raine,
   Till our days wark be done.
  Fairweill, for wee ar at the flicht.
  Placebo rewll our Roy at richt:
  We sall be heir man or midnicht,
   Thocht wee marche with the Mone.

Heir sall thay depairt singand mirrelly.

392 *deid* death   393 *tuik* took   *skaith* harm   394 *lever* had rather
395 *tume* virgin   398 *feirie* active   405 *cunye* money   406 *sunyie* delay
407 *lunyie* back   413 *at the flicht* in a hurry

WANTONNES: Pastyme with pleasance and greit
      prosperitie,
  Be to yow Soveraine Sensualitie.

SENSUALITIE: Sirs, ye ar welcum: quhair go ye? eist or
      west?

WANTONNES: In faith I trow we be at the farrest.   420

SENSUALITIE: Quhat is your name? I pray you, Sir,
      declair.

WANTONNES: Marie, Wantonnes, the King[i]s secretair.

SENSUALITIE: Quhat King is that quhilk hes sa gay a
      boy?

WANTONNES: Humanitie that richt redoutit Roy,
  Quhilk dois commend him to yow hartfullie,
  And sends yow heir ane ring with ane rubie,
  In takin that abuife all creatour,
  He hes chosen yow to be his paramour:
  He bade me say that he will be bot deid,
  Without that ye mak haistelie remeid.   430

SENSUALITIE: How can I help him althocht he suld
      forfair?
  Ye ken richt weill I am na medcinair.

SOLACE: Yes, lustie ladie, thocht he war never sa seik,
  I wait ye beare his health into your breik:
  Ane kis of your sweit mow, in ane morning,
  Till his seiknes micht be greit comforting;
  And als he maks yow supplicatioun,
  This nicht to mak with him collatioun.

SENSUALITIE: I thank his grace of his benevolence.
  Gude sirs, I sall be reddie evin fra hand: 440
  In me thair sall be fund na negligence,
  Baith nicht and day, quhen his grace will demand.
  Pas ye befoir and say I am cummand,
  And thinks richt lang to haif of him ane sicht:

419 *eist* east   427 *takin* token   431 *forfair* perish
432 *medcinair* doctor   433 *seik* sick   434 *into* in   *breik* buttocks
438 *collatioun* meal

And I to Venus do mak ane faithfull band,
That in his arms I think to ly all nicht.

WANTONNES: That sal be done, bot yit or I hame pas,
  Heir I protest for Hamelynes your las.
SENSUALITIE: Scho salbe at command, sir, quhen ye will:
  I traist scho sall find yow flinging your fill.   450

WANTONNES: Now hay for joy and mirth I dance,
  Tak thair ane gay gamond of France:
  Am I nocht worthie till avance,
    That am sa gude a page,
  And that sa spedelie can rin
  To tyst my maister unto sin?
  The fiend a penny he will win
    Of this his mariage.
I rew richt sair, be sanct Michell,
Nor I had pearst hir my awin sell: 460
For quhy yon king, be Bryd[i]s bell,
    Kennis na mair of ane cunt
Nor dois the noveis of ane freir.
It war bot almis to pull my eir
That wald not preif yon gallant geir:
    Fy that I am sa blunt.
I think this day to win greit thank,
Hay, as ane brydlit cat I brank:
Alace I have wreistit my schank,
    Yit I gang be Sanct Michaell.   470
Quhilk of my leggis, sirs, as ye trow,
Was it that I did hurt evin now?
Bot quhairto sould I speir at yow?
    I think thay baith ar haill.

---

445 *band* bond   448 *protest* lay claim to   450 *flinging* capering
452 *gamond* caper   456 *tyst* tempt   460 *pearst* pierced
462 *Kennis* knows   463 *noveis* novice   468 *brydlit* bridled   *brank* prance
473 *speir* ask

[Wantonness returns to the King.]

Gude morrow Maister, be the Mes.
REX: Welcum, my minyeon Wantonnes;
  How hes thow sped in thy travell?
WANTONNES: Rycht weill, be him that herryit hell:
  Your erand is weill done.
REX: Then, Wantonnes, how weill is mee,   480
  Thow hes deservit baith meit and fie,
    Be Him that maid the Mone.
  Thair is ane thing that I wald speir;
  Quhat sall I do, quhen scho cums heir?
  For I knaw nocht the craft perqueir
    Of luifers gyn:
  Thaifoir at lenth ye mon me leir,
    How to begin.
WANTONNES: To kis hir, and clap hir, sir, be not
      affeard;
  Sho will not schrink, thocht ye kis hir ane span within
    the baird.   490
  Gif ye think that sho think[i]s shame, then hyd the
    bairn[i]s eine
  With hir taill, and tent hir weil, ye wait quhat I meine.
  Will ye leif me, sir, first for to go to,
  And I sall leirne yow all kewis how to do?
REX: God forbid, Wantonnes, that I gif the leife:
  Thou art over perillous ane page sic practik[i]s to
    preife.
WANTONNES: Now sir, preife as ye pleis, I se hir
      cumand;
  Use your self gravelie, wee sall by yow stand.

*Heir sall Sensualitie cum to the King and say

477 *travell* labour   478 *herryit* harrowed   481 *meit* meat   *fie* fee
485 *perqueir* by heart   486 *gyn* skill   487 *leir* teach   489 *clap* caress
492 *tent* (v) probe   494 *kewis* appropriate things   496 *preife* prove

SENSUALITIE: O Queene Venus, unto thy celsitude
 I gif gloir, honour, laud and reverence: 500
 Quha grantit me sic perfite pulchritude,
 That princes of my persone have pleasance.
 I mak ane vow with humbill observance,
 Richt reverentlie thy Tempill to visie,
 With sacrifice unto thy deitie.

 Till everie stait I am so [a]greabill,
 That few or nane refuses me at all:
 Paipis, Patriarks or Prelats venerabill,
 Common pepill and Princes temporall,
 Ar subject all to me Dame Sensuall.   510
 Sa sall it be ay quhill the warld indures,
 And speciallie quhair youthage hes the cures.
  Quha knawis the contrair?
 I traist few in this companie,
 Wald thay declair the veritie,
 How thay use Sensualitie,
  Bot with me maks repair.
 And now my way I man avance
 Unto ane Prince of great puissance,
 Quhom young men hes in governance,   520
  Rolland into his rage.
 I am richt glaid, I yow assure,
 That potent Prince to get in cure,
 Quhilk is of lustines the luir,
 And greitest of curage.

   Heir sall scho mak reverence and say

O potent Prince of pulchritude preclair,
God Cupido preserve your celsitude:

499 *celsitude* majesty 506 *stait* estate, rank 518 *man* must
523 *in cure* into my power 524 *luir* lure, attraction

466

And Dame Venus mot keip your court from cair,
As I wald sho suld keip my awin hart-blud.
REX: Welcum to me peirles in pulchritude,   530
  Welcum to me thow sweiter nor the lamber.
  Quhilk hes maid me of all dolour denude.
  Solace, convoy this ladie to my chamber.

*Heir sall scho pass to the chalmer and say

SENSUALITIE: I gang this gait with richt gude will.
  Sir Wantonnes, tarie ye stil:
  And Hamelines the cap yeis fill,
    And beir him cumpanie.
[HAMELINES:] That sall I do, withoutin dout,
  And he and I sall play cap'out.
WANTONNES: Now ladie len me that batye tout: 540
    Fill in for I am dry.
  Your dame be this trewlie,
  Hes gotten upon the gumis.
  Quhat rak thocht ye and I
  Go iunne our iusting lumis.
HAMELINES: Content I am with [richt] gude will,
  Quhen ever ye ar reddie,
  [All] your pleasure to fulfill.
WANTONNES: Now weill said, be Our Ladie.
  Ile bair my maister cumpanie,   550
  Till that I may indure:
  Gif ye be quisland wantounlie,
  We sall fling on the flure.

*Heir sall thay pass all to the chalmer and Gude
Counsale sall say

531 *nor* than   532 *denude* free   536 *cap* cup   *yeis* you shall
540 *len* give   *batye tout* drinking cup   552 *quisland* whistling

GUDE COUNSALL: Immortall God, maist of magnificence,
    Quhais Majestie na clark can comprehend,
    Must save yow all that givis sic audience,
    And grant yow grace him never till offend,
    Quhik on the Croce did willinglie ascend,
    And sched his pretious blude on everie side:
    Quhais pitious passioun from danger yow defend,   560
    And be your gratious governour and gyde.
    Now my gude freinds considder I yow beseik
    The caus maist principall of my cumming:
    Princis or Potestatis ar nocht worth ane leik,
    Be thay not gydit be my gude governing.
    Thair was never Empriour, Conqueror nor King,
    Without my wisdome that micht thair wil avance.
    My name is Gude Counsall without feinyeing;
    Lords for lack of my lair ar brocht to mischance.

Finallie for conclusioun,   570
Quha halds me at delusioun
Sall be brocht to confusioun:
    And this I understand.
For I have maid my residence,
With hie Princes of greit puissance,
In Ingland, Italie and France,
    And monie uther land.
Bot out of Scotland, wa, alace,
I haif bene fleimit lang tyme space,
That garris our gyders all want grace,   580
    And die befoir thair day:
Becaus thay lychtlyit Gude Counsall,
Fortune turnit on thame hir saill,
Quhilk brocht this realme to meikill baill
    Quha can the contrair say?
My Lords, I came nocht heir to lie:

555 *Quhais* whose   562 *beseik* beseech   564 *leik* leek   569 *lair* lore
579 *fleimit* banished   580 *gyders* steersmen, rulers
582 *lychtlyit* made light of   584 *baill* woe

How happinit yow into this place?
FLATTERIE: Now be my saul evin on a cace.
  I come in sleipand at the port,
  Or evir I wist amang this sort.
  Quhair is Dissait, that limmer loun?
FALSET: I left him drinkand in the toun;
  He will be heir incontinent.   650
FLATTERIE: Now be the Haly Sacrament,
  Thay tydingis comforts all my hart:
  I wait Dissait will tak my part.
  He is richt craftie as ye ken,
  And counsallour to the merchand-men:
  Let us ly doun heir baith and spy
  Gif wee persave him cummand by.

      [*Enter Dissait.*]

DISSAIT: Stand by the gait that I may steir.
  Aisay, Koks bons, how cam I heir?
  I can not mis to tak sum feir,   660
    Into sa greit ane thrang.
  Marie! heir ane cumlie congregatioun;
  Quhat ar ye, sirs, all of ane natioun?
  Maisters, I speik be protestatioun,
    In dreid ye tak me wrang.
  Ken ye not, sirs, quhat is my name?
  Gude faith, I dar not schaw it for schame:
  Sen I was clekit of my dame,
    Yit was I never leill:
  For Katie Unsell was my mother,   670
  And Common Theif my father-brother:
  Of sic freindship I had ane fither,
    Howbeit I can not steill.

645 *cace* chance 646 *sleipand* slipping *port* gate
648 *limmer* wicked 660 *feir* companions 668 *clekit* born, hatched
669 *leill* loyal 670 *Unsell* unhallowed

Bot yit I will borrow and len,
As be my cleathing ye may ken
That I am cum of nobill men:
 And als I will debait
That querrell with my feit and hands.
And I dwell amang the merchandſ:
My name gif onie man demands,   680
 Thay call me Dissait.
Bon-jour, brother, with all my hart:
Heir am I cum to tak your part,
 Baith into gude and evill.
I met Gude Counsall be the way,
Quha pat me in ane felloun fray:
 I gif him to the Devill.

FALSET: How chaipit ye, I pray yow tell?
DISSAIT: I slipit into ane bordell,
 And hid me in a bawburds bed: 690
 Bot suddenlie hir schankis I sched,
 With hoch hurland amang hir howis:
 God wait gif wee maid monie mowis.
 How came ye heir, I pray yow tell me?
FALSET: Marie, to seik King Humanitie.
DISSAIT: Now be the gude ladie that me bair,
 That samin hors is my awin mair:
 Now with our purpois let us mell:
 Quhat is your counsall, I pray yow tell?
 Sen we thrie seiks yon nobill king,   700
 Let us devyse sum subtill thing:
 And als I pray you as my brother,
 That we ilk ane be trew to uther.
 I mak ane vow with all my hart,
 In gude and evill to tak your part.

674 *len* lend   675 *cleathing* clothing   677 *debait* contest
686 *felloun* terrible   *fray* fear   688 *chaipit* escaped   689 *bordell* brothel
690 *bawburds* whore's   698 *mell* be concerned

I pray to God nor I be hangit,
Bot I sall die or ye be wrangit.

FALSET: Quhat is thy counsall that wee do?
DISSAIT: Marie, sirs, this is my counsall lo:
    Till tak our tyme, quhill wee may get it,   710
    For now thair is na man to let it:
    Fra tyme the King begin to steir him,
    Marie Gude Counsall I dreid cum neir him,
    Ane be we knawin with Correctioun,
    It will be our confusioun.
    Thairfoir, my deir brother, devyse
    To find sum toy of the new gyse.

FLATTERIE: Marie, I sall finde ane thousand wyles:
    Wee man turne our claithis, and change our stiles,
    And disagyse us, that na man ken us.   720
    Hes no man clarkis cleathing to len us?
    And let us keip grave countenance,
    As wee war new cum out of France.
DISSAIT: Now, be my saull, that is weill devysit.
    Ye sall se me sone disagysit.
FALSET: And as sall I, man, be the Rude:
    Now sum gude fallow lan me ane hude.

*Heir sall Flattry help his twa marrowis.

DISSAIT: Now am I buskit and quha can spy,
    The Deuill stik me, gif this be I?
    If this be I, or not, I can not weill say,   730
    Or hes the Feind or Farie-folk borne me away?

706 *nor* lest   711 *let* (v) hinder   719 *stiles* appearance   727 *lan* lend
727 SD *marrowis* companions   728 *buskit* disguised

FALSET: And gif my hair war up in ane how,
    The feind ane man wald ken me, I trow:
    Quhat sayis thou of my gay garmoun?
DISSAIT: I say thou luiks evin like ane loun.
    Now brother Flatterie, quhat do ye?
    Quhat kynde of man schaip ye to be?
FLATTERIE: Now be my faith, my brother deir,
    I will gang counterfit the Freir.
DISSAIT: A Freir? Quhairto? Ye can not preiche.   740
FLATTERIE: Quhat rak man! I can richt weill fleich.
    Perchance Ile cum [to] that honour,
    To be the King[i]s confessour.
    Pure Freirs are free at any feast,
    And marchellit ay amang the best.
    Als God hes lent to them sic graces,
    That Bischops puts them in thair places,
    Out-throw thair Dioceis to preiche,
    Bot ferlie nocht, howbeit thay fleich:
    For schaw thay all the veritie,   750
    Thaill want the Bischops charitie.
    And thocht the corne war never sa skant,
    The gudewyfis will not let Freirs want:
    For quhy thay ar thair confessours,
    Thair heavinlie prudent counsalours.
    Thairfoir the wyfis plainlie taks thair parts,
    And shawis the secreits of thair harts
    To Freirs with better will I trow,
    Nor thay do to thair bed-fallow.
DISSAIT: And I reft anis ane Freirs coull,   760
    Betuix Sanct-Johnestoun and Kinnoull:
    I sall gang fetch it, gif ye will tarie.
FLATTERIE: Now play me that of companarie.
    Ye saw him nocht, this hundreth yeir,
    That better can counterfeit the Freir.
DISSAIT: Heir is thy gaining, all and sum:
    That is ane koull of Tullilum.

732 *how* coif   734 *garmoun* garment   741 *rak* matters   *fleich* flatter
760 *reft* stole   *coull* cowl   763 *companarie* good fellowship

FLATTERIE: Quha hes ane portouns for to len me?
The feind ane saull I trow will ken me.

FALSET: Now gang thy way quhair ever thow will,   770
Thow may be fallow to Freir Gill:
Bot with Correctioun gif wee be kend,
I dreid wee mak ane schamefull end.

FLATTERIE: For that mater I dreid nathing;
Freiris ar exemptit fra the King:
And freiris will reddie entries get,
Quhen Lords ar haldin at the get.

FALSET: Wee man do mair yit, be Sanct James,
For wee mon all thrie change our names.
Hayif me and I sall baptize thee.   780

DISSAIT: Be God and thair-about may it be.
How will thou call me, I pray the tell?

FALSET: I wait not how to call my sell.

DISSAIT: Bot yit anis name the bairn[i]s name.

FALSET: Discretioun, Discretioun, in God[i]s name.

DISSAIT: I neid nocht now to cair for thrift,
Bot quhat salbe my Godbairne gift?

FALSET: I gif yow all the Deuilis of hell.

DISSAIT: Na, brother, hauld that to thy sel.
Now sit doun, let me baptise the: 790
I wad not quhat thy name sould be.

FALSET: Both yit anis name the bairn[i]s name.

DISSAIT: Sapience, in ane warld[i]s-schame.

FLATTERIE: Brother Dissait, cum baptize me.

DISSAIT: Then sit doun lawlie on thy kne.

FLATTERIE: Now brother name the bairn[i]s name.

DISSAIT: Devotioun, in the Deuillis name.

FLATTERIE: The deuill resave the, lurdoun loun;
Thow hes wet all my new schawin croun.

DISSAIT: Devotioun, Sapience, and Discretioun,   800
Wee thre may rewll this regioun.
Wee sall find monie craftie things,
For to begyll ane hundreth kingis.

768 *portouns* breviary   777 *get* gate   780 *Hayif* christen
787 *Godbairne* godchild   795 *lawlie* meekly   799 *schawin* shaven

For thow can richt weil crak and clatter,
And I sall feinye, and thow sall flatter.
FLATTERIE: Bot I wald have, or wee depairtit,
Ane drink to mak us better hartit.

Now the King sall cum fra his chamber.

DISSAIT: Weill said, be him that herryit hell,
I was evin thinkand that my sell.
Now till wee get the Kings presence   810
Wee will sit doun and keip silence.
I se ane yeoman; quhat ever be,
Ile wod my lyfe, yon same is he.
Feir nocht brother, bot hauld yow still,
Till wee have hard quhat is his will.
REX: Now quhair is Placebo and Solace?
Quhair is my minyeoun Wantonnes?
Wantonnes, hoaw, cum to me sone.
WANTONNES: Quhy cryit ye, sir, till I had done?
REX: Quhat was ye doand tell me that?   820
WANTONNES: Mary, leirand how my father me gat.
I wait nocht how it stands but doubt.
Me think the warld rinnis round about.
REX: And sa think I, man, be my thrift:
I see fyfteine Mones in the lift.
[WANTONNES: Lat Hamelines, my lass, allane.
Scho bendit up ay twa for ane.]
HAMELINES: Gat ye nocht quhilk ye desyrit?
Sir, I beleif that ye ar tyrit.
DANGER: Bot, as for Placebo and Solace,   830
I held them baith in mirrines.
[Howbeid I maid it sumthing tewch,
I fand thame chalmer-glew annewch.

804 *crak* boast 805 *feinye* dissemble 813 *wod* (v) wager
825 *Mones* moons *lift* sky 832 *tewch* tough
833 *chalmer-glew* intercourse *annewch* enough

SOLLACE: Mary, thow wald gar ane hundreth tyre;
   Thow hes ane cunt lyke ane quaw-myre.
DANGER: Now fowll fall yow, it is na bourdis,
   Befoir ane king to speik fowll wourdis.
   Or evir ye cum that gait agane,
   To kiss my cloff ye salbe fane.]
SOLACE: Now schaw me sir, I yow exhort,   840
   How ar ye of your luif content?
   Think ye not this ane mirrie sport?
REX: Yea, that I do in verament.
   Quhat bairnis ar yon upon the bent?
   I did nocht se them all this day.
WANTONNES: Thay will be heir incontinent,
   Stand still and heir quhat thay will say.

Now the vycis cums and maks salutatioun saying –

DISSAIT: Laud, honor, gloir, triumph and victory
   Be to your maist excellent Maiestie.
REX: Ye ar welcum gude freind[i]s, be the Rude: 850
   Appeirandlie ye seime sum men of gude.
   Quhat ar your names, tell me without delay.
DISSAIT: Discretioun, sir, is my name, perfay.
REX: Quhat is your name, sir, with the clipit croun?
FLATTERIE: But dout my name is callit Devotioun.
REX: Welcum Devotioun, be Sanct Jame:
   Now sirray, tell quhat is your name.
FALSET: Marie, sir, thay call me ... quhat call thay me?
   [I wat not weill, but gif I lie.]
REX: Can ye nocht tell quhat is your name?   860
FALSET: I kend it quhen I cam fra hame.
REX: Quhat gars ye can nocht schaw it now?
FALSET: Marie, thay call me thin-drink, I trow.
REX: Thin-drink! Quhat kynde of name is that?

834 *gar ... tyre* make ... tire   835 *quaw-myre* quagmire
836 *bourdis* joke   839 *cloff* cleavage   854 *clipit* shorn

477

DISSAIT: Sapiens, thow servis to beir ane plat.
    Me think thow schawis the not weill-wittit.
FALSET: Sypeins, sir, Sypeins, marie now ye hit it.
FLATTERIE: Sir, gif ye pleis to let [me] say,
    His name is Sapientia.
FALSET: That same is it, be Sanct Michell.   870
REX: Quhy could thou not tell it thy sell?
FALSET: I pray your grace, appardoun me,
    And I sall schaw the veritie:
    I am sa full of Sapience,
    That sumtyme I will tak ane trance:
    My spreit wes reft fra my bodie,
    Now heich abone the Trinitie.
REX: Sapience suld be ane man of gude.
FALSET: Sir, ye may ken that be my hude.
REX: Now have I Sapience and Discretioun,   880
    How can I faill to rewll this regioun?
    And Devotioun to be my confessour:
    Thir thrie came in ane happie hour.
    Heir I mak the my secretar,
    And thou salbe my thesaurar,
    And thow salbe my counsallour
    In sprituall things and confessour.
FLATTERIE: I sweir to yow, sir, be Sanct An,
    Ye met never with ane wyser man,
    For monie a craft, sir, do I can   890
        War thay weill knawin:
    Sir, I have na feill of flattrie,
    Bot fosterit with Phil[o]sophie,
    Ane strange man in Astronomie,
        Quhilk salbe schawin.

FALSET: And I have greit intelligence
    In quelling of the quintessence:
    Bot to preif my experience,

865 *beir* receive   *plat* smack   866 *weill-wittit* clever witted
885 *thesaurar* treasurer

Sir, len me fourtie crownes,
To mak multiplicatioun.   900
And tak my obligatioun,
Gif wee mak fals narratioun,
    Hauld us for verie lownes.

DISSAIT: Sir, I ken be your physnomie
    Ye sall conqueis, or els I lie,
    Danskin Denmark, and [all] Almane,
    Spittelfeild, and the realme of Spane.
    Ye sall have at your governance
    Ranfrow and all the realme of France,
    Yea Rugland and the toun of Rome,   910
    Castorphine and al christindome.
    Quhairto, sir, be the Trinitie,
    Ye ar ane verie Apersie.

FLATTERIE: Sir, quhen I dwelt in Italie
    I leirit the craft of Palmistrie.
    Schaw me the lufe, sir, of your hand,
    And I sall gar yow understand
    Gif your grace be infortunat,
    Or gif ye be predestinat.
    I see ye will have fyfteine queenes   920
    And fyfteine scoir of concubeines.
    The Virgin Marie saife your grace,
    Saw ever man sa quhyte ane face,
    Sa greit ane arme, sa fair ane hand;
    Thairs nocht sic ane leg in al this land.
    War ye in armis, I think na wonder
    Howbeit ye dang doune fyfteine hunder.
DISSAIT: Now be my saull, thats trew thow sayis,
    Wes never man set sa weill his clais:

902 *Gif* if   904 *physnomie* physiognomy   905 *conqueis* conquer
913 *Apersie* incomparable   916 *lufe* palm   927 *dang* strike
929 *clais* clothes

Thair is na man in Christintie
Sa meit to be ane king as ye.
FALSET: Sir, thank the Haly Trinitie,
 That send us to your cumpanie:
 For God nor I gaip in ane gallows,
 Gif ever ye fand thrie better fallows.
REX: Ye ar richt welcum, be the Rude,
 Ye seime to be thrie men of gude.

Heir sall Gude Counsell schaw himself in the feild.

Bot quha is yon that stands sa still?
Ga spy and speir quhat is his will.
And, gif he yearnis my presence,   940
Bring him to mee with diligence.
DISSAIT: That sall we do, be God[i]s breid;
 We's bring him eather quick or deid.
REX: I will sit still heir and repois.
 Speid yow agane to me my jois.
FALSET: Ye hardlie sir, keip yow in clois
 And quyet till wee cum againe.
 Brother, I trow be cok[i]s toes,
 Yon bairdit bogill cums fra ane traine.
DISSAIT: Gif he dois sa he salbe slaine. 950
 I doubt him nocht, nor yit ane uther:
 Trowit I that he come for ane traine,
 Of my freindis I sould rais ane futher.
FLATTERIE: I doubt full sair, be God him sell,
 That yon auld churle be Gude Counsell:
 Get he anis to the Kings presence,
 We thrie will get na audience.
DISSAIT: That matter I sall tak on hand,
 And say it is the Kings command

935 *fand* found 940 *yearnis* wishes for 944 *repois* rest 945 *jois* joys
946 *hardlie* by all means *clois* secret 949 *bairdit* bearded
bogill rogue *traine* trick

That he anone devoyd this place, 960
And cum nocht neir the King[i]s grace:
And that under the paine of tressoun.

FLATTERIE: Brother, I hauld your counsell ressoun.
Now let is heir quhat he will say:
Auld lyart beard, gude day, gude day.

GUDE COUNSALL: Gude day againe, sirs, be the rude,
The Lord mot make yow men of gude.

DISSAIT: Pray nocht for us to Lord nor Ladie,
For we ar men of gude alreadie.
Sir, schaw to us quhat is your name. 970

GUDE COUNSALL: Gude Counsell thay call me at hame.

FALSET: Quhat says thow carle, ar thow Gude Counsell?
Swyith pak the sone, unhappie unsell.
Gif ever thou cum this gait againe,
I vow to God thou sall be slaine.

GUDE COUNSALL: I pray yow, sirs, gif me licence
To cum anis to the Kings presence,
To speik bot two words to his grace.

FLATTERIE: Swyith, hursone carle, devoyd this place.

GUDE COUNSALL. Brother, I ken yow weill aneuch, 980
Howbeit ye mak it never sa teuch:
Flattrie, Dissait and Fals-report,
That will not suffer to resort
Gude Counsall to the Kings presence.

DISSAIT: S[w]yith, hursun carle, gang pak the hence:
Gif ever thou cum this gait agane,
I vow to God thou sall be slane.

Heir sall thay hurle away Gude Counsall

[GOOD COUNSALL:] Sen at this tyme I can get na
presence,
Is na remeid bot tak in patience.
Howbeit Gude Counsall haistelie be nocht hard 990

965 *lyart* grey   973 *Swyith* quickly   *pak* go   987 SD *hurle* drive

With young Princes yit sould thay noch[t] be skard:
Bot, quhen youthheid hes blawin his wanton blast,
Then sall Gude Counsall rewll him at the last.

Now the Vycis gangs to ane counsall.

FLATTERIE: Now quhill Gude Counsall is absent,
Brother, wee mon be diligent:
And mak betwix us sikker bands,
Quhen vacands fallis in onie lands,
That everie man help weill his fallow.

DISSAIT: I had deir brother, be Alhallow,
Sa ye fische nocht within our bounds.   1000
FLATTERIE: That sall I nocht be God[i]s wounds,
Bot I sall plainlie tak your partis.
FALSET: Sa sall wee thyne with all our hartis.
Bot haist us quhill the King is young.
Let everie man keip weill ane toung,
And in ilk quarter have ane spy
Us till adverteis haistelly
Quhen ony casualities
Sall happin into our countries.
And let us mak provisioun,   1010
Or he cum to discretioun:
Na mair he waits now nor ane sant
Quhat thing it is to haif or want.
Or he cum till his perfyte age,
We sall be sikker of our wage:
And then let everie carle craif uther.
DISSAIT: That mouth speik mair my awin deir brother.
For God nor I rax in ane raip,
Thow may gif counsall to the Paip.

992 *youthheid* youth   996 *sikker* certain   997 *vacands* vacancies
1007 *adverteis* warn   1018 *rax* stretch

Now thay returne to the King.

REX: Quhat gart you bid sa lang fra my presence?   1020
  I think it lang since ye depairtit thence.
  Quhat man was yon with ane greit boustous beird?
  Me thocht he maid yow all thrie very feard.
DISSAIT: It was ane laidlie lurdan loun,
  Cumde to break buithis into this toun.
  Wee have gart bind him with ane poill,
  And send him to the theifis hoill.
REX: Let him sit thair with ane mischance,
  And let us go to our pastance.
WANTONNES: Better go revell at the rackat,   1030
  Or ellis go to the hurlie hackat,
  Or then to schaw our curtlie corsses,
  Ga se quha best can rin thair horsses.
SOLACE: Na, soveraine, or wee farther gang,
  Gar Sensualitie sing ane sang.

*Heir sall the Ladies sing ane sang, the King sall ly
doun amang the Ladies, and then Veritie sall enter.*

VERITIE: *Diligite Iustitiam qui iudicatis terram.*
  Luif Justice ye quha hes ane judges cure
  In earth, and dreid the awful judgement
  Of Him that sall cum judge baith rich and pure,
  Rycht terribilly with bludy wound [i]s rent.   1040
  That dreidfull day into your harts imprent;
  Belevand weill how and quhat maner ye
  Use Justice heir til uthers, thair at lenth
  That day but doubt sa sall ye judgit be.

1022 *boustous* rough   1024 *laidlie* loathly   1025 *Cumde* come
buithis shops   1026 *poill* pole   1030 *rackat* rackets   1032 *curtlie* courtly
corsses ?horsemanship   1039 *pure* poor   1043 *heir* here

Wo than, and duill be to yow Princes all,
Sufferand the pure anes for till be opprest:
In everlasting burnand fyre ye sall
With Lucifer richt dulfullie be drest.
Thairfoir in tyme for till eschaip that nest,
Feir God; do law and justice equally   1050
Till everie man; se that na puir opprest
Up to the hevin on yow ane vengence cry.
Be just judges without favour or fead,
And hauld the ballance evin till everie wicht.
Let not the fault be left into the head,
Then sall the members reulit be at richt.
For quhy subjects to follow day and nicht
Thair governours, in vertew and in vyce.
Ye ar the lamps that sould schaw them the licht
To leid them on this sliddrie rone of yce.   1060
Mobile mutatur semper cum principe vulgus.
And gif ye wald your subjectis war weill gevin,
Then verteouslie begin the dance your sell,
Going befoir, then they anone I wein,
Sall follow yow, eyther till hevin or hell:
Kings sould of gude exempils be the well.
Bot gif that your strands be intoxicate,
In steid of wyne thay drink the poyson fell:
Thus pepill follows ay thair principate.
Sic luceat lux vestra coram hominibus ut videant opera
vestra bona.   1070
And specially ye Princes of the Preist[i]s,
That of peopill hes spiritual cuir,
Dayly ye sould revolve into your breistis
How that thir haly words ar still maist sure.
In verteous lyfe gif that ye do indure,
The pepill wil tak mair tent to your deids
Then to your words; and als baith rich and puir
Will follow yow baith in your warks and words.

1045 *duill* sorrow   1046 *anes* ones   *till* to   1049 *eschaip* escape
1053 *fead* enmity   1054 *wicht* man   1064 *wein* think
1067 *strands* streams   *intoxicate* poisoned

Heir sal Flatterie spy Veritie with ane dum
countenance.

Gif men of me wald have intelligence,
Or knaw my name – thay call me Veritie.   1080
Of Christis law I have experience,
And hes oversaillit many stormie sey.
Now am I seikand King Humanitie,
For of his grace I have gude esperance
Fra tyme that he acquaintit be with mee,
His honour and heich gloir I sall avance.

Heir sall Veritie pas to hir sait.

DISSAIT: Gude day, father, quhair have ye bene?
Declair till us of your novels.
FLATTERIE: Thair is now lichtit on the grene
Dame Veritie, be buiks and bels.   1090
Bot cum scho to the Kings presence
Thair is na buit for us to byde.
Thairfoir I red us all go hence.
FALSET: That will we nocht yit, be Sanct Bryde:
But wee sall ather gang or ryde
To Lords of Spritualitie,
And gar them trow yon bag of pryde
Hes spokin manifest heresie.

Heir thay cum to the Spritualitie.

FLATTERIE: O reverent fatheris of the Sprituall stait,
Wee counsall yow be wyse and vigilant: 1100

1081 *experience* knowledge   1082 *sey* sea   1088 *novels* news
1089 *lichtit* arrived   1090 *buiks* books   1092 *buit* advantage
1097 *trow* believe

Dame Veritie hes lychtit now of lait,
And in hir hand beirand the New Testament.
Be scho ressavit but doubt wee ar bot schent:
Let hir nocht ludge thairfoir into this land,
And this wee reid yow do incontinent,
Now quhill the King is with his luif sleipand.

SPRITUALITIE: Wee thank yow freinds of your
      benevolence:
It sall be done evin as ye have devysit.
Wee think ye serve ane gudlie recompence,
Defendand us that wee be nocht supprysit.   1110
In this mater wee man be weill advysit,
Now quhill the King misknawis the Veritie.
Be scho ressavit then wee will be deprysit.
Quhat is your counsell, brother, now let se?

ABBOT: I hauld it best that wee incontinent
Gar hauld hir fast into captivitie,
Unto the thrid day of the Parlament,
And then accuse hir of hir herisie:
Or than banische hir out of this cuntrie,
For with the King gif Veritie be knawin,   1120
Of our greit gloir wee will degradit be,
And all our secreits to the commouns schawin.

PERSONE: Ye se the King is yit effeminate,
And gydit be Dame Sensualitie,
Rycht sa with young counsall intoxicate,
Swa at this tyme ye haif your libertie.
To tak your tyme I hauld it best for me,
And go distroy all thir Lutherians:
In speciall yon ladie Veritie.

1103 *ressavit* received   1109 *serve* deserve
1112 *misknawis* does not know   1113 *deprysit* disgraced
1123 *effeminate* besotted by women   1127 *hauld* consider

SPRITUALITIE: Schir Persone, ye sall be my commissair   1130
    To put this mater till executioun.
    And ye sir Freir, becaus ye can declair
    The haill processe, pas with him in commissioun.
    Pas all togidder with my braid bennisoun,
    And gif scho speiks against our libertie,
    Then put hir in perpetuall presoun,
    That scho cum nocht to King Humanitie.

> *Heir sall thay pas to Verity.*

PERSONE: Lustie Ladie, we wald faine understand,
    Quhat earand ye haif in this regioun.
    To preich or teich quha gaif to yow command,   1140
    To counsall Kingis how gat ye commissioun?
    I dreid without ye get ane remissioun,
    And syne renunce your new opiniones,
    The sprituall stait sall put yow to perdition,
    And in the fyre will burne yow flesche and bones.

VERITIE: I will recant nathing that I have schawin:
    I have said nathing bot the veritie.
    Bot with the King fra tyme that I be knawin,
    I dreid ye spaiks of Spritualitie
    Sall rew that ever I came in this cuntrie: 1150
    For gif the Veritie plainlie war proclamit,
    And speciallie to the Kings Maiestie,
    For your traditions ye wilbe all defamit.

> *Heir the Vycis gais to the Sprituall Estait and lyis
> upoun Veretie desiring hir to be put in captivitie
> quhilk is done with diligence.*

1143 *syne* soon   *renunce* give up   1149 *spaiks* spokes
1153 *traditions* deceptions

487

FLATTERIE: Quhat buik is that, harlot, into thy hand?
  Out walloway, this is the New Testment,
  In Englisch toung, and printit in England,
  Herisie, herisie, fire, fire, incontinent.
VERITIE: Forsuith, my freind, ye have ane wrang
          judgement,
  For in this buik thair is na heresie,
  Bot our Christs word, baith dulce and redolent,   1160
  And springing well of sinceir veritie.
DISSAIT: Cum on your way: for all your yealow locks,
  Your vantoun words but doubt ye sall repent.
  This nicht ye sall forfair ane pair of stocks,
  And syne the morne be brocht to thoill judgement.
VERITIE: Four our Christs saik I am richt weill content
  To suffer all thing that sall pleis his grace;
  Howbeit ye put ane thousand to torment,
  Ten hundreth thowsand sall rise into thair place.

Veritie sits doun on hir knies and sayis

Get up, thow sleipis all too lang, O Lord,   1170
And mak sum ressonabill reformatioun
On them that dois tramp doun thy gracious word,
And hes ane deidlie indignatioun
At them quha maks maist trew narratioun.
Suffer me not, Lord, mair to be molest.
Gude Lord, I mak the supplicatioun,
With thy unfreinds let me nocht be supprest:
  Now Lords do as ye list,
  I have na mair to say.
FLATTERIE: Sit doun and tak yow rest,   1180
  All nicht till it be day.

1160 *dulce* sweet   1162 *yealow* yellow   1163 *vantoun* wanton
1164 *forfair* wear out, ?endure 1165 *syne* afterwards, then *thoill* suffer
1177 *unfreinds* enemies

Thay put Veritie in the stocks and returne to Spritualite.

DISSAIT: My Lord, wee have with diligence
    Bucklit up weill yon bledrand baird.
SPRITUALITIE: I think ye serve gude recompence;
    Tak thir ten crowns for your rewaird.
VERITIE: The Prophesie of the Propheit Esay
    Is practickit, alace, on mee this day,
    Quha said the veritie sould be trampit doun
    Amid the streit, and put in strang presoun.
    His fyve and fyftie chapter quha list luik,   1190
    Sall find thir word[i]s writtin in his Buik.
    Richt sa Sanct Paull wrytis to Timothie,
    That men sall turne thair earis from veritie.
    Bot in my Lord God I have esperance;
    He will provide for my deliverance.
    Bot ye Princes of Spritualitie,
    Quha sould defend the sinceir veritie,
    I dreid the plagues of Iohnes Revelatioun
    Sall fal upon your generatioun.
    I counsall yow this misse t'amend,   1200
    Sa that ye may eschaip that fatall end.

*Heir sall entir Chaistetie and say

CHASTITIE: How lang sall this inconstant warld indure,
    That I sould baneist be sa lang, alace:
    Few creatures or nane takis on me cure,
    Quhilk gars me monie nicht ly harbrieles.
    Thocht I have past all yeir fra place to place,
    Amang the Temporal and Spirituall staits,
    Nor amang Princes I can get na grace,
    Bot boustuouslie am halden at the getis.

1183 *bledrand* raving   *baird* bard   1189 *streit* street
1205 *harbrieles* without shelter   1209 *boustuouslie* roughly   *getis* gates

DILIGENCE: Ladie, I pray yow schaw [to] me your name.   1210
  It dois me noy, your lamentatioun.
CHASTITIE: My freind, thairof I neid not to think shame;
  Dame Chastitie, baneist from town to town.
DILIGENCE: Then pas to ladies of Religioun,
  Quhilk maks thair vow to observe Chastitie:
  Lo, quhair thair sits ane Priores of renown
  Amang the rest of Spritualitie.

CHASTITIE: I grant yon Ladie hes vowit Chastitie,
  For hir professioun thairto sould accord:
  Scho maid that vow for ane Abesie,   1220
  Bot nocht for Christ Jesus our Lord.
  Fra tyme that they get thair vows, I stand for'd,
  Thay banische hir out of thair cumpanie:
  With Chastitie thay can mak na concord
  Bot leids thair lyfis in Sensualitie.
  I sall observe your counsall gif I may:
  Cum on and heir quhat yon Ladie will say.

Chastitie passis to the Ladie Priores and sayis

My prudent lustie Ladie Priores,
Remember how ye did vow Chastitie:
Madame, I pray yow of your gentilnes   1230
That ye wald pleis to haif of me pitie,
And this ane nicht to gif me harberie:
For this I mak yow supplicatioun.
Do ye nocht sa, Madame, I dreid perdie,
It will be caus of depravatioun.

PRIORES: Pas hynd, Madame, be Christ ye cum nocht
    heir,

    1211 *noy* (v) trouble   1222 *for'd* for it   1234 *perdie* by God
    1236 *hynd* hence

Ye ar contrair to my cumplexioun.
Gang seik ludging at sum auld Monk or Freir,
Perchance thay will be your protectioun.
Or to Prelats mak your progressioun,   1240
Quhilks ar obleist to yow als weill as I.
Dame Sensuall hes gevin directioun
Yow till exclude out of my cumpany.

CHASTITIE: Gif ye wald wit mair of the veritie,
  I sall schaw yow be sure experience,
  How that the Lords of Sprituality
  Hes baneist me, alace, fra thair presence.

Chastitie passes to the Lords of Spritualitie.

My Lords, laud, gloir, triumph and reverence
Mot be unto your halie Sprituall stait.
I yow beseik of your benevolence   1250
To harbry mee that am sa desolait.
Lords, I have past throw mony uncouth schyre,
Bot in this land I can get na ludgeing.
Of my name gif ye wald haif knawledging,
Forsuith my Lords, thay call me Chastitie.
I yow beseik of your graces bening,
Gif me ludging this nicht for charitie.
SPRITUALITIE: Pas on Madame we knaw yow nocht:
  Or be him that the warld [hes] wrocht,
  Your cumming sall be richt deir coft   1260
    Gif ye mak langer tarie.
ABBOT: But doubt wee will baith leif and die
  With our luif Sensualitie.

1237 *cumplexioun* temperament   1240 *progressioun* way
1241 *obleist* pledged   1251 *harbry* (v) shelter   1252 *uncouth* strange
schyre shire   1253 *ludgeing* lodging   1256 *bening* kind
1260 *coft* bought

Wee will haif na mair deall with the
    Then with the Queene of Farie.
PERSONE: Pas hame amang the Nunnis and dwell,
    Quhilks ar of Chastitie the well.
I traist thay will with Buik and bell
    Ressave yow in thair closter.

CHASTITIE: Sir, quhen I was the Nunnis amang,   1270
    Out of thair dortour thay mee dang,
And wald nocht let me bide sa lang
    To say my Pater Noster.
I se na grace thairfoir to get.
I hauld it best or it be lait,
For till go prove the Temporall stait,
    Gif thay will mee resaif.
Gud-day, my Lord Temporalitie,
And yow merchant of gravitie:
Ful faine wald I have harberie,   1280
    To ludge amang the laif.

TEMPORALITIE: Forsuith wee wald be weil content
    To harbrie yow with gude intent,
War nocht we haif impediment:
    For quhy we twa ar maryit.
Bot wist our wyfis that ye war heir,
Thay wald mak all this town on steir:
Thairfoir we reid yow rin areir,
    In dreid ye be miscaryit.

[*Chastity approaches the craftsmen*]

1264 *deall* to do with 1269 *closter* cloister
1271 *dortour* dormitory *dang* beat 1281 *laif* remainder
1288 *rin* run *areir* into confusion

CHASTITIE: Ye men of craft of greit ingyne,   **1290**
 Gif me harbrie, for Christis pyne,
 And win Gods bennesone and myne,
  And help my hungrie hart.
SOWTAR: Welcum, be him that maid the Mone,
 Till dwell with us till it be June.
 We sall mend baith your hois and schone,
  And plainlie tak your part.
TAYLOUR: Is this fair Ladie Chastitie?
 Now welcum, be the Trinitie.
 I think it war ane great pitie   **1300**
  That thou sould ly thairout.
 Your great displeasour I forthink.
 Sit doun, Madame, and tak ane drink,
 and let na sorrow in yow sink,
  Bot let us play cap'out.
SOWTAR: Fill and play cap'out,
 For I am wonder dry.
 The Deuill snyp aff thair snout,
 That haits this company.

Heir sall thay gar Chestety sit down and drink.
[*Enter Jennie, Tailor's Wife, and Sowtar's Wife.*]

JENNIE: Hoaw mynnie, mynnie, mynnie.   **1310**
TAYLOURS WYFE: Quhat wald thow, my deir dochter
   Jennie?
 Jennie my Joy, quhair is thy dadie?
JENNIE: Mary, drinkand with ane lustie Ladie,
 Ane fair young mayden cled in quhyte,
 Of quhom my dadie taks delyte.
 Scho hes the fairest forme of face,
 Furnischit with all kynd of grace.

1290 *ingyne* ability 1291 *pyne* pain 1292 *bennesone* blessing
1296 *hois* hose 1302 *forthink* regret 1308 *snyp* cut
1309 *haits* hates 1310 *mynnie* mother

I traist gif I can reckon richt,
Scho schaips to ludge with him all nicht.

SOWTARS WYFE: Quhat dois the Sowtar my gudman?   1320

JENNIE: Mary, fillis the cap and turnes the can.
Or he cum hame be God I trow
He will be drunkin lyke ane sow.

TAYLOURS WYFE: This is ane greit dispyte, I think,
For to resave sic ane kow-clink.
Quhat is your counsell that wee do?

SOWTARS WYFE: Cummer, this is my counsall, lo:
Ding ye the tane, and I the uther.

TAYLOURS WYFE: I am content, be Gods mother.
I think for mee thay huirsone smaiks   1330
Thay serve richt weill to get thair paiks.
Quhat master feind neids all this haist?
For it is half ane yeir almaist
Sen ever that loun laborde my ledder.

SOWTARS WYFE: God nor my trewker mence ane tedder,
For it is mair nor fourtie dayis,
Sen ever he cleikit up my clayis:
And last quhen I gat chalmer glew,
That foull Sowter began till spew.
And now thay will sit doun and drink   1340
In company with ane kow-clink.
Gif thay haif done us this dispyte,
Let us go ding them till thay dryte.

Heir the wifis sall chase away Chastitie.

TAYLOURS WYFE: Go hence, harlot, how durst thow be
        sa bauld
To ludge with our gudemen but our licence?

1321 *cap* cup   1325 *kow-clink* whore   1327 *Cummer* gossip
1330 *thay* those   *smaiks* contemptible fellows
1331 *paiks* deserved thrashings   1343 *dryte* (v) excrete
1345 *but* without

494

I mak ane vow to him that Judas sauld,
This rock of myne sall be thy recompence.
Schaw me thy name, dudron, with diligence.
CHASTITIE: Marie, Chastitie is my name, be Sanct Blais.
TAYLOURS WYFE: I pray God nor he work on the
        vengence, 1350
  For I luifit never Chastitie all my dayes.

SOWTARS WYFE: Bot my gudeman, the treuth I sall the
        tell,
Gars mee keip Chastitie sair agains my will.
Becaus that monstour hes maid sic ane mint
With my bedstaf that dastard beirs ane dint.
And als I vow cum thow this gait againe,
Thy buttoks salbe beltit be Sanct Blaine.

Heir sall thay speik to thair gudemen and ding them.

TAYLOURS WYFE: Fals hurson carle, but dout thou sall
        forthink,
That evar thow eat or drink with yon kow-clink.
SOWTARS WYFE: I mak ane vow to Sanct Crispine, 1360
  Ise be revengit on that graceles grume:
And to begin the play tak thair ane flap.
SOWTAR: The feind ressave the hands that gaif mee that.
SOWTARS WYFE: Quhat now, huirsun, begins thow for
        til ban?
Tak thair ane uther upon thy peild harne-pan.
Quhat now cummer, will thow nocht tak my part?
TAYLOURS WYFE: That sal I do, cummer, with all my
        hart.

1347 *rock* distaff 1348 *dudron* slut 1354 *mint* mess 1357 *beltit* beaten
1361 *Ise* I shall *grume* ugly fellow 1364 *ban* curse
1365 *peild* bald *harne-pan* head

Heir sall thay ding thair gudemen, with silence.

TAYLOUR: Alace, gossop, alace! How stands with yow?
    Yon cankart carling, alace, hes brokin my brow.
    Now weils yow, Preists, now weils yow all your lifes,   1370
    That ar nocht weddit with sic wickit wyfes.
SOWTAR: Bischops ar blist howbeit that thay be waryit,
    For thay may fuck thair fill and be unmaryit.
    Gossop, alace, that blak band we may wary,
    That ordanit sic puir men as us to mary.
    Quhat may be done bot tak in patience?
    And on all wyfis we'ill cry ane loud vengence.

Heir the wyfis stand be the watter syde and say

SOWTARS WYFE: Sen of our cairls we have the victorie,
    Quhat is your counsell, cummer, that be done?
TAYLOURS WYFE: Send for gude wine and hald our
        selfis merie,   1380
    I hauld this ay best, cummer, be Sanct Clone.
SOWTARS WYFE: Cummer, will ye draw aff my hois and
        schone,
    To fill the Quart I sall rin to the toun.
TAYLOURS WYFE: That sal I do, be him that maid the
        Mone,
    With all my hart, thairfoir, cummer, sit doun.
    Kilt up your claithis abone your waist,
    And speid yow hame againe in haist,
    And I sall provyde for ane paist,
      Our corsses to comfort.
SOWTARS WYFE: Then help me for to kilt my clais.   1390
    Quhat gif the padoks nip my tais?

1369 *cankart* spiteful   *carling* old woman   1370 *weils* is well with
1372/4 *wary(it)* curse(d)   1374 *band* bond   1386 *Kilt* (v) tuck
1388 *paist* pastry   1391 *padoks* frogs   *tais* toes

I dreid to droun heir, be Sanct Blais,
   Without I get support.

*Sho lifts up hir clais above hir waist and enters in the
water.*

Cummer, I will nocht droun my sell.
Go east about the nether mill.
TAYLOURS WYFE: I am content, be Bryd[i]s bell,
   To gang with yow quhair ever ye will.

Heir sall thay depairt and pas to the Palgeoun.

DILIGENCE TO CHASTITIE: Madame, quhat gars yow
      gang sa lait?
  Tell me, how ye have done debait,
  With the Temporall and Spirituall stait?   1400
   Quha did yow maist kyndnes?
CHASTITIE: In faith I fand bot ill and war,
  Thay gart mee stand fra thame askar:
  Evin lyk ane begger at the bar,
   And fleimit mair and lesse.
DILIGENCE: I counsall yow but tarying,
  Gang tell Humanitie the King.
  Perchance hee of his grace bening
   Will mak to yow support.
CHASTITIE: Of your counsell I am content,   1410
  To pas to him incontinent,
  And my service till him present,
   In hope of sum comfort.

Heir sall thay pas to the King.

1397 SD *Palgeoun* pavilion   1402 *war* worse   1403 *askar* at a distance
1405/17 *fle(i)mit* banished

DILIGENCE: Hoaw Solace, gentil Solace, declair unto the
   King
 How thair is heir ane Ladie fair of face,
 That in this cuntrie can get na ludging;
 Bot pitifullie flemit from place to place,
 Without the king of his speciall grace
 As ane servand hir in his court resaif.
 Brother Solace, tell the King all the cace,   1420
 That scho may be resavit amang the laif.
SOLACE: Soverane, get up and se ane hevinlie sicht,
 Ane fair Ladie in quhyt abuilyement.
 Scho may be peir unto ane king or knicht,
 Most lyk ane angell be my judg[e]ment.
REX: I sall gang se that sicht incontinent.
 Madame, behauld gif ye have knawledging
 Of yon Ladie, or quhat is hir intent,
 Thairefter wee sall turne but tarying.
SENSUALITIE: Sir, let me se quhat yon mater may meine, 1430
 Perchance that I may knaw hir be hir face:
 But doubt this is Dame Chastitie, I weine.
 Sir, I and scho cannot byde in ane place:
 But gif it be the pleasour of your grace
 That I remaine into your company,
 This woman richt haistelie gar chase,
 That scho na mair be sene in this cuntry.
REX: As evir ye pleis, sweit hart, sa sall it be,
 Dispone hir as ye think expedient:
 Evin as ye list to let hir live or die,   1440
 I will refer that thing to your judgement.
SENSUALITIE: I will that scho be flemit incontinent,
 And never to cum againe in this cuntrie:
 And gif scho dois but doubt scho sall repent,
 As als perchance a duilfull deid sall die.
 Pas on, sir Sapience and Discretioun,
 And banische hir out of the Kings presence.

1419 *servand* servant 1421 *laif* rest 1423 *abuilyement* clothing
1439 *Dispone* deal with 1445 *duilfull* sorrowful

DISCRETIOUN: That sall we do, Madame, be Gods
       passioun:
  Wee sall do your command with diligence,
  And at your hand serve gudely recompence.   **1450**
  Dame Chastitie, cum on, be not agast;
  We sall rycht sone, upon your awin expence,
  Into the stocks your bony fute mak fast.

*Heir sall they harll Chastitie to the stoks and scho
sall say*

[CHASTITIE:] I pray yow, sirs, be patient,
  For I sall be obedient
    Till do quhat ye command,
  Sen I se thair is na remeid,
  Howbeit it war to suffer deid,
    Or flemit furth of the land.
I wyte the Empreour Constantine,   **1460**
  That I am put to sic ruine,
    And baneist from the Kirk:
  For sen he maid the Paip ane King,
  In Rome I could get na ludging,
    Bot heidlangs in the mirk.
Bot Ladie Sensualitie
Sensyne hes gydit this cuntrie,
    And monie of the rest.
And now scho reulis all this land,
And hes decryit at hir command,   **1470**
    That I suld be supprest.
Bot all comes for the best,
Til him that lovis the Lord:
Thocht I be now molest
I traist to be restorde.

1453 *bony* bonny   *fute* foot   1460 *wyte* blame
1465 *heidlangs* headlong   1467 *Sensyne* since then
1470 *decryit* decreed

Heir sall they put hir in the stocks.

Sister, alace, this is ane cairful cace,
That we with Princes sould be sa abhorde.
VERITIE: Be blyth, sister. I trust within schort space
That we sall be richt honorablie restorde,
And with the King we sall be at concorde,   1480
For I heir tell Divyne Correctioun
Is new landit, thankit be Christ our Lord.
I wait hee will be our protectioun.

H[e]ir sall enter Corrections Varlet.

VARLET: Sirs, stand abak and hauld yow coy,
I am the King Correctiouns Boy,
     Cum heir to dres this place:
Se that ye mak obedience
Untill his nobill excellence
     Fra tyme ye se his face.
For he maks reformatiouns   1490
Out-throw all Christin natiouns,
     Quhair he finds great debaits.
And sa far as I understand,
He sall reforme into this land
     Evin all the Thrie Estaits.
God furth of heavin hes him send
To punische all that dois offend
     Against his Majestie,
As lyks him best to tak vengence,
Sumtyme with sword and pestilence   1500
     With derth and povertie.
Bot quhen the peopill dois repent,
And beis to God obedient,
     Then will he gif them grace:

1476 *cairful* distressful   1484 *coy* quiet   1491 *Out-throw* throughout

Bot thay that will nocht be correctit,
Rycht sudanlie will be dejectit,
   And fleimit from his face.
Sirs, thocht wee speik in generall,
Let na man into speciall
   Tak our words at the warst: 1510
Quhat ever wee do, quhat ever wee say,
I pray yow tak it all in play,
   And judg ay to the best.
For silence I protest
   Baith of Lord, Laird and Ladie.
Nor I will rin but rest
   And tell that all is ready.

DISSAIT: Brother, heir ye yon proclamatioun?
I dreid full sair of reformatioun,
   Yon message make me mangit.   1520
Quhat is your counsell to me tell,
Remaine wee heir be God him-sell
   Wee will be all thre hangit.

FLATTERIE: Ile gang to Spritualitie,
And preich out-throw his dyosie,
   Quhair I will be unknawin.
Or keip me closse into sum closter,
With mony piteous *Pater Noster*,
   Till all thir blasts be blawin.
DISSAIT: Ile be weill treitit, as ye ken,   1530
With my maisters, the merchand men,
   Quhilk can mak small debait.
Ye ken richt few of them that thryfes,
Or can begyll the landwart wyfes,
   But me thair man Dissait.
Now, Falset, quhat sall be thy schift?

1506 *dejectit* thrown out   1508 *thocht* though
1520 *mangit* confused   1525 *dyosie* diocese   1527 *closse* (adj) close
1533 *thryfes* thrive   1534 *landwart* country   1536 *schift* plan

FALSET: Na cuir thow nocht, man, for my thrift.
　　Trows thou that I be daft?
　Na, I will leif ane lustie lyfe,
　Withoutin ony sturt and stryfe,　　　　　　　　　　1540
　　Amang the men of craft.

FLATTERIE: I na mair will remaine besyd yow,
　Bot counsell yow rycht weill to gyde yow:
　　Byd nocht on Correctioun.
　Fair-weil, I will na langer tarie.
　I pray the alrich Queene of Farie
　　To be your protectioun.

DISSAIT: Falset, I wald wee maid ane band.
　Now quhill the King is yit sleipand,
　　Quhat rak to steill his box?　　　　　　　　　　　1550
FALSET: Now weill said, be the Sacrament:
　I sall it steill incontinent,
　　Thocht it had twentie lox.

Heir sall Falset steill the Kings box with silence.

Lo heir the box, now let us ga,
　This may suffice for our rewairds.
DISSAIT: Yea that it may, man, be this day,
　It may weill mak of landwart lairds.
　Now let us cast away our clais,
　In dreid sum follow on the chase.
FALSET: Rycht weill devysit, man, be Sanct Blais.　　1560
　Wald God wee war out of this place!

Heir sall thay cast away thair conterfit clais.

1540 *sturt* discord　1546 *alrich* elvish

DISSAIT: Now sen thair is na man to wrang us,
  I pray yow, brother, with my hart,
  Let us ga part this pelf amang us,
  Syne haistely we sall depart.

FALSET: Trows thou to get als mekill as I?
  That sall thow nocht, I staw the box:
  Thou did nathing bot luikit by,
  Ay lurkeand lyke ane wylie fox.

DISSAIT: Thy heid sall beir ane cuppill of knox,   1570
  Pellour, without I get my part
  Swith, huirsun smaik, ryfe up the lox
  Or I sall stick the throuch the hart.

     Heir sall thay fecht with silence.

FALSET: Alace, for ever my eye is out!
  Walloway, will na man red the men?
DISSAIT: Upon thy craig tak thair ane clout,
  To be courtesse I sall the ken.
  Fair-weill, for I am at the flicht,
  I will nocht byde on ma demands:
  And wee twa meit againe this nicht,   1580
  Thy feit salbe w[i]rth fourtie hands.

    Heir sal Dissait rin away with the box throuch the
    water. [*Correction enters.*]

1564 *pelf* booty   1567 *staw* stole   1568 *luikit* watched
1571 *Pellour* thief   1572 *Swith* quickly   *smaik* fellow
ryfe break open   1573 SD *fecht* fight   1575 *red* divide, separate
1576 *craig* neck   1577 *ken* teach   1578 *flicht* flight

DIVYNE CORRECTIOUN: *Beati qui esuriunt et sitiunt*
   Justitiam.

Thir ar the words of the redoutit Roy,
The Prince of Peace above all King[i]s King,
Quhilk hes me sent all cuntries to convoye,
And all misdoars dourlie to doun thring.
I will do nocht without the conveining
Ane Parleament of the Estait[i]s all:
In thair presence I sall but feinyeing
Iniquitie under my sword doun thrall.   1590
Thair may no Prince do act[i]s honorabill,
Bot gif his counsall thairto will assist.
How may he knaw the thing maist profitabil
To follow vertew and vycis to resist
Without he be instructit and solist?
And quhen the King stands at his counsell sound,
Then welth sall wax and plentie as he list,
And policie sall in his realme abound.
Gif ony list my name for till inquyre,
I am callit Divine Correctioun.   1600
I fled throch mony uncouth land and schyre,
To the greit profit of ilk Natioun.
Now am I cum into this regioun
To teill the ground that hes bene lang unsawin,
To punische tyrants for thair transgressioun,
And to caus leill men live upon thair awin.
Na realme nor land but my support may stand,
For I gar kings live into royaltie.
To rich and puir I beir bane equall band,
That thay may live into thair awin degrie.   1610
Quhair I am nocht is no tranqu[i]llitie,
Be me tratours and tyrants ar put doun:
Quha thinks na schame of thair iniquitie
Till thay be punisched be mee, Correctioun.
Quhat is ane King? Nocht bot ane officiar,

1585 *convoye* manage, administer 1586 *dourlie* fiercely
thring throw 1587 *conveining* convening 1590 *thrall* (v) subject
1595 *solist* solicited 1604 *teill* till *unsawin* unsown

To caus his leiges live in equitie:
And under God to be ane punischer
Of trespassours against his Majestie.
Bot quhen the King dois live in tyrannie,
Breakand Justice for feare or affectioun,   1620
Then is his realme in weir and povertie,
With schamefull slaughter but correctioun.
I am ane judge richt potent and seveir,
Cum to do justice monie thowsand myle.
I am sa constant baith in peice and weir,
Na bud nor favour may my sicht oversyle.
Thair is thairfoir richt monie in this Ile
Of my repair but doubt that dois repent:
Bot verteous men I traist sall on me smyle,
And of my cumming sall be richt weill content.   1630

GUDE COUNSELL: Welcum, my Lord, welcum ten
                thousand tyms
    Till all faithfull men of this regioun:
    Welcum for till correct all falts and cryms
    Amang this cankred congregatioun.
    Louse Chastitie I mak supplicatioun;
    Put till fredome fair Ladie Veritie,
    Quha be unfaithfull folk of this natioun
    Lyis bund full fast into captivitie.
CORRECTIOUN: I mervel, Gude Counsell, how that may
                be,
    Ar ye nocht with the King familiar?   1640
GUDE COUNSELL: That I am nocht, my Lord, full wa is
                me,
    Bot lyke ane begger am halden at the bar:
    Thay play bo-keik evin as I war ane skar.
    Thair came thrie knaves in cleithing counterfeit,
    And fra the King thay gart me stand affar,
    Quhais names war Flattrie, Falset and Dissait.

1616 *leiges* subjects   1621 *weir* war   1626 *bud* bribe   *oversyle* beguile
1635 *Louse* (v) release   1643 *skar* scarecrow, fright

505

Bot quhen thay knaves hard tell of your cumming,
Thay staw away ilk ane ane sindrie gait,
And cuist fra them thair counterfit cleithing.
For thair leving full weill thay can debait: 1650
The merchandmen thay haif resavit Dissait;
As for Falset, my Lord, full weill I ken
He will be richt weill treitit air and lait
Amang the maist part of the craft[i]s men;
Flattrie hes taine the habite of ane Freir,
Thinkand to begyll Spiritualitie.

CORRECTIOUN: But doubt, my freind, and I live half ane
      yeir,
  I sall search out that great iniquitie.
  Quhair lyis yon Ladyes in captivitie?
  How now, sisters? Quha hes yow sa disgysit?   1660
VERITIE: Unfaithfull members of iniquitie
  Dispytfullie, my Lord, hes us supprysit.

CORRECTIOUN: Gang put yon Ladyis to thair libertie
  Incontinent, and break doun all the stocks:
  But doubt thay ar full deir welcum to mee.
  Mak diligence, me think ye do bot mocks.
  Speid hand, and spair nocht for to break the locks
  And tenderlie tak them up be the hand.
  Had I them heir, thay knaves suld ken my knocks
  That them opprest and baneist aff the land.   1670

     Thay tak the Ladyis furth of the stocks, and
     Veritie sall say

VERITIE: Wee thank you, sir, of your benignitie.
  Bot I beseik your majestie royall
  That ye wald pas to King Humanitie,

1648 *staw* stole   *sindrie* different   *gait* way   1649 *cuist* cast
1650 *leving* living   1653 *air* early

And fleime from him yon Ladie Sensuall,
And enter in his service Gude Counsell,
For ye will find him verie counsalabill.
CORRECTIOUN: Cum on, sisters, as ye haif said I sall,
And gar him stand with yow thrie firme and stabill.

*Correctioun passis towards the King, with Veritie,
Chastitie and Gude Counsell.*

WANTONNES: Solace, knawis thou not quhat I se?
Ane knicht or ellis ane king thinks me,   1680
With wantoun wings as he wald fle.
    Brother, quhat may this meine?
I understand nocht be this day,
Quhidder that he be freind or fay:
Stand still and heare quhat he will say,
    Sic ane I haif nocht seine.

SOLACE: Yon is ane stranger, I stand forde.
He semes to be ane lustie lord.
Be his heir-cumming for concorde,
    And be kinde till our King,   1690
He sall be welcome to this place,
And treatit with the Kingis grace.
Be it nocht sa we sall him chace
    And to the divell him ding.

PLACEBO: I reid us put upon the King,
And walkin him of his sleiping.
Sir, rise and se ane uncouth thing.
    Get up, ye ly too lang.

1674 *fleime* banish   1676 *counsalabill* full of good advice
1684 *fay* foe   1686 *seine* seen   1696 *walkin* awaken

SENSUALITIE: Put on your hude, Johne-Fule, ye raif.
How dar ye be so pert, sir knaif,   1700
To tuich the King? Sa Christ me saif,
    Fals huirsone, thow sall hang.

CORRECTIOUN: Get up, sir King, ye haif sleipit aneuch
Into the armis of Ladie Sensual.
Be suir that mair belangis to the pleuch,
As efterward perchance rehears I sall.
Remember how the King Sardanapall,
Amang fair Ladyes tuke his lust sa lang,
Sa that the maist part of his leiges al
Rebeld, and syne him duilfully doun thrang.   1710

Remember how, into the tyme of Noy
For the foull stinck and sin of lechery,
God be my wande did al the warld destroy.
Sodome and Gomore richt sa full rigorously,
For that vyld sin war brunt maist cruelly.
Thairfoir I the command incontinent,
Banische from the that huir Sensualitie,
Or els but doubt rudlie thow sall repent.

REX: Be quhom have ye sa greit authoritie?
Quha dois presume for til correct ane King?   1720
Knaw ye nocht me, greit King Humanitie,
That in my regioun royally dois ring?

CORRECTIOUN: I have power greit Princes to doun
        thring,
That lives contrair the Majestie Divyne:
Against the treuth quhilk plainlie dois maling,
Repent they nocht I put them to ruyne.

1705 *pleuch* plough 1710 *Rebeld* rebelled 1715 *brunt* burnt
1725 *maling* malign

I will begin at thee quhilk is the head
And mak on the first reformatioun:
Thy Leiges than will follow the but pleid.
Swyith harlot, hence without dilatioun.   1730

SENSUALITIE: My Lord, I mak yow supplicatioun,
Gif me licence to pas againe to Rome:
Amang the Princes of that natioun,
I lat yow wit my fresche beautie with blume.
Adew, Sir King, I may na langer tary:
I cair nocht that als gude luife cums as gais,
I recommend yow to the Queene of Farie.
I se ye will be gydit with my fais,
As for this king, I cure him nocht twa strais:
War I amang Bischops and Cardinals,   1740
I wald get gould, silver and precious clais:
Na earthlie joy but my presence avails.

Heir sall scho pas to Spiritualitie.

My Lord[i]s of the Sprituall stait,
Venus preserve yow air and lait:
For I can mak na mair debait,
    I am partit with your King;
And am baneischt this regioun,
Be counsell of Correctioun:
Be ye nocht my protectioun,
    I may seik my ludgeing.   1750

SPIRITUALITIE: Welcum, our dayis darling,
    Welcum with all our hart:
Wee all but feinyeing
Sall plainly tak your part.

1734 *blume* bloom   1736 *gais* goes   1738 *fais* foes   1739 *strais* straws
1753 *but feinyeing* without deceiving

*Heir sal the Bishops, Abbots and Persons kis the
Ladies.*

CORRECTIOUN: Sen ye ar quyte of Sensualitie,
Resave into your service Gude Counsall:
And richt sa this fair Ladie Chastitie,
Till ye mary sum Queene of blude-royall.
Observe then Chastitie matrimoniall,
Richt sa resave Veritie be the hand,   1760
Use thair counsell your fame sall never fall,
With thame thairfoir mak ane perpetuall band.

*Heir sall the King resave Gude Counsell, Veritie, and
Chastitie.*

Now, sir, tak tent quhat I will say,
Observe thir same baith nicht and day,
And let them never part yow fray.
    Or els withoutin doubt,
Turne ye to Sensualitie,
To vicious lyfe and rebaldrie,
Out of your realme richt schamefullie,
    Ye sall be ruttit out.   1770
As was Tarquine, the Romane King,
Quha was for his vicious living,
And for the schamefull ravisching
    Of the fair chaist Lucres,
He was regraidit of his croun,
And baneist aff his regioun:
I maid on him correctioun,
    As stories dois expres.

1755 *quyte* quit   1763 *tent* notice   1770 *ruttit* rooted
1775 *regraidit* degraded

REX: I am content to your counsall t'inclyne,
 Ye beand of [so] gude conditioun.   1780
 At your command sall be all that is myne,
 And heir I gif yow full commissioun,
 To punische faults and gif remissioun.
 To all vertew I salbe consociabill,
 With yow I sall confirme ane unioun,
 And at your counsall stand ay firme and stabill.

*The King imbraces Correction with a humbil
countenance.*

CORRECTIOUN: I counsall yow incontinent,
 To gar proclame ane Parliament
  Of all the Thrie Estatits.
 That thay be heir with diligence,   1790
 To mak to yow obedience,
  And syne dres all debaits.

REX: That salbe done but mair demand,
 Hoaw Diligence cum fra heir fra hand,
  And tak your informatioun:
 Gang warne the Spiritualitie,
 Rycht sa the Temporalitie,
  Be oppin proclamatioun,
 In gudlie haist for to compeir
 In thair maist honorabill maneir,   1800
  To gif us thair counsals:
 Quha that beis absent to them schaw,
 That thay sall underly the law,
  And punischt be that fails.

1780 *beand* being 1784 *consociabill* ?agreeable 1799 *compeir* appear
1802 *schaw* show

DILIGENCE: Sir, I sall baith in bruch and land,
  With diligence do your command,
    Upon my awin expens:
  Sir, I have servit yow all this yeir,
  Bot I gat never ane dinneir
    Yit for my recompence.   1810

REX: Pas on, and thou salbe regairdit,
  And for thy service weill rewairdit,
    For quhy with my consent,
  Thou sall have yeirly for thy hyre,
  The teind mussellis of the Ferrie Myre,
    Confirmit in Parliament.

DILIGENCE: I will get riches throw that rent,
  Efter the day of Dume:
  Quhen in the colpots of Tranent,
    Butter will grow on brume.   1820
  All nicht I had sa meikill drouth,
    I micht nocht sleip ane wink:
  Or I proclame ocht with my mouth,
    But doubt I man haif drink.

CORRECTIOUN: Cum heir, Placebo and Solace,
  With your companyeoun Wantonnes,
    I knaw weill your conditioun:
  For tysting King Humanitie
  To resave Sensualitie,
    Ye man suffer punitioun.   1830

WANTONNES: We grant, my lord, we have done ill,
  Thairfoir wee put us in your will.
    Bot wee haife bene abusit:

1805 *bruch* borough   1809 *dinneir* penny   1820 *brume* broom
1821 *drouth* thirst   1823 *ocht* anything   1828 *tysting* enticing

For in gude faith, sir, wee beleifit,
That lecherie had na man greifit,
  Becaus it is sa usit.

PLACEBO: Ye se how Sensualitie,
  With Principals of ilk cuntrie,
    Bene glaidlie lettin in,
  And with our Prelatis mair and les.   1840
  Speir at my Ladie Priores,
    Gif lechery be sin.

SOLACE: Sir, wee sall mend our conditioun,
  Sa ye give us remissioun,
    Bot give us live to sing:
  To dance, to play at chesse and tabils,
  To reid stories and mirrie fabils,
    For pleasure of our King.

CORRECTIOUN: Sa that ye do na uther cryme,
  Ye sall be pardonit at this tyme,   1850
    For quhy as I suppois
  Princes may sumtyme seik solace
  With mirth and lawfull mirrines,
    Thair spirits to rejoyis.
  And richt sa halking and hunting,
  Ar honest pastimes for ane King
    Into the tyme of peace:
  And leirne to rin ane heavie spear,
  That he into the tyme of wear,
    May follow at the cheace.   1860

REX: Quhair is Sapience and Discretioun?
  And quhy cums nocht Devotioun nar?

1835 *greifit* harmed   1846 *tabils* backgammon   1855 *halking* hawking
1858 *rin* thrust   1860 *cheace* hunting   1862 *nar* near

VERITIE: Sapience, sir, was ane verie loun,
And Discretioun was nathing war:
The suith, sir, gif I wald report,
Thay did begyle your Excellence,
And wald not suffer to resort
Ane of us thrie to your presence.

CHASTITIE: Thay thrie war Flattrie and Dissait,   1870
And Falset, that unhappie loun,
Against us thrie quhilk maid debait
And banischt us from town to town.
Thay gart us twa fall into sowne,
Quhen thay us lockit in the stocks:
That dastart knave, Discretioun,
Full thrifteouslie did steill your box.

REX: The Deuill tak them sen thay ar gane,
Me thocht them ay thrie verie smaiks.
I mak ane vow to Sanct Mavane,
Quhen I them finde thays bear thair paiks.   1880
I se they have playit me the glaiks.
Gude Counsall, now schaw me the best,
Quhen I fix on yow thrie my staiks,
How I sall keip my realme in rest.

GUDE COUNSALL: *Initium sapientiae est timor Domini.*
Sir, gif your hienes yearnis lang to ring,
First dread your God abuif all uther thing.
For ye ar bot ane mortall instrument,
To that great God and King Omnipotent.
Preordinat be his divine Majestie,   1890
To reull his peopill intill unitie.
The principall point, sir, of ane kings office

1865 *suith* truth 1873 *sowne* swoon 1876 *thrifteouslie* profitably
1883 *staiks* supports 1886 *yearnis* longs *ring* reign

Is for to do to everilk man justice,
And for to mix his justice with mercie
But rigour, favour or parcialitie.
Forsuith, it is na littill observance,
Great Regions to have in governance.
Quha ever taks on him that kinglie cuir,
To get ane of thir twa he suld be suir:
Great paine and labour and that continuall,   1900
Or ellis to have defame perpetuall.
Quha guydis weill they win immortall fame,
Quha the contrair, they get perpetuall schame:
Efter quhais death but dout ane thousand yeir
Thair life at lenth rehearst sall be perqueir.
The Chroniklis to knaw I yow exhort,
Thair sall ye finde baith gude and evill report:
For everie Prince efter his qualitie,
Thocht he be deid, his deids sall never die.
Sir, gif ye please for to use my counsall,   1910
Your fame and name sall be perpetuall.

Heir sall the messinger Diligence returne and cry a
Hoyʒes, a Hoyʒes, a Hoyʒes, and say

[DILIGENCE:] At the command of King Humanitie,
I wairne and charge all members of Parliament,
Baith Sprituall Stait and Temporalite,
That till his Gracè thay be obedient,
And speid them to the Court incontinent,
In gude ordour arrayit royally.
Quha beis absent or inobedient,
The Kings displeasure thay sall underly.

And als I mak yow exhortatioun,   1920
Sen ye haif heard the first pairt of our play,

1893 *everilk* every   1904 *quhais* whose   1905 *rehearst* related
perqueir by heart   1919 *underly* endure

Go tak ane drink and mak collatioun,
Ilk man drink till his marrow, I yow pray.
Tarie nocht lang, it is lait in the day.
Let sum drink ayle and sum drink claret wine:
Be great Doctors of Physick I heare say
That michtie drink comforts the dull ingine.

And ye Ladies that list to pisch,
Lift up your taill, plat in ane disch,
And gif that your mawkine cryis quhisch,   1930
    Stop in ane wusp of stray.
Let nocht your bladder burst I pray yow,
For that war evin aneuch to slay yow:
For yit thair is to cum, I say yow,
    The best pairt of our play.

The END of the first part of the Satyre.

1922 *collatioun* refreshment   1923 *marrow* companion
1927 *ingine* intelligence   1930 *mawkine* pudendum
quhisch 'whish'(onomatopoeia)   1931 *wusp* wisp

Now sall the pepill mak collatioun, then beginnis the
Interlude, the Kings, Bischops, and principall
players being out of their seats.

[*Enter Pauper, met by Diligence.*]

PAUPER, THE PURE MAN: Of your almis gude folks for
       Gods luife of heavin,
  For I have motherless bairns either sax or seavin.
  Gif ye'ill gif me na gude for the luife of Jesus,
  Wische me the richt way till Sanct Androes.
DILIGENCE: Quhair have wee gottin this gudly
       companyeoun?   1940
  Swyith out of the feild, fals raggit loun.
  God wait gif heir be ane weill keipit place,
  Quhen sic ane vilde begger carle may get entres.
  Fy on yow officiars that mends nocht thir failyies,
  I gif yow all till the deuill baith Provost and Bailyies.
  Without ye cum and chase this carle away,
  The deuill a word ye'is get mair of our play.
  Fals huirsun raggit carle, quhat deuil is that thou rugs?
PAUPER: Quha Devil maid the ane gentill man that wald
       not cut thy lugs?
DILIGENCE: Quhat now? Me thinks the carle begins to
       crack.   1950
  Swyith carle, away – or be this day Ise break thy back.

1937 *sax* six   1939 *Wische* direct   1943 *entres* entrance
1944 *failyies* failings   1948 *rugs* pulls   1949 *lugs* ears

*Heir sall the Carle clim up and sit in the Kings
tchyre.*

Cum doun, or be Gods croun, fals loun, I sall slay the.
PAUPER: Now sweir be thy brunt schinis. The Deuill ding
 them fra the.
Quhat say ye till thir court dastards? be thay get hail
 clais,
Sa sune do thay leir to sweir and trip on thair tais.
DILIGENCE: Me thocht the carle callit me knave evin in
 my face.
Be Sanct Fillane, thou salbe slane, bot gif thou ask
 grace.
Loup doun or be the gude Lord thow sall los thy heid.

PAUPER: I sal anis drink or I ga thocht thou had sworne
 my deid.

Heir Diligence castis away the ledder.

DILIGENCE: Loup now gif thou list, for thou hes lost the
 ledder. 1960
PAUPER: It is full weil thy kind to loup and licht in a
 ledder.
Thou sal be faine to fetch agane the ledder or I loup.
I sall sit heir into this tcheir till I have tumde the stoup.

Heir sall the Carle loup aff the scaffald.

1951 SD *tchyre* chair   1953 *brunt* wounded   *schinis* shins
1954 *hail* whole   1955 *leir* learn   1957 *bot gif* unless   1958 *Loup* leap
1963 *tumde* emptied   *stoup* drink

DILIGENCE: Swyith, begger bogill, haist the away.
  Thow art over pert to spill our play.
PAUPER: I will not gif for al your play worth an sowis
      fart,
  For thair is richt lytill play at my hungrie hart.
DILIGENCE: Quhat Devill ails this cruckit carle?
PAUPER: Marie,
    meikill sorrow:
  I can not get, thocht I gasp to beg nor to borrow.
DILIGENCE: Quhair, deuill, is this thou dwels, or quhats
     thy intent?   1970
PAUPER: I dwell into Lawthiane ane myle fra Tranent.
DILIGENCE: Quhair wald thou be, carle, the suth to me
     schaw?
PAUPER: Sir, evin to Sanct Androes for to seik law.
DILIGENCE: For to seik law in Edinburgh was the neirest
     way.
PAUPER: Sir, I socht law thair this monie deir day,
  Bot I culd get nane at Sessioun nor Seinye:
  Thairfoir the mekill dum Deuill droun all the meinye.
DILIGENCE: Shaw me thy mater, man, with al the
     circumstances,
  How that thou hes happinit on thir unhappie chances.
PAUPER: Gude-man will ye gif me your charitie,   1980
  And I sall declair yow the black veritie.
  My father was ane auld man and ane hoir,
  And was of age fourscoir of yeirs and moir,
  And Mald my mother was fourscoir and fyfteine,
  And with my labour I did thame baith susteine.
  Wee had ane meir that caryit salt and coill,
  And everie ilk yeir scho brocht us hame ane foill.
  Wee had thrie ky that was baith fat and fair,
  Nane tydier into the toun of Air.
  My father was sa waik of blude and bane   1990
  That he deit, quhairfoir my mother maid great maine.

1964 *bogill* goblin   1965 *spill* spoil   1968 *cruckit* deformed
1977 *meinye* company   1982 *hoir* hoary   1983 *moir* more   1986 *coill* coal
1987 *foill* foal   1989 *tydier* in better condition   1991 *maine* moan

Then scho deit within ane day or two,
And thair began my povertie and wo.
Our gude gray meir was baittand on the feild,
And our lands laird tuik hir for his hyreild.
The Vickar tuik the best cow be the head,
Incontinent quhen my father was deid.
And quhen the Vickar hard tel how that my mother
Was dead, fra-hand he tuke to him ane uther.
Then Meg my wife did murne both evin and morow   2000
Till at the last scho deit for verie sorow:
And quhen the Vickar hard tell my wyfe was dead,
The thrid cow he cleikit be the head.
Thair umest clayis that was of rapploch gray,
The Vickar gart his Clark bear them away.
Quhen all was gaine I micht mak na debeat
Bot with my bairns past for till beg my meat.
Now have I tald yow the blak veritie,
How I am brocht into this miserie.

DILIGENCE: How did the person, was he not thy gude
        freind?   2010
PAUPER: The devil stick him, he curst me for my teind
And halds me yit under that same proces
That gart me want the Sacrament at Pasche.
In gude faith, sir, thocht he wald cut my throt,
I have na geir except ane Inglis grot,
Quhilk I purpois to gif ane man of law.

DILIGENCE: Thou art the daftest fuill that ever I saw.
Trows thou, man, be the law to get remeid
Of men of kirk? Na, nocht till thou be deid.

PAUPER: Sir, be quhat law tell me quhaifoir or quhy   2020
That ane Vickar sould tak fra me thrie ky?

1994 *baittand* grazing   1995 *hyreild* tribute   2003 *cleikit* clutched
2004 *umest* uppermost   *clayis* clothes   *rapploch* coarse, undyed
2011 *teind* tithe   2013 *Pasche* Easter   2015 *geir* goods   *grot* groat

DILIGENCE: Thay have na law exceptand consuetude,
  Quhilk law to them is sufficient and gude.
PAUPER: Ane consuetude against the common weill,
  Sould be na law I think, be sweit Sanct Geill.
  Quhair will ye find that law tell gif ye can
  To tak thrie ky fra ane pure husband man?
  Ane for my father and for my wyfe ane uther,
  And the thrid cow he tuke for Mald my mother.

DILIGENCE: It is thair law all that they have in use,   2030
  Thocht it be cow, sow, ganer, gryse, or guse.

PAUPER: Sir, I wald speir at yow ane questioun:
  Behauld sum prelats of this regioun,
  Manifestlie during thair lustie lyfis,
  Thay swyfe ladies, madinis and uther mens wyfis,
  And sa thair cunts thay have in consuetude.
  Quidder say ye that law is evill or gude?
DILIGENCE: Hald thy toung man, it seims that thou war
      mangit,
  Speik thou of Preists, but doubt thou will be hangit.
PAUPER: Be him that buir the cruell croun of thorne,   2040
  I cair nocht to be hangit evin the morne.
DILIGENCE: Be sure of Preistis thou will get na support.
PAUPER: Gif that be trew the feind resave the sort.
  Sa sen I se I get na uther grace,
  I will ly doun and rest mee in this place.

Pauper lyis doun in the feild. Pardoner enters.

PARDONER: *Bona dies, Bona dies.*
  Devoit peopill, gude day I say yow.

2022 *consuetude* custom   2031 *ganer* gander   *gryse* pig   *guse* goose
2038 *mangit* stupid   2040 *buir* (v) bore   2043 *sort* group, lot

Now tarie any lytill quhyll I pray yow,
 Till I be with yow knawin:
Wait ye weill how I am namit?   2050
Ane nobill man and undefamit
 Gif all the suith war schawin.
I am Sir Robert Rome-raker,
Ane perfite publicke pardoner
 Admittit be the Paip.
Sirs, I sall schaw yow for my wage
My pardons and my pilgramage,
 Quhilk ye sall se and graip.
I give to the devill with gude intent
This unsell wickit New Testament,   2060
 With them that it translaitit:
Sen layik men knew the veritie,
Pardoners gets no charitie,
 Without that thay debait it
Amang the wives with wrinks and wyles,
As all my marrowis, men begyles,
 With our fair fals flattrie:
Yea, all the crafts I ken perqueir,
As I was teichit be ane Freir
 Callit Hypocrisie.   2070
Bot now, allace, our greit abusioun
Is cleirlie knawin till our confusioun,
 That we may sair repent:
Of all credence now am I quyte,
For ilk man halds me at dispyte,
 That reids the New Test'ment.
Duill fell the braine that hes it wrocht,
Sa fall them that the Buik hame brocht:
 Als I pray to the Rude
That Martin Luther that fals loun,   2080
Black Bullinger and Melancthoun,
 Had bene smorde in their cude.

2058 *graip* grasp   2060 *unsell* unhallowed   2062 *layik* laic, lay
2065 *wrinks* tricks   2074 *quyte* free from   2077 *fell* overcome
2082 *smorde* smothered   *cude* baptismal cloth

Be him that buir the crowne of thorne,
I wald Sanct Paull had never bene borne,
   And als I wald his buiks
War never red into the kirk,
Bot amangs freirs into the mirk,
   Or riven amang ruiks.

Heir sall he lay doun his geir upon ane buird and say

My patent pardouns ye may se,
Cum fra the Cave of Tartarie   2090
   Weill seald with oster-schellis.
Thocht ye have no contritioun,
Ye sall have full remissioun,
   With help of Buiks and bellis.
Heir is ane relict lang and braid,
Of Fine Macoull the richt chaft blaid,
   With teith and al togidder:
Of Collings cow heir is ane horne,
For eating of Makconnals corne
   Was slaine into Baquhidder.   2100
Heir is ane coird baith great and lang,
Quhilk hangit Johne the Armistrang,
   Of gude hemp soft and sound:
Gude halie peopill I stand for'd,
Quha ever beis hangit with this cord,
   Neids never to be dround.
The culum of Sanct Bryd[i]s kow,
The gruntill of Sanct Antonis sow,
   Quhilk buir his haly bell:
Quha ever he be heiris this bell clinck,   2110
Gif me ane ducat for till drink,
   He sall never gang to hell,
Without he be of Baliell borne.

2088 *riven* torn   *ruiks* rooks   2088 SD *buird* board
2096 *chaft blaid* jaw bone   2107 *culum* anus   2108 *gruntill* snout

Maisters trow ye that this be scorne?
　Cum win this pardoun, cum.
Quha luifis thair wyfis nocht with thair hart
I have power them for till part:
　Me think yow deif and dum.
Hes naine of yow curst wickit wyfis,
That halds yow into sturt and stryfis?　　　　2120
　Cum tak my dispensatioun.
Of that cummer I sall mak yow quyte,
Howbeit your selfis be in the wyte,
　And mak ane fels narratioun.
Cum win the pardoun now let se,
For meill, for malt, or for monie,
　For cok, hen, guse or gryse:
Of relicts heir I have ane hunder.
Quhy cum ye nocht? This is ane wonder.
　I trow ye be nocht wyse.　　　　2130

[*Enter Sowtar, followed by his Wife.*]

SOWTAR: Welcum hame, Robert Rome-raker,
　Our halie patent pardoner:
　　Gif ye have dispensatioun,
To pairt me and my wickit wyfe,
And me deliver from sturt and stryfe,
　I mak yow supplicatioun.

PARDONER: I sall yow pairt but mair demand,
　Sa I get mony in my hand,
　　Thairfoir let se sum cunye.

SOWTAR: I have na silver be my lyfe,　　　　2140
　Bot fyve schillings and my schaipping knyfe,
　　That sall ye have but sunye.

2120 *sturt* vexation　2123 *wyte* wrong　2128 *hunder* hundred
2139 *cunye* coin　2141 *schaipping* shaping　2142 *sunye* delay

PARDONER: Quhat kynd of woman is thy wyfe?

SOWTAR: Ane quick devill, sir, ane storme of stryfe,
　　Ane frog that fyles the winde:
　Ane fistand flag, a flagartie fuffe,
　At ilk ane pant scho lets ane puffe,
　　And hes na ho behind.
　All the lang day scho me dispyts,
　And all the nicht scho flings and flyts,　　　　　2150
　　Thus sleip I never ane wink:
　That Cockatrice, that commoun huir,
　The mekill Devill may nocht induir
　　Hir stuburnnes and stink.

SOWTARS WIFE: Theif carle, thy words I hard rycht
　　　　weill.
　In faith my freindschip ye sall feill,
　　And I the fang.

SOWTAR: Gif I said ocht, Dame, be the Rude,
　Except ye war baith fair and gude,
　　God, nor I hang.　　　　　　　　　　　2160

PARDONER: Fair dame, gif ye wald be ane wower,
　To part yow twa I have ane power.
　Tell on, ar ye content?

SOWTARS WYFE: Ye, that I am with all my hart
　Fra that fals huirsone till depart,
　　Gif this theif will consent.
　Causses to part I have anew,

2145 *fyles* defiles　2147 *ilk* each　2148 *ho* hold, control
2150 *flyts* scolds

Becaus I gat na chamber-glew,
   I tell yow verely.
I mervell nocht, sa mot I lyfe,
Howbeit that swingeour can not swyfe,
   He is baith cauld and dry.

2170

PARDONER: Quhat wil ye gif me for your part?
[SOWTARS WYFE:] Ane cuppill of sarks with all my hart,
   The best claith in the land.

PARDONER: To part sen ye ar baith content,
   I sall yow part incontinent,
     Bot ye mon do command.
My will and finall sentence is,
Ilk ane of yow uthers arsse kis:
Slip doun your hois, me thinkis the carle is glaikit,
Set thou not by howbeit scho kisse and slaik it.

2180

> *Heir sall scho kis his arsse with silence.*

Lift up his clais, kis hir hoill with your hart.
SOWTAR: I pray yow sir forbid hir for to fart.

> *Heir sall the Carle kis hir arsse with silence.*

PARDONER: Dame, pas ye to the east end of the toun,
And pas ye west evin lyke ane cuckald loun.
Go hence, ye baith, with Baliels braid blissing.
Schirs, saw ye ever mair sorrowles pairting?

> *[Exeunt Sowtar and Wife.]*
> *Heir sal the Boy cry aff the hill.*

2171 *swingeour* rogue   *swyfe* copulate   2172 *cauld* cold
2174 *sarks* shirts   2181 *glaikit* foolish   2182 *slaik* slake, quench

WILKIN: Hoaw maister, haow, quhair ar ye now?

PARDONER: I am heir, Wilkin Widdiefow.   2190

WILKIN: Sir, I have done your bidding,
   For I have fund ane great hors-bane,
   Ane fairer saw ye never nane,
      Upon Dame Fleschers midding.
   Sir, ye may gar the wyfis trow,
   It is ane bane of Sanct Bryds cow,
      Gude for the fever quartane:
   Sir, will ye reull this relict weill,
   All the wyfis will baith kis and kneill,
      Betuixt this and Dumbartane.   2200

PARDONER: Quhat say thay of me in the toun?
WILKIN: Sum sayis ye ar ane verie loun:
   Sum sayis *Legatus natus*:
   Sum sayis y'ar ane fals Saracene,
   And sum sayis ye ar for certaine
      Diabolus incarnatus.
   Bot keip yow fra subjectioun,
   Of the curst King Correctioun:
      For be ye with him fangit.
   Becaus ye ar ane Rome-raker,   2210
   And commoun publick cawsay-paker,
      But doubt ye will be hangit.

PARDONER: Quhair sall I ludge into the toun?
WILKIN: With gude kynge Christiane Anderson,
      Quhair ye will be weill treatit.
   Gif ony limmer yow demands,

2194 *midding* dung-heap   2197 *quartane* on the fourth day
2198 *relict* relic   2209 *fangit* caught   2211 *cawsay-paker* street walker
2216 *limmer* rogue

527

Scho will defend yow with hir hands,
  And womanlie debait it.
Bawburdie says, be the Trinitie,
That scho sall beir yow cumpanie,   2220
  Howbeit ye byde ane yeir.

PARDONER: Thou hes done weill, be Gods mother.
  Tak ye the taine and I the t'other,
    Sasall we mak greit cheir.

WILKIN: I reid yow speid yow heir,
  And mak na langer tarie.
  Byde ye lang thair but weir,
  I dreid your weird yow warie.

Heir sall Pauper rise and rax him.

PAUPER: Quhat thing was yon that I hard crak and cry?
  I have bene dreamand and dreveland of my ky.   2230
  With my richt hand my haill bodie I saine,
  Sanct Bryd, Sanct Bryd, send me my ky againe.
  I se standa[n]d yonder ane halie man,
  To mak me help let me se gif he can.
  Halie maister, God speid yow and gude morne.

PARDONER: Welcum to me thocht thou war at the horne.
  Cum win the pardoun and syne I sall the saine.
PAUPER: Wil that pardoun get me my ky againe?
PARDONER: Carle of thy ky I have nathing ado.
  Cum win my pardon and kis my relicts to.   2240

    2219 *Bawburdie* whore   2223 *taine* the one
    2230 *dreveland* talking nonsense   2231 *saine* make sign of the cross
    2236 *at the horne* outlawed

Heir sall he saine him with his relictis.

PARDONER: Now lows thy pursse and lay doun thy
    offrand,
  And thou sall have my pardon evin fra-hand.
  With raipis and relicts I sall the saine againe,
  Of gut or gravell thou sall never have paine.
  Now win the pardon limmer, or thou art lost.
PAUPER: My haly father, quhat wil that pardon cost?
PARDONER: Let se quhat mony thou bearest in thy bag.
PAUPER: I have ane grot heir bund into ane rag.
PARDONER: Hes thou na uther silver bot ane groat?
PAUPER: Gif I have mair, sir, cum and rype my coat.   2250
PARDONER: Gif me that grot man, gif thou hest na mair.
PAUPER: With all my heart, maister, lo tak it thair.
  Now let me se your pardon with your leif.
PARDONER: Ane thousand yeir of pardons I the geif.
PAUPER: Ane thousand yeir? I will not live sa lang.
  Delyver me it maister and let me gang.
PARDONER: Ane thousand yeir I lay upon thy head,
  With *totiens quotiens*: now mak me na mair plead,
  Thou hast resaifit thy pardon now already.
PAUPER: Bot I can se na thing, sir, be Our Lady.   2260
  Forsuith maister I trow I be not wyse,
  To pay ere I have sene my marchandryse.
  That ye have gottin my groat full sair I rew.
  Sir, quhidder is your pardon black or blew?
  Maister, sen ye have taine fra me my cunyie,
  My marchandryse schaw me, withouttin sunyie.
  Or to the Bischop I sall pas and pleinyie
  In Sanct Androis, and summond yow to the seinyie.
PARDONER: Quhat craifis the carle? Me thinks thou art
    not wise.
PAUPER: I craif my groat or ellis my marchandrise.   2270

2241 *lows* loosen   2244 *gut* gout   2250 *rype* rip   2264 *quhidder* whether
2265 *cunyie* coin   2266 *sunyie* hesitation   2267 *pleinyie* complain
2268 *seinyie* ecclesiastical court   2269 *craifis* craves

PARDONER: I gaif the pardon for ane thowsand yeir.
PAUPER: How shall I get that pardon? Let me heir.
PARDONER: Stand still and I sall tell [thee] the haill storie,
 Quhen thow art deid and gais to Purgatorie,
 Being condempit to paine a thowsand yeir,
 Then sall thy pardoun the releif but weir.
 Now be content. Ye ar ane mervelous man.
PAUPER: Sall I get nathing for my grot quhill than?
PARDONER: That sall thou not, I mak it to yow plaine.
PAUPER: Na? Than gossop, gif me my grot againe.   2280
 Quhat say ye, maisters? Call ye this gude resoun
 That he sould promeis me ane gay pardoun,
 And he resave my money in his stead,
 Syne mak me na payment till I be dead?
 Quhen I am deid I wait full sikkerlie,
 My sillie saull will pas to Purgatorie.
 Declair me this: now God nor Baliell bind the
 Quhen I am thair curst carle, quhair sall I find the?
 Not into heavin, bot rather into hell:
 Quhen thou are thair thou can not help thy sel.   2290
 Quhen will thou cum my dolours till abait?
 Or I the find my hippis will get ane hait.
 Trowis thou butchour that I will by blind lambis?
 Gif me my grot. The devill dryte in thy gambis.
PARDONER: Suyith stand abak, I trow this man be
    mangit.
 Thou gets not this carle, thocht thou suld be hangit.
PAUPER: Gif me my grot weill bund into ane clout,
 Or be Gods breid Robin sall beir ane rout.

Heir sal they fecht with silence, and Pauper sal cast
doun the buird, and cast the relicts in the water.

2273 *haill* whole 2276 *but* without *weir* doubt 2278 *quhill* until
2285 *sikkerlie* without doubt 2286 *sillie* simple, good
2292 *hait* heating 2294 *dryte* excrete *gambis* tricks 2298 *rout* blow
2298 SD *fecht* fight

DILIGENCE: Quhat kind of daffing is this al day?
Suyith smaiks out of the feild, away.
Into ane presoun put them sone,
Syne hang them quhen the play is done.

2300

[*Exeunt Pardoner and Pauper.*]

2299 *daffing* fooling   2300 *smaiks* wretches

[PART TWO]

Heir sall Diligence mak his Proclamatioun.

Famous peopill tak tent, and ye sall se
The Thrie Estaitis of this natioun
Cum to the Court with ane strange gravitie.
Thairfoir I mak yow supplicatioun:
Till ye have heard our haill narratioun
To keip silence and be patient I pray yow.
Howbeit we speik be adulatioun,
Wee sall say nathing bot the suith I say yow.   2310
Gude verteous men that luifis the veritie,
I wait thay will excuse our negligence:
Bot vicious men denude of charitie,
As feinyeit fals flattrand Saracens,
Howbeit thay cry on us ane loud vengence,
And of our pastyme make ane fals report,
Quhat may wee do bot tak in patience,
And us refer unto the faithfull sort?
Our Lord Jesus, Peter nor Paull,
Culd not compleis the peopill all,   2320
 Bot sum war miscontent:
Howbeit thay schew the veritie,
Sum said that it war heresie,
 Be thair maist fals judgement.

Heir sall the Thrie Estaitis cum fra the palyeoun,
gangand backwart led be thair vyces.

2313 *denude of* without   2314 *feinyeit* claimed, told   2320 *compleis* please
2324 SD *palyeoun* pavilion

WANTONNES: Now braid benedicite,
   Quhat thing is yon that I se?
     Luke, Solace, my hart.
SOLACE: Brother Wantonnes, quhat thinks thow?
   Yon ar the Thrie Estaitis I trow,
     Gangand backwart. 2330

WANTONNES: Backwart, backwart? Out. Wallaway.
   It is greit schame for them I say
     Backwart to gang.
   I trow the King Correctioun
   Man mak ane reformatioun,
     Or it be lang.
   Now let us go and tell the King.

     Pausa

   Sir, wee have sene ane mervelous thing,
     Be our judgement:
   The Thrie Estaitis of this regioun 2340
   Ar cummand backwart, throw this toun
     To the Parlament.

REX: Backwart, backwart, how may that be?
   Gar speid them haistelie to me,
     In dreid that thay ga wrang.

PLACEBO: Sir, I se them yonder cummand,
   Thay will be heir evin fra hand,
     Als fast as thay may gang.

   2327 *Luke* look   2344 *Gar speid them* make them hurry

GUDE COUNSELL: Sir, hald you stil and skar them nocht,
   Till ye persave quhat be thair thocht,   2350
      And se quhat men them leids.
And let the King Correctioun
Mak ane scharp inquisitioun,
      And mark them be the heids.
Quhen ye ken the occasioun,
That maks them sic persuasioun,
      Ye may expell the caus:
Syne them reforme as ye think best,
Sua that the realme may live in rest,
      According to Gods lawis.   2360

> *Heir sall the Thrie Estaitis cum and turne thair faces*
> *to the King.*

SPIRITUALITIE: Gloir, honour, laud, triumph and
          victorie
  Be to your michtie prudent excellence.
Heir ar we cum all the Estait[i]s Thrie,
Readie to mak our dew obedience,
At your command with humbill observance,
As m[a]y pertene to Spiritualitie,
With counsell of the Temporalitie.

TEMPORALITIE: Sir, we with michtie curage at command
  Of your superexcellent Majestie,
Sall mak service baith with our hart and hand,   2370
And sall not dreid in thy defence to die:
Wee ar content but doubt that wee may se
That nobill heavinlie King Correctioun,
Sa he with mercie mak punitioun.

2349 *skar* (v) scare   2351 *leids* (v) leads   2366 *pertene* pertain

MERCHAND: Sir, we ar heir your Burgessis and
        Merchands:
  Thanks be to God that we may se your face,
  Traistand wee may now into divers lands,
  Convoy our geir with support of your grace.
  For now I traist wee sall get rest and peace,
  Quhen misdoars ar with your sword overthrawin   2380
  Then may leil merchands live upon thair awin.

REX: Welcum to me my prudent Lord[i]s all,
  Ye ar my members suppois I be your head:
  Sit doun that we may with your just counsall,
  Aganis misdoars find soveraine remeid,
  Wee sall nocht spair for favour nor for feid,
  With your avice to mak punitioun,
  And put my sword to executioun.

CORRECTIOUN: My tender freinds, I pray yow with my
        hart
  Declair to me the thing that I wald speir.   2390
  Quhat is the caus that ye gang all backwart?
  The veritie thairof faine wald I heir.

SPIRITUALITIE: Soveraine, we have gaine sa this mony a
        yeir.
  Howbeit ye think we go undecently,
  Wee think wee gang richt wonder pleasantly.
DILIGENCE: Sit down my Lords into your proper places:
  Syne let the King consider all sic caces.
  Sit down, sir scribe, and sit doun dampster to,
  And fence the Court as ye war wont to do.

    *Thay ar set doun and Gude Counsell sal pas to his
    seat.*

2386 *feid* enmity   2393 *gaine* gone   2399 *fence* establish

REX: My prudent Lord[i]s of the Thrie Estaitis, 2400
   It is our will abuife all uther thing
   For to reforme all them that maks debaits,
   Contrair the richt quhilk daylie dois maling,
   And thay that dois the Common-weil doun thring.
   With help and counsell of King Correctioun,
   It is our will for to mak punisching,
   And plaine oppressours put to subjectioun.

SPIRITUALITIE: Quhat thing is this, sir, that ye have
      devysit?
   Schirs, ye have neid for till be weill advysit.
   Be nocht haistie into your executioun, 2410
   And be nocht our extreime in your punitioun.
   And gif ye please to do sir as wee say,
   Postpone this Parlament till ane uther day.
   For quhy? the peopill of this regioun
   May nocht indure extreme correctioun.

CORRECTIOUN: Is this the part, my Lords, that ye will
      tak
   To mak us supportatioun to correct?
   It dois appeir that ye ar culpabill,
   That ar nocht to Correctioun applyabill.
   Suyith, Diligence, ga schaw it is our will, 2420
   That everilk man opprest geif in his bill.
DILIGENCE: All maneir of men I wairne that be opprest,
   Cum and complaine and thay salbe redrest.
   For quhy it is the nobill Princes will,
   That ilk compleiner sall gif in his bill.

[*Enter John the Commonwealth.*]

2401 *abuife* above   2403 *maling* malign   2404 *thring* throw
2411 *our* over   2421 *bill* account

536

JOHNE THE COMMON-WEILL: Out of my gait, for Gods
        saik let me ga:
Tell me againe, gude maister, quhat ye say.
DILIGENCE: I warne al that be wrangouslie offendit,
Cum and complaine and thay sall be amendit.
JOHN: Thankit be Christ that buir the croun of thorne   2430
For I was never sa blyth sen I was borne.
DILIGENCE: Quhat is thy name, fallow? That wald I feil.
JOHN: Forsuith thay call me Johne the Common-weil.
Gude maister, I wald speir at you ane thing:
Quhair traist ye I sall find yon new cumde King?
DILIGENCE: Cum over, and I sall schaw the to his grace.
JOHNE: Gods bennesone licht on that luckie face.
Stand by the gait, let se gif I can loup:
I man rin fast in cace I get ane coup.

Heir sall Johne loup the stank or els fall in it.

DILIGENCE: Speid the away, thou taryis all to lang.   2440
JOHNE: Now be this day I may na faster gang.
JOHNE *to the King*: Gude day, gud day, grit God saif baith
        your graces,
Wallie, wallie fall thay twa weill fairde faces.
REX: Shaw me thy name, gude man, I the command.
JOHNE: Marie Johne the Common-weil of fair Scotland.
REX: The Common-weil hes bene amang his fais.
JOHNE: Ye, sir. That gars the Common-weil want clais.
REX: Quhat is the caus the Common-weil is crukit?
JOHNE: Becaus the Common-weill hes bene overlukit.
REX: Quhat gars the luke sa with ane dreirie hart?   2450
JOHNE: Becaus the Thrie Estaits gangs all backwart.
REX: Sir Common-weill, knaw ye the limmers that them
        leids?

2428 *wrangouslie* wrongfully   2432 *feil* know   2437 *bennesone* blessing
2438 *loup* leap   2439 *coup* tumble   2439 SD *stank* ditch
2443 *Wallie* good luck   2448 *crukit* lame   2449 *overlukit* neglected

JOHNE: Thair canker cullours I ken them be the heads:
  As for our reverent fathers of Spiritualitie,
  Thay ar led be Covetice and cairles Sensualitie.
  And as ye se Temporalitie hes neid of correctioun,
  Quhilk hes lang tyme bene led be publick oppressioun:
  Loe quhair the lóun lyis lurkand at his back.
  Get up! I think to se thy craig gar ane raip crack.
  Loe heir is Falset and Dissait weill I ken,   2460
  Leiders of the merchants and sillie crafts-men.
  Quhat mervell thocht the Thrie Estaits backwart gang,
  Quhen sic an vyle cumpanie dwels them amang,
  Quhilk hes reulit this rout monie deir dayis,
  Quhilk gars John the Common-weill want his warme
    clais?
  Sir, call them befoir yow and put them in ordour,
  Or els John the Common-weil man beg on the bordour.
  Thou feinyeit Flattrie, the feind fart in thy face:
  Quhen ye was guyder of the Court we gat litill grace
  Ryse up Falset and Dissait without ony sunye,   2470
  I pray God nor the devils dame dryte on thy grunye.
  Behauld as the loun lukis evin lyke a thief:
  Monie wicht warkman thou brocht to mischief.
  My soveraine Lord Correctioun, I mak yow
    supplication,
  Put thir tryit truikers from Christis congregation.

CORRECTIOUN: As ye have devysit but doubt it salbe
    done.
  Cum heir, my Sergeants, and do your debt sone.
  Put thir thrie pellours into pressoun strang,
  Howbeit ye sould hang them ye do them na wrang.

FIRST SERGEANT: Soveranę Lords, wee sall obey your
    commands: 2480

2453 *canker* corrupt   *cullours* specious arguments   2459 *craig* neck
2468 *feinyeit* (adj) dissembling   2470 *sunye* delay   2471 *grunye* snout
2473 *wicht* brave   2475 *tryit* convicted   *truikers* thieves

Brother, upon thir limmers lay on thy hands!
Ryse up sone loun! Thou luiks evin lyke ane lurden:
Your mouth war meit to drink an wesche jurden.

SECUND SERGEANT: Cum heir, gossop, cum heir, cum
    heir.
Your rackles lyfe ye sall repent:
Quhen was ye wont to be sa sweir?
Stand still and be obedient.

FIRST SERGEANT: Thair is nocht in all this toun –
Bot I wald nocht this taill war tald –
Bot I wald hang him for his goun,   2490
Quhidder that it war Laird or laid.
I trow this pellour be spur-gaid.
Put in thy hand into this cord.
Howbeit I se thy skap skyre skaid,
Thou art ane stewat I stand foird.

Heir sall the Vycis be led to the stocks.

SECUND SERGEANT: Put in your leggis into the stocks,
For ye had never ane meiter hois.
Thir stewats stinks as thay war broks.
Now ar ye sikker I suppois.

Pausa.

My Lords, wee have done your commands.   2500
Sall wee put Covetice in captivitie?

2483 *meit* fitting   *wesche jurden* full chamber pot   2486 *sweir* unwilling
2491 *Quhidder* whether   *laid* ploughboy   2492 *spur-gaid* galled by spurs
2495 *stewat* stinkard   *foird* for it   2497 *meiter* better   *hois* hose
2498 *broks* badgers

CORRECTION: Ye, hardlie lay on them your hands,
  Rycht sa upon Sensualitie.
SPIRITUALITIE: Thir is my Grainter and my
        Chalmerlaine,
  And hes my gould and geir under hir cuiris.
  I mak ane vow to God I sall complaine
  Unto the Paip how ye do me injuris.
COVETICE: My reverent fathers, tak in patience,
  I sall nocht lang remaine from your presence.
  Thocht for ane quhyll I man from yow depairt,   2510
  I wait my spreit sall remaine in your hart,
  And quhen this King Correctioun beis absent,
  Then sall we twa returne incontinent.
  Thairfoir adew ...
SPIRITUALITIE: Adew, be Sanct Mavene.
  Pas quhair ye will, we ar twa naturall men.
SENSUALITIE: Adew my Lord ...
SPIRITUALITIE: Adew, my awin sweit
    hart.
  Now duill fell me that wee twa man depart.
SENSUALITIE: My Lord, howbeit this parting dois me
    paine,
  I traist in God we sal meit sone agane.
SPIRITUALITIE: To cum againe I pray yow do your
    cure: 2520
  Want I yow twa I may nocht lang indure.

*Heir sal the Sergeants chase them away, and thay
sal gang to the seat of Sensualitie.*

TEMPORALITIE: My Lords, ye knaw the Thrie Estaits
  For Common-weill suld mak debaits.
  Let now amang us be devysit
  Sic actis that with gude men be praysit,
  Conforming to the common law,

2504 *Grainter* granary steward   2511 *spreit* spirit   2515 *naturall* kindred

For of na man we sould stand aw.
And for till saif us fra murmell,
Schone Diligence, fetch us Gude Counsell,
For quhy he is ane man that knawis   2530
Baith the Cannon and Civil lawis.
DILIGENCE: Father, ye man incontinent
Passe to the Lords of Parliament,
For quhy thay ar determinat all,
To do na thing by your counsall.
GUDE COUNSAL: That sal I do within schort space,
Praying the Lord to send us grace,
For till conclude or wee depart,
That they may profeit efterwart.
Baith to the Kirk and to the King,   2540
I sall desyre na uther thing.

Pausa.

My Lords, God glaid the cumpanie.
Quhat is the caus ye send for me?
MERCHAND: Sit doun and gif us your counsell,
How we sall slaik the greit murmell
Of pure peopill that is weill knawin,
And as the Common-weill hes schawin.
And als wee knaw it is the Kings will,
That gude remeid be put thairtill.
Sir Common-weill, keip ye the bar: 2550
Let nane except your-self cum nar.

JOHNE: That sall I do as I best can:
I sall hauld out baith wyfe and man.
Ye man let this puir creature
Support me for till keip the dure.

2528 *murmell* unrest   2539 *efterwart* afterwards   2542 *glaid* make glad
2545 *slaik* ease   2551 *nar* near   2555 *dure* door

I knaw his name full sickerly,
He will complaine als weill as I.

GUDE COUNSALL: My worthy Lords, sen ye have taine
       on hand
Sum reformatioun to mak into this land,
And als ye knaw it is the King[i]s mynd,   2560
Quha till the Common-weil hes ay bene kynd,
Thocht reif and thift wer stanchit weill aneuch,
Yit sumthing mair belangis to the pleuch.
Now into peace ye sould provyde for weirs,
And be sure of how mony thowsand speirs,
The King may be quhen he hes ocht ado,
For quhy, my Lords, this is my ressoun lo.
The husband-men and commons thay war wont,
Go in the battell formest in the front.
Bot I have tint all my experience,   2570
Without ye mak sum better diligence:
The Common-weill mon uther wayis be styllit,
Or be my faith the King wilbe begyllit.
Thir pure commouns daylie as ye may se,
Declynis doun till extreme povertie:
For sum ar hichtit sa into thair maill,
Thair winning will nocht find them water kaill.
How Prelats heichts thair teinds it is well knawin,
That husband-men may not weill hald thair awin,
And now begins ane plague amang them new,   2580
That gentill men thair steadings taks in few.
Thus man may pay great ferme or lay thair steid,
And sum ar plainlie harlit out be the heid,
And ar distroyit without God on them rew.

PAUPER: Sir, be Gods breid that taill is verie trew.

2564 *weirs* wars   2570 *tint* lost   2572 *styllit* honoured
2578 *heichts* raise   *teinds* tithes   2581 *steadings* farm buildings
few tribute   2582 *ferme* rent   *lay* ?lose   *steid* farm

It is weill kend I had baith nolt and hors,
Now all my geir ye se upon my cors.

CORRECTION: Or I depairt I think to mak ane ordour.
JOHNE: I pray yow, sir, begin first at [the] bordour.
    For how can we fend us aganis Ingland,   2590
    Quhen we can nocht within our native land,
    Destroy our awin Scots common traitor theifis,
    Quha to leill laborers daylie dois mischeifis?
    War I ane king, my Lord, be God[i]s wounds,
    Quha ever held common theifis within thair bounds –
    Quhairthrow that dayly leilmen micht be wrangit –
    Without remeid thair chiftanis suld be hangit,
    Quhidder he war ane knicht, ane Lord or Laird,
    The Devill draw me to hell and he war spaird.

TEMPORALITIE: Quhat uther enemies hes thou let us
      ken?   2600
JOHNE: Sir, I compleine upon the idill men,
    For quhy, sir, it is Gods awin bidding,
    All Christian men to wirk for thair living.
    Sanct Paull, that pillar of the Kirk,
    Sayis to the wretchis that will not wirk,
    And bene to vertews [labour] laith,
    Qui non laborat non manducet.
    This is in Inglische toung or leit,
    'Quha labouris nocht he sall not eit'.
    This bene against the strang beggers,   2610
    Fidlers, pypers, and pardoners,
    Thir jugglars, jestars, and idill cuitchours,
    Thir carriers and thir quintacensours,
    Thir babil-beirers and thir bairds,
    Thir sweir swyngeours with Lords and Lairds

2586 *nolt* cattle   2596 *Quhairthrow* so that   *leilmen* loyal men
2606 *laith* unwilling   2608 *leit* language   2612 *cuitchours* gamblers
2613 *carriers* jugglers   2614 *babil-beirers* fools   *bairds* bards
2615 *sweir* lazy   *swyngeours* scoundrels

Ma then thair rent[i]s may susteine,
Or to thair profeit neidfull bene,
Quhillk bene ay blythest of discords,
And deidly feid amang thar Lords.
For then they sleutchers man be treatit,　　　　2620
Or els thair querrels undebaitit.
This bene against thir great fat Freiris,
Augustenes, Carmeleits and Cordeleirs,
And all uthers that in cowls bene cled,
Quhilk labours nocht and bene weill fed.
I mein nocht laborand Spirituallie,
Nor for thair living corporallie,
Lyand in dennis lyke idill doggis,
I them compair to weil fed hoggis.
I think they do them selfis abuse,　　　　2630
Seing that thay the warld refuse:
Haifing profest sic povertie,
Syne fleis fast fra necessitie.
Quhat gif thay povertie wald professe,
And do as did Diogenes,
That great famous philosophour,
Seing in earth bot vaine labour,
Alutterlie the warld refusit
And in ane tumbe himself inclusit,
And leifit on herbs and water cauld　　　　2640
Of corporall fude na mair he wald?
He trottit nocht from toun to toun
Beggand to feid his carioun.
Fra tyme that lyfe he did profes
The wa[r]ld of him was cummerles.
Rycht sa of Marie Magdalene,
And of Mary th'Egyptiane,
And of auld Paull the first hermeit:
All thir had povertie compleit.
Ane hundreth ma I micht declair,　　　　2650

2619 *feid* feud　　　2621 *undebaitit* not contended　　　2628 *dennis* dens
2638 *Alutterlie* utterly　　　2640 *leifit* lived　　　2645 *cummerles* untroubled
2650 *ma* more

Bot to my purpois I will fair,
Concluding sleuthfull idilnes,
Against the Common-weill expresse.

CORRECTIOUN: Quhom upon ma will ye compleine?

JOHNE: Marie, on ma and ma againe.
For the pure peopill cryis with cairis,
The infetching of Justice airis:
Exercit mair for covetice,
Then for the punisching of vyce.
Ane peggrell theif that steillis ane kow   2660
Is hangit: bot he that steillis ane bow,
With als meikill geir as he may turs,
That theif is hangit be the purs.
Sic pykand peggrall theifis ar hangit,
Bot he that all the warld hes wrangit,
Ane cruell tyrane, ane strang transgressour,
Ane common publick plaine oppressour,
By buds may he obteine favours
Of tresurers and compositours.
Thocht he serve greit punitioun,   2670
Gets easie compositioun:
And throch laws consistoriall
Prolixt, corrupt and perpetuall,
The common peopill ar put sa under,
Thocht thay be puir it is na wonder.

CORRECTIOUN: Gude Johne I grant all that is trew,
Your infortoun full sair I rew.
Or I pairt aff this natioun,
I sall mak reformatioun.
And als, my Lord Temporalitie,   2680
I yow command in tyme that ye
Expell oppressioun aff your lands.
And als I say to yow merchands,
Gif ever I find be land or sie,

2660 *peggrell* paltry   2661 *bow* farm   2662 *turs* carry
2664 *pykand* thieving   2668 *buds* bribes   2669 *compositours* grafters
2672 *consistoriall* diocesan   2677 *infortoun* misfortune   *sair* sorely
2684 *sie* sea

Dissait be in your cumpanie,
Quhilk ar to Common-weill contrair,
I vow to God I sall not spair
To put my sword to executioun,
And mak on yow extreme punitioun.
Mairover, my Lord Spiritualitie, 2690
In gudlie haist I will that ye
Set into few your temporall lands
To men that labours with thair hands,
Bot nocht to ane gearking gentill man,
That nether will he wirk, nor can,
Quhair throch the policy may incresse.

TEMPORALITIE: I am content, sir, be the messe,
Swa that the Spiritualitie
Sets thairs in few als weill as wee.

CORRECTIOUN: My Spirituall Lords ar ye content? 2700
SPIRITUALITIE: Na, na, wee man tak advysement.
In sic maters for to conclude
Ouir haistelie, we think nocht gude.
CORRECTIOUN: Conclude ye nocht with the
Common-weil
Ye salbe punischit be Sanct Geill.

Heir sall the Bischops cum with the Freir.

SPIRITUALITIE: Schir, we can schaw exemptioun
Fra your temporall punitioun,
The quhilk wee purpois till debait.

CORRECTIOUN: Wa than, ye think to stryve for stait.
My Lords, quhat say ye to this play? 2710

2692 *few* freehold   2694 *gearking* foppish   2709 *stait* supremacy

546

TEMPORALITIE: My soveraine Lord, we will obay,
    And tak your part with hart and hand,
    Quhat ever ye pleis us to command.

*Heir sal the Temporal Stait sit doun on thair kneis
and say*

Bot wee beseik yow, Soveraine,
Of all our cryms that ar bygaine
To gif us ane remissioun,
And heir wee mak to yow conditioun,
The Common-weill for till defend,
From hence-forth till our lives end.

CORRECTIOUN: On that conditioun I am content   2720
    Till pardon yow sen ye repent;
    The Common-weill tak be the hand
    And mak with him perpetuall band.

*Heir sall the Temporal Staits, to wit, the Lords and
Merchands imbreasse Johne the Common-weill.*

Johne, have ye ony ma debaits
Against the Lords of Spirituall Staits?
JOHNE: Na, sir, I dar nocht speik ane word:
    To plaint on Preistis it is na bourd.

CORRECTIOUN: Flyt on thy fow fill I desyre the,
    Swa that thou schaw bot the veritie.

2715 *bygaine* gone by   2724 *debaits* contention   2727 *bourd* joke
2728 *Flyt* complain   *fow* full

JOHNE: Grandmerces, then I sall nocht spair, 2730
　First to compleine on the Vickair.
　The pure Cottar being lyke to die,
　Haifand young infants, twa or thrie
　And hes twa ky but ony ma,
　The Vickar most haif ane of thay,
　With the gray frugge that covers the bed,
　Howbeit the wyfe be purelie cled.
　And gif the wyfe die on the morne,
　Thocht all the bairns sould be forlorne,
　The uther kow he cleiks away 2740
　With the pure cot of raploch gray.
　Wald God this custome war put doun,
　Quhilk never was foundit be ressoun.

TEMPORALITIE: Ar all thay tails trew that thou telles?

PAUPER: Trew sir, the Divill stick me elles.
　For be the halie Trinitie,
　That same was practeisit on me.
　For our Vickar, God give him pyne,
　Hes yit thrie tydie kye of myne:
　Ane for my father, and for my wyfe ane uther, 2750
　And the thrid cow he tuke for Mald my mother.
JOHNE: Our Persone heir he takis na uther pyne,
　Bot to ressave his teinds and spend them syne.
　Howbeit he be obleist be gude ressoun,
　To preich the Evangell to his parochoun.
　Howbeit thay suld want preiching sevintin yeir,
　Our Persoun will not want ane scheif of beir.

PAUPER: Our bishops with thair lustie rokats quhyte,
　Thay flow in riches royallie and delyte:

2730 *spair* spare　2736 *frugge* coverlet　2740 *cleiks* seizes
2741 *cot* coat　*raploch* coarse woollen cloth　2749 *tydie* fat
2754 *obleist* obliged　2755 *parochoun* parish　2757 *scheif* tithe
beir barley　2758 *rokats* rochets

Lyke Paradice bene thair palices and places,   2760
And wants na pleasour of the fairest faces.
Als thir Prelates hes great prerogatyves,
For quhy thay may depairt ay with thair wyves,
Without ony correctioun or damnage,
Syne tak ane uther wantoner but mariage.
But doubt I wald think it ane pleasant lyfe,
Ay on quhen I list to part with my wyfe,
Syne tak ane uther of far greiter bewtie.
Bot ever alace, my Lords, that may not be,
For I am bund alace in mariage;   2770
Bot thay lyke rams rudlie in thair rage,
Unpysalt rinnis amang the sillie yowis,
Sa lang as kynde of nature in them growis.

PERSON: Thou lies, fals huirsun raggit loun:
Thair is na Preists in all this toun,
That ever usit sic vicious crafts.

JOHNE: The feind ressave thay flattrand chafts:
Sir Dominie, I trowit ye had be dum.
Quhair Devil gat we this ill fairde blaitie bum?
PERSON: To speik of Preists be sure it is na bourds: 2780
Thay will burne men now for rakles words,
And all thay words ar herisie in deid.

JOHNE: The mekil feind resave the saul that leid.
All that I say is trew thocht thou be greifit,
And that I offer on they pallet to preif it.

SPIRITUALITIE: My Lords, quhy do ye thoil that lurdun
      loun
Of Kirk-men to speik sic detractioun?

2764 *damnage* fine   2772 *Unpysalt* unpizzled   *sillie* simple   *yowis* ewes
2777 *chafts* jaws   2779 *ill fairde* ill favoured   *blaitie bum* lazy fellow
2780 *bourds* joke   2781 *rakles* careless   2782 *thay* those
2783 *leid* lied   2784 *greifit* grieved   2785 *pallet* head   2786 *thoil* suffer

I let yow wit, my Lords, it is na bourds,
Of Prelats for till speik sic wantoun words.

Heir Spritualitie fames and rages.

Yon villaine puttis me out of charitie.   2790

TEMPORALITIE: Quhy, my Lord, sayis he ocht bot
       verity?
Ye can nocht stop ane pure man for till pleinye,
Gif he hes faltit, summond him to your Seinye.

SPIRITUALITIE: Yea, that I sall: I sall mak greit God a
       vow
He sall repent that he spak of the kow.
I will not suffer sic words of yon villaine.

PAUPER: Than gar gif me my thrie fat ky againe.

SPIRITUALITIE: Fals carle, to speik to me stands thou not
       aw?

PAUPER: The feind resave them that first devysit that
       law.
Within an houre efter my dade was deid   2800
The Vickar had my kow hard be the heid.

PERSON: Fals huirsun carle, I say that law is gude,
Becaus it hes bene lang our consuetude.

2789 SD *fames* foams (at the mouth) 2792 *pleinye* complain
2793 *faltit* lied *Seinye* Session 2803 *consuetude* custom

550

PAUPER: Quhen I am Paip that law I sal put doun:
   It is ane sair law for the pure commoun.
SPIRITUÁLITIE: I mak an vow thay words thou sal
        repent.
GUDE COUNSALL: I yow requyre, my Lords, be patient.
   Wee came nocht heir for disputatiouns:
   Wee came to make gude reformatiouns.
   Heirfoir of this your propositioun,   2810
   Conclude and put to executioun.

MERCHAND: My Lords, conclud that al the temporal lands
   Be set in few to laboreris with thair hands,
   With sic restrictiouns as sall be devysit,
   That thay may live and nocht to be supprysit
   With ane ressonabill augmentatioun:
   And quhen thay heir ane proclamatioun,
   That the Kings grace dois mak him for the weir,
   That thay be reddie with harneis, bow and speir.
   As for myself, my Lord, this I conclude.   2820

GUDE COUNSALL: Sa say we all your ressoun be sa gude.
   To mak an Act on this we ar content.

JOHNE: On that, sir Scribe, I tak an instrument.
   Quhat do ye of the corspresent and kow?

GUDE COUNSALL: I wil conclude nathing of that as now
   Without my Lord of Spiritualitie
   Thairto consent with all this haill cleargie.
   My Lord Bischop, will ye thairto consent?

2815 *supprysit* surprised   2816 *augmentatioun* increase of dignity
2824 *corspresent* funeral gift to officiating priest

SPIRITUALITIE: Na, na, never till the day of Judgement.
   Wee will want nathing that wee have in use,   2830
   Kirtil, nor kow, teind lambe, teind gryse nor guse.

TEMPORALITIE: Forsuith, my Lord, I think we suld
        conclude,
   Seing this kow ye have in consuetude.
   Wee will decerne heir that the King[i]s grace
   Sall wryte unto the Paipis holines:
   With his consent be proclamatioun,
   Baith corspresent and cow we sall cry doun.

SPIRITUALITIE: To that, my Lords, wee plainlie
        disassent:
   Noter, thairof I tak ane instrument.

TEMPORALITIE: My Lord, be him that al the warld hes
        wrocht,   2840
   Wee set nocht by quhider ye consent or nocht:
   Ye ar bot ane Estait and we ar twa,
   Et ubi maior pars ibi tota.

JOHNE: My Lords, ye haif richt prudentlie concludit.
   Tak tent now how the land is clein denudit
   Of gould and silver quhilk daylie gais to Rome,
   For buds, mair then the rest of Christindome.
   War I ane King, sir, be coks passioun,
   I sould gar mak ane proclamatioun,
   That never ane penny sould go to Rome at all,   2850
   Na mair then did to Peter nor to Paull
   Do ye nocht sa, heir for conclusioun
   I gif yow all my braid black malesoun.

2831 *Kirtil* gown   *gryse* pig   2834 *decerne* (v) decree
2839 *Noter* notary   2853 *malesoun* curse

MERCHANT: It is of treuth, sirs, be my Christindome,
　　That mekil of our money gais to Rome.
　　For we merchants, I wait, within our bounds,
　　Hes furneist Preists ten hundreth thowsand punds
　　For thair finnance; nane knawis sa weill as wee.
　　Thairfoir, my Lords, devyse sum remedie.
　　For throw thir playis and thir promotioun,　　　　　2860
　　Mair for denners nor for devotioun,
　　Sir Symonie hes maid with them ane band,
　　The gould of weicht thay leid out of the land.
　　The Common-weil thair throch bein[g] sair opprest:
　　Thairfoir devyse remeid as ye think best.

GUDE COUNSALL: It is schort tyme sen ony benefice
　　Was sped in Rome except greit Bischopries.
　　Bot now for ane unworthie Vickarage,
　　Ane Preist will rin to Rome in pilgrimage.
　　Ane cavell, quhilk was never at the scule,　　　　　2870
　　Will rin to Rome and keip ane Bischops mule,
　　And syne cum hame with mony colorit crack,
　　With ane buirdin of benefices on his back:
　　Quhilk bene against the law, ane man alane
　　For till posses ma benefices nor ane.
　　Thir greit commends I say withoutin faill
　　Sould nocht be given bot to the blude royall.
　　Sa I conclude, my Lords, and sayis for me,
　　Ye sould annull all this pluralitie.

SPIRITUALITIE: The Paip hes given us dispensatiouns.　　2880

GUDE COUNSALL: Yea, that is be your fals narratiouns.
　　Thocht the Paip for your pleasour will dispence,

2860 *playis* pleas　2861 *denners* coins, money
2863 *weicht* weight　*leid* take　2870 *cavell* low fellow　*scule* school
2872 *colorit* elaborate　*crack* (n) boast　2873 *buirdin* burden

I trow that can nocht cleir your conscience.
Advyse, my Lords, quhat ye think to conclude.

TEMPORALITIE: Sir, be my faith, I think it verie gude,
   That fra hence furth na Preistis sall pas to Rome,
   Becaus our substance thay do still consume.
   For pleyis and for thair profeit singulair,
   Thay haif of money maid this realme bair.
   And als I think it best be my advyse,   2890
   That ilk Preist sall haif bot ane benefice.
   And gif thay keip nocht that fundatioun,
   It sall be caus of deprivatioun.

MERCHANT: As ye haif said, my Lord, we wil consent:
   Scribe, mak an act on this incontinent.

GUDE COUNSALL: My Lords, thair is ane thing yit
        unproponit,
   How Prelats and Preistis aucht to be disponit.
   This beand done we have the les ado.
   Quhat say ye, sirs? This is my counsall, lo,
   That or wee end this present Parliament,   2900
   Of this mater to tak rype advysement.
   Mark weill, my Lords, thair is na benefice
   Given to ane man bot for ane gude office.
   Quha taks office and syne thay can nocht us it,
   Giver and taker I say ar baith abusit.
   Ane Bischops office is for to be ane preichour,
   And of the law of God ane publick teachour.
   Rycht sa the Persone unto his parochoun,
   Of the Evangell sould leir them ane lessoun.
   Thair sould na man desyre sic dignities,   2910
   Without he be abill for that office.

2896 *unproponit* undiscussed   2897 *disponit* dealt with
2901 *rype* considered   2904 *us* use

And for that caus I say without leising,
Thay have thair teinds and for na uther thing.

SPIRITUALITIE: Freind, quhair find ye that we suld
      prechours be?
GUDE COUNSALL: Luik quhat Sanct Paul wryts unto
      Timothie
 Tak thair the Buik: let se gif ye can spell.
SPIRITUALITIE: I never red that, thairfoir reid it your sel.

   Counsall sall read thir wordis on ane Buik:
     Fidelis sermo, si quis Episcopatum desiderat, bonum
     opus desiderat. Oportet [ergo] eum irreprehensibilem
     esse, unius uxoris virum, sobrium, prudentem,   2920
     ornatum, pudicum, hospitalem, doctorem: non
     vinolentum, non percussorem: sed modestum.
  That is – This is a true saying, If any man desire the office of
  a Bishop, he desireth a worthie worke: a Bishop therefore
  must be unreproveable, the husband of one wife, &c.

SPIRITUALITIE: Ye temporall men, be him that heryit
      hell,
 Ye are ovir peart with sik maters to mell.

TEMPORALITIE: Sit still, my Lord, ye neid not for till
      braull,
 Thir ar the verie words of th'Apostill Paull.

SPIRITUALITIE: Sum sayis be him that woare the croun
      of thorne,   2930
 It had been gude that Paull had neir bene borne.

   2912 *leising* telling lies   2916 *spell* read
   2927 *peart* presumptuous   *mell* be concerned

GUDE COUNSALL: Bot ye may knaw, my Lord, Sanct
        Pauls intent:
  Schir, red ye never the New Testament?

SPIRITUALITIE: Na sir, be him that our Lord Jesus
        sauld,
  I red never the New Testament nor Auld.
  Nor ever thinks to do sir be the Rude,
  I heir freiris say that reiding dois na gude.
GUDE COUNSALL: Till yow to reid them I think it is na
        lack,
  For anis I saw them baith bund on your back:
  That samin day that ye was consecrat.   2940
  Sir, quhat meinis that?
SPIRITUALITIE: The feind stick them that wat.
MERCHANT: Then befoir God how can ye be excusit
  To haif ane office and waits not how to us it?
  Quhairfoir war gifin yow all the temporal lands,
  And all thir teinds ye haif amang your hands?
  Thay war givin yow for uther causses, I weine,
  Nor mummil Matins and hald your clayis cleine.
  Ye say to the Appostils that ye succeid,
  Bot ye schaw nocht that into word nor deid.
  The law is plaine: our teinds suld furnisch teichours.   2950

GUDE COUNSALL: Yea, that it sould, or susteine prudent
        preichours.
PAUPER: Sir, God nor I be stickit with ane knyfe,
  Gif ever our Persoun preichit in all his lyfe.

PERSONE: Quhat devil raks the of our preiching undocht?
PAUPER: Think ye that ye suld have the teinds for nocht?
PERSONE: Trowis thou to get remeid, carle, of that thing?

2941 *wat* know   2947 *mummil* mumble   2954 *undocht* ignoramus

PAUPER: Yea, be Gods breid, richt sone war I ane King.
PERSONE: Wald thou of Prelats mak deprivatioun?

PAUPER: Na, I suld gar them keip thair fundatioun,
    Quhat devill is this? Quhom of sould Kings stand aw   2960
    To do the thing that they sould be the law?
    War I ane King, be coks deir passioun,
    I sould richt sone mak reformatioun,
    Failyeand thairof your grace sould richt sone finde,
    That Preists sall leid yow lyke ane bellie blinde.

JOHNE: Quhat gif King David war leivand in thir dayis
    The quhilk did found sa mony gay Abayis?
    Or out of Heavin quhat gif he luikit doun,
    And saw the great abominatioun,
    Amang thir Abesses and thir Nunries,   2970
    Thair publick huirdomes and thair harlotries?
    He wald repent he narrowit sa his bounds,
    Of yeirlie rent thriescoir of thowsand pounds.
    His successours maks litill ruisse I ges,
    Of his devotioun or of his holiness.

ABBASSE: How dar thou, carle, presume for to declair,
    Or for to mell the with sa heich a mater?
    For in Scotland thair did yit never ring,
    I let the wit, and mair excellent King.
    Of holines he was the verie plant,   2980
    And now in heavin he is ane michtfull Sanct,
    Becaus that fyftein Abbasies he did found,
    Quhair-throw great riches hes ay done abound
    Into our Kirk and daylie yit abunds.
    Bot kings now I trow few Abbasies founds.
    I dar weill say thou art condempnit in hel,

2964 *Failyeand* failing   2974 *ruisse* praise   2981 *michtfull* mighty

That dois presume with sic maters to mell.
Fals huirsun carle, thou art ovir arrogant
To iudge the deids of sic ane halie Sanct.

JOHNE: King James the First Roy of this regioun   2990
Said that he was ane sair Sanct to the croun.
I heir men say that he was sumthing blind,
That gave away mair nor he left behind.
His successours that halines did repent,
Quhilk gart them do great inconvenient.

ABBAS: My Lord Bishop, I mervel how that ye
Suffer this carle for to speik heresie!
For be my faith, my Lord, will ye tak tent,
He servis for to be brunt incontinent.
Ye can nocht say bot it is heresie,   3000
To speik against our law and libertie.

SPIRITUALITIE: *Sancte Pater*, I mak yow supplicatioun:
Exame yon carle syne mak his dilatioun.
I mak ane vow to God omnipotent,
That bystour salbe brunt incontinent.
[FLATTERIE:] Venerabill father, I sall do your command:
Gif he servis deid I sall sune understand.

Pausa.

Fals huirsun carle, schaw furth thy faith.
JOHNE: Me think ye speik as ye war wraith.
To yow I will nathing declair,   3010
For ye ar nocht my ordinair.

2999 *servis* deserves   *brunt* burnt   3003 *Exame* examine
dilatioun amplification   3005 *bystour* boaster

FLATTERIE: Quhom in trowis thou, fals monster mangit?
JOHNE: I trow to God to se the hangit.
  War I ane King, be coks passioun,
  I sould gar mak ane congregatioun,
  Of all the freirs of the four ordours,
  And mak yow vagers on the bordours.
  Schir, will ye give me audience,
  And I sall schaw your excellence,
  Sa that your grace will give me leife   3020
  How into God that I beleife.

CORRECTIOUN: Schaw furth your faith and feinye nocht.

JOHNE: I beliefe in God that all hes wrocht,
  And creat everie thing of nocht;
  And in his Son our Lord Iesu,
  Incarnat of the Virgin trew,
  Quha under Pilat tholit passioun
  And deit for our Salvatioun;
  And on the thrid day rais againe,
  As halie scriptour schawis plane.   3030
  And als, my Lord, it is weill kend,
  How he did to the heavin ascend,
  And set him doun at the richt hand,
  Of God the Father I understand;
  And sall cum judge on Dumisday –
  Quhat will ye mair, sir, that I say?
CORRECTIOUN: Schaw furth the rest: this is na game.

JOHNE: I trow *Sanctam Ecclesiam,*
  Bot nocht in thir Bischops nor thir Freirs,
  Quhilk will for purging of thir neirs,   3040

3012 *mangit* confused, mad   3017 *vagers* vagrants
3022 *feinye* dissemble   3028 *deit* died   3031 *kend* known
3036 *mair* more   3040 *neirs* kidneys

Sard up the ta raw and doun the uther:
The mekill Devill resave the fidder.

CORRECTIOUN: Say quhat ye will, sirs, be Sanct Tan,
Me think Johne ane gude Christian man.

TEMPORALITIE: My Lords, let be your disputatioun.
Conclude with firm deliberatioun
How Prelats fra thyne sall be deponit.

MERCHAND: I think for me evin as ye first proponit,
That the Kings grace sall gif na benefice,
Bot till ane preichour that can use that office.   3050
The sillie sauls that bene Christis scheip
Sould nocht be givin to gormand wolfis to keip.
Quhat bene the caus of all the heresies,
Bot the abusioun of the prelacies?
Thay will correct and will nocht be correctit,
Thinkand to na prince thay wil be subiectit.
Quhairfoir I can find na better remeid,
Bot that thir kings man take it in thair heid,
That thair be given to na man bischopries,
Except thay preich out-throch thair diosies,   3060
And ilk persone preich in his parochon:
And this I say for finall conclusion.

TEMPORALITIE: Wee think your counsall is verie gude,
As ye have said wee all conclude.
Of this conclusioun, Noter, wee mak ane act.

SCRYBE: I wryte all day bot gets never ane plack.

3041 *Sard* copulate   *ta raw* one row   3066 *plack* coin worth 4d.

PAUPER: Och, my Lords for the Halie Trinitie,
Remember to reforme the consistorie.
It hes mair neid of reformatioun
Nor Ploutois court, sir, be coks passioun. 3070

PERSONE: Quhat caus hes thou fals pellour for to
pleinye?
Quhair was ye ever summond to thair seinye?

PAUPER: Marie, I lent my gossop my mear to fetch hame
coills
And he hir drounit into the querrell hollis.
And I ran to the Consistorie for to pleinye,
And thair I happinit amang ane greidie meinye.
Thay gave me first ane thing thay all *citandum*,
Within aucht dayis I gat bot *lybellandum*,
Within ane moneth I gat *ad opponendum*,
In half ane yeir I gat *interloquendum*, 3080
And syne I gat, how call ye it? *ad replicandum*:
Bot I could never ane word yit understand him.
And than thay gart me cast out many plackis,
And gart me pay for four and twentie actis.
Bot or thay came half gait to *concludendum*,
The feind ane plack was left for to defend him.
Thus thay postponit me twa yeir with thair traine,
Syne *hodie ad octo* bad me cum againe;
And than thir ruiks thay roupit wonder fast,
For sentence silver thay cryit at the last. 3090
Of *pronunciandum* thay maid me wonder faine,
Bot I gat never my gude gray meir againe.

TEMPORALITIE: My Lords, we mon reforme thir
consistory lawis,
Quhais great defame above the heavins blawis.

3073 *mear* mare *coills* coals 3074 *querrell hollis* quarry holes
3076 *greidie* greedy 3078 *aucht* eight 3087 *traine* trickery
3089 *ruiks* rooks *roupit* croaked

I wist ane man in persewing ane kow,
Or he had done he spendit half ane bow.
Sa that the kings honour wee may avance,
Wee will conclude, as they have done in France,
Let Sprituall maters pas to Spritualitie,
And Temporall maters to Temporalitie.   3100
Quha failyeis of this sall cost them of thair gude;
Scribe, mak ane act for sa wee will conclude.

SPIRITUALITIE: That act, my Lords, plainlie I will
      declair:
It is againis our profeit singulair.
Wee will nocht want our profeit, be Sanct Geill.

TEMPORALITIE: Your profeit is against the
      Common-weil.
It salbe done by Lords as ye have wrocht:
We cure nocht quhidder ye consent or nocht.
Quhairfoir servis then all thir Temporall Judges?
Gif temporall maters sould seik at yow refuges.   3110
My Lord, ye say that ye ar Sprituall,
Quhairfoir mell ye than with things temporall?
As we have done conclude sa sall it stand,
Scribe, put our Acts in ordour evin fra hand.
SPRITUALITIE: Till all your Acts plainlie I disassent,
Notar, thairof I tak ane instrument.

*Heir sall Veritie and Chastitie mak thair plaint at
the bar.*

VERITIE: My Soverane, I beseik your excellence
Use Justuce on Spritualitie.
The quhilk to us hes done great violence,

3096 *bow* herd

Becaus we did rehers the veritie.   3120
Thay put us close into captivitie,
And sa remanit into subjectioun:
Into great langour and calamitie,
Till we ar fred be King Correctioun.

CHASTITIE: My Lord, I haif great caus for to complaine,
I could get na ludging intill this land:
The Spirituall Stait had me sa at disdaine,
With Dame Sensuall thay have maid sic ane band,
Amang them all na freindschip, sirs, I fand,
And quhen I came the nobill [nunnis] amang,   3130
My lustie Lady Priores fra hand:
Out of dortour durlie scho me dang.

VERITIE: With the advyse, sir, of the Parliament,
Hairtlie we mak yow supplicatioun:
Cause King Correctioun tak incontinent
Of all this sort examinatioun.
Gif thay be digne of deprivatioun,
Ye have power for to correct sic cases:
Chease the maist cunning Clerks of this natioun,
And put mair prudent pastours in thair places.   3140
My prudent Lords, I say that pure craftsmen,
Abufe sum Prelats ar mair for to commend:
Gar exame them and sa ye sall sune ken,
How thay in vertew Bischops dois transcend.

SCRIBE: Thy life and craft mak to thir King[i]s kend,
Quhat craft hes thow, declair that to me plaine.

TAILYEOUR: Ane tailyour, sir, that can baith mak and
      mend:
I wait nane better into Dumbartane.

3123 *langour* distress   3128 *band* agreement   3132 *dortour* dormitory
durlie fiercely   *dang* drove   3139 *Chease* choose

563

SCRIBE: Quhairfoir of tailyeours beir[i]s thou the styl?

TAILYEOUR: Becaus I wait is nane within ane myll,　　3150
　　Can better use that craft as I suppois:
　　For I can mak baith doublit coat and hois.

SCRIBE: How cal thay you, sir, with the schaiping knife?

SOWTAR: Ane sowtar sir, nane better into Fyfe.

SCRIBE: Tel me quhairfoir ane sowtar ye ar namit?

SOWTAR: Of that surname I neid nocht be aschamit,
　　For I can mak schone brotekins and buittis.
　　Gif me the coppie of the King[i]s cuittis,
　　And ye sall se richt sune quhat I can do:
　　Heir is my lasts and weill wrocht ledder to.　　3160
GUDE COUNSALL: O Lord my God, this is an mervelous
　　　　　thing
　　How sic misordour in this realme sould ring.
　　Sowtars and tailyeours thay ar far mair expert
　　In thair pure craft and in thair handie art,
　　Nor ar our Prelatis in thair vocatioun:
　　I pray yow, sirs, mak reformatioun.

VERITIE: Alace, alace, quhat gars thir temporal Kings
　　Into the Kirk of Christ admit sic doings?
　　My Lords, for lufe of Christ[i]s passioun,
　　Of thir ignorants mak deprivatioun,　　3170

3149 *styl* appearance　3150 *myll* mile　3154 *sowtar* cobbler
3157 *brotekins* high boots　*buittis* boots　3158 *cuittis* ankles
3160 *ledder* leather

Quhilk in the court can do bot flatter and fleich,
And put into thair places that can preich.
Send furth and seik sum devoit cunning Clarks,
That can steir up the peopill to gude warks.

CORRECTIOUN: As ye have done, Madame, I am content
Hoaw Diligence pas hynd incontinent,
And seik out-throw all towns and cities:
And visie all the universities.
Bring us sum Doctours of Divinitie,
With licents in the law and theologie,   3180
With the maist cunning Clarks in all this land.
Speid sune your way, and bring them heir fra hand.

DILIGENCE: Quhat gif I find sum halie provinciall?
Or minister of the gray freiris all?
Or ony freir that can preich prudentlie,
Sall I bring them with me in cumpanie?
CORRECTIOUN: Cair thou nocht quhat estait sa ever he
        be,
Sa thay can teich and preich the veritie.
Maist cunning Clarks with us is best beluifit,
To dignitie thay salbe first promuifit.   3190
Quhidder thay be Munk, Channon, Preist or Freir,
Sa thay can preich faill nocht to bring them heir.

DILIGENCE: Than fair-weill, sir, for I am at the flicht.
I pray the Lord to send yow all gude nicht.

Heir sall Diligence pas to the Palyeoun.

3171 *fleich* cajole   3176 *hynd* hence   3178 *visie* visit
3180 *licents* licentiates to preach   3183 *provinciall* religious leader
3189 *beluifit* beloved   3190 *promuifit* promoted
3191 *Quhidder* whether

TEMPORALITIE: Sir, we beseik your soverane celsitude
Of our dochtours to have compassioun,
Quhom wee may na way marie be the Rude,
Without wee mak sum alienatioun
Of our land for thair supportatioun.
For quhy? the markit raisit bene sa hie   3200
That Prelats dochtours of this natioun,
Ar maryit with sic superfluitie.
Thay will nocht spair to gif twa thowsand pound,
With thair docthtours to ane nobill man:
In riches sa thay do superabound.
Bot we may nocht do sa, be Sanct Allane,
Thir proud Prelats our dochters sair may ban,
That thay remaine at hame sa lang unmaryit:
Schir, let your Barrouns do the best thay can,
Sum of our dochtours, I dreid, salbe miscaryit.   3210

CORRECTIOUN: My Lord your complaint is richt
        ressonabill,
And richt sa to our dochtours profitabill:
I think or I pas aff this natioun,
Of this mater till mak reformatioun.

Heir sall enter Common Thift.

THIFT: Ga by the gait man, let me gang.
How Devill came I into this thrang?
With sorrow I may sing my sang,
    And I be taine.
For I have run baith nicht and day,
Throw speid of fut I gat away,   3220
Gif I be kend heir, wallaway,
    I will be slaine.

3195 *celsitude* majesty   3196 *dochtours* daughters

PAUPER: Quhat is thy name, man, be thy thrift?
THIFT: Huirsun, thay call me Common Thift:
　For quhy I had na uther schift,
　　Sen I was borne.
In Eusdaill was my dwelling place,
Mony ane wyfe gart I cry alace;
At my hand thay gat never grace,
　　Bot any forlorne.　　　　　　　　　　　　　　3230
Sum sayis ane king is cum amang us,
That purpois to head and hang us:
Thai is na grace gif he may fang us
　　Bot on an pin.
Ring he, we theifis will get na gude,
I pray God and the Halie Rude,
He had bene smoird into his cude,
　　And all his kin.
Get this curst King me in his grippis,
My craig will wit quat weyis my hippis:　　　　3240
The Devill I gif his toung and lippis,
　　That of me tellis.
Adew, I dar na langer tarie,
For be I kend thay will me carie,
And put me in ane fierie farie,
　　I se nocht ellis.
I raife. Be him that herryit hell,
I had almaist forget my sell:
Will na gude fallow to me tell,
　　Quhair I may finde　　　　　　　　　　　　3250
The Earle of Rothus best haiknay,
That was my earand heir away:
He is richt starck as I heir say
　　And swift as winde.
Heir is my brydill and my spurris,
To gar him lance ovir land and furris:

3230 *forlorne* lost　3232 *head* behead　3233 *fang* catch
3237 *smoird* smothered　*cude* baptismal cloth　3245 *fierie* great
farie confusion　3247 *raife* rave　3251 *haiknay* hackney (horse)
3253 *starck* strong　3256 *furris* furrows

Micht I him get to Ewis-durris,
   I tak na cuir.
Of that hors micht I get ane sicht,
I haife na doubt yit or midnicht,   3260
That he and I sould tak the flicht
   Throch Dysert Mure.
Of cumpanarie tell me, brother,
Quhilk is the richt way to the Strother:
I wald be welcum to my mother,
   Gif I micht speid.
I wald gif baith my coat and bonet
To get my Lord Lindesayis broun Jonet:
War he beyond the watter of Annet,
   We sould nocht dreid.   3270

[*Enter Oppression.*]

Quhat now Oppressioun my maister deir!
Quhat mekill Devill hes brocht yow heir?
Maister, tell me the caus perqueir,
   Quhat is that ye have done.

OPPRESSIOUN: Forsuith, the Kings maiestie
Hes set me heir as ye may se:
Micht I speik Temporalitie,
   He wald me releife sone.
I beseik yow, my brother deir,
Bot halfe ane houre for to sit heir: 3280
Ye knaw that I was never sweir
   Yow to defend.
Put in your leg into my place,
And heir I sweir, be God[i]s grace,
Yow to releife within schort space,
   Syne let yow wend.

3263 *cumpanarie* good fellowship   2368 *Jonet* jennet (small horse)
3281 *sweir* unwilling

THIFT: Than maister deir, gif me your hand,
    And mak to me ane faithfull band,
    That ye sall cum agane fra hand
      Withoutin faill.   3290

OPPRESSIOUN: Tak thair my hand richt faithfullie
    Als I promit the verelie,
    To gif to the ane cuppill of kye
      In Liddisdaill.

      *Heir sall Common Thift put his feit in the stokkis
      and Oppressioun sall steill away and betra him.*

[OPPRESSIOUN: Bruder, tak patience in thy pane
    Ffor I sweir the, be Sanct Fillane,
    We twa sall nevir meit agane
      In land nor toun.
THIFT: Maister, will ye not keip conditioun,
    And put me forth of this suspitioun?   3300

OPPRESSIOUN: Na, nevir quhill I get remissioun.
    A-dew to my companyeoun:
    I sall commend the to my dame.
THIFT: Adew than, in the divillis name,
    For to be fals thinkis thow na schame,
      To leif me in this pane?
    Thow art ane loun, and that ane liddir.
OPPRESSIOUN: Bo, man. I will go to Baquihiddir.
    It sall be Pasche, be Goddis moder
      Or evir we meit agane.]   3310
    Haif I nocht maid ane honest schift,
    That hes betrasit Common Thift?

    3307 *liddir* lazy   3309 *Pasche* Easter

For thair is nocht under the lift
 Ane curster cors:
I am richt sure that he and I
Within this hal[f] yeir craftely
Hes stolen ane thowsand scheip and ky,
 By meiris and hors.
Wald God I war baith sound and haill,
Now liftit into Liddisdaill: 3320
The Mers sould find me beif and kaill,
 Quhat rak of bread:
War I thair liftit with my lyfe,
The Devil sould stick me with ane knyfe
And ever I come againe to Fyfe
 Quhill I war dead.
Adew, I leife the Devill amang yow,
That in his fingers he may fang yow,
With all leill men that dois belang yow.
 For I may rew   3330
That ever I came into this land,
For quhy ye may weill understand,
I gat na geir to turne my hand:
 Yit anis adew.

[Exit Oppression.]
Heir sall Diligence convoy the thrie Clarks.

DILIGENCE: Sir, I have brocht unto your Excellence,
 Thir famous Clarks of greit intelligence:
 For to the common peopill thay can preich,
 And in the Scuilis in Latine toung can teich.
 This is ane Doctour of Divinitie,
 And thir twa Licents men of gravitie.   3340
 I heare men say their conversatioun
 Is maist in divine contemplatioun.

3314 *curster* more vicious   3318 *meiris* mares   3327 *leife* leave
3334 SD *convoy* bring

DOCTOUR: Grace, peace and rest from the hie Trinitie
    Mot rest amang this godlie cumpanie:
    Heir ar we cumde as your obedients,
    For to fulfil your iust commandements.
    Quhat evir it please your Grace us to command,
    Sir, it sall be obeyit evin fra-hand.
REX: Gud freinds, ye ar richt welcome to us all:
    Sit down all thrie and geif us your counsall.   3350
CORRECTIOUN: Sir, I give yow baith counsal and
           command,
    In your office use exercitioun:
    First that ye gar search out throch all your land,
    Quha can nocht put to executioun
    Thair office efter the institutioun
    Of godlie lawis conforme to thair vocatioun:
    Put in thair places men of gude conditioun,
    And this ye do without dilatioun.
    Ye ar the head, sir, of this congregatioun,
    Preordinat be God Omnipotent,   3360
    Quhilk hes me send to mak yow supportatioun,
    Into the quhilk I salbe diligent.
    And quha-saever beis inobedient,
    And will nocht suffer for to be correctit,
    Thay salbe all deposit incontinent,
    And from your presence they sall be deiectit.
GUDE COUNSALL: Begin first at the Spritualtie,
    And tak of them examinatioun,
    Gif they can use their divyne dewetie.
    And als I mak yow supplicatioun,   3370
    All thay that hes thair offices misusit,
    Of them make haistie deprivatioun:
    Sa that the peopill be na mair abusit.
CORRECTIOUN: Ye ar ane Prince of Spritualitie.
    How have ye usit your office, now let se?

SPIRITUALITIE: My Lords, quhen was thair ony Prelats
        wont

3352 *exercitioun* vigorous effort   3358 *dilatioun* delay

Of thair office till ony king mak count?
Bot of my office gif ye wald have the feill,
I let yow wit I have usit it weill.
For I tak in my count twyse in the yeir,   3380
Wanting nocht of my teind ane boll of beir.
I gat gude payment of my temporall lands,
My buttock-maill, my coattis and my offrands,
With all that dois perteine my benefice:
Consider now, my Lord, gif I be wyse.
I dar nocht marie contrair the common law,
Ane thing thair is my Lord that ye may knaw.
Howbeit I dar nocht plainlie spouse ane wyfe,
Yit concubeins I have had four or fyfe.
And to my sons I have givin rich rewairds,   3390
And all my dochters maryit upon lairds.
I let yow wit my Lord I am na fuill,
For quhy I ryde upon ane amland muill.
Thair is na Temporall Lord in all this land,
That maks sic cheir I let yow understand.
And als, my Lord, I gif with gude intentioun,
To divers Temporall Lords ane yeirlie pensioun
To that intent that thay with all thair hart,
In richt and wrang sal plainlie tak my part.
Now have I tauld yow, sir, on my best ways,   3400
How that I have exercit my office.

CORRECTIOUN: I weind your office had bene for til
       preich,
And Gods law to the peopill teich:
Quhairfoir weir ye that mytour ye me tell?

SPIRITUALITIE: I wat nocht, man, be him that herryit
       hel.

3378 *feill* experience   3381 *boll* measure   *beir* barley
3383 *buttock-maill* fine for fornication   *coattis* tax for proving will
offrands offerings   3393 *amland* ambling   *muill* mule
3404 *mytour* mitre

CORRECTIOUN: That dois betakin that ye with gude
      intent,
  Sould teich and preich the Auld and New Testament.

SPIRITUALITIE: I have ane freir to preiche into my
      place:
  Of my office ye heare na mair quhill Pasche.

CHASTITIE: My Lords, this Abbot and this Priores   3410
  Thay scorne thair gods: this is my reason quhy
  Thay beare an habite of feinyeit halines,
  And in thair deid thay do the contrary:
  For to live chaist thay vow solemnitly,
  Bot fra that thay be sikker of thair bowis
  Thay live in huirdome and in harlotry.
  Examine them, sir, how thay observe thair vowis.

CORRECTIOUN: Sir Scribe, ye sall at Chastities requeist
  Pas and exame yon thrie in gudlie haist.

SCRIBE: Father Abbot, this counsall bids me speir   3420
  How ye have usit your Abbay thay wald heir.
  And als thir Kings hes givin to me commissioun
  Of your office for to mak inquisitioun.
ABBOT: Tuiching my office, I say to yow plainlie,
  My monks and I, we leif richt easelie:
  Thair is na monks from Carrick to Carraill,
  That fairs better and drinks mair helsum aill.
  My Prior is ane man of great devotioun:
  Thairfoir daylie he gets ane double portioun.
SCRIBE: My Lords, how have ye keipit your thrie vows?   3430
ABBOT: Indeid richt weill till I gat hame my bows.

    3409 *quhill* until   3412 *feinyeit* pretended   3415 *sikker* safe
    bowis papal bulls   3427 *helsum* wholesome

In my Abbay quhen I was sure professour,
Then did I leife as did my predecessour.
My paramours is baith als fat and fair,
As ony wench into the toun of Air.
I send my sons to Pareis to the scullis,
I traist in God that thay salbe na fuillis.
And all my douchters I have weill providit,
Now judge ye gif my office be weill gydit.

SCRIBE: Maister Person, schaw us gif ye can preich.   3440

PERSONE: Thocht I preich not I can play at the caiche.
I wait thair is nocht ane amang yow all,
Mair ferilie can play at the fut-ball;
And for the carts, the tabils and the dyse,
Above all persouns I may beir the pryse.
Our round bonats we mak them now four-nuickit,
Of richt fyne stuiff, gif yow list cum and luik it.
Of my office I have declarit to the:
Speir quhat ye pleis, ye get na mair of me.

SCRIBE: Quhat say ye now, my Ladie Priores?   3450
How have ye usit your office can ye ges?
Quhat was the caus ye refusit herbrie
To this young lustie Ladie Chastitie?

PRIORES: I wald have harborit hir with gude intent,
Bot my complexioun thairto wald not assent:
I do my office efter auld use and wount,
To your Parliament I will mak na mair count.

VERITIE: Now caus sum of your cunning Clarks
Quhilk ar expert in heavinlie warks,
And men fulfillit with charitie   3460
That can weill preiche the veritie,
And gif to sum of them command
Ane sermon for to make fra-hand.

CORRECTIOUN: As ye have said I am content
To gar sum preich incontinent.

3432 *professour* one who has taken vows   3443 *ferilie* nimbly
3444 *carts* cards   *tabils* backgammon   3446 *four-nuickit* four cornered
3452 *herbrie* shelter

Pausa.

Magister Noster, I ken how ye can teiche,
Into the scuillis and that richt ornatlie:
I pray yow now that ye wald please to preiche,
In Inglisch toung land folk to edifie.
DOCTOUR: Soverane, I sall obey yow humbillie,   3470
With ane schort sermon presentlie in this place:
And schaw the word of God unfeinyeitlie,
And sinceirlie as God will give me grace.

Heir sall the Doctour pas to the pulpit and say
Si vis ad vitam ingredi, serva mandata.
Devoit peopill, Sanct Paull the preichour sayis
The fervent luife and fatherlie pitie,
Quhilk God almichtie hes schawin mony wayis
To man in his corrupt fragilitie,
Exceids all luife in earth, sa far that we
May never to God mak recompence conding: 3480
As quha sa lists to reid the veritie,
In Halie Scripture he may find this thing.
Sic Deus dilexit mundum.
Tuiching nathing the great prerogative,
Quhilk God to man in his creatioun lent:
How man of nocht creat superlative
Was to the image of God omnipotent.
Let us consider that speciall luife ingent,
God had to man quhen our foir-father fell,
Drawing us all in his loynis immanent,   3490
Captive from gloir in thirlage to the hel.
Quhen Angels fell thair miserabil ruyne

3467 *ornatlie* ornately   3472 *unfeinyeitlie* without deception
3480 *conding* condign   3488 *ingent* immense   3490 *loynis* loins
immanent indwelling   3491 *thirlage* bondage

Was never restorit: bot for our miserie,
The Son of God, secund persone divyne,
In ane pure Virgin tuke humanitie.
Syne for our saik great harmis suffered he
In fasting, walking, in preiching, cauld and heit,
And at the last ane schamefull death deit he,
Betwix twa theifis on croce he yeild the spreit.
And quhair an drop of his maist precious blude   3500
Was recompence sufficient and conding,
Ane thowsand warlds to ransoun from that wod
Infernall feind, Sathan, notwithstanding
He luifit us sa that for our ransoning,
He sched furth all the blude of his bodie,
Riven, rent and sair wondit quhair he did hing,
Naild on the croce on the Mont Calvery.
Et copiosa apud eum redemptio.
O cruell death, be the the venemous
Dragon, the Devill infernall lost his pray: 3510
Be the the stinkand mirk contageous,
Deip pit of hell mankynd escaipit fray:
Be the the port of Paradice alsway
Was patent maid unto the heavin sa hie:
Opinnit to man and maid ane reddie way,
To gloir eternall with th'Haly Trinitie.
And yit for all this luife incomparabill,
God askis na rewaird fra us againe
Bot luife for luife. In his command, but fabill,
Conteinit ar all haill the lawis ten: 3520
Baith ald and new and commandements ilk ane.
Luife bene the ledder quhilk hes bot steppis twa,
Be quhilk we may clim up to lyfe againe,
Out of this vaill of miserie and wa.
Diliges Dominum Deum tuum ex toto corde tuo, et
proximum tuum sicut teipsum: in his duobus mandatis, &c.
The first step suithlie of this ledder is
To luife thy God as the fontaine and well

3502 *wod* mad   3513 *port* gate   *alsway* forever   3514 *patent* open
3515 *Opinnit* opened   3522 *bene* well

Of luife and grace: and the secund I wis,
To luife thy nichtbour as thou luifis thy sell.   3530
Quha tynis ane stop of thir twa gais to hel,
Bot he repent and turne to Christe anone.
Hauld this na fabill, the halie Evangell
Bears in effect thir word[i]s everie one.
Si vis ad vitam ingredi, serva mandata Dei.
Thay tyne thir steps all thay quha ever did sin
In pryde, invy, in ire and lecherie,
In covetice, or ony extreme win,
Into sweirnes, or into gluttonie;
Or quha dois nocht the deid[i]s of mercie,   3540
Gif hungrie meit and gif the naikit clayis.

PERSONE: Now walloway! Thinks thou na schame to lie?
I trow the Devill a word is trew thou sayis.
Thou sayis thair is bot twa steppis to the heavin,
Quha failyeis them man backwarts fall in hell:
I wait it is ten thowsand mylis and sevin,
Gif it be na mair I do it upon thy sell.
Schort-leggit men I se be Bryd[i]s bell,
Will nevir cum thair, thay steppis bene sa wyde.
Gif thay be the words of the Evangell,   3550
The Sprituall men hes mister of ane gyde.

ABBOT: And I beleif that cruikit men and blinde
Sall never get up upon sa hich ane ledder.
By my gude faith I dreid to ly behinde,
Without God draw me up into ane tedder.
Quhat and I fal, than I will break my bledder.
And I cum thair this day the Devill speid me,
Except God make me lichter nor ane fedder,
Or send me doun gude widcok wingis to flie.

3530 *nichtbour* neighbour   3531 *tynis* loses   *stop* step
3538 *win* (n) profit   3539 *sweirnes* sloth   3545 *failyeis* fails
3551 *mister* need   3555 *tedder* rope   3556 *bledder* bladder

PERSONE: Cum doun, dastart, and gang sell draiff,   3560
I understand nocht quhat thow said.
Thy words war nather corne nor caiff,
I walde thy toung againe war laide.
Quhair thow sayis pryde is deidlie sin,
I say pryde is bot honestie:
And covetice of warldlie win
Is bot wisdome, I say for me:
Ire, hardines and gluttonie
Is nathing ellis but lyfis fude:
The naturall sin of lecherie   3570
Is bot trew luife: all thir ar gude.

DOCTOR: God and the Kirk hes givin command
That all gude Christian men refuse them.

PERSONE: Bot war thay sin I understand
We men of Kirk wald never use them.
DOCTOUR: Brother, I pray the Trinitie
Your faith and charitie to support,
Causand yow knaw the veritie,
That ye your subjects may comfort.
To your prayers peopill I recommend   3580
The rewlars of this nobill regioun:
That our Lord God his grace mot to them send,
On trespassours to mak punitioun.
Prayand to God from feinds yow defend,
And of your sins to gif yow full remissioun:
I say na mair – to God I yow commend.

> *Heir Diligence spyis the Freir roundand to the*
> *Prelate.*

3560 *draiff* draff, hogwash   3562 *caiff* chaff
3586 SD *roundand* whispering

DILIGENCE: My lords, I persave that the Sprituall Stait
  Be way of deid purpois to mak debait:
  For be the counsall of yon flattrand freir,
  Thay purpois to mak all this toun on steir.   3590

FIRST LICENT: Traist ye that thay wilbe inobedient
  To that quhilk is decreitit in Parliament?

DILIGENCE: Thay se the Paip with awfull ordinance
  Makis weir against the michtie King of France:
  Richt sa thay think that prelats suld nocht sunyie
  Be way of deid defend thair patrimonie.

FIRST LICENT: I pray the, brother, gar me understand
  Quhair ever Christ possessit ane fut of land.

DILIGENCE: Yea, that he did, father, withoutin fail,
  For Christ Jesus was King of Israell.   3600

FIRST LICENT: I grant that Christ was King abufe al
        kings,
  Bot he mellit never with temporall things:
  As he hes plainlie done declair him sell,
  As thou may reid in his Halie Evangell:
  Birds hes thair nests, and tod[i]s hes thair den,
  Bot Christ Jesus, the Saviour of men,
  In all this warld hes nocht ane penny braid,
  Quhair on he may repois his heavinlie head.

DILIGENCE: And is that trew?

FIRST LICENT: Yes, brother, be Alhallows:
  Christ Jesus had na propertie bot the gallows,   3610
  And left not quhen he yeildit up the Spreit
  To by himself ane simpill winding-scheit.

DILIGENCE: Christs successours I understand
  Thinks na schame to have temporall land.
  Father, thay have na will I yow assure,
  In this warld to be indigent and pure.
  Bot, sir, sen ye ar callit sapient,
  Declair to me the caus with trew intent
  Quhy that my lustie Ladie Veritie

3587 *persave* perceive   3592 *decreitit* decreed   3595 *sunyie* (v) hesitate
3602 *mellit* concerned himself with   3605 *todis* foxes
3607 *braid* in breadth

Hes nocht bene weill treatit in this cuntrie? 3620
BATCHELER: Forsuith, quhair Prelats uses the counsall
  Of beggand freirs in monie regioun,
  And thay Prelats with Princes principall,
  The veritie but doubt is trampit doun,
  And Common-weill put to confusioun.
  Gif this be trew to yow I me report:
  Thairfoir my lords mak reformatioun,
  Or ye depart, hairtlie I yow exhort.
  Sirs, freirs wald never I yow assure
  That ony Prelats usit preiching: 3630
  And Prelats tuke on them that cure,
  Freirs wald get nathing for thair fleiching.
  Thairfoir I counsall yow fra hand,
  Banische yon freir out of this land,
    And that incontinent.
  Do ye nocht sa withoutin weir,
  He will mak all this toun on steir,
    I knaw his fals intent.
  Yon Priores withoutin fabill,
  I think scho is nocht profitabill 3640
    For Christis regioun.
  To begin reformatioun,
  Mak of them deprivatioun,
    This is my opinioun.

FIRST SERGEANT: Sir, pleis ye that we twa invaid them,
  And ye sall se us sone degraid them
    Of cowll and chaplarie.
CORRECTIOUN: Pas on. I am richt weill content.
  Syne banische them incontinent
    Out of this cuntrie. 3650
FIRST SERGEANT: Cum on, sir freir, and be nocht fleyit,
  The King our maister mon be obeyit,

3622 *monie* many   3632 *fleiching* flattering   3636 *weir* doubt
3645 *invaid* despoil   3646 *degraid* strip   3647 *chaplarie* scapulary
3651 *fleyit* frightened

Bot ye sall have na harme.
Gif ye wald travell fra toun to toun,
I think this hude and heavie goun
    Will hald your wambe ovir warme.
FLATTERIE FREIR: Now quhat is this that thir monster
        meins?
I am exemptit fra Kings and Queens,
    And fra all humane law.
SECUND SERGEANT: Tak ye the hude and I the gown.   3660
This limmer luiks als lyke ane lown,
    As any that ever I saw.

FIRST SERGEANT: Thir freirs to chaip punitioun
Haulds them at their exemptioun,
    And na man will obey:
Thay ar exempt I yow assure
Baith fra Paip, Kyng and Empreour,
    And that maks all the pley.

SECUND SERGEANT: On Duimsday, quhen Christ sall say
    Venite benedicti,   3670
The Freirs will say without delay
    Nos sumus exempti.

Heir sall thay spuilye Flattrie of the Freirs habite.

GUDE COUNSALL: Sir, be the Halie Trinitie,
This same is feinyeit Flattrie,
    I ken him be his face.
Beleivand for to get promotioun,
He said that his name was Devotioun,
    And sa begylit your gracce.

3656 *wambe* stomach   3663 *chaip* escape   3672 SD *spuilye* strip
3674 *feinyeit* deceiving

FIRST SERGEANT: Cum on, my Ladie Priores,
    We sall leir yow to dance,   3680
And that within ane lytill space,
    Ane new pavin of France.

      Heir sall thay spuilye the Priores and scho sall have
      ane kirtill of silk under hir habite.

Now brother be the Masse,
By my judgement I think
This halie Priores
    Is turnit in ane cowclink.

PRIORES: I gif my freinds my malisoun,
    That me compellit to be ane nun,
        And wald nocht let me marie.
It was my freind[i]s greadines   3690
That gart me be ane Priores:
        Now hartlie them I warie.
Howbeit that nunnis sing nichts and dayis,
Thair hart waitis nocht quhat thair mouth sayis,
        The suith I yow declair.
Makand yow intimatioun,
To Christis congregatioun,
        Nunnis ar nocht necessair.
Bot I sall do the best I can,
And marie sum gude honest man,   3700
        And brew gude aill and tun.
Mariage, be my opinioun,
It is better religioun,
        As to be freir or nun.

FLATTERIE FREIR: My Lords, for Gods saik let not
        hang me,

3682 *pavin* pavane   3692 *warie* curse   3701 *tun* put in casks

582

Howbeit that widdiefows wald wrang me.
   I can mak na debait
To win my meat at pleuch nor harrowis,
Bot I sall help to hang my marrowis,
   Both Falset and Dissait.

CORRECTIOUN: Than pas thy way and greath the gallous,   3710
Syne help for to hang up thy fellowis:
   Tha gets na uther grace.

FLATTERIE: Of that office I am content,
   Bot our Prelates I dread repent,
    Be I fleimde from thair face.

Heir sall Flattrie sit besyde his marrowis.

DISSAIT: Now, Flattrie, my auld companyeoun,
   Quhat dois yon King Correctioun?
    Knawis thou nocht his intent?
   Declair to us of thy novellis.   3720
FLATTERIE: Ye'ill all be hangit, I se nocht ellis,
   And that incontinent.

DISSAIT: Now walloway, will ye gar hang us?
   The Devill brocht yon curst King amang us,
    For mekill sturt and stryfe.

FLATTERIE: I had bene put to deid amang yow,
   War nocht I tuke on hand till hang yow,
    And sa I saifit my lyfe.
I heir them say thay will cry doun,
All freirs and nunnis in this regioun,   3730

3706 *widdiefows* rascal   3708 *pleuch* plough   3711 *greath* prepare
3716 *fleimde* banished   3725 *sturt* discord

So far as I can feill,
Becaus thay ar nocht necessair,
And als thay think thay ar contrair
To Johne the Common-weill.

Heir sal the Kings and the Temporal Stait round
togider.

CORRECTIOUN: With the advice of King Humanitie,
Heir I determine with rype advysement,
That all thir Prelats sall deprivit be,
And be decreit of this present Parliament,
That thir thrie cunning clark[i]s sapient
Immediatlie thair places sall posses,   3740
Becaus that they have bene sa negligent
Suffring the word of God for till decres.

REX HUMANITAS: As ye have said but dout it salbe done:
Pas to and mak this interchainging sone.

The Kings servants lays hands on the thrie Prelats
and says

WANTONNES: My Lords, we pray yow to be patient,
For we will do the Kings commandement.

SPRITUALITIE: I mak ane vow to God and ye us handill,
Ye salbe curst and gragit with buik and candill:
Syne we sall pas unto the Paip and pleinyie,
And to the Devill of hell condemne this meinye,   3750

3734 SD *round* (v) whisper   3738 *decreit* decreed   3747 *handill* touch
3748 *gragit* excommunicated

For quhy sic reformatioun as I weine
Into Scotland was never hard nor seine.

*Heir sall thay spuilye them with silence and put thair
habite on the thrie Clarks.*

MERCHANT: We mervell of yow paintit sepulturis,
That was sa bauld for to accept sic cuiris,
With glorious habite rydand upon your muillis,
Now men may se ye ar bot verie fuillis.

SPRITUALITIE: We say the Kings war greiter fuillis nor we,
That us promovit to sa great dignitie.

ABBOT: Thair is ane thowsand in the kirk but doubt,
Sic fuillis as we gif thay war weill socht out.   3760
Now, brother, sen it may na better be,
Let us ga soup with Sensualitie.

Heir sall thay pas to Sensualitie.

SPRITUALITIE: Madame, I pray you mak us thrie gude
                    cheir,
We cure nocht to remaine with yow all yeir.
SENSUALITIE: Pas fra us fuillis be him that hes us wrocht,
Ye ludge nocht heir becaus I knaw yow nocht.
SPRITUALITIE: Sir Covetice, will ye also misken me?
I wait richt weill ye wil baith gif and len me.
Speid hand my freind, spair nocht to break the lockis:
Gif me ane thowsand crouns out of my box.   3770

3758 *promovit* promoted   3767 *misken* refuse to know   3768 *len* lend

585

COVETICE: Quhairfoir, sir fuil, gif yow ane thowsand
    crowns?
  Ga hence. Ye seime to be thrie verie lowns.
SPRITUALITIE: I se nocht els, brother, withoutin faill,
  Bot this fals warld is turnit top ovir taill.
  Sen all is vaine that is under the lift,
  To win our meat we man mak uther schift.
  With our labour except we mak debait,
  I dreid full sair we want baith drink and meat.
PERSONE: Gif with our labour we man us defend,
  Then let us gang quhair we war never kend.   3780
SPRITUALITIE: I wyte thir freirs that I am thus abusit,
  For by thair counsall I have bene confusit.
  Thay gart me trow it suffysit allace,
  To gar them plainlie preich into my place.
ABBOT: Allace, this reformatioun I may warie,
  For I have yit twa dochters for to marie:
  And thay ar baith contractit be the Rude,
  And waits nocht how to pay thair tocher-gude.
PERSONE: The Devill mak cair for this unhappie chance,
  For I am young and thinks to pas to France,   3790
  And tak wages amang the men of weir,
  And win my living with my sword and speir.

*The Bischop, Abbot, Persone, and Priores depairts
altogidder.*

GUDE COUNSALL: Or ye depairt, sir, aff this regioun,
  Gif Johne the Common-weill ane gay garmoun;
  Becaus the Common-weill hes bene overluikit,
  That is the caus that Common-weill is cruikit.
  With singular profeit he hes bene sa supprysit,
  That he is baith cauld, naikit and disgysit.

3775 *lift* air   3788 *tocher-gude* dowry   3791 *weir* war
3794 *garmoun* robe   3796 *cruikit* lame   3798 *disgysit* disfigured

CORRECTIOUN: As ye have said, father, I am content.
  Sergeants, gif Johne ane new abuilyement   3800
  Of sating, damais or of the velvot fyne.
  And gif him place in our Parliament syne.

> *Heir sal thay cleith Johne the Common-weil*
> *gorgeouslie and set him doun amang them in the*
> *Parliament.*

All verteous peopill now may be rejoisit,
Sen Common-weill hes gottin ane gay garmoun,
And ignorants out of the Kirk deposit:
Devoit Doctours and Clark[i]s of renoun,
Now in the Kirk sall have dominioun:
And Gude Counsall with Ladie Veritie
Ar profest with our King[i]s Majestie.
Blist is that realme that hes ane prudent King,   3810
Quhilk dois delyte to heir the veritie,
Punisching thame that plainlie dois maling
Contrair the Common-weill and equitie.
Thair may na peopill have prosperitie,
Quhair ignorance hes the dominioun,
And common-weil be tirants trampit doun.

> *Pausa.*

Now, maisters, ye sall heir incontinent
At great leysour in your presence proclamit
The Nobill Act[i]s of our Parliament,
Of quhilks we neid nocht for to be aschamit.   3820
Cum heir trumpet and sound your warning tone,
That ever man may knaw quhat we have done.

3800 *abuilyement* dress   3801 *sating* satin   *damais* damask
3809 *profest* have taken service   3812 *maling* evil   3818 *leysour* leisure

*Heir sall Diligence with the Scribe and the trumpet
pas to the pulpit and proclame the Actis.*

[DILIGENCE:]
  The First Act:
  It is devysit be thir prudent King[i]s,
  Correctioun and King Humanitie,
  That thair leigis induring all thair ringis,
  With the avyce of the Estait[i]s Thrie,
  Sall manfullie defend and fortifie
  The Kirk of Christ and his religioun,
  Without dissimulance or hypocrisie,
  Under the paine of thair punitioun.   3830
    2 Als thay will that the Act[i]s honorabill,
  Maid be our Prince in the last Parliament,
  Becaus thay ar baith gude and profitabill,
  Thay will that everie man be diligent
  Them till observe with unfeinyeit intent.
  Quha disobeyis inobedientlie
  Be thir lawis but doubt thay sall repent,
  And painis conteinit thairin sall underly.
    3 And als the Common-weil for til advance,
  It is statute that all the Temporall lands   3840
  Be set in few, efter the forme of France,
  Till verteous men that labours with thair hands:
  Resonabillie restrictit with sic bands
  That they do service nevertheles
  And to be subject ay under the wands,
  That riches may with policie incres.
    4 Item, this prudent Parliament hes devysit,
  Gif Lords halds under thair dominioun
  Theifis, quhair throch puir peopil bein supprisit,
  For them thay sall make answeir to the croun,   3850
  And to the pure mak restitutioun,
  Without thay put them in the judges hands,
  For thair default to suffer punitioun,

  3825 *ringis* reigns   3835 *unfeinyeit* true, genuine

Sa that na theifis remaine within thair lands.
   5 To that intent that Justice sould incres,
It is concludit in this Parliament,
That into Elgin or into Innernesse,
Sall be ane sute of Clark[i]s sapient,
Togidder with ane prudent Precident
To do justice in all the Norther Airtis,   3860
Sa equallie without impediment,
That thay neid nocht seik justice in thir pairts.
   6 With licence of the Kirk[i]s halines,
That justice may be done continuallie,
All the maters of Scotland mair and les,
To thir twa famous saits perpetuallie
Salbe directit becaus men seis plainlie
Thir wantoun nunnis ar na way necessair
Till Common-weill, nor yit to the glorie
Of Christ[i]s Kirk, thocht thay be fat and fair.   3870
And als that fragill ordour feminine
Will nocht be missit in Christs religioun,
Thair rents usit till ane better fyne,
For common-weill of all this regioun.
Ilk Senature for that erectioun,
For the uphalding of thair gravitie,
Sall have fyve hundreth mark of pensioun:
And also bot twa sall thair nummer be.
Into the North saxteine sall thair remaine,
Saxtein rycht sa in our maist famous toun   3880
Of Edinburgh to serve our Soveraine,
Chosen without partiall affectioun
Of the maist cunning Clarks of this regioun;
Thair Chancellar chosen of ane famous Clark,
Ane cunning man of great perfectioun,
And for his pensioun have ane thowsand mark.
   7 It is devysit in this Parliament,
From this day furth na mater temporall
Our new Prelats thairto hes done consent
Cum befoir Judges Consistoriall,   3890
  3873 *fyne* end

Quhilk hes bene sa prolixt and partiall
To the great hurt of the communitie.
Let Temporall men seik Judges Temporall,
And Sprituall men to Spritualitie.
    8 Na benefice beis giffin in tyme cumming,
Bot to men of gude eruditioun,
Expert in the Halie Scripture and cunning
And that they be of gude conditioun,
Of publick vices but suspitioun,
And qualefiet richt prudentlie to preich,   3900
To thair awin folk baith into land and toun,
Or ellis in famous scuillis for to teich.
    9 And als becaus of the great pluralitie
Of ignorant Preists ma then ane legioun,
Quhair throch of teicheouris the heich dignitie
Is vilipendit in ilk regioun,
Thairfoir our Court hes maid provisioun
That na B[i]shops mak teichours in tyme cumming,
Except men of gude eruditioun,
And for preistheid qualefeit and cunning.   3910
Siclyke as ye se in the borrows toun
Ane tailyeour is nocht sufferit to remaine
Without he can mak doublet, coat and gown,
He man gang till his prenteischip againe:
Bischops sould nocht ressave me think certaine
Into the Kirk except ane cunning Clark.
Ane idiot preist Esay compaireth plaine
Till ane dum dogge that can nocht byte nor bark.
    10 From this day furth se na Prelats pretend,
Under the paine of inobedience,   3920
At Prince or Paip to purchase ane command
Againe the kow becaus it dois offence.
Till ony Preist we think sufficience
Ane benefice for to serve God withall.
Twa Prelacies sall na man have from thence,
Without that he be of the blude royall.

3904 *ma* more   3906 *vilipendit* of little value   3910 *cunning* knowing
3911 *Siclyke* such   *borrows toun* borough

11 Item, this prudent counsall hes concludit,
Sa that our haly Vickars be nocht wraith,
From this day furth thay salbe cleane denudit
Baith of corspresent, cow and umest claith,
To pure commons becaus it hath done skaith. 3930
And mairover we think it lytill force,
Howbeit the Barrouns thairto will be laith,
From thine-furth thay sall want thair hyrald hors.

12 It is decreit that in this Parliament
Ilk Bischop, Minister, Priour and Persoun,
To the effect thay may tak better tent
To saulis under thair dominioun,
Efter the forme of thair fundatioun,
Ilk Bischop in his Diosie sall remaine: 3940
And everilk Persone in his parachoun,
Teiching thair folk from vices to refraine.

13 Becaus that clarks our substance dois consume
For bils and proces of thair prelacies,
Thairfoir thair sall na money ga to Rome
From this day furth [f]or any benefice,
Bot gif it be for greit Archbischopries.
As for the rest na money gais at all,
For the incressing of thair dignities,
Na mair nor did to Peter nor to Paull. 3950

14 Considering that our Preists for the maist part
Thay want the gift of Chastitie we se,
Cupido hes sa perst them throch the hart,
We grant them licence and frie libertie,
That thay may have fair virgins to thair wyfis,
And sa keip matrimoniall Chastitie,
And nocht in huirdome for to leid thair lyfis.

15 This Parliament richt sa hes done conclude
From this day forth our Barrouns Temporall
Sall na mair mix thair nobil ancient blude 3960
With bastard bairns of Stait Spirituall:
Ilk Stait amang thair awin selfis marie sall.

3928 *wraith* angry 3931 *skaith* harm 3933 *laith* loath
3934 *thine-furth* thenceforward 3962 *Ilk* every

Gif Nobils marie with the Spritualitie,
From thyne subject thay salbe, and all
Sal be degraithit of thair Nobilitie,
And from amang the Nobils cancellit,
Unto the tyme thay by thair libertie
Rehabilit be the civill magistrate.
And sa sall marie the Spiritualitie:
Bischops with bischops sall mak affinitie,   3970
Abbots and Priors with the Priores,
As Bischop Annas in Scripture we may se
Maryit his dochter on Bischop Caiphas.
    Now have ye heard the Act[i]s honorabill,
Devysit in this present Parliament,
To Common-weill we think [it] agreabill.
All faithful folk sould heirof be content
Them till observe with hartlie trew intent.
I wait nane will against our Acts rebell,
Nor till our law be inobedient,   3980
Bot Plutois band the potent prince of hell.

Heir sall Pauper cum befoir the King and say

PAUPER: I gif yow my braid bennesoun,
    That hes givin Common-weill a goun.
    I wald nocht for ane pair of plackis,
    Ye had nocht maid thir nobill Actis.
    I pray to God and sweit Sanct Geill
    To gif yow grace to use them weill:
    Wer thay weill keipit I understand,
    It war great honour to Scotland.
    It had bene als gude ye had sleipit,   3990
    As to mak Acts and be nocht keipit.
    Bot I beseik yow for allhallows,
    To heid Dissait and hang his fellows,

3965 *degraithit* degraded   3968 *Rehabilit* restored
3982 *bennesoun* blessing   3993 *heid* behead

And banische Flattrie aff the toun,
For thair was never sic ane loun.
That beand done I hauld it best
That everie man ga to his rest.
CORRECTIOUN: As thou hes said it salbe done:
Suyith, Sergeants, hang yon swingeours sone.

*Heir sal the Sergeants lous the presoners out of the
stocks and leid them to the gallows.*

FIRST SERGEANT: Cum heir, sir Theif, cum heir, cum
     heir.   4000
  Quhen war ye wont to be sa sweir?
  To hunt cattell ye war ay speidie,
  Thairfoir ye sall weave in ane widdie.
THIFT: Man I be hangit? Allace, allace,
  Is thair nane heir may get me grace?
  Yit or I die gif me ane drink.
FIRST SERGEANT: Fy, huirsun carle. I feil ane stink.
THIFT: Thocht I wald nocht that it war wittin,
  Sir, in gude faith I am bedirtin:
  To wit the veritie gif ye pleis   4010
  Louse doun my hois, put in your neis.
FIRST SERGEANT: Thou art ane limmer I stand foird.
  Slip in thy head into this coird:
  For thou had never ane meiter tippit.
THIFT: Allace, this is ane fellon rippit.

   Pausa

The widdifow wairdanis tuke my geir,
And left me nether hors nor meir:

3999 *swingeours* rogues 4003 *weave* hang, wave about *widdie* halter
4008 *wittin* known 4009 *bedirtin* incontinent 4011 *neis* nose
4012 *foird* forward 4014 *tippit* rope 4015 *fellon rippit* ?bad go
4016 *widdifow* rogue *wairdanis* wardens

Nor earthlie gude that me belangit,
Now walloway I man be hangit.
   Repent your lyfis, ye plaine oppressours,   4020
All ye misdoars and transgressours:
Or ellis gar chuse yow gude confessours,
   And mak yow forde.
For gif ye tarie in this land,
And cum under Correctiouns hand:
Your grace salbe I understand,
   Ane gude scharp coird.
Adew, my bretheren common theifis,
That helpit me in my mischeifis.
Adew Grosars, Nicksons and Bellis,   4030
Oft have we run out-thoart the fellis.
Adew Robsonis, Hansles and Pyilis,
That in our craft hes mony wylis.
Lytils, Trumbels and Armestrangs,
Adew all theifis that me belangs,
Tailyeour[i]s, Curwings and Elwands,
Speidie of fut and wicht of hands,
The Scottis Ewisdaill and the Graimis,
I have na tyme to tell your namis:
With King Correctioun and ye be fangit,   4040
Beleif richt weill ye wilbe hangit.
FIRST SERGEANT: Speid hand man with thy clitter
      clatter.

THIFT: For Gods saik, sir, let me mak watter.
   Howbeit I have bene cattel-gredie,
   It schamis to pische into an widdie.

Heir sal Thift be drawin up or his figour.

4023 *mak yow forde* get you gone
4031 *out-thoart* throughout *fellis* fells   4037 *wicht* clever
4040 *fangit* taken

SECUND SERGEANT: Cum heir, Dissait, my
  companyeoun;
 Saw ever ane man lyker ane loun
  To hing upon ane gallows?

DISSAIT: This is aneuch to make me mangit,
 Duill fell me that I man be hangit,   4050
  Let me speik with my fallows.
 I trow wan-fortune brocht me heir:
 Quhat mekill feind maid me sa speidie?
 Sen it was said it is sevin yeir
 Than I sould weave into ane widdie.
 I leirit my maisters to be gredie.
 Adew, for I se na remeid:
 Luke quhat it is to be evil-deidie.
SECUND SERGEANT: Now in this halter slip thy heid.
 Stand still, me think ye draw aback.   4060
DISSAIT: Allace, maister, ye hurt my crag.
SECUND SERGEANT: It will hurt better, I woid ane plak,
 Richt now quhen ye hing on ane knag.

DISSAIT: Adew my maisters, merchant men,
 I have yow servit as ye ken,
  Truelie baith air and lait.
 I say to yow for conclusioun,
 I dreid ye gang to confusioun,
  Fra tyme ye want Dissait.
 I leirit yow merchants mony ane wyle,   4070
 Upalands wyfis for to begyle,
  Upon ane markit-day.
 And gar them trow your stuffe was gude,
 Quhen it was rottin be the Rude,
  And sweir it was nocht sway.

4049 *mangit* mad 4052 *wan-fortune* ill-fortune
4058 *evil-deidie* active in evil 4062 *woid* wager 4063 *knag* gallows tree
4066 *air* early 4071 *Upalands* upland

I was ay roundand in your ear,
And leirit yow for to ban and sweir,
   Quhat your geir cost in France:
Howbeit the Devill ane word was trew.
Your craft gif King Correctioun knew,   4080
   Wald turne yow to mischance.
I leirit yow wyllis many fauld,
To mix the new wyne and the auld,
   That faschioun was na follie:
To sell richt deir and by gude-chaip,
And mix ry-meill amang the saip,
   And saiffrone with oyl-dolie.
Forget nocht ocker I counsall yow,
Mair than the vicker dois the kow,
   Or Lords thair doubill maill.   4090
Howbeit your elwand be too skant,
Or your pound-wecht thrie unces want,
   Think that bot lytill faill.
Adew the greit Clan Jamesone,
The blude royal of Clappertoun,
   I was ay to yow trew:
Baith Andersone and Patersone,
Above them all Thome Williamsone,
   My absence ye will rew.
Thome Williamsone, it is your pairt   4100
To pray for me with all your hairt,
   And think upon my warks:
How I leirit yow ane gude lessoun,
For to begyle in Edinburgh toun
   The Bischop and his Clarks.
Ye young merchants may cry allace,
For wanting of your wonted grace:
   Yon curst King ye may ban.
Had I leifit bot halfe ane yeir,
I sould have leirit yow crafts perqueir,   4110

4076 *roundand* whispering   4085 *gude-chaip* very cheap
4088 *ocker* usury   4090 *maill* rent   4091 *elwand* measure
4092 *unces* ounces   4110 *perqueir* by heart

To begyle wyfe and man.
How may ye merchants mak debait
Fra tyme ye want your man Dissait?
   For yow I mak great cair:
Without I ryse fra deid to lyfe,
I wait weill ye will never thryfe,
   Farther nor the fourth air.

Heir sal Dissait be drawin up or ellis his figure.

FIRST SERGEANT: Cum heir, Falset, and mense the
     gallows:
Ye man hing up amang your fallows,
   For your cankart conditioun.   4120
Monie ane trew man ye have wrangit,
Thairfoir but doubt ye salbe hangit,
   But mercie or remissioun.

FALSET: Allace, man I be hangit to?
   Quhat mekill Devill is this ado?
     How came I to this cummer?
My gude maisters, ye craft[i]s men,
Want ye Falset full weill I ken,
   Ye will all die for hunger
Ye men of craft may cry allace,   4130
Quhen ye want me ye want your grace:
   Thairfoir put into wryte
My lessouns that I did yow leir.
Howbeit the commons eyne ye bleir,
   Count ye nocht that ane myte.
Find me ane Wobster that is leill,
Or ane Walker that will nocht steill,
   Thair craftines I ken:

4117 *air* heir   4118 *mense* grace   4120 *cankart* wicked
4126 *cummer* distress   4134 *bleir* blur

Or ane Millair that hes na falt,
That will nather steill meall nor malt, 4140
  Hauld them for halie men.
At our fleschers tak ye na greife,
Thocht thay blaw leane mutton and beife,
  That thay seime fat and fair:
Thay think that practick bot ane mow,
Howbeit the Devill a thing it dow,
  To thame I leirit that lair.
I lairit Tailyeours in everie toun,
To schaip fyve quarters in ane goun,
  In Angus and in Fyfe: 4150
To uplands Tailyeours I gave gude leife,
To steill ane sillie stump or sleife,
  Unto Kittok his wyfe.
My gude maister Andro Fortoun,
Of Tailyeours that may weir the croun,
  For me he will be mangit:
Tailyeour Baberage, my sone and air,
I wait for me will rudlie rair,
  Fra tyme he se me hangit.
The barfit Deacon Jamie Ralfe, 4160
Quha never yit bocht kow nor calfe,
  Becaus he can nocht steall:
Willie Cadyeoch will make na plead,
Howbeit his wyfe want beife and bread,
  Get he gude barmie aill.
To the brousters of Cowper toun,
I leife my braid black malesoun,
  Als hartlie as I may:
To make thinne aill thay think na falt,
Of mekill burne and lytill malt, 4170
  Agane the market-day.
And thay can mak withoutin doubt,
Ane kynde of aill thay call Harns-out,

4139 *falt* fault   4142 *fleschers* ?butchers   4143 *blaw* inflate
4145 *mow* joke   4146 *dow* avails   4160 *barfit* barefoot
4170 *burne* warm water

Wait ye how thay mak that?
Ane curtill queine, ane laidlie lurdane,
Of strang wesche scho will tak ane jurdane,
    And settis in the gyle-fat.
Quha drinks of that aill, man or page,
It will gar all his harnis rage,
    That jurdane I may rew: 4180
It gart my heid rin hiddie giddie,
Sirs, God not I die in ane widdie,
    Gif this taill be nocht trew.
Speir at the sowtar Geordie Sillie,
Fra tyme that he had fild his bellie,
    With this unhelthsum aill.
Than all the Baxters will I ban,
That mixes bread with dust and bran,
    And fyne flour with beir maill.
Adew, my maisters, Wrichts and Maissouns,   4190
I have neid to leir you few lessouns:
    Ye knaw my craft perqueir.
Adew, blak-smythis and lorimers,
Adew, ye crafty cordiners,
    That sellis the schone over deir.
Gold-smythis, fair-weill above them all,
Remember my memoriall,
    With mony ane sittill cast.
To mix set ye nocht by twa preinis,
Fyne ducat gold with hard gudlingis,   4200
    Lyke as I leirnit yow last.
Quhen I was ludgit upaland,
The schiphirds maid with me ane band,
    Richt craftelie to steill:
Than did I gif ane confirmatioun,
To all the schiphirdis of this natioun,
    That they sould never be leill,

4175 *curtill* skittish   *laidlie* ugly   4176 *wesche* urine
jurdane chamber-pot   4177 *settis* put   *gyle-fat* brewing-vat
4189 *maill* meal   4198 *sittill* crafty   *cast* stratagem   4199 *preinis* pins
4200 *gudlingis* guilders

And ilk ane to reset ane uther.
I knaw fals schiphirds fyftie fidder,
　　War thair ca[u]teleinis kend,　　　　　　　　4210
How thay mak in thair conventiouns,
On montans far fra ony touns,
　　To let them never mend.
Amang crafts-men it is ane wonder,
To find ten leill amang ane hunder:
　　The treuth I to yow tell.
Adew, I may na langer tarie,
I man pas to the King of Farie,
　　Or ellis the rycht to hell.

Heir sall he luke up to his fallows hingand.

Wais me for the, gude Common Thift,　　　　　　4220
Was never man maid ane mair honest schift,
　　His leifing for to win.
Thair was nocht ane in all Lidsdaill,
That ky mair craftelie culd staill,
　　Quhair thou hings on that pin.
Sathan ressave thy saull, Dissait.
Thou was to me ane faithfull mait,
　　And als my father brother.
Duill fell the sillie merchant men,
To mak them service weill I ken,　　　　　　　　4230
　　Thaill never get sic ane uther.

Heir sall thay festin the coard to his neck with ane
dum countenance: thairefter he sall say

4208 *reset* harbour against the law　　4209 *fidder* load
4210 *cauteleinis* tricks　　4215 *hunder* hundred　　4220 *Wais* Woe is
4222 *leifing* living　　4224 *staill* steal

Gif any man list for to be my mait,
Cum follow me for I am at the gait.
Cum follow me, all catyfe covetous Kings,
Reavers but richt of uthers realmis and rings,
Togidder with all wrangous conquerours,
And bring with yow all publick oppressours.
With Pharao King of Egiptians,
With him in hell salbe your recompence.
All cruell schedders of blude innocent,   4240
Cum follow me or ellis rin and repent.
Prelats that hes ma benefeits nor thrie,
And will nocht teich nor preiche the veritie.
Without at God in tyme thay cry for grace,
In hiddeous hell I sall prepair thair place.
Cum follow me, all fals corruptit Judges,
With Pontius Pilat I sall prepair your ludges.
All ye officials that parts men with thair wyfis,
Cum follow me, or els gang mend your lyfis:
With all fals leiders of the constrie law,   4250
With wanton scribs and clarks intill ane raw,
That to the puir maks mony partiall traine,
Syne *hodie ad octo* bids them cum againe.
And ye that taks rewairds at baith the hands,
Ye sall with me be bund in Baliels bands.

Cum follow me, all curst unhappie wyfis,
That with your gudemen dayly flytis and stryfis,
And quyetlie with rybalds makes repair,
And taks na cure to make ane wrangous air.
Ye sal in hel rewairdit be, I wein,   4260
With Jesabell of Israell the Queene.
I have ane curst unhappie wyfe my sell,
Wald God scho war befoir me into hell:
That bismair war scho thair withoutin doubt,
Out of hell the Devill scho wald ding out.

4235 *Reavers* thieves   4236 *wrangous* wrongful   4250 *constrie* consistory
4257 *flytis* quarrels   4259 *air* heir   4264 *bismair* bawd

Ye maryit men evin as ye luife your lyfis,
Let never preists be hamelie with your wyfis.
My wyfe with preists sho doith me greit onricht,
And maid me nine tymes cuckald on ane nicht.
Fairweil, for I am to the widdie wend,　　　　　　　　4270
For quhy Falset maid never ane better end.

*Heir sal he be heisit up, and not his figure, and ane
Craw or an Ke salbe castin up, as it war his saull.*

FLATTERIE: Have I nocht chaipit the widdie weil?
　Yea, that I have, be sweit Sanct Geill,
　　For I had nocht bene wrangit,
　Becaus I servit be Alhallows,
　Till have bene merchellit amang my fellowis,
　　And heich above them hangit.
　I maid far ma falts nor my maits,
　I begylde all the Thrie Estaits,
　　With my hypocrisie.　　　　　　　　　　　　　4280
　Quhen I had on my freirs hude,
　All men beleifit that I was gude:
　　Now judge ye gif I be.
　Tak me ane rackles rubiator,
　Ane theif, ane tyrane or ane tratour,
　　Of everie vyce the plant.
　Gif him the habite of ane freir,
　The wyfis will trow withoutin weir,
　　He be ane verie Saint.
　I knaw the cowle and skaplarie,　　　　　　　　4290
　Genners mair hait nor charitie,
　　Thocht thay be blak or blew.
　Quhat halines is thair within,
　Ane wolfe cled in ane wedders skin?

4268 *onricht* wrong　4276 *merchellit* marshalled
4284 *rackles* reckless　*rubiator* libertine　4286 *plant* novice
4291 *Genners* begets　4294 *wedders* wether's

Judge ye gif this be trew.
Sen I have chaipit this firie farie,
Adew, I will na langer tarie
  To cumber yow with my clatter.
Bot I will with ane humbill spreit,
Gang serve the Hermeit of Lareit,   4300
  And leir him for till flatter.

  [*Exit Flattery.*]
  Heir sal enter Foly.

FOLY: Gude day, my Lords, and als God saine.
  Dois na man bid gude day againe?
  Quhen fuillis ar fow then ar thay faine,
    Ken ye nocht me?
  How call thay me can ye nocht tell?
  Now be him that herryit hell,
  I wait nocht how thay call my sell,
    Bot gif I lie.

DILIGENCE: Quhat brybour is this that maks sic beiris?   4310
FOLY: The feind ressave that mouth that speir[i]s:
  Gude man ga play you with your feiris,
    With muck upon your mow.

DILIGENCE: Fond fuill, quhair hes thou bene sa lait?
FOLY: Marie, cummand throw the Schogait.
  Bot thair hes bene ane great debait,
    Betwixt me and ane sow.
  The sow cryit guff, and I to ga,
  Throw speid of fute I gat awa,
  Bot in the midst of the cawsa,   4320
    I fell into ane midding.

4296 *firie farie* great confusion   4302 *saine* bless   4304 *fow* drunk
4310 *brybour* rascal   *beiris* tumult   4312 *feiris* tumult
4313 *mow* mouth   4318 *guff* grunt   *to ga* ran away   4320 *cawsa* road
4321 *midding* midden

Scho lap upon me with ane bend,
Quha ever the middings sould amend,
God send them ane mischevous end,
    For that is both Gods bidding.
As I was pudlit thair God wait,
Bot with my club I maid debait:
Ise never cum againe that gait,
    I sweir yow be Alhallows.
I wald the officiars of the toun,   4330
That suffers sic confusioun,
That thay war harbreit with Mahown,
    Or hangit on ane gallows.
Fy, fy, that sic ane fair cuntrie,
Sould stand sa lang but policie:
I gif them to the Devill hartlie,
    That hes the wyte.
I wald the Provost wald tak in heid,
Of yon midding to make remeid,
Quhilk pat me and the sow at feid,   4340
    Quhat may I do bot flyte?

REX: Pas on, my servant Diligence,
    And bring yon fuill to our presence.

DILIGENCE: That sall be done but tarying.
    Foly, ye man ga to the King.

FOLY: The King, quhat kynde of thing is that?
    Is yon he with the goldin hat?

DILIGENCE: Yon same is he, cum on thy way.

4322 *lap* leaped   *bend* bound   4326 *pudlit* in a puddle
4337 *wyte* blame   4340 *feid* enmity

FOLY: Gif ye be King, God [gif] yow gude day:
    I have ane plaint to make to yow.   4350

REX: Quhom on, Folie?
FOLIE: Marie, on ane sow.
    Sir, scho hes sworne that scho sall sla me,
    Or ellis byte baith my balloks fra me.
    Gif ye be King, be Sanct Allan,
    Ye sould do justice to ilk man.
    Had I nocht keipit me with my club,
    The sow had drawin me in ane dub.
    I heir them say thair is cum to the toun,
    Ane king callit Correctioun.
    I pray yow tell me quhilk is he.   4360

DILIGENCE: Yon with the wings. May [thou] nocht se?

FOLIE: Now wallie fall that weill fairde mow!
    Sir, I pray yow correct yon sow,
    Quhilk with hir teith but sword or knyfe,
    Had maist have reft me of my lyfe:
    Gif ye will nocht mak correctioun,
    Than gif me your protectioun
    Of all swyne for to be skaithles,
    Betuix this toun and Innernes.
DILIGENCE: Foly, hes thou ane wyfe at hame?   4370
FOLY: Yea, that I have, God send hir schame.
    I trow be this scho is neir deid:
    I left ane wyfe bindand hir heid.
    To schaw hir seiknes I think schame:
    Scho hes sic rumbling in hir wambe,
    That all the nicht my hart overcasts,
    With bocking and with thunder-blasts.

4357 *dub* puddle   4362 *wallie fall* good luck to . . .   4365 *maist* almost
4368 *skaithles* unharmed   4373 *bindand* binding   4377 *bocking* retching

DILIGENCE: Peradventure scho be with bairne.

FOLIE: Allace, I trow scho be forfaine.
   Scho sobbit and scho fell in sown,   4380
   And than thay rubbit hir up and doun.
   Scho riftit, routit and maid sic stends,
   Scho yeild and gaid at baith the ends,
   Till scho had castin ane cuppill of quarts,
   Syne all turnit to ane rickill of farts.
   Scho blubert, bockit and braikit still,
   Hir arsse gaid evin lyke ane wind-mill.
   Scho stumblit and stutterit with sic stends,
   That scho recantit at baith ends.
   Sik dismell drogs fra hir scho schot,   4390
   Quhill scho maid all the fluir on flot.
   Of hir hurdies scho had na hauld,
   Quhill scho had twmed hir monyfauld.

DILIGENCE: Better bring hir to the leitches heir.
FOLIE: Trittill trattill, scho may nocht steir:
   Hir verie buttoks maks sic beir,
      It skars baith foill and fillie.
   Scho bocks sik bagage fra hir breist,
   He wants na bubbils that sittis hir neist,
   And ay scho cryis a preist, a preist,   4400
      With ilk a quhillie lillie.

DILIGENCE: Recoverit scho nocht at the last?
FOLIE: Yea, bot wit ye weil scho fartit fast.
   Bot quhen scho sichis my hart is sorie.

4379 *forfaine* passed away 4382 *riftit* belched *routit* bellowed
stends (n) leaps 4385 *rickill* noise   4386 *blubert* sobbed
braikit broke wind 4390 *dismell* dismal *drogs* excrement
4391 *fluir* floor *flot* flood 4392 *hurdies* buttocks 4393 *twmed* emptied
4397 *skars* scars *foill* foal

DILIGENCE: Bot drinks scho ocht?

FOLIE: Ye, be Sanct Marie,
    Ane quart at anis it will nocht tarie,
      And leif the Devill a drap:
    Than sic flobbage scho layis fra hir,
    About the wallis, God wait sic wair,
    Quhen it was drunkin I gat to skair,   4410
      The lickings of the cap.

DILIGENCE: Quhat is in that creill, I pray the tell.

FOLIE: Marie, I have folie hats to sell.

DILIGENCE: I pray the sell me ane or tway.

FOLIE: Na, tarie quhill the market-day.
    I will sit doun heir, be Sanct Clune,
    And gif my babies thair disiune.
    Cum heir gude Glaiks, my dochter deir:
    Thou salbe maryit within ane yeir,
    Upon ane freir of Tillilum.   4420
    Na, thou art nather deaf nor dum.
    Cum hidder Stult, my sone and air,
    My joy thou art, baith gude and fair:
    Now sall I fend yow as I may,
    Thocht ye cry lyke ane ke all day.

*Heir sal the bairns cry keck lyke ane ke, and he sal
put meat into thair mouth.*

DILIGENCE: Get up Folie, but tarying,
    And speid yow haistelie to the King.
    Get up! Me think the carle is dum.

FOLIE: Now bum balerie, bum, bum.

4408 *flobbage* slime   4410 *skair* share   4411 *cap* cup
4412 *creill* basket   4417 *disiune* breakfast   4425 SD *ke* jackdaw

DILIGENCE: I trow the trucour lyis in ane trance.   4430
   Get up, man, with ane mirrie mischance,
   Or be Sanct Dyonis of France,
     Ise gar the want thy wallet:
   Its schame to se man how thow lyis.

FOLIE: Wa; yit agane. Now this is thryis:
   The Devill wirrie me and I ryse,
     Bot I sall break thy pallet.
   Me think my pillok will nocht ly doun:
   Hauld doun your head, ye lurdon loun.
   Yon fair las with the sating goun   4440
     Gars yow thus bek and bend.
   Take thair ane neidill for your cace.
   Now for all the hiding of your face,
   Had I yow in ane quyet place,
     Ye wald nocht waine to flend.
   Thay bony armis thats cled in silk,
   Ar evin als wantoun as any wilk,
   I wald forbeir baith bread and milk
     To kis thy bony lippis.
   Suppois ye luke as ye war wraith,   4450
   War ye at quyet behand ane claith,
   Ye wald not stick to preife my graith,
     With hobling of your hippis.
   [Be God, I ken yow weill annewch:
   Ye ar fane, thocht ye mak it twich.
   Think ye not on into the sewch
     Besyd the quarrell hoillis?
   Ye wan fra me baith hoiss and schone,
   And gart me mak mowis to the mone,
   And ay lap on your courss abone.   4460
DILIGENCE: Thow mon be dung with poillis.]

4430 *trucour* deceiver   4436 *wirrie* worry   4438 *pillok* penis
4441 *bek* nod   4445 *waine* think   *flend* flee   4446/9 *bony* bonny
4447 *wilk* whelk   4452 *graith* manhood   4453 *hobling* dancing
4455 *twich* touch   4456 *sewch* divide   4461 *poillis* poles

Suyith harlot, haist the to the King,
And let allane thy trattilling.
Le heir is Folie, sir, alreadie,
Ane richt sweir swingeour, be Our Ladie.
FOLIE: Thou art not half sa sweir thy sell,
Quhat meins this pulpit, I pray the tell.
DILIGENCE: Our new Bischops hes maid ane preiching,
Bot thou heard never sic pleasant teiching:
Yon Bischop will preich throch the coast.   4470
FOLIE: Than stryk ane hag into the poast,
For I hard never in all my lyfe,
Ane Bischop cum to preich in Fyfe.
Gif Bischops to be preichours leiris,
Wallaway quhat sall word of freiris?
Gif Prelats preich in brugh and land,
The sillie freirs, I understand,
Thay will get na mair meall nor malt,
Sa I dreid freirs sall die for falt.
Sen sa is that yon nobill King,   4480
Will mak men Bischops for preiching:
Quhat say ye, sirs, hauld ye nocht best
That I gang preich amang the rest?
Quhen I have preichit on my best wayis,
Then will I sell my merchandise,
To my bretherin and tender maits,
That dwels amang the Thrie Estaits.
For I have heir gude chaifery,
Till any fuill that lists to by.

Heir sall Foly hing up his hattis on the pulpet and say

God sen I had ane Doctours hude.   4490
REX: Quhy Folie, wald thou mak ane preiching?

4463 *trattilling* prating   4471 *hag* notch   4475 *word* become
4476 *brugh* town   4488 *chaifery* merchandise

FOLIE: Yea, that I wald sir, be the Rude,
    But eyther flattering or fleiching.
REX: Now, brother, let us heir his teiching,
    To pas our tyme and heir him raife.
DILIGENCE: He war far meiter for the kitching,
    Amang the pottis, sa Christ me saife.
    Fond Foly, sall I be thy Clark,
    And answeir the ay with amen?

FOLIE: Now at the beginning of my wark,   4500
    The feind ressave that graceles grim.

    Heir sal Folie begin his sermon, as followis

    Stultorum numerus infinitus.
Salomon, the maist sapient King,
In Israell quhan he did ring,
Thir word[i]s in effect did write,
The number of fuillis ar infinite.
I think na schame sa Christ me saife,
To be ane fuill amang the laife,
Howbeit ane hundreth stands heir by,
Perventure als great fuillis as I.   4510
    Stultorum [*numerus infinitus.*]
I have of my genelogie,
Dwelland in everie cuntrie,
Earles, Duiks, Kings, and Empriours,
With mony guckit Conquerours:
Quhilk dois in folie perseveir,
And hes done sa this many yeir.
Sum seiks to warldlie dignities,
And sum to sensuall vanities:
Quhat vails all thir vaine honour[i]s,   4520
Nocht being sure to leife twa houris?

    4495 *raife* rave   4501 *grim* ugly face   4515 *guckit* foolish
    4521 *leife* live

Sum greidie fuill dois fill ane box,
Ane uther fuill cummis and breaks the lox,
And spends that uther fuillis hes spaird,
Quhilk never thocht on them to wairde.
Sum dois as thay sould never die,
Is nocht this folie, quhat say ye?
    Sapientia huius mundi stultitia est apud Deum.
Becaus thair is sa many fuillis
Rydand on hors and sum on muillis: 4530
Heir I have b[r]ocht gude chafery,
Till ony fuill that lists to by.
And speciallie for the Thrie Estaits,
Quhair I have mony tender maits:
Quhilk causit them as ye may se,
Gang backwart throw the haill cuntrie.
Gif with my merchandise ye list to mell,
Heir I have folie hattis to sell.
Quhairfoir is this hat wald ye ken?
Marie, for insatiabill merchant men!   4540
Quhen God hes send them abundance
Ar nocht content with sufficiance.
Bot saillis into the stormy blastis,
In winter to get greater castis:
In mony terribill great torment,
Against the Acts of Parliament.
Sum tynis thair geir, and sum ar drounde:
With this sic merchants sould be crounde.

DILIGENCE: Quhom to schaips thou to sell that hude?
  I trow to sum great man of gude.   4550

FOLIE: This hude to sell richt faine I wald,
  Till him that is baith auld and cald,
  Reddie till pas to hell or heavin,

    4524 *spaird* spared   4525 *wairde* guard   4544 *castis* profits
    4547 *tynis* lose

And hes fair bairn[i]s sax or seavin,
And is of age fourscoir of yeir,
And taks ane lasse to be his peir,
Quhilk is nocht fourteine yeir of age,
And joynis with hir in mariage,
Geifand hir traist that scho nocht wald
Rycht haistelie mak him cuckald.   4560
Quha maryes beand sa neir thair dead,
Set on this hat upon his head.

DILIGENCE: Quhat hude is that, tell me, I pray the?

FOLIE: This is ane haly hude, I say the;
    This hude is ordanit I the assure,
    For Sprituall fuillis that taks in cure
    The saullis of great Diosies,
    And regiment of great Abesies,
    For gredines of warldlie pelfe,
    Than can nocht justlie gyde them selfe.   4570
    Uthers sauls to saife it settis them weill,
    Syne sell thair awin saullis to the Devil.
    Quha ever dois sa, this I conclude,
    Upon his heid set on this hude.
DILIGENCE: Foly is thair ony sic men
    Now in the Kirk that thou can hen?
    How sall I ken them?

FOLIE: Na keip that clois:
    Ex operibus eorum cognoscetis eos.
    And fuillis speik of the Prelacie,
    It will be hauldin for herisie.   4580
REX: Speik on hardlie. I gif the leife.
FOLIE: Than my remissioun is in my sleife.

    4554 sax six   4556 peir companion   4569 pelfe gain
    4577 clois secret   4580 hauldin considered   4582 sleife sleeve

Will ye leife me to speik of kings?
REX: Yea: hardlie speik of all kin things.
FOLIE: Conforming to my first narratioun,
  Ye ar all fuillis, be Cok[i]s passioun.

DILIGENCE: Thou leis. I trow this fuill be mangit.
FOLIE: Gif I lie, God nor thou be hangit:
  For I have heir I to the tell,
  Ane nobill cap imperiell,   4590
  Quhilk is nocht ordanit bot for doings,
  Of Empreours, of Duiks and Kings.
  For princelie and imperiall fuillis,
  Thay sould have luggis als lang as muillis.
  The pryde of Princes withoutin faill,
  Gars all the warld rin top ovir taill.
  To win them warldlie gloir and gude,
  Thay cure nocht schedding of saikles blude.
  Quhat cummer have ye had in Scotland,
  Be our auld enemies of Ingland?   4600
  Had nocht bene the support of France,
  We had bene brocht to great mischance.
  Now I heir tell the Empreour,
  Schaippis for till be ane Conquerour,
  And is muifing his ordinance
  Against the nobill King of France.
  Bot I knaw nocht his just querrell,
  That he hes for till mak battell.
  All the Princes of Almanie,
  Spaine, Flanders and Italie,   4610
  This present yeir ar in ane flocht:
  Sum sall thair wages find deir bocht.
  The Paip with bombard, speir and scheild,
  Hes send his armie to the feild.
  Sanct Peter, Sanct Paull nor Sanct Androw,
  Raisit never sic ane oist I trow.

  4594 *luggis* ears   4598 *saikles* innocent   4611 *flocht* commotion
  4616 *oist* host

Is this fraternall charitie,
Or furious folie, quhat say ye?
Thay leird nocht this at Christis scuillis:
Thairfoir I think them verie fuillis.   4620
I think it folie, be Gods mother,
Ilk Christian Prince to ding doun uther:
Becaus that this hat sould belang them,
Gang thou and part it evin amang them.
The Prophesie, withouttin weir,
[Of] Marling beis compleit this yeir
For my gudame the Gyre Carling,
Leirnde me the Prophesie of Marling:
Quhairof I sall schaw the sentence,
Gif ye will gif me audience.   4630

Flan fran resurgent, simul Hispan viribus urgent
Dani vastabunt, Vallones valla parabunt
Sic tibi nomen in a mulier cacavit in olla.
Hoc epulum comedes . . .

DILIGENCE: Marie, this is ane il savorit dische.
FOLIE: Sa be this Prophesie plainlie appeirs,
That mortall weirs salbe amang freirs:
Thay sall nocht knaw weill in thair closters,
To quhom thay sall say thair *Pater Nosters.*
Wald thay fall to and fecht with speir and sheild,   4640
The feind mak cuir quhilk of them win the feild.
Now of my sermon have I maid ane end.
To Gilly-mouband I yow all commend,
And I yow all beseik richt hartfullie,
Pray for the saull of gude Cacaphatie,
Quhilk laitlie drownit himself into Lochleavin,
That his sweit saull may be above in heavin.

DILIGENCE: Famous peopil, hartlie I yow requyre,
This lytill sport to tak in patience:

4637 *weirs* wars

We traist to God, and we leif ane uther yeir,   4650
Quhair we have failit we sall do diligence,
With mair pleasure to mak yow recompence,
Becaus we have bene sum part tedious,
With mater rude, denude of eloquence,
Likewyse perchance, to sum men odious.

[Adew, we will mak no langar tary,
Prayand to Jesu Chryst, oure salviour,
That he be requeist of his moder Mary,
He do preserve this famous awditour,
Withowt that grittar materis do incure: 4660
For your plesour we sall devyse ane sport,
Plesand till every gentill creatour,
To raise your spreitis to plesour and confort.]
Now let ilk man his way avance,
Let sum ga drink and sum ga dance.
Menstrell, blaw up ane brawll of France;
    Let se quha hobbils best.
For I will rin, incontinent,
To the tavern or ever I stent,
And pray to God Omnipotent,   4670
    To send yow all gude rest.

Rex sapiens aeterne Deus genitorque benigne
Sit tibi perpetuo gloria, laus et honor.

4659 *awditour* audience   4660 *grittar* greater   *incure* occur

NOTES

NOTES

THE CASTLE OF PERSEVERANCE

The Banns. These stanzas are apparently intended to give advance notice of performance. They briefly outline the plot of the play, giving a number of insights into the theological background. J. Bennett thought that the style indicated composition by a different author, and he rightly drew attention to the inconsistencies between the Banns and events in the play ('*The Castle of Perseverance*: Redactions, Place and Date', *Medieval Studies* 24, 1962, pp. 141–52). It should be noted that there are no indications within the play itself that it was taken on tour.

1. *Glorious God*. The imagery of the first stanza, with its reference to the glory of God and the creation gives some hint of the mystery plays whose composition was almost contemporary.

25. *fre arbritracion*. The morality play, if it is to present a truly Christian view, and if it is to have a dramatic action which has surprise and a significant sequence of events, must give Man the freedom to choose. The action is well managed in that although we may suspect that Man will make the right choice, his salvation is affected by a number of uncertainties.

29. The configuration of the World, the Devil, and the Flesh is widespread in theological writings, and appears in *Mankind* at l. 884. But in our play the writer makes a great dramatic effect of the three enemies by giving them scaffolds, and making them command groups of sins. The latter relationship is not original, however, for a sermon entitled *Per Propriam Sanguinem*, written by John Gregory before 1404, has the World shooting with arrows of Covetousness and Avarice, The Devil with Pride, Anger, and Envy, and the Flesh with Gluttony, Lechery, and Sloth: cf. M. W. Bloomfield, *The Seven Deadly Sins*, East Lansing, Michigan, 1952, p. 213. See also ibid., pp. 131, 141; and 'one could hardly deal with the World, the Flesh, and the Devil in the late fourteenth century without at least thinking about the deadly sins', p. 200.

34. *Bakbytynge*. Slander was conventionally associated with Envy, cf. *Piers Plowman*, B text, Passus V, ll. 89, and 130.

37. *gun.* 'begin' – often used as an auxiliary verb with little more function than to mark a past tense.

44. *Concyens.* This character does not appear in the list of parts, nor in the play itself. The Banns are thus inconsistent with the play at this point.

52. cf. ll. 1713–4. The play has no title in the manuscript. The figure of the castle is widespread in medieval literature. The definitive study is R. Cornelius, *The Figurative Castle*, Bryn Mawr, 1930, and there is much detail in Bloomfield, op. cit., (see his index under 'castle'). None of the parallels or possible sources so far revealed has a castle called Perseverance, but the image of a castle defended by virtues against vices (sometimes the seven deadly sins) appears in *Sawles Ward* 1200–25; *The Ancren Riwle* c. 1225; R. Grosseteste, *Chasteau d'amour* c. 1230; *Cursor Mundi* 1300–25; William Langland, *Piers Plowman* c. 1377 (B text, Passus XX). One of the earliest parallels is the Castle of Wisdom in a sermon by Hugo of St Victor (d. 1141) which shelters a prodigal child and withstands attacks by temptations (Bloomfield, op. cit., p. 318). Although our author's use of the idea of the castle links him with his theological and literary predecessors, his choice of perseverance, and his realization of the dramatic possibilities of the castle are clearly important and successful.

82. *And . . . fayle.* 'And convinces him to fall short of his obligation.' In the text there is no hint that Man experiences poverty while he is in the Castle.

92. *Secundus*, Eccles: *Primus*, MS. The speech heads are in the wrong order for the rest of the Banns in the manuscript, and are reversed here.

108. *scyfftyd.* 'shared'. Eccles refers to the use of this word in a Lincolnshire will of 1451.

124. The intercession by Our Lady is not enacted in the play; instead the divine mercy is aroused by the debate of the Four Daughters. The lost ending of *The Pride of Life* apparently also showed Our Lady's intercession, see *T.I.*, p. 46, ll. 97–100.

127. *mowthys confession.* 'spoken confession'. The salvation of Man in this play turns upon confession which acknowledges guilt: contrast Bale's critical attitude to this in *King Johan*, below p. 655.

134. No name in MS here or at ll. 145, 148. Probably the intention was that the players fitted in the name of the village or town required. But in view of the huge cast one must wonder whether there were performances at many different places.

154. *lendys*, MS.: *lende*, Eccles.

156. Trumpets are used in the battle, below l. 1909.

160. The call for silence is conventional, cf. *The Pride of Life*, ll. 1–12 (*T.I.* p. 43).

170. This alliterated list is a conventional boast; see Eccles for some further details.

Assarye Assyria; *Acaye* Achaia; *Almayne* Germany; *Cavadoyse* Calvados; *Capadoyse* Cappadocia; *Cananee* Canaan; *Brabon* Brabant; *Burgoyne* Burgundy; *Bretayne* Brittany; *Galys* Galicia; *Gryckysch See* Aegean Sea; *Masadoyne* Macedonia; *Freslonde* Friesland; *Normande* Normandy; *Pynceras* land of the Pincenarii in Thrace; *Pygmayne* land of the Pigmies; *Trage* ?Thrace; *Dreye Tre* The Dry Tree in Eden; *Rodys* Rhodes.

184. *Ther . . . warne.* 'There is no man in the world who will reject my wisdom.'

188. *be . . . derne.* 'by the most secret valleys', (tag).

201. *Carlylle.* Chosen for its remoteness.

202. As the plan indicates, Belyal is equipped with fireworks.

211. *Envye . . . wyth.* 'Envy shall go quickly to war in my company'.

213. *dene.* 'den', i.e. his 'lair' on the scaffold.

235. *Brod brustun-gutte.* 'broad fat-guts', lit. 'burst guts'.

250. *lent am I lowe.* 'I am deeply committed'.

262. *Thou . . . drepe.* 'Though I am changed into dust, dissolving into rubbish'.

271. *on hylle.* Addressed to some of the spectators apparently on a hill, or a raised part of the audience.

316. *strete and stalle.* Alliterative tag, 'everywhere', cf. ll. 532, 574.

333. *be grevys grene.* 'by green groves'; ?'by green pastures', (tag).

362. *Divicias . . . Domine.* 'Give me neither riches nor poverty, O Lord', *Prov.* 30 8 (all references to A.V.).
This is the first of many scriptural quotations which are usually extra to the verse structure. In this edition the lines are numbered in sequence: Eccles and Bevington do not number them. Some of the quotations are placed on the right-hand side of the text in the manuscript, as though they were meant as a learned commentary (e.g. ll. 3193, 3279), but this is not true of all cases (e.g. ll. 362, 412). Probably they were not all meant to be delivered in performance.

371. *late bedys be.* 'leave your prayer beads alone'.

392. Note the concern for riches: this is a preparation for the late impact of Avarice upon Man.

400. This anticipates the character Lust-and-Liking (l. 471).

412. *Homo . . . peccabis.* 'Man, remember thine end, and thou shalt never do amiss', *Ecclesiasticus* 7 36.

442–3. *And thou . . . lord-lyche.* 'And I do not care if I am false, provided that I can live like a lord.'

457. S D The music marks the end of the first sequence, and perhaps allows time for the actors to move about.

471. *Lust-Lykyng.* This is one character, Voluptas or Pleasure, who like Stulticia and Garcio is a servant of World (cf. the list of characters, and ll. 523, 526, and 530).

482. *be londys lawe.* 'by the law of the land'.

492. S D *Tunc . . . pariter. descendit* MS. 'Then they shall descend into the place together.'

505. *Non . . . habundo.* 'There is no rich man in the world who says he has enough.'

520. *Sapiencia . . . Domini.* 'Wisdom comes from the Lord', cf. *Ecclesiasticus* I I.

532. *be downys drye.* 'by barren hills', (tag).

548. *fast . . . thrywe.* 'quickly he begins to thrive'.

556. *Metys . . . trye.* 'He shall have choice meat and drink.'

557. *of lofte.* 'of high position', or 'on high', referring to Lechery on Flesh's scaffold.

574. *Be . . . broun.* 'by woods and brown hillsides', (tag).

578. S D *Tunc . . . Voluptas.* 'Then Lust-Liking, Folly, Bad Angel and Man shall go to World, and Lust-Liking shall say.'

589. *wede.* 'clothing'. The intention is that Man be clothed anew in garments provided by World, cf. l. 628. Such changes became an important convention in the moralities and interludes, cf. *Magnyfycence*, l. 2010, and l. 2406.

592. *betyn . . . bryth.* 'adorned with bright ornaments like coins'.

618. S D *Tunc . . . Mundum.* 'Then Man shall ascend to World.'

651. The entry of Backbiter draws attention away from World's scaffold, Southern, op. cit., p. 164.

657–8. *Ya . . . mende.* 'Yes, my mind is full of false tales, loud lies held on a leash.'

666. *lende.* 'loins'; perhaps the meaning is that he has a powerful supply of lies.

671. *renne . . . whele.* 'prosper', cf. l. 1078.

685. *Bakbytere . . . spronge.* 'Backbiter appears far and wide'.

705. cf. l. 592.

758. *And . . . bette.* 'and yet live in a much better way'.

762. *at . . . mette.* 'from your own words'.

779. *Flepergebet.* Flibbertigibbet, name for Backbiter as a gossip, see *Notes and Queries* 203, 1958, p. 98–9.

790. *to . . . kende.* 'to follow my natural inclination'.

805. *at hert.* 'seriously'.

806. Proverbial, cf. *Towneley 2, The Killing of Abel,* (*E.M.P.* p. 83, l. 84).

808. *pyke . . . lys.* 'pick off your own lice', cf. *Piers Plowman,* B text, Passus V, l. 195–9.

812. *podys prys.* 'to the value of toads'.

847. *but . . . why.* 'unless you have good reason'.

854. *sotel of sleytys.* 'clever in trickery'.

870. *Caton.* Dionysius Cato, third-century author of *Disticha de Moribus ad Filium,* a collection of moral hexameters much used in the medieval period; see W. J. Chase, *The Distichs of Cato,* Madison, 1922.

871. *Labitur . . . longo.* '(Wealth) which is brought forth over a long time slips quickly away', *Disticha* 2 17.

876–9. This passages indicates shows how near man is to damnation, cf. *Matthew* 25 41–6.

884. *si dedero.* 'If I give, I expect money in return', Eccles.

911. *Wondyr . . . houte.* 'I heard wonderfully loud shouts made from the hill'. The hill is presumably the raised scaffold of Avarice.

939. *Whanne . . . stonys.* 'When you move, or glare, or stumble on stones'.

944. *Wyth . . . gast.* 'In order to terrify a certain man with our fearful appearance'.

974–5. *I rape . . . kynde.* 'With all speed I hasten to control (them) and to hamper (them) as is my nature'.

993. Thus Sloth helps Lechery.

1014. SD *Tunc . . . Superbia.* 'Then Pride, Wrath, Envy, Gluttony, Lechery, and Sloth shall go to Avarice, and Pride shall say'.

1058. *Kast . . . kettys.* 'make wretched carrion of them'.

1064. *crakows.* Pointed toes. This fashion in shoes was at its height in the years 1382–1425, and thus the word gives some evidence for the date of composition of the play.

1072. *schelfe.* Not traced.

1078. *Whyl . . . whel.* 'While I rejoice in favourable circumstances', cf. l. 671.

1127. *On the hey name.* 'In the name of God': here a blasphemy.

1140. *rote and rynde.* 'root and bark', i.e. 'source'.

1150. *on lofte.* i.e. into Avarice's scaffold.

1204. *Lykynge . . . lende.* 'Pleasure is found in thy loins'.

1224–5. *Penaunce . . . make.* 'Penance which is imposed at confession is ignored, and I make sure of that.'

1248. *at . . . met.* 'as much as I please'.

1310–11. *Why ... pale.* 'Why, pale from painful stabs, do you lament in your heart?'

1341. SD *Tunc ... dicet Confessio.* 'Then they (Confession and Penitence) shall go to Man, and Confession shall say'.

1354. *Palme Sunday.* It was necessary to take Easter communion, and to be shriven beforehand. According to Man, Sloth says that to confess on Palm Sunday is really much too early ('be-tyme'), Good Friday would be soon enough.

1374. *We ... everychone.* 'We have all eaten garlick', not traced as a proverb, but cf. 'and ginger shall be hot i' the mouth', *Twelfth Night* II 3 103.

1379. *That* MS.: *But* Eccles.

1384. *launce.* cf. Death's lance, l. 2830.

1386. *Sorwe of hert.* Sorrow of heart is a sign of true repentance demanded by the penitential rite.

1450. SD *Tunc ... Confessionem. descendit* MS. 'Then he shall descend to Confession.'

1453. *Ye ... scho.* 'You are preparing a wretched fate for Man'.

1507. *Quantum peccasti.* 'In so far as you have sinned'.

1511. *Vitam male continuasti.* 'You have maintained your life evilly'.

1520. *Quicquid gesisti.* 'Whatever your conduct has been'.

1524. *Vicium quodcumque fecisti.* 'Whatever fault you have committed'.

1533. *Noli peccare.* 'Do not sin (again)', cf. *John* 5 14.

1537. *Posius noli viciare.* 'Preferably do not condemn', cf. *John* 8 11 where Christ is reluctant to condemn the woman taken in adultery: cf. marginal note to *Ludus Coventriae* 24, 'nolo mortem peccatoris'.

1606. One leaf missing here, probably containing speeches by Meekness and Patience.

1616–17. cf. St Paul, 1 *Corinthians* 13 1–3.

1621. *Take ... refeccyon.* 'Eat moderately'.

1630–1. *Who-so ... a-store.* 'Whoever eats or drinks more than is wise for his proper estate ...'

1637. *Quia ... possunt.* 'Because those who live in the flesh cannot please God', *Romans* 8 8.

1651. *Osiositas ... malum.* 'Idleness brings forth all evil', cf. *Ecclesiasticus* 33 27.

1670–3. cf. *Luke* 12 33–4; *Matthew* 6 19–21.

1678–9. *Dame ... wreche.* 'Dame Meekness, through your power, I will avoid evil vengeance.'

1704. *Cum ... et cetera.* 'Thou shalt be holy in company with the holy, etc.', *Psalm* 18 26.

1704. SD *Tunc intrabit.* 'Then he shall enter.'

1714. *Qui . . . . erit.* 'He that endureth to the end shall be saved', *Matthew* 10 22.

1714. SD *Tunc . . . dicet Humilitas.* 'Then shall they sing "O Eternal King Most High," and Humility shall say'.

1720. *dyen dos ?* 'dying potion'. ?Vinegar at the crucifixion.

1751. *Seynt Jamys of Galys.* St James of Galicia.

1754. SD *Tunc . . . Belial.* 'Then he shall go to Belial.'

1760. *be . . . hothe.* 'by woods and heath', (tag).

1775. SD *Tunc . . . Iram,* Eccles: *Tunc vocavit Superbia . . .* MS. The word *vocavit* is difficult to decipher. The emended version means 'Then he shall call Pride, Envy, and Wrath'; see A. Henry, *N. and Q.,* 210, 1965, p. 448.

1786. SD *Et . . . terram.* 'And he shall beat them on the ground.' Presumably he descends from his scaffold to make the beating more effective.

1799. SD *Ad Carnem.* 'To Flesh.'

1820. SD *Tunc . . . Luxuriam.* 'Then Flesh shall shout to Gluttony, Sloth and Lechery.'

1831. SD *Tunc . . . placeam: verberavit* MS. 'Then he shall beat them into the place.' Again the beating is given at ground level.

1844. SD *Ad Mundum.* 'To World.'

1847. *I founde* MS.: *ifounde* Eccles.

1861. SD *Tunc . . . Avariciam.* 'Then he shall blow with a horn to Avarice.'

1864. *Lowde* MS.: *Lewde* Eccles.

1872. SD *Tunc . . . eum. verberavit* MS. 'Then he shall beat him.'

1895–6. *Yerne . . . schonde.* 'Quickly let my banner flutter on high and let us prepare shame and ruin.'

1907. SD *Tunc . . . Demon.* 'Then World, Avarice and Folly shall go to the Castle with the banner, and the Devil shall say'.

1911. *Tho . . . merre.* 'To destroy the intention of those maidens'.

1938. *Golyas.* Goliath, the Philistine giant slain by David, 1 *Samuel* 17.

1950. *gogmagog.* British giant, probably from *Ezekiel* 38 39.

1951. *I wagge . . . wyt.* 'I make to move with a weight', like a clock.

1954–5. *Wyth . . . flode.* 'With care so as to crack that castle, and shatter it into the water.' *flode* means the moat round the stage castle.

1977. SD *Tunc . . . placeam.* 'Then they shall descend into the place.'

1978. SD *Malus . . . Belyal.* 'The Bad Angel shall say to Belial'.

1978. *heyward.* 'One who guards fences and enclosures', *N.E.D.* *herawd* Eccles, 'herald'.

1979. *to . . . dote.* 'to stupefy those damsels'.

1982. *penon . . . rowte.* 'pennant which brings rags and ruin'.

1983. *Do . . . mote.* 'Cause this wench Meekness to dwindle to a speck.'

1990. SD *Ad Carnem.* 'To Flesh.'

1994. *Gere . . . gerys.* 'Equip yourself with armour'.

1999. SD *Ad Mundum.* 'To World.'

2009. *To . . . kave.* 'For man there is prepared a cave full of misery'. *ben* MS.: *thei* Eccles.

2011. *Mankynd . . . wave.* 'In order to make Man roll and twist with misery'.

2017. *Omne . . . insideritis.* 'Count it all joy when ye fall into divers temptations', *James* 1 2.

2031. *Delectare . . . tui.* 'Delight in the Lord and he shall give to you the desires of your heart', *Psalm* 37 4.

2033. *Prymrose . . . parlasent.* Hitherto unexplained this elliptical line may be construed 'O precious first flowers, stir yourselves willingly'. (Cf. *Play* v. Primary meaning 'to bestir or busily occupy oneself', *N.E.D.*)

2037. *Rode . . . i-rent.* 'red as a rose torn from its branch'.

2064. They will defend themselves with flowers, cf. ll. 2159, 2235–7.

2079. *To . . . rede.* 'I commend you to hasten with blows on all sides'.

2106. *Desposuit . . . cetera.* 'He hath put down the mighty from their seat, etc.', *Luke* 1 52.

2120. *Qui . . . cetera.* 'For whosoever exalteth himself shall be abased', *Luke* 14 11.

2124. *stourys* MS.: *stonys* Eccles.

2128. *wyld fere.* Wildfire, inflammable material used as a weapon of war.

2133. *Thou . . . motyhole. modyr* 'wench'. *motyhole* 'dusty hole' Eccles; but cf. *mort* (or *mot*) sb⁴, 'loose woman, harlot', *N.E.D.*

2138. *Quia . . . operatur.* 'For the wrath of man worketh not the righteousness of God', *James* 1 20.

2164. *hore clowte.* 'old rag'; but cf. *clout* sb² 'clod of earth' *N.E.D.*

2178. *Ve . . . venit.* 'Woe to that man by whom the offence cometh', *Matthew* 18 7.

2213. SD *Tunc pugnabunt diu.* 'Then they shall fight for a long time'. The Vices have conventional weapons, but the roses used by the Virtues in reply inflict painful wounds, cf. ll. 2226, 2237–8.

2243. *let . . . bord.* 'make an attack'.

2285. *bred.* 'bread', i.e. the body of Christ.

2293. *Cum . . . cetera.* 'When he had fasted forty days etc.', *Matthew* 4 2.

2301. *schet undyr schawe.* 'shut under the earth'.

2310. *pyssynge pokys.* 'sexual organs'.

2320. *Mater . . . concupiscentias.* 'Mother and Virgin, extinguish fleshly lusts.'

2336-7. *For . . . sede.* 'For you will not subdue Mankind to sully him with sinful semen.'

2352. *iij mens songys.* Songs for men written in three parts.

2382. *Nunc . . . labora. hora* MS.: *ora* Eccles. 'Now read, now pray, now learn, and now toil,' (untraced).

2386. *And . . . a-ray.* 'and strike blows in a warlike fashion'.

2395. SD *Tunc pugnabunt diu.* cf. l. 2213 note. In this round of the contest, Gluttony and Sloth are beaten, and Lechery is drenched.

2427. SD *Ad Mundum.* 'To World.'

2439. *galows Canwyke.* Canwick Hill, S.E. of Lincoln, was the site of the gallows in medieval times. This reference implies local knowledge, perhaps indicating that the author or the play has association with Lincoln, but the text was written by a scribe who used linguistic forms from Norfolk.

2445 ff. Avarice does not seek to prevail by violence but by persuasion: he aims at offering Man the consolation of riches in his old age. Man should really persevere after the first temptation, but Avarice misleads him.

2453. *Seynt Gyle.* St Giles, the patron saint of Edinburgh.

2471. *Maledicti . . . temporis.* 'Cursed are the covetous of this generation.'

2482-4. cf. 'For the love of money is the root of all evil', 1 *Timothy* 6 10.

2501. *colde* MS.: *olde* Eccles.

2513. *Markys.* Marks, coins worth two-thirds of £1 sterling.

2532. *bok of kendys.* The Book of Nature, i.e. *De Naturis Rerum* by Alexander Neckam (Nequam) 1157-1217 (see *D.N.B.*).

2557-8. *It . . . hyde.* 'It is sensible, for all eventualities, to hide some property somewhere.'

2575. SD *Tunc . . . Avariciam. descendit* MS. 'Then he shall descend to Avarice.'

2579. The Virtues may not interfere since Man must be allowed to exercise free will.

2590. *He . . . helve.* 'He had the axe by the handle', i.e. he had the opportunity of making his own decision, even though he made a bad one.

2613. *can hys wyt*. 'can think for himself'.

2619. *Mundus . . . eius*. 'The world passes away and the lust thereof.'
1 *John* 2 17.

2632. *And . . . fodyr*. 'And let him remain in Death's company'.

2633. *Et . . . suas*. 'And thus they leave their wealth to others.'
Psalm 49 10.

2647. *Non . . . eius*. 'His glory shall not descend after him.' *Psalm*
49 17.

2661. *Avarus . . . pecunia*. 'The miser shall not be satisfied with
money', cf. *Ecclesiasticus* 5 10.

2671 ff. After the anxieties expressed by the Virtues, the tone of the
Bad Angel's speech, with its abuse and vulgarity, clarifies his evil intention.

2715. *Wyth . . . awake*. 'He will wake up through my "good"
plans'.

2722 ff. In contrast to the siege, the action now becomes very intimate, only Avarice and Man being concerned.

2729–30. *More . . . terage*. 'Take possession, indeed, of more wealth
than is legally yours.'

2765. Man's action here is contrary to that enjoined by the parable
of the talents, *Matthew* 25 14–30.

2775. This is the last speech by Avarice, who presumably withdraws
to his scaffold.

2801. For the influence of the sermon on the presentation of Death,
'goddys mesangere', see G. R. Owst, *Literature and Pulpit in Medieval
England*, Oxford, 1962, pp. 531–6. In the following lines Death presents the characteristics of his role: he comes to rich and poor, and is to
be seen as part of God's response to Man's immorality. R. Potter sees
the coming of Death as an essential part of the penitential doctrine of
the play, *The English Morality Play*, 1975, pp. 20–21.
Presumably Death was dressed to resemble a skeleton.

2833. *In . . . bed*. 'I prepare a bed for them underground.'

2838. *grete pestelens* refers to the plague.

2843. cf. *The Pride of Life*, ll. 361–2 (*T.I.* p. 57).

2862. *I . . . schappe*. 'I shall make a horrible appearance out of
you.'

2912. *In . . . a-syse*. 'His way ends in sorrow.'

2915. *be-hett* MS.: *behott* Eccles.

2931. *in . . . wounde*. 'clad in (fine) clothes'.

2943. SD *Tunc . . . Genus*. 'Then he shall go to Man.'

2991. *I-Wot-Nevere-Whoo*. 'I do not know who', i.e. his name indicates that he is impersonal and callous.

3009. *Tesaurizat . . . ea.* 'He heapeth up riches and knoweth not who shall gather them.' *Psalm* 39 6.

3031. Man's final appeal for mercy means that there is hope of salvation.

3031. SD This is not in the manuscript, but the instruction on the plan reads 'Mankyndeis bed schal be undyr the castel and ther schal the sowle lye undyr the bed tyl he schal ryse and pleye.'

3032. *Anima.* Southern, op. cit., p. 210, misreads this as *Domina:* cf. the speech head *Avaricia* in Bevington op. cit., l. 2726.

3053. One leaf of about two hundred lines missing. The action may have shown the Bad Angel asserting his rights over the Soul against the Good Angel. After the lacuna the Bad Angel is speaking.

3071. *he* MS.: *I* Eccles.

3084. 'He[re] aperith the sowle' added by a later hand in the right-hand margin before this line.

3118. Here the Bad Angel begins to beat the Soul, and continues until l. 3144.

3120–1. *in . . . redempcio.* 'In hell there is no redemption', cf. *Job* 7 9.

3137. *in peynnys plow.* ?'subject to hardship'. *peymys* MS. is incomprehensible.

3146. He takes the Soul on his back and carries him off to Hell. This is the first known example of a persistent convention which was still being echoed as a comic device in the sixteenth century: cf. the Vice rides off on the Devil's back in *Like Will to Like* (*T.I.* p. 362).

3153. The plan indicates that the Four Daughters are to wear mantles: Mercy in white, Justice in red, Truth in green, and Peace in black. Eccles (p. 184n.) interprets the colours: white for purity, red as a justice's robes, green for everlasting truth, and black for mourning for man.

'Thei schal pleye in the place al togedyr tyl they brynge up the sowle', (plan). This, as Southern suggests (op. cit., p. 212), implies that their action takes place on the open playing space, and that they do not leave it until they take the Soul from the Devil's scaffold at l. 3630 (cf. l. 3254 note).

For the debate see *Psalm* 85 10 'Mercy and Truth are met together: Righteousness and Peace have kissed each other.' The reconciliation of the Daughters symbolized the establishment of the divine will. It appeared as a theme in theological literature, and in the drama as in *Ludus Coventriae* Play XI, and in the later interlude *Respublica* Act V Scene 4 (*T.I.* p. 248–9). In our play the action is reduced to a very direct exchange of points of view in a debate. There is very little physical action, and one must suppose that the coming of forgiveness is a penitential ritual. J. Bennett proposes that the Debate is a redaction of an earlier version still reflected in the Banns, in which mercy was obtained by the intercession of the Virgin. There are indeed differences in dramatic and poetic style between the Debate and the rest of the play, but the evidence so far adduced by Bennett does not point conclusively to a revision whether by the original author or another.

3188. *Unusquisque ... portabit.* 'For every man shall bear his own burden.' *Galatians* 6 5.

3193. *Non ... celorum.* 'Not everyone that saith unto me Lord, Lord, shall enter into the kingdom of heaven.' *Matthew* 7 21.

3254. SD *Tunc ... Veritas. ascendet ... dixit* MS. 'Then they shall ascend to the Father all together, and Verity shall say'. Southern doubts this stage direction, proposing that the debate be conducted in front of God's scaffold and not on it, op. cit., pp. 212–14.

3279. *Quoniam ... dilexisti.* 'Since thou hast desired the truth.' Cf. *Psalm* 51 6.

3293. *Aurum ... bibisti.* 'Thou hast thirsted for gold, and gold hast thou drunk.'

3299–3301. *moriendo ... reprehendo.* 'when dying, too late in penitence, I condemn such a death.'

3306. The warning here is against sinning in anticipation of forgiveness, cf. ll. 3199–3202.

3312. *Quia ... eternum.* 'Because his truth endureth for ever', *Psalm* 117 2.

3313–14. *Tendit ... supernum.* 'man goes to Hell (and) never comes to heaven.'

3323–4. *Unnethe ... thynge.* 'He can scarcely give you thanks for anything at all.'

3342–3. *O Pater ... nostra.* 'O Father of mercies and God of all comfort, who comforteth us in all our tribulation.' 2 *Corinthians* 1 3–4.

3370–1. *Si ... fuisset.* 'If old Adam had not fallen through sinning, the Mother (Mary) would never have been pregnant for the nativity.' This particular form of the well-known doctrine of the fortunate fall has not been traced: cf. *Piers Plowman* B text V l. 491.

3380. *Passus ... Poncio.* 'suffered under Pontius Pilate'.

3384. *Scitio.* 'I thirst.' *John* 19 28. Christ's cry on the cross is interpreted as a thirst for souls.

3385. *Scilicet ... animarum.* 'That is, for the health of souls.'

3389. *Consummatum est.* 'It is finished.' *John* 19 30.

3394. *Aqua ... redempcionis.* 'The water of baptism and the blood of redemption'.

3398. *Est ... salvacionis.* 'is the cause of salvation'.

3407. *Quia . . . servabo.* 'Because thou hast said, "My mercy I will keep".' Cf. *Psalm* 89 28.

3411. *Misericordias . . . cantabo.* 'I will sing of the mercies of the Lord for ever.' *Psalm* 89 1.

3416. *Justicias . . . dilexit.* 'The just Lord loves justice.' *Psalm* 11 7.

3426. *Quia . . . dereliquit.* 'Because he has forgotten God who formed thee', cf. *Deuteronomy* 32 18.

3435. *Sicut justi tui.* 'in the manner of your virtuous servants'.

3439. *Quia . . . sui.* 'Because he is unmindful of the Lord his creator', cf. *Deuteronomy* 32 18.

3441. *formydiste . . . face.* 'and madest him in thine own image'.

3479. *Letabitur . . . vindictam.* 'The righteous shall rejoice when he seeth vengeance.' *Psalm* 58 10.

3493. *Et . . . eius.* 'And his tender mercies are over all his works.' *Psalm* 145 9.

3507. *Et . . . cetera.* 'And his mercy is on them that fear him from generation to generation.' *Luke* 1 50.

3510. This theme appears in the *York Plays*, see *Judgement Day* ll. 325–332. (*E.M.P.* pp. 643–4); it derives from *Matthew* 25 41–6.

3522–6. *boun . . . soun . . . doun.* In interpreting the MS. abbreviation for these words, I follow the suggestion by E. Talbot Donaldson (*TLS*, 16/v/75, p. 542). Eccles and Bevington read *bonn . . . sonn . . . donn.*

3560–61. *Misericordia . . . sunt.* See note to l. 3153.

3575. *Hic . . . honestas.* 'Here is peace, here is goodness, here is glory, and here is virtue for ever.'

3589–90. *Et . . . mansiones.* 'And we ask, O Lord, for your compassion, so that you will deign to grant to him bright and quiet resting-places.'

3595. *Tanquam . . . es.* 'Thou wast led as a sheep (to the slaughter)', cf. *Acts* 8 32.

3596. *gutte . . . a-dounn.* ?'blood, pouring out, ran down'.

3604. SD *Pater . . . trono.* 'The Father sitting on His throne'. *Ego . . . affliccionis.* 'I think the thoughts of peace and not of affliction.' Cf. *Jeremiah* 29 11.

3618. *Misericordia . . . terra.* 'The earth is filled with the mercy of the Lord.' *Psalm* 33 5. SD *Dicet filiabus.* 'He shall say to his daughters'.

3630. SD *Tunc . . . dicet Pax.* 'Then they shall ascend to the Bad Angel all together, and Peace shall say'.

3638. SD *Tunc . . . tronum.* 'Then they shall ascend to the throne.'

In the final sequence it is probable that God, the daughters and Man are all on God's scaffold, above the audience.

3640. cf. *The Pride of Life*, l. 264 (*T.I.* p. 53).

3643. SD *Pater ... Iudicio.* 'The Father, sitting in Judgement.' The York Cycle ends with God's judgement and mercy, God making the last speech (*E.M.P.* p. 644–5).

Sicut ... maris. 'Like a spark (of fire) in the middle of the sea (so is all the impiety of man to the mercy of God).' Also cited in *Piers Plowman* B text Passus V l. 291; see note p. 171 in the edition by J. A. W. Bennett, Oxford, 1972.

3657–8. *Ego ... eruere.* 'I shall kill and I shall make alive, I shall wound and I shall heal, and there is no one who can tear himself from my hand.' *Deuteronomy* 32 39.

3659 ff. The style of this stanza, particularly its alliterated list of nobles and prelates, recalls and contrasts with the empty boasts of World, Devil and Flesh, ll. 157–274.

3672. *Ecce ... pastoris.* 'Behold, I shall require my flock from the hand of the shepherd.' *Ezekiel* 34 10.

3677. The works of mercy are enumerated in *Matthew* 25 35–36, where the scene of God's judgement is foretold. The Gospel account is also the basis for a more detailed version in the York *Judgement* (see *E.M.P.* pp. 642–5).

3686–7. *Et ... eternum.* 'And those who do good things shall go into eternal life, but those who do evil shall go into eternal fire.' Cf. *Matthew* 25 46.

3700. *Te Deum laudamus.* 'We praise thee, O God.' Ancient Latin hymn in thanksgiving for deliverance, sung regularly at Matins. The Towneley *Judgement Day* ends with this hymn. It was also associated in the liturgical drama with the Resurrection Play.

1–7. 'All things – whether of high or low estate in the world – are subject to man's reason. There is sooner or later an appropriate time for wealth, whose use is a good test of wisdom: only a fool is at odds with the proper use of wealth. But today men are so badly disposed that wealth is employed worse than anything else.' The leading theme established here is the proper use of wealth and the need for wisdom in managing it. The purpose of the play is to demonstrate this idea: it is not meant to suggest that wealth in itself is improper.

5. Proverbial, cf. 'A fool and his money are soon parted', Tilley, F452. For the importance of proverb and *sententia*, see R. S. Kinsman, 'Skelton's *Magnyfycence*: The Strategy of the "Olde Sayde Saw"', *S.P.* 63, 1966, pp. 99–125. The idea of the Fool is later elaborated into the characters of Fansy and Foly.

16. Sad Cyrcumspeccyon is referred to l. 311, and eventually appears in the action at l. 2418. He is the embodiment of reason in the play.

17. *made . . . lure.* 'Trained to come to the lure' (false prey used in falconry).

19. *But . . . subjeccyon.* i.e. instead of controlling wealth, reason is subjected to wilfulness.

24. *Lyberte* is not necessarily an evil; indeed he must be related to the freedom of the will which is a fundamental doctrine of the morality plays. However he needs to be controlled by the right principles, and tends to be misused, cf. l. 73 and l. 2113.

42. *advertysment, Cam.: advertence,* Ramsay, from rhyme with l. 45.

59–60. *Somwhat . . . debarre.* 'I could adduce something to obstruct your conception.'

73 ff. Lyberte's case is that he should not be subject to the restraint of law.

80. SD *Hic intrat Measure.* 'Here Measure enters.' Following a convention of the moralities he already knows the substance of the argument he interrupts.

90. Skelton was a stylist of great distinction. The comment here on language is a hint of his conscious exploitation of many different types of vocabulary and rhythm. Here the intention is to be crisp and rapid; cf. Magnyfycence's comment at l. 1531.

114. *Oracius.* Horace, *Odes* 2 10 –
    aurecam quisquis mediocritatem diligit . . .

'whoever loves the golden mean . . .' (ll. 5–6), and cf. 'The heart that is well prepared for the changes of fate hopes in adversity, and fears in prosperity', (ll. 13–15). W. O. Harris shows that these ideas were much used by medieval theologians and moralists to support the notion that the kingly virtue of Fortitude or Magnanimity was able to meet good and bad fortune with equanimity, (*Skelton's 'Magnyfycence' and the Cardinal Virtues Tradition*, Chapel Hill, 1965, pp. 139–44). Measure is thus an essential support for Magnyfycence.

Note the change back to the more formal rime royal.

118–9. *I ponder . . . opynyon.* 'I weigh everything carefully: all things are managed by measure, as in the beginning of the world, showing divine judgement.'

125. *Measure is treasure.* Proverbial, Tilley M805.

136. *rest.* 'means of stopping a horse', *N.E.D.* sb 3.

144. *That . . . behynde.* 'If that which was first should now be last.'

146. *cut . . . clothe.* Proverbial, Tilley C433, 'to act with abandon'.

147. The action of the play is thus seen to be dependent upon the exercise of free will. Magnyfycence must exercise his free will, and in this respect he is allied to the heroes of earlier moral plays, cf. *Castle of Perseverance*, l. 25 and note.

152–3. This anticipates the later action of the play: cf. ll. 1955 ff. and 2284 ff.

159–60. Thus Welthe and Lyberte controlled by Measure are fitting for the king. The statement of this theoretical equilibrium brings to an end the first part of the play, and the real action can now begin. Note that Lyberte specifically refers to a 'prynce' – the play is concerned with princely virtues.

162. SD *Hic . . . Magnyfycence.* 'Here Magnyfycence enters.'

211. *Had I wyste.* 'If only I had known!' Proverbial, cf. l. 1395.

213. *Bycause . . . Measure.* 'Assuming that Measure is exercised'.

216. *Se* Dyce: *So* Cam.

238. Magnyfycence subjects Lyberte to Measure, and thus begins well. The attack of the vices succeeds by a breach in this arrangement.

239. SD *Itaque . . . Felicitate.* 'And so let Measure leave the place with Lyberte, and Magnyfycence remain with Felycyte.'

240–50. This short episode is a good example of morality technique: it reminds the audience of Lyberte's instability, and shows that Magnyfycence is aware of it even though he disregards it shortly.

250. SD *Hic . . . Fansy.* 'Here Fansy comes in.' There is no indication to the audience of his name until the comedy with Counterfet Countenaunce at l. 325 ff. He tells Magnyfycence that his name is Largesse (l. 270). Fansy is the foolish madness which is substituted for

reason – hence the trick of the supposed letter from Cyrcumspeccyon, and Fansy's role in creating aliases (l. 518 ff.). He is distinctly stupid, 'brain-sick', and is attired as a Fool (cf. l. 1047).

254. *Here . . . forsyth.* 'There is no one here cares . . .'

258. *Jacke of the Vale.* A yokel, also mentioned in Skelton's *Mannerly Margery Milk and Ale*, l. 7 *et seq.*

260. *Me . . . bled.* Proverbial, Tilley D608.

280. *Kynge Lewes of Fraunce.* Identified by Ramsay as Louis XII, 1498–1515, to whom Henry's sister Mary was betrothed in 1514 in splendour. Ramsay suggests that Louis' reputation for largess derives from the celebrations (p. xxiii). This seems a more likely identification than that with Louis XI, 1461–83 by L. Winser, 'Skelton's *Magnyfycence*', *Renaissance Quarterly* 23, 1970, pp. 14–25: this would put the composition of the play back to c. 1500.

289. Perhaps an indication that Fansy was a boy or dwarf.

291. *colyca passyo.* colic.

293. *Dauncaster cuttys.* Horses from Doncaster, with tails cut short.

294. *wylde . . . buttes.* The bolt (heavy arrow) was often thought of as the weapon of a fool: cf. 'a fool's bolt is soon shot', Tilley F515.

300. *wyse . . . pole.* Proverbial, cf. 'Fools lade the water and wise men catch the fish', Tilley F538.

303. *Go . . . nedys.* 'Go and shake yourself, you dog, hey, since you must do so!'

309. *wrytynge.* He presents a letter which turns out to be a forgery.

311. *Sad Cyrcumspeccyon* eventually appears at l. 2418.

324. SD *Hic . . . manu.* 'Here let him [Magnyfycence] act as though he is quietly reading the letter. Meanwhile let Counterfet Countenaunce arrive singing and hopping, and when he sees Magnyfycence let him draw back for a moment. But after a short delay let Counterfet Countenaunce approach Magnyfycence looking at him and speaking from a distance: and Fansy motions him to silence with his hand.' Counterfet Countenaunce is a trickster and a forger (cf. l. 403 ff.).

328. *Flemynge.* Men from Flanders were seen as comic figures, blustering and often drunk, cf. note to l. 747 below.

343. *Pountesse.* Pontoise, but it is not clear why Skelton settled upon this.

344. *taken me.* 'committed to me'.

350. Speech heads as Dyce: *Cam.* attributes the whole line to Fansy.

352. *They . . . hande.* 'They arrested me on suspicion.'

357–8. *Freer Tucke . . . hole.* Ramsay (p. xcviii–xcix) suggests that Friar Tuck was descended from the boy bishop, and associates Fansy as the Fool with Friar Tuck as folk figures.

The *pylery* (pillory) had holes through which the head and hands were fixed. The *stole* (l. 359) is a strip of linen worn as a vestment.

360. *sere ... marke.* i.e. 'brand him'.

364. *as ... hyght.* 'in accordance with my name'.

365. Perhaps an indication that this was an evening performance.

381. *blannched ... bene.* For this *non sequitur* see B. J. Whiting, *Proverbs in the Earlier English Drama*, Cambridge, Mass., 1938, p. 86.

384–5. *otes ... grotes.* Ramsay reversed these words.

395. SD *Hic ... Countenaunce.* 'Here let Magnyfycence go away with Fansy, and Counterfet Countenaunce enters.' After the entry at l. 324 Fansy forced him to remain unseen. He now attempts to speak to Fansy who brushes him aside.

403. This striking image indicates that Counterfet Countenaunce perceives that Magnyfycence is well caught. It is the first of a series of references to flies. Some of them seem concerned with the idea that flies were evil, perhaps devils (ll. 503, and 1193, where eating a fly is mentioned). Others (ll. 413, 470, 1710, 1889) are proverbial, meaning 'of no value': cf. Tilley F396.

406. *put the stone.* i.e. to waste time.

408. *bastarde ryme.* The following monologue, ll. 410–493, is written in a variation of rime royal, seven-line stanzas with only one rhyme instead of three.

423. *Tyburne.* Tyburn, near Marble Arch, used for public executions until 1783.

427. *Counterfet ... playes.* 'By trickery appear to be in earnest.'

432. *grese.* i.e. grease (as in grease one's palm): proverbial, Tilley M397.

435. *sande* Ramsay: *founde, Cam.* Sugar was expensive at the time.

441. *fayty bone geyte.* for *fait à bon get* 'elegant' (Dyce). The line perhaps means 'use counterfeit language in an elegant way'.

443. *A counte ... resayte.* 'To give a false account of what has been received.'

448. Proverbial?

457. *Margery Mylke Ducke, mermoset.* Perhaps the actor here teases someone conspicuously dressed in the audience. The name appears in *The Tunning of Elinor Rummyng* l. 418 where the woman is a coarse drunkard. *Mermoset* is a term of affection.

467. *pevysshe pope holy.* Early uses of 'peevish' imply dislike or distaste (*N.E.D.*). *pope holy* 'hypocrite'. *pope* is hard to decipher in *Cam.*

470. *flye.* cf. l. 403.

476/7. *Coll, Annot.* common names.

490. *benedicite.* 'Bless ye.' The blessing is used as a cover for greed.

493. SD *Hic . . . Conveyaunce. properantur . . . famina multa, Cam.* 'Here let Fansy come in quickly with Counterfet Counteraunce, talking by turns very vigorously: at length when Counterfet Counteraunce is perceived let Crafty Conveyaunce say . . .' Crafty Conveyaunce is one who deceives by cunning use of legal or official means.

503. *ete a flye.* cf. l. 403.

507. *heyre parent.* 'heir apparent'.

518. The use of aliases is a conventional part of the strategy of deception in morality plays. All six villains in *Magnyfycence* adopt them, and usually the name indicates how the evil is to operate, cf. ll. 270, 674, 681, 765, and 1310.

523. *lytell of stature.* Implies that Fansy is a boy or a dwarf.

525–6. Speech heads as Dyce: reversed in *Cam.*

532. *underneth a shrowde.* 'in secrecy'.

535. *dysceyved.* 'tricked'. Ramsay has *dyscryved,* 'discovered'.

559. *elbowe . . . ake.* Proverbial, often seen as a sign of foreboding, Tilley E98.

572. SD *Hic . . . ambulando.* 'Here let Clokyd Colousyon enter with a lofty expression, pacing up and down.' Clokyd Colousyon's superior manner is enhanced by his heavy (?ecclesiastical) outer cloak. He is a conspirer and manipulator, and he works by flattery and hypocrisy.

579. *jurde hayte.* Not explained.

583. An example of the persistent abuse of Foly by the other villains, cf. l. 608. Usually he is mocked for his stupidity.

586. *ratches.* The ratch, or rache, was a hunting dog which hunted by scent, and was thus useless against hares.

605. *Syr John Double-Cloke, Cam.: Cope,* Ramsay (for rhyme). The name suggests that he is disguised as a priest, and that he wears a heavy black cloak which is too small for him (l. 607).

609. *cloked for the rayne.* 'an expedient in every difficulty', proverbial, Tilley·C417.

630–1. Speech heads thus in Ramsay: *Cam.* gives both lines to Crafty Conveyaunce.

642. *Craftely . . . save.* 'so cunningly as to preserve the appearance of virtue.'

649. *pystell of a postyke.* ?'a backdoor epistle', (cf. *Lat,* posticum).

665. *Cam.* omits speech head, supplied by Dyce.

671. *owle flyght.* Time when owls fly, night-time.

674. *Good Demeynaunce.* This suggests a proper manner of behaviour.

675. *Calys.* Calais was still an English possession. The oath suggests that Counterfet Countenaunce has, like Fansy, come from France.

688. SD *Hic deambulat.* 'Here he takes a walk', cf. l. 691.

690. *occupy the place.* He is alone in the acting area, and his speech is arranged to fill in time.

727. *favell.* 'Flattery'. Favell is a character in Skelton's *Bowge of Court*, and is said to be 'full of flattery', (l. 134).

744. SD *Hic . . . cantando.* 'Here let Courtly Abusyon come in singing.' He is extravagantly dressed – gold ornaments on his boots, wide sleeves, French fashions. He brings disaster upon all who use him, offering the trap of extravagance and courtly ambition.

745. *Huffa . . . huffa.* This seems to be meaningless bluster.

747. *Rutty . . . heyda.* This boastful song is preserved in British Museum MS. 5465, in a version which may have been written out by Skelton. N. C. Carpenter suggests that the chanson 'Roti bouilli joyeulx' perhaps originated in Brabant, and there is some evidence for associating it with the Flemish knight (rutterkin) who made his money in the wool trade and aspired to life at Court ('Skelton and Music: Roty Bully Boys', *Review of English Studies*, N.S.6, 1955, p. 279–84).

748. *De . . . vous.* 'Of what country are you?'

748. SD *Et . . . ironice. exiat beretrum cronice, Cam.* 'And he shall pretend to take off his cap ironically.'

749. *Decke your hofte.* 'Cover your head'.

lowce. Lice are proverbially worthless.

750. *Say . . . dawce.* 'Can you sing *Ventre très douce?'*

751. *Wyda, wyda.* 'Yes, yes.'

758. *Jacke Hare.* Dyce mentions a poem by Lydgate which names Jack Hare as a slovenly lad who turns the spit. (vol. 2, p. 211–12).

765. *Thy . . . swanne.* 'Your slippers stamp clumsily, yet you dance like a swan.'

778. SD From here until l. 1966 most of the stage directions are in English (cf. Intro. p. 40).

781. This line is given to Clokyd Colusyon in *Cam.*

armys of the dice, a dicer's oath.

814. *ofte . . . frayes.* 'often peace takes the place of quarrels', but the quarrel just enacted is a conventional piece of stage villainy.

843. *poynte devyse.* 'perfectly', cf. l. 1540.

910. *Tyborne checke.* A choke at Tyburn, the hangman's rope.

912. *stow.* Call for a hawk by falconers, cf. Skelton's *Ware the Hawk* l. 73, but since the bird is an owl (cf. l. 1005) the word is incongruous.

913. *out of harre.* 'out of order', lit. 'off the hinge'.

922. *Marche hare.* Proverbial, usually 'mad as . . .' Tilley H148.

926. *hawke of the towre.* Noble hawk.

927. *malarde fat.* To catch mallards.

938. This is the first sign of Magnyfycence's decline: Lyberte's escape from Measure is critical.

944. *dyvyls date.* 'time of the devil' (tag): cf. *Piers Plowman* B text, Passus II l.112.

952. *checked ... consayte.* 'checked (as in chess) out of his reason.'

970. *There ... foule.* 'If you are ugly, there are many who look worse.' Pun on *fowl/foul*.

975. *Jesse.* Jesus.

982–3. *Tyne ... Kent.* i.e. North to South, West to East.

986–7. *How ... behynde.* i.e. the owl can fly both with and against the wind.

988. *Barbyd.* A barb was worn on or below the chin as a sign of mourning, and was part of a nun's habit.

998–9. *Pease ... sease.* 'Peace, man, peace, I think we should stop.' Perhaps he was about to say something impertinent.

1002. *tenter hokys.* 'tenter hooks', sharp hooks for holding cloth on a frame called a tenter.

1005. *Tewyt.* (*Teuyt, Cam.*) He hoots at the owl.

1007. *The devyll ... whyt.* ?'The devil have every bit', (tag).

1027. *Plucke ... tyle.* 'Pull down lead from roofs, and thatch with tiles.'

1029. *Make ... mat.* Making a windmill out of a mat is an example of Fansy's foolish ideas. Also in *Against Venemous Tongues*, l. 13.

1043. SD *Hic ... similia. quesiendo, Cam.* 'Here let Foly come in shaking a bauble, and making much ado by beating drums and such like.' From this stage direction Foly appears to be in fool's costume. He represents trivial and empty ideas (his alias is Conceit), and he shows himself to be clever in outwitting Fansy and Crafty Conveyaunce.

1050. *lyppes ... eyen.* Proverbial for foolish blindness, cf. *Youth*, l. 217 (*T.I.*, p. 122) and Tilley L330.

1055. Foly's cur, like Fansy's owl, is an excellent spur to comic business (cf. Launce's dog, Crab, in *Two Gentlemen of Verona* III iii).

1057. *Mackemurre.* Probably Macmurrough, the Irish family, Kings of Leinster in the fifteenth century.

1061. *coughe me a dawe.* 'prove me a fool', (*N.E.D. Cough* v 6).

1062. *Cokermowthe* is in Cumbria.

1070 ff. Indications that Fansy was small in stature.

1083/4. *dogge ... hogge* Dyce: *hogge ... dogge, Cam.*

1105. It may be that this by-play with purses arises partly because a large purse was a traditional item of fool's costume.

1118. *Chysshe*. Pet name?

1122. *Anwyke ... Aungey*. Alnwick, Northumberland, and perhaps Anjou in France.

1136. *pultre ... catell*. 'poultry ... livestock': grandiose words for Fansy's bird and Foly's dog.

1143. *Nil ... nyfyls*. An attempt to decline *nihil* 'nothing' as in a school lesson.

anglice. 'in English'. *nyfyls*. 'nothings'.

1155. *Est snavi snago*. Not explained: ?Latin.

vilis imago. 'a horrible appearance', ('shrewde face'). The two lines are clumsy hexameters. *Cam*. prints 'Versus' between them.

1156. *Grimbaldus*. identified as a henchman of Dudley and Simpson, Henry VII's agents. (Winser, op. cit., p. 23).

1176. *doteryll*. dotterel (*Eudromias morinellus*), kind of plover, said to be very stupid, and very easily caught.

1180. *gave me a blurre*. perhaps 'befouled me' or 'insulted me'.

1192. *Cocke Wat*. 'playing the fool', cf. *Against Venemous Tongues*, l. 15.

1193. *Yes, yet*. Ramsay: *Yet yes*, Cam.

gnat. cf. l. 403.

1198. *Regardes, voyes*. 'Look, watch closely': like a modern conjuror, he asks for close attention.

1205. *John a Bonam* appears in the *Hunting of the Hare* (Dyce). Bonhommes were friars, and the name was also given to the Albigenses.

1210. *rode of Wodstocke Parke*. The *rode* is the rood or cross, and the oath refers to the park at Woodstock in Oxfordshire which was a favourite royal residence in medieval times.

1233–4. *tappet* Dyce: *tap*, Cam. For a similar lecherous practice see *Agaynst Garnesche* l. 75.

1268. *Symkyn Tytyvell and Pers Pykthanke*. cf. *Colin Clout* l. 418 ff. Titivillus was the devil who picked up gossip and unwonted scraps of conversation as well as lost syllables at Mass (cf. *Mankind* where he is the chief devil). A Pickthank is a flatterer or a sycophant.

1278. *shroudly towchyd*. 'shrewdly, cunningly mentioned'.

1302–4. *And I ... nought*. Obscure. *gadde* ?goad. The passage may be read 'And I Foly bring them to painful realization of what has been, with this retrospect I make them mad, and bring them from what was something to sheer shaking nought.'

1320. *Who ... fat?* 'Who is master of the mashing-vat for malt?'

1326. *Away the mare.* The phrase, which also appears in *Elinor Rumming* l. 110, is thought by Dyce to be part of a ballad. Proverbial, Tilley M645.

1342. *hoby ... dare.* The hobby (hawk) was used to catch larks by inducing them to fall into a stupor of fear (*dare*).

1387. Reason has lost control of Magnyfycence with Lyberte's release.

1404. *eten sauce.* 'to have found favour', proverbial, Tilley S100, cf. *Bowge of Court* l. 72.

Taylers Hall. Merchant Tailors' Hall in Broad Street Ward of the City of London: it has been on the site of 30 Threadneedle Street since 1313.

1420. *appetyte* – note Magnyfycence's assertion of will here.

1427. *Jacke a Thrommys.* Skelton's other references to Jack a Thrum (*Agaynst Garnesche* l. 204, *Colin Clout* l. 284, and *Garden of Laurell* l. 209) are all suggestive of ignorant and drunken preaching, or of collecting scraps of theology in an unlearned way. To interpret Jack a Thrum's Bible would therefore be an act of foolish ingenuity.

1429. *Loke ... kay. bay, Cam.* 'Put you under lock and key.'

1459. Magnyfycence's boast recalls the tyrants of the mystery cycles. But Skelton's wide reading gives much greater depth. The challenge to Fortune is particularly dangerous, and is as important as the challenge to pride expressed at the end of each stanza.

1466. *Alexander.* Alexander III of Macedon (356–323 B.C.), called 'the Great', conqueror of the East as far as India.

1473. *Syrus.* Cyrus the Great, founder of the Persian Empire, conquered Babylon in 539 BC., and in the next year released the Jews from captivity and allowed them to return to Palestine.

1480. *Porcenya.* Porsena, King of Clusium in Etruria, and supporter of King Tarquinius against the Romans.

1482. *Cesar July.* Julius Caesar, 100–44 B.C.

1487. *Cato.* Marcus Porcius Cato (234–149 B.C.) or his grandson M. P. Cato Uticensis (95–46 B.C.); both famed for valour and noble principles.

1488. *Daryus.* Darius the Great, who ruled the Persian Empire 522–486 B.C.

1494. *Hercules.* Greek hero who, armed with his club, carried out twelve labours at the behest of Eurystheus. The last of these was to bring Cerberus, the three-headed dog, to earth from hell.

1496. *Thesius.* Theseus of Athens who was detained by Pluto in hell, and had to be rescued by Hercules. The two heroes and Cerberus are mentioned in *Philip Sparrow* l. 84–91.

1500. *To me . . . sene.* 'It must be appropriate for all princes to bow to me.'

1501. *Cherlemayne.* Charles the Great, King of the Franks, 742/3–814.

1502. *Arthur.* King Arthur of Albion, the British chieftain who fought against the Saxons in the sixth century, and whose deeds were celebrated for years afterwards in the Arthurian Cycles.

1503. *Basyan.* Antoninus Bassianius Caracalla, Emperor 211–17, who increased the tax on inheritance.

1504. *Aleryeus.* Alaric, c. 370–410, leader of the Visigoths, and conqueror of the city of Rome.

1508. *Galba,* Servius Sulpicius, Emperor 68–9, assassinated by his soldiers.

1509. *Nero,* Caius Claudius, Emperor 54–68, killed his mother, and after many other crimes killed himself.

1510. *Vaspasyan.* Titus Flavius Vespasianus, Emperor 69–79. Dyce quotes a poem which indicates that there was a legend that his name derived from the Latin word for wasp (*vespa*); wasps having supposedly built a nest in his nose.

1511. *Hanyball.* Hannibal the Carthaginian general (247–183 B.C.) who invaded Italy and threatened the gates of Rome in 217 B.C.

1512. *Cypyo.* Publius Cornelius Scipio (236–184 B.C.) given the title 'Africanus' for his conquest of Carthage in 202 B.C.

1514. *frounce . . . foretop.* Ramsay suggests 'curl the hair', but perhaps it means 'wrinkle their brows for them' in consternation.

1531. *Pullyshyd . . . ornacy.* 'Your ornate language is polished and lively': another example of Skelton's awareness of stylistic effects, cf. l. 90 and note. Here the style is 'aureate' as befits the pretensions of Courtly Abusyon.

1540. *Poynt devyse.* cf. l. 843 note.

1545 ff. In this passage Skelton has adapted the morality tradition to his particular requirements. In urging Magnyfycence to enjoy Carnall Delectacyon he is leading him towards Lechery and Wrath. See Wyll (l. 1595) and Lust-and-Lykyng (l. 1607).

1553. *asure inde blewe.* 'azure indigo blue', (pleonastic).

1555. *leyre* Dyce: *heyre* Cam.

1556. *relucent as carbuncle.* 'bright as a carbuncle', (red precious stone).

1562. *Phylyp Sparowe.* Term of affection: sparrows were noted for lechery. Cf. Skelton's poem *Phyllyp Sparowe,* written before 1508.

1581. *fortresse of the holde.* 'stronghold'.

1586. *omnis ... potest.* 'every woman is a whore if it can be concealed.'

1607. 'Lust and Lykynge' is a character in *The Castle of Perseverance.*

1608. *wrastynge and wrythynge.* Obscure, perhaps physical movement 'twisting and writhing', perhaps metaphorical 'seizing by extortion and cunning'.

1612. This picture of assumed rage may be a hit at Henry VIII, but if it is Skelton has justified it most carefully in his moral scheme.

1614. *Call ... candell.* As an emetic.

1624. *hole ... troute.* Proverbial, Tilley T536.

1629 ff. The following episode is a good example of deception. Clokyd Colusyon pretends to Measure that he will speak to Magnyfycence in his interest; in fact the words do him harm, and Measure ends up worse than he began.

1666–7. *subscrybe ... recorde.* 'sign a legal undertaking'.

1692. SD *Hic ... elatissimo.* 'Here let Colusion introduce Measure, while Magnyfycence stares with a lordly expression.'

1710. *all ... all.* 'when all is summed up.'

1756. *vergesse.* Liquor of crab apples used in cooking for its sourness.

1783–8. This speech confirms that he has capitulated to the evils around him: the moment of truth is at hand, and he approaches it in ignorance, cf. ll. 1797–8.

1815. *lyme rodde.* lime twig, normally used for bird catching.

1819 ff. This kind of nonsense becomes a characteristic of Vices in later Interludes (cf. *Apius and Virginia,* in *T.I.,* pp. 313–15). Here the extravagant stupidity is a sign that Magnyfycence has lost all true gravity.

1824. *a losell ... lurden.* 'one good for nothing lead another', (Dyce).

1836–40. *bytter.* 'bittern'. *snyte.* 'snipe'. This list of birds is perhaps an adaptation of the literary convention used by Chaucer in *The Parlement of Foules,* ll. 336–64, and from earlier lists in the works of Marie de France and Alain de Lille.

1876. For the various conventions combined in Adversyte's character see Intro. p. 44.

1877. *quyte ... mede.* 'give you your reward.'

1912. *with* Dyce: *to, Cam.*

1928–9. Proverbial, cf. *Proverbs* 23 14–15.

1941. *prynt ... pen.* 'I record them'.

1966. SD *Hic ... stratum.* 'Here let him approach to lift Magnyfycence and he shall put him on the strewn place.' Perhaps on the rushes strewn over the middle of the hall, and now a convenient place for a pauper.

1988–9. Poverte tries to persuade Magnyfycence to pray for forgiveness, but he persists in lamenting his fate. This leads to the disaster of Wanhope and attempted suicide. Harris sees this as the second temptation to which Magnyfycence (Fortitude) succumbs: as the trial by adversity which complements the trial by prosperity. Harris is probably right in general terms, but dramatically this second episode is handled with much less emphasis than the first, and it is very much shorter.

2016. *shertes of Raynes.* Rennes, in Brittany, was well known for fine linen from which shirts were made.

2026. *dawnsyth varyaunce.* 'takes it by turns to be opposite'.

2031. *yesterday ... agayne.* Proverbial, Tilley Y31.

2037. SD *Discedendo ... verba* Dyce: *Disidendo, Cam.* 'As he goes let him say these words'.

2044. *in manus tuas.* 'into Thy hands (O Lord, I commend my spirit)'. Last prayer before hanging.

2068. *on the le.* The refrain from a song.

2084. *may holde to tacke.* 'may not endure'.

2089. *totum ... hawe.* 'all in all is worth nothing', cf. Tilley H221.

2095. *to ... harre.* cf. l. 913 and note.

2098. *jackenapes.* 'pert upstart', originally a pet name for a monkey.

2106. *bounde in a mat.* i.e. wearing poor clothing.

2113ff. Lyberte, who may be said to have prompted Magnyfycence's errors earlier, now turns upon him and rehearses the mistakes made: this is a convention of morality plays.

2124. *patchynge ... sharde.* 'for patching a broken pot.'

2136. *That ... brydyll.* 'to give too much freedom'. Proverbial, Tilley B671.

2140. *prechynge ... Hyll.* Euphemism for last words before execution on Tower Hill.

2150. SD *Hic ... populum.* 'Here let someone blow on a horn from the back, behind the people.'

2159. Magnyfycence remains silent until his interruption at l. 2237. There is considerable dramatic advantage in having him miserably overhear the self-congratulation of the villains.

2173. *lay ... pate.* 'clout you on the head', (slang). The brawl which follows is typical of groups of stage vices.

2187. *wrynge ... brake.* Perhaps 'I shal wring all your 'be' on the wrack', referring to 'be' in ll. 2182, 2184.

2234. *Your trymynge . . . tangyd.* 'your silly devices must be made effective by me', (*N.E.D.* trimtram, tang v¹ 2 b).

2236. Magnyfycence has presumably been present throughout this scene, and can contain himself no longer.

2260. *requiem eternam.* 'eternal rest' (from the Mass for the Dead): but the intention is mocking.

2263. *halfe strete.* The stews in Southwark.

2265. *motton.* Slang for 'prostitute'.

2272. *clappyd with a coloppe.* 'beaten with a lump of meat'.

2276. SD *Et . . . loco.* 'And let them leave the place in a hurry.'

2283. SD *Hic . . . Dyspare.* 'Here Dyspare enters.' Worse than the arrival of Adversyte, this episode threatens Magnyfycence's life and soul.

2308. SD *Hic . . . Myschefe.* 'Here Myschefe enters.'

2323. *Cam.* attributes this line to Magnyfycence.

2324. SD *Hic . . . dicat.* 'Here Good Hope enters, while Dyspayre and Myschefe run away; suddenly let Good Hope wrench the sword from him and say'.

2337. *Wanhope.* i.e. want of hope, despair, especially despair of the mercy of God.

2345. This is the beginning of Magnyfycence's restoration through repentance.

2347. *gumme of Arabe.* Gum arabic, from the acacia tree.

2384. SD *Hic . . . Redresse.* 'Here Redresse enters.'

2401. SD *Et exiat.* 'And let him go out.'

2406. SD *Magnyfycence . . . indumentum.* 'Let Magnyfycence accept the robe.' The change of clothing is a stage convention, cf. Craik, op. cit., p. 73 ff.

2418. Sad Cyrcumspeccyon is the embodiment of reason in the play. His arrival is a sign that the moral order is restored.

2439. *letter.* cf. l. 309 ff.

2456. *And . . . forfende.* 'And I forbid you those who are crafty and corrupt.'

2456. SD *Hic . . . Perseveraunce.* 'Here Perseveraunce enters.' Perseveraunce in this play is necessary to the moral scheme, for it is the means by which Magnyfycence (Fortitude) is to endure the tests of adversity and prosperity.

2468. *Faythfull* Dyce: *Faytfully, Cam.*

2510. *sekernesse* Dyce: *sekenesse, Cam.* cf. l. 2517. 'sickness' seems unlikely in this context.

2519 ff. Skelton here adds to his themes of the danger of flattery and the need for kingly judgement in wealth a powerful reminder of mutability.

2556. *Ensordyd.* 'defiled'. *Ensorbyd* 'sucked' (Dyce).

2568. *Amen.* Thus the play ends with a prayer, but it is interesting that it is not a prayer for the King as the custom was in later years.

1. SD There is no stage direction in MS. King John's first speech appears to be an introductory soliloquy. There has been some speculation as to whether a Prologue has been lost.

10–13. *granfather.* Perhaps Henry V, the Holy Roman Emperor, to whom John was distantly related by marriage. His father was Henry II, and his brother Richard I, Coeur-de-Lyon (l. 13).

16. *Yerlond.* John was granted the Lordship of Ireland in 1177 when he was ten years old.

Angoye. Henry II inherited Anjou from his father, and Normandy from his mother.

21. SD. No stage direction in MS. England's opening words indicate that she must have overheard some of the end of John's speech.

34. *Matt.* 13 13–14, and 15 14.

42. SD. Not in MS. *Sedwsyon* substituted as speech heading for *Kynge Johan* by scribe A.

54. *Collessyans. Colossians* 4 6. 'Let your speech be always with grace, seasoned with salt, that ye may know how ye ought to answer every man.' Earlier Biblical translations read 'powdred' for 'seasoned' (Adams): Sedition's word 'spycer' (l. 50) is a play on 'powder'.

64–5. *Luke* 20 46–7.

66. *syde cotys.* These were long coats with full skirts used by actors, and especially by fools.

71. *wyld bore of Rome.* The Pope; cf. l. 86.

86. *aper de sylva.* 'the boar out of the wood', *Psalm* 80 13.

97. *Quodcumque ligaveris.* 'Whatsoever thou shalt bind (on earth shall be bound in heaven . . .)' *Matt.* 16 19. E. S. Miller, 'The Roman Rite in Bale's *King John*', *PMLA*, 64, 1949, pp. 802–22, sees this as an important passage in the protracted parody of the confessional. By means of confession, Bale thought that the Pope was able to exercise political control.

117–18. *John* 1 1.

130–2. *Esaye. Isaiah* 1 17, 'Pursue justice, and champion the oppressed, give the orphan his rights, plead the widow's cause', *N.E.B.*

141. *be fast and swer.* 'firmly and surely.'

155. SD. This is the first stage direction concerned with a change of costume for doubling, see Appendix 1.

175. *goose go barefote*. Proverbial, to give shoes to a goose is a pointless exercise. Cf. Tilley, G354.

199. *Syre John*. Usually a contemptuous reference to a priest.

202. *cutt shoes*. sandals, as worn by monks.

215. *Spruse*. Prussia. *Berne* emended for *Beirne* (?Bohemia, Adams). The list of places is reminiscent of the Vice's travels.

227. *short ther hornys*. Perhaps equivalent to modern 'Cut them down to size.'

233-4. *Hector*, son of King Priam and champion of Troy in the *Iliad*.

> *Diomedes*, one of the bravest of the Greeks at Troy, who fought against Hector and Aeneas.

> *Achylles*, Greek hero at Troy and slayer of Hector.

244. *Argus* had a hundred eyes, of which only two slept at any time.

262. *Gesse at a ventur*. 'Have a guess . . .'

264. *benedicite*. 'Bless me.' The words of the penitent at confession. Because of its secrecy, confession permitted sedition to flourish, cf. the conspiracy described in l. 272-3.

296. Sedition eventually disguises himself as the monk Stephen Langton (l. 984).

304-5. *lecherous . . . relygyous*. This is an example of the conventional slip of the Vice whereby he reveals his evil nature, cf. Clergy ll. 512-514.

312. SD. This is scribe A's marginal addition, see Appendix 1.

326. *by the waye . . . shall*. 'By the way that my soul shall go', i.e. to heaven.

335. Bale's charge is that the clergy do not interpret Scripture as they should, but indulge in conspiracy.

369. *Babulon*. Babylon. *Revelation* 17 gives an account of the fall of the Whore of Babylon: this was commonly taken as a vision of the fall of Rome by Protestant polemicists.

415. *popetly playes*. Presumably 'popish ceremonies', but this could be a reference to dramatic productions encouraged by the church as a teaching activity.

420. *Mortuaryes*. Gifts to the clergy from the estate of dead parishioners.

422. *cowrtes of baudrye*. ?assemblies of vain finery, perhaps a reference to ceremonial vestments.

423. *trentalls*. Sets of thirty requiem masses.

Scalacely messys. Masses associated with St Bernard's vision of the ladder to heaven.

434-5. *Astitit . . . varietate*. Psalm 44 10 (*Vulgate*), 45 10 (A.V.).

442ff. The list which follows is not without antiquarian interest and forms part of Bale's prolonged attempt to denigrate the monastic orders. The sources have been discussed by T. B. Blatt, *The Plays of John Bale*, Copenhagen, 1968, Appendix I, pp. 235–43. Bale wrote two lists in MS. Bodley 73 (*c.* 1525), and these formed the basis for the first version in *King Johan*. Additions in Bale's hand, ll. 447–58, derive to a large extent from F. Lambertus, *In Regulam Minoritarum*, 1523. Though not all the items have been identified, it now seems likely that, however exotic they may appear, few are entirely fictitious.

Grandy Montensers followers of St Stephen Grandmont, established c. 1076 in France.

Benedictyns founded by St Benedict, the patriarch of western monks, and established at Monte Cassino c. 529.

Primonstratensers founded by St Norbert 1119, called White Canons.

Bernardes founded by St Bernard of Clairvaux c. 1115.

Gylbertynys founded by Gilbert of Sempringham, Lincs, following the Augustinian Rule.

Jacobytes French order of preaching friars (Dominican).

Mynors Friars Minor, established by St Francis.

Whyght Carmes Carmelites, White Friars: cf. Mt Carmel.

Augustynis Black Friars, Augustinian Canons, founded c. 1060.

Sanbonites third of the minor orders.

Cluniackes Cluniacs, branch of Benedictines founded at Cluny in France in 910; important in N. of England.

Carthusyans, founded by St Bruno at the Grand Chartreuse near Grenoble in 1084.

Heremytes hermits, *auncors* anchorites, perhaps individuals rather than established orders.

Rodyans Knights Hospitallers, with their fortress at Rhodes and later at Malta.

Crucifers ?cross-bearers.: name refers to emblem worn on the habit.

Lucifers founded by Lucifer, Bishop of Cagliari in fifth century.

Brigettes Bridgetines, founded by St Bridget of Sweden, 1344.

Ambrosyanes followers of the Ambrosian Liturgy, after St Ambrose.

Stellifers ?star bearers.

Ensifers ?sword bearers.

Purgatoryanes ?believers in Purgatory.

Sophyanes ?after St Sophia.

Indianes named after St Thomas of India.

Camaldulensers founded by St Romauld near Florence, 1012.

Jesuytes 'Jesuit' was a term of contempt for some time before it was applied to the Society of Jesus founded by St Ignatius Loyola in 1540. It is not clear whether Bale has the Order in mind. One should note that the word is here part of an insertion probably added after 1540.

Joannytes mentioned by Lambertus.

Clarimontensers not traced.

Clarynes Minoresses, founded by St Clare and St Francis of Assisi, c. 1212.

Columbynes ?after St Columba who founded an Irish order in the seventh century.

Templers military order founded by Baldwin II of Jerusalem.

New Ninivytes mentioned by Lambertus.

Rufyanes ?Rufinus (?340–410), theologian, monk, friend and opponent of Jerome.

Tercyanes Franciscans, Third Order founded by St Francis.

Lorytes not traced.

Lazarytes Lazar, leper: also called Magdalenites by Lambertus.

Hungaryes mentioned by Lambertus.

Teutonyckes military order founded 1191 at Acre, and later campaigning in E. Prussia.

Hospitelers cf. Rodyans.

Honofrynes mentioned by Lambertus.

Basyles St Basil founded a monastery in Pontus c. 360. His Rule influenced St Benedict, and also Greek monasticism. There were houses in Italy and Sicily.

Bonhams Bonhommes, begging friars who came to England in the thirteenth century.

Sclavons mentioned by Lambertus.

Celestynes founded by Pope Celestine V in 1254 from St Bernard's order.

Paulynes known in 1310.

Hieronymytes Augustinians, called after St Jerome, founded in Kent, 1375.

Monkes of Josaphathes Valleye named after a Carmelite monastery, and mentioned in *The Image of Ipocrisy*, (attributed to Skelton), together with *Bretherne of the Black Alleye.*

Fulgynes Black Monks.

Flamynes perhaps included to suggest pagan origin for the clergy, cf. *Vestals*, (Blatt).

Donates ancient sect.

Dimysynes not traced.

Canons of St Mark not traced.

Vestals ?an order of chastity.

Monyals ?those who live alone.

466. The morality tradition frequently shows that the Devil can cite Scripture: here Bale modifies the convention for a polemical purpose, overlooking, perhaps, that he himself was formidable in the use of Scripture in controversy.

483. *cormerantes*. Cormorants, proverbially greedy birds.

522. *Loth. Genesis* 19 15–26.

556. S. D. Scribe A wrote *dyssymalacyon* first, and corrected to *Sedewsyon*. Probably he realized that his projected doubling plan was running into difficulties, see Appendix 1.

579. *Angoye.* There was no historical gift of Anjou to Arthur.

580. *abbeye . . . graunge.* Proverbial, suggesting impoverishment due to bad husbandry.

609. *Matt* 17 24–7, 22 15–22.

627. Sedition's entry and his first speech show a number of common Vice characteristics: notably his familiar style of speech, his frank villainy, his reference to the stews and to possible hanging, and his search for companion villains. The scene which follows keeps up the Vice convention: as in the mocking echo (l. 640), the suggestion of brawling (l. 651), the playing on words, particularly Latin and French, the showing off in strange clothes (l. 724), the moral demonstration (ll. 760–76), the carrying of Sedition which recalls the Vice's custom of riding on the Devil's back (see Nichol Newfangle, l. 1212 SD, *Like Will to Like*, in *T.I.*, p. 362), the singing (l. 828), the taking of aliases (l. 983 SD). All these features indicate that Bale was well aware of the growing popularity of the Vice on the Tudor stage in the 1530s. Bale's particular contribution is to use him in religious controversy.

639–41. *Sancte . . . nobis.* 'O holy Dominican, pray for us.
                O holy bald monk, I curse you.
                O holy Franciscan, pray for us.'

643–4. *Pater . . . sanctyficetur.* 'Our Father . . . who art in heaven . . . hallowed be . . .'

647. A grotesque nose was part of the Vice's costume; cf. 'bottle-nosed knave'.

650. *A Johanne . . . Domine.* 'Free us, O Lord, from the evil King John.'

668. *Par . . . plesaunce.* 'By my faith, my friend, I (am) entirely at your service.'

680. *Benno.* Eleventh-century Bavarian bishop who sided with the Pope against the Emperor.

708. *imagys . . . Savyer.* Images of the Holy Spirit and of Christ as Saviour.

715. *bryng . . . boxe.* 'to bring this trick to fruition'. Bale's mockery of Latin refers to the controversy about vernacular services and translations of the Bible.

726–9. Dissimulation is dressed in a monastic habit of many colours deriving from the costumes of the different orders he mentions.

749. *gam.* cf. *Castle of Perseverance*, ll. 2688, 2697, 3644–6; *Magnyfycence* ll. 2566–7. The use of 'game' here is a particularly illuminating example of the medieval sense that drama was a game: 'It played action in *game* – not in *ernest* – within a world set apart, established by convention and obeying rules of its own', V. A. Kolve, *The Play Calle*

Corpus Christi, 1966, p. 32. Dissimulation sees the sequence which demonstrates the allegorical connections between him and his fellows (ll. 763–897) as a 'game'.

764–5. *Super ... aliena.* 'By the rivers of Babylon we hanged our instruments (upon trees). How shall we sing a good song in a strange land?' *Psalm* 137 1–4 *(Vulgate* 136). The choice of this quotation is ironic since these two villains will not sing a good song but a corrupt one.

766. *placebo.* The Office of the Dead.

767. *vadam et videbo.* 'I shall go and see (him).' *Genesis* 45 28.

802. S D This action, clearly reminiscent of the Devil bearing the Vice on his back, is the visual culmination of the moral demonstration in this sequence. The allegory is that Dissimulation, who came from the Devil (l. 779), brings in first Private Wealth. The latter, in turn, brings in Usurped Power, who later turns out to be the Pope (l. 833), and all three together are then told to carry Sedition. The moral demonstration, characteristic of the morality play, is turned again into a polemical one by the concentration upon the Pope after l. 833.

803. *I am* Collier: *thu art* MS.

805. St Antony was one of the earliest leaders of monasticism; he flourished in Egypt in the third century.

807. *Awsten ... Gregory.* St Augustine of Hippo.(354–430) inspirer of monastic discipline. St Ambrose (c. 340–397) Bishop of Milan, liturgist. St Jerome (c. 347–420) defender of monasticism, and biblical scholar of great eminence. Pope Saint Gregory I, the Great (540–604).

828. The cementing of an alliance, or the hatching of a plot are frequently cues for song in the Vice tradition, cf. *Mankind* l. 327.

837–8. Usurped Power is clearly not dressed as the Pope as yet, cf. l. 983 S D. The allegory is that Usurped Power can appear in different forms of which that of the Pope is the most immediate. This protean quality, or trickery, is shared by Sedition who is sometimes a monk, and sometimes Stephen Langton, the Archbishop, cf. T. W. Craik, *The Tudor Interlude*, p. 88–9.

848. *A pena et culpa.* Formula of Confession, '(Free from) punishment and blame'. The doctrinal point here is that no man can release sinners from blame; it is God's prerogative. Usurped Power, the Pope, therefore acts beyond his competence at l. 861, cf. Miller, op. cit., p. 807.

851. *dobyll bere.* 'have a double helping', or perhaps 'at double strength'.

891. Dissimulation's message is to reveal that the Clergy is under pressure from John to produce more taxes, and also that the Church's

right of benefit of clergy is being challenged. His terror of the Pope, and the coarse joke at l. 893–5 maintain the feeling against the Pope.

898. *leve yowr gawdes*. Perhaps the 'gam' (l. 749 and note) is now ending.

907. *No . . . cary*. 'Keep on taking in (money and wealth); let none go from you.'

932–3. The Interdict in 1208 and the Excommunication in 1209 were carried out by three bishops of whom William of London and Eustace of Ely were two. Adams (pp. 37 and 134) makes it clear that the error derives from one of Bale's sources, the English *Brut*, cxlvii.

937. Stephen Langton had been known to Innocent for some years before the latter became Pope. Innocent appears to have put him forward as a compromise candidate between the claims of John de Gray, Bishop of Norwich, the choice of King John, and Reginald, sub-prior of Canterbury, the choice of some of the monks at Canterbury.

943. *hym* must refer to John: Norwich was attempting to gain the primacy, according to Dissimulation's interpretation, by flattering the King.

959. *indeucte*. 'inducted', taken through the ceremonial conferring rights and profits.

  intronyȝate enthroned as a bishop (obs. *enthronize N.E.D.*).

967. *cléne remyssion* would remove all guilt for ever, without fear of Purgatory. Thus the Church is using forgiveness as a political bribe.

983. SD. The stage direction requires the abstract characters now to assume disguises as though they were historical people. The conspiracy has been hatched by abstractions and Bale now moves into a quasi-historical mode for the dramatic ceremony of excommunication.

991–1011. These lines were added by Bale on a separate sheet (MS p. 23). Perhaps this was, as Collier suggests, to give time for the change of costume, but the fiercely anti-Catholic tone of the insertion is to be noted. Between the early and late versions Bale's bitterness intensified.

998–9. *He . . . heresye*. 'He will ensure that the ritual ceremonies of the Church – matins, the canonical hours, the mass, and evensong – will overwhelm the truth of the Scriptures by creating fear of heresy.'

1008. *Albygeanes*. The Albigensian sect, centred on Albi in Southern France, criticized the corruption of the priesthood from the eleventh century. Innocent III ordered the Cistercians to preach a crusade against them in 1209. The campaign against them, pursued by the Inquisition into the fourteenth century, led to their eventual extinction.

1013. *Laternense*. The Fourth Lateran Council held at Rome in 1215 by Innocent III has been considered to be the high point of the medieval

Papacy. From it flowed the condemnation of the Albigensians and other heresies, the episcopal Inquisition, and the preaching of a new crusade. The Lateran was the palace of the Laterni family, and became a papal church and residence.

1028. *Mea ... culpa.* 'Through my fault, my most grievous fault.' Part of the Act of Contrition.

1029. *pro ... Maria.* 'on behalf of God and Holy Mary.'

1035. *crosse ... candle.* This is a dramatic version of an excommunication. The actions embodied are reversing the cross (l. 1036); closing up the book, probably the Missal (l. 1038–9); blowing out the candle (l. 1040); ringing the bell (l. 1042–3). Possibly there is confusion between the interdiction, which prevented the holding of services, and the excommunication, withdrawing the Church's protection from John himself (Adams, p. 167); but it is hard to accept that Bale was unable to distinguish between the two. The 'confusion' is more probably a matter of dramatic expediency.

1045. *ember dayes.* Four periods of fasting and prayer, one for each season of the year.

1056. *Pandulphus.* Private Wealth is to take this alias. Pandulphus, the Papal Legate, never became a Cardinal, but he is so identified later in the play.

1057. *Raymundus.* Not identified historically; this alias for Dissimulation is not developed further by Bale.

1082. *fower beggyng orderes.* The mendicant orders arose at the beginning of the thirteenth century: Franciscans (Grey Friars), Dominicans (Black Friars), Carmelites (White Friars), and Augustinian Hermits.

1086. The Interpreter's speech appears in the manuscript in Bale's autograph as MS. p. 26. It is marked for insertion at the end of the Pope's speech, l. 1085 on MS. p. 27. The stage direction has thus to be split so as to separate the Pope's exit and the entry of Sedition and Nobility. MS. p. 26 concludes with Bale's *Finit Actus Primus*, suggesting that the text of scribe A was not divided into acts. If Bale appeared in this play as he did in some of his other work, it is likely that he would have assumed the role of the Interpreter.

1087–8. *myrrour ... magistrate.* Perhaps a nod by Bale at the very successful and influential collection of stories *A Mirror for Magistrates* which appeared in 1555 and 1559.

1107–13. *Exodus* 12–18, *Joshua* 1 12.

1114–15. 1 *Samuel* 17. This interpretation of the historical events in terms of scriptural parallel reflects Bale's attitude to history. The contemporary achievements of Henry VIII are anticipated by the earlier Biblical ones. It has been suggested that this reflects a cyclic view of history as found in the treatment of historical events in the mystery cycles: see S. J. Kahrl, *The Traditions of Medieval English Drama* 1974, pp. 130–1.

1136. *Good Perfeccyon.* Here Sedition, appearing as a monk, takes on an allegorical alias so as to hear the confession of Nobility. His object is 'to barter indulgence for treason,' (Miller, p. 811).

1140. *umfrey* not identified.

1149–50. *Benedicite . . . amen.* 'Bless ye. In the name of the Lord Pope, Amen.' This is another parody of the confession. Sedition, wearing his stole (l. 1148), sits to hear Nobility's confession, but he should do so in the name of the Father, Son, and Holy Ghost, not of the Lord Pope.

1155. *The workes . . . slepte.* 'I have slumbered instead of carrying out my charitable obligations.'

1159. *so mote I the.* 'As I may thrive.'

1161. *dyrge.* The antiphon used in the Roman Office of the Dead.

1178. cf. *Romans* 13 1.

1182. *damnacyon.* Nobility has perhaps realized that the confession is not legitimate, but Sedition brings him to order by the threat of damnation.

1186. *Auctoritate . . . te.* 'By the authority of the pontiff of Rome, I absolve you'. Not by the authority of God.

1205. *interdyte* put under interdiction. Sedition (Stephen Langton) and Private Wealth (Pandulphus) are come to execute the Papal decree.

1215–30. This passage contains much polemical rubbish. The purpose is to use scraps of superstition, scandal, and miscellaneous trivia to discredit the use of relics – a satirical intention which goes back to pre-Reformation literature, as in Chaucer's Pardoner. From a dramatic point of view Clergy and Civil Order are made traitors by Sedition's false absolution.

Barnabe. St Barnabas, apostle, known for his generous nature.

Myhelles. St Michael, archangel.

Twyde. Not traced.

Haylys. The blood of Christ kept in a vial at Hayles Abbey in Gloucestershire was said to be invisible to sinners. The vial is reputed to have been a conjuror's device which could be made to appear red on payment of an appropriate sum.

Job. For the sores inflicted upon Job by Satan see *Job* 1 7–8.

Fandigo. ?Fantinus, tenth-century Greek Abbot.

Blythe. ?Blitharius, seventh-century Scot who worked in France. His relics were disturbed by sixteenth-century Calvinists.

Johan Shornes. Not traced.

Jesse. The 'Tree of Jesse' was widely used as a representation of Christ's genealogy in church ornament and in literature. Jesse was the father of David.

Rabart. Not traced.

Darvell Gathyron. Derfel Gadarn, a large wooden image of a saint, was brought to London from Wales and burnt at Smithfield on 22 May 1538. The passage is thus a useful pointer for dating.

1284. *Forty . . . clarke.* Thomas à Becket, murdered in Canterbury Cathedral, 29 December 1170.

1304. Pandulf, as Papal Legate, reached England in 1211 with the purpose of increasing the pressure on John. In the play he repeats the excommunication at l. 1358, and receives the submission of the King at l. 1728 (historically at Dover in 1213). Bale telescopes these events, partly because of his sources, and partly in order to concentrate the dramatic impact of the Cardinal.

1343. *Salomon. Proverbs* 16 10.

1346–7. *Matthew* 22 21.

1354. *Belles prystes.* Priests of Baal, *I Kings* 18 17–40.

1366. *Seynt Assys.* St Asaph.

1378–81. The stage direction and these four lines are written in Bale's hand from bottom to top in the margin of MS. p. 32. Sedition is to call 'from outside the place'. Dramatically the problem arises whether the audience is supposed to know that it is Sedition who shouts. If he had a peculiar voice, or if he was seen in some way outside the playing area, the moral point would be made that the Cardinal is promoting Sedition. But equally Sedition may be kept offstage because he is changing his costume in order to double. The addition might be said to give extra support to King John's subsequent references to the Devil (ll. 1382, 1387).

1398. In the following sequence, ll. 1398–1533, Bale seeks to justify King John's position by extensive reference to scriptural authority. Unlike most other heroes of morality plays, King John is not subjected to temptation.

1407. *Ecclesiastes* 10 20.

1408. *Powle. Romans* 13 1–2.

1410. *Cyrinus. Luke* 2 1–5.

1412. *Matthew* 17 27.

1436–7. *Balaam. Numbers* 23 8, 24 13.

1459. *leven pharesayycall.* cf. *I Corinthians* 5 6–8. 'the leaven of corruption and wickedness'. *N.E.D.* 'leaven' sb.1.c.

1460–2. *Susan.* The story of Susannah, tempted by the Elders, is told in the apocryphal *History of Susannah*: 'It is better for me to fall into your hands and not do it, than to sin in the sight of the Lord', (v. 23).

1467. *nunc reges intelligite.* 'Be wise now, O Kings', *Psalm* 2 10.

1498–9. *Pawle. II Corinthians* 2 5–8.

1501–4. *Powle. Romans* 13 1–6.

1512. *Josaphat.* Jehoshaphat, King of Judah, 2 *Chronicles* 19 4–11.

1513. *Ezechias.* Hezekiah, King of Judah, 2 *Kings* 18–20 passim.

1515. *Machabees.* See *Apocrypha*, 1 *Machabees* 4 41–51.

1528–9. *Dathan and Abiron.* Dathan and Abiram rebelled against the authority of Moses, and were destroyed. *Numbers* 16 1–35.

1531. *Beyng . . . fere.* 'Because you are accursed you make me afraid, truly.'

1572. *spowse.* 'God hym-selfe' l. 109: her case is that Catholicism separates from God because it is not the true religion.

1600. *Peccavi, mea culpa.* 'I have sinned, the fault is mine.'

1605. *Phelype.* The Pope had instructed Philip to move against King John in pursuance of the excommunication in 1211. Pandulf, the Papal Legate, was also to threaten deposition.

1632–9. Alexander of Scotland had been subdued by King John in 1209, but there seems little historical evidence of a conspiracy involving Scotland, France, Portugal, and the Scandinavian armies.

1644–5. *Jubyle.* Sedition's proclamation of a Jubilee meant that there would be a year of remission during which plenary indulgence might be obtained by those fighting against King John. Miller, op. cit., p. 812.

1665. After this line, which is the tenth line of MS. p. 38, there begins Bale's major revision of the earlier text copied by Scribe A, see Appendix 2. The dramatic effect of the first long insertion is to elaborate Sedition's part, making him more of a Vice – he tells the truth and laughs (ll. 1682–94) – and to strengthen King John's role as the protector of England.

1692–3. *Cantate . . . Confitebor . . . Iubilate.* 'Sing ye . . . I will confess . . . Rejoice.'

1698. *Solon.* Wise man and lawgiver in Athens in the sixth century B.C. He legislated against loose living, and condemned theatrical fiction.

1728. John's submission occurred at Ewell near Dover on 13 May 1213.

1729–31. Adams makes it clear that Bale took several details from *The Brut*: notably the actual words of the submission, and Pandulf's retention of the crown for five days – from chap. cl; and the tribute of one thousand marks – from chap. cli.

1758. S D Sedition must leave the stage here as he is to return as Stephen Langton at l. 1783.

1785. *meteropolytan* metropolitan, the chief bishop of a country or province.

1789–1800. *Confiteor . . . amen.* 'I confess to the Lord Pope, and to all his cardinals, and to you, that I have sinned too much by demanding tax from the church, through my fault. Thus I pray the most holy Lord Pope, and all his prelates, and you, to pray for me. May the almighty Pope have pity on you, and release you from all your faults, and free you from suspension, excommunication, and interdiction, and restore you to your kingdom.
Amen.
Our Lord Pope absolves you, and I absolve you through his authority, and by the authority of the Apostles Peter and Paul given to me in this behalf, from all your heresies, and I restore you to crown and kingdom, in the name of the Lord Pope, amen.'

Miller points out that this sequence is 'abridgement, adaptation, and parody' of the *Confiteor*, the *Misereatur* and the absolution after excommunication, particularly in the substitution of the Pope, Cardinals, and Langton for God, the saints and the Virgin, op. cit., p. 813.

1818. *pryme.* The first of the Canonical Hours of worship, usually 6 a.m.

1830. *cruettes.* Small vessels used for wine or water at Mass.

1855. *Annas, Cayphas.* Caiaphas was the High Priest, and Annas his father-in-law, *John* 18 13, 14. Both characters appear in the Mystery Cycles: see R. Woolf, *The English Mystery Plays*, 1972, pp. 250–4.

1858–60. Bale took the episode of the forging cleric, here called Treason, from *The Brut*, chap. cl. Bale maintains sympathy for John at this point in the play by making him unable to act against wicked clergy.

1883. *Peter Pomfrete.* A contemporary holy man who forecast King John's loss of the crown, and whom John executed saying that the prophecy had not been fulfilled.

1899. *Maister Morres.* Maurice Morganensis, fl. 1210; but his works are lost. Bale may have the story from Giraldus Cambrensis, *De Instructione Principium*: see J. H. P. Pafford, 'Two Notes on Bale's *Kyng Johan*', *M.L.R.* 56, 1961, pp. 553–5.

1902. *Destruet . . . plaga.* 'The king of kings shall destroy this kingdom with a double misfortune.'

1922. Tilley, B94: cf. 'Not to know which to shun, or to chuse, which to leave or which to take.'

1928. *Julyane.* Richard's wife was Berengaria. She is called Julyan in *The Brut*, chap. cliii.

1956. SD *In . . . dicens.* 'Falling upon his knees, he shall worship God, saying . . .'

1957. *David. II Samuel* 7 25–9.

1964. *placebo.* Vespers in the Office of the Dead. He presumably means that he will not receive any financial advantage from her death.

1975. *Saynt Loe . . . Legearde.* St Louis . . . St Leger.

1976. *Saynt Antonyes hogge.* Saint Anthony contended with the hog who represented sensual indulgence.

2002. *wyldefyer.* Highly inflammable material used in warfare.

2043. *Swynsett.* Cistercian Abbey at Swineshead, Lincolnshire: this is given as the place of King John's death by some early authorities, including *The Brut,* chap clv.

2061. SD *Flectit genua.* 'He bends his knee.'

2069. *Gualo.* Guala Bicchieri, Papal Legate.

2076. *Otto.* Emperor, excommunicated 1210.

2109. *malmesaye . . . ypocras. Malmsey* – strong sweet wine originally from Monemvasia in Greece. *Caprick* – liquid made from nasturtium seeds, used for pickling. *Tyre* – strong sweet wine. *Ypocras* – spiced wine, supposedly of medicinal value.

2128. *Scala Celi.* see l. 423 note.

2129. *Enoch . . . Heli.* Enoch (*Genesis* 5 24) and Elijah (2 *Kings* 2 11) were taken into heaven by the Lord.

2195. *Polydorus.* Polydore Vergil (1470?–1555?) *Anglicae Historiae Libri,* Basle, 1534.

2198. *Leylande.* John Leland (1506–52) King Henry's Antiquary. He was commissioned to search out documents in ecclesiastical libraries from 1533, and in doing so made a journey throughout England and Wales. It is thought that Bale used his work, much of which remained in manuscript. The 'slumbre' may refer to his insanity from 1550 until his death.

2201–3. *Sigebertus.* Sigbert of Gemblours (1030?–1112), Belgian chronicler whose works were continued anonymously.

Vincentius. Vincent of Beauvais (1190?–1264?), *Speculum Historiale,* Venice, 1494.

Nauclerus, John Nauclerus, *Memorabilium omnis aetatis et omnium gentium chronicii commentarii,* Tubingen, 1516.

Giraldus Cambrensis, (1146–1226?) *Topographia Hibernia.*

Mathu Parys, Historia Anglorum, thirteenth century.

Paulus Phrigio, (1483?–1543) *Chronicorum regum regnorumque omnium catalogum,* Basle, 1534.

Johan Maior, (1467–1550) *Historia Maioris Britanniae,* Paris, 1521.

Hector Boethius, (1456?–1536) *Scotorum historiae a prima gentis origine*, Paris, 1527.
This formidable list shows the depth of Bale's interest in the material available upon King John. Adams (op. cit., pp. 27–31) questions whether all the authors are as favourable as Bale suggests, and it may be that the importance of this passage is that it seeks to build up King John's virtues.

2212. *Yppeswych, Donwych, and Berye.* Ipswich, Dunwich, and Bury St Edmunds are all in Suffolk, Bale's native county.

2217. The old London Bridge was built between 1179 and 1209, and remained in use until 1831.

2227. *Ecclesiastes* 10 20.

2231. *Saynt Hierome.* St Jerome, c. 342–420, biblical scholar: but the reference is untraced.

2237–9. *Proverbs* 16 10.

2244. *Proverbs* 22 11.

2245. *Cleros.* See *N.E.D.* The derivation is from the Greek meaning 'Lot, heritage'. Matthias, the additional apostle, was chosen by lot, *Acts* 1 23–6.

2251. *Clerus.* A worm-like spider mentioned by Aristotle.

2262. *Aioth. Judges* 3 12–36.

2263. *Esdras.* Ezra obtained permission to restore parts of Jerusalem, *Ezra* 7.

2268. *Mantuan.* Baptista Spagnuoli of Mantua (1448–1516), author of anti-clerical Eclogues, some of which were translated by Alexander Barclay in 1514.

2273. *Chrysostome.* St John Chrysostom (347–407), bishop of Constantinople.

2279. *Anneus Seneca. Epistulae Morales* 83.

2291. 2 *Samuel* 1 2–16, not 'the Seconde of Kynges' (l. 2294).

2300. *hatefull* is written above *odyouse* and may have been intended by Bale as a substitution.

2345. *Omnes Una.* 'All together.'

2351. *Romans* 13 1–2.

2366. The story of the young man, the Amalekite, is given in 2 *Samuel* 1 2–16, not in 'Kynges' (l. 2365).

2372. *Isboset.* The murder of Ishbosheth, son of Saul, and David's revenge upon the murderers is told in 2 *Samuel* 4 5–12.

2410. *levyathan.* Sea monster, *Isaiah* 27 1, *Psalm* 104 26, *Job* 3 8. Some authors suggest the crocodile.

2417–8. *caro ... celestis.* 'Flesh and blood hath not revealed it unto thee, but my heavenly Father', *Matthew* 16 17.

2419. *of carnall generacyon.* 'by means of human procreation'.

2444. *goo ... flyes.* 'will go hunting for nothing.'

2456. The stave of music is copied from fol. 57 of the manuscript.

2506. *playe Pasquyll.* 'write lampoons', *N.E.D.*

2514–5. A reference to the great uprising of 1536 in the North of England.

2525. *playe boo pepe.* From a game involving hiding one's eyes; cf. *King Lear* 1 4 184.

2531. *Sacramentaryes.* Those denying the doctrine of the Real Presence in the Eucharist.

2532. *Anabaptystes.* This is the first of three references to the Anabaptists (cf. ll. 2626–31, 2678–81). The sect, which began in 1521 at Zwickau in Germany, was perhaps the most radical of many Reformation sects. The denial of the validity of infant baptism was only one aspect of their beliefs which challenged Catholicism; their reliance upon a literal interpretation of the Bible was unacceptable. Politically their criticism of the process of law and government caused much uneasiness. The sect took over Munster in 1532, and held it against siege until 1535. The intention was that Munster should become the centre of the world's conversion to the new doctrines which were fanatically proclaimed during these years.

Bale's reaction is interesting in that both Sedition, who expresses the Catholic view, and Imperial Majesty, the Protestant monarch, condemn the sect. Sedition says that any subject who criticizes the priesthood can be accused of being an Anabaptist and so destroyed; Imperial Majesty, at ll. 2626–30, sees the affair at Munster as planting pestilent seeds. In common with many other Protestant Reformers, therefore, Bale repudiated the radicalism of the Anabaptists. The personal excesses of the leaders did little to recommend them.

It is notable that the third reference at ll. 2678–81, indicates that Elizabeth I has taken action against them as advocated by Imperial Majesty at ll. 2626–30. Adams (op. cit., p. 23–4) reasonably concludes that Bale's transcription must have been made after Elizabeth's Proclamation of 22 September 1560; the passage spoken by Imperial Majesty was probably composed somewhat earlier.

2535. *Newgate ... Marshall-see.* Two London prisons: Newgate was to the north-west of the City; the Marshalsea was south of the river in Southwark.

2564. *Kyrye (eleison).* 'Lord, (have mercy):' petition from the Mass.

2566. *paxe.* Osculatory: representation of the Crucifixion, kissed as part of Church ceremonial.

2579. *Tyburne.* One of the traditional places of execution, near to the modern Marble Arch.

2605–6. *Brute . . . Cassius.* Marcus Junius Brutus, and Caius Cassius, conspirators who murdered Caesar in 44 B.C., and died at Philippi in 42 B.C.

2606. *Catilyne.* Lucius Sergius Catilina conspired against the Republic and was killed in battle in 63 B.C.

Absolon. Absalom rebelled against his father King David, 2 *Samuel* 13–19.

2620. The Pharisees, Sadducees and Essenes were influential Jewish sects at the time of Christ.

2629. See ll. 2532 and note.

2645. SD *Hic . . . osculatur.* 'here the king kisses them all.'

2659. *Their . . . passes.* 'The trickery of the confession surpasses all other kinds of treachery.'

2675–7. *Revelation* 7 2–4.

2678. *Danyels sprete.* i.e. in the spirit of Daniel, the purifier: cf. ll. 2532 and note.

2686. *Nestor.* Greek hero, present at Troy and famous for his longevity.

2689. *Helias.* Perhaps a reference to Elijah's triumphs over false gods, 1 *Kings* 18, and 2 *Kings* 1.

2691. *Thus . . . Johan.* For the division of the play into Books or Acts, see Introduction p. 48.

Proclamatioun. This Proclamation (the *Cupar Banns*) refers only to the performance of 1552 at Cupar, Fife. No doubt it was specially written for it. Bannatyne included it in his manuscript version (*Bann. MS.*), but it was omitted by Robert Charteris in his printed text (*1602*). See Introduction p. 58.

1. *Nuntius.* The Messenger who opens the play with the Proclamation. He stays in the acting area through the whole of the *Banns*. Possibly the role was performed by the actor playing Diligence.

2. *prince.* Rex Humanitas, King Humanity.

11. *Sevint . . . June.* It is clear from l. 271 that this is Whit Tuesday; the latter fell on 7 June in 1552.

14. *hour of sevin.* 'seven o'clock in the morning'. The order for drink at eleven o'clock (l. 16) suggests that the play at Cupar took four hours to perform. A modern production of three-fifths of the complete text took two and a half hours (Kinsley, p. 20).

17. *Castell Hill.* Probably the open air playing space in Cupar, later called the Playfield, see Introduction p. 59–60.

25. *Cotter.* A cotter was a peasant who paid the rent on his cottage by labour.

29. *Johnne Willamsoun.* Hamer, vol. IV, p. 146, notes a John Williamson in 1531 at Cupar. Many of the named people in the play have been identified in Cupar and its surroundings.

30. *Thocht . . . rair.* 'though all the cattle should bellow'.

39. *dreifland in diseiss.* 'chattering in discomfort'.

45. *Withowt the Constry law.* 'Outside the law of the Church'.

46–8. *Nor . . . daw.* 'Unless I be stuck with a knife, the day shall never dawn when I wed any other wife.'

50. *Sanct Fillane.* St Fillan, eighth-century saint.

55. *as effeiris.* 'as is becoming'. The 'chastity' of priests and other religious celibates is much in question in the play. It was probably a conventional theme, but Lindsay is not slow to exploit it for homiletic and dramatic purposes.

88. *paik thy cote.* 'beat your coat', i.e. beat him.

101. *Fynlaw of the Fute Band.* Findlaw of the Foot Band; a braggadocio.

125. *Pynky Craiggis.* Battle of Pinkie Crags (or Cleuch), fought in

663

1547, six miles east of Edinburgh, in which the English inflicted heavy losses upon the Scots.

140–1. *I tak ... heid.* 'I undertake before I leave this place to frighten the boaster with a sheep's head.'

147. SD These three characters anticipate the Three Estates.

162. *this.* The grotesque penis of the Fool, common to classical and folk drama. Cf. l. 4438 ff.

196. *Want we weir heir.* 'If we do not have war here'.

215. *cry keip.* 'call out that you are safe'.

218. *jufflane Jok.* ?'bumbling fool'.

224. *holland claith.* linen cloth from Holland. The shift she is making soon becomes another way of deceiving him: while she pretends to fit him, the Fool returns the key, (l. 225 SD).

240. *Golias.* Goliath, cf. I *Samuel* 17.

242. *Gray steill.* according to an old story the wicked Sir Graysteel was conquered by Sir Grime.

243. *Kynneill.* Kinneil, Linlithgowshire.

245. *Bews.* Sir Bevis, subject of a thirteenth-century poem.

246. *Hector.* mightiest champion of Troy.

Gawyne. Gawain, one of the bravest of King Arthur's knights.

250. *In ... filii.* 'In the name of the Father, and of the Son ...' – the words were used to frighten away devils.

251. *Gy.* Guy of Warwick, subject of a medieval romance, originally French.

252. *Marling.* Merlin, the Celtic wizard, who appeared in Arthurian legend.

253. *Gyr garling.* Gyre Carling, she-ghost, or witch, who reputedly lived on Christian flesh.

257. *Gowmakmorne.* Gow (or Gaul) MacMorne, legendary Gaelic hero, perhaps of Irish origin.

271–2. *Witsone tysday ... June.* cf. l. 11 and note.

275. *teme your bleddir.* 'empty your bladder'.

1. SD The action requires an acting area with several centres of interest, though it is not clear how they relate to one another. The King's throne is probably the focal point. It stands upon a scaffold (l. 1963 SD), and has a ladder leading up to it (l. 1959 SD). There is a pond or ditch, which acts as a barrier at times (ll. 1377 SD, 1581 SD). From time to time actors withdraw to the Pavilion at the end of a sequence (l. 1397) or for sexual encounters (The Fool and Bessy, *Banns* l. 175 SD; the King and Sensuality, l. 533 SD). During much of the play, particularly during the Second Part, some of the characters

sit on their seats and watch the action, taking a part only when necessary: seats are mentioned for the Three Estates themselves, and for
Verity and Good Counsel. At various points a gallows, a bar as in a
court of justice, and a pulpit for sermons are required.

It should be borne in mind that the *1602* text is closest to the performance of 1554 at the Greenside. The circumstances at Castle Hill,
Cupar, to which the *Banns* are closest, and in the Lyon Chalmer at
Linlithgow would have been rather different. In the case of the latter,
for instance, the *Nootes* preserved by Eure give no indication of the
water, the bar, the pulpit, or the gallows.

All the stage directions in *1602* are included. Occasionally I have
incorporated directions from *Bann MS.* marking them with (*), and I
have added a few of my own where it seemed appropriate, placing them
in brackets.

1. The opening speech by Diligence is spoken in an alliterative style
reminiscent of other medieval plays where a powerful effect was sought,
cf. *The Chester Cycle*, Play 1.

13. *Pausa.* The pause is required to make sure that the audience is
duly settled.

26. *That . . . beiris.* 'Innocent people have been brought to their
deaths.'

56. *certaine houris.* Charteris indicates that the play lasted nine hours,
though this contained a break for a meal. Modern productions are
nearer four, cf. Banns, l. 14 and note.

69. *hand for hand.* 'in full agreement'.

81. *haifing na mateir.* 'having no material substance'.

107. *for ocht he can.* 'for all that he can do about it'.

110. *Placebo.* 'I shall please' (Latin): a character representing flattering advice to the King.

156. *Peiblis on the Greine.* Perhaps an allusion to 'Peblis to the Play',
attributed to James I of Scotland, 1394–1437.

161. *bowis.* Arches or town gates. Such a haunt would enable her to
be generally available.

183. *The feind . . . faster.* 'by the devil I could get along no faster'.

185. *Of wyfes . . . fidder.* 'fifteen loads of women'.

222. *The quhilk . . . till.* 'which you gave to me'.

224. *Tanquam tabula rasa.* 'like a scraped tablet', i.e. innocent and
unmarked.

233–4. Proverbial: Tilley, D311, S33.

249. *In nomine Domini.* 'In the name of the Lord'.

261. *Bamirrinoch.* Cistercian Abbey at Balmerino, Fife.

269. *Omnia probate.* 'Prove all thinge', cf. 1 *Thessalonians* 5 21.

299. *Danger*. This character represents false circumspection, cf. ll. 305–6.

312. *Fund-Jonet*. A male character, an associate of Danger.

320. *Sen . . . spair*. 'Since then, by the devil, you spare no man'.

326. The song was probably sung here: the King notices it.

334. S.D. (*) marks stage directions from *Bann. MS*.

389. *With siching . . . schent*. 'I am completely destroyed by sighing sorely' – the lover's hyperbole.

400. *Till gar . . . rout*. 'to make our purses cry out', i.e. spare no expense.

404. *back or eadge*. Proverbial: 'come what may', Tilley B12, B15.

416. SD They walk about the stage as though on a long journey – a common convention for changing the action from one place to another. They encounter Sensuality, and arrange for her to approach the King at l. 493.

461. *Brydis*. St Bride, or St Bridget, d. 525. Patroness of Ireland. Restored stolen cattle, and therefore often represented with a cow beside her. Presumably the bell is a cow-bell.

464–5. *It . . . geir*. 'It were a kindness to twist my ear (like a donkey) if I were not able to try out that tempting woman.'

469. *Alace . . . schank*. 'Alas, I have twisted my leg': comic business consequent upon his capering about from l. 451.

490. *baird*. white linen covering, probably for the breast.

492. *taill*. the train of the skirt.

505. *deitie*. Bann: *Dyosie 1602* (for 'diocese').

512. *quhair . . . cures*. 'where youth has charge'.

533. The King and Sensuality, ushered by Diligence, and Wantonness with Homeliness withdraw, probably to the Pavilion.

539. *play cap'out*. 'drink deep'.

543. *Hes . . . gumis*. 'has had sexual intercourse'.

544–5. *Quhat . . . lumis*. 'why should not we two engage in sexual encounter' *lumis* – tools, implements.

601. SD Good Counsel now waits, perhaps withdrawing to his seat until l. 937.

stormested at the May. 'storm-bound at the Isle of May, in the Forth'.

607. Flatterie's journeys are a common Vice convention, and one shared with the Fool in the Folk-drama.

624. *braikand like ane brok*. 'breaking wind like a badger'.

635. *Wa sair the Devill, 1602*: *Wa serve the divill*, Bann. MS.: *Wa fair*, Kinsley.

671. *father-brother*. 'father's brother'.

691–3. *Bot . . . mowis.* 'But suddenly I parted her legs with my thigh driving among her hollows: God knows we had a great time.'

731. *Farie-folk.* The Fairies, i.e. evil spirits. He associates his disguise as a friar with evil possession.

761. *Sanct-Johnestoun.* Perth.

Kinnoull. on the Tay, east of Perth.

767. *koull of Tullilum.* cowl of Tullilum, a Carmelite monastery west of Perth.

778. *Sanct James.* St James the Greater, Apostle: his shrine at Compostella in Spain was an important centre for pilgrims in the Middle Ages.

785–805. The christening is a comic episode which underlines the taking of aliases, a common feature in the Vice convention.

810. At this point *Bann. MS.* has a further stage direction:
  'Heir sall thay drink and the King sall cum furth of his chalmer and call for Wantones.'
This is followed by another after l. 815:
  'Heir the king hes bene with his concubyne and theireftir returns to his yung cumpany.'
These two directions indicate that at Cupar the setting included at least two locations.

826. The passages in brackets are supplied from *Bann. MS.*

897. *quelling . . . quintessence.* 'in extracting the quintessence'. The latter was the substance of which, according to medieval philosophy, the heavenly bodies were composed. Its extraction was one of the objectives of alchemy.

906–912. *Danskin.* probably an adjective, 'Danish'. *Almane* Germany. *Spittelfeild* Spittalfields, Perthshire. *Ranfrow* Renfrew. *Rugland* Rutherglen, Lanarkshire. *Castorphine* Costorphine, Edinburgh.

937. SD *feild.* Good Counsel is meant to appear at a distance, and he is noticed by the King and the Vices.

980. Good Counsel is not deceived by the disguises of the Vices.

994. The Vices' conference is clearly separated from the King and the Court.

1008. *casualities.* 'unexpected events' or possibly 'unexpected financial opportunities'.

1031. *hurlie hackat.* a game in which the participants slid down a slope on a sledge.

1036. *Diligite . . . terram.* 'Love justice, ye who judge the earth', *Wisdom* 1 1 (*Apocrypha*).

1060. *sliddrie rone of yce.* 'slippery patch of ice'.

1061. *Mobile . . . vulgus.* 'The unstable common people are always changed with their leader.' Hamer traces this to Claudian, *Panegrycus de Quarto Consolatii Honorii Augusti*, l. 302, and he suggests that the line was not uncommon in medieval literature.

1070. *Sic . . . bona.* 'Let your light so shine before men that they may see your good works', *Matthew* 5 16.

1094. *Sanct Bryde.* cf. l. 461.

1098. The members of the Spirituality have their own seats, as does Temporality, l. 1278.

1102. Verity is thus clearly aligned with the New Testament in English, and with the Reformation.

1128. *Lutherians.* Followers of Martin Luther, i.e. Protestants.

1186. The reference to *Isaiah* 55 should perhaps be 59 14.

1192. 2 *Timothy* 4 4.

1198. *Revelation* 15.

1305. *cap'out.* cf. l. 539.

1309. S D The Sowtar and the Tailor are seated as at an Inn, perhaps near the seat of Temporality.

1334. *laborde my ledder.* 'mounted me'.

1335. *nor . . . tedder.* 'lest my deceiver grace the (gallows) rope'.

1337. *cleikit up my clayis.* 'pulled up my clothes'.

1338. *chalmer glew.* sexual intercourse.

1349. *Sanct Blais.* St Blasius, martyred 316.

1354–5. *Becaus . . . dint.* 'because that monster (Chastity) has so en-feebled my husband's virility the wretch there bears the marks of my rage.' The comedy of this scene relies largely upon the supposed effemi-nacy of the Tailors and Cobblers.

1357. *Sanct Blaine.* Seventh-century Scottish saint.

1360. *Sanct Crispine.* Patron of Shoemakers; d. Soissons 287.

1381. *Sanct Clone.* St Cluanus, sixth-century Irish abbot.

1398. The action now returns to the King's throne.

1446. Discretion is Dissait in disguise, cf. l. 785: Sapience is Falset, cf. l. 793.

1475. Verity is put in the stocks with Chastity, cf. l. 1670 SD.

1550. *Quhat rak . . .* 'What is it worth . . .?'

1558. They remove their disguises.

1581. *Thy feit . . . hands.* 'Your running will be much better than your fighting.'

1582. Correctioun is apparently winged like an angel, cf. l. 4361. *Beati . . . Iustitiam.* 'Blessed are they who hunger and thirst for justice', *Matthew* 5 6.

1627–8. *Thair . . . repent.* 'There are therefore many in this island who without doubt will repent my coming here.'

1643. *bo-keik*. cf. *Kynge Johan*, l. 2525, and note.

1705. *mair . . . pleuch*. 'there is more to be done'.

1707. *Sardanapall*. Sardanapalus, King of Assyria, ninth century B.C., famed for effeminacy and voluptuousness.

1711. *Noy*. Noah, *Genesis* 6–8.

1714. *Sodome and Gomore*. The destruction of Sodom and Gomorrah: see *Genesis* 18 and 19.

1727–30. *I . . . dilatioun*. 'I will begin with thee, who art the head, and make reformation starting with thee: thy subjects will then follow thee without making excuses. Hence quickly, harlot (Sensuality), without any delay.' *1602* has a full stop after *harlot*.

1771. *Tarquine*. Sextus Tarquinius ravished Lucretia (Lucres, l. 1774). She revealed the crime and killed herself: Sextus was murdered, and his family lost its political influence.

1784. *consociabill 1602*; *consonable Bann. MS*.

1815. *The teind . . . Myre*. 'the tithe mussels of the Ferry Mire'. Hamer suggests that this is illusory (like the pleasures of Wigan Pier).

1819. *colpots of Tranent*. The coalpits of Tranent, east of Edinburgh: but an income from butter grown on broom there is nonsense.

1879. *Sanct Mavane*. St Mevenna, d. 617, founded abbey of St Meen in Brittany.

1881. *playit . . . glaiks*. 'cheated me'.

1885. *Initium . . . Domini*. 'The fear of the Lord is the beginning of wisdom', *Psalm* 111 10.

1904–5. *Efter . . . perqueir*. 'After whose death, their life (and shame) shall no doubt be recalled exactly and in detail for over a thousand years'.

1911. *Hoyzes*. 'oyez' – 'listen'; the traditional shout of ushers and criers.

1927. *Bann. MS*. here repeats ll. 70–7 above.

1935. *1602* gives this break: the following stage direction indicates that the audience took refreshment. Presumably the Kyngs and Bishops are characters who leave their seats together with the chief actors.

1939. *Sanct Androes*. St Andrews, in the eastern part of Fife. It was an ecclesiastical centre, and Lindsay probably studied at its university.

1945. *Provost and Bailyies*. The mayor and chief magistrates.

1957. *Sanct Fillane*. see *Banns.*, l. 50 and note.

1971. *Lawthiane*. Lothian.
Tranent. cf. l. 1819.

1976. *Seinye*. Consistory Court.

1989. *Air*. Ayr, on the West coast.

2004. *umest clayis.* the bed-cover, made of coarse undyed cloth, was seized by the priest on the death of a parishioner.

2025. *Sanct Geill.* St Giles, patron saint of Edinburgh.

2047. *Bona dies.* 'Good day'.

2081. *Bullinger*, Heinrich, (1504–75), Protestant pastor at Zurich.
Melancthoun, Philip, (1497–1560), scholar and reformer, close associate of Luther.

2090. *Cave.* perhaps *Cane* – 'Khan' (Hamer).

2096. *Fine Macoull.* Finn MacCoul, legendary Gaelic giant.

2099. *Makconnals.* MacConnal ?of Kyntyre.

2100. *Baquhidder.* Balquidder in West Perthshire.

2102. *Johne the Armistrang.* John Armstrong, freebooter from Langholm, was hanged by James V, near Hawick in 1529.

2108. *Sanct Antonis sow.* see *King Johan*, l. 1976 and note.

2113. *Baliell.* Belial, cf. *Castell*, 1.

2146. *Ane fistand . . . fuffe.* 'a fighting whore, a sluttish stinkard'.

2152. *Cockatrice.* A serpent, also called the Basilisk, able to kill with a look, and hatched from a cock's egg.

2168. *chamber-glew.* cf. l. 1339.

2188. SD Both *Bann. MS.* and *1602* refer in this stage direction to 'the Hill': in the case of the former, at Cupar, Wilkin would be below the performing area, but at Edinburgh the hill may have been Calton Hill, which overlooks the Greenside.

2190. *Widdiefow.* one who fills a widdie, a halter.

2200. *Dumbartane.* Dumbarton, west of Glasgow, on the Clyde.

2203. *Legatus natus.* a bishop exercising papal authority.

2206. *Diabolus incarnatus.* the Devil incarnate.

2227–8. *Byde . . . warie.* 'If you stay there for long, without doubt I fear your fate will curse you.'

2258. *totiens quotiens.* Probably has little meaning, perhaps 'as many times as necessary'.

2324. SD The Three Estates come from the Pavilion, and Wantonness notices that they are walking backwards.

2398. *dampster.* official who pronounces doom or judgement.

2399. SD The King and the Estates are now seated as at a Parliament, with officials present (the Sergeants and the Scribe).

2453. The allegory of the Three Estates who enter backwards at l. 2324 is here completed by John's explanation that Spirituality is led by Covetousness and Sensuality, Temporality by Public Oppression, and the Merchants and Craftsmen by Falset and Dissait. His revelation leads to the stocking of the Vices (ll. 2495–2503), but Covetousness and

Sensuality escape to the safety of Spirituality's seat (l. 2521). For Flattery see l. 3005 and note below.

2459. *gar ... crack.* 'cause a (hangman's) rope to break'.

2494. *I se ... skaid.* 'I see that your scalp is scabby with scirrhus'.

2514. *Mavene.* cf. l. 1879.

2521. SD Sensuality and Covetousness, who are indispensable to Spirituality, take refuge in his seat.

2562. *Thocht ... aneuch.* 'Though robbery and theft were properly brought to an end'.

2563. *Yit ... pleuch.* 'There is more to be done.'

2576. *sum ... maill.* 'Some have their rents raised so high ...'

2607. *Qui ... manducet.* 'The man who will not work shall not eat', 2 *Thessalonians* 3 10.

2613. *quintacensours.* Those who seek the quintessence, cf. l. 897 and note.

2620. *For ... treatit.* 'For those idlers must be dealt with.'

2623. *Augustenes, Carmeleits.* see *Kynge Johan* l. 422 ff. and note.
       Cordeleirs. Franciscan Friars.

2635. *Diogenes.* Cynic philosopher who lived in Athens. Reputedly he lived in a tub, and made a display of poverty and misery. He died in 324 B.C., aged 96.

2647. *Mary th'Egyptiane.* Converted from a life of dissipation, she lived in the desert and died in 421.

2648. *Paull.* Paul the Hermit, supposedly lived ninety years in the desert, and died in 342.

2657. *The infetching ... airis.* 'the deceiving of the courts of Justice'. *airis.* assizes.

2705. *Sanct Geill.* cf. l. 2025.

2843. *Et ubi ... tota.* 'And where the greater part is, there the whole shall be'.

2876. *commends. in commendam* – 'in trust': benefice given in trust for life, or until another incumbent was appointed.

2917ff. *Buik.* Bible. The passage comes from 1 *Timothy* 3 1–3. Lindsay's translation might be completed thus – '... sober, wise, distinguished, virtuous, hospitable, learned; not given to violence, not one who strikes blows, but able to exercise restraint'.

2965. *bellie blinde.* blindfold player in blindman's bluff.

2966. *King David.* David I (1084–1153), King of Scots, founder of many religious houses.

3002. *Sancte Pater.* 'O holy father', addressed to Flatterie in his disguise as Devotion.

3006. *1602* text gives these lines to Spirituality. I follow Hamer. Presumably Flatterie is not stocked at l. 2543. He is disguised as a friar (cf. ll. 3657–79).

3007. *Gif . . . deid.* 'If he deserves death'.

3011. *ordinair.* Ordinary – ecclesiastical official with legal jurisdiction.

3038. *Sanctam Ecclesiam.* 'in the Holy Church', but he leaves out '*Catholicam*', and switches to a sharp attack on the clergy.

3043. *Sanct Tan.* ?St Anne.

3070. *Ploutois.* Pluto, the god who ruled in the classical Hades.

3077–91. *citandum . . . lybellandum . . . ad opponendum . . . interloquendum . . . ad replicandum . . . hodie ad octo . . . pronunciandum.* These were the phrases by which the documents in a law-suit were known. The satire is directed against the cumbersomeness of the process: summons, first plea, reply, intermediate decree, defendant's reply, delay of one week, judgment.

3105. *Sanct Geill.* cf. l. 2025.

3145. *Thy . . . kend.* 'Make your life and craft known to these kings'. The interest shifts here to the common men (cf. l. 3141).

3148. *Dumbartane.* cf. l. 2200.

3194. Diligence goes to the pavilion to summon the learned preachers, cf. l. 3334 S D.

3206. *Sanct Allane.* St Allan, or St Eilan, sixth-century Breton saint.

3227. *Eusdaill.* The valley of the River Ewes, Dumfriesshire. John Armstrong lived there (cf. l. 2102).

3240. *My craig . . . hippis.* 'my neck will learn the weight of my hips', (by hanging).

3251. *Earle of Rothus.* Earl of Rothes, Sheriff of Fife, died 1558. Perhaps he was present at the Cupar performance when many local names were mentioned.

3257. *Ewis-durris.* The pass ('doors') between the valley of the Teviot flowing north, and that of the Ewes flowing south.

3262. *Dysert Mure.* Dysart Moor. Dysart is on the Fifeshire coast, and the Moor lies between the Earl's house at Leslie and the sea.

3264. *Strother.* Struthers, south of Cupar.

3269. *watter of Annet.* River Annet, Perthshire, tributary of the R. Teith, about fifty miles west of Cupar.

3294. *Liddisdaill.* Liddisdale, a few miles east of the R. Ewes, and roughly parallel to it. Notorious for thieves.

3296. *Sanct Fillane.* cf. l. 1959.

3321. *Mers.* The Merse, part of Berwickshire, often subjected to raids from the freebooters who lived further up the border dales.

3426. *from Carrick to Carraill.* from Carrick, Argyllshire (west coast), to Crail, Fifeshire (east coast).

3441. *caiche.* hand tennis.

3446. *four-nuickit.* four cornered, in fashionable style.

3474. *Si vis ... mandata.* 'If you wish to enter life, keep the commandments', *Matthew* 19 17.

3483. *Sic ... mundum.* 'So God loved the world ...' *John* 3 16.

3508. *Et ... redemptio.* 'and with (the Lord) there is plenteous redemption', *Psalm* 130 7.

3525–6. *Diliges ... mandatis.* from three verses of Christ's teaching before Jerusalem: 'Thou shalt love the Lord thy God with all thy heart ... and thy neighbour as thyself ... on these two commandments hang all the law and the prophets', *Matthew* 22 37, 39, 40.

3535. *Si vis ... Dei.* cf. l. 3474 and note.

3560. Addressed to the Doctor.

3594. *King of France.* Perhaps a reference to a campaign fought by the Papal army against Henry II of France in 1551–2: see A. J. Mill, 'Representations of Lyndsay's *Satyre of the Thrie Estaitis*', *PMLA* 47, 1932, p. 641.

3605–8. *Luke* 9 58.

3670–2. *Venite ... exempti.* To the scriptural welcome 'Come, blessed ones' (*Matthew* 25 34), the friars will give their habitual response, 'we are specially excused'.

3716. Flatterie now joins Dissait and Falset.

3726. Flatterie's desertion is characteristic of the Vice's callousness.

3744. SD *thrie Prelats.* The Bishop, the Abbot and the Priest. At l. 3752 SD their habits are removed and given to the Doctor and the two Licentiates. Under their ecclesiastical garments they are dressed as Fools, l. 3765.

3752. The three clerks are the Doctor and the two Licentiates summoned by Diligence, ll. 3339–40.

3753. *paintit sepulturis.* 'whited sepulchres', hypocrites.

3806 ff. The anti-episcopal movement was not really successful until the political crisis of 1559–60. For an account of the religious changes foreshadowed here see J. D. Mackie, *A History of Scotland*, Penguin Books, 1964, pp. 142–63.

3822. SD The Proclamation of the Fifteen Acts is a remarkable programme of ecclesiastical reform. It reflects Lindsay's deep concern with the abuses of the Kirk, and at the same time reveals the diplomat's care in choosing a compromise. In his version of 1568 Bannatyne omitted ll. 3817–3991, and it may be that his introductory remark applies – 'levand (omitting) the grave mater thairof becaws the samyne abuse is weill reformit in Scotland, praysit be God'.

3838. *And painis ... underly.* 'and shall be subject to the penalties contained therein'.

3845. *ay ... wands.* 'always under due restraint'.

3857–60. *That ... Airtis.* 'That there shall be at Elgin or Inverness a company of wise and learned men, together with a prudent president, to do justice in the northern region'.

3866. *twa famous saits.* Presumably Inverness or Elgin. The intention seems to be to use the wealth of nunneries to support the new judicial system in the north.

3908. Lindsay accepts the Bishops, but under a reformed Kirk.

3917. *Isaiah* 56 10.

3930. cf. l. 1990.

3934. *hyrald hors.* death tax of a beast, due to a landlord.

3972. *Annas.* cf. *Kynge Johan*, l. 1855 and note.

3986. *Sanct Geill.* St Giles, cf. l. 2025.

4030. *Grosars.* This list of names seems to consist of family names from the Border where theft was notorious.

4045. SD *figour.* A dummy could be used, but the implication is that the actor *might* enact the death.

4086–7. *And mix ... oyl-dolie.* Both are methods of adulteration: ryemeal in the soap, and saffron, a colouring substance, in the olive oil.

4094. *Jamesone.* A Fifeshire family. Most of the family names which follow have been traced to the Cupar area: Hamer, op. cit, IV, pp. 144–8.

4095. *Clappertoun 1602* (town near Linlithgow): *Cowpar Town*, *Bann. MS.*

4127 ff. Falset turns his satire on to craftsmen – Webster (weaver), Walker (fuller), Miller, Butcher, Tailor, Brewster, Sowtar, Baxter, Wright, Mason, Blacksmith, Lorimer (harness), Cordwainer (leather), Goldsmith.

4173. *Harns-out. Harns* – brains: a drink to knock out the brains.

4223. *Lidsdaill.* cf. l. 3294.

4253. *hodie ad octo.* 'a week from today'.

4261. *Jesabell.* Jezebel, wife of King Ahab: she worshipped Baal, and opposed Elijah, 1 *Kings* 16–18.

4271. SD The crow or jackdaw represents his soul, as a thief.

4273. *Sanct Geill.* cf. l. 2025.

4300. *Hermeit of Lareit.* A notorious chapel at Loretto, near Musselburgh.

4301. With Dissait, Falset and Thift hanged, Flatterie, like some other morality Vices, lives to fight another day.

4315. *Schogait.* This street has not been identified: *Bann. MS.* names the Bonnygait, still the main street in Cupar.

4332. *Mahown.* Mahound, Mahomet – common name for Devil in plays.

4354. *Sanct Allan.* cf. l. 3206.

4369. *Innernes.* Inverness.

4399. *He . . . neist.* 'He who sits next to her shall find filth enough'.

4401. *quhillie lillie.* A retching noise.

4416. *Sanct Clune.* St Cluanus, Irish abbot, sixth century.

4420. *Tillilum.* cf. l. 777 and note.

4432. *Dynois.* St Denis, or Dionysius, martyred near Paris, third century.

4456–7. *sewch . . . hoillis.* 'furrow by the quarry holes', perhaps obscene.

4502. *Stultorum numerus infinitus.* 'The number of Fools is infinite'. This appears in *N.E.B.* as 'what is not there cannot be counted', *Ecclesiastes*, 1 15.

4528. *Sapientia . . . Deum.* 'the wisdom of this world is folly in God's sight', I *Corinthians* 3 19.

4538. Folly has a collection of fool's hats, one for each type of fool.

4578. *Ex operibus . . . eos.* 'You will recognize them by their fruits', *Matthew* 7 20.

4605. *muifing his ordinance.* 'moving his armies'.

4613. *bombard.* a small brass gun.

4626. *Marling.* Merlin, cf. Banns l. 252.

4627. *Gyre Carling.* cf. Banns. l. 253.

4631. *Flan . . . comedes.* partly a quotation from Merlin's prophecy of the destruction of the Britons, and partly a ridiculous jingle.

4643. *Gilly-mouband.* A Fool paid at the court of James V in 1527 (Hamer).

4645. *Cacaphatie.* ?a Fool's name.

4666. *Menstrell . . . France.* The Minstrel, perhaps a piper, is to play a French dance.

4672–3. *Rex . . . honor.* 'Let there be everlasting glory, praise, and honour to thee, O wise King, eternal God, kindly Father.'

APPENDIX I.
DOUBLING IN *MAGNYFYCENCE* AND *KING JOHAN*

THESE two plays are of interest since they both show a practical interest in doubling. There is little doubt that doubling was a necessity for writers working on plays to be performed by small professional companies.

Unfortunately we have no contemporary indications about how playwrights set out their doubling schemes, and it is therefore necessary to devise a means of showing how the various roles could interlock. I have set out two schemes which answer strictly to the texts, but there are places where an alternative arrangement is possible.

The case of *Magnyfycence* is the simpler of the two. There are never more than four actors on the stage at any one time. But the play is so closely plotted that it appears essential that there should be five actors available: when the scheme comes under stress, one actor would be making ready offstage for a new phase in the plot. This is particularly necessary in the sequence from ll.1159 to 1456. The actor playing Crafty Conveyaunce is on stage at the same time as the actor playing Fansy during ll.1159–1326. He could not therefore appear at l. 1409 as Fansy. During this time the other three actors are necessary for the roles of Magnyfycence, Felycyte and Lyberte.

The roles from l. 2284 to the end of the play need not necessarily be distributed in the way shown here. Indeed four actors could manage the seven roles quite successfully if Dyspare were doubled with Redresse (for example). However the earlier passage does suggest that five is the inevitable number. This distribution gives to Actor 1 the role of Magnyfycence, and to Actor 2 that of Fansy*, these two being the chief parts. At worst the other actors would then have to play six or seven roles.

As *King Johan* was first written c. 1538 and revised by 1561, its composition occurred in that period when doubling was the general practice. There are two reasons for supposing that the play was arranged for doubling: the action is so con~olled that there are never more than

---

*N.B. If the actor playing Fansy really was a dwarf, he could not be used in doubling.

Fig. 1 Doubling scheme for *Magnyfycence*

	1	2	3	4	5
line 1			Fel		
24			Fel		Lyb
81			Fel	Meas	Lyb
163	Mag		Fel	Meas	Lyb
240	Mag		Fel		
251	Mag	Fan	Fel		
325	Mag	Fan			Cou Coun
396		Fan			Cou Coun
403					Cou Coun
494		Fan		Cra Con	Cou Coun
573		Fan	Clo Col	Cra Con	Cou Coun
689			Clo Col		
745			Clo Col		C Ab
779			Clo Col	Cra Con	C Ab
825					C Ab
912		Fan			C Ab
968		Fan			
1044		Fan			Foly
1159		Fan		Cra Con	Foly
1327				Cra Con	
1375	Mag		Fel	Cra Con	Lyb
1401	Mag		Fel		Lyb
1409	Mag	Fan	Fel		Lyb
1457	Mag				
1515	Mag				C Ab
1629	Mag		Clo Col	Meas	C Ab
1726	Mag		Clo Col		
1797	Mag				
1803	Mag				Foly
1843	Mag	Fan			Foly
1851	Mag	Fan			
1873	Mag	Fan	Adv		
1875	Mag		Adv		
1953	Mag		Adv	Pov	
1955	Mag			Pov	
2048	Mag				
2064	Mag				Lyb
2153	Mag				

Fig. 1 (*continued*)

line	1	2	3	4	5
2160	(Mag)		Clo Col	Cra Con	
2198	Mag		Clo Col	Cra Con	Cou Coun
2277	Mag				
2284	Mag				Dys
2309	Mag		Mys		Dys
2325	Mag			G H	
2385	Mag			G H	Red
2402	Mag				Red
2419	Mag		S Cyrc		Red
2457	Mag		S Cyrc	Pers	Red
	(1)	(1)	(6)	(5)	(6)

five actors on stage at any one time, and the text contains a number of instructions which require the actors to change costume in readiness for a subsequent appearance. Fig. 2 indicates the truth of the first statement: the maximum of five actors is used only three times and for relatively short periods (ll. 1809–1919, 2318–2363, and 2457–92).

The question of the number of actors has been discussed by several critics, notably T. W. Craik and B. B. Adams*. Their concensus is as follows (aliases in brackets) –

Actor A: Nobility, Private Wealth, (Cardinal)
     B: England, Clergy
     C: Sedition, (Stephen Langton, Good Perfection)
     D: Civil Order, Commonalty, Dissimulation
     E: King John, Imperial Majesty
     F: Usurped Power, (Pope), Treason, Verity.

There is nothing intrinsically unsound about this arrangement, but since the purpose of doubling was to make the use of actors as economical as possible, it is clearly advantageous for a play to be actable by five rather than six. It follows from the chart that the parts would be played by five in this way –

*T. W. Craik, *The Tudor Interlude*, pp. 32–3 and n. 17; B. B. Adams, *John Bale's 'King Johan'*, pp. 8–12, 43–7. and 'Doubling in Bale's *King Johan*', *S.P.* 62, 1965, pp. 111–120. Craik remarks that four of Bale's other surviving plays could be played by five actors.

Actor 1: King John, Imperial Majesty
     2: England, Clergy, Usurped Power, (Pope)
     3: Sedition, (Stephen Langton, Good Perfection), Verity
     4: Nobility, Private Wealth, (Cardinal)
     5: Civil Order, Dissimulation, (Simon), Commonalty, Treason.

The role of the Interpreter is generally thought to have been played by Bale himself on the analogy of his appearance in his other plays. If need arose, however, it could be played by a number of actors; B (most likely), C or E; and 1 (most likely), 3 or 5.

The presence of stage directions which actually mention the changes actors are to make is rare: it both supports the general contention that doubling did take place, and raises a few problems about the mechanics of it. There are eight places in the text where the actors are told to change their costumes –

155 England change to Clergy
312 Sedition to Civil Order
556 Civil Order to Sedition (Dissimulation deleted)
983 Usurped Power to the Pope
    Private Wealth to the Cardinal
    Sedition to a monk, actually Stephen Langton
1061 Cardinal to Nobility
1397 Cardinal to Nobility
1490 Clergy to England
    Civil Order to Commonalty
1533 Nobility to Cardinal.

Two further cases occur in the rejected pages of the text written out by Scribe A –

P.*2 A24 Go owt Ynglond and dresse for Dyssymulacyon.
    A45 Here the Cardynall go owt and d[resse] for Nobelyte.

It is significant that all these are to be found in the part written out by Scribe A. When Bale expanded the second part of the play he appears to have taken no special notice of these directions, even though he must have seen them, and even though his expansion continues to respect the doubling plan for a minimum of five actors.

Of these ten examples, then, one (l. 983) is not an instruction for doubling; it is merely meant to tell the actors to assume aliases which the text demands be thoroughly understood by the audience since they carry homiletic or satiric significance: it was certainly copied from the original text. Seven of the rest (ll. 155, 312, 556, 1061, 1397, A24, A45) are either clearly marginal additions or are added with a measure of irregularity to an existing stage direction. Only two (ll. 1490, 1533) can be said to be indisputably part of the copy at its first transcription and can therefore be assumed to have been in Scribe A's exemplar. This suggests that the seven were added after Scribe A had copied the whole of his text when he felt the need to regularize the position, or perhaps – and this conjecture is admittedly difficult to substantiate – he was trying to reduce the number of actors from five to four. In support of the latter it is notable that there are never five actors on stage in that part of the play copied by Scribe A, as reference to Fig. 2 indicates.

In his efforts to indicate the scheme for doubling Scribe A made three interesting errors. The actor playing Sedition cannot become Civil Order at l. 312 since both characters are on stage at ll. 1191–1275, and similarly the actor playing Sedition cannot become Dissimulation at A24 since both characters appear on stage together in the deleted passage, A103 ff. Moreover, the Scribe actually changed his mind at l. 556 where he first wrote that Civil Order was to change to Dissimulation, and then cancelled Dissimulation, substituting Sedition, which, we have seen, is inconsistent.

One may sum up this rather complicated situation by saying that it appears that there is nothing in the whole text which is incompatible with its being designed from the very first to be played by five actors. Scribe A perhaps tried to revise the text after he had copied it to make it actable by four, but he got into difficulties which he was unable to resolve. Bale ignored Scribe A's notes for doubling, except that his final version was not inconsistent with five actors as a minimum. This was probably his original intention when he first composed the play before Scribe A made the A-text.

Fig. 2 Doubling scheme for *King Johan*

line		1	2	3	4	5
	1	J				
	22	J	E			
	43	J	E	S		
	156	J		S		
	313	J				
	314	J			N	
	334	J	C		N	
	375	J	C	(CO)	N	CO

Fig. 2 (*continued*)

	1	2	2	4	5
line 557–626		C		N	
627			S		
639			S		D
764		UP	S	PW	D
984					D
1026		P	SL	Cd	D
1062		P	SL		D
1066		P			D
1074–1085		P			
1086–1120					Int
1121			SL	N	
1191–1275		C	SL		CO
1276	J				
1304	J			PW	
1378	J		(S) off	PW	
1380	J			PW	
1398	J				
1418	J				CO
1430	J	C			CO
1446	J	C		N	CO
1491	J			N	
1534	J	E			Cm
1598	J	E		Cd	Cm
1610	J	E		Cd	Cm
1644	J	E	S	Cd	
(1666	Major revision begins here)				
1682			S	Cd	
1703	J	E	S	Cd	
1759	J	E		Cd	
1783	J	E	SL	Cd	
1809	J	E	SL	Cd	T

Fig. 2 (*continued*)

	I	2	3	4	5
1920	J	E	SL	Cd	
1984			SL	Cd	
2006			SL		
2008–			SL		D
2049					
2050	J	E			
2094	J	E			D
2123	J	E	S		D
2138–	J	E			
2192					
2193			V		
2218		C	V	N	CO
2318	IM	C	V	N	CO
2364	IM	C		N	CO
2457	IM	C	S	N	CO
2593	IM	C		N	
2611	IM	C		N	CO
2650–		C		N	CO
2691					

APPENDIX 2.
BALE'S REVISION OF LL. 1666–1803

AT l. 1665 on MS. p. 38 Bale apparently decided that the modifications
he wished to make were more far-reaching than could be managed in
the ways he had used in earlier places in the text. These more radical
alterations were incorporated in the following way –

1. He wrote a long passage on MS. pp. 39 and 40, and marked it with
the symbol O, showing that it was to be inserted after l. 1665. This
comprises ll. 1666 to 1724.

2. The text then goes back to MS. p. 38 at l. 1725 for thirty lines to
l. 1754. At this point another four lines written by Bale on MS. p. 40
and marked A are to be inserted. These are ll. 1755–8.

3. MS. p. 38 is then resumed at l. 1759, and the text continues to the
foot of the sheet at l. 1764.

4. There are two sheets with the text written by Scribe A which are
not numbered in the manuscript. These were the original A-text continuation after MS. p. 38 and probably became separated as a result of
Bale's revision. Three of the four sides are crossed out, but the first
sheet, usually now called *1, is largely uncancelled, and from it Bale
intended that the equivalent of thirty-five lines should follow l. 1764.

5. Bale wrote out another brief insertion of four lines on MS. p. 40,
marking them B for insertion after the eighth line on *1. The thirty-five
lines from *1 and the four lines of insertion B make up ll. 1765 to
1803.

6. On *1 at l. 1803 Bale put the letter C in the margin. He then began
his own rewriting of the text on MS. p. 41, marking C by the top line
which thus becomes l. 1804. The text continues from MS. p. 41 in
Bale's handwriting uninterrupted to the end of the play.

The A-text which consists of MS. pp. 1 to 38, and the two unnumbered sheets, are roughly folio in size: Bale's changes are all the more
noticeable because he used quarto sheets for the two pages of insertions
(MS. pp. 39 and 40) and for his own continuous rewriting on MS. p. 41
and the following sheets.

The relationship between the five pages embodying the changes can
be represented thus –

A-text (Folio size)		Bale's revisions (Quarto size)
MS. p. 38	1656–1665	
	1666–1724	MS. pp. 39 and part of 40, insert O
MS. p. 38	1725–1754	
	1755–1758	MS. p. 40, insert A
MS. p. 38	1759–1764	
unnumbered page *1	1765–1772	
	1773–1776	MS. p. 40, insert B
unnumbered page *1	1777–1803	
	1804 et seq.	MS. p. 41, marked C

Perhaps the changes to Sedicyon's part (ll. 1681–1700, and l. 1757) are a reflection of a change of theatrical convention. In the years between 1538 and 1558 the Vice's part became more popular, and showed considerable development. It may be that by the time he made his revisions Bale saw that his Vice could be made more up-to-date; and we must also bear in mind that Sedicyon's last scene (ll. 2656–2592) falls into that section of the text for which the earlier version is now lost. It is interesting to note that R. Pineas emphasizes the importance of the growth of the Vice's part in the plays concerned with anti-Catholic propaganda (*Tudor and Early Stuart Anti-Catholic Drama*, pp. 46–7).

GLOSSARY

a have
a in
a he
abavyd amazed
abeye, abyn pay
ableth empowers
abone, aboif, abuife above
abuilyement, abylement clothing
abusyons abuses
acomberyd encumbered
advertence notice
advertysement advice, attention
af off
affyaunce faith
affynyte kin
aforse exert
agryse tremble
air early
air heir
akale cold
aknowe acknowledge
alevyn eleven
alkynnys all kinds of
allege call upon
alrich elvish
als as
alowde received
altrycacyon argument
alutterlie utterly
alyde allied
amense remedy
amland ambling
amonge at the same time
anes, anis once
annewch enough

antetyme text, theme
apayed contented
appellacyon appeal
appose argue
arayes clothing
arecte refer
asay try
aslake lessen
asoly, assoyle forgive
assayes matters
assys asses
astore restore
asyse measure
atenyde grieved
attemperaunce moderation
atwynne in two, asunder
aucht eight
avale bring low
avertyce warn
aw all
award protection
awin own
awreke perform
axe ask
ayere heir
ayle (v) troubles

B

bace low
backes bats
baggys bagpipes
baillis woes
baittand grazing
bale torment, ill
ballyd bald

band bond
bane summons
bane, banne ruin, curse
banis bones
barfit, berfote barefoot
basnetys helmets
basse kiss
baston staff
bate, bayte strife
batell bargain
bawburd whore
bayte temptation
be by
becked beaked
becometh befits
bede prayer beads
bede (v) offer, present
be-dene at once
bedyth threatens
befole ridicule
beguith began
begynner originator
behalfe matter
be-hetyn promised
be-hyth promise, tell
beir barley
beiris tumult
beltit beaten
beluifit beloved
belys bellies
bemys trumpets
bende bondage
bende band
bening benign
bennesonne blessing
be-nome benumbed
berdys taken away
berewarde bearward
beseik beg
beste beast
betake send
bete cure

bette better
be-tyde happening
bewray(e) reveal
beg suffer, pray
bismair bawd
blad blade
blaynes swellings
ble complexion, condition
bledrand raving
bleir blur
blemysh discredit
blent blinded
bleryn weep
bleykyn grow/make pale
blo (v) blow
blodyr blubber
bloo blue
blother gabble
blubert sobbed
blyfe joyful
blynne stop, refrain from
blysse strike
blyve quickly
bobaunce pomp
bobbyd bounced
bobbyd mocked
bocher butcher
bock retch
bocke book
bogill goblin
boll(e), boule bowl, measure
bolnyd, bolnynge swollen, swelling
bone boon, prayer, request
bonne beauty
bore boar
bote cure, remedy
boun quickly
bourdis joke
bourys dwelling
boustous rough
bow herd
bowde drunk, fool

688

bowget pouch
boystows(ly) fierce(ly)
brace embrace
brede broad
breik buttocks
brenne burn
bresse embrace
brestyn, brestyth burst
brevyate abbreviate
brewe (v) ease
breyde make
broche pierce
brodde spike
brok badger
brothel(l) wretch, lecher
browne prepared
browth brought
bruch borough
brue cause
brunt burned, wounded
brybaunce plundering
bryboury pilfering
brydlit bridled
brymly fiercely
bryst breast
bryth brightly
bud bribe
buird board
buirdin burden
buit advantage
buittis boots
bultyn fornicate
buske prepare
buskyth hurries
but without
but gif, but if unless
by buy
bycchys bitches
bycherye wickedness
bygaine gone by
byggyngys dwellings
byll dwell

bynne stall
bystour boaster
bysytyth assails

C

cace, dress, habit
caiff chaff
cairful distressful
calke calculate
callet whore
cankard evil, spiteful
canker corrupt
cap cup
capasyte understanding
capcyose great
carbuckyls tumours
carless careless
carling crone
carpynge words
carriers jugglers
carts cards
cast stratagem
castis profits
casuall precarious
catel(l) property
cauteles, cawtelles tricks
cauteleinis tricks
cavell low fellow
cawsa road
cawth wrapped
cawth caught
ceiss cease
celsitude majesty
chafer merchandise
chaip(it) escape(d)
chalmer chamber
chalmer-glew intercourse
chanons canons
chase chose
checke taunt, quarrel
chefe foremost

689

cheiss choose
ches quarrelling
chesun, reason, cause
cheve thrive
chevysaunce booty
chocke thrust
chyncherde miser
clad clod
clais clothes
clappyd thrust
clatter argue
clatteryd rattled
cleikit clutched
clekit born
clenly innocently
clepe kiss
cleymyth claims
clipit shorn
clois secret
clokys clutches
clonge decayed
clos imprisonment
clourys, clowrys the ground
clowtes, clowtys clothes, rags
cloyed obstructed
cloyners cheats
clynge waste
clyvyn ruin
coft bought
coill(is) coal(s)
collatioun meal
colys coals, fires
comberaunce temptation; distress
commaunde commend
commens the common people
commodyteys possessions
common (n) speech; (v) speak
commynnalte community
commyned of discussed
comonynge conversing
compast brought about
compeir appear

complectyon, complexion nature
compositours grafters
conding condign
conquies conquer
consayte idea
consuetude custom
contryvyd controlled
convaye contrive, remove
convenit gathered
conventeth summon
convenyent suitable
convoye manage
coryen drubbed
coryous sensitive
cost(e) manner
costys habits
cote house
coull cowl
counsolabill full of good advice
countenaunce restraint
coup tumble
coveyth cravest
cowche cower
cowchyd expressed
coy quiet
crackis (n) boasts
craifis craves
craig neck
crake boast
crase shelter
creil(l) basket
crofte enclosure
crokys (v) bends, curves
croysyd crucified
cruikit deformed, lame
cruyse pot
crysme baptismal cloth
cuculled cowled
cude baptismal cloth
cue penny
cuir, cure care
cuitchours gamblers

cuittis ankles
cullours specious arguments
cukke excrete
cummer gossip
cummer distress
cummerles untroubled
cumplexioun temperament
cumpanarie good fellowship
cunne know
cunning knowing
cunye money
curate parish priest
curtlie courtly
cust kissed
custrell base fellow

D

dagges shreds
daggeswane coarse coverlet
daile sorrow
dalyaunce favour
dalys valleys
damais damask
dang beat, drove
dapyrly elegantly
dawe fool
dawnt become tame
day (v) die
dayl(e) deal
debaits contention
debatements strife
decerne decree
declare reveal
decreitit decreed
decryit decreed
dectyd decked
ded did
dees dais
defarre defer
defende forbid
degraid strip

degraithit degraded
dejectit thrown out
deit dead
del deal
dele grief
delfe pierce
delle put
delyaunce delay
dempte judged
denne valley
dennis dens
denners, dinneir penny, money
dent blow
deperte separate
deprave defame
deprysit disgraced
dere (v) harm, hurt
derke dark
derne secluded
derogacyon disparagement
des seat
deseytys deception
desseyvabyll deceiving
dessyer desire
deth-drawth death-blow
deunesse rights
dever duty
dewte duty
dilatioun delay
discommendeth censures
diseiss discomfort
disgysit disfigured
disiune breakfast
displeisit displeased
dispone deal with
distayne defile
do cause (to)
dochtours daughters
dogge jog
dole grief
dolfully cruelly
dolorrouse painful

doo doe
dorter, dortour dormitory
dourlie, durlie fiercely
dow avails
dow dough
dowght fear
dowtyd feared
draf(fe) filth, refuse
dreifland raving
drenche drown
drenkelyd drowned
drepe, drepyn droop, dropped
dreveland talking nonsense
drouth thirst
dryftes purposes
dryte excrete
drywe hasten
dub puddle
ducke bob
dudron slut
duile sorrow
duilfull sorrowful
dur door
durke lie in wait
durynge lasting
dyffame defame
dykys ditches
dyme tithe
dynge (v) beat
dynge noble, worthy
dyosie diocese
dys dice
dyscayte deceit
dyscryve probe
dyscuste considered
dyser scoffer
dysordereth corrupts
dyspent spent
dysseyved deceived
dystaunce disagreement, discord
dyth placed, prepare(d)
dyth save

E

effecte substance
effeminate besotted by women
eird earth
eiss ease
eist east
elevand measure
ell(es) else
elmes-dede charitable acts
endytynge accusation
enprise power
ensense arise
ensewthe follows
entent care
envyronnyd surrounded
erdyn petition, errand
ere ear
eryth inherit
estates ranks
everilk every
every everyone
everychon everyone
exercitioun vigorous action
experyence trial, test, knowledge
eyne eyes
eyr heir
eysyl vinegar

F

factes crimes
facyon sect
fadde fed
failyies, failyeand failing(s)
fais foes
falssed falsehood
faltit led
fane banner
fane glad
fang(it) catch, caught
fantasye caprice

fare go, walk
fare far
farle, farly wonderful
farme rent
farmerye infirmary
faulle fall
faunt child
fawchyn cut
fawe glad
fay foe
fayne glad
fayne pretend
faytour deceiver
fecht fight
fedder feather
fee feudal benefice
fefarme subject to rent
feffe, feffyd endow, invested
feid enmity
feil know, find out
  einye dissemble
feinyeit claimed
feir companion(s)
feirie active
feldys fields
sele marry
fell(e) fierce
fellaue fellow
fellone terrible, foul
felloun terrible
fellyd struck down
felyie fail
fence establish
fended defended
fer far
fer fair
fere fear
fere (v) frighten
fere companion
ferlie (v) wonder
ferne distant
fese incite

fesycyan physician
fesyl break wind
feterel deceiver
fette device
few tribute
fewte loyalty
fidder load
firy wonderful
flappyn beat
flappys blows
flawnes flat cakes
fleiche flatter
fleimit banished
flene flay
flery fawn
flete float, run
flete abound
fleyd, fleyit frightened
flicht flight
flocht commotion
flode stream
florchyd decorated
fluir floor
flyte, flyts scold(s), quarrel(s)
fode deceive
fogge go, jog
foill foal
foird forward
folde earth
fole fool
folw follow
fon fool
fonde tempt, try
fonnyshe foolish
forberyn give up
forfair perish, suffer, wear out
forfende forbid
forfett misdeed
forlor(n)e lost
forseth matters
fothyr company
forthynk cause to regret, regret

fortynable fortunate
foul full
fow drunk, full
fowe clean out
foyson plenty
fra-hand at once
frawt(h) endowed
fray fear
frayed bruised
freke man, fellow
frelie, frely noble, nobly
frenchepe friendship
frete make angry
frete gnaw
freyne request
froskys frogs
froward(e) perverse
froyter refectory
frubyssher furbisher
frugge coverlet
fryke daring
fud fellow
funteston font
furde furred
furderance aid
furris furrows
fute foot
fyle wretched
fyles defiles
fynd fiend
fyth strife, fight

G

gadlyngys wretches
gaist ghost
gait way
gald galled
gale speech
gall sensitive spot
gambis tricks
gamond caper

gamyn sport, pleasure
ganer gander
ganestand withstand
gapyn gape
gar cause to
garde made, caused
gardevaunce chest
garris causes
gastful dreadful
gastyd terrified
gaude, gawde(s) trick(s)
gay go
gearking foppish
geegaw trifle
ger(e) matter, device
gest fellow
gevyt (v) give, care
geyn-went way back
gif, give if
glaid make glad
glaikit foolish
gle pleasure
glede fire
glede kite
glent glittering
glose gloss
gobet morsel
gonge privy
gore wretch
gost, goost spirit
gostly spiritual
govyn given
graip grasp
graith manhood
grame fret
graythyd dressed
greath prepare
grede, gredyn call
greffe grief
greidie greedy
greifit harmed
grenne gnash the teeth

694

gres(s) grass
grese grease
grewaunse distress
grittor greater
grocchyn, grucche, grwcchyn moan
groge grudge
grom man
grope grasp, clasp, examine
gropyd seized
grot groat
gruntill snout
gryffys groves
grylle fierce
grynde gnash
grype clutch
gryse pig
grysly frightful
guare swear
guckit foolish
gud good
gudlingis guilders
gut goat
gyldar guilder
gylle guile
gylyd tricked
gyn rack
gyn(ne) skill, contrivance
gynne (v) contrive
gyse fashion

H

hafter sharper
hag notch
haif have
hail(l) whole
hais hoarse
hait hot
haits hates
hakle feathers
hale hall
halking hawking

hals(e) (n) neck
halse (v) embrace
haltynge limping
handill touch
happe, happys fortune
happyd fortuned
harbrie, herbrie shelter
harbrieles without shelter
hard mean
hard(e) heard
hardlie by all means, certainly
haryed dragged
hatte be called
hauld consider
hauntyth inhabits
hawe hawthorn berry
hawte haughty
hay enclosed land
hayif christen
hed heed
heich high
heid (v) behead
heid head
heidlangs headlong
helde obey
hele health, well-being
hele hide
helsum wholesome
hende handsome
hendly graciously
hent taken
her here
herde hard
herdely firmly
here hear
herne nook
herryit harrowed
herynge hearing
herys ears
hes has
hest command
het promised

hete heat
heve-ryche kingdom of heaven
hevynes grief
heynyd exalted
hobby hunt
hod hood
hooddypeke fool
hodys hoods
hois hose
hokys hooks
hokys people
hole whole
hollys woods
holt wood
homlyest most familiar
hooly wholly
hordys treasures
how hoary
howe stop
howtyth proclaim
huckill hip
hugger mugger secretly
huir whore
huksters buttocks
hurle drive
hy haste
hyen raise
hyge (v) go
hyghte am called
hyle, hyll shelter
hyll hell
hynd hence
hyreild tribute
hyt high

I, J

i, in into
jagge slash
jaggynge slashing
jangelynge chattering
jangle chatter

japes tricks
javell wretch
iche I
ichon everyone
ient beautiful
jet, jettys fashion(s)
jette swagger
je~ter swaggerer
ilk(e) each, every
i-ment set
incure occur
indewer, indouer endure
indygth arrests
infortoun misfortune
ingent immense
ingrosed arranged
ingyne ability
inow(gh) enough
interdyght interdict
intere whole
intill into
in into
intoxicate poison(ed)
intymate reveal
invaid despoil
inwyt secret
iote jot
jous, jows juice
joynted dismembered
i-pyth adorned
irchoun brat
irke resent
Ise I shall
juelys ornaments
jurden chamber pot
jwelles jewels
i-wys indeed, certainly

K

kachyn bring
kaity mistress, lover

696

karke distress
karpyn cry out
kayes keys
kayserys emperors
ke jackdaws
kelen ease
kempys champions
ken, kenne direct, instruct, teach
kene brave
kennis knows
kevere recover
kewe mew
keyes, kyes keys
keyser emperor
kirtill shirt, gown
knag gallows tree
knappe blow
knapskaw head-piece
knet tied
knokylbonyarde clumsy fellow
knowledge acknowledge
knyth tied
koltys colts
koure cower
kowclink whore
krake noise
kuik cook
ky cow
kyd famous
kylt killed
kynde nature, natural
kyth make plain
kyth loins
kytte cut

L

lace dress
lac(c)he strike, attack
lacke blame
laid ploughboy
laidlie loathly

laif remainder, rest
lair lore
laith loath
lake pit
lakkis reproaches
lan lend
landwart country
langour distress
lante lent, given
lap leaped
lapped wrapped
lathe by-path
lawe leave
lawe low
lawit humble, lay
lawlie meekly
lawnde glade
lawth caught
lay fallow
laykys games
lazars lepers
leche physician
ledder leather
ledrouns rascals
leene (v) lean
lefe willing
leids (v) leads
leif (v) live
leife leave
leife live
leik leek
leill loyal
leir(is) learn, teach
leising telling lies
leit language
lely truly
lelys lilies
lemand shining
len give
len lende
lende (v) stay
lende loins

697

lendys attend
lengar longer
lepe leap
lere teach, learn
lere, leyre face
leryth teaches
les control
lese (v) loose, lose
lesse joy
let(te) stop, hinder, omit
lete think
leve believe, consider
leve pleasant
leve (v) stop
levene lightning, light
levyng living
levyn (v) live
lewde ignorant
ley lay
leye flame
leye place
leye fallow
leyke, leykyn rejoice, play
leysour leisure
leyst lest
lichit arrived
lift air
limmer wicked
lofly willing
lokys looks
loller heretic
long belong
lopys leaps
lore lost
lore, loore learning, teaching
lose destroy
losengerys flatterers
losyll lout
lot(h)ly horrible
louce loose
loun lout
loup, leap

louse, lows (v) release
loute submit, bow
lowe (v) humble
lowghtes louts
lufe palm
lufe love
luffely willing
luge prison
lugs ears
luikit watched
luker money
lurdane vagabond
lydderyns rascals
lyfte banish
lykynge joyful
lynde lime tree
lyre skin
lysis liest
lyste stripe
lyt(h) little
lyth light, bright
lyth nimble
lyther withered
lythyr lazy, wicked
lyvely living
lywe live

M

mad made
maddynge madness
mae more
magry in spite of
maill rent
maill meal
maine moan
mair more
male bag, pack
malesoun curse
maling malign
malypert impudent
mamerynge muttering

mamockes scraps
man must
manerly in a courtly way
mangit confused, mad
marmoll ulcer
marrowis companions
mary marrow
mase mace
masked, maskyd enmeshed
maskeryd bewildered
masyd confused
mat mate
maysterfeest bound to a master
maystery, mastrye clever device
mear mare
medelyth mingles
medyll be concerned with
meinye, meynye company
meir more
meit meet
meiter better
mekill, mekyl, mykyl great, much
mel meal
mell(e) be concerned with
mende thought
mendement amendment
menge mix
mengyth troubles
mense grace
menschepe honour
ment spoken
menys mediation
mere sole
mes-crede the Creed
mese group
mesels lepers
meselynge bespotted
metely moderately
metes food
mevyn move
meyne middle voice
meyntener defender

midding midden
mint miss
mister need
moch much
mod mind, mood
moderys young women
moght moth
molde earth, ground
mone grief
mone moon
monie many
monyeon minion
morowe morning
morttmayne right
mossell morsel, dish
mot(e) may
mow joke
mow(e) mouth
mowle ground
mowynge grimacing
muill mule
murmell unrest
mustyr muster
myche much
mydylerd earth
mykyl see *mekill*
mynne less
myrieast merriest
mysbede ill-treat
myscheved destroyed
myskaryed led astray
mysteryes secrets
myth power
myth mite
mytour mitre

N

nar near
negarde miser
neirs kidneys
neis nose

nen, nyn nor
nerhand almost
nest next
nevene mention
nichtbour neighbour
nocht not
nolt cattle
nones nuns
noppe nap
norche nourish
nors nurse
not (v) do not know
noter notary
nout nothing
novels news
nowghty wicked
nowth nothing
noy (v) trouble
noyfull harmful
nyce extravagant, foolish
nyfte nephew
nyth night

O

obleist pledged
occacyon cause
ocker usury
of off
offent offended
offrands offerings
oist host
on one
onethys scarcely
onpursed robbed
onricht wrong
ony any
or before
ore grace
os as
ost host
othyrwhyle sometimes

our over
outewronge squeezed
out-thoart throughout
out-throw throughout
overhande upper hand
overluikit neglected
oversyght authority
oversyle beguile
overthynke cause to regret
overwharte irritable
ovyrblyve too eagerly
ovyrlad overcome
ovyrlyt too little
owe own
ower over
owr hour
owse role

P

pace pass on
padoks frogs
pagent part
paiks beatings
pairt part
paist pastry
pak go
palgeoun pavilion
palle robe
pangeth hurts
parasent willingly
parcell part (of the argument)
parcellys parts
parell peril
parochoun parish
partryche partridge
passe rely
passynge exceptionally
pastaunce pastime
patent open
patlet ruff
pawment pavement

pea, pese peace
peggrell paltry
peild, pyld bald
peke peep
pelf booty
pellours, pelowryis thief, despoilers
pend written
pende limit
penne plume
peradvertaunce close attention
pere pear
perquier by heart
pertly quickly
pete pity
petyeth, pyttyth grieves
pevyshness obstinacy
peyryth injures
physnomie portrait
pillok penis
placebo vespers for the dead
plashes puddles
playis pleas
pleinyie complain
plenarly fully
plete plead
pleuch plough
plyth pledge
podys toads
pollynge extortion
polytyke crafty
pomped pampered
popetty popish
poppynge blabbing
portas portable breviary
porte bearing, reputation
portouns breviary
pose shove
powder mix
powdyr smoke
practyse skill, treachery
prane prawn
praye prey

prece (v) press
precely seriously
preclair famous
prehemynens superior rank
preif prove
preinis pins
prekyd, pryckyd dressed
premye gift
prene (v) pierce
prest neat
pretend offer
preve secret
probate test
proctors stewards
promosyon promotion
promuifit promoted
pronge device
propyrtes stage properties
pryers priors
prys value
puer pure
punchyd punished
pundyr balance
pure poor
purveaunce provision
pycke, pick pitch
pyke go
pykand thieving
pylt thrust out
pynde tormented
pystyl epistle
pyth, pytte placed
pythe decorated

Q

quartane on the fourth day
quassynge drinking
quecke quickly
queysy causing sickness
quha who
quhair where

quhair-throw so that, through which
quhais whose
quhilk who, which
quhill until
quhite, *quhyt* white
quidder whether
quiotose quiet
quisland whistling
quoman pudenda
quyckes tenderest parts
quyte acquit, quit
quyth reward
qwed bad
qweyntly cunningly

R

rabyll rabble
rad readily
rafte deprived
raife rave
rair roar
rak, *rek* counts, is of value
rakle haste
rammyshe wild
ranke corrupt
rapely hastily
rapploch undyed cloth
rappockys wretches
rappys blows, strokes
rapyn, *rapyth* hurries, hasten(s)
ravener plunderer
rawe row
rawyn rave
rayle rail
reavers thieves
rechate horn call
reche give
reckys cares
red divide
red decided

redders punishment
rede advise
refrayne ask
reft stole
rehabilit restored
rele uproar
renne run
reporte refer
repryvable reprovable
res haste
respyth respite
rerage debt
rere rare
ressaif receive
retchlesse heedless
revin ruined
revme realm
rewe regret
rewly grievous
rewthe pitifulness
reyne rain down
reyse raise
rickill noise
riftit belched
ringand reigning
ringis reigns
rink run
rochettes, *rokats* surplices
rode rod, punishment
ronne run
ropys ropes
ros boast
rote root
rothyr, *rodyr* rudder
round(and) whisper(ing)
roupit croaked
rout blow
route (v) associate
route roar, resound
route, *rowte* crowd
routit bellowed
row raw

rowe row, line
rowne whisper
rowt took notice of
rowtynge violent
rowtys blows
rubiator libertine
ruble crush
rudyes redness
ruffle swagger, rage
ruggynge gnawing
rugs pulls
ruik rook
ruitit rooted
ruisse praise
rung reigned
russheth rustles
ruste decay
rutter gallant
ruttingly ostentatiously
ryall royal
ryfe break open
ryn run
rynge roar
rynnand running
ryth right
ryve generous

S

sad serious, sober
saikles innocent
saine, saynt (v) bless
sair sore
sale hall
sallett helmet
salve remedy
same together
sangis songs
sare sore sorrow
sark shift, shirt
sating satin
saun without

saw wise saying
sawe (v) sow
sawte assault
sax six
scathe harm
scelpe blow
schade pour
schawe ground
schawin shaven
scheif tithe
schelve shield
schenchepe harm
schende (v) abuse
schent destroyed
schere cut off
schete protect
schetyn hit, shoot
scheve thrive
schift plan
schiris sirs
scho shoe
schonde (n) ruin, disgrace
schorn made
schreve shriven
schrewdness wickedness
schryftes penances
schryve forgive
schryves sheriffs
schylde (v) shield
schylle shrilly
schyttyth shut
scrypp bag
se seat
seasit seated
seasyd possessed of
seasyne season
sedycyous seditious
seik sick
seinyie ecclesiastical court
seke sick
sekernesse security
seketours, sekkatours executors

sel(e) time, moment
selkowth wonderful
sell self
selle seat
sely, wretched, humble
sen, sensyne since
sen seeing
sendel fine silk
sentence opinion
senyes signs
sequester excommunicate
serdyn serve
ses cease
sese, sesyd endow(ed)
set sat
sete seat
seth(e) (v) watch, notice
sett sit
sett care
settis put ·
sewche divide
sey sea
seyn to say
seyng seeing
sheppes ships
shevere shiver, split
sho, scho she
shone soon
shyt shut
sic such
sicht sight
sickerly surely
siclyke such
sie sea
sie see
sikker certain
sillie simple
sindrie various
sittil crafty
skaith, skathe harm
skallyd scurvy, scabby
skape escape

skelp blow
skelpe (v) strike
skerre scare
skoutys, skowte, skowtys whore(s)
skoymose reluctant
skyll (v) matter
skyl(le) (adj) wise, right
skylle (n) argument, reason, craft
slaik ease
slake abate
slauterman executioner
slawe lazy
slayght crafty
sle, slea slay
sleife sleeve
sleper deceitful
sleyt skill
slo slough, evil
sloo slay
sloppe gown
slydder slippery
slypper slippery
slyve sleeve
smaiks contemptible fellow
smater chatter
smeke smoke
smete struck
smodyr fumes
smorde smothered
snelle vigorously
sojet subject
solempe ceremonious
soloyen, solwyd sully, sullied
sompe swamp
sonde country
sonde sand
sonde sending
sondys messages
sone, soun soon
sonsy lucky
sophysteres false reasoners
sort group

sowme sum
sowne swoon
sowtar, sowter shoemaker
spaiks spokes
spedde learned
speir ask
spell speak
spell expel
spell read
spence expenditure
spense store
sperd shut up
spere stripling
spere, speare close, lock
spete point
spetously shamefully
spill(e), spylle destroy, spoil
sportaunce indulgence
sportour companion
spot disgrace
spouse-breche adultery
spreit, sprete spirit
spretuallte spirituality
spud knife
spuilye strip
spynne move
squat cowering
stacker stagger
staikis supports
stail steal
stait estate, rank
stakyr stagger
stank ditch
stark(e) perfect, unqualified;
    clumsy, rigid
staunche firm
staw stole
steadings farm buildings
steke shut up
stel steel
stends (n) leaps
stere stir up

sterracles spectacle shows
sterve die
stevene petition
stewat stinkard
stodye study
stondeth agrees
stordy fierce
store restore
stoup (n) drink
straiks blows
strais straws
strayghtly, streytly strictly
strywyth strives
stuffe provide
sturt vexation
stuse stews
stye path
styllit honoured
stynteth stops
styrt escape
styrte leap
suer sure
suith truth
sunyie delay
suppell mollify
supplye beg
supportacyon help
swa so
swart dark
sweir sloth
sweirness unwilling, lazy
swer sure
swet(e) sweat
swingeour rogue
swot sweat
swote sweet
swyfe, swyve copulate
swynke drink deep
swyth(e) quickly
sy saw
syh sigh
syke such

syke stream
synesoon afterwards
syth appearance
syth sit
sythyn since
syttynge suitable

T

tabils backgammon
tache arrest
tais toes
tale concern
tall tale
tan arrived, reached
tan taken
tapperes tapers
tappet tapestry
tappster barmaid
tappyn strike
tapytys tapestries
tawth instructed
tchyre chair
te(e) go
tedder rope
teill till
teind tithe
tene (v) harm
teneful painful
tent heed
tent tenth
tent (v) probe
ter tar
terage soil
tere tear
tereste earthly
tetter skin disease
tewch tough
tey(e) bind
thame them
than then
thay those

the(e) thrive
thedom prosperity
thende prosperous, blessed
ther their
thine-furth thenceforward
thir these
thirlage bondage
tho those
thocht though
thoil(l) suffer
thorwe throughout
thost dung
thou though, although
thouth thought
thoutys, thowth thought
thrall subject
thring sorrow
throwe time
thrist push
thwyte whittle
till to
tippit rope
to also
to two
tol(e) sword, weapon, equipment
tocher-gude dowry
todis foxes
tollyth entice
tone to the one
to-rase cut to pieces
tothyr the other
tottys devils
towart free
towte rump
tradicyons teaching
traditions deceptions
traine trick
trase dance
trat hag
trattle chatter
traytery treachery
trebelen sound shrilly

trebyllys trebles
trecchyn deceive
tremle quiver
trompouris deceivers
trost safe
trotte march
trouth truth
truikers thieves
trusse, trussyd packed
try (adj) choice
trye tested
tryist trust
tryit convicted
tuik took
tumde emptied
tume virgin
turmentry torment
turmoyle (v) agitate
turs carry
tway two
tydie fat
tyle obtain
tyllyth draws, entices
tymbyr (v) build
tympanye swelling
tyned pronged
tynis loses
tynt lost
tyre head-dress
tyst tempt
tysyd enticed
tysyke phthisis
tyth, tytly quickly
tythands tidings
tythe pay tithes

U

umest uppermost
unblyst cursed
underly endure
underne mid-morning

underset supported
undocht ignoramus
undyrfonge receive
undyscuste without legal authority
unfeinyeit true
unhende unfitting, unready
unproponit undiscussed
unquert wicked
unsell unhallowed
unslye foolish
unthende unhealthy
unwolde infirm
up upon
upseasynge taking possession of
ure habit
uryd disposed
us use

V

vagers vagrants
vagys strayings
varyaunce dispute
vaunce advance
vayle benefit
velyarde old man
venym poisonous
veryaunce difference
vilependit of little value
voyde escape
vyre bolt

W

wa woe
wache guard
wage reward, payment
waine think
wairde guard
wait wet
wait know
wall flow

wallie good luck
walter stagger
waltyr float
wambe stomach
wambleth heaves
wane reluctant
wanfortune ill-fortune
wanne when
wappyn strike
war worse
wardon warden pears
war(e) were
ware goods
warely cunningly
warie, wary curse, swear
warlo devil
wat know
wawe go
wawys waves
weche which
wed pledged
wede clothing
wedred withered
wedyr whither
weicht weight
weils is well with
wein think
weir war
weir doubt
welde (v) conduct
wele prosperity
welle boil
welny almost
wene think
wenne pleasure
werd world
were defend
werne prevent, stop
weryed wearied
wete, weten, wetyn, wote know
wey weigh
weye-went by-way

weyin measure
weyl wail
weytys weights
whou, whow how
whwtynge shouting
whyt jot
wicht brave
wicht man
widdie halter
widdiefows rascals
wische direct
wist knew
wod, woid wager
wod(e), wood mad
wokys week
wold possess
won vow
wonde, rod, control
wonde, wondyn wrapped, clothed
wonne dwell
wont fashion
wonys places
worch work
wormes snakes
wortes vegetables
woste knowest
wrake ruin, pain
wrangit wronged
wrangous wrongful
wrast trick
wreche vengeance
wrekyn destroy
wrenchys deceits, tricks
wrethe (v) angers
wrinks tricks
wroken fulfilled
wrothsome angry
wryen twist
wryght correct
wryngyth wrings
wunte custom
wurde word

wusp wisp
wycke wickedness
wyle snare
wyll well
wynche kick
wynde go
wynke blink
wynne joy
wyst knew
wyt (v) know
wyt wise
wyte (n) wrong
wyte, wyth, wytyn blame
wyth(e) person, creature
wyth(ly), wytly quickly
wytsave vouchsafe
wytys men, people

Y
Y I
yare ready

yarke beat
ydder udder
yearnis longs
yeid went
yeis you shall
yelpe boast
yende end
yene, yone that
yep vigorous
yerne quickly
yeve give, care
yewle howl
yle aisle
yne eyes
yolde submitted
yowis yews
yynge young
yyt yet

MORE ABOUT PENGUINS, PELICANS,
PEREGRINES AND PUFFINS

For further information about books available from Penguins please write to Dept EP, Penguin Books Ltd, Harmondsworth, Middlesex UB7 ODA.

In the U.S.A.: For a complete list of books available from Penguins in the United States write to Dept DG, Penguin Books, 299 Murray Hill Parkway, East Rutherford, New Jersey 07073.

In Canada: For a complete list of books available from Penguins in Canada write to Penguin Books Canada Ltd, 2801 John Street, Markham, Ontario L3R 1B4.

In Australia: For a complete list of books available from Penguins in Australia write to the Marketing Department, Penguin Books Australia Ltd, P.O. Box 257, Ringwood, Victoria 3134.

In New Zealand: For a complete list of books available from Penguins in New Zealand write to the Marketing Department, Penguin Books (N.Z.) Ltd, Private Bag, Takapuna, Auckland 9.

In India: For a complete list of books available from Penguins in India write to Penguin Overseas Ltd, 706 Eros Apartments, 56 Nehru Place, New Delhi 110019.

PERSUASION
JANE AUSTEN

Edited by D. W. Harding

Persuasion, published posthumously in 1818, is Jane Austen's last novel. Like the earlier works it is a tale of love and marriage, told with the irony, insight, and sane evaluation of human conduct which sets her writing apart. But the starting-point is a new one, the tone a little more sombre. Anne Elliott and Captain Wentworth have met and separated years before. Their reunion forces a recognition of the false values that drive them apart. The characters who embody these values are the objects of some of the most withering satire that Jane Austen ever wrote.

This edition also includes Austen-Leigh's valuable work, *A Memoir of Jane Austen*.

Also published:

EMMA
MANSFIELD PARK
SENSE AND SENSIBILITY
LADY SUSAN/THE WATSONS/SANDITON
NORTHANGER ABBEY
PRIDE AND PREJUDICE

JANE EYRE
CHARLOTTE BRONTË

Edited by Q. D. Leavis

Since its publication in 1847 *Jane Eyre* has never ceased to be one of the most widely read of English novels. Transmuted by the rare Brontë imagination, the romance of Jane and Rochester takes on a strange and unforgettable atmosphere that lifts it above the level of mere melodrama. But Charlotte Brontë intended more. She portrayed the refusal of a spirited and intelligent woman to accept her appointed place in society with unusual frankness and with a passionate sense of the dignity and needs of her sex. Q. D. Leavis's introduction brings out the revolutionary qualities of the book and its author's creation of something that would 'be true to the experience of the whole woman and . . . convey a sense of life's springs and undercurrents'.

THE NEW PELICAN GUIDE
TO ENGLISH LITERATURE

Edited by Boris Ford

Authoritative, stimulating and accessible, the original seven-volume *Pelican Guide to English Literature* has earned itself a distinguished reputation. Now enlarged to nine titles this popular series has been wholly revised and updated.

What this work sets out to offer is a guide to the history and traditions of English literature, a contour-map of the literary scene. Each volume includes these standard features:

(i) An account of the social context of literature in each period.

(ii) A general survey of the literature itself.

(iii) A series of critical essays on individual writers and their works – each written by an authority in their field.

(iv) Full appendices including short author biographies, listings of standard editions of authors' works, critical commentaries and titles for further study and reference.

The *Guide* consists of the following volumes:

'The best and most lively general survey of English literature available to schools, students and general readers' – *The Times Educational Supplement*

THE LIFE AND ADVENTURES OF MARTIN CHUZZLEWIT

Charles Dickens

Edited by P. N. Furbank

Martin Chuzzlewit (1843–4) is Charles Dicken's comic masterpiece – an opinion shared by Dickens himself who, when he began the novel 'never had so much confidence in his powers', and when he had finished it was convinced it was 'in a hundred points immeasurably the best of my stories'. A study of selfishness and hypocrisy, the plot of *Martin Chuzzlewit* moves from the sunniest farcicality to the grimmest reaches of criminal psychology, from the domestic and parochial villainy of Mr Pecksniff to the public villainy of the Anglo-Bengalee Assurance Company. The novel is peopled with such superb Dickensian characters as Mrs Gamp, Poll Sweedlepipe, Montague Tiggs, Chevy Slyme and the Chuzzlewit brothers and, as P. N. Furbank writes in his introduction, Dickens 'certainly never wrote in higher spirits'.

Also published:

DAVID COPPERFIELD

GREAT EXPECTATIONS

LITTLE DORRIT

OLIVER TWIST

HARD TIMES

DOMBEY AND SON

BLEAK HOUSE

A TALE OF TWO CITIES

AMERICAN NOTES

BARNABY RUDGE

THE CHRISTMAS BOOKS

THE MYSTERY OF EDWIN DROOD

THE OLD CURIOSITY SHOP

OUR MUTUAL FRIEND

PICKWICK PAPERS

MIDDLEMARCH

George Eliot

Edited by W. J. Harvey

Middlemarch (1871–2) is perhaps the masterpiece of a writer who is now recognized as a major literary figure of the nineteenth century. Virginia Woolf hailed as 'one of the few English novels written for adult people' this magnificent work in which George Eliot paints a luminous and spacious landscape of life in a provincial town. With sure and subtle touch she draws together the links of the rural network: Dorothea, a modern St Teresa; Dr Lydgate, the young doctor defeated by self and circumstance; Rosamond, that masterly study in triviality and egoism, and the unprepossessing and doomed banker, Bulstrode. Indeed, in her analysis of human nature George Eliot achieved what Dr Leavis has called 'a Tolstoyan depth and reality'.

Also published:

SILAS MARNER

DANIEL DERONDA

FELIX HOLT

SCENES OF CLERICAL LIFE

ENGLISH AND AMERICAN LITERATURE IN PENGUINS

☐ *Emma* **Jane Austen**

'I am going to take a heroine whom no one but myself will much like,' declared Jane Austen of Emma, her most spirited and controversial heroine in a comedy of self-deceit and self-discovery.

☐ *Tender is the Night* **F. Scott Fitzgerald**

Fitzgerald worked on seventeen different versions of this novel, and its obsessions – idealism, beauty, dissipation, alcohol and insanity – were those that consumed his own marriage and his life.

☐ *The Life of Johnson* **James Boswell**

Full of gusto, imagination, conversation and wit, Boswell's immortal portrait of Johnson is as near a novel as a true biography can be, and still regarded by many as the finest 'life' ever written. This shortened version is based on the 1799 edition.

☐ *A House and its Head* **Ivy Compton-Burnett**

In a novel 'as trim and tidy as a hand-grenade' (as Pamela Hansford Johnson put it), Ivy Compton-Burnett penetrates the facade of a conventional, upper-class Victorian family to uncover a chasm of violent emotions – jealousy, pain, frustration and sexual passion.

☐ *The Trumpet Major* **Thomas Hardy**

Although a vein of unhappy unrequited love runs through this novel, Hardy also draws on his warmest sense of humour to portray Wessex village life at the time of the Napoleonic wars.

☐ *The Complete Poems of Hugh MacDiarmid*

☐ Volume One
☐ Volume Two

The definitive edition of work by the greatest Scottish poet since Robert Burns, edited by his son Michael Grieve, and W. R. Aitken.

ENGLISH AND AMERICAN LITERATURE IN PENGUINS

☐ *Main Street* **Sinclair Lewis**

The novel that added an immortal chapter to the literature of America's Mid-West, *Main Street* contains the comic essence of Main Streets everywhere.

☐ *The Compleat Angler* **Izaak Walton**

A celebration of the countryside, and the superiority of those in 1653, as now, who love *quietnesse, vertue* and, above all, *Angling*. 'No fish, however coarse, could wish for a doughtier champion than Izaak Walton' – Lord Home

☐ *The Portrait of a Lady* **Henry James**

'One of the two most brilliant novels in the language', according to F. R. Leavis, James's masterpiece tells the story of a young American heiress, prey to fortune-hunters but not without a will of her own.

☐ *Hangover Square* **Patrick Hamilton**

Part love story, part thriller, and set in the publands of London's Earls Court, this novel caught the conversational tone of a whole generation in the uneasy months before the Second World War.

☐ *The Rainbow* **D. H. Lawrence**

Written between *Sons and Lovers* and *Women in Love, The Rainbow* covers three generations of Brangwens, a yeoman family living on the borders of Nottinghamshire.

☐ *Vindication of the Rights of Woman*
Mary Wollstonecraft

Although Walpole once called her 'a hyena in petticoats', Mary Wollstonecraft's vision was such that modern feminists continue to go back and debate the arguments so powerfully set down here.

ENGLISH AND AMERICAN
LITERATURE IN PENGUINS

☐ *Nostromo* **Joseph Conrad**

In his most ambitious and successful novel Conrad created an entire imaginary republic in South America. As he said, 'you shall find there according to your deserts: encouragement, consolation, fear, charm – all you demand – and, perhaps, also that glimpse of truth for which you forgot to ask.'

☐ *A Passage to India* **E. M. Forster**

Centred on the unsolved mystery at the Marabar Caves, Forster's masterpiece conveys, as no other novel has done, the troubled spirit of India during the Raj.

These books should be available at all good bookshops or newsagents, but if you live in the UK or the Republic of Ireland and have difficulty in getting to a bookshop, they can be ordered by post. Please indicate the titles required and fill in the form below.

NAME _____ BLOCK CAPITALS

ADDRESS _____

_____

Enclose a cheque or postal order payable to The Penguin Bookshop to cover the total price of books ordered, plus 50p for postage. Readers in the Republic of Ireland should send £1R equivalent to the sterling prices, plus 67p for postage. Send to: The Penguin Bookshop, 54/56 Bridlesmith Gate, Nottingham, NG1 2GP.

You can also order by phoning (0602) 599295, and quoting your Barclaycard or Access number.

Every effort is made to ensure the accuracy of the price and availability of books at the time of going to press, but it is sometimes necessary to increase prices and in these circumstances retail prices may be shown on the covers of books which may differ from the prices shown in this list or elsewhere. This list is not an offer to supply any book.

This order service is only available to residents in the UK and the Republic of Ireland.